Temporal Power

A Study in Supremacy

Marie Corelli

Contents

TEMPORAL POWER

A STUDY IN SUPREMACY

by

Marie Corelli

CHAPTER I
THE KING'S PLEASAUNCE

IN the beginning," so we are told, "God made the heavens and the earth." The statement is simple and terse; it is evidently intended to be wholly comprehensive. Its decisive, almost abrupt tone would seem to forbid either question or argument. The old-world narrator of the sublime event thus briefly chronicled was a poet of no mean quality, though moved by the natural conceit of man to give undue importance to the earth as his own particular habitation. The perfect confidence with which he explains 'God' as making 'two great lights, the greater light to rule the day, the lesser light to rule the night,' is touching to the verge of pathos; and the additional remark which he throws in, as it were casually,—'He made the stars also,' cannot but move us to admiration. How childlike the simplicity of the soul which could so venture to deal with the inexplicable and tremendous problem of the Universe! How self-centred and sure the faith which could so arrange the work of Infinite and Eternal forces to suit its own limited intelligence! It is easy and natural to believe that 'God,' or an everlasting Power of Goodness and Beauty called by that name, 'created the heavens and the earth,' but one is often tempted to think that an altogether different and rival element must have been concerned in the making of Man. For the heavens and the earth are harmonious; man is a discord. And not only is he a discord in himself, but he takes pleasure in producing and multiplying discords. Often, with the least possible amount of education, and on the slightest provocation, he mentally sets Himself, and his trivial personal opinion on religion, morals, and government, in direct opposition to the immutable laws of the Universe, and the attitude he assumes towards the mysterious Cause and

Original Source of Life is nearly always one of three things; contradiction, negation, or defiance. From the first to the last he torments himself with inventions to outwit or subdue Nature, and in the end dies, utterly defeated. His civilizations, his dynasties, his laws, his manners, his customs, are all doomed to destruction and oblivion as completely as an ant-hill which exists one night and is trodden down the next. Forever and forever he works and plans in vain; forever and forever Nature, the visible and active Spirit of God, rises up and crushes her puny rebel.

There must be good reason for this ceaseless waste of human life,—this constant and steady obliteration of man's attempts, since there can be no Effect without Cause. It is, as if like children at a school, we were set a certain sum to do, and because we blunder foolishly over it and add it up to a wrong total, it is again and again wiped off the blackboard, and again and again rewritten for our more careful consideration. Possibly the secret of our failure to conquer Nature lies in ourselves, and our own obstinate tendency to work in only one groove of what we term 'advancement,'—namely our material self- interest. Possibly we might be victors if we would, even to the very vanquishment of Death!

So many of us think,—and so thought one man of sovereign influence in this world's affairs as, seated on the terrace of a Royal palace fronting seaward, he pondered his own life's problem for perhaps the thousandth time.

"What is the use of thinking?" asked a wit at the court of Louis XVI. "It only intensifies the bad opinion you have of others,—or of yourself!"

He found this saying true. Thinking is a pernicious habit in which very great personages are not supposed to indulge; and in his younger days he had avoided it. He had allowed the time to take him as it found him, and had gone with it unresistingly wherever it had led. It was the best way; the wisest way; the way Solomon found most congenial, despite its end in 'vanity and vexation of spirit.' But with the passing of the years a veil had been dropped over that path of roses, hiding it altogether from his sight; and another veil rose inch by inch before him, disclosing a new and less joyous prospect on which he was not too-well-pleased to look.

The sea, stretching out in a broad shining expanse opposite to him, sparkled dancingly in the warm sunshine, and the snowy sails of many yachts and pleasure-boats dipped now and again into the glittering waves like white birds skimming over the tiny flashing foam-crests. Dazzling and well-nigh blinding to his eyes were the burning glow and exquisite radiance of colour which seemed melted like gold and sapphire into that bright half-circle of water and sky,—beautiful, and full of a dream-like evanescent quality, such as marks all the loveliest scenes and impressions of our life on earth. There was a subtle scent of violets in the air,—and a gardener, cutting sheafs of narcissi from the edges of the velvety green banks which rolled away in smooth undulations upward from the terrace to the wider extent of the palace pleasaunce beyond, scattered such perfume with his snipping shears as might have lured another Proserpine from Hell. Cluster after cluster of white blooms, carefully selected for the adornment of the Royal apartments, he laid beside him on the grass, not presuming to look in the direction where that other Workman in the ways of life sat silent and absorbed in thought. That other, in his own long-practised manner, feigned not to be aware of his dependant's proximity,—and in this fashion they twain—human beings made of the same clay and relegated, to the same dust— gave sport to the Fates by playing at Sham with Heaven and themselves. Custom, law, and all the paraphernalia of civilization, had set the division and marked the boundary between them,—had forbidden the lesser in world's rank to speak to the greater, unless the greater began conversation,—had equally forbidden the greater to speak to the lesser lest such condescension should inflate the lesser's vanity so much as to make him obnoxious to his fellows. Thus,—of two men, who, if left to nature would have been merely—men, and sincere enough at that,—man himself had made two pretenders,—the one as gardener, the other as—King! The white narcissi lying on the grass, and preparing to die sweetly, like sacrificed maiden-victims of the flower-world, could turn true faces to the God who made them,— but the men at that particular moment of time had no real features ready for God's inspection,—only masks.

"C'est mon metier d'etre Roi!" So said one of the many dead and gone martyrs on the rack of sovereignty. Alas, poor soul, thou would'st have been happier in any other 'metier' I warrant! For kingship is a profession which cannot be abandoned for a change of humour, or cast aside in light indifference and independence because a man is bored by it and would have something new. It is a routine and drudgery to which some few are born, for which they are prepared, to which they must devote their span of life, and in which they must die. "How shall we pass the day?" asked a weary Roman emperor, "I am even tired of killing my enemies!"

'Even' that! And the strangest part of it is, that there are people who would give all their freedom and peace of mind to occupy for a few years an uneasy throne, and who actually live under the delusion that a monarch is happy!

The gardener soon finished his task of cutting the narcissi, and though he might not, without audacity, look at his Sovereign-master, his Sovereign-master looked at him, furtively, from under half-closed eyelids, watching him as he bound the blossoms together carefully, with the view of giving as little trouble as possible to those whose duty it would be to arrange them for the Royal pleasure. His work done, he walked quickly, yet with a certain humble stealthiness,—thus admitting his consciousness of that greater presence than his own,— down a broad garden walk beyond the terrace towards a private entrance to the palace, and there disappeared.

The King was left alone,—or apparently so, for to speak truly, he was never alone. An equerry, a page-in-waiting,—or what was still more commonplace as well as ominous, a detective,—lurked about him, ever near, ever ready to spring on any unknown intruder, or to answer his slightest call.

But to the limited extent of the solitude allowed to kings, this man was alone,— alone for a brief space to consider, as he had informed his secretary, certain documents awaiting his particular and private perusal.

The marble pavilion in which he sat had been built by his father, the late King, for his own pleasure, when pleasure was more possible than it is now. Its slender Ionic columns, its sculptured friezes, its painted ceilings, all expressed a gaiety, grace and beauty gone from the world, perchance for ever. Open on three sides to the living picture of the ocean, crimson and white roses clambered about it, and tall plume-like mimosa shook fragrance from its golden blossoms down every breath of wind. The costly table on which this particular Majesty of a nation occasionally wrote his letters, would, if sold, have kept a little town in food for a year,—the rich furs at his feet would have bought bread for hundreds of starving families,—and every delicious rose that nodded its dainty head towards him with the breeze would have given an hour's joy to a sick child. Socialists say this kind of thing with wildly eloquent fervour, and blame all kings in passionate rhodomontade for the tables, the furs and the roses,—but they forget— it is not the sad and weary kings who care for these or any luxuries,— they would be far happier without them. It is the People who insist on having kings that should be blamed,—not the monarchs themselves.

A king is merely the people's Prisoner of State,—they chain him to a throne,—they make him clothe himself in sundry fantastic forms of attire and exhibit his person thus decked out, for their pleasure,— they calculate, often with greed and grudging, how much it will cost to feed him and keep him in proper state on the national premises, that they may use him at their will,—but they seldom or never seem to remember the fact that there is a Man behind the King!

It is not easy to govern nowadays, since there is no real autocracy, and no strong soul likely to create one. But the original idea of sovereignty was grand and wise;—the strongest man and bravest, raised aloft on shields and bucklers with warrior cries of approval from the people who voluntarily chose him as their leader in battle,—their utmost Head of affairs. Progress has demolished this ideal, with many others equally fine and inspiring; and now all kings are so, by right of descent merely. Whether they be infirm or palsied, weak or wise, sane or crazed, still are they as of old elected; only no more as the Strongest, but simply as the Signposts of a traditional bygone authority. This King however, here written of, was not deficient in either mental or physical attributes. His outward look and bearing betokened him as far more fit to be lifted in triumph on the shoulders of his battle-heroes, a real and visible Man, than to play a more or less cautiously inactive part in the modern dumb-show of Royalty. Well- built and muscular, with a compact head regally poised on broad shoulders, and finely formed features which indicated in their firm modelling strong characteristics of pride, indomitable resolution and courage, he had an air of rare and reposeful dignity which made him much more impressive as a personality than many of his fellow- sovereigns. His expression was neither foolish nor sensual,—his clear dark grey eyes were sane and steady in their regard and had no tricks of shiftiness. As an ordinary man of the people his appearance would have been distinctive,—as a King, it was remarkable.

He had of course been called handsome in his childhood,—what heir to a Throne ever lived that was not beautiful, to his nurse at least?—and in his early youth he had been grossly flattered for his cleverness as well as his good looks. Every small attempt at witticism,—every poor joke he could invent, adapt or repeat, was laughed at approvingly in a chorus of admiration by smirking human creatures, male and female, who bowed and bobbed up and down before the lad like strange dolphins disporting themselves on dry land. Whereat he grew to despise the dolphins, and no wonder. When he was about seventeen or eighteen he began to ask odd questions of one of his preceptors, a learned and ceremonious personage who, considering the extent of his certificated wisdom, was yet so singularly servile of habit and disposition that he might have won a success on the stage as Chief Toady in a burlesque of Court life. He was a pale, thin old man, with a wizened face set well back amid wisps of white hair, and a scraggy throat which asserted its working muscles visibly whenever he spoke, laughed or took food. His way of shaking hands expressed his moral flabbiness in the general dampness, looseness and limpness of the act,—not that he often shook hands with his pupil, for though that pupil was only a boy made of ordinary flesh and blood like other boys, he was nevertheless heir to a Throne, and in strict etiquette even friendly liberties were not to be too frequently taken with such an Exalted little bit of humanity. The lad himself, however, had a certain mischievous delight in making him perform this courtesy, and being young and vigorous, would often squeeze the old gentleman's hesitating fingers in his strong clasp so energetically as to cause him the severest pain. Student of many philosophies as he was, the worthy pedagogue would have cried out, or sworn profane oaths in his agony, had it been any other than the 'Heir- Apparent' who thus made him wince with torture,—but as matters stood, he merely smiled—and bore it. The young rascal of a prince smiled too,—taking note of his obsequious hypocrisy, which served an inquiring mind with quite as good a field for logical speculation as any problem in Euclid. And he went on with his questions,—questions, which if not puzzling, were at least irritating enough to have secured him a rap on the knuckles from his tutor's cane, had he been a grocer's lad instead of the eldest son of a Royal house.

"Professor," he said on one occasion, "What is man?"

"Man," replied the professor sedately, "is an intelligent and reasoning being, evolved by natural processes of creation into his present condition of supremacy."

"What is Supremacy?"

"The state of being above, or superior to, the rest of the animal creation."

"And is he so superior?"

"He is generally so admitted."

"Is my father a man?"

"Assuredly! The question is superfluous."

"What makes him a King?"

"Royal birth and the hereditary right to his great position."

"Then if man is in a condition of supremacy over the rest of creation, a king is more than a man if he is allowed to rule men?"

"Sir, pardon me!—a king is not more than a man, but men choose him as their ruler because he is worthy."

"In what way is he worthy? Simply because he is born as I am, heir to a throne?"

"Precisely."

"He might be an idiot or a cripple, a fool or a coward,—he would still be King?"

"Most indubitably."

"So that if he were a madman, he would continue to hold supremacy over a nation, though his groom might be sane?"

"Your Royal Highness pursues the question with an unwise flippancy;"— remonstrated the professor with a pained, forced smile. "If an idiot or a madman were unfortunately born to a throne, a regency would be appointed to control state affairs, but the heir would, in spite of natural incapability, remain the lawful king."

"A strange sovereignty!" said the young prince carelessly. "And a still stranger patience in the people who would tolerate it! Yet over all men,—kings, madmen, and idiots alike,—there is another ruling force, called God?"

"There is a force," admitted the professor dubiously—"But in the present forward state of things it would not be safe to attempt to explain the nature of that force, and for the benefit of the illiterate masses we call it God. A national worship of something superior to themselves has always been proved politic and necessary for the people. I have not at any time resolved myself as to why it should be so; but so it is."

"Then man, despite his 'supremacy' must have something more supreme than himself to keep him in order, if it be only a fetish wherewith to tickle his imagination?" suggested the prince with a touch of satire,— "Even kings must bow, or pretend to bow, to the King of kings?"

"Sir, you have expressed the fact with felicity;" replied the professor gravely—"His Majesty, your august father, attends public worship with punctilious regularity, and you are accustomed to accompany him. It is a rule which you will find necessary to keep in practice, as an example to your subjects when you are called upon to reign."

The young man raised his eyebrows deprecatingly, with a slight ironical smile, and dropped the subject. But the learned professor as in duty bound, reported the conversation to his pupil's father; with the additional observation that he feared, he very humbly and respectfully feared, that the developing mind of the prince appeared undesirably disposed towards discursive philosophies, which were wholly unnecessary for the position he was destined to occupy. Whereupon the King took his son to task on the subject with a mingling of kindness and humour.

"Do not turn philosopher!" he said—"For philosophy will not so much content you with life, as with death! Philosophy will chill your best impulses and most generous enthusiasms,—it will make you over-cautious and doubtful of your friends,— it will cause you to be indifferent to women in the plural, but it will hand you over, a weak and helpless victim to the *one* woman,—when she comes,—as she is bound to come. There is no one so hopelessly insane as a philosopher in love! Love women, but not *a* woman!"

"In so doing I should follow the wisest of examples,—yours, Sir!" replied the prince with a familiarity more tender than audacious, for his father was a man of fine presence and fascinating manner, and knew well the extent of his power to charm and subjugate the fairer sex,— "But I have a fancy that love,—if it exists anywhere outside the dreams of the poets,—is unknown to kings."

The monarch bent his brows frowningly, and his eyes were full of a deep and bitter melancholy.

"You mistake!" he said slowly—"Love,—and by that name I mean a wholly different thing from Passion,—comes to kings as to commoners,—but whereas the commoner may win it if he can, the king must reject it. But it comes,—and leaves a blank in the proudest life when it goes!"

He turned away abruptly, and the conversation was not again resumed. But when he died, those who prepared his body for burial, found a gold chain round his neck, holding the small medallion portrait of a woman, and a curl of soft fair hair. Needless to say the portrait was not that of the late Queen-Consort, who had died some years before her Royal spouse, nor was the hair hers,—but when they brought the relic to the new King, he laid it back with his own hands on his father's lifeless breast, and let it go into the grave with him. For, being no longer the crowned Servant of the State, he had the right as a mere dead man, to the possession of his love-secret.

So at least thought his son and successor, who at times was given to wondering whether if, like his father, he had such a secret he would be able to keep it as closely and as well. He thought not. It would be scarcely worth while. It can only be the greatest love that is always silent,—and in the greatest,—that is, the ideal and self-renouncing love,—he did not believe; though in his own life's experience he had been given a proof that such love is possible to women, if not to men. When he was about twenty, he had loved, or had imagined he loved, a girl,—a pretty creature, who did not know him as a prince at all, but simply as a college student. He used to walk with her hand in hand through the fields by the river, and gather wild flowers for her to wear in her little white bodice. She had shy soft eyes, and a timid, yet trusting look, full of tenderness and pathos. Moved by a romantic sense of honour and chivalry, he promised to marry her, and thereupon wrote an impulsive letter to his father informing him of his intention. Of course he was summoned home from college at once,—he was reminded of his high destiny—of the Throne that would be his if he lived to occupy it,—of the great and serious responsibilities awaiting him,— and of how impossible it was that the Heir-Apparent to the Crown should marry a commoner.

"Why not?" he cried passionately—"If she be good and true she is as fit to be a queen as any woman royally born! She is a queen already in her own right!"

But while he was being argued with and controlled by all the authorities concerned in king's business, his little sweetheart herself put an end to the matter. Her parents told her all unpreparedly, and with no doubt unnecessary harshness, the real position of the college lad with whom she had wandered in the fields so confidingly; and in the bewilderment of her poor little broken heart and puzzled brain, she gave herself to the river by whose flowering banks she had sworn her maiden vows,—though she knew it not,—to her future King; and so, drowning her life and love together, made a piteous exit from all difficulty. Before she went forth to die, she wrote a farewell to her Royal lover, posting the letter herself on her way to the river, and, by the merest chance he received it without a spy's intervention. It was but one line, scrawled in a round youthful hand, and blotted with many tears.

"Sir—my love!—forgive me!"

It would be unwise to say what that little scrap of ill-formed writing cost the heir to a throne when he heard how she had died,—or how he raged and swore and wept. It was the first Wrong forced on him as Right, by the laws of the realm; and he was young and generous and honest, and not hardened to those laws then. Their iniquity and godlessness appeared to him in plain ugly colours undisguised. Since that time he had perforce fallen into the habit and routine of his predecessors, though he was not altogether so 'constitutional' a sovereign as his father had been. He had something of the spirit of one who had occupied his throne five hundred years before him; when strength and valour and wit and boldness, gave more kings to the world than came by heritage. He did unconventional things now and then; to the grief of flunkeys, and the alarm of Court parasites. But his kingdom was of the South, where hot blood is recognized and excused, and fiery temper more admired than censured, and where,—so far as social matters went,—his word, whether kind, cold, or capricious, was sufficient to lead in any direction that large flock of the silly sheep of fashion who only exist to eat, and to be eaten. Sometimes he longed to throw himself back into bygone centuries and stand as his earliest ancestor stood, sword in hand, on a height overlooking the battle- field, watching the swaying rush of combat,—the glitter of spears and axes—the sharp flight of arrows—the tossing banners, the grinding chariots, the flying dust and carnage of men! There was something to fight for in those days,—there was no careful binding up of wounds,— no provision for the sick or the mutilated,—nothing, nothing, but 'Victory or Death!' How much grander, how much finer the old fierce ways of war than now, when any soldier wounded, may write the details of his bayonet-scratch or bullet-hole to the cheap press, and the surgeon prys about with Rontgen-ray paraphernalia and scalpel, to discover how much or how little escape from dissolution a man's soul has had in the shock of contest with his foe! Of a truth these are paltry days!—and paltry days breed paltry men. Afraid of sickness, afraid of death, afraid of poverty, afraid of offences, afraid to think, afraid to speak, Man in the present era of his boasted 'progress' resembles nothing so much as a whipped child,—cowering under the outstretched arm of Heaven and waiting in whimpering terror for the next fall of the scourge. And it is on this point especially, that the monarch who takes part in this unhesitating chronicle of certain thoughts and movements hidden out of sight,—yet deeply felt in the under-silences of the time,—may claim to be unconventional;—he was afraid of nothing,—not even of himself as King!

CHAPTER II
MAJESTY CONSIDERS AND RESOLVES

THE little episode of his first love, combined with his ungovernable fury and despair at its tragic conclusion, had of course the natural result common in such a case, to the fate of all who are destined to occupy thrones. A marriage was 'arranged' for him; and pressing reasons of state were urged for the quick enforcement and carrying out of the 'arrangement.' The daughter of a neighbouring potentate was elected to the honour of his alliance,—a beautiful girl with a pale, cold clear- cut face and brilliant eyes, whose smile penetrated the soul with an icy chill, and whose very movement, noiseless and graceful as it was, reminded one irresistibly of slowly drifting snow. She was attended to the altar, as he was, by all the ministers and plenipotentiaries of state that could possibly be gathered together from the four quarters of the globe as witnesses to the immolation of two young human lives on the grim sacrificial stone of a Dynasty; and both prince and princess accepted their fate with mutually silent and civil resignation. Their portraits, set facing each other with a silly smile, or taken in a linked arm-in-arm attitude against a palatial canvas background, appeared in every paper published throughout the world, and every scribbler on the Press took special pains to inform the easily deluded public that the Royal union thus consummated was 'a romantic love- match.' For the People still have heart and conscience,—the People, taken in the rough lump of humanity, still believe in love, in faith, in the dear sweetness of home affections. The politicians who make capital out of popular emotion, know this well enough,—and are careful to play the tune of their own personal interest upon the gamut of National Sentiment in every stump oration. For how terrible it would be if the People of any land learned to judge their preachers and teachers by the lines of fact alone! Inasmuch as fact would convincingly prove to them that their leaders prospered and grew rich, while they stayed poor; and they might take to puzzling out reasons for this inadequacy which would inevitably cause trouble. For this, and divers other motives politic, the rosy veil of sentiment is always delicately flung more or less over every new move on the national debating-ground,—and whether marriageable princes and princesses love or loathe each other, still, when they come to wed, the words 'romantic love-match' must be thrown in by an oblig-ing Press in order to satisfy the tender scruples of a people who would certainly not abide the thought of a Royal marriage contracted in mutual aversion. Thus much soundness and right principle there is at least, in what some superfine persons call the 'common' folk,—the folk whose innermost sense of truth and straightforward-ness, not even the proudest statesman dare outrage.

But with what unuttered and unutterable scorn the youthful victims of the Royal pairing accepted the newspaper-assurances of the devoted tenderness they entertained for each other! With what wearied impatience both prince and prin-cess received the 'Wedding Odes' and 'Epithalamiums,' written by first-class and no-class versifiers for the occasion! What shoals of these were cast aside unread, to occupy the darkest dingiest corner of one of the Royal 'refuse' libraries! The writ-ers of such things expected great honours, no doubt, each and every man-jack of them,—but apart from the fact that the greatest literature has always lived without any official recognition or endowment from kings,—being in itself the supremest sovereignty,—poets and rhymesters alike never seem to realize that no one is, or can be, so sickened by an 'Ode' as the man or woman to whom it is written!

The brilliant marriage ceremony concluded, the august bride and bridegroom took their departure, amid frantically cheering crowds, for a stately castle standing high among the mountains, a truly magnificent pile, which had been placed at their disposal for the 'honeymoon' by one of the wealthiest of the King's subjects,—and there, as soon as equerries, grooms-in-waiting, flunkeys, and every other sort of indoor and outdoor retainer would consent to leave them alone together, the Royal wife came to her Royal husband, and asked to be allowed to speak a few words on the subject of their marriage, 'for the first and last time,' said she, with a straight glance from the cold moonlight mystery of her eyes. Beautiful at all times, her beauty was doubly enhanced by the regal attitude and expression she unconsciously assumed as she made the request, and the prince, critically studying her form and features, could not but regard himself as in some respects rather particularly favoured by the political and social machinery which had succeeded in persuading so fair a creature to resign herself to the doubtful destiny of a throne. She had laid aside her magnificent bridal-robes of ivory satin and cloth-of-gold,—and appeared before him in loose draperies of floating white, with her rich hair unbound and rippling to her knees.

"May I speak?" she murmured, and her voice trembled.

"Most assuredly!"—he replied, half smiling—"You do me too much honour by requesting the permission!"

As he spoke, he bowed profoundly, but she, raising her eyes, fixed them full upon him with a strange look of mingled pride and pain.

"Do not," she said, "let us play at formalities! Let us be honest with each other for to-night at least! All our life together must from henceforth be more or less of a masquerade, but let us for to-night be as true man and true woman, and frankly face the position into which we have been thrust, not by ourselves, but by others."

Profoundly astonished, the prince was silent. He had not thought this girl of nineteen possessed any force of character or any intellectual power of reasoning. He had judged her as no doubt glad to become a great princess and a possible future queen, and he had not given her credit for any finer or higher feeling.

"You know,"—she continued—"you must surely know—" here, despite the strong restraint she put upon herself, her voice broke, and her slight figure swayed in its white draperies as if about to fall. She looked at him with a sense of rising tears in her throat,—tears of which she was ashamed,—for she was full of a passionate emotion too strong for weeping—a contempt of herself and of him, too great for mere clamour. Was he so much of a man in the slow thick density of his brain she thought, as to have no instinctive perception of her utter misery? He hastened to her and tried to take her hands, but she drew herself away from him and sank down in a chair as if exhausted.

"You are tired!" he said kindly—"The tedious ceremonial—the still more tedious congratulations,—and the fatiguing journey from the capital to this place have been too much for your strength. You must rest!"

"It is not that!"—she answered—"not that! I am not tired,—but—but— I cannot say my prayers tonight till you know my whole heart!"

A curious reverence and pity moved him. All day long he had been in a state of resentful irritation,—he had loathed himself for having consented to marry this girl without loving her,—he had branded himself inwardly as a liar and hypocrite when he had sworn his marriage vows 'before God,' whereas if he truly believed in God, such vows taken untruthfully were mere blasphemy;—and now she herself, a young thing tenderly brought up like a tropical flower in the enervating hot-house atmosphere of Court life, yet had such a pure, deep consciousness of God in her, that she actually could not pray with the slightest blur of a secret on her soul! He waited wonderingly.

"I have plighted my faith to you before God's altar to-day," she said, speaking more steadily,—"because after long and earnest thought, I saw that there was no other way of satisfying the two nations to which we belong, and cementing the friendly relations between them. There is no woman of Royal birth,—so it has been pointed out to me—who is so suitable, from a political point of view, to be your wife as I. It is for the sake of your Throne and country that you must marry—and I ask God to forgive me if I have done wrong in His sight by wedding you simply for duty's sake. My father, your father, and all who are connected with our two families desire our union, and have assured me that, it is right and good for me to give up my life to yours. All women's lives must be martyred to the laws made by men,—or so it seems to me,—I cannot expect to escape from the general doom apportioned to my sex. I therefore accept the destiny which transfers me to you as a piece of human property for possession and command,—I accept it freely, but I will not say gladly, because that would not be true. For I do not love you,—I cannot love you! I want you to know that, and to feel it, that you may not ask from me what I cannot give."

There were no tears in her eyes; she looked at him straightly and steadfastly. He, in his turn, met her gaze fully,—his face had paled a little, and a shadow of pained regret and commiseration darkened his handsome features.

"You love someone else?" he asked, softly.

She rose from her chair and confronted him, a glow of passionate pride flushing her cheeks and brow.

"No!" she said—"I would not be a traitor to you in so much as a thought! Had I loved anyone else I would never have married you,—no!— though you had been ten times a prince and king! No! You do not understand. I come to you heartwhole and passionless, without a single love-word chronicled in my girlhood's history, or a single incident you may not know. I have never loved any man, because from my very childhood I have hated and feared all men! I loathe their presence— their looks—their voices—their manners,—if one should touch my hand in ordinary courtesy, my instincts are offended and revolted, and the sense of outrage remains with me for days. My mother knows of this, and says I am 'unnatural,'—it may be so. But unnatural or not, it is the truth; judge therefore the extent of the sacrifice I make to God and our two countries in giving myself to you!"

The prince stood amazed and confounded. Did she rave? Was she mad? He studied her with a curious, half-doubting scrutiny, and noted the composure of her attitude, the cold serenity of her expression,—there was evidently no hysteria, no sur-excitation of nerves about this calm statuesque beauty which in every line and curve of loveliness silently mutinied against him, and despised him. Puzzled, yet fascinated, he sought in his mind for some clue to her meaning.

"There are women" she went on—"to whom love, or what is called love, is necessary,—for whom marriage is the utmost good of existence. I am not one of these. Had I my own choice I would live my life away from all men,—I would let nothing of myself be theirs to claim,—I would give all I am and all I have to God, who made me what I am. For truly and honestly, without any affectation at all, I look upon marriage, not as an honour, but a degradation!"

Had she been less in earnest, he might have smiled at this, but her beauty, intensified as it was by the fervour of her feeling, seemed transfigured into something quite supernatural which for the moment dazzled him.

"Am I to understand—" he began.

She interrupted him by a swift gesture, while the rich colour swept over her face in a warm wave.

"Understand nothing"—she said,—"but this—that I do not love you, because I can love no man! For the rest I am your wife; and as your wife I give myself to you and your nation wholly and in all things— save love!"

He advanced and took her hands in his.

"This is a strange bargain!" he said, and gently kissed her.

She answered nothing,—only a faint shiver trembled through her as she endured the caress. For a moment or two he surveyed her in silence,—it was a singular and novel experience for him, as a future king, to be the lawful possessor of a woman's beauty, and yet with all his sovereignty to be unable to waken one thrill of tenderness in the frozen soul imprisoned in such exquisite flesh and blood. He was inclined to disbelieve her assertions,—surely he thought, there must be emotion, feeling, passion in this fair creature, who, though she seemed a goddess newly descended from inaccessible heights of heaven was still *only* a woman? And upon the whole he was not ill- pleased with the curious revelation she had made of herself. He preferred the coldness of women to their volcanic eruptions, and would take more pains to melt the snow of reserve than to add fuel to the flame of ardour.

"You have been very frank with me," he said at last, after a pause, as he loosened her hands and moved a little apart from her—"And whether your physical and mental hatred of my sex is a defect in your nature, or an exceptional virtue, I shall not quarrel with it. I am myself not without faults; and the chiefest of these is one most common to all men. I desire what I may not have, and covet what I do not possess. So! We understand each other!"

She raised her eyes—those beautiful deep eyes with the moonlight glamour in them,—and for an instant the shining Soul of her, pure and fearless, seemed to spring up and challenge to spiritual combat him who was now her body's master. Then, bending her head with a graceful yet proud submission, she retired.

From that time forth she never again spoke on this, or any other subject of an intimate or personal nature, with her Royal spouse. Cold as an iceberg, pure as a diamond, she accepted both wifehood and motherhood as martyrdom, with an evident contempt for its humiliation, and without one touch of love for either husband or children. She bore three sons, of whom the eldest, and heir to the throne was, at the time this history begins, just twenty. The passing of the years had left scarcely a trace upon her beauty, save to increase it from the sparkling luminance of a star to the glory of a full-orbed moon of loveliness,—and she had easily won a triumph over all the other women around her, in the power she possessed to command and retain the admiration of men. She was one of those brilliant creatures who, like the Egyptian Cleopatra, never grow old,—for she was utterly exempt from the wasting of the nerves through emotion. Her eyes were always bright and clear; her skin dazzling in its whiteness, save where the equably flowing blood flushed it with tenderest rose,—her figure remained svelte, lithe and graceful in all its outlines. Finely strung, yet strong as steel in her temperament, all thoughts, feelings and events seemed to sweep over her without affecting or disturbing her mind's calm equipoise. She lived her life with extreme simplicity, regularity, and directness, thus driving to despair all would-be scandal-mongers; and though many gifted and famous men fell madly in love with their great princess, and often, in the extremity of a passion which amounted to disloyalty, slew themselves for her sake, she remained unmoved and pitiless.

Her husband occasionally felt some compassion for the desperate fellows who thus immolated themselves on the High Altar of her perfections, though it must be admitted that he received the news of their deaths with tolerable equanimity, knowing them to have been fools, and as such, better out of the world than in it. During the first two or three years of his marriage he had himself been somewhat of their disposition, and as mere man, had tried by every means in his power to win the affection of his beautiful spouse, and to melt the icy barrier which she, despite their relations with each other, had resolutely kept up between herself and him. He had made the attempt, not because he actually loved her, but simply because he desired the satisfaction of conquest. Finding the task hopeless, he resigned himself to his fate, and accepted her at the costly valuation she set upon herself; though for pastime he would often pay court to certain ladies of easy virtue, with the vague idea that perhaps the spirit of jealousy might enter that cold shrine of womanhood where no other demon could force admission, and wake up the passions slumbering within. But she appeared not to be at all aware of his many and open gallantries; and only at stray moments, when her frosty flashing glance fell upon him engaged in some casual flirtation, would a sudden smarting sense of injury make him conscious of her contempt.

But he could reasonably find no fault with her, save the fault of being fault-less. She was a perfect hostess, and fulfilled all the duties of her exalted position with admirable tact and foresight,—she was ever busy in the performance of good and charitable deeds,—she was an excellent mother, and took the utmost personal care that her sons should be healthily nurtured and well brought up,—she never interfered in any matter of state or ceremony,—she simply seemed to move as a star moves, shining over the earth but having no part in it. Irresponsive as she was, she nevertheless compelled admiration,—her husband himself admired her, but only as he would have admired a statue or a painting. For his was an impulsive and generous nature, and his marriage had kept his heart empty of the warmth of love, and his home devoid of the light of sympathy. Even his children had been born more as the sons of the nation than his own,—he was not conscious of any very great affection for them, or interest in their lives. And he had sought to kindle at many strange fires the heavenly love-beacon which should have flamed its living glory into his days; so it had naturally chanced that he had spent by far the larger portion of his time on the persuasion of mere Whim,—and as vastly inferior women to his wife had made him spend it.

But at this particular juncture, when the curtain is drawn up on certain scenes and incidents in his life-drama, a change had been effected in his opinions and surroundings. For eighteen years after his marriage, he had lived on the first step of the Throne as its next heir; and when he passed that step and ascended the Throne itself, he seemed to have crossed a vast abyss of distance between the Old and the New. Behind him the Past rolled away like a cloud vanishing, to be seen no more,— before him arose the dim vista of wavering and uncertain shadows, which no matter how they shifted and changed,—no matter how many flashes of sunshine flickered through them,—were bound to close in the thick gloom of the inevitable end,— Death. This is what he was chiefly thinking of, seated alone in his garden-pavilion facing the sea on that brilliant southern summer morning,—this,—and with the thought came many others no less sad and dubious,—such as whether for example, his eldest son might not already be eager for the crown?— whether even now, though he had only reigned three years, his people were not more or less dissatisfied under his rule?

His father, the late King, had died suddenly,—so suddenly that there was neither help nor hope for him among the hastily summoned physicians. Stricken numb and speechless, he kept his anguished eyes fixed to the last upon his son, as one who should say—"Alas, and to thee also, falls this curse of a Crown!" Once dead, he was soon forgotten,—the pomp of the Royal obsequies merely made a gala-day for the light-hearted Southern populace, who hailed the accession of their new King with as much gladness as a child, who, having broken one doll, straightway secures another as good, if not better. As Heir-Apparent the succeeding sovereign had won great popularity, and was much more generally beloved than his father had been,—so that it was on an extra high wave of jubilation and acclamation that he and his beautiful consort were borne to the Throne.

Three years had passed since then; and so far his reign had been untroubled by much difficulty. Difficulty there was, but he was kept in ignorance of it,—troubles were brooding, but he was not informed of them. Things likely to be disagreeable were not conveyed to his ears,— and matters which, had he been allowed to examine into them, might have aroused his indignation and interference, were diplomatically hushed up. He was known to possess much more than the limited intelligence usually apportioned to kings; and certainly, as his tutor had said of him in his youth, he was dangerously "disposed towards discursive philosophies." He was likewise accredited with a conscience, which many diplomats consider to be a wholly undesirable ingredient in the moral composition of a reigning monarch. Therefore, those who move a king, as in the game of chess, one square at a time and no more,—were particularly cautious as to the 'way' in which they moved him. He had shown himself difficult to manage once or twice; and interested persons could not pursue their usual course of self-aggrandisement with him, as he was not susceptible to flattery. He had a way of asking straight questions, and what was still worse, expecting straight answers, such as politicians never give.

Nevertheless he had, up to the present, ruled his conduct very much on the lines laid down by his predecessors, and during his brief reign had been more or less content to passively act in all things as his ministers advised. He had bestowed honours on fools because his ministers considered it politic,—he had given his formal consent to the imposition of certain taxes on his people, because his ministers had judged such taxes necessary,—in fact he had done everything he was expected to do, and nothing that he was not expected to do. He had not taken any close personal thought as to whether such and such a political movement was, or was not, welcome to the spirit of the nation, nor had he weighed intimately in his own mind the various private interests of the members of his Government, in passing, or moving the rejection of, any important measure affecting the well-being of the community at large. And he had lately,—perhaps through the objectionable 'discursive philosophies' before mentioned,—come to consider himself somewhat of a stuffed Dummy or figure-head; and to wonder what would be the result, if with caution and prudence, he were to act more on his own initiative, and speak as he often thought it would be wise and well to speak? He was but forty-five years old,—in the prime of life, in the plenitude of health and mental vigour,—was he to pass the rest of his days guarded by detectives, flunkeys and physicians, with never an independent word or action throughout his whole career to mark him Man as well as Monarch? Nay, surely that would be an insult to the God who made him! But the question which arose in his mind and perplexed him was, How to begin? How, after passive obedience, to commence resistance? How to break through the miserable conventionalism, the sordid commonplace of a king's surroundings? For it is only in medieval fairy-tales that kings are permitted to be kingly.

Yet, despite custom and usage, he was determined to make a new departure in the annals of modern sovereignty. Three years of continuous slavery on the tread-mill of the Throne had been sufficient to make him thirst for freedom,—freedom of speech,—freedom of action. He had tacitly submitted to a certain ministry because he had been assured that the said ministry was popular,—but latterly, rumours of discontent and grievance had reached him,—albeit indistinctly and incoherently,—and he began to be doubtful as to whether it might not be the Press which supported the existing state of policy, rather than the People. The Press! He began to consider of what material this great power in his country was composed. Originally, the Press in all countries, was intended to be the most magnificent institution of the civilized world,—the voice of truth, of liberty, of justice—a voice which in its clamant utterances could neither be bribed nor biassed to cry out false news. Originally, such was meant to be its mission;—but nowadays, what, in all honesty and frankness, is the Press? What was it, for example, to this king, who from personal knowledge, was able to practically estimate and enumerate the forces which controlled it thus:—Six, or at the most a dozen men, the proprietors and editors of different newspapers sold in cheap millions to the people. Most of these newspapers were formed into 'companies'; and the managers issued 'shares' in the fashion of tea merchants and grocers. False news, if of a duly sensational character, would sometimes send up the shares in the market,—true information would equally, on occasion, send them down. These premises granted, might it not follow that for newspaper speculators, the False would often prove more lucrative than the True? And, concerning the persons who wrote for these newspapers,—of what calling and election were they? Male and female, young and old, they were generally of a semi-educated class lacking all distinctive ability,—men and women who were, on an average, desperately poor, and desperately dissatisfied. To earn daily bread they naturally had to please the editors set in authority over them; hence their expressed views and opinions on any subject could only be counted as *nil*, being written, not independently, but under the absolute control of their employers. Thus meditating, the King summed up the total of his own mental argument, and found that the vast sounding 'power of the Press' so far as his own dominion was concerned, resolved itself into the mere trade monopoly of the aforesaid leading dozen men. What he now proposed to himself to discover among other things, was,—how far and how truly these dozen tradesmen voiced the mind of the People over whom he was elected to reign? Here was a problem, and one not easy to solve. But what was very plain and paramount to his mind was this,—that he was thoroughly sick and tired of being no more than a 'social' figure in the world's affairs. It was an effeminate part to play. It was time, he considered, that he should intelligently try his own strength, and test the nation's quality.

"If there is corruption in the state," he said to himself, "I will find its centre! If I am fooled by my advisers then I will be fooled no longer. With whatsoever brain and heart and reason and understanding the Fates have endowed me, I will study the ways, the movements, the desires of my people, and prove myself their friend, as well as their king. Suppose they misunderstand me?—What matter!—Let the nation rise against me an' it will, so that I may, before I die, prove myself worthy of the mere gift of manhood! To-day"—and, rising from his chair, he advanced a step or two and faced the sea and sky with an unconscious gesture of invocation; "To-day shall be the first day of my real monarchy! To-day I begin to reign! The past is past,—for eighteen long years as prince and heir to the throne I trifled away my time among the follies of the hour, and laughed at the easy purchase I could make of the assumed 'honour' of men and women; and I enjoyed the liberty and license of my position. Since then, for three years I have been the prisoner of my Parliament,—but now—now, and for the rest of the time granted to me on earth, I will live my life in the belief that its riddle must surely meet with God's own explanation. To me it has become evident that the laws of Nature make for Truth and Justice; while the laws of man are framed on deception and injustice. The two sets of laws contend one against the other, and the finite, after foolish and vain struggle, succumbs to the infinite,—better therefore, to begin with the infinite Order than strive with the finite Chaos! I, a mere earthly sovereign, rank myself on the side of the Infinite,— and will work for Truth and Justice with the revolving of Its giant wheel! My people have seen me crowned,—but my real Coronation is to- day— when I crown myself with my own resolve!"

His eyes flashed in the sunshine;—a rose shook its pink petals on the ground at his feet. In one of the many pleasure-boats skimming across the sea, a man was singing; and the words he sang floated distinctly along on the landward wind.

> "Let me be thine, O love,
> But for an hour! I yield my heart and soul
> Into thy power,—Let me be thine, O Love of mine,
> But for an hour!"

The King listened, and a faint shadow darkened the proud light on his face.

"'But for an hour!'" he said half aloud—"Yes,—it would be enough! No woman's love lasts longer!"

CHAPTER III
A NATION OR A CHURCH?

AN approaching step echoing on the marble terrace warned him that he was no longer alone. He reseated himself at his writing-table, and feigned to be deeply engrossed in perusing various documents, but a ready smile greeted the intruder as soon as he perceived who it was,— one Sir Roger de Launay, his favourite equerry and intimate personal friend.

"Time's up, is it, Roger?" he queried lightly,—then as the equerry bowed in respectful silence—"And yet I have scarcely glanced at these papers! All the same, I have not been idle—I have been thinking."

Sir Roger de Launay, a tall handsome man, with an indefinable air of mingled good-nature and lassitude about him which suggested the possibility of his politely urging even Death itself not to be so much of a bore about its business, smiled doubtfully. "Is it a wise procedure, Sir?" he enquired—"Conducive to comfort I mean?"

The King laughed.

"No—I cannot say that it is! But thought is a tonic which sometimes restores a man's enfeebled self-respect. I was beginning to lose that particular condition of health and sanity, Roger!—my self-respect was becoming a flaccid muscle—a withering nerve;—but a little thought- exercise has convinced me that my mental sinews are yet on the whole strong!"

Sir Roger offered no reply. His eyes expressed a certain languid wonderment; but duty being paramount with him, and his immediate errand being to remind his sovereign of an appointment then about due, he began to collect the writing materials scattered about on the table and put them together for convenient removal. The smile on the King's face deepened as he watched him.

"You do not answer me, De Launay,"—he resumed, "You think perhaps that I am talking in parables, and that my mind has been persuaded into a metaphysical and rambling condition by an hour's contemplation of the sunlight on the sea! But come now!—have you not yourself felt a longing to break loose from the trammels of conventional routine,—to be set free from the slavery of answering another's beck and call,—to be something more than my attendant and friend——"

"Sir, more than your friend I have never desired to be!" said Sir Roger, simply.

The King extended his hand with impulsive quickness, and Sir Roger as he clasped it, bent low and touched it with his lips. There was no parasitical homage in the act, for De Launay loved his sovereign with a love little known at courts; loyally, faithfully, and without a particle of self-seeking. He had long recognized the nobility, truth and courage which graced and tempered the disposition of the master he served, and knew him to be one, if not the only, monarch in the world likely to confer some lasting benefit on his people by his reign.

"I tell you," pursued the King, "that there is something in the mortal composition of every man which is beyond mortality, something which clamours to be heard, and seen, and proved. We may call it conscience, intellect, spirit or soul, and attribute its existence, to God, as a spark of the Divine Essence, but whatever it is, it is in every one of us; and there comes a moment in life when it must flame out, or be quenched forever. That moment has come to me, Roger,—that something in me must have its way!"

"Your Majesty no doubt desires the impossible!"—said Sir Roger with a smile, "All men do,—even kings!"

"'Even kings!'" echoed the monarch—"You may well say 'even' kings! What are kings? Simply the most wronged and miserable men on earth! I do not myself put in a special claim for pity. My realm is small, and my people are, for aught I can learn or am told of them, contented. But other sovereigns who are my friends and neighbours, live, as it were, under the dagger's point,—with dynamite at their feet and pistols at their heads,—all for no fault of their own, but for the faults of a system which they did not formulate. Conspirators on the threshold— poison in the air,—as in Russia, for example!—where is the joy or the pride of being a King nowadays?"

"Talking of poison," said Sir Roger blandly, as he placed the last document of those he had collected, neatly in a leather case and strapped it—"Your Majesty may perhaps feel inclined to defer giving the promised audience to Monsignor Del Fords of the Society of Jesus?"

"By Heaven, I had forgotten him!" and the King rose. "This is what you came to remind me of, Roger? He is here?"

De Launay bowed an assent.

"Well! We have kept a messenger of Mother Church waiting our pleasure, —and not for the first time in the annals of history! But why do you associate his name with poison?"

"Really, Sir, the connection is inexplicable,—unless it be the memory of a religious lesson-book given to me in my childhood. It was an illustrated treasure, and one picture showed me the Almighty in the character of an old gentleman seated placidly on a cloud, smiling;— while on the earth below, a priest, exactly resembling this Del Fortis, poured a spoonful of something,—poison—or it might have been boiling lead—down the throat of a heretic. I remember it impressed me very much with the goodness of God."

He maintained a whimsical gravity as he spoke, and the King laughed.

"De Launay, you are incorrigible! Come!—we will go within and see this Del Fortis, and you shall remain present during the audience. That will give you a chance to improve your present impression of him. I understand he is a very brilliant and leading member of his Order,— likely to be the next Vicar-General. I know his errand,—the papers concerning his business are there—," and he waved his hand towards the leather case Sir Roger had just fastened—"Bring them with you!"

Sir Roger obeyed, and the King, stepping forth from the pavilion, walked slowly along the terrace, watching the sparkling sea, the flowering orange-trees lifting their slender tufts of exquisitely scented bloom against the clear blue of the sky, the birds skimming lightly from point to point of foliage, and the white-sailed yachts dipping gracefully as the ocean rose and fell with every wild sweet breath of the scented wind. Pausing a moment, he presently took out a field-glass and looked through it at one of the finest and fairest of these pleasure-vessels, which, as he surveyed it, suddenly swung round, and began to scud away westward.

"The Prince is on board?" he asked.

"Yes, Sir," replied De Launay—"His Royal Highness intends sailing as far as The Islands, and remaining there till sunset."

"Alone, as usual?"

"As usual, Sir, alone, save for his captain and crew."

The King walked on in silence for a minute. Then he paused abruptly.

"I do not like it, De Launay!"—he said decisively—"I do not like his abnormal love of solitude. Books are all very well—poetry is in its way excellent,—music, as we are told 'hath charms'—but the boy broods too much, and stays away too much from Court. What woman attracts him?"

Sir Roger's eyes opened wide as the King turned suddenly round upon him with this question.

"Woman, Sir? I know of none. The Prince is but twenty——"

"At twenty," said the King,—"boys love—the wrong girl. At thirty they marry—the wrong woman. At forty they meet the only true and fitting soul's companion,—and cry for the moon till the end! My son is in the first stage, or I am much mistaken,—he loves—the wrong girl!"

He walked on,—and De Launay followed, with a vague sense of amusement and disquietude in his mind. What had come to his Royal master, he wondered? His ordinary manner had changed somewhat,—he spoke with less than the customary formality, and there was an expression of freedom and authority, combined with a touch of defiance in his face, that was altogether new to the observation of the faithful equerry.

Arrived at the palace, and passing through one of the long and spacious painted corridors, lit by richly coloured mullioned windows from end to end, the King came face to face with a lady-in-waiting carrying a large cluster of Madonna lilies. She drew aside, with a deep reverence, to allow him to pass; but he stopped a moment, looking at the great gorgeous white flowers faint with fragrance, and at the slight retiring figure of the woman who held them.

"Are these for the chapel, Madame?" he asked.

"No, Sir! For the Queen."

'For the Queen!' A quick sigh escaped him. He still stood, caught by a sudden abstraction, looking at the dazzling whiteness of the snowy blooms, and thinking how fittingly they would companion his beautiful, cold, pure Queen Consort, who had never from her marriage day uttered a word of love to him, or given him a glance of tenderness. Their rich odours crept into his warm blood, and the bitter old sense of unfulfilled longing, longing for affection, for comprehension, for all that he had not possessed in his otherwise brilliant life, vexed and sickened him. He turned away abruptly, and the lady-in-waiting, having curtsied once more profoundly, passed on with her glistening sheaf of bloom and disappeared vision-like in a gleam of azure light falling through one of the further and higher casements. The King watched her disappear, the meditative line of sadness still puckering his brow, then, followed by his equerry, he entered a small private audience chamber, where Sir Roger de Launay notified an attendant gentleman usher that his Majesty was ready to receive Monsignor Del Fortis.

During the brief interval occupied in waiting for his visitor's approach, the King selected certain papers from those which Sir Roger had brought from the garden pavilion and placed them in order on the table.

"For the past six months," he said "I have had this Jesuit's name before me, and have been in twenty minds a month about granting or refusing what his Society demands. The matter has been discussed in the Press, too, with the usual pros and cons of hesitation, but it is the People I am thinking of, the People! and I am just now in the humour to satisfy a Nation rather than a Church!"

De Launay said nothing. His opinion was not asked.

"It is a case in which the temporal overbalances the spiritual," continued the King—"Which plainly proves that the spiritual must be lacking in some essential point somewhere. For if the spiritual were always truly of God, then would it always be the strongest. The question which brings Monsignor Del Fortis here as special emissary of the Vicar-General of the Society of Jesus, is simply this: Whether or no a certain site in a particularly fertile tract of land belonging chiefly to the Crown, shall be granted to the Jesuits for the purpose of building thereon a church and monastery with schools attached. It seems a reasonable request, set forth with an apparently religious intention. Yet more than forty petitions have been sent in to me from the inhabitants of the towns and villages adjacent to the lands, imploring me to refuse the concession. By my faith, they plead as eloquently as though asking deliverance from the plague! It is a curious dilemma. If I grant the people's request I anger the priests; if I satisfy the priests I anger the people."

"You mentioned a discussion in the Press, Sir—" hinted Sir Roger.

"Oh, the Press is like a weathercock—it turns whichever way the wind of speculation blows. One day it is 'for,' another 'against.' In this particular case it is diplomatically indifferent, except in one or two cases where papal money has found its way into the newspaper offices."

At that moment the door was flung open, and Monsignor Del Fortis was ceremoniously ushered into the presence of his Majesty. At the first glance it was evident that De Launay had reasonable cause for associating the mediaeval priestly torturer pictured in his early lesson-book with the unprepossessing personage now introduced. Del Fortis was a dark, resentful-looking man of about sixty, tall and thin, with a long cadaverous face, very strongly pronounced features and small sinister eyes, over which the level brows almost met across the sharp bridge of nose. His close black garb buttoned to the chin, outlined his wiry angular limbs with an almost painful distinctness, and the lean right hand which he placed across his breast as he bowed profoundly to the King, looked more like the shrunken hand of a corpse than that of a living man. The King observed him attentively, but not with favour; while thoughts, strange, and for him as a constitutional monarch audacious, began to move in the undercurrents of his mind, stirring him to unusual speech and action. Sir Roger, retiring to the furthest end of the room stood with his back against the door, a fine upright soldierly figure, as motionless as though cast in bronze, though his eyes showed keen and sparkling life as they rested on his Royal master, watching his every gesture, as well as every slightest movement on the part of his priestly visitor.

"You are welcome, Monsignor Del Fortis,"—said the King, at last breaking silence.—"To save time and trouble, I may tell you that I need no explanation of the nature of your business."

The Jesuit bowed with an excessive humility.

"You wish me to grant to your Society," continued the monarch—"that portion of the Crown lands named in your petition, to be held in your undisputed possession for a long term of years,—and in order to facilitate my consent to this arrangement, your Vicar-General has sent you here to furnish the full details of your building scheme. Am I so far correct?"

The priest's dark secretive eyes glittered craftily a moment as he raised them to the open and tranquil countenance of the sovereign,— then once again he bowed profoundly.

"Your Majesty has, with your customary care and patience, fully studied the object of my errand"—he replied in a clear thin, somewhat rasping voice, which he endeavoured to make smooth and conciliatory—"But it is impossible that your Majesty, immersed every day in the affairs of state, should have found time to personally go through the various papers formally submitted to your consideration. Therefore, the Vicar- General of our Order considered that if the present interview with your Majesty could be obtained, I, as secretary and treasurer for the proposed new monastery, might be able to explain the spiritual, as well as the material advantages to be gained by the use of the lands for the purpose mentioned."

He spoke slowly, enunciating each word with careful distinctness.

"The spiritual part of the scheme is of course the most important to you!"—said the King with a slight smile,—"But material advantages are never entirely overlooked, even by holy men! Now I am merely a 'temporal' sovereign; and as such, I wish to know how your plan will affect the people of the neighbouring town and district. What are your intentions towards them? Their welfare is my chief concern; and what I have to learn from you is,—How do you propose to benefit them by maintaining a monastery, church and schools in their vicinity?"

Again Del Fortis gave a furtive glance upward. Seeing that the King's eyes were steadily fixed upon him, he quickly lowered his own, and gave answer in an evidently prepared manner.

"Sir, the people of the district in question are untaught barbarians. It is more for their sakes,—more for the love of gathering the lost sheep into the fold, than for our own satisfaction, that we seek to pitch our tents in the desert of their ignorance. They, and their children, are the prey of heathenish modern doctrines, which alas!— are too prevalent throughout the whole world at this particular time,— and, as they are at present situated, no restraint is exercised upon them for the better controlling of their natural and inherited vices. Unless the gentle hand of Mother Church is allowed to rescue these, her hapless and neglected ones; unless she has an opportunity afforded her of leading them out of the darkness of error into the light of eternal day—"

He broke off, his eloquence being interrupted by a gesture from the King.

"There is a Government school in the town,"—said the monarch, referring to one or two documents on the table before him.—"There is also a Free Public Library, and a Free School of Art. Thus it does not seem that education is quite neglected."

"Alas, Sir, such education is merely disastrous!" said Del Fortis, with a deep sigh,—"Like the fruit on the tree of knowledge in the Garden of Eden, it brings death to the soul!"

"You condemn the Government methods?" asked the King coldly.

The Jesuit moved uneasily, and a dull flush reddened his pale skin.

"Far be it from me, Sir, as a poor servant of the Church, to condemn lawful authorities,—yet we should not forget that the Government is temporal and changeable,—the Church is spiritual and changeless. We cannot look for entire success in a scheme of popular education which is not formulated under the guidance or the blessing of God!"

The King leaned forward a little in his chair, and surveyed him fixedly.

"How do you know that it is not formulated under the guidance and blessing of God?" he asked suddenly—"Has the Almighty given you His special opinion and confidence on the matter?"

Monsignor Del Fortis started indignantly.

"Sir! Your Majesty——"

De Launay made a step forward, but the King motioned him back. Accordingly he resumed his former position, but his equable temperament was for once seriously disturbed. He saw that his Royal master was evidently bent on speaking his mind; and he knew well what a dangerous indulgence that is for all men who desire peace and quietness in their lives.

"I am aware of what you would say," pursued the King—"You would say that the Church—your Church—is the only establishment of the kind which receives direct inspiration from the Creator of Universes. But I do not feel justified in limiting the control of the Almighty to one special orbit of Creed. You tell me that a government system of education for the people is a purely temporal movement, and that, as such, it is not blessed by the guidance of God. Yet the Pope seeks 'temporal' power! It is explained to us of course that he seeks it in order that he may unite it to the spiritual in his own person,— theoretically for the good of mankind, if practically for the advancement of his own particular policy. But have you never thought,

Monsignor, that the marked severance of what you call 'temporal' power, from what you equally call 'spiritual' power, is God's work? Inasmuch as nothing can be done without God's will; for even if there is a devil (which I am inclined to doubt) he owes his unhappy existence to God as much as I do!"

He smiled; but Del Fortis stood rigidly silent, his head bent, and one hand folded tight across his breast, an attitude Sir Roger de Launay always viewed in every man with suspicion, as it suggested the concealment of a weapon.

"You will admit" pursued the King, "that the action of human thought is always progressive. Unfortunately your Creed lags behind human thought in its onward march, thus causing the intelligent world to infer that there must be something wrong with its teaching. For if the Church had always been in all respects faithful to the teaching of her Divine Master, she would be at this present time the supreme Conqueror of Nations. Yet she is doing no more nowadays than she did in the middle ages,—she threatens, she intimidates, she persecutes all who dare to use for a reasonable purpose the brain God gave them,—but she does not help on or sympathize with the growing fraternity and civilization of the world. It is impossible not to recognize this. Yet I have a profound respect for each and every minister of religion who honestly endeavours to follow the counsels of Christ,"—here he paused,—then added with slow and marked emphasis—"in whose Holy Name I devoutly believe for the redemption of whatever there is in me worth redeeming; —nevertheless my first duty, even in Christ, is plainly to the people of the country over which I am elected to rule."

The flickering shadow of a smile passed over the Jesuit's dark features, but he still kept silence.

"Therefore," went on the King—"it is my unpleasant task to be compelled to inform you, Monsignor, that the inhabitants of the district your Order seeks to take under its influence, have the strongest objection to your presence among them. So strong indeed is their aversion towards your Society, that they have petitioned me in numerous ways, (and with considerable eloquence, too, for 'untaught barbarians') to defend them from your visitation. Now, to speak truly, I find they have all the advantages which modern advancement and social improvement can give them,—they attend their places of public worship in considerable numbers, and are on the whole decent, God-fearing, order-loving subjects to the Throne,—and more

I do not desire for them or for myself. Criminal cases are very rare in the district,—and the poor are more inclined to help than to defraud each other. All this is so far good,—and, I should imagine,—not displeasing to God. In any case, as their merely temporal sovereign, I must decline to give your Order any control over them."

"You refuse the concession of land, Sir?" said Del Fortis, in a voice that trembled with restrained passion.

"To satisfy those of my subjects who have appealed to me, I am compelled to do so," replied the King.

"I pray your Majesty's pardon, but a portion of the land is held by private persons who are prepared to sell to us——"

A quick anger flashed in the King's eyes.

"They shall sell to me if they sell at all,"—he said,—"I repeat, Monsignor, the fact that the law-abiding people of the place have sought their King's protection from priestly interference;—and,—by Heaven!—they shall have it!"

There was a sudden silence. Sir Roger de Launay drew a sharp breath,— his habitual languor of mind was completely dissipated, and he studied the inscrutable face of Del Fortis with deepening suspicion and disfavour. Not that there was the slightest sign of wrath or dismay on the priest's well-disciplined countenance;—on the contrary, a chill smile illumined it as he spoke his next words with a serious, if somewhat forced composure.

"Your Majesty is, without doubt, all powerful in your own particular domain of society and politics," he said—"But there is another Majesty higher than yours,—that of the Church, before which dread and infallible Tribunal even kings are brought to naught——"

"Monsignor Del Fortis," interrupted the King, "We have not met this morning, I presume, to indulge in a religious polemic! My power is, as you very truly suggest, merely temporal—yours is spiritual. Yours should be the strongest! Go your way now to your Vicar-General with the straight answer I have given you,—but if by your 'spiritual' power you can persuade the people who now hate your Society, to love it,—to demand it,—to beg that you may be permitted to found a colony among them,—why, in that case, come to me again, and I will grant you the land. I am not prejudiced one way or the other, but I will not hand over any of my subjects to the influence of priestcraft, so long as they desire me to defend them from it."

Del Fortis still smiled.

"Pardon me, Sir, but we of the Society of Jesus are your subjects also, and we judge you to be a Christian and Catholic monarch——"

"As I am, most assuredly!" replied the King—"Christian and Catholic are words which, if I understand their meaning, please me well! 'Christian' expresses a believer in and follower of Christ,—'Catholic' means universal, by which, I take it, is intended wide, universal love and tolerance without sect, party, or prejudice. In this sense the Church is not Catholic—it is merely the Roman sect. Nor are you truly my subjects, since you have only one ruler, the Supreme Pontiff,—with whom I am somewhat at variance. But, as I have said, we are not here to indulge in argument. You came to proffer a request; I have given you the only answer I conceive fitting with my duty;—the matter is concluded."

Del Fortis hesitated a moment,—then bowed low to the ground;—anon, lifting himself, raised one hand with an invocative gesture of profound solemnity.

"I commend your Majesty to the mercy of God, that He may in His wisdom, guard your life and soften your heart towards the ministers of His Holy Religion, and bring you into the ways of righteousness and peace! For the rest, I will report your Majesty's decision to the Vicar-General."

"Do so!"—rejoined the King—"And assure him that the decision is unalterable,—unless the inhabitants of the place concerned desire to have it revoked."

Again Del Fortis bowed.

"I humbly take my leave of your Majesty!"

The monarch looked at him steadfastly as he made another salutation, and backed out of the presence-chamber. Sir Roger de Launay opened the door for him with alacrity, handing him over into the charge of an usher with the whispered caution to see him well off the Royal premises; and then returning to his sovereign, stood "at attention." The King noted his somewhat troubled aspect, and laughed.

"What ails you, De Launay?" he asked—"You seem astonished that for once I have spoken my mind?"

"Sir, to speak one's mind is always dangerous!"

"Dangerous—danger!—What idle words to make cowards of men! Danger—of what? There is only one danger—death; and that is sure to come to every man, whether he be a hero or a poltroon."

"True,—but——"

"But—what? De Launay, if you love me, do not look at me with so expostulatory an air! It does not become your inches! Now listen!—when the next press reporter comes nosing round for palace news, let him be told that the King has refused permission to the Jesuits to build on any portion of the Crown lands demanded for the purpose. Let this be made known to Press and People—the sooner the better!"

"Sir," murmured De Launay—"We live in strange times——"

"Why, there you speak most truly!" said the King, with emphasis—"We do live in strange times—the very strangest perhaps, since Aeneas Sylvius wrote concerning Christendom. Do you remember the words he set down so long ago?—'It is a body without a head,—a republic without laws or magistrates. The pope or the emperor may shine as lofty titles, as splendid images,—but they are unable to command, and no one is willing to obey!' History thus repeats itself, De Launay;—and yet with all its past experience, the Roman Church does not seem to realize that it is powerless against the attacks of intellectual common sense. Faith in God,—a high, perfect, pure faith in God, and a simple following of the Divine Teacher of God's command, Christ;—these things are wise and necessary for all nations; but, to allow human beings to be coerced by superstition for political motives, under the disguise of religion, is an un-Christian business, and I for one will have no part in it!"

"You will lay yourself open to much serious misconstruction, Sir," said De Launay.

"Let us hope so, Roger!" rejoined the King with a smile—"For if I am never misunderstood, I shall know myself to be a fool! Come,—do not look so glum!—I want you to help me."

"To help you, Sir?" exclaimed De Launay eagerly,—"With my life, if you demand it!"

The King rested one hand familiarly on his shoulder.

"I would rather take my own life than yours, De Launay!" he said—"No, —whatever difficulties I get myself into, you shall not suffer! But—as I told you a while ago,—there is something in me that must have its way. I am sick to death of conventionalities,—you must help me to break through them! You are right in saying that we live in strange times;—they are strange times!—and they may perchance be all the better for a strange King!"

CHAPTER IV
SEALED ORDERS

SOME hours later on, Sir Roger de Launay, having left his Sovereign's presence, and being off duty for a time, betook himself to certain apartments in the west wing of the palace, where the next most trusted personage to himself in the confidence of the King, had his domicile,— Professor von Glauben, resident physician to the Royal Household. Heinrich von Glauben was a man of somewhat extraordinary character and individuality. In his youth he had made a sudden meteoric fame for his marvellous skill and success in surgery, as also for his equally surprising quickness and correctness in diagnosing obscure diseases and tracing them to their source. But, after creating a vast amount of discussion and opposition among his confreres, and almost reaching that brilliant point of triumph when his originality and cleverness were proved great enough to win him a host of enemies, he all at once threw up the game as it were, and, resigning the favourable opportunities of increasing distinction offered him in his native Germany, accepted the comparatively retired and private position he now occupied. Some said it was a disappointment in love which had caused his abrupt departure from the Fatherland,—others declared it was irritation at the severe manner in which his surgical successes had been handled by the medical critics,—but whatever the cause, it soon became evident that he had turned his back on the country of his birth for ever, and that he was apparently entirely satisfied with the lot he had chosen. His post was certainly an easy and pleasant one,—the members of the Royal family to which his services were attached were exceptionally healthy, as Royal families go; and he was seldom in more than merely formal attendance, so that he had ample time and opportunity to pursue those deeper forms of physiological study which had excited the wrath and ridicule of his contemporaries, as well as to continue the writing of a book which he intended should make a stir in the world, and which he had entitled "The Moral and Political History of Hunger."

"For," said he—"Hunger is the primal civilizer,—the very keystone and foundation of all progress. From the plain, prosy, earthy fact that man is a hungry animal, and must eat, has sprung all the civilization of the world! I shall demonstrate this in my book, beginning with the scriptural legend of Adam's greed for an apple. Adam was evidently hungry at the moment Eve tempted him. As soon as he had satisfied his inner man, he thought of his outer,—and his next idea was, naturally, tailoring. From this simple conjunction of suggestions, combined with what 'God' would have to say to him concerning his food-experiment and fig-leaf apron, man has drawn all his religions, manners, customs and morals. The proposition is self-evident,—but I intend to point it out with somewhat emphasised clearness for the benefit of those persons who are inclined to arrogate to themselves the possession of superior wisdom. Neither brain nor soul has placed man in a position of Supremacy,—merely Hunger and Nakedness!"

The Professor was now about fifty-five, but his exceptionally powerful build and robust constitution gave him the grace in appearance of many years younger, though perhaps the extreme composure of his temperament, and the philosophic manner in which he viewed all circumstances, whether pleasing or disastrous, may have exercised the greatest influence in keeping his eyes clear and clean, and his countenance free of unhandsome wrinkles. He was more like a soldier than a doctor, and was proud of his resemblance to the earlier portraits of Bismarck. To see him in his own particular 'sanctum' surrounded by weird-looking diagrams of sundry parts of the human frame, mysterious phials and stoppered flasks containing various liquids and crystals, and all the modern appliances for closely examining the fearful yet beautiful secrets of the living organism, was as if one should look upon a rough and burly giant engaged in some delicate manipulation of mosaics. Yet Von Glauben's large hand was gentler than a woman's in its touch and gift of healing,—no surgeon alive could probe a wound more tenderly, or with less pain to the sufferer,—and the skill of that large hand was accompanied by the penetrative quality of the large benevolent brain which guided it,—a brain that could encompass the whole circle of the world in its observant and affectionate compassion.

"Ach!—who is there that can be angry with anyone?—impatient with anyone,—offended with anyone!" he was wont to say—"Everybody suffers so much and so undeservedly, that as far as my short life goes I have only time for pity—not condemnation!"

To this individual, as a kind of human calmative and tonic combined, Sir Roger de Launay was in the habit of going whenever he felt his own customary tranquillity at all disturbed. The two were great friends;— friends in their mutual love and service of the King,—friends in their equally mutual but discreetly silent worship of the Queen,—and friends in their very differences of opinion on men and matters in general. De Launay, being younger, was more hasty of judgment and quick in action; but Von Glauben too had been known to draw his sword with unexpected rapidity on occasion, to the discomfiture of those who deemed him only at home with the scalpel. Just now, however, he was in a particularly non-combative and philosophic mood; he was watching certain animalculae wriggling in a glass tube, the while he sat in a large easy-chair with slippered feet resting on another chair opposite, puffing clouds of smoke from a big meerschaum,—and he did not stir from his indolent attitude when De Launay entered, but merely looked up and smiled placidly.

"Sit down, Roger!" he said,—then, as De Launay obeyed the invitation, he pushed over a box of cigars, and added—"You look exceedingly tired, my friend! Something has bored you more than usual? Take a lesson from those interesting creatures!" and he pointed with the stem of his pipe to the bottled animalculae— "They are never bored,—never weary of doing mischief! They are just now living under the pleasing delusion that the glass tube they are in is a man, and that they are eating him up alive. Little devils! Nothing will exhaust their vitality till they have gorged themselves to death! Just like a great many human beings!"

"I am not in the mood for studying animalculae," said De Launay irritably, as he lit a cigar.

"No? But why not? They are really quite as interesting as ourselves!"

"Look here, Von Glauben, I want you to be serious—"

"My friend, I am always serious," declared the Professor—"Even when I laugh, I laugh seriously. My laughter is as real as myself."

"What would you think,"—pursued De Launay—"of a king who freely expressed his own opinions?"

"I should say he was a brave man," answered the Professor; "He would certainly deserve my respect, and he should have it. Even if the laws of etiquette were not existent, I should feel justified in taking off my hat to him."

"Never from henceforth wear a hat at all then," said De Launay—"It will save you the trouble of continually doffing it at every glimpse of his Majesty!"

Von Glauben drew his pipe from his mouth and gazed blankly at the ceiling for a few moments in silence. "His Majesty?" he presently murmured—"Our Majesty?"

"Yes; our Majesty—our King"—replied De Launay—"For some inscrutable reason or other he has suddenly adopted the dangerous policy of speaking his mind. What now?"

"What now? Why nothing particular just now,—unless you have something to tell me. Which, judging from your entangled expression of eye, I presume you have."

De Launay hesitated a moment. The Professor saw his hesitation.

"Do not speak, my friend, if you think you are committing a breach of confidence," he said composedly—"In the brief affairs of this life, it is better to keep trouble on your own mind than impart it to others."

"Oh, there is no breach of confidence;" said De Launay, "The thing is as public as the day, or if it is not public already, it soon will be made so. That is where the mischief comes in,—or so I think. Judge for yourself!" And in a few words he gave the gist of the interview which had taken place between the King and the emissary of the Jesuits that morning.

"Nothing surprises me as a rule,"—said the Professor, when he had heard all—"But if anything could prick the sense of astonishment anew in me, it would be to think that anyone, king or commoner, should take the trouble to speak truth to a Jesuit. Why, the very essence of their carefully composed and diplomatic creed, is to so disguise truth that it shall be no more recognisable. Myself, I believe the Jesuits to be the lineal descendants of those priests who served Bel and the Dragon. The art of conjuring and deception is in their very blood. It is for the Jesuits that I have invented a beautiful new verb,—'To hypocrise.' It sounds well. Here is the present tense,—'I hypocrise, Thou hypocrisest, He hypocrises:—We hypocrise, You hypocrise, They hypocrise.' Now hear the future. 'I shall hypocrise, Thou shalt hypocrise, He shall hypocrise; We shall hypocrise, You shall hypocrise, They shall hypocrise.' There is the whole art of Jesuitry for you, made grammatically perfect!"

De Launay gave a gesture of impatience, and flung away the end of his half-smoked cigar.

"Ach! That is a sign of temper, Roger!" said Von Glauben, shaking his head—"To lift one's shoulders to the lobes of one's ears, and waste nearly the half of an exceedingly expensive and choice Havana, shows nervous irritation! You are angry, my friend—and with me!"

"No I am not," replied De Launay, rising from his chair and beginning to pace the room—"But I do not profess to have your phlegmatic disposition. I feel what I thought you would feel also,—that the King is exposing himself to unnecessary danger. And I know what you do not yet know, but what this letter will no doubt inform you,"—and he drew an envelope bearing the Royal seal from his pocket and handed it to the Professor—"Namely,—that his Majesty is bent on rushing voluntarily into various other perils, unless perhaps, your warning or advice may hinder him. Mine has no effect,—moreover I am bound to serve him as he bids."

"Equally am I also bound to serve him;"—said Von Glauben, "And gladly and faithfully do I intend to perform my service wherever it may lead me!" Whereupon, shaking himself out of his recumbent position, like a great lion rolling out of his lair, he stood upright, and breaking the seal of the envelope he held, read its contents through in silence. Sir Roger stood opposite to him, watching his face in vain for any sign of astonishment, regret or dismay.

"We must do as he commands,"—he said simply as he finished reading the letter and folded it up for safe keeping—"There is no other way; not for me at least. I shall most assuredly be at the appointed place, at the appointed hour, and in the appointed manner. It will be a change; certainly lively, and possibly beneficial!"

"But the King's life—"

"Is in God's keeping!" said Von Glauben,—"Believe me, Roger, no harm comes undeservedly to a brave man with a good conscience! It is a bad conscience which invites mischief. I am a great believer in the law of attraction. The good attracts the good,—the bad, the bad. That is why truthful persons are generally lonely—because nearly all the world's inhabitants are liars!"

"But the King—" again began Sir Roger.

"The King is a man!" said Von Glauben, with a flash of pride in his eyes—
"Which is more than I will say for most kings! Who shall blame him for asserting
his manhood? Not I! Not you! Who shall blame him for seeking to know the real
position of things in the country he governs? Not I! Not you! Our business is to
guard and defend him—with our own lives, if necessary,—we shall do that with
a will, Roger, shall we not?" And with an impulsive quickness of action, he took a
sword from a stand of weapons near him, drew it from its scabbard and kissing the
hilt, held it out to De Launay who did the same—"That is understood! And for the
rest, Roger my friend, take it all lightly and easily—as a farce!—as a bit of human
comedy, with a great actor cast for the chief role. We are only supers, you and I, but
we shall do well to stand near the wings in case of fire!"

He drew himself up to his great height and squared his shoulders,—then smiled
benevolently.

"I believe it will be all very amusing, Roger; and that your fears for the safety of
his Majesty will be proved groundless. Remember, Court life is excessively dull,—
truly the dullest form of existence on earth,—it is quite natural that he who is the
most bored by it should desire some break in the terrible monotony!"

"The monotony will certainly be broken with a vengeance, if the King contin-
ues in his present humour!"—said De Launay grimly.

"Possibly! And let us hope the comfortable self-assurance and complacency of
a certain successful Minister may be somewhat seriously disturbed!" rejoined Von
Glauben,—"For myself, I assure you I see sport!"

"And I scent danger,"—said De Launay—"For if any mischance happen to the
King, the Prince is not ripe enough to rule."

A slight shadow darkened the Professor's open countenance. He looked fixedly
at Sir Roger, who met his gaze with equal fixity.

"The Prince,"—he said slowly—"is young—"

"And rash—" interposed De Launay.

"No. Pardon me, my friend! Not rash. Merely honest. That is all! He is a very
honest young man indeed. It is unfortunate that he is so; a ploughman may be honest if he likes, but a prince—never!"

De Launay was silent.

"I will now destroy a world"—continued Von Glauben, "Kings, emperors, popes, councillors and common folk, can all perish incontinently,—as— being myself for the present the free agent of the Deity concerned in the matter,—I have something else to do than to look after them,"—and he took up the glass vessel containing the animalculae he had been watching, and cast it with its contents into a small stove burning dimly at one end of the apartment,—"Gone are their ambitions and confabulations for ever! How easy for the Creator to do the same thing with us, Roger! Let us not talk of any special danger for the King or for any man, seeing that we are all on the edge of an eternal volcano!"

De Launay stood absorbed for a moment, as if in deep thought. Then rousing himself abruptly he said:—

"You will not see the King, and speak with him before to-morrow night?"

"Why should I?" queried the Professor. "His wish is a command which I must obey. Besides, my good Roger, all the arguments in the world will not turn a man from having his own way if he has once made up his own mind. Advice from me on the present matter would be merely taken as an impertinence. Moreover I have no advice to give,—I rather approve of the plan!"

Sir Roger looked at him; and noting the humorous twinkle in his eyes smiled, though somewhat gravely.

"I hope, with you, that the experiment may only prove an amusing one," he said—"But life is not always a farce!"

"Not always, but often! When it is not a farce it is a tragedy. And such a tragedy! My God! Horrible—monstrous—cruel beyond conception, and enough to make one believe in Hell and doubt Heaven!"

He spoke passionately, in a voice vibrating with strong emotion. De Launay glanced at him wonderingly, but did not speak.

"When you see tender young children tortured by disease," he went on,— "Fair and gentle women made the victims of outrage and brutality— strong men killed in their thousands to gain a little additional gold, an extra slice of empire,—then you see the tragic, the inexplicable, the crazy cruelty of putting into us this little pulse called Life. But I try not to think of this—it is no use thinking!"

He paused,—then in his usual quiet tone said:

"To-morrow night, then, my friend?"

"To-morrow night," rejoined De Launay,—"Unless you receive further instructions from the King."

At that moment the clear call of a trumpet echoing across the battlements of the palace denoted the hour for changing the sentry. "Sunset already!" said Von Glauben, walking to the window and throwing back the heavy curtain which partially shaded it, "And yonder is Prince Humphry's yacht on its homeward way."

De Launay came and stood beside him, looking out. Before them the sea glistened with a thousand tints of lustrous opal in the light of the sinking sun, which, surrounded by mountainous heights of orange and purple cloud, began to touch the water-line with a thousand arrowy darts of flame. The white-sailed vessel on which their eyes were fixed, came curtseying over the waves through a perfect arch of splendid colour, like a fairy or phantom ship evoked from a poet's dream.

"Absent all day, as he has been," said De Launay, "his Royal Highness is punctual to the promised hour of his return."

"He is, as I told you, honest;" said Von Glauben, "and it is possible his honesty will be his misfortune."

De Launay muttered something inaudible in answer, and turned to leave the apartment.

Von Glauben looked at him with an affectionate solicitude.

"What a lucky thing it is you never married, Roger! Otherwise you would now be going to tell your wife all about the King's plans! Then she, sweet creature, would go to confession,—and her confessor would tell a bishop,—and a bishop would tell a cardinal,—and a cardinal would tell a confidential monsignor,—and the confidential monsignor would tell the Supreme Pontiff,—and so all the world would be ringing with the news started by one little pretty wagging tongue of a woman!"

A faint flush coloured De Launay's bronzed cheek, but he laughed.

"True! I am glad I have never married. I am still more glad—of circumstances"— he paused,—then went on, "which have so chanced to me that I shall never marry." He paused again—then added—"I must be gone, Von Glauben! I have to meet Prince Humphry at the quay with a message from his Majesty."

"Surely," said the Professor, opening his eyes very wide, "The Prince is not to be included in our adventure?"

"By no means!" replied De Launay,—"But the King is not pleased with his son's frequent absences from Court, and desires to speak with him on the matter."

Von Glauben looked grave.

"There will be some little trouble there," he said, with a half sigh— "Ach! Who knows! Perhaps some great trouble!"

"Heaven forbid!" ejaculated Sir Roger,—"We live in times of peace. We want no dissension with either the King or the people. Till to-morrow night then?"

"Till to-morrow night!" responded Von Glauben, whereupon Sir Roger with a brief word of farewell, strode away.

Left to himself, the Professor still stood at his window watching the approach of the Prince's yacht, which came towards the shore with such swift and stately motion through the portals of the sunset, over the sparkling water.

"Unfortunate Humphry!" he muttered,—"What a secret he has entrusted me with! And yet why do I call him unfortunate? There should be nothing to regret— and yet—! Well! The mischief was done before poor Heinrich von Glauben was consulted; and if poor Heinrich were God and the Devil rolled into one strange Eternal Monster, he could not have prevented it! What is done, can never be undone!"

CHAPTER V
"IF I LOVED YOU!"

A singular pomp is sometimes associated with the announcement that my Lord Pedigree, or Mister Nobody has 'had the honour of dining' with their Majesties the King and Queen. Outsiders read the thrilling line with awe and envy,—and many of them are foolish enough to wish that they also were Lords Pedigree or Misters Nobody. As a matter of sad and sober fact, however, a dinner with royal personages is an extremely dull affair. 'Do not speak unless you are spoken to,' is a rule which, however excellent and necessary in Court etiquette, is apt to utterly quench conversation, and render the brightest spirits dull and inert. The silent and solemn movements of the Court flunkeys,—the painful attitudes of those who are *not* 'spoken to'; the eager yet laboured smiles of those who *are* 'spoken to ';—the melancholy efforts at gaiety—the dread of trespassing on tabooed subjects—these things tend to make all but the most independent and unfettered minds shrink from such an ordeal as the 'honour' of dining with kings. It must, however, be conceded that the kings themselves are fully aware of the tediousness of their dinner parties, and would lighten the boredom if they could; but etiquette forbids. The particular monarch whose humours are the subject of this 'plain unvarnished' history would have liked nothing better than to be allowed to dine in simplicity and peace without his conversation being noted, and without having a flunkey at hand to watch every morsel of food go into his mouth. He would have liked to eat freely, talk freely, and conduct himself generally with the ease of a private gentleman.

All this being denied to him, he hated the dinner-hour as ardently as he hated receiving illuminated addresses, and the freedom of cities. Yet all things costly and beautiful were combined to make his royal table a picture which would have pleased the eyes and taste of a Marguerite de Valois. On the evening of the day on which he had determined, as he had said to himself, to 'begin to reign,' it looked more than usually attractive. Some trifling chance had made the floral decorations more tasteful—some amiable humour of the providence which rules daily events, had ordained that two or three of the prettiest Court ladies should be present;— Prince Humphry and his two brothers, Rupert and Cyprian, were at table,—and though conversation was slow and scant, the picturesqueness of the scene was not destroyed by silence. The apartment which was used as a private dining-room when their Majesties had no guests save the members of their own household, was in it- self a gem of art and architecture,—it had been designed and painted from floor to ceiling by one of the most famous of the dead and gone masters, and its broad windows opened out on a white marble loggia fronting the ocean, where festoons of flowers clambered and hung, in natural tufts and trails of foliage and blossom, mingling their sweet odours with the fresh scent of the sea. Amid all the glow and delicacy of colour, the crowning perfection of the perfect environment was the Queen-Consort, lovelier in her middle-age than most women in their teens. An ex- quisite figure of stateliness and dignity, robed in such hues and adorned with such jewels as best suited her statuesque beauty, and attended by ladies of whose more youthful charms she was never envious, having indeed no cause for envy, she was a living defiance to the ravages of time, and graced her royal husband's dinner-table with the same indifferent ease as she graced his throne, unchanging in the dazzling light of her physical faultlessness. He, looking at her with mingled impatience and sadness, almost wished she would grow older in appearance with her years, and lose that perfect skin, white as alabaster,—that glittering but cold luminance of eye. For experience had taught him the worthlessness of beauty unaccompanied by tender- ness, and fair faces had no longer the first attraction for him. His eldest son, Prince Humphry, bore a strong resemblance to himself,—he was tall and slim, with a fine face, and a well-built muscular figure; the other two younger princes, Rupert and Cyprian, aged respectively eighteen and sixteen, were like their mother,—beautiful in form and feature, but as indifferent to all tenderness of thought and sentiment as they were full of splendid health and vigour. And, despite the fact that the composition and surroundings of his household were, to all outward appearances, as satisfactory as a man in his position could expect them to be, the King was intellectually and spiritually aware of the emptiness of the shell he called 'home.'

Love was lacking; his beautiful wife was the ice-wall against which all waves of feeling froze as they fell into the stillness of death. His sons had been born as the foals of a racing stud might be born,—merely to continue the line of blood and succession. They were not the dear offspring of passion or of tenderness. The coldness of their mother's nature was strongly engendered in them, and so far they had never shown any particular affection for their parents. The princes Rupert and Cyprian thought of nothing all day but sports and games of skill; they studied serious tasks unwillingly, and found their position as sons of the reigning monarch, irksome, and even ridiculous. They had caught the infection of that diseased idea which in various exaggerated forms is tending to become more or less universal, and to work great mischief to nations,—namely, that 'sport' is more important than policy, and that all matters relating to 'sport,' are more worth attention than wisdom in government. Of patriotism, or love of country they had none; and laughed to scorn the grand old traditions and sentiments of national glory and honour, which had formerly inspired the poets of their land to many a wild and beautiful chant of battle or of victory. How to pass the day—how best to amuse themselves—this was their first thought on waking every morning,—football, cricket, tennis and wrestling formed their chief subjects of conversation; and though they had professors and tutors of the most qualified and certificated ability, they made no secret of their utter contempt for all learning and literature. They were fine young animals; but did less with the brains bestowed upon them than the working bee who makes provision of honey for the winter, or the swallow that builds its nest under warmly sheltered eaves.

Prince Humphry, however, was of a different nature. From a shy, somewhat unmanageable boy, he had developed into a quiet, dreamy youth, fond of books, music, and romantic surroundings. He avoided the company of his brothers whenever it was possible; their loud voices, boisterous spirits and perpetual chatter concerning the champions of this or that race or match, bored him infinitely, and he was at no pains to disguise his boredom. During the last year he seemed to have grown up suddenly into full manhood,—he had begun to assert his privileges as

Heir- Apparent, and to enjoy the freedom his position allowed him. Yet the manner of his enjoyment was somewhat singular for a young man who formed a central figure in the circle of the land's Royalty,—he cared nothing at all for the amusements and dissipations of the time; he merely showed an abnormal love of solitude, which was highly unflattering to fashionable society. It was on this subject that the King had decided to speak with him,—and he watched him with closer attention than usual on this particular evening when his habit of absenting himself all day in his yacht had again excited comment. It was easy to see that the Prince had been annoyed by the message Sir Roger de Launay had conveyed to him on his arrival home,—a message to the effect that, as soon as dinner was concluded, he was required to attend his Majesty in private; and all through the stately and formal repast, his evident irritation and impatience cast a shadow of vague embarrassment over the royal party,—with the exception of the princes Rupert and Cyprian, who were never embarrassed by anything, and who were more apt to be amused than disquieted by the vexation of others. Welcome relief was at last given by the serving of coffee,—and the Queen and all her ladies adjourned to their own apartments. With their departure the rest of the circle soon dispersed, there being no special guests present; and at a sign from De Launay, Prince Humphry reluctantly followed his father into a small private smoking-room adjacent to the open loggia, where the equerry, bowing low, left the two together.

For a moment the King kept silence, while he chose a cigar from the silver box on the table. Then, lighting it, he handed the box courteously to his son.

"Will you smoke, Humphry?"

"Thanks, Sir,—no."

The King seated himself; Prince Humphry remained standing.

"You had a favourable wind for your expedition today;" said the monarch at last, beginning to smoke placidly—"I observe that The Islands appear to have won special notice from you. What is the attraction? The climate or the scenery?"

The Prince was silent.

"I like fine scenery myself,—" continued the King—"I also like a change of air. But variation in both is always desirable,—and for this, it is unwise to go to the same place every day!"

Still the Prince said nothing. His father looked up and studied his face attentively, but could guess nothing from its enigmatical expression.

"You seem tongue-tied, Humphry!" he said—"Come, sit down! Let us talk this out. Can you not trust me, your father, as a friend?"

"I wish I could!" answered the young man, half inaudibly.

"And can you not?"

"No. You have never loved me!"

The King drew his cigar from his mouth, and flicking off a morsel of ash, looked at its end meditatively.

"Well—no!—I cannot say honestly that I have. Love,—it is a ridiculous word, Humphry, but it has a meaning on certain occasions!— love for the children of your mother is an impossibility!"

"Sir, I am not to blame for my mother's disposition."

"True—very true. You are not to blame. But you exist. And that you do exist is a fact of national importance. Will you not sit down?"

"At your command, Sir!" and the Prince seated himself opposite his father, who having studied his cigar sufficiently, replaced it between his lips and went on smoking for a few minutes before he spoke again. Then he resumed:—

"Your existence, I repeat, Humphry, is a fact of national importance. To you falls the Throne when I have done with it, and life has done with me. Therefore, your conduct,—your mode of life—your example in manners—concern, not me, so much as the nation. You say that you cannot trust me as a friend, because I have never loved you. Is not this a somewhat childish remark on your part? We live in a very practical age—love is not a necessary tie between human beings as things go nowadays;—the closest bond of friendship rests on the basis of cash accounts."

"I am perfectly aware of that!" said the Prince, fixing his fine dark eyes full on his father's face—"And yet, after all, love is such a vital necessity, that I have only to look at you, in order to realize the failure and mistake of trying to do without it!"

The King gave him a glance of whimsical surprise.

"So!—you have begun to notice what I have known for years!" he said lightly— "Clever young man! What fine fairy finger is pointing out to you my deficiencies, while supplying your own? Do you learn to estimate the priceless value of love while contemplating the romantic groves and woodlands of The Islands? Do you read poetry there?—or write it? Or talk it?"

Prince Humphry coloured,—then grew very pale.

"When I misuse my time, Sir," he said—"Surely it will then be needful to cat-echise me on the manner in which I spend it,—but not till then!"

"Fairly put!" answered the King—"But I have an idea—it may be a mistaken idea,—still I have it—that you *are* misusing your time, Humphry! And this is the cause of our present little discussion. If I knew that you occupied yourself with the pleasures befitting your age and rank, I should be more at ease."

"What do you consider to be the pleasures befitting my age and rank?" asked the Prince with a touch of satire; "Making a fool of myself generally?"

The King smiled.

"Well!—it would be better to make a fool of yourself generally than particu-larly! Folly is not so harmful when spread like jam over a whole slice of bread,—but it may cause a life-long sickness, if swallowed in one secret gulp of sweetness!"

The Prince moved uneasily.

"You think I am catechising you,—and you resent it—but, my dear boy, let me again remind you that you are in a manner answerable to the nation for your ac-tions; and especially to that particular section of the nation called Society. Society is the least and worst part of the whole community—but it has to be considered by such servants of the public as ourselves. You know what James the First of England wrote concerning the 'domestic regulations' on the conduct of a prince and future king? 'A king is set as one on a stage, whose smallest, actions and gestures all the people gazinglie do behold; and, however just in the discharge of his office, yet if his behaviour be light or dissolute, in indifferent actions, the people, who see but the outward part, conceive preoccupied conceits of the king's inward intention, which although with time, the trier of all truth, will evanish by the evidence of the con-trarie effect, yet, *interim patitur justus*, and prejudged conceits will, in the meantime, breed contempt, the mother of rebellion and disorder.' Poor James of the 'goggle eyes and large hysterical heart' as Carlyle describes him! Do you not agree with his estimate of a royal position?"

"I am not aware, Sir, that my behaviour can as yet be called light or dissolute;" replied the Prince coldly, with a touch of hauteur.

"I do not call it so, Humphry"—said the King—"To the best of my knowledge, your conduct has always been most exemplary. But with all your excessive decorum, you are mysterious. That is bad! Society will not endure being kept in the dark, or outside the door of things, like a bad child! It wants to be in the room, and know everything and everybody. And this reminds me of another point on which the good English James offers sound advice. 'Remember to be plaine and sensible in your language; for besides, it is the tongue's office to be the messenger of the mind, it may be thought a point of imbecilitie of spirit, in a king to speak obscurely, much more untrewly, as if he stood in awe of any in uttering his thoughts.' That is pre-cisely your mood at the present moment, Humphry,—you stand 'in awe'—of me or of someone else,—in 'uttering your thoughts.'"

"Pardon me, Sir,—I do not stand in awe of you or of anyone;" said the Prince composedly—"I simply do not choose to 'utter my thoughts' just now."

The King looked at him in surprise, and with a touch of admiration. The defiant air he had unconsciously assumed became him,—his handsome face was pale, and his dark eyes coldly brilliant, like those of his beautiful mother, with the steel light of an inflexible resolve.

"You do not choose?" said the King, after a pause—"You decline to give any ex-planation of your long hours of absence?—your constant visits to The Islands, and your neglect of those social duties which should keep you at Court?"

"I decline to do so for the present," replied the young man decisively; "I can see no harm in my preference for quietness rather than noise,— for scenes of na-ture rather than those of artificial folly. The Islands are but two hours sail from this port,—little tufts of land set in the sea, where the coral-fishers dwell. They are beautiful in their natural adornment of foliage and flower;—I go there to read—to dream—to think of life as a better, purer thing than what you call 'society' would make it for me; you cannot blame me for this?"

The King was silent.

"If it is your wish,"—went on the Prince—"that I should stay in the palace more, I will obey you. If you desire me to be seen oftener in the capital, I will en-deavour to fulfil your command, though the streets stifle me. But, for God's sake, do not make me a puppet on show before my time,—or marry me to a woman I hate, merely for the sake of heirs to a wretched Throne!"

The King rose from his chair, and, walking towards the garden, threw the rest of his cigar out among the foliage, where the burning morsel shone like a stray glowworm in the green. Then he turned towards his son;—his face was grave, almost stern.

"You can go, Humphry!" he said;—"I have no more to say to you at present. You talk wildly and at random, as if you were, by some means or other, voluntarily bent upon unfitting yourself for the position you are destined to occupy. You will do well, I think, to remain more in evidence at Court. You will also do well to be seen at some of the different great social functions of the day. But I shall not coerce you. Only—consider well what I have said!—and if you have a secret"— he paused, and then repeated with emphasis—"I say, if you have a secret of any kind, be advised, and confide in me before it is too late! Otherwise you may find yourself betrayed unawares! Good-night!"

He walked away without throwing so much as a backward glance at the Prince, who stood amazed at the suddenness and decision with which he had brought the conversation to a close; and it was not till his tall figure had disappeared that the young man began to realize the doubtful awkwardness of the attitude he had assumed towards one who, both as parent and king, had the most urgent claim in the world upon his respect and obedience. Impatient and angry with himself, he crossed the loggia and went out into the garden beyond. A young moon, slender as a bent willow wand, gleamed in the clear heavens among hosts of stars more brilliantly visible than itself, and the soft air, laden with the perfume of thousands of flowers, cooled his brain and calmed his nerves. The musical low murmur of the sea, lapping against the shore below the palace walls, suggested a whole train of pleasing and poetical fancies, and he strolled along the dewy grass paths, under tangles of scented shrubs and arching boughs of pine, giving himself up to such idyllic dreams of life and life's fairest possibilities, as only youthful and imaginative souls can indulge in. He was troubled and vexed by his father's warning, but not sufficiently to pay serious heed to it. His 'secret' was safe so far;—and all he had to do, so he considered, was to exercise a little extra precaution.

"There is only Von Glauben,"—he thought, "and he would never betray me. Besides it is a mere question of another year—and then I can make all the truth known."

The lovely long-drawn warble of a nightingale broke the stillness around him with a divine persistence of passion. He listened, standing motionless, his eyes lifted towards the dark boughs above him, from whence the golden notes dropped liquidly; and his heart beat quickly as he thought of a voice sweeter than that of any heavenly-gifted bird, a face fairer than that of the fabled goddess who on such a night as this descended from her silver moon-car to enchant Endymion;—and he murmured half aloud—

"Who would not risk a kingdom—ay! a thousand kingdoms!—for such happiness as I possess! It is a foolish, blind world nowadays, that forgets the glory of its youth,—the glow, the breath, the tenderness of love!—all for amassing gold and power! I will not be of such a world, nor with it;—I will not be like my father, the slave of pomp and circumstance;—I will live an unfettered life—yes!—even if I have to resign the throne for the sake of freedom, still I will be free!"

He strolled on, absorbed in romantic reverie, and the nightingale's song followed him through the winding woods down to the shore, where the waves made other music of their own, which harmonised with the dreamy fancies of his mind.

Meanwhile, the King had sought his consort in her own apartments. Walking down the great corridor which led to these, the most beautiful rooms in the palace, he became aware of the silvery sound of stringed instruments mingling with harmonious voices,—though he scarcely heeded the soft rush of melody which came thus wafted to his ears. He was full of thoughts and schemes,—his son's refusal to confide in him had not seriously troubled him, because he knew he should, with patience, find out in good time all that the young Prince had declined to explain,—and his immediate interest was centred in his own immediate plans.

On reaching the ante-room leading to the Queen's presence-chamber, he was informed that her Majesty was listening to a concert in the rosery. Thither he went unattended,—and passing through a long suite of splendid rooms, each one more sumptuously adorned than the last, he presently stepped out on the velvet greensward of one of the most perfect rose gardens in the world—a garden walled entirely round with tall hedges of the clambering flowers which gave it its name, and which were trailed up on all sides, so as to form a ceiling or hanging canopy above. In the centre of this floral hall, now in full blossom, a fountain tossed up one tall column of silver spray; and at its upper end, against a background of the dainty white roses called "Felicite perpetuelle" sat the Queen, in a high chair of carved ivory, surrounded by her ladies. Delicious music, performed by players and singers who were hidden behind the trees, floated in voluptuous strains upon the air, and the King, looking at the exquisite grouping of fair women and flowers, lit by the coloured lamps which gleamed here and there among the thick foliage, wondered to himself how it chanced, that amid surroundings which were calculated to move the senses to the most refined and delicate rapture, he himself could feel no quickening pulse, no touch of admiration. These open-air renderings of music and song were the Queen's favourite form of recreation;—at such times alone would her proud face soften and her eyes grow languid with an unrevealed weight of dreams. But should her husband, or any one of his sex break in upon the charmed circle, her pleasure was at once clouded,—and the cold hauteur of her beautiful features became again inflexibly frozen. Such was the case now, when perceiving the King, she waved her hand as a sign for the music to cease; and with a glance of something like wonderment at his intrusion, saluted him profoundly as he entered the precincts of her garden Court. But for once he did not pause as usual, on his way to where she sat,—but lightly acknowledging the deep curtseys of the ladies in attendance, he advanced towards her and raising her hand in courtly homage to his lips, seated himself carelessly in a low chair at her feet.

"Let the music go on!" he said; "I am here to listen."

The Queen looked at him,—he met her eyes with an expression that she had never seen on his face before.

"Suffer me to have my way!" he said to her in a low tone—"Let your singers finish their programme; afterwards do me the favour to dismiss your women, for I must speak with you alone."

She bent her head in acquiescence; and re-seated herself on her ivory throne. The sign was given for the continuance of the music, and the King, leaning back in his chair, half closed his eyes as he listened dreamily to the harmonious throbbing of harps and violins around him, in the stillness of the languid southern night. His hand almost brushed against his wife's jewelled robes—the scent of the great lilies on her breast was wafted to him with every breath of air, and he thought—"All this would be Paradise,—with any other woman!" And while he so thought, the clear tenor voice of one of the unseen singers rang out in half gay, half tender tones:

> If I loved you, and you loved me,
> How happy this little world would be—

The light of the day, the dancing hours,
The skies, the trees, the birds and flowers,
Would all be part of our perfect gladness;—
And never a note of pain or sadness
Would jar life's beautiful melody
If I loved you, and you loved me!

'If I loved you!' Why, I scarcely know
How if I did, the time would go!—
I should forget my dreary cares,
My sordid toil, my long despairs,
I should watch your smile, and kneel at your feet,
And live my life in the love of you, Sweet!—
So mad, so glad, so proud I should be,
If I loved you, and you loved me!

'If you loved me!' Ah, nothing so strange
As that could chance in this world of change!—
As well expect a planet to fall,
Or a Queen to dwell in a beggar's hall—
But if you did,—romance and glory
Might spring from our lives' united story,
And angels might be less happy than we—
If I loved you and you loved me!

'If I loved you and you loved me!'
Alas, 't is a joy we shall never see!
You are too fair—I am too cold;—
We shall drift along till we both grow old,
Till we reach the grave, and gasping, die,
Looking back on the days that have passed us by,
When 'what might have been,' can no longer be,—
When I lost you, and you lost me!

The song concluded abruptly, and with passion;—and the King, turning on his elbow, glanced with a touch of curiosity at the face of his Queen. There was not a flicker of emotion on its fair cold calmness,— not a quiver on the beautiful lips, or a sigh to stir the quiet breast on which the lilies rested, white and waxen, and heavily odorous. He withdrew his gaze with a half smile at his own folly for imagining that she could be moved by a mere song to any expression of feeling,—even for a moment,—and allowed his glance to wander unreservedly over the forms and features of the other ladies in attendance who, conscious of his regard, dropped their eyelids and blushed softly, after the fashion approved by the heroines of the melodramatic stage. Whereat he began to think of the tiresome sameness of women generally; and their irritating habit of living always at two extremes,—either all ardour, or all coldness.

"Both are equally fatiguing to a man's mind," he thought impatiently— "The only woman that is truly fascinating is the one who is never in the same mind two days together. Fair on Monday, plain on Tuesday, sweet on Wednesday, sour on Thursday, tender on Friday, cold on Saturday, and in all moods at once on Sunday,—that being a day of rest! I should adore such a woman as that if I ever met her, because I should never know her mind towards me!"

A soft serenade rendered by violins, with a harp accompaniment, was followed by a gay mazurka, played by all the instruments together,—and this finished the musical programme.

The Queen rose, accepting the hand which the King extended to her, and moved with him slowly across the rose-garden, her long snowy train glistering with jewels, and held up from the greensward by a pretty page, who, in his picturesque costume of rose and gold, demurely followed his Royal lady's footsteps,—and so amid the curtseying ladies-in-waiting and other attendants, they passed together into a private boudoir, at the threshold of which the Queen's train-bearer dropped his rich burden of perfumed velvet and gems, and bowing low, left their Majesties together.

Shutting the door upon him with his own hand, the King drew a heavy portiere across it,—and then walking round the room saw that every window was closed,— every nook secure. The Queen's boudoir was one of the most sacred corners in the whole palace,—no one, not even the most intimate lady of the Court in personal attendance on her Majesty, dared enter it without special permission; and this being the case, the Queen herself was faintly moved to surprise at the extra precaution her husband appeared to be taking to ensure privacy. She stood silently watching his movements till he came up to her, and bowing courteously, said:—

"I pray you, be seated, Madam! I will not detain you long."

She obeyed his gesture, and sank down in a chair with that inimitable noiseless grace which made every attitude of hers a study for an artist, and waited for his next words; while he, standing opposite to her, bent his eyes upon her face with a certain wistfulness and appeal.

"I have never asked you a favour," he began—"and—since the day we married,—I have never sought your sympathy. The years have come and gone, leaving no visible trace on either you or me, so far as outward looks go,—and if they have scarred and wrinkled us inwardly, only God can see those scars! But as time moves on with a man,—I know not how it is with a woman,—if he be not al-together a fool, he begins to consider the way in which he has spent, or is spending his life,— whether he has been, or is yet likely to be of any use to the world he lives in,—or if he is of less account than the blown froth of the sea, or the sand on the shore. Myriads and myriads of men and women are no more than this—no more than midges or ants or worms;—but every now and then in the course of centu-ries, one man does stand forth from the million,—one heart does beat courageously enough to send the firm echo of its pulsations through a long vista of time,—one soul does so exalt and inspire the rest of the world by its great example that we are, through its force reminded of something divine,—something high and true in a low wilderness of shams!"

He paused; the Queen raised her beautiful eyes, and smiled strangely.

"Have you only just now thought of this?" she said.

He flushed, and bit his lip.

"To be perfectly honest with you, Madam, I have thought of nothing worth thinking about for many years! Most men in my position would probably make the same confession. Perhaps had you given me any great work to do for your sake I should have done it! Had *you* inspired me to achieve some great conquest, either for myself or others, I should no doubt have conquered! But I have lived for twenty-one years in your admirable company without being commanded by you to do any-thing worthy of a king;—I am now about to command Myself!—in order to leave some notable trace of my name in history."

While he thus spoke, a faint flush coloured the Queen's cheeks, but it quickly died away, leaving her very pale. Her fingers strayed among the great jewels she wore, and toyed unconsciously with a ruby talisman cut in the shape of a heart, and encircled with diamonds. The King noted the flash of the gems against the white-ness of her hand, and said:

"Your heart, Madam, is like the jewel you hold!—clear crimson, and full of fire,—but it is not the fire of Heaven, though you may perchance judge it to be so. Rather is it of hell!—(I pray you to pardon me for the roughness of this suggestion!)—for one of the chief crimes of the devil is unconquerable hatred of the human race. You share Satan's aversion to man!—and strange indeed it is that even the most sympathetic companionship with your own sex cannot soften that aver-sion! However, we will not go into this;—the years have proved you true to your own temperament, and there is nothing to be said on the matter, either of blame or of praise. As I said, I have never asked a favour of you, nor have I sought the sympa-thy which it is not in your nature to give. I have not even claimed your obedience in any particular strictness of form; but that is my errand to you to-night,— indeed it is the sole object of this private interview,—to claim your entire, your unfaltering, your implicit obedience!"

She raised her head haughtily.

"To what commands, Sir?" she asked.

"To those I have here written,—" and he handed her a paper folded in two, which she took wonderingly, as he extended it. "Read this carefully!—and if you have any objections to urge, I am willing to listen to you with patience, though scarcely to alter the conditions laid down."

He turned away, and walked slowly through the room, pausing a moment to whistle to a tiny bird swinging in a gilded cage, that perked up its pretty head at his call and twittered with pleasure.

"So you respond to kindness, little one!" he said softly,—"You are more Christ-like in that one grace than many a Christian!"

He started, as a light touch fell on his shoulder, and he saw the Queen standing beside him. She held the paper he had given her in one hand, and as he looked at her enquiringly she touched it with her lips, and placed it in her bosom.

"I swear my obedience to your instructions, Sir!" she said,—"Do not fear to trust me!"

Gently he took her hands and kissed them.

"I thank you!" he said simply.

For a moment they confronted each other. The beautiful cold woman's eyes drooped under the somewhat sad and searching gaze of the man.

"But—your life!—" she murmured.

"My life!" He laughed and dropped her hands. "Would you care, Madam, if I were dead? Would you shed any tears? Not you! Why should you? At this late hour of time, when after twenty-one years passed in each other's close company we are no nearer to each other in heart and soul than if the sea murmuring yonder at the foot of these walls were stretching its whole width between us! Besides—we are both past our youth! And, according to certain highly instructed scientists and philosophers, the senses and affections grow numb with age. I do not believe this theory myself—for the jejune love of youth is as a taper's flame to the great and passionate tenderness of maturity, when the soul, and not the body, claims its due; when love is not dragged down to the vulgar level of mere cohabitation, after the fashion of the animals in a farmyard, but rises to the best height of human sympathy and intelligent comprehension. Who knows!—I may experience such a love as that yet,— and so may you!"

She was silent.

"Talking of love,"—he went on—"May I ask whether our son,—or rather the nation's son, Humphry,—ever makes you his confidante?"

"Never!" she replied.

"I thought not! We do not seem to be the kind of parents admired in moral story-books, Madam! We are not the revered darlings of our children. In fact, our children have the happy disposition of animal cubs,—once out of the nursing stage, they forget they ever had parents. It is quite the natural and proper thing, born as they were born,—it would never do for them to have any over-filial regard for us. Imagine Humphry weeping for my death, or yours! What a grotesque idea! And as for Rupert and Cyprian,—it is devoutly to be hoped that when we die, our funerals may be well over before the great cricket matches of the year come on, as otherwise they will curse us for having left the world at an inconvenient season!" He laughed. "How sentiment has gone out nowadays, or how it seems to have gone out! Yet it slumbers in the heart of the nation,—and if it should ever awaken,— well!—it will be dangerous! I asked you about Humphry, because I imagine he is entangled in some love-affair. If it should be agreeable to your humour to go with me across to The Islands one day this week, we may perhaps by chance discover the reason of his passion for that particular kind of scenery!"

The Queen's eyes opened wonderingly.

"The Islands!" she repeated,—"The Islands? Why, only the coral-fishers live there,—they have a community of their own, and are jealous of all strangers. What should Humphry do there?"

"That is more than I can tell you," answered the King,—"And it is more than he will himself explain. Nevertheless, he is there nearly every day,—some attraction draws him, but what, I cannot discover. If Humphry were of the soul of me, as he is of the body of me, I should not even try to fathom his secret,—but he is the nation's child—heir to its throne—and as such, it is necessary that we, for the nation's sake, should guard him in the nation's interests. If you chance to learn anything of the object of his constant sea-wanderings, I trust you will find it coincident with your pleasure to inform me?"

"I shall most certainly obey you in this, Sir, as in all other things!" she replied.

He moved a step or two towards her.

"Good-night!" he said very gently, and detaching one of the lilies from her corsage, took it in his own hand. "Good-night! This flower will remind me of you;—white and beautiful, with all the central gold deep hidden!"

He looked at her intently, with a lingering look, half of tenderness, half of re-gret, and bowing in the courtliest fashion of homage, left her presence.

She remained alone, the velvet folds of her train flowing about her feet, and the jewels on her breast flashing like faint sparks of flame in the subdued glow of the shaded lamplight. She was touched for the first time in her life by the consciousness of something infinitely noble, and altogether above her in her husband's nature. Slowly she drew out the paper he had given her from her bosom and read it through again—and yet once again. Almost unconsciously to herself a mist gathered in her eyes and softened into two bright tears, which dropped down her fair cheeks, and lost themselves among her diamonds.

"He is brave!" she murmured—"Braver than I thought he could ever be—"

She roused herself sharply from her abstraction. Emotions which were beyond her own control had strangely affected her, and the humiliating idea that her moods had for a moment escaped beyond her guidance made her angry with herself for what she considered mere weakness. And passing quickly out of the boudoir, in the vague fear that solitude might deepen the sense of impotence and failure which insinuated itself slowly upon her, like a dull blight creeping through her heart and soul, she rejoined her ladies, the same great Queen as ever, with the same look of indifference on her face, the same chill smile, the same perfection of loveliness, unwithered by any visible trace of sorrow or of passion.

CHAPTER VI
SERGIUS THORD

THE next day the heavens were clouded; and occasional volleys of heavy thunder were mingled with the gusts of wind and rain which swept over the city, and which lashed the fair southern sea into a dark semblance of such angry waves as wear away northern coasts into bleak and rocky barrenness. It was disappointing weather to multitudes, for it was the feast-day of one of the numerous saints whose names fill the calendar of the Roman Church,—and a great religious procession had been organized to march from the market-place to the Cathedral, in which two or three hundred children and girls had been chosen to take part. The fickle bursts of sunshine which every now and again broke through the lowering sky, decided the priests to carry out their programme in spite of the threatening storm, in the hope that it would clear off completely with the afternoon. Accordingly, groups of little maidens, in white robes and veils, began to assemble with their flags and banners at the appointed hour round the old market cross, which,—grey and crumbling at the summit,—bent over the streets like a withered finger, crook'd as it were, in feeble remonstrance at the passing of time,— while glimpses of young faces beneath the snowy veils, and chatter of young voices, made brightness and music around its frowning and iron-bound base. Shortly before three o'clock the Cathedral bells began to chime, and crowds of people made their way towards the sacred edifice in the laughing, pushing, gesticulating fashion of southerners, to whom a special service at the Church is like a new comedy at the theatre,—women with coloured kerchiefs knotted over their hair or across their bosoms—men, more or less roughly clad, yet all paying compliment to the Saint's feast-day by some extra smart touch in their attire, if it were only a pomegranate flower or orange-blossom stuck in their hats, or behind their ears. It was a mixed crowd, all of the working classes, who are proverbially called 'the common,' as if those who work, are not a hundred times more noble than those who do nothing! A few carriages, containing some wealthy ladies of the nobility, who, to atone for their social sins, were in the habit of contributing largely to the Church, passed every now and again through the crowd, but taken as a spectacle it was simply a 'popular' show, in which the children of the people took part, and where the people themselves were evidently more amused than edified.

While the bells were ringing the procession gradually formed;—a dozen or more priests leading,—incense-bearers and acolytes walking next,— and then the long train of little children and girls carrying their symbolic banners, following after. The way they had to walk was a steep, winding ascent, through tortuous streets, to the Cathedral, which stood in the centre of a great square on an eminence which overlooked the whole city, and as soon as they started they began to sing,—softly at first, then more clearly and sweetly, till gradually the air grew full of melody, rising and falling on the capricious gusts of wind which tore at the gilded and emblazoned banners, and tossed the white veils of the maidens about like wreaths of drifting snow. Two men standing on the Cathedral hill, watched the procession gradually ascending—one tall and heavily-built, with a dark leonine head made more massive-looking by its profusion of thick and unmanageable hair— the other lean and narrow-shouldered, with a peaked reddish-auburn beard, which he continually pulled and twitched at nervously as though its growth on his chin was more a matter of vexation than convenience. He was apparently not so much interested in the Church festival as he was in his companion's face, for he was perpetually glancing up at that brooding countenance, which, half hidden as it was in wild hair and further concealed by thick moustache and beard, showed no expression at all, unless an occasional glimpse of full flashing eyes under the bushy brows, gave a sudden magnetic hint of something dangerous and not to be trifled with.

"You do not believe anything you hear or read, Sergius Thord!" he said —"Will you twist your whole life into a crooked attitude of suspicion against all mankind?" He who was named Sergius Thord, lifted himself slowly from the shoulders upwards, the action making his great height and broad chest even more apparent than before. A gleam of white teeth shone under his black moustache.

"I do not twist my life into a crooked attitude, Johan Zegota," he replied. "If it is crooked, others have twisted it for me! Why should I believe what I hear, since it is the fashion to lie? Why should I accept what I read, since it is the business of the press to deceive the public? And why do you ask me foolish questions? You should be better instructed, seeing that your creed is the same as mine!"

"Have I ever denied it?" exclaimed Zegota warmly—"But I have said, and I say again that I believe the news is true,—and that these howling hypocrites,—" this with an angry gesture of his hand towards the open square where the chanting priests who headed the procession were coming into view—"have truly received an unlooked-for check from the King!"

Sergius Thord laid one hand heavily on his shoulder.

"When the King—when any king—does anything useful in the world, then you may hang me with your own hands, Zegota! When did you ever hear, except in myths of the past, of a monarch who cared for his people more than his crown? Tell me that! Tell me of any king who so truly loved the people he was called upon to govern, that he sacrificed his own money, as well as his own time, to remedy their wrongs?—to save them from unjust government, to defend them from cruel taxation?—to see that their bread was not taken from their mouths by foreign competition?—and to make it possible for them to live in the country of their birth in peace and prosperity? Bah! There never was such a king! And that this man,—who has for three years left us to the mercy of the most accursed cheat and scoundrel minister that ever was in power,—has now declared his opposition to the Jesuits', is more than I will or can believe."

"If it were true?"—suggested Zegota, with a more than usually vicious tug at his beard.

"If it were true, it would not alter my opinion, or set aside my intention," replied Thord,—"I would admit that the King had done one good deed before going to hell! Look! Here come the future traitresses of men—girls trained by priests to deceive their nearest and dearest! Poor children! They know nothing as yet of the uses to which their lives are destined! If they could but die now, in their innocent faith and stupidity, how much better for all the world!"

As he spoke, the wind, swooping into the square, and accompanied by a pattering gust of rain, fell like a fury upon the leaders of the religious procession and tore one of the great banners out of the hands of the priest who held it, beating it against his head and face with so much force that he fell backward to the ground under its weight, while from a black cloud above, a flash of lightning gleamed, followed almost instantaneously by a loud clap of thunder, which shook the square with a mighty reverberation like that of a bursting bomb. The children screamed,—and ran towards the Cathedral pellmell; and for a few moments there ensued indescribable confusion, the priests, the people, and the white-veiled girls getting mixed together in a wild hurly- burly. Sergius Thord suddenly left his companion's side, and springing on a small handcart that stood empty near the centre of the square, his tall figure rose up all at once like a dark apparition above the heads of the assembled crowd, and his voice, strong, clear, and vibrating with passion, rang out like a deep alarm bell, through all the noise of the storm.

"Whither are you going, O foolish people? To pray to God? Pray to Him here, then, under the flash of His lightning!—in the roll of His thunder!—beneath His cathedral-canopy of clouds! Pray to Him with all your hearts, your brains, your reason, your intelligence, and leave mere lip-service and mockery to priests; and to these poor children, who, as yet, know no better than to obey tyrants! Would you find out God? He is here—with me,—with you!—in the earth, in the sky, in the sun and storm! Whenever Truth declares a living fact, God speaks,— whenever we respond to that Truth, God hears! No church, no cathedral contains His presence more than we shall find it here—with us—where we stand!"

The people heard, and a great silence fell upon them. All faces were turned toward the speaker, and none appeared to heed the great drops of fast-falling rain. One of the priests who was trying to marshal the scattered children into their former order, so that they might enter the Cathedral in the manner arranged for the religious service, looked up to see the cause of the sudden stillness, and muttered a curse under his breath. But even while the oath escaped his lips, he gave the signal for the sacred chanting to be resumed, and in another moment the 'Litany of the Virgin' was started in stentorian tones by the leaders of the procession. Intimidated by the looks, as well as by the commands of the priests, the girls and children joined in the chanting with tremulous voices, as they began to file through the Cathedral doors and enter the great nave. But a magnetic spell, stronger than any invocation of the Church, had fallen upon the crowd, and they all stood as though caught in the invisible web of some enchanter, their faces turned upwards to where Thord's tall figure towered above them. His eyes glittered as he noted the sudden hush of attention which prevailed, and lifting his rough cap from his head, he waved it towards the open door of the Cathedral, through which the grand strains of the organ rolling out from within gave forth solemn invitation:—

"Sancta Dei Genitrix, Ora pro nobis!"

sang the children, as they passed in line under the ancient porch, carved with the figures of forgotten saints and bishops, whose stone countenances had stared at similar scenes through the course of long centuries.

"Sancta Dei Genitrix, ora pro nobis!" echoed Sergius Thord—"Do you hear it, O men? Do you hear it, O women? What does it teach you? 'Holy Mother of God!' Who was she? Was she not merely a woman to whom God descended? And what is the lesson she gives you? Plainly this—that men should be as gods, and women as the mothers of gods! For every true and brave man born into the world has God within him,—is made of God, and must return to God! And every woman who gives birth to one such, true, brave man, has given a God-incarnated being to the world! 'Sancta Dei Genitrix!' Be all as mothers of gods, O women! Be as gods, O men! Be as gods in courage, in truth, in wisdom, in freedom! Suffer not devils to have command of you! For devils there are, as there are gods;—evil there is, as there is good. Fiends are born of women as gods are—and yet evil itself is of God, inasmuch as without God there can be neither evil nor good. Let us help God, we His children, to conquer evil by conquering it in ourselves—and by refusing to give it power over us! So shall God show us all goodness,—all pity! So shall He cease to afflict His children; so will He cease to torture us with undeserved sorrows and devilish agonies, for which we are not to blame!"

He paused. The singing had ceased; the children's procession had entered the Cathedral, and the doors still stood wide open. But the people remained outside, crowded in the square, and gathering momentarily in greater numbers.

"Look you!" cried Sergius Thord—"The building which is called the Sanctuary of God, stands open—why do you not all enter there? Within are precious marbles, priceless pictures, jewels and relics—and a great altar raised up by the gifts of wicked dead kings, who by money sought to atone for their sins to the people.

There are priests who fast and pray in public, and gratify all the lusts of appetite in private. There are poor and ignorant women who believe whatsoever these priests tell them—all this you can see if you go inside yonder. Why do you not go? Why do you remain with me?"

A faint murmur, like the rising ripple of an angry sea, rose from the crowd, but quickly died away again into silence.

"Shall I tell you why you stay?" went on Thord,—"Because you know I am your friend—and because you also know that the priests are your enemies! Because you know that I tell you the truth, and that the priests tell you lies! Because you feel that all the promises made to you of happiness in Heaven cannot explain away to your satisfaction the causes of your bitter suffering and poverty on earth! Because you are gradually learning that the chief business of priestcraft is to deceive the people and keep them down,—down, always down in a state of wretched ignorance. Learn, learn all you can, my brothers—take the only good thing modern government gives you—Education! Education is thrown at us like a bone thrown to a dog, half picked by others and barely nourishing—but take it, take it, friends, for in it you shall find the marrow of vengeance on your tyrants and oppressors! The education of the masses means the downfall of false creeds,—the ruin of all false priests! For it is only through the ignorance of the many that tyrannical dominion is given into the hands of the few! Slavish submission to a corrupt government would be impossible if we all refused to be slaves. O friends, O brothers, throw off your chains! Break down your prison doors! Some good you have done already—be brave and strong to do more! Press forward fearlessly and strive for liberty and justice! To-day we are told that the King has refused crown-lands to the Jesuits. Shall we be told to-morrow that the King has dismissed Carl Perousse from office?"

A long wild shout told how this suggestion had gone straight home to the throng.

"Shall we be told this, I ask? No! Ten thousand times no! The refusal of the King to grant the priests any wider dominion over us is merely an act of policy inspired by terror. The King is afraid! He fears the people will revolt against the Church, and so takes part with them lest there should be trouble in the land, but he never seems to think there may be another kind of revolt against himself! His refusal to concede more place for the accursed practice of Jesuitry is so far good; but his dismissal of

Perousse would be still better!"

A perfect hurricane of applause from the people gave emphatic testimony to the truth of these words.

"What is this man, Carl Perousse?" he went on—"A man of the people— whose oaths were sworn to the people,—whom the people themselves brought into power because he promised to remain faithful to them! He is false,—a traitor and political coward! A mere manufacturer of kitchen goods, who through our folly was returned to this country's senate;—and through our still further credulity is now set in almost complete dominion over us. Well! We have suffered and are suffering for our misplaced belief in him;—the question is, how long shall we continue to suffer? How long are we to be governed by the schemes of Carl Perousse, the country's turncoat,—the trafficker in secret with Jew speculators? It is for you to decide! It is for you to work out your own salvation! It is for you to throw off tyranny, and show yourselves free men of reason and capacity! Just as the priests chant long prayers to cover their own iniquity, so do the men of government make long speeches to disguise their own corruption. You know you cannot believe their promises. Neither can you believe the press, for if this is not actually bought by Perousse, it is bribed. And you cannot trust the King; for he is as a house divided against itself which must fall! Slave of his own passions, and duped by women, what is he but a burden to the State? Justice and power should be on the side of kings,—but the days are come when self-interest and money can even buy a throne! O men, O women, rouse up your hearts and minds to work for yourselves, to redress wrongs,—to save your country! Rouse up in your thousands, and with your toil-worn hands pull down the pillars of iniquity and vice that overshadow and darken the land! Fight against the insolent pride of wealth which strives to crush the poor; rouse, rouse your hearts!— open your eyes and see the evils which are gathering thick upon us!—and like the lightnings pent up in yonder clouds, leap forth in flame and thunder, and clear the air!"

A burst of frantic acclamation from the crowd followed this wild harangue, and while the loud roar of voices yet echoed aloft, a band of armed police came into view, marching steadily up from the lower streets of the city. Sergius Thord smiled as he saw them approach.

"Yonder comes the Law!" he said—"A few poor constables, badly paid, who if they could find anything better to do than to interfere with their fellow-men would be glad of other occupation! Before they come any nearer, disperse yourselves, my friends, and so save them trouble! Go all to your homes and think on my words;—or enter the Cathedral and pray, those who will—but let this place be as empty of you in five minutes as though you never had been here! Disperse,—and farewell! We shall meet again!"

He leaped down from his position and disappeared, and in obedience to his command the crowd began to melt away with almost miraculous speed. Before the police could reach the centre of the square, there were only some thirty or forty people left, and these were quietly entering the Cathedral where the service for the saint whose feast day was being celebrated was now in full and solemn progress.

For one instant, on the first step of the great porch, Sergius Thord and his companion, Johan Zegota, met,—but making a rapid sign to each other with the left hand, they as quickly separated,—Zegota to enter the Cathedral, Thord to walk rapidly down one of the narrowest and most unfrequented streets to the lower precincts of the city.

The afternoon grew darker, and the weather more depressing, and by the time evening closed in, the rain was pouring persistently. The wind had ceased, and the thunder had long since died away, its force drenched out by the weight of water in the clouds. The saint's day had ended badly for all concerned;—many of the children who had taken part in the procession had been carried home by their parents wet through, all the pretty white frocks and veils of the little girls having been completely soaked and spoilt by the unkind elements. A drearier night had seldom gloomed over this fair city of the southern sea, and down in the quarters of the poor, where men and women dwelt all huddled miserably in overcrowded tenements, and sin and starvation kept hideous company together, the streets presented as dark and forbidding an aspect as the heavy skies blackly brooding above. Here and there a gas- lamp flared its light upon the drawn little face of some child crouching asleep in a doorway, or on the pinched and painted features of some wretched outcast wending her way to the den she called 'home.' The loud brutal laughter of drunken men was mingled with the wailing of half-starved and fretful infants, and the mean, squalid houses swarmed with the living spawn of every vice and lust in the calendar of crime. Deep in the heart of the so-called civilized, beautiful and luxurious city, this 'quarter of the poor,' the cancer of the social body, throbbed and ate its destructive way slowly but surely on, and Sergius Thord, who longed to lay a sharp knife against it and cut it out, for the health of the whole community, was as powerless as Dante in hell to cure the evils he witnessed. Yet it was not too much to say that he would have given his life to ease another's pain,—as swiftly and as readily as he would have taken life without mercy, in the pursuit of what he imagined to be a just vengeance.

"How vain, after all, is my labour!" he thought—"How helpless I am to move the self-centred powers of the Government and the Throne! Even were all these wretched multitudes to rise with me, and make havoc of the whole city, should we move so much as one step higher out of the Gehenna of poverty and crime? Almost I doubt it!"

He walked on past dark open doorways, where some of the miserable inhabitants of the dens within, stood to inhale the fresh wet air of the rainy night. His tall form was familiar to most of them,—if they were considered as wolves of humanity in the sight of the law, they were all faithful dogs to him; doing as he bade, running where he commanded, ready at any moment to assemble at any given point and burn and pillage, or rob and slay. There were no leaders in the political government,—but this one leader of the massed poor could, had he chosen, have burned down the city. But he did not choose. He had a far- sighted, clear brain,—and though he had sworn to destroy abuses wherever he could find them, he moved always with caution; and his plans were guided, not by impulse alone, but by earnest consideration for the future. He was marked out by the police as a dangerous Socialist; and his movements were constantly tracked and dodged, but so far, he had done nothing which could empower his arrest. He was a free subject in a free country; and provided he created no open disturbance he had as much liberty as a mission preacher to speak in the streets to those who would stop to listen. He paused now in his walk at the door of one house more than commonly dingy and tumble-down in appearance, where a man lounged outside in his shirt-sleeves, smoking.

"Is all well with you, Matsin?" he asked gently.

"All is well!" answered the man called Matsin,—"better than last night. The child is dead."

"Dead!" echoed Thord,—"And the mother——"

"Asleep!" answered Matsin. "I gave her opium to save her from madness. She was hungry, too—the opium fed her and made her forget!"

Thord pushed him gently aside, and went into the house. There on the floor lay the naked body of a dead child, so emaciated as to be almost a skeleton; and across it, holding it close with one arm, was stretched a woman, half clothed, her face hidden in her unbound dark hair, breathing heavily in a drugged sleep. Great tears filled Thord's eyes.

"God exists!" he said,—"And He can bear to look upon a sight like this! If I were God, I should hate myself for letting such things be!"

"Perhaps He does hate Himself!" said the man Matsin, who had also come in, and now looked at the scene with sullen apathy—"That may be the cause of all our troubles! I don't understand the ways of God; or the ways of man either. I have done no harm. I married the woman—and we had that one child. I worked hard for both. I could not get sufficient money to keep us going; I did metal work—very well, so I was told. But they make it all abroad now by machinery—I cannot compete. They don't want new designs they say—the old will serve. I do anything now that I can— but it is difficult. You, too,—you starve with us!"

"I am poor, if that is what you mean," said Thord,—"but take all I have to-night, Matsin—" and he emptied a small purse of silver coins into the man's hand. "Bury the poor little innocent one;—and comfort the mother when she wakes. Comfort her!—love her!—she needs love! I will be back again to-morrow."

He strode away quickly, and Matsin remained at his door turning over the money in his hand.

"He will sacrifice something he needs himself, for this," he muttered. "Yet that is the man they say the King would hang if ever he got hold of him! By Heaven!— the King himself should hang first!"

Meanwhile Sergius Thord went on, slackening his pace a little as he came near his own destination, a tall and narrow house at the end of the street, with a single light shining in one of the upper windows. There was a gas-lamp some few paces off, and under this stood a man reading, or trying to read, a newspaper by its flickering glare. Thord glanced at him with some suspicion—the stranger was too near his own lodging for his pleasure, for he was always on his guard against spies. Approaching more closely, he saw that though the man was shabbily attired in a rough pilot suit, much the worse for wear, he nevertheless had the indefinable look and bearing of a gentleman. Acting on impulse, as he often did, Thord spoke to him.

"A rough night for reading by lamplight, my friend!" he said.

The man looked up, and smiled.

"Yes, it is, rather! But I have only just got the evening paper."

"Any special news?"

"No—only this—" and he pointed to a bold headline—"The King *versus* The Jesuits."

"Ah!" said Thord, and he studied the looks and bearing of the stranger with increasing curiosity. "What do you think of it?"

"What do I think? May I ask, without offence, what *you* think?"

"I think," said Thord slowly, "that the King has for once in his life done a wise thing."

"'For once in his life!'" repeated the stranger dubiously—"Then I presume your King is, generally speaking, a fool?"

"If you are a subject of his—" began Thord slowly——

"Thank Heaven, I am not! I am a mere wanderer—a literary loafer—a student of men and manners. I read books, and I write them too,—this will perhaps explain the eccentricity of my behaviour in trying to read under the lamplight in the rain!"

He smiled again, and the smile was irresistibly pleasant. Something about him attracted Thord, and after a pause he asked:

"If you are, as you say, a wanderer and a stranger in this town, can I be of service to you?"

"You are very kind!" said the other, turning a pair of deep, dark, grey meditative eyes upon him,—"And I am infinitely obliged to you for the suggestion. But I really want nothing. As a matter of fact, I am waiting for two friends of mine who have just gone into one of the foul and filthy habitations here, to see what they can do for a suddenly bereaved family. The husband and father fell dead in the street before our eyes,—and those who picked him up said he was drunk, but it turned out that he was merely starved,— *merely*!—you understand? Merely starved! We found his home,—and the poor widow is wailing and weeping, and the children are crying for food. I confess myself quite unable to bear the sight, and so I have sent all the money I had about me to help them for to-night at least. By my faith, they are most hopelessly, incurably miserable!"

"Their lot is exceedingly common in these quarters," said Thord, sorrowfully. "Day after day, night after night, men, women and children toil, suffer and die here without ever knowing what it is to have one hour of free fresh air, one day of rest and joy! Yet this is a great city,—and we live in a civilized country!" He smiled bitterly, then added—"You have done a good action; and you need no thanks, or I would thank you; for my life's work lies among these wretched poor, and I am familiar with their tragic histories. Good-night!"

"Pray do not go!" said the stranger suddenly—"I should like to talk to you a little longer, if you have no objection. Is there not some place near, where we can go out of this rain and have a glass of wine together?"

Sergius Thord stood irresolute,—gazing at him, half in liking, half in distrust.

"Sir," he said at last, "I do not know you—and you do not know me. If I told you my name, you would probably not seek my company!"

"Will you tell it?" suggested the stranger cheerfully—"Mine is at your service— Pasquin Leroy. I fear my fame as an author has not reached your ears!"

Thord shook his head.

"No. I have never heard of you. And probably you have never heard of me. My name is Sergius Thord."

"Sergius Thord!" echoed the stranger; "Now that is truly remarkable! It is a happy coincidence that we should have met to-night. I have just seen your name in this very paper which you caught me reading—see!— the next heading under that concerning the King and the Jesuits— 'Thord's Rabble.' Are not you that same Thord?"

"I am!" said Thord proudly, his eyes shining as he took the paper and perused quickly the few flashy lines which described the crowd outside the Cathedral that afternoon, and set him down as a crazy Socialist, and disturber of the peace, "And the 'rabble' as this scribbling fool calls it, is the greater part of this city's population. The King may intimidate his Court; but I, Sergius Thord, with my 'rabble' can intimidate both Court and King!"

He drew himself up to his full majestic height—a noble figure of a man with his fine heroic head and eagle-like glance of eye,—and he who had called himself

Pasquin Leroy, suddenly held out his hand.

"Let me see more of you, Sergius Thord!" he said,—"You are the very man for me! They say in this paper that you spoke to a great multitude outside the Cathedral this afternoon, and interfered with the religious procession; they also say you are the head of a Society called the Revolutionary Committee;—now let me work for you in some department of *that* business!"

"Let you work for me?" echoed Thord astonished—"But how?"

"In this way—" replied the other—"I write Socialistic works,—and for this cause have been expelled from my native home and surroundings. I have a little money—and some influence,—and I will devote both to your Cause. Will you take me, and trust me?"

Thord caught his extended hand, and looked at him with a kind of fierce intentness.

"You mean it?" he said in thrilling tones—"You mean it positively and truly?"

"Positively and truly!" said Leroy—"If you are working to remedy the frightful evils abounding in this wretched quarter of the poor, I will help you! If you are striving to destroy rank abuses, I ask nothing better than to employ my pen in your service. I will get work on the press here—I will do all I can to aid your purposes and carry out your intentions. I have no master, so am free to do as I like; and I will devote myself to your service so long as you think I can be of any use to you."

"Wait!" said Thord—"You must not be carried away by a sudden generous impulse, simply because you have witnessed one scene of the continual misery that is going on here daily. To belong to our Committee means much more than you at present realize, and involves an oath which you may not be willing to take! And what of the friends you spoke of?"

"They will do what I do," replied Leroy—"They share my fortunes— likewise my opinions;—and here they come,—so they can speak for themselves," this, as two men emerged from a dark street on the left, and came full into the lamplight's flare—"Axel Regor, Max Graub—come hither! Fortune has singularly favoured us to-night! Let me present to you my friend—" and he emphasized the word, "Sergius Thord!"

Both men started ever so slightly as the introduction was performed, and Thord looked at them with fresh touches of suspicion here and there lurking in his mind. But he was brave; and having once proceeded in a given direction was not in the habit of turning back. He therefore saluted both the new-comers with grave courtesy.

"I trust you!" he then said curtly to Leroy, "and I think you will not betray my trust. If you do, it will be the worse for you!"

His lips parted in a slight sinister smile, and the two who were respectively called Axel Regor and Max Graub, exchanged anxious glances. But Leroy showed no sign of hesitation or alarm.

"Your warning is quite unnecessary, Sergius Thord," he said,—"I pledge you my word with my friendship—and my word is my bond! I will also hold myself responsible for my companions."

Thord bent his head in silent recognition of this assurance.

"Then follow me, if such is your desire," he said—"Remember, there is yet time to go in another direction, and to see me no more; but if you once do cast in your lot with mine the tie between us is indissoluble!"

He paused, as though expecting some recoil or hesitation on the part of those to whom he made this statement, but none came. He therefore strode on, and they followed, till arriving at the door of the tall, narrow house, where the light in the highest window gleamed like a signal, he opened it with a small key and entered, holding it back courteously for his three new companions to enter with him. They did so, and he closed the door. At the same moment the light was extinguished in the upper window, and the outside of the house became a mere wall of dense blackness in the driving rain.

CHAPTER VII
THE IDEALISTS

U P a long uncarpeted flight of stairs, and into a large lofty room on the
second storey, Thord led the way for his newly-found disciples to follow.
It was very dark, and they had to feel the steps as they went, their guide
offering neither explanation nor apology for the Cimmerian shades of
gloom. Stumbling on hands and knees they spoke not a word; though once Max
Graub uttered something like an oath in rough German; but a whisper from Leroy
rebuked and silenced him, and they pursued their difficult ascent until, arriving
at the room mentioned, they found themselves in the company of about fifteen to
twenty men, all sitting round a table under two flaring billiard lamps, suspended
crookedly from the ceiling. As Thord entered, these men all rose, and gave him
an expressive sign of greeting with the left hand, the same kind of gesture which
had passed between him and Zegota on the Cathedral steps in the morning. Zegota
himself was one of their number. There was also another personage in the room
who did not rise, and who gave no sign whatever. This was a woman, who sat in the
embrasure of a closed and shuttered window with her back to the whole company.
It was impossible to say whether she was young or old, plain or handsome, for she
was enveloped in a long black cloak which draped her from shoulder to heel. All
that could be distinguished of her was the white nape of her neck, and a great twist
of dead gold hair. Her presence awakened the liveliest interest in Pasquin Leroy,
who found it impossible to avoid nudging his companions, and whispering—

"A woman! By Heaven, this drama becomes interesting!"

But Axel Regor and Max Graub were seemingly not disposed to levity, and they offered no response to their lighter minded comrade beyond vague hasty side-looks of alarm, which appeared to amuse him to an extent that threatened to go beyond the limits of caution. Sergius Thord, however, saw nothing of their interchange of glances for the moment,— he had other business to settle. Addressing himself at once to the men assembled, he said.—

"Friends and brothers! I bring you three new associates! I have not sought them; they have sought me. On their own heads be their destinies! They offer their names to the Revolutionary Committee, and their services to our Cause!"

A low murmur of approbation from the company greeted this announcement. Johan Zegota advanced a little in front of all the rest.

"Every man is welcome to serve us who will serve us faithfully," he said. "But who are these new comrades, Sergius Thord? What are they?"

"That they must declare for themselves," said Thord, taking a chair at the head of the table which was evidently his accustomed place—"Put them through their examination!"

He seated himself with the air of a king, his whole aspect betokening an authority that would not be trifled with or gainsaid.

"Gott in Himmel!"

This exclamation burst suddenly from the lips of the man called Max Graub.

"What ails you?" said Thord, turning full upon him his glittering eyes that flashed ferocity from under their shaggy brows—"Are you afraid?"

"Afraid? Not I!" protested Graub—"But, gentlemen, think a moment! You speak of putting us—myself and my friends—through an examination! Why should you examine us? We are three poor adventurers—what can we have to tell?"

"Much, I should imagine!" retorted Zegota—"Adventurers are not such without adventures! Your white hairs testify to some experience of life."

"My white hairs— *my* white hairs!" exclaimed Graub, when a touch from Axel Regor apparently recalled something to his mind for he began to laugh—"True, gentlemen! Very true! I had forgotten! I have had some adventures and some experiences! My good friend there, Pasquin Leroy, has also had adventures and experiences,—so have we all! Myself, I am a poor German, grown old in the service of a bad king! I have been kicked out of that service—Ach!—just for telling the truth; which is very much the end of all truth telling, is it not? Tell lies,—and kings will reward you and make you rich and great!—but tell truth, and see what the kings will give you for it! Kicks, and no halfpence! Pardon! I interrupt this so pleasant meeting!"

All the men present looked at him curiously, but said nothing in response to his outburst. Johan Zegota, seating himself next to Sergius Thord, opened a large parchment volume that lay on the table, and taking up a pen addressed himself to Thord, saying—

"Will you ask the questions, or shall I?"

"You, by all means! Proceed in the usual manner."

Whereupon Zegota began.—

"Stand forth, comrades!"

The three strangers advanced.

"Your names? Each one answer separately, please!"

"Pasquin Leroy!"

"Axel Regor!"

"Max Graub!"

"Of what nationality, Pasquin Leroy?"

Leroy smiled. "Truly I claim none!" he said; "I was born a slave."

"A slave!"

The words were repeated in tones of astonishment round the room.

"Why, yes, a slave!" repeated Leroy quietly. "You have heard of black slaves,— have you not heard of white ones too? There are countries still, where men purchase other men of their own blood and colour;— tyrannous governments, which force such men to work for them, chained to one particular place till they die. I am one of those,—though escaped for the present. You can ask me more of my country if you will; but a slave has no country save that of his master. If you care at all for my services, you will spare me further examination on this subject!"

Zegota looked enquiringly at Thord.

"We will pass that question," said the latter, in a low tone.

Zegota resumed—

"You, Axel Regor—are you a slave too?"

Axel Regor smiled languidly.

"No! I am what is called a free-born subject of the realm. I do what I like, though not always how I like, or when I like!"

"And you, Max Graub?"

"German!" said that individual firmly; "German to the backbone— Socialist to the soul!—and an enemy of all ruling sovereigns,— particularly the one that rules *me*!"

Thord smiled darkly.

"If you feel inclined to jest, Max Graub, I must warn you that jesting is not suited to the immediate moment."

"Jesting! I never was more in earnest in my life!" declared Graub,— "Why have I left my native country? Merely because it is governed by Kaiser Wilhelm!"

Thord smiled again.

"The subject of nationality seems to excite all three of you," he said, "and though we ask you the question *pro forma*, it is not absolutely necessary that we should know from whence you come. We require your names, and your oath of fealty; but before binding yourselves, I will read you our laws, and the rules of membership for this society; rules to which, if you join us, you are expected to conform."

"Suppose, for the sake of argument," said Pasquin Leroy,—"that after hearing the rules we found it wisest to draw back? Suppose my friends, —if not myself,— were disinclined to join your Society;—what would happen?"

As he asked the question a curious silence fell upon the company, and all eyes were turned upon the speaker. There was a dead pause for a moment, and then Thord replied slowly and with emphasis:—

"Nothing would happen save this,—that you would be bound by a solemn oath never to reveal what you had heard or seen here to-night, and that you would from henceforth be tracked every day and hour of your life by those who would take care that you kept your oath!"

"You see!" exclaimed Axel Regor excitedly, "There is danger——"

"Danger? Of what?" asked Pasquin Leroy coldly;—"Of death? Each one of us, and all three of us would fully merit it, if we broke our word! Gentlemen both!"— and he addressed his two companions, "If you fear any harm may come to yourselves through joining this society, pray withdraw while there is yet time! My own mind is made up; I intend to become familiar with the work of the Revolutionary Committee, and to aid its cause by my personal service!"

A loud murmur of applause came from the company. Axel Regor and Max Graub glanced at Leroy, and saw in his face that his decision was unalterable.

"Then we will work for the Cause, also," said Max Graub resignedly. "What you determine upon, we shall do, shall we not, Axel?"

Axel Regor gave a brief assent.

Sergius Thord looked at them all straightly and keenly.

"You have finally decided?"

"We have!" replied Leroy. "We will enrol ourselves as your associates at once."

Whereupon Johan Zegota rose from his place, and unlocking an iron safe which stood in one corner of the room, took out a roll of parchment and handed it to Thord, who, unfolding it, read in a clear though low voice the following:—

"We, the Revolutionary Committee, are organized as a Brotherhood, bound by all the ties of life, death, and our common humanity, to destroy the abuses, and redress the evils, which self-seeking and tyrannous Governments impose upon the suffering poor.

"*Firstly:* We bind ourselves to resist all such laws as may in any degree interfere with the reasonable, intellectual, and spiritual freedom of man or woman.

"*Secondly:* We swear to agitate against all forms of undue and excessive taxation, which, while scarcely affecting the rich, make life more difficult and unendurable to the poor.

"*Thirdly:* We protest against the domination of priestcraft, and the secret methods which are employed by the Church to obtain undue influence in Governmental matters.

"*Fourthly:* We are determined to stand firmly against the entrance of foreign competitors in the country's trade and business. All heads and ruling companies of firms employing foreigners instead of native workmen, are marked out by us as traitors, and are reserved for traitors' punishment.

"*Fifthly:* We are sworn to exterminate the existing worthless Government, and to replace it by a working body of capable and intelligent men, elected by the universal vote of the entire country. Such elections must take place freely and openly, and no secret influence shall be used to return any one person or party to power. Those attempting to sway opinion by bribery and corruption, will be named to the public, and exposed to disgrace and possible death.

"*Sixthly:* We are resolved to unmask to the public the duplicity, treachery, and self-interested motives of the Secretary of State, Carl Perousse.

"*Seventhly:* We are sworn to bring about such changes as shall elevate a Republic to supreme power, and for this purpose are solemnly pledged to destroy the present Monarchy."

"These," said Sergius Thord, "are the principal objects of our Society's work. There are other points to be considered, but these are sufficient for the present. I will now read the rules, which each member of our Brotherhood must follow if he would serve us faithfully."

He turned over another leaf of the parchment scroll he held, and continued, reading very slowly and distinctly:

"*Rule 1.*—Each member of the Revolutionary Committee shall swear fidelity to the Cause, and pledge himself to maintain inviolable secrecy on all matters connected with his membership and his work for the Society.

"*Rule 2.*—No member shall track, follow, or enquire into the movements of any other member.

"*Rule 3.*—Once in every month all members are expected to meet together at a given place, decided upon by the Chief of the Committee at the previous meeting, when business will be discussed, and lots drawn, to determine the choice of such members as may be fitted to perform such business.

"*Rule 4.*—No member shall be bound to give his address, or to state where he travels, or when or how he goes, as in all respects save that of his membership he is a free man.

"*Rule 5.*—In this same respect of his membership, he is bound to appear, or to otherwise report himself once a month at the meeting of the Committee. Should he fail to do so either by person, or by letter satisfactorily explaining his absence, he will be judged as a traitor, and dealt with accordingly.

"*Rule 6.*—In the event of any member being selected to perform any deed involving personal danger or loss to himself, the rest of the members are pledged to shelter him from the consequences of his act, and to provide him with all the necessaries of life, till his escape from harm is ensured and his safety guaranteed."

"You have heard all now," said Thord, as he laid aside the parchment scroll;

"Are you still willing to take the oath?"

"Entirely so!" rejoined Pasquin Leroy cheerfully; "You have but to administer it."

Here a man, who had been sitting in a dark corner apart from the table, with his head buried in his hands, suddenly looked up, showing a thin, fine, eager face, a pair of wild eyes, and a tumbled mass of dark curly hair, plentifully sprinkled with grey.

"Ah!" he cried,—"Now comes the tragic moment, when the spectators hold their breath, and the blue flame is turned on, and the man manages the lime-light so that its radiance shall fall on the face of the chief actor—or Actress! And the bassoons and 'cellos grumble inaudible nothings to the big drum! Administer the oath, Sergius Thord!"

A smile went the round of the company.

"Have you only just wakened up from sleep, Paul Zouche?" asked Zegota.

"I never sleep," answered Zouche, pushing his hair back from his forehead;—"Unless sleep compels me, by force, to yield to its coarse and commonplace persuasion. To lie down in a shirt and snore the hours away! Faugh! Can anything be more gross or vulgar! Time flies so quickly, and life is so short, that I cannot afford to waste any moment in such stupid unconsciousness. I can drink wine, make love, and kill rascals—all these occupations are much more interesting than sleeping. Come, Sergius! Play the great trick of the evening! Administer the oath!"

A frowning line puckered Thord's brows, but the expression of vexation was but momentary. Turning to Leroy again he said:

"You are quite ready?"

"Quite," replied Leroy.

"And your friends——?"

Leroy smiled. "They are ready also!"

There followed a pause. Then Thord called in a clear low tone—

"Lotys!"

The woman sitting in the embrasure of the window rose, and turning round fully confronted all the men. Her black cloak falling back on either side, disclosed her figure robed in dead white, with a scarlet sash binding her waist. Her face, pale and serene, was not beautiful; yet beauty was suggested in every feature. Her eyes seemed to be half closed in a drooping indifference under the white lids, which were fringed heavily with dark gold lashes. A sculptor might have said, that whatever claim to beauty she had was contained in the proud poise of her throat, and the bounteous curve of her bosom, but though in a manner startled by her appearance, the three men who had chanced upon this night's adventure were singularly disappointed in it. They had somehow expected that when that mysterious cloaked feminine figure turned round, a vision of dazzling beauty would be disclosed; and at the first glance there was nothing whatever about this woman that seemed particularly worthy of note. She was not young or old—possibly between twenty-eight or thirty. She was not tall or short; she was merely of the usual medium height,—so that altogether she was one of those provoking individuals, who not seldom deceive the eye at first sight by those ordinary looks which veil an extraordinary personality.

She stood like an automatic figure, rigid and silent,—till Sergius Thord signed to his three new associates to advance. Then with a movement, rapid as a flash of lightning, she suddenly drew a dagger from her scarlet girdle, and held it out to them. Nerved as he was to meet danger, Pasquin Leroy recoiled slightly, while his two companions started as if to defend him. As she saw this, the woman raised her drooping eyelids, and a pair of wonderful eyes shone forth, dark blue as iris-flowers, while a faint scornful smile lifted the corners of her mouth. But she said nothing.

"There is no cause to fear!" said Sergius Thord, glancing with a touch of derision in his looks from one to the other, "Lotys is the witness of all our vows! Swear now after me upon this drawn dagger which she holds,—lay your right hands here upon the blade!"

Thus adjured, Pasquin Leroy approached, and placed his right hand upon the shining steel.

"I swear in the name of God, and in the presence of Lotys, that I will faithfully work for the Cause of the Revolutionary Committee,—and that I will adhere to its rules and obey its commands, till all shall be done that is destined to be done! And may the death I deserve come suddenly upon me if ever I break my vow!"

Slowly and emphatically Pasquin Leroy repeated this formula after Sergius Thord, and his two companions did the same, though perhaps less audibly. This ceremony performed, the woman called Lotys looked at them steadfastly, and the smile that played on her lips changed from scorn to sweetness. The dark blue iris-coloured eyes deepened in lustre, and flashed brilliantly from under their drowsy lids,—a rosy flush tinted the clear paleness of her skin, and like a statue warming to life she became suddenly beautiful.

"You have sworn bravely!" she said, in a low thrilling voice. "Now sign and seal!"

As she spoke she lifted her bare left arm, and pricked it with the point of the dagger. A round, full drop of blood like a great ruby welled up on the white skin. All the men had risen from their places, and were gathered about her;—this 'taking of the oath' was evidently the dramatic event of their existence as a community.

"The pen, Sergius!" she said.

Thord approached with a white unused quill, and a vellum scroll on which the names of all the members of the Society were written in ominous red. He handed these writing implements to Leroy.

"Dip your pen here," said Lotys, pointing to the crimson drop on her arm, and eyeing him still with the same half-sweet, half-doubting smile—"But when the quill is full, beware that you write no treachery!"

For one second Leroy appeared to hesitate. He was singularly unnerved by the glances of those dark blue eyes, which like searchlights seemed to penetrate into every nook and cranny of his soul. But his recklessness and love of adventure having led him so far, it was now too late to retract or to reconsider the risks he might possibly be running. He therefore took the quill and dipped it into the crimson drop that welled from that soft white flesh.

"This is the strangest ink I have ever used!" he said lightly,—"but— at your command, Madame———!"

"At my command," rejoined Lotys, "your use of it shall make your oath indelible!"

He smiled, and wrote his name boldly 'Pasquin Leroy' and held out the pen for his companions to follow his example.

"Ach Gott!" exclaimed Max Graub, as he dipped the pen anew into the vital fluid from a woman's veins—"I write my name, Madame, in words of life, thanks to your condescension!"

"True!" she answered,—"And only by your own falsehood can you change them into words of death!"

Signing his name 'Max Graub,' he looked up and met her searching gaze. Something there was in the magnetic depth of her eyes that strangely embarrassed him, for he stepped back hastily as though intimidated. Axel Regor took the pen from his hand, and wrote his name, or rather scrawled it carelessly, almost impatiently,—showing neither hesitation nor repugnance to this unusual method of subscribing a document.

"You are acting on compulsion!" said Lotys, addressing him in a low tone; "Your compliance is in obedience to some other command than ours! And—you will do well to remain obedient!"

Axel Regor gave her an amazed glance,—but she paid no heed to it, and binding her arm with her kerchief, let her long white sleeve fall over it.

"So, you are enrolled among the sons of my blood!" she said, "So are you bound to me and mine!" She moved to the further end of the table and stood there looking round upon them all. Again the slow, sweet, half-disdainful smile irradiated her features. "Well, children!—what else remains to do? What next? What next can there be but drink—smoke —talk! Man's three most cherished amusements!"

She sat down, throwing back her heavy cloak on either side of her. Her hair had come partly unbound, and noticing a tress of it falling on her shoulder, she drew out the comb and let it fall altogether in a mass of gold-brown, like the tint of a dull autumn leaf, flecked here and there with amber. Catching it dexterously in one hand, she twisted it up again in a loose knot, thrusting the comb carelessly through.

"Drink—smoke—talk, Sergius!" she repeated, still smiling; "Shall I ring?"

Sergius Thord stood looking at her irresolutely, with the half-angry, half-pleading expression of a chidden child.

"As you please, Lotys!" he answered. Whereupon she pressed an invisible spring under the table, which set a bell ringing in some lower quarter of the house.

"Pasquin Leroy, Axel Regor, Max Graub!" she said—"Take your places for to-night beside me—newcomers are always thus distinguished! And all of you sit down! You are grouped at present like hungry wolves waiting to spring. But you are not really hungry, except for something which is not food! And you are not waiting for anything except for permission to talk! I give it to you—talk, children! Talk yourselves hoarse! It will do you good! And I will personate supreme wisdom by listening to you in silence!"

A kind of shamed laugh went round the company,—then followed the scuffling of feet, and grating of chairs against the floor, and presently the table was completely surrounded, the men sitting close up together, and Sergius Thord occupying his place at their head.

When they were all seated, they formed a striking assembly of distinctly marked personalities. There were very few mean types among them, and the stupid, half-vague and languid expression of the modern loafer or 'do nothing' creature, who just for lack of useful work plots mischief, was not to be seen on any of their countenances. A certain moroseness and melancholy seemed to brood like a delayed storm among them, and to cloud the very atmosphere they breathed, but apart from this, intellectuality was the dominant spirit suggested by their outward looks and bearing. Plebeian faces and vulgar manners are, unfortunately, not rare in representative gatherings of men whose opinions are allowed to sway the destinies of nations, and it was strange to see a group of individuals who were sworn to upset existing law and government so distinguished by refined and even noble appearance. Their clothes were shabby,—their aspect certainly betokened long suffering and contention with want and poverty, but they were, taken all together, a set of men who, if they had been members of a recognized parliament or senate, would have presented a fine collection of capable heads to an observant painter. As soon as they were gathered round the table under the presidency of Sergius Thord at one end, and the tranquil tolerance of the mysterious Lotys at the other, they broke through the silence and reserve which they had carefully maintained till their three new comrades had been irrecoverably enrolled among them, and conversation went on briskly. The topic of 'The King *versus* the Jesuits' was one of the first they touched upon, Sergius Thord relating for the benefit of all his associates, how he had found Pasquin Leroy reading by lamplight the newspaper which reported his Majesty's refusal to grant any portion of Crown lands to the priests, and which also spoke of 'Thord's Rabble.'

"Here is the paper!" said Leroy, as he heard the narration; "Whoever likes to keep it can do so, as a memento of my introduction to this Society!"

And he tossed it lightly on the table.

"Good!" exclaimed Paul Zouche; "Give it to me, and I will cherish it as a kind of birthday card! What a rag it is! 'Thord's Rabble' eh! Sergius, what have you been doing that this little flea of an editor should jump out of his ink-pot and bite you? Does he hurt much?"

"Hurt!" Thord laughed aloud. "If I had money enough to pay the man ten golden coins a week where his present employer gives him five, he would dance to any tune I whistled!"

"Is that so?" asked Leroy, with interest.

"Do you not know that it is so?" rejoined Thord. "You tell me you write Socialistic works—you should know something concerning the press."

"Ah!" said Max Graub, nodding his head sagely, "He does know much, but not all! It would need more penetration than even *he* possesses, to know all! Alas!—my friend was never a popular writer!"

"Like myself!" exclaimed Zouche, "I am not popular, and I never shall be. But I know how to make myself reputed as a great genius, and all the very respectable literary men are beginning to recognize me as such. Do you know why?"

"Because you drink more than is good for you, my poor Zouche!" said Lotys tranquilly; "That is one reason!"

"Hear her!" cried Zouche,—"Does she not always, like the Sphinx, propound enigmas! Lotys,—little, domineering Lotys, why in the name of Heaven should I secure recognition as a poet, through drunkenness?"

"Because your vice kills your genius," said Lotys; "Therefore you are quite safe! If you were less of a scamp you would be a great man,— perhaps the greatest in the country! That would never do! Your rivals would never forgive you! But you are a hopeless rascal, incapable of winning much honour; and so you are compassionately recognized as somebody who might do something if he only would—that is all, my Zouche! You are an excellent after-dinner topic with those who are more successful than yourself; and that is the only fame you will ever win, believe me!"

"Now by all the gods and goddesses!" cried Paul—"I do protest——"

"After supper, Zouche!" interrupted Lotys, as the door of the room opened, and a man entered, bearing a tray loaded with various eatables, jugs of beer, and bottles of spirituous liquors,—"Protest as much as you like then,—but not just now!"

And with quick, deft hands she helped to set the board. None of the men offered to assist her, and Leroy watching her, felt a sudden sense of annoyance that this woman should seem, even for a moment, to be in the position of a servant to them all.

"Can I do nothing for you?" he said, in a low tone—"Why should you wait upon us?"

"Why indeed!" she answered—"Except that you are all by nature awkward, and do not know how to wait properly upon yourselves!"

Her eyes had a gleam of mischievous mockery in them; and Leroy was conscious of an irritation which he could scarcely explain to himself. Decidedly, he thought, this Lotys was an unpleasant woman. She was 'extremely plain,' so he mentally declared, in a kind of inward huff,— though he was bound to concede that now and then she had a very beautiful, almost inspired expression. After all, why should she not set out jugs and bottles, and loaves of bread, and hunks of ham and cheese before these men? She was probably in their pay! Scarcely had this idea flashed across his mind than he was ashamed of it. This Lotys, whoever she might actually be, was no paid hireling; there was something in her every look and action that set her high above any suspicion that she would accept the part of a salaried *comedienne* in the Socialist farce. Annoyed with himself, though he knew not why, he turned his gaze from her to the man who had brought in the supper, —a hunchback, who, notwithstanding his deformity, was powerfully built, and of a countenance which, marked as it was with the drawn pathetic look of long-continued physical suffering, was undeniably handsome. His large brown eyes, like those of a faithful dog, followed every movement of Lotys with anxious and wistful affection, and Leroy, noticing this, began to wonder whether she was his wife or daughter? Or was she related in either of these ways to Sergius Thord? His reflections were interrupted by a slight touch from Max Graub who was seated next to him.

"Will you drink with these fellows?" said Graub, in a cautious whisper —"Expect to be ill, if you do!"

"You shall prescribe for me!" answered Leroy in the same low tone—"I faithfully promise to call in your assistance! But drink with them I must, and will!"

Graub gave a short sigh and a shrug, and said no more. The hunchback was going the round of the table, filling tall glasses with light Bavarian beer.

"Where is the little Pequita?" asked Zouche, addressing him—"Have you sent her to bed already, Sholto?"

Sholto looked timorously round till he met the bright reassuring glance of Lotys, and then he replied hesitatingly—

"Yes!—no—I have not sent the little one to bed;—she returned from her work at the theatre, tired out—quite tired out, poor child! She is asleep now."

"Ha ha! A few years more, and she will not sleep!" said Zouche—"Once in her teens—"

"Once in her teens, she leaves the theatre and comes to me," said Lotys, "And you will see very little of her, Zouche, and you will know less! That will do, Sholto! Good-night!"

"Good-night!" returned the hunchback—"I thank you, Madame!—I thank you, gentlemen!"

And with a slight salutation, not devoid of grace, he left the room.

Zouche was sulky, and pushing aside his glass of beer, poured out for himself some strong spirit from a bottle instead.

"You do not favour me to-night, Lotys," he said irritably—"You interrupt and cross me in everything I say!"

"Is it not a woman's business to interrupt and cross a man?" queried Lotys, with a laugh,—"As I have told you before, Zouche, I will not have Sholto worried!"

"Who worries him?" grumbled Zouche—"Not I!"

"Yes, you!—you worry him on his most sensitive point—his daughter," said Lotys;—"Why can you not leave the child alone? Sholto is an Englishman," she explained, turning to Pasquin Leroy and his companions —"His history is a strange one enough. He is the rightful heir to a large estate in England, but he was born deformed. His father hated him, and preferred the second son, who was straight and handsome. So Sholto disappeared."

"Disappeared!" echoed Leroy—"You mean——"

"I mean that he left his father's house one morning, and never returned. The clothes he wore were found floating in the river near by, and it was concluded that he had been drowned while bathing. The second son, therefore, inherited the property; and poor Sholto was scarcely missed; certainly not mourned. Meanwhile he went away, and got on board a Spanish trading boat bound for Cadiz. At Cadiz he found work, and also something that sweetened work—love! He married a pretty Spanish girl who adored him, and—as often happens when lovers rejoice too much in their love—she died after a year's happiness. Sholto is all alone in the world with the little child his Spanish wife left him, Pequita. She is only eleven years old, but her gift of dancing is marvellous, and she gets employment at one of the cheap theatres here. If an influential manager could see her performance, she might coin money."

"The influential manager would probably cheat her," said Zouche,— "Things are best left alone. Sholto is content!"

"Are you content?" asked Johan Zegota, helping himself from the bottle that stood near him.

"I? Why, no! I should not be here if I were!"

"Discontent, then, is your chief bond of union?" said Axel Regor, beginning to take part in the conversation.

"It is the very knot that ties us all together!" said Zouche with enthusiasm.— "Discontent is the mother of progress! Adam was discontented with the garden of Eden,—and found a whole world outside its gates!"

"He took Eve with him to keep up the sickness of dissatisfaction," said Zegota; "There would certainly have been no progress without *her*!"

"Pardon,—Cain was the true Progressivist and Reformer," put in Graub; "Some fine sentiment of the garden of Eden was in his blood, which impelled him to offer up a vegetable sacrifice to the Deity, whereas Abel had already committed murder by slaying lambs. According to the legend, God preferred the 'savour' of the lambs, so perhaps,—who knows!—the idea that the savour of Abel might be equally agreeable to Divine senses induced Cain to kill him as a special 'youngling.' This was a Progressive act,—a step beyond mere lambs!"

Everyone laughed, except Sergius Thord. He had fallen into a heavy, brooding silence, his head sunk on his breast, his wild hair falling forward like a mane, and his right hand clenched and resting on the table.

"Sergius!" called Lotys.

He did not answer.

"He is in one of his far-away moods,"—said one of the men next to Axel Regor,—"It is best not to disturb him."

Paul Zouche, however, had no such scruples. "Sergius!" he cried,—"Come out of your cloud of meditation! Drink to the health of our three new comrades!"

All the members of the company filled their glasses, and Thord, hearing the noise and clatter, looked up with a wild stare.

"What are you doing?" he asked slowly;—"I thought some one spoke of Cain killing Abel!"

"It was I," said Graub—"I spoke of it—irreverently, I fear,—but the story itself is irreverent. The notion that 'God,' should like roast meat is the height of blasphemy!"

Zouche burst into a violent fit of laughter. But Thord went on talking in a low tone, as though to himself.

"Cain killing Abel!" he repeated—"Always the same horrible story is repeated through history—brother against brother,—blood crying out for blood—life torn from the weak and helpless body—all for what? For a little gold,—a passing trifle of power! Cain killing Abel! My God, art Thou not yet weary of the old eternal crime!"

He spoke in a semi-whisper which thrilled through the room. A momentary hush prevailed, and then Lotys called again, her voice softened to a caressing sweetness.

"Sergius!"

He started, and shook himself out of his reverie this time. Raising his hand, he passed it in a vague mechanical way across his brow as though suddenly wakened from a dream.

"Yes, yes! Let us drink to our three new comrades," he said, and rose to his feet. "To your health, friends! And may you all stand firm in the hour of trial!"

All the company sprang up and drained their glasses, and when the toast was drunk and they were again seated, Pasquin Leroy asked if he might be allowed to return thanks.

"I do not know," he said with a courteous air, "whether it is permissible for a newly-enrolled associate of this Brotherhood to make a speech on the first night of his membership,—but after the cordial welcome I and my comrades, strangers as we are, have received at your hands, I should like to say a few words—if, without breaking any rules of the Order, I may do so."

"Hear, hear!" shouted Zouche, who had been steadily drinking for the last few moments,—"Speak on, man! Whoever heard of a dumb Socialist! Rant—rant! Rant and rave!—as I do, when the fit is on me! Do I not, Thord? Do I not move you even to tears?"

"And laughter!" put in Zegota. "Hold your tongue, Zouche! No other man can talk at all, if you once begin!"

Zouche laughed, and drained his glass.

"True!—my genius is of an absorbing quality! Silence, gentlemen! Silence for our new comrade! 'Pasquin' stands for the beginning of a jest—so we may hope he will be amusing,—'Leroy' stands for the king, and so we may expect him to be non-political!"

CHAPTER VIII
THE KING'S DOUBLE

A S Leroy rose to speak, there was a little commotion. Max Graub upset his glass, and seemed to be having a struggle under the table with Axel Regor.

"What ails you?" said Leroy, glancing at his friends with an amazed air—"Are you quarrelling?"

"Quarrelling!" echoed Max Graub, "Why, no—but what man will have his beer upset without complaint? Tell me that!"

"You upset it!" said Regor angrily—"I did not."

"You did!" retorted Graub, "and because I pushed you for it, you showed me a pistol in your pocket! I object to be shown a pistol. So I have taken it away. Here it is!" and he laid the weapon on the table in front of him.

A look of anger darkened Leroy's brows.

"I was not aware you carried arms," he said coldly.

Sergius Thord noticed his annoyance.

"There is nothing remarkable in that, my friend!" he interposed—"We all carry arms,—there is not one of us at this table who has not a loaded pistol,—even Lotys is no exception to this rule."

"Now by my word!" said Graub, "*I* have no loaded pistol,—and I will swear Leroy is equally unarmed!"

"Entirely so!" said Leroy quietly—"I never suspect any man of evil intentions towards me."

As he said this, Lotys leaned forward impulsively and stretched out her hand,—a beautiful hand, well-shaped and white as a white rose petal.

"I like you for that!"—she said—"It is the natural attitude of a brave man!"

A slight colour warmed his bronzed skin as he took her hand, pressed it gently, and let it go again. Axel Regor looked up defiantly.

"Well, I *do* suspect every man of evil intentions!" he said, "So you may all just as well know the worst of me at once! My experience of life has perhaps been exceptionally unpleasant; but it has taught me that as a rule no man is your friend till you have made it worth his while!"

"By favours bestowed, or favours to come?" queried Thord, smiling,—"However, without any argument, Axel Regor, I am inclined to think you are right!"

"Then a weapon is permissible here?" asked Graub.

"Not only permissible, but necessary," replied Thord. "As members of this Brotherhood we live always prepared for some disaster,—always on our guard against treachery. Comrades!" and raising his voice he addressed the whole party. "Lay down your arms, all at once and together!"

In one instant, as if in obedience to a military order, the table was lined on either side with pistols. Beside these weapons, there was a goodly number of daggers, chiefly of the small kind such as are used in Corsica, encased in leather sheaths. Pasquin Leroy smiled as he saw Lotys lay down one of those tiny but deadly weapons, together with a small silver-mounted pistol.

"Forewarned is forearmed!" he said gaily;—"Madame, if I ever offend, I shall look to you for a happy dispatch! Gentlemen, I have still to make my speech, and if you permit it, I will speak now,—unarmed as I am,— with all these little metal mouths ready to deal death upon me if I happen to make any observation which may displease you!"

"By Heaven! A brave man!" cried Zouche; "Thord, you have picked up a trump card! Speak, Pasquin Leroy! We will forgive you, even if you praise the King!"

Leroy stood silent for a moment, as if thinking. His two companions looked up at him once or twice in unquestionable alarm and wonderment, but he did not appear to be conscious of their observation. On the contrary, some very deeply seated feeling seemed to be absorbing his soul,—and it was perhaps this suppressed emotion which gave such a rich vibrating force to his accents when he at last spoke.

"Friends and Brothers!" he said;—"It is difficult for one who has never experienced the three-fold sense of Liberty, Equality and Fraternity until to-night, to express in the right manner the sense of gratitude which I, a complete stranger to you, feel for the readiness and cordiality of the welcome you have extended to me and my companions, accepting us without hesitation, as members of your Committee, and as associates in the work of the Cause you have determined to maintain. It is an Ideal Cause,—I need not tell you that! To rescue and protect the poor from the tyranny of the rich and strong, was the mission of Christ when He visited this earth; and it would perhaps be unwise on my part, and discouraging to yourselves, to remind you that even He has failed! The strong, the selfish, and the cruel, still delight in oppressing their more helpless fellows, despite the theories of Christianity. And it is perfectly natural that it should be so, seeing that the Christian Church itself has become a mere system of money-making and self-advancement."

A burst of applause interrupted him. Eyes lightened with eager enthusiasm, and every face was turned towards him. He went on:—

"To think of the great Founder of a great Creed, and then to consider what his pretended followers have made of Him and His teaching, is sufficient to fill the soul with the sickness of despair and humiliation! To remember that Christ came to teach all men the Gospel of love,—and to find them after eighteen hundred years still preferring the Gospel of hate,—is enough to make one doubt the truth of religion altogether! The Divine Socialist preached a creed too good and pure for this world; and when we try to follow it, we are beaten back on all sides by the false conventionalities and customs of a sacerdotal system grown old in self-seeking, not in self-sacrifice. Were Christ to come again, the first thing He would probably do would be to destroy all the churches, saying: 'I never knew you: depart from me ye that work iniquity!' But till He does come again, it rests with the thinkers of the time to protest against wrongs and abuses, even if they cannot destroy them,—to expose falsehood, even if they cannot utterly undo its vicious work. Seeing, however, that the greater majority of men are banded on the side of wealth and material self- interest, it is unfortunately only a few who remain to work for the cause of the poor, and for such equal rights of justice as you—as we— in our present Association claim to be most worthy of man's best efforts. It may be asked by those outside such a Fraternity as ours,— 'What do they want? What would they have that they cannot obtain?' I would answer that we want to see the end of a political system full of bribery and corruption,—that we desire the disgrace and exposure of such men as those, who, under the pretence of serving the country, merely line their own coffers out of the taxes they inflict upon the people;—and that if we see a king inclined to favour the overbearing dominance of a political party governed by financial considerations alone,—a party which has no consideration for the wider needs of the whole nation, we from our very hearts and souls desire the downfall of that king!"

A low, deep murmur responded to his words,—a sound like the snarl of wolves, deep, fierce, and passionate. A close observer might perhaps have detected a sudden pallor on Leroy's face as he heard this ominous growl, and an involuntary clenching of the hand on the part of Axel Regor. Max Graub looked up.

"Ah so, my friends! You hate the King?"

No answer was vouchsafed to this query. The interruption was evidently unwelcome, all eyes being still fixed on Leroy. He went on tranquilly:

"I repeat—that wherever and whenever a king—any king—voluntarily and knowingly, supports iniquity and false dealing in his ministers, he lays himself open to suspicion, attack, and dethronement! I speak with particular feeling on this point, because, apart from whatever may be the thoughts and opinions of these who are assembled here to-night, I have a special reason of my own for hating the King! That reason is marked on my countenance! I bear an extraordinary resemblance to him, —so great indeed, that I might be taken for his twin brother if he had one! And I beg of you, my friends, to look at me long and well, that you make no error concerning me, for, being now your comrade, I do not wish to be mistaken for your enemy!"

He drew himself up, lifting his head with an air of indomitable pride and grace which well became him. An exclamation of surprise broke from all present, and Sergius Thord bent forward to examine his features with close attention. Every man at the table did the same, but none regarded him more earnestly or more searchingly than Lotys. Her wonderful eyes seemed to glow and burn with strange interior fires, as she kept them steadily fixed upon his face.

"Yes—you are strangely like the King!" she said—"That is,—so far as I am able to judge by his portraits and coins. I have never seen him."

"I *have* seen him,"—said Sergius Thord, "though only at a distance. And I wonder I did not notice the strange resemblance you bear to him before you called my attention to it. Are you in any way related to him?"

"Related to him!" Leroy laughed aloud. "No! If the late King had any bastard sons, I am not one of them! But I pray you again all to carefully note this hateful resemblance,—a resemblance I would fain rid me of—for it makes me seem a living copy of the man I most despise!"

There was a pause,—during which he stood quietly, submitting himself to the fire of a hundred wondering, questioning, and inquisitorial eyes without flinching.

"You are all satisfied?" he then asked; "You, Sergius Thord,—my chief and commander,—you, and all here present are satisfied?"

"Satisfied?—Yes!" replied Thord; "But sorry that your personality resembles that of a fool and a knave!"

A strange grimace distorted the countenance of Max Graub, but he quickly buried his nose and his expression together in a foaming glass of beer.

"You cannot be so sorry for me as I am for myself!" said Leroy, "And now to finish the few words I have been trying to say. I thank you from my heart for your welcome, and for the trust you have reposed in me and my companions. I am proud to be one of you; and I promise that you shall all have reason to be glad that I am associated with your Cause! And to prove my good faith, I undertake to set about working for you without a day's delay; and towards this object, I give you my word that before our next meeting something shall be done to shake the political stronghold of Carl Perousse!"

Sergius Thord sprang up excitedly.

"Do that," he said, "and were you a thousand times more like the King than you are, you shall be the first to command our service and honour!"

Loud acclamation followed his words, and all the men gathered close up about Leroy. He looked round upon them, half-smiling, half-serious.

"But you must tell me what to do!" he said. "You must explain to me why you consider Perousse a traitor, and how you think it best his treachery should be proved. For, remember, I am a stranger to this part of the country, and my accidental resemblance to the King does not make me his subject!"

"True!" said Paul Zouche,—his eyes were feverishly bright and his cheeks flushed—"To be personally like a liar does not oblige one to tell lies! To call oneself a poet does not enable one to write poetry! And to build a cathedral does not make one a saint! To know all the highways and byways of the Perousse policy, you must penetrate into the depths and gutter-slushes of the great newspaper which is subsidised by the party to that policy! And this is difficult—exceedingly difficult, let me assure you, my bold Pasquin! And if you can perform such a 'pasquinade' as shall take you into these Holy of Holy purlieus of mischief and money-making, you will deserve to be chief of the Committee, instead of Sergius! Sergius talks—he will talk your head off!—but he does nothing!"

"I do what I can,"—said Thord, patiently. "It is true I have no access to the centres of diplomacy or journalism. But I hold the People in the hollow of my hand!"

He spoke with deep and concentrated feeling, and the power of his soul looked out eloquently from the darkening flash of his eyes. Leroy studied his features with undisguised interest.

"If you thus hold the People," he said,—"Why not bid them rise against the evil and tyranny of which they have cause to complain?"

Thord shook his head.

"To rouse the People," he replied, "would be worse than to rouse a herd of starving lions from their forest dens, and give them freedom to slay and devour! Nay!—the time is not yet! All gentle means must be tried; and if these fail—why then—!"

He broke off, but his clenched hand and expressive glance said the rest.

"Why do you not use the most powerful of all the weapons ever invented for the destruction of one's enemies—the Pen?" asked Max Graub. "Start a newspaper, for example, and gibbet your particular favourite Carl Perousse therein!"

"Bah! He would get up a libel case, and advertise himself a little more by that method!" said Zegota contemptuously; "And besides, a newspaper needs unlimited capital behind it. We have no rich friends."

"Rich friends!" exclaimed Lotys suddenly; "Who speaks of them—who needs them? Rich friends expect you to toady to them; to lick the ground under their feet; to fawn and flatter and lie, and be anything but honest men! The rich are the vulgar of this world;—no one who has heart, or soul, or sense, would condescend to seek friendships among those whose only claim to precedence is the possession of a little more yellow metal than their neighbours."

"Nevertheless, they and their yellow metal are the raw material, which Genius may as well use to pave its way through life," said Zegota. "Lotys, you are too much of an idealist!"

"Idealist! And you call yourself a realist, poor child!" said Lotys with a laugh; "I tell you I would sooner starve than accept favour or assistance from the merely rich!"

"Of course you would!" said Zouche, "And is not that precisely the reason why you are set in dominion over us all? We men are not sure of ourselves—but—Heaven knows why!—we are sure of You! I suppose it is because you are sure of yourself! For example, we men are such wretched creatures that we cannot go long without our food,—but you, woman, can fast all day, and scorn the very idea of hunger. We men cannot bear much pain,—but you,—woman,—can endure suffering of your own without complaint, while attending to our various lesser hurts and scratches. Wherefore, just because we feel you are above us in this and many other things, we have set you amongst us as a warning Figurehead, which cries shame upon us if we falter, and reminds us that you, a woman, can do, and probably will do, what we men cannot. Imagine it! You would bear all things for love's sake!—and, frankly speaking, we would bear nothing at all, except for our own immediate and particular pleasure. For that, of course, we would endure everything till we got it, and then—pouf!—we would let it go again in sheer weariness and desire for something else! Is it not so, Sergius?"

"I am glad you know yourself so well!" said Thord gloomily. "Personally, I am not prepared to accept your theory."

"Men are children!" said Lotys, still smiling; "And should be treated as children always, by women! Come, little ones! To bed, all of you! It is growing late, and the rain has ceased."

She went to the window, and unbarring the shutters, opened it. The streets were wet and glistening below, but the clouds had cleared, and a pale watery moon shone out fitfully from the misty sky.

"Say good-night, and part;" she continued. "It is time! This day month we will meet here again,—and our new comrades will then report what progress they have made in the matter of Carl Perousse."

"Tell me," said Leroy, approaching her, "What would you do, Madame, if you had determined, on proving the corruption and falsehood of this at present highly-honoured servant of the State?"

"I should gain access to his chief tool, David Jost, by means of the Prime Minister's signet," said Lotys,—"If I could get the signet!— which I cannot! Nor can you! But if I could, I should persuade Jost to talk freely, and so betray himself. He and Carl Perousse move the Premier and the King whichever way they please."

"Is that so—?" began Leroy, when he was answered by a dozen voices at once:—

"The King is a fool!"

"The King is a slave!"

"The King accepts everything that is set before him as being rightly and wisely ordained,—and never enquires into the justice of what is done!"

"The King assumes to be the friend of the People, but if you ask him to do anything for the People, you only get the secretary's usual answer— 'His Majesty regrets that it is impossible to take any action in the matter'!"

"Wait!—wait!—" said Leroy, with a gesture which called for a moment's silence; "The question is,— *Could* the King do anything if he would?"

"I will answer that!" said Lotys, her eyes flashing, her bosom heaving, and her whole figure instinct with pride and passion; "The King could do everything! The King could be a man if he chose, instead of a dummy! The King could cease to waste his time on fools and light women!—and though he is, and must be a constitutional Monarch, he could so rule all social matters as to make them the better,—not the worse for his influence! There is nothing to prevent the King from doing his most kingly duty!"

Leroy looked at her for a moment in silence.

"Madame, if the King heard your words he might perhaps regret his many follies!" he said courteously;—"But where Society is proved worse, instead of better for a king's influence, is it not somewhat too late to remedy the evil? What of the Queen?"

"The Queen is queen from necessity, not from choice!" said Lotys;—"She has never loved her husband. If she had loved him, perhaps he might,— through her,— have loved his people more!"

There was a note of pathos in her voice that was singularly tender and touching. Anon, as if impatient with herself, she turned to Sergius Thord.

"We must disperse!" she said abruptly; "Daybreak will be upon us before we know it, and we have done no business at all this evening. To enrol three new associates is a matter of fifteen minutes; the rest of our time has been wasted!"

"Do not say so, Madame!" interposed Max Graub, "You have three new friends—three new 'sons of your blood,' as you so poetically call them,—though, truly, I for one am more fit to be your grandfather! And do you consider the time wasted that has been spent in improving and instructing your newly-born children?"

Lotys turned upon him with a look of disdain.

"You are a would-be jester;" she said coldly; "Old men love a jest, I know, but they should take care to make it at the right time, and in the right place. They should not play with edge-tools such as I am, though I suppose, being a German, you think little or nothing of women?"

"Madame!" protested Graub, "I think so much of women that I have never married! Behold me, an unhappy bachelor! I have spared any one of your beautiful sex from the cruel martyrdom of having to endure my life-long company!"

She laughed—a pretty low laugh, and extended her hand with an air of queenly condescension.

"You are amusing!" she said,—"And so I will not quarrel with you! Good-night!"

"Auf wiedersehn!" and Graub kissed the white hand he held. "I shall hope you will command me to be of service to you and yours, ere long!"

"In what way, I wonder," she asked dubiously; "What can you do best? Write? Speak? Or organize meetings?"

"I think," said Graub, speaking very deliberately, "that of all my various accomplishments, which are many—as I shall one day prove to you—I can poison best!"

"Poison!"

The exclamation broke simultaneously from all the company. Graub looked about him with a triumphant air.

"Ah so,—I know I shall be useful," he said; "I can poison so very beautifully and well! One little drop—one, little microbe of mischief—and I can make all your enemies die of cholera, typhoid, bubonic plague, or what you please! I am what is called a Christian scientific poisoner—that is a doctor! You will find me a most invaluable member of this Brotherhood!"

He nodded his head wisely, and smiled. Sergius Thord laid one hand heavily on his shoulder.

"We shall find you useful, no doubt!" he said, "But mark me well, friend! Our mission is not to kill, but to save!—not to poison, but to heal! If we find that by the death of one traitor we can save the lives of thousands, why then that traitor must die. If we know that by killing a king we destroy a country's abuses, that king is sent to his account. But never without warning!—never without earnest pleading that he whom the laws of Truth condemn, may turn from the error of his ways and repent before it is too late. We are not murderers;—we are merely the servants of justice."

"Exactly!" put in Paul Zouche; "You understand? We try to be what God is not,—just!"

"Blaspheme not, Zouche!" said Thord; "Justice is the very eye of God!— the very centre and foundation of the universe."

Zouche laughed discordantly.

"Excellent Sergius! Impulsive Sergius!—with big heart, big head and no logic! Prove to me this eternal justice! Where does it begin? In the creation of worlds without end, all doomed to destruction, and therefore perfectly futile in their existence? In the making of man, who lives his little day with the utmost difficulty, pain and struggle, and is then extinguished, to be heard of no more? The use of it, my Sergius!—point out the use of it! No,—there is no man can answer me that! If I could see the Creator, I would ask Him the question personally—but He hides Himself behind the great big pendulum He has set swinging—tick—tock!—tick—tock! Life—Death!—Life—Death!—and never a reason why the clock is set going! And so we shall never have justice,—simply because there is none! It is not just or reasonable to propound a question to which there is no answer; it is not just or reasonable to endow man with all the thinking powers of brain, and all the imaginative movements of mind, merely to turn him into a pinch of dust afterwards. Every generation, every country strives to get justice done, but cannot,—merely for the fact that God Himself has no idea of it, and therefore it is naturally lacking in His creature, man. Our governing-forces are plainly the elements. No Divine finger stops the earthquake from engulfing a village full of harmless inhabitants, simply because of the injustice of such utter destruction! See now!— look at the eyes of

Lotys reproaching me! You would think they were the eyes of an angel, gazing at a devil in the sweet hope of plucking him out of hell!"

"Such a hope would be vain in your case, Zouche," said Lotys tranquilly; "You make your own hell, and you must live in it! Nevertheless, in some of the wild things you say, there is a grain of truth. If I were God, I should be the most miserable of all beings, to look upon all the misery I had myself created! I should be so sorry for the world, that I should put an end to all hope of immortality by my own death."

She made this strange remark with a simplicity and wistfulness which were in striking contrast to the awful profundity of the suggestion, and all her auditors, including the half-tipsy Zouche, were silent.

"I should be so sorry!" she repeated; "For even as a mortal woman my pity for the suffering world almost breaks my heart;—but if I were God, I should have all the griefs of all the worlds I had made to answer for,—and such an agony would surely kill me. Oh,—the pain, the tears, the mistakes, the sins, the anguish of humanity! All these are frightful to me! I do not understand why such misery should exist! I think it must be that we have not enough love in the world; if we only loved each other faithfully, God might love us more!"

Her eyes were wet; she caught her breath hard, and smiled a little difficult smile. Something in her soul transfigured her face, and made it for the moment exquisitely lovely, and the men around her gazed at her in evidently reverential silence. Suddenly she stretched out both her hands:

"Good-night, children!"

One by one the would-be-fierce associates of the Revolutionary Committee bent low over those fair hands; and then quietly saluting Sergius Thord, as quietly left the room, like schoolboys retiring from a class where the lessons had been more or less badly done. Paul Zouche was not very steady on his feet, and two of his comrades assisted him to walk as he stumbled off, singing somewhat of a ribald rhyme in *mezza-voce*. Pasquin Leroy and his two friends were the last to go. Lotys looked at them all three meditatively.

"You will be faithful?" she said.

"Unto death!" answered Leroy.

She came close up to him, placing one hand on his arm, and glanced meaningly towards Sergius Thord, who was standing at the threshold watching Zouche stumbling down the dark stairs.

"Sergius is a good man!" she said; "One of the mistaken geniuses of this world,—savage as a lion, yet simple as a child! Whoever, and whatever you are, be true to him!"

"He is dear to you?" said Leroy on a sudden impulse, catching her hand; "He is more to you than most men?"

She snatched away her hand, and her eyes lightened first with wrath, then with laughter.

"Dear to me!" she echoed,—"to Me? No one man on earth is dearer to me than another! All are alike in my estimation,—all the same barbaric, foolish babes and children—all to be loved and pitied alike! But Sergius Thord picked me out of the streets when I was no better than a stray and starving dog,—and like a dog I serve him—faithfully! Now go!"

She stretched out her hand in an attitude of command, and there was nothing for it but to obey. They therefore repeated their farewells, and in their turn, went out, one by one, down the tortuous staircase. Sholto, the hunchback, was below, and he let them out without a word, closing and barring the door carefully behind them. Once in the street and under the misty moonlight, Pasquin Leroy nodded a careless dismissal to his companions.

"You will return alone?" enquired Max Graub.

"Quite alone!" was the reply.

"May I not follow you at a distance?" asked Axel Regor.

Leroy smiled. "You forget! One of the rules we have just sworn to conform to, is—'No member shall track, follow or enquire into the movements of any other member.' Go your ways! I will thank you both for your services to-morrow."

He turned away rapidly and disappeared. His two friends remained gazing somewhat disconsolately after him.

"Shall we go?" at last said Max Graub.

"When you please," replied Axel Regor irritably,—"The sooner the better for me! Here we are probably watched,—we had best go down to the quay, and from thence——"

He did not finish his sentence, but Graub evidently understood its conclusion—

and they walked quickly away together in quite an opposite direction to that in which Leroy had gone.

Meanwhile, up in the now closed and darkened house they had left behind them, Lotys stood looking at Sergius Thord, who had thrown himself into a chair and sat with his elbows resting on the table, and his head buried in his hands.

"You make no way, poor Sergius!" she said gently. "You work, you write, you speak to the people, but you make no way!"

He looked up fiercely.

"I do make way!" he said; "How can you doubt it? A word from me, and the massed millions would rise as one man!"

"And of what use would that be?" enquired Lotys. "The soldiers would fire on the people, and there would be riot and bloodshed, but no actual redress for wrong. You work vainly, Sergius!"

"If I could but kill the King!" he muttered.

"Another king would succeed him," she said. "And after all, if you only knew it, the King may be a miserable man enough—far more miserable, perhaps, than any of us imagine ourselves to be. No, Sergius!—I repeat it, you work vainly! You have made me the soul of an Ideal which you will never realise? Tell me, what is it you yourself would have, out of all your work and striving?"

He looked at her with great, earnest, burning eyes.

"Power!" he said. "Power to change the mode of government; power to put down the tyranny of priestcraft—power to relieve the oppressed, and reward the deserving—power to make of you, Lotys, a queen among women!"

She smiled.

"I am a queen among men, Sergius, and that suffices me! How often must I tell you to do nothing for my sake, if it is for my sake only? I am a very simple, plain woman, past my youth, and without beauty—I deserve and demand nothing!"

He raised himself, and stretched out his arms towards her with a gesture of entreaty.

"You deserve all that a man can give you!" he said passionately. "I love you, Lotys! I have always loved you ever since I found you a little forsaken child, shivering and weeping on the cold marble steps of the Temesvar place in Buda. I love you!—you know I have always loved you!—I have told you so a hundred times,—I love you as few men love women!"

She regarded him compassionately, and with a touch of wistful sorrow in her eyes. Her black cloak fell away on either side of her in two shadowy folds, disclosing her white-robed form and full bosom, like a pearl in a dark shell.

"Good-night, Sergius!" she said simply, and turned to go.

He gave an exclamation of anger and pain.

"That is all you say—'Good-night'!" he muttered. "A man gives you his heart, and you set it aside with a cold word of farewell! And yet—and yet—you hold all my life!"

"I am sorry, Sergius," she said, in a gentle voice; "very sorry that it is so. You have told me all this before; and I have answered you often, and always in the same way. I have no love to give you, save that which is the result of duty and gratitude. I do not forget!—I know that you rescued me from starvation and death—though sometimes I question whether it would not have been better to have let me die. Life is worth very little at its utmost best; nevertheless, I admit I have had a certain natural joy in living, and for that I have to thank you. I have tried to repay you by my service—"

"Do not speak of that," he said hurriedly; "I have done nothing! You are a genius in yourself, and would have made your way anywhere,— perhaps better without me."

She smiled doubtfully.

"I am not sure! The trick of oratory does not carry one very far,—not when one is a woman! Good-night again, Sergius! Try to rest,—you look worn out. And do not think of winning power for my sake; what power I need I will win for myself!"

He made no answer, but watched her with jealous eyes, as she moved towards the door. On the threshold she turned.

"Those three new associates of yours—are they trustworthy, think you?"

He gave a gesture of indifference.

"I do not know! Who is there we can absolutely trust save ourselves? That man, Leroy, is honest,—of that I am confident,—and he has promised to be responsible for his friends."

"Ah!" She paused a moment, then with another low breathed 'good-night' she left the room.

He looked at the door as it closed behind her—at the chair she had left vacant.

"Lotys!" he whispered.

His whisper came hissing softly back to him in a fine echo on the empty space, and with a great sigh he rose, and began to turn out the flaring lamps above his head.

"Power!—Power!" he muttered—"She could not resist it! She would never be swayed by gold,—but power! Her genius would rise to it—her beauty would grow to it like a rose unfolding in the sun! 'Past youth, and without beauty' as she says of herself! My God! Compare the tame pink- and-white prettiness of youth with the face of Lotys,—and that prettiness becomes like a cheap advertisement on a hoarding or a match- box! Contrast the perfect features, eyes and hair of the newest social 'beauty,'—with the magical expression, the glamour in the eyes of Lotys,—and perfection of feature becomes the rankest ugliness! Once in a hundred centuries a woman is born like Lotys, to drive men mad with desire for the unattainable—to fire them with such ambition as should make them emperors of the world, if they had but sufficient courage to snatch their thrones—and yet,—to fill them with such sick despair at their own incompetency and failure, as to turn them into mere children crying for love—for love!—only love! No matter whether worlds are lost, kings killed, and dynasties concluded, love!—only love!—and then death!—as all sufficient for the life of a man! And only just so long as love is denied—just so long we can go on climbing towards the unreachable height of greatness,—then—once we touch love, down we fall, broken-hearted; but—we have had our day!"

The room was now in darkness, save for the glimmer of the pale moon through the window panes, and he opened the casement and looked out. There was a faint scent of the sea on the air, and he inhaled its salty odour with a sense of refreshment.

"All for Lotys!" he murmured. "Working for Lotys, plotting, planning, scheming for Lotys! The government intimidated,—the ministry cast out,—the throne in peril,—the people in arms,—the city in a blaze,— Revolution and Anarchy doing their wild work broad-cast together,— all for Lotys! Always a woman in it! Search to the very depth of every political imbroglio,—dig out the secret reason of every war that ever was begun or ended in the world,—and there we shall find the love or the hate of a woman at the very core of the business! Some such secrets history knows, and has chronicled,—and some will never be known,—but up to the present there is not even a religion in the world where a Woman is not made the beginning of a God!"

He smiled somewhat grimly at his own fanciful musings, and then, shutting the window, retired. The house was soon buried in profound silence and darkness, and over the city tuneful bells rang the half- hour after midnight. Four miles distant from the 'quarter of the poor,' and high above the clustering houses of the whole magnificent metropolis, the Royal palace towered whitely on its proud eminence in the glimmer of the moon, a stately pile of turrets and pinnacles; and on the battlements the sentries walked, pacing to and fro in regular march, with regular changes, all through the night hours. Half after midnight! 'All's well!' Three-quarters, and still 'All's well' sounded with the clash of steel and a tinkle of silvery chimes. One o'clock struck,—and the drifting clouds in heaven cleared fully, showing many brilliant stars in the western horizon,—and a sentry passing, as noiselessly as his armour and accoutrements would permit, along the walled battlement which protected and overshadowed the windows of the Queen's apartments, paused in his walk to look with an approving eye at the clearing promise of the weather. As he did so, a tall figure, wrapped in a thick rain-cloak, suddenly made its unexpected appearance through a side door in the wall, and moved rapidly towards a turret which contained a secret passage leading to the Queen's boudoir,—a private stairway which was never used save by the Royal family. The sentry gave a sharp warning cry.

"Halt! Who goes there?"

The figure paused and turned, dropping its cloak. The pale moonlight fell slantwise on the features, disclosing them fully.

"T is I! The King!"

The soldier recoiled amazed,—and quickly saluted. Before he could recover from his astonishment he was alone again. The battlement was empty, and the door to the turret-stairs,—of which only the King possessed the key,—was fast locked; and for the next hour or more the startled sentry remained staring at the skies in a sort of meditative stupefaction, with the words still ringing like the shock of an alarm- bell in his ears:

"'T is I! The King!"

CHAPTER IX
THE PREMIER'S SIGNET

THE next day the sun rose with joyous brightness in a sky clear as crystal. Storm, wind, and rain had vanished like the flying phantoms of an evil dream, and all the beautiful land sparkled with light and life in its enlacing girdle of turquoise blue sea. The gardens of the Royal palace, freshened by the downpour of the past night, wore their most enchanting aspect,—roses, with leaves still wet, dropped their scented petals on the grass,—great lilies, with their snowy cups brimming with rain, hung heavily on their slim green stalks, and the air was full of the deliciously penetrating odour of the mimosa and sweetbriar. Down one special alley, where the white philadelphus, or 'mock orange' grew in thick bushes on either side, intermingled with ferns and spruce firs, whose young green tips exhaled a pungent, healthy scent that entered into the blood like wine and invigorated it, Sir Roger de Launay was pacing to and fro with a swinging step which, notwithstanding its ease and soldierly regularity, suggested something of impatience, and on a rustic seat, above which great clusters of the philadelphus-flowers hung like a canopy, sat Professor von Glauben, spectacles on nose, sorting a few letters which he had just taken from his pocket for the purpose of reading them over again carefully one by one. He was a very particular man as regarded his correspondence. All letters that required answering he answered at once,—the others, as he himself declared, 'answered themselves' in silence.

"There is no end to the crop of fools in this world," he was fond of saying;— "Glorious, precious fools! I love them all! They make life worth living—but sometimes I am disposed to draw the line at letter- writing fools. These persons chance to read a book—my book for example,—that particularly clever one I wrote on the possibilities of eternal life in this world. They at once snatch their pens and write to say that they are specially deserving of this boon, and wish to live for ever—will I tell them how? And these are the very creatures I will not tell how—because their perpetual existence would be a mistake and a nuisance! The individuals whose lives are really valuable never ask anyone how to make them so."

He looked over his letters now with a leisurely indifference. The morning's post had brought him nothing of special importance. He glanced from his reading now and again at De Launay marching up and down, but said nothing till he had quite finished with his own immediate concerns. Then he removed his spectacles from his nose and put them by.

"Left—Right—Left—Right—Left—Right! Roger, you remind me of my drilling days on a certain flat and dusty ground at Coblentz! The Rhine!—the Rhine! Ah, the beautiful Rhine! So dirty—so dull—with its toy castles, and its big, ugly factory chimneys, and its atrociously bad wine! Roger, I beseech you to have mercy upon me, and leave off that marching up and down,—it gets on my nerves!"

"I thought nothing ever got on your nerves," answered Sir Roger, stopping abruptly—"You seem to take serious matters coolly enough!"

"Serious matters demand coolness," replied Von Glauben. "We should only let steam out over trifles. Have you seen his Majesty this morning?"

"Yes. I am to see him again at noon."

"When do you go off duty?"

"Not for a month, at least."

"Much may happen in that month," said the Professor sententiously; "*Your* hair may grow white with the strangeness of your experiences!"

Sir Roger met his eyes, and they both laughed.

"Though it is no laughing matter," resumed Von Glauben. "Upon my soul as a German,—if I have any soul of that nationality,—I think it may be a serious business!"

"You have come round to my opinion then," said De Launay. "I told you from the first that it was serious!"

"The King does not think it so," rejoined Von Glauben. "I was summoned to his presence early this morning, and found him in the fullest health and highest spirits."

"Why did he send for you then?" enquired De Launay.

"To feel his pulse and look at his tongue! To make a little game of me before he stepped out of his dressing-gown! And I enjoyed it, of course,—one must always enjoy Royal pleasantries! I think, Roger, his Majesty wishes this entire affair treated as a pleasantry,—by us at any rate, however seriously he may regard it himself."

De Launay was silent for a minute or two, then he said abruptly:

"The Premier is summoned to a private audience of the King at noon."

"Ah!" And Von Glauben drew a cluster of the overhanging philadelphus flowers down to his nose and smelt them approvingly.

"And"—went on De Launay, speaking more deliberately, "this afternoon their Majesties sail to The Islands——"

Von Glauben jumped excitedly to his feet.

"Not possible!"

Sir Roger looked at him with a dawning amusement beginning to twinkle in his clear blue eyes.

"Quite possible! So possible, that the Royal yacht is ordered to be in readiness at three o'clock. Their Majesties and suite will dine on board, in order to enjoy the return sail by moonlight."

The Professor's countenance was a study. Anxiety and vexation struggled with the shrewd kindness and humour of his natural expression, and his suppressed feelings found vent in a smothered exclamation, which sounded very much like the worst of blasphemous oaths used in dire extremity by the soldiers of the Fatherland.

"What ails you?" demanded De Launay; "You seem strangely upset for a man of cool nerve!"

"Upset? Who—what can upset me? Nothing! Roger, if I did not respect you so much, I should call you an ass!"

Sir Roger laughed.

"Call me an ass, by all means," he said, "if it will relieve your feelings;—but in justice to me, let me know why you do so! What is my offence? I give you a piece of commonplace information concerning the movements of the Court this afternoon, and you jump off your seat as if an adder had bitten you. Why?"

"I have the gout," said Von Glauben curtly.

"Oh!" And again Sir Roger laughed. "That last must have been a sharp twinge!"

"It was—it was! Believe me, my excellent Roger, it was exceedingly severe!" His brow smoothed, and he smiled. "See here, my dear friend!— you know, do you not, that boys will be boys, and men will be men?"

"Both are recognised platitudes," replied Sir Roger, his eyes still twinkling merrily; "And both are frequently quoted to cover our various follies!"

"True, true! But I wish to weigh more particularly on the fact that men will be men! I am a man, Roger,—not a boy!"

"Really! Well, upon my word, I should at this moment take you for a raw lad of about eighteen,—for you are blushing, Von Glauben!—actually blushing!"

The Professor drew out a handkerchief, and wiped his brow.

"It is a warm morning, Roger," he said, with a mildly reproachful air; "I suppose I am permitted to feel the heat?" He paused—then with a sudden burst of impatience he exclaimed: "By the Emperor's head! It is of no use denying it—I am very much put out, Roger! I must get a boat, and slip off to The Islands at once!"

Sir Roger stared at him in complete amazement.

"You? You want to slip off to The Islands? Why, Von Glauben——!"

"Yes—yes,—I know! You cannot possibly imagine what I want to go there for! You wouldn't suppose, would you, that I had any special secrets— an old man like me;—for instance, you would not suspect me of any love secrets, eh?" And he made a ludicrous attempt to appear sentimental. "The fact is, Roger,—I have got into a little scrape over at The Islands—" here he looked warmer and redder than ever;— "and I want to take precautions! You understand—I want to take care that the King does not hear of it—Gott in Himmel! What a block of a man you are to stand there staring open-mouthed at me! Were you never in love yourself?

"In love? In love!—you,—Professor? Pray pardon me—but—in love? Am I to understand that there is a lady in your case?"

"Yes!—that is it," said Von Glauben, with an air of profound relief; "There is a lady in my case;—or my case, speaking professionally, is that of a lady. And I shall get any sort of a sea-tub that is available, and go over to those accursed Islands without any delay!"

"If the King should send for you while you are absent—" began De Launay doubtfully.

"He will not send. But if he should, what of it? I am known to be somewhat eccentric—particularly so in my love of hard work, fresh air and exercise—besides, he has not commanded my attendance. He will not, therefore, be surprised at my absence. I tell you, Roger,—I *must* go! Who would have expected the King to take it into his head to visit The Islands without a moment's warning! What a freak!"

"And here comes the reason of the freak, if I am not very much mistaken," said De Launay, lowering his voice as an approaching figure flung its lengthy shadow on the path,—"Prince Humphry!"

Von Glauben hastily drew back, De Launay also, to allow the Prince to pass. He was walking slowly, and reading as he came. Looking up from his book he saw, them, and as they saluted him profoundly, bade them good-day.

"You are up betimes, Professor," he said lightly; "I suppose your scientific wisdom teaches you the advantage of the morning air."

"Truly, Sir, it is more healthful than that of the evening," answered Von Glauben in somewhat doleful accents.—"For example, a sail across the sea with the morning breeze, is better than the same sort of excursion in the glamour of the moon!"

Prince Humphry looked steadfastly at him, and evidently read something of a warning, or a suggestion, in his face, for he coloured slightly and bit his lip.

"Do you agree with that theory, Sir Roger," he said, turning to De Launay.

"I have not tested it, Sir," replied the equerry, "But I imagine that whatever Professor von Glauben asserts must be true!"

The young man glanced quickly from one to the other, and then with a careless air turned over the pages of the book he held.

"In the earlier ages of the world," he said,—"men and women, I think, must have been happier than they are now, if this book may be believed. I find here written down—What is it, Professor? You have something to say?"

"Pardon me, Sir," said Von Glauben,—"But you said—'If this book may be believed.' I humbly venture to declare that no book may be believed!"

"Not even your own, when it is written?" queried the Prince with a smile; "You would not like the world to say so! Nay, but listen, Professor,—here is a thought very beautifully expressed—and it was written in an ancient language of the East, thousands of years before we, in our quarter of the world, ever dreamt of civilization.—'Of all the sentiments, passions or virtues which in their divers turns affect the life of a man, the influence and emotion of Love is surely the greatest and highest. We do not here speak of the base and villainous craving of bodily appetite; but of that pure desire of the unfettered soul which beholding perfection, straight-way and naturally flies to the same. This love doth so elevate and instruct a man, that he seeketh nothing better than to be worthy of it, to attempt great deeds and valiantly perform them, to confront foul abuses, and most potently destroy them,—and to esteem the powers and riches of this world as dross, weighed against this rare and fiery talisman. For it is a jewel which doth light up the heart, and make it strong to support all sorrow and ill fortune with cheerfulness, knowing that it is in itself of so lasting a quality as to subjugate all things and events unto its compelling sway.' What think you of this? Sir Roger, there is a whole volume of comprehension in your face! Give some word of it utterance!"

Sir Roger looked up.

"There is nothing to say, Sir," he replied; "Your ancient writer merely expresses a truth we are all conscious of. All poets, worthy the name, and all authors, save and except the coldest logicians, deem the world well lost for love."

"More fools they!" said Von Glauben gruffly; "Love is a mere illusion, which is generally destroyed by one simple ceremony—Marriage!"

Prince Humphry smiled.

"You have never tried the cure, Professor," he said, "But I daresay you have suffered from the disease! Will you walk with me?"

Von Glauben bowed a respectful assent; and the Prince, with a kindly nod of dismissal to De Launay, went on his way, the Professor by his side. Sir Roger watched them as they disappeared, and saw, that at the furthest end of the alley, when they were well out of ear-shot, they appeared to engage in very close and confidential conversation.

"I wonder," he mused, "I wonder what it all means? Von Glauben is evidently mixed up in some affair that he wishes to keep secret from the King. Can it concern Prince Humphry? And The Islands! What can Von Glauben want over there?"

His brief meditation was interrupted by a soft voice calling.

"Roger!"

He started, and at once advanced to meet the approaching intruder, his sister,

Teresa de Launay, a pretty brunette, with dark sparkling eyes, one of the favourite ladies of honour in attendance on the Queen.

"What were you dreaming about?" she asked, as he came near, "And what is the Prince doing with old Von Glauben?"

"Two questions at once, Teresa!" he said, stooping his tall head to kiss her; "I cannot possibly answer both in a breath! But answer me just one—What are you here for?"

"To summon *you*!" she answered. "The Queen desires you to wait upon her immediately."

She fixed her bright eyes upon him as she spoke, and an involuntary sigh escaped her, as she noted the touch of pallor that came on his face at her words.

"Where is her Majesty?" he asked.

"Here—close at hand—in the arbour. She spied you at a distance through the trees, and sent me to fetch you."

"You had best return to her at once, and say that I am coming."

His sister looked at him again, and hesitated—he gave a slight, vexed gesture of impatience, whereupon she hurried away, with flying footsteps as light as those of a fabled sylph of the woodlands. He watched her go, and for a moment an expression came into his eyes of intense suffering—the look of a noble dog who is suddenly struck undeservedly by an unkind master.

"She sends for me!" he muttered; "What for? To amuse herself by reading every thought of my life with her cold eyes? Why can she not leave me alone?"

He walked on then, with a quiet, even pace, and presently reaching the end of the alley, came out on a soft stretch of greensward facing a small ornamental lake and fountain. Here grew tall rushes, bamboos and flag-flowers—here, too, on the quiet lake floated water-lilies, white and pink, opening their starry hearts to the glory of the morning sun. A quaintly shaped, rustic arbour covered with jasmine, faced the pool, and here sat the Queen alone and unattended, save by Teresa de Launay, who drew a little apart as her brother, Sir Roger, approached, and respectfully bent his head in the Royal presence. For quite a minute he stood thus in dumb attention, his eyes lowered, while the Queen glanced at him with a curious expression, half of doubt, half of commiseration. Suddenly, as if moved by a quick impulse, she rose—a stately, exquisite figure, looking even more beautiful in her simple morning robe of white cashmere and lace, than in all the glory of her Court attire,—and extended her hand. Humbly and reverentially he bent over it, and kissed the great jewel sparkling like a star on the central finger. As he then raised his eyes to her face she smiled;—that smile of hers, so dazzling, so sweet, and yet so cold, had sent many men to their deaths, though she knew it not.

"I see very little of you, Sir Roger," she said slowly, "notwithstanding your close attendance on my lord the King. Yet I know I can command your service!"

"Madam," murmured De Launay, "my life——"

"Oh, no," she rejoined quickly, "not your life! Your life, like mine, belongs to the King and the country. You must give all, or not at all!"

"Madam, I do give all!" he answered, with a look in his eyes of mingled pain and passion; "No man can give more!"

She surveyed him with a little meditative, almost amused air.

"You have strong feelings, Sir Roger," she said; "I wonder what it is like—to *feel*?"

"If I may dare to say so, Madam, I should wish you to experience the sensation," he returned somewhat bitterly; "Sometimes we awaken to emotions too late—sometimes we never awaken. But I think it is wisest to experience the nature of a storm, in order to appreciate the value of a calm!"

"You think so?" She smiled indulgently. "Storm and calm are to me alike! I am affected by neither. Life is so exceedingly trivial an affair, and is so soon over, that I have never been able to understand why people should ever trouble themselves about anything in it."

"You may not always be lacking in this comprehension, Madam," said Sir Roger, with a certain harshness in his tone, yet with the deepest respect in his manner; "I take it that life and the world are but a preparation for something greater, and that we shall be forced to learn our lessons in this preparatory school before we leave it, whether we like it or no!"

The slight smile still lingered on her beautiful mouth,—she pulled a spray of jasmine down from the trailing clusters around her, and set it carelessly among the folds of her lace. Sir Roger watched her with moody eyes. Could he have followed his own inclination, he would have snatched the flower from her dress and kissed it, in a kind of fierce defiance before her very eyes. But what would be the result of such an act? Merely a little contemptuous lifting of the delicate brows—a slight frown on the fair forehead, and a calm gesture of dismissal. No more—no more than this; for just as she could not be moved to love, neither could she be moved to anger. The words of an old song rang in his ears:—

> She laughs at the thought of love—
> Pain she scorns, and sorrow she sets aside—
> My heart she values less than her broidered glove,
>   She would smile if I died!

"You are a man, Sir Roger de Launay," she said after a pause, "And man- like, you propound any theory which at the moment happens to fit your own particular humour. I am, however, entirely of your opinion that this life is only a term of preparation, and with this conviction I desire to have as little to do with its vile and ugly side as I can. It is possible to accept with gratitude the beautiful things of Nature, and reject the rest, is it not?"

"As you ask me the question point-blank, Madam, I say it is possible,— it can be done,—and you do it. But it is wrong!"

She raised her languid eyelids, showing no offence.

"Wrong?"

"Wrong, Madam!" repeated Sir Roger bluntly; "It is wrong to shut from your sight, from your heart, from your soul the ugly side of Nature;— to shut your ears to the wants—the pains—the tortures—the screams— the tears, and groans of humanity! Oh, Madam, the ugly side has a strange beauty of its own that you dream not of! God makes ugliness as he makes beauty; God created the volcano belching forth fire and molten lava, as He created the simple stream bordered with meadow flowers! Why should you reject the ugly, the fierce, the rebellious side of things? Rather take it into your gracious thoughts and prayers, Madam, and help to make it beautiful!"

He spoke with a force which surprised himself—he was carried away by a passion that seemed almost outside his own identity. She looked at him curiously.

"Does the King teach you to speak thus to me?" she asked.

De Launay started,—the hot colour mounting to his cheeks and brow.

"Madam!"

"Nay, no excuse! I understand! It is your own thought; but a thought which is no doubt suddenly inspired by the King's actions," she went on tranquilly; "You are in his confidence. He is adopting new measures of domestic policy, in which, perchance, I may or may not be included—as it suits my pleasure! Who knows!" Again the little musing smile crossed her countenance. "It is of the King I wish to speak to you."

She glanced around her, and saw that her lady-in-waiting, Teresa de Launay, had discreetly wandered by herself to the edge of the water- lily pool, and was bending over it, a graceful, pensive figure in the near distance, within call, but certainly not within hearing.

"You are in his confidence," she repeated, drawing a step nearer to him, "and—so am I! You will not disclose his movements—nor shall I! But you are his close attendant and friend,—I am merely—his wife! I make you responsible for his safety!"

"Madam, I pray you pardon me!" exclaimed De Launay; "His Majesty has a will of his own,—and his sacred life is not in my hands. I will defend him to the utmost limit of human possibility,—but if he voluntarily runs into danger, and disregards all warning, I, as his poor servant, am not to blame!"

Her eyes, brilliant and full of a compelling magnetism, dwelt upon him steadfastly.

"I repeat my command," she said deliberately, "I make you responsible! You are a strong man and a brave one. If the King is rash, it is the duty of his servants to defend him from the consequences of his rashness; particularly if that rashness leads him into danger for a noble purpose. Should any mischance befall him, let me never see your face again! Die yourself, rather than let your King die!"

As she spoke these words she motioned him away with a grand gesture of dismissal, and he retired back from her presence in a kind of stunned amazement. Never before in all the days of her social sway as Crown- Princess, had she ever condescended to speak to him on any matter of confidence,—never during her three years of sovereignty as Queen- Consort had she apparently taken note, or cared to know any of the affairs connected with the King, her husband. The mere fact that now her interest was roused, moved De Launay to speechless wonderment. He hardly dared raise his eyes to look at her, as she turned from him and went slowly, with her usual noiseless, floating grace of movement, towards the water-lily pool, there to rejoin her attendant, Teresa de Launay, who at the same time advanced to meet her Royal mistress. A moment more, and Queen and lady of honour had disappeared together, and De Launay was left alone. A little bird, swinging on a branch above his head, piped a few tender notes to the green leaves and the sunlit sky, but beyond this, and the measured plash of the fountain, no sound disturbed the stillness of the garden.

"Upon my word, Roger de Launay," he said bitterly to himself, "you are an ass sufficiently weighted with burdens! The love of a Queen, and the life of a King are enough for one man's mind to carry with any degree of safety! If it were not for the King, I think I should leave this country and seek some other service—but I owe him much,—if only by reason of my own heart's folly!"

Impatient with himself, he strode away, straight across the lawn and back to the palace. Here he noticed just the slightest atmosphere of uneasiness among some of the retainers of the Royal household,—a vague impression of flurry and confusion. Through various passages and corridors, attendants and pages were either running about with extra haste, or else strolling to and fro with extra slowness. As he turned into one of the ante-chambers, he suddenly confronted a tall, military-looking personage in plain civilian attire, whom he at once recognized as the Chief of the Police.

"Ah, Bernhoff!" he said lightly, "any storms brewing?"

"None that call for particular attention, Sir Roger," replied the individual addressed; "But I have been sent for by the King, and am here awaiting his pleasure."

Sir Roger showed no sign of surprise, and with a friendly nod passed on. He began to find the situation rather interesting.

"After all," he argued inwardly, "there is nothing to hinder the King from being a social autocrat, even if he cannot by the rules of the Constitution be a political one. And we should do well to remember that politics are governed entirely by social influence. It is the same thing all over the world—a deluded populace—a social movement which elects a parliament and ministry—and then the result,—which is, that this or that party hold the reins of government, on whichever side happens to be most advantageous to the immediate social and financial whim. The people are the grapes crushed into wine for their rulers' drinking; and the King is merely the wine-cup on the festal board. If he once begins to be something more than that cup, there will be an end of revelry!"

His ideas were not without good foundation in fact. Throughout all history, where a strong man has ruled a nation, whether for good or ill, he has left his mark; and where there has been no strong man, the annals of the time are vapid and uninteresting. Governments emanate from social influences. The social rule of the Roman Emperors bred athletes, heroes, and poets, merely because physical strength and courage, combined with heroism and poetic perception were encouraged by Roman society. The social rule of England's Elizabeth had its result in the brilliant attainments of the many great men who crowded her Court— the social rule of Victoria, until the death of the Prince Consort, bred gentle women and chivalrous men. In all these cases, the reigning monarchs governed society, and society governed politics. Politics, indeed, can scarcely be considered apart from society, because on the nature and character of society depend the nature and character of politics. If society is made up of corrupt women and unprincipled men, the spirit of political government will be as corrupt and unprincipled as they. If any King, beholding such a state of things, were to suddenly cut himself clear of the corruption, and to make a straight road for his own progress—clean and open—and elect to walk in it, society would follow his lead, and as a logical consequence politics would become honourable. But no monarchs have the courage of their opinions nowadays,—if only one sovereign of them all possessed such courage, he could move the world!

The long bright day unwound its sunny hours, crowned with blue skies and fragrant winds, and the life and movement of the fair city by the sea was gay, incessant and ever-changing. There was some popular interest and excitement going on down at the quay, for the usual idle crowd had collected to see the Royal yacht being prepared for her afternoon's cruise. Though she was always kept ready for sailing, the King's orders this time had been sudden and peremptory, and, consequently, all the men on board were exceptionally hard at work getting things in immediate readiness. The fact that the Queen was to accompany the King in the afternoon's trip to The Islands, where up to the present she had never been, was a matter of lively comment,—her extraordinary beauty never failing to attract a large number of sight- seers.

In the general excitement, no one saw Professor von Glauben quietly enter a small and common sailing skiff, manned by two ordinary fishermen of the shore, and scud away with the wind over the sea towards the west, where, in the distance on this clear day, a gleaming line of light showed where The Islands lay, glistening like emerald and pearl in the midst of the dark blue waste of water. His departure was unnoticed, though as a rule the King's private physician commanded some attention, not only by reason of his confidential post in the Royal household, but also on account of certain rumours which were circulated through the country concerning his wonderful skill in effecting complete cures where all hope of recovery had been abandoned. It was whispered, indeed, that he had discovered the 'Elixir of Life,' but that he would not allow its properties to be made known, lest as the Scripture saith, man should 'take and eat and live for ever.' It was not advisable— so the Professor was reported to have said—that all men should live for ever,—but only a chosen few; and he, at present, was apparently the privileged person who alone was fitted to make the selection of those few. For this and various other reasons, he was generally looked at with considerable interest, but this morning, owing to the hurried preparations for the embarking of their Majesties on board the Royal yacht, he managed to escape from even chance recognition,—and he was well over the sea, and more than half-way to his destination before the bells of the city struck noon.

Punctual to that hour, a close carriage drove up to the palace. It contained no less a personage than the Prime Minister, the Marquis de Lutera,—a dark, heavy man, with small furtive eyes, a ponderous jaw, and a curious air of seeming for ever on an irritable watch for offences. His aspect was intellectual, yet always threatening; and his frigid manner was profoundly discouraging to all who sought to win his attention or sympathy. He entered the palace now with an easy, not to say assertive deportment, and as he ascended the broad staircase which led to the King's private apartments, he met the Chief of the Police coming down. This latter saluted him, but he barely acknowledged the courtesy, so taken by surprise was he at the sight of this administrative functionary in the palace at so early an hour. However, it was impossible to ask any questions of him on the grand staircase, within hearing of the Royal lackeys; so he continued on his way upstairs, with as much dignity as his heavily-moulded figure would permit him to display, till he reached the upper landing known as the 'King's Corridor,' where Sir Roger de Launay was in waiting to conduct him to his sovereign's presence. To him the Marquis addressed the question:

"Bernhoff has been with the King?"

"Yes. For more than an hour."

"Any robbery in the palace?"

De Launay smiled.

"I think not! So far as I am permitted to be cognisant of events, there is nothing wrong!"

The Marquis looked slightly perplexed.

"The King is well?"

"Remarkably well—and in excellent humour! He is awaiting you, Marquis,—permit me to escort you to him!"

The carved and gilded doors of the Royal audience-chamber were thereupon flung back, and the Marquis entered, ushered in by De Launay. The doors closed again upon them both; and for some time there was profound silence in the King's corridor, no intruder venturing to approach save two gentlemen-at-arms, who paced slowly up and down at either end on guard. At the expiration of about an hour, Sir Roger came out alone, and, glancing carelessly around him, strolled to the head of the grand staircase, and waited patiently there for quite another thirty minutes. At last the doors were flung open widely again, and the King himself appeared, clad in easy yachting attire, and walking with one hand resting on the arm of the Marquis de Lutera, who, from his expression, seemed curiously perturbed.

"Then you will not come with us, Marquis?" said the King, with an air of gaiety; "You are too much engrossed in the affairs of Government to break loose for an afternoon from politics for the sake of pleasure? Ah, well! You are a matchless worker! Renowned as you are for your studious observation of all that may tend to the advancement of the nation's interests—admired as you are for the complete sacrifice of all your own advantages to the better welfare of the country, I will not (though I might as your sovereign), command your attendance on this occasion! I know the affairs you have in hand are pressing and serious!"

"They will be more than usually so, Sir," said the Marquis in a low voice; "for if you persist in maintaining your present attitude, the foreign controversy in which we are engaged can scarcely go on. But your action will be questioned by the Government!"

The King laughed.

"Good! By all means question it, my dear Marquis! Prove me an unconstitutional monarch, if you like, and put Humphry on the throne in my place,—but ask the People first! If they condemn me, I am satisfied to be condemned! But the present political difference between ourselves and a friendly nation must be arranged without offence. There does not exist at the moment any reasonable cause for fanning the dispute into a flame of war."—He paused, then resumed—"You will not come with us?"

"Sir, if you will permit me to refuse the honour on this occasion———"

"The permission is granted!" replied the King, still smiling; "Farewell, Marquis! We are not in the habit of absenting ourselves from our own country, after the fashion of certain of our Royal neighbours, who shall be nameless; and we conceive it our duty to make ourselves acquainted with the habits and customs of all our subjects in all quarters of our realm. Hence our resolve to visit The Islands, which, to our shame be it said, we have neglected until now. We expect to derive both pleasure and instruction from the brief voyage!"

"Are the islanders aware of your intention, Sir?" enquired the Marquis.

"Nay—to prepare them would have spoilt our pleasure!" replied the King. "We will take them by surprise! We have heard of certain countries, whose villages and towns have never seen the reigning sovereign,—and though we have been but three years on the throne, we have resolved that no corner of our kingdom shall lack the sunlight of our presence!" He gave a mirthful side-glance at De Launay. Then, extending his hand cordially, he added: "May all success attend your efforts, Marquis, to smooth over this looming quarrel between ourselves and our friendly trade-rivals! I, for one, would not have it go further. I shall see you again at the Council during the week."

As the premier's hand met that of his Sovereign, the latter exclaimed suddenly:

"Ah!—I thought I missed a customary friend from my finger; I have forgotten my signet-ring! Will you lend me yours for to-day, Marquis?"

"Sir, if you will deign to wear it!" replied the Marquis readily, and at once slipping off the ring in question, he handed it to the King, who smilingly accepted it and put it on.

"A fine sapphire!" he said approvingly; "Better, I think, than my ruby!"

"Sir, your praise enhances its value," said De Lutera bowing profoundly; "I shall from henceforth esteem it priceless!"

"Well said!" returned the King, "And rightly too!—for diplomacy is wise in flattering a king to the last, even while meditating on his possible downfall! Adieu, Marquis! When we next meet, I shall expect good news!"

He descended the staircase, closely attended by De Launay, and passed at once into a larger room of audience, where some notable persons of foreign distinction were waiting to be received. On the way thither, however, he turned to Sir Roger for a moment, and held up the hand on which the Marquis de Lutera's signet flashed like a blue point of flame.

"Behold the Premier's signet!" he said with a smile; "Methinks, for once, it suits the King!"

CHAPTER X

THE ISLANDS

SURROUNDED by a boundless width of dark blue sea at all visible points of view, The Islands, lovely tufts of wooded rock, trees, and full- flowering meadowlands, were situated in such a happy position as to be well out of all possibility of modern innovation or improvement. They were too small to contain much attraction for the curious tourist; and though they were only a two-hours' sail from the mainland, the distance was just sufficiently inconvenient to keep mere sight-seers away. For more than a hundred years they had been almost exclusively left to the coral-fishers, who had made their habitation there; and the quaint, small houses, and flowering vineyards and gardens, dotted about in the more fertile portions of the soil, had all been built and planned by a former race of these hardy folk, who had handed their properties down from father to son. They were on the whole, a peaceable community. Coral-fishing was one of the chief industries of the country, and the islanders passed all their days in obtaining the precious product, cleansing, and preparing it for the market. They were understood to be extremely jealous of strangers and intruders, and to hold certain social traditions which had never been questioned or interfered with by any form of existing government, because in themselves they gave no cause for interference, being counted among the most orderly and law- abiding subjects of the realm. Very little interest was taken in their doings by the people of the mainland,—scarcely as much interest, perhaps, as is taken by Londoners in the inhabitants of Orkney or Shetland. One or two scholars, a stray botanist here and there, or a few students fond of adventure, had visited the place now and again, and some of these had brought back enthusiastic accounts of the loveliness of the natural scenery, but where a whole country is beautiful, little heed is given to one small corner of it, particularly if that corner is difficult of access, necessitating a two hours' sail across a not always calm sea. Vague reports were current that there was a strange house on The Islands, built very curiously out of the timbers and spars of wrecked vessels. The owner of this abode was said to be a man of advanced age, whose history was unknown, but who many years ago had been cast ashore from a great shipwreck, and had been rescued and revived by the coral-fishers, since when, he had lived among them, and worked with them. No one knew anything about him beyond that since his advent The Islands had been more cultivated, and their inhabitants more prosperous; and that he was understood to be, in the language or dialect of the country, a 'life-philosopher.' Whereat, hearing these things by chance now and then, or seeing a scrappy line or two in the daily press when active reporters had no murders or suicides to enlarge upon, and wanted to 'fill up space,' the gay aristocrats or 'smart set' of the metropolis laughed at their dinner-parties and balls, and asked one another inanely, "What is a 'life-philosopher'?"

In the same way, when a small volume of poetry, burning as lava, wild as a storm-wind, came floating out on the top of the seething soup of current literature, bearing the name of Paul Zouche, and it was said that this person was a poet, they questioned smilingly, "Is he dead?" for, naturally, they could not imagine these modern days were capable of giving birth to a living specimen of the *genus* bard. For they, too, had their motor-cars from France and England;—they, too, had their gambling-dens secreted in private houses of high repute,— they, too, had their country-seats specially indicated as free to such house-parties as wished to indulge in low intrigue and unbridled licentiousness; they, too, weary of simple Christianity, had their own special 'religions' of palmistry, crystal-gazing, fortune-telling by cards, and Esoteric 'faith-healing.' The days were passing with them— as it passes with many of their 'set' in other countries,—in complete forgetfulness of all the nobler ambitions and emotions which lift Man above the level of his companion Beast. For the time is now upon us when what has formerly been known as 'high' is of its own accord sinking to the low, and what has been called the 'low' is rising to the high. Strange times!—strange days!—when the tradesman can scorn the duchess on account of her 'dirty mind'—when a certain nobleman can get no honest labourers to work on his estate, because they suspect him of 'rooking' young college lads;—and when a church in a seaport town stands empty every Sunday, with its bells ringing in vain, because the congregation which should fill it, know that their so-called 'holy man' is a rascal! All over the world this rebellion against Falsehood,—this movement towards Truth is felt,—all over the world the people are growing strong on their legs, and clear in their brains;—no longer cramped and stunted starvelings, they are gradually developing into full growth, and awaking to intelligent action. And wherever the dominion of priestcraft has been destroyed, there they are found at their best and bravest, with a glimmering dawn of the true Christian spirit beginning to lighten their darkness,—a spirit which has no race or sect, but is all-embracing, all-loving, and all-benevolent;—which 'thinketh no evil,' but is so nobly sufficing in its tenderness and patience, as to persuade the ob-stinate, govern the unruly, and recover the lost, by the patient influence of its own example. On the reverse side of the medal, wherever we see priestcraft dominant, there we see ignorance and corruption, vice and hypocrisy, and such a low standard of morals and education as is calculated to keep the soul a slave in irons, with no possibility of any intellectual escape into the 'glorious liberty of the free.'

The afternoon was one of exceptional brilliance and freshness, when, punctu-ally at three o'clock, the Royal yacht hoisted sail, and dipped gracefully away from the quay with their Majesties on board, amid the cheers of an enthusiastic crowd. A poet might have sung of the scene in fervid rhyme, so pretty and gay were all the surroundings,—the bright skies, the dancing sea, the flying flags and streamers, and the soft music of the Court orchestra, a band of eight players on stringed instru-ments, which accompanied the Royal party on their voyage of pleasure. The Queen stood on deck, leaning against the mast, her eyes fixed on the shore, as the vessel swung round, and bore away towards the west;—the people, elbowing each other, and climbing up on each other's shoulders and on the posts of the quay, merely to get a passing glimpse of her beauty, all loyally cheering and waving their hats and handkerchiefs, were as indifferent to her sight and soul as an ant-heap in a garden walk. She had accustomed her mind to dwell on things beyond life, and life itself had little interest for her. This was because she had been set among the shams of worldly state and ceremonial from her earliest years, and being of a profound and thoughtful nature, had grown up to utterly despise the hollowness and hypocrisy of her surroundings. In extenuation of the coldness of her temperament, it may be said that her rooted aversion to men arose from having studied them too closely and accurately. In her marriage she had fulfilled, or thought she had fulfilled, a mere duty to the State—no more; and the easy conduct of her husband during his apprenticeship to the throne as Heir-Apparent, had not tended in any way to show her anything particularly worthy of admiration or respect in his character. And so she had gone on her chosen way, removed and apart from his,—and the years had flown by, and now she was,—as she said to herself with a little touch of contempt,—'old—for a woman!'—while the King remained 'young,—for a man! 'This was a mortifying reflection. True, her beauty was more perfect than in her youth, and there were no signs as yet of its decay. She knew well enough the extent of her charm,—she knew how easily she could command homage wherever she went,—and knowing, she did not care. Or rather—she had not cared. Was it possible she would ever care, and perhaps at a time when it was no use caring? A certain irritability, quite foreign to her usual composure, fevered her blood, and it arose from one simple admission which she had been forced to make to herself within the last few days, and this was, that her husband was as much her kingly superior in heart and mind as he was in rank and power. She had never till now imagined him capable of performing a brave deed, or pursuing an independently noble course of action. Throughout all the days of his married life he had followed the ordinary routine of his business or pleasure with scarce a break,— in winter to his country seat on the most southern coast of his southern land,—in spring to the capital,—in full summer to some fashionable 'bath' or 'cure,'—in autumn to different great houses for the purpose of shooting other people's game by their obsequious invitation,—and in the entire round he had never shown himself capable of much more than a flirtation with the prettiest or the most pushing new beauty, or a daring ride on the latest invention for travelling at lightning speed. She had noticed a certain change in him since he had ascended the throne, but she had attributed this to the excessive boredom of having to attend to State affairs.

Now, however, all at once and without warning, this change had developed into what was evidently likely to prove a complete transformation—and he had surprised her into an involuntary, and more or less reluctant admiration of qualities which she had never hitherto suspected in him. She had consented to join him on this occasion in his trip to The Islands, in order to try and fathom the actual drift of his intentions,—for his idea that their son, Prince Humphry, had yielded to some particular feminine attraction there, piqued her curiosity even more than her interest. She turned away now from her observation of the shore, as it receded on the horizon and became a mere thin line of light which vanished in its turn as the vessel curtsied onward; and she moved to the place prepared for her accommodation—a sheltered corner of the deck, covered by silken awnings, and supplied with luxurious deck chairs and footstools. Here two of her ladies were waiting to attend upon her, but none of the rougher sex she so heartily abhorred. As she seated herself among her cushions with her usual indolent grace, she raised her eyes and saw, standing at a respectful distance from her, a distinguished personage who had but lately arrived at the Court, from England,—Sir Walter Langton, a daring traveller and explorer in far countries,—one who had earned high distinction at the point of the sword. He had been presented to her some evenings since, among a crowd of other notabilities, and she had, as was her usual custom with all men, scarcely given him a passing glance. Now as she regarded him, she suddenly decided, out of the merest whim, to call him to her side. She sent one of her ladies to him, charged with her invitation to approach and take his seat near her. He hastened to obey, with some surprise, and no little pleasure. He was a handsome man of about forty, sun-browned and keen of eye, with a grave intellectual face after the style of a Vandyk portrait, and a kindly smile; and he was happily devoid of all that unbecoming officiousness and obsequiousness which some persons affect when in the presence of Royalty. He bowed profoundly as the Queen received him, saying to him with a smile:—

"You are a stranger here, Sir Walter Langton!—I cannot allow you to feel solitary in our company!"

"Is it possible for anyone to feel solitary when you are near, Madam?" returned Sir Walter gallantly, as he obeyed the gesture with which she motioned him to be seated;—"You must be weary of hearing that even your silent presence is sufficient to fill space with melody and charm! And I am not altogether a stranger; I know this country well, though I have never till now had the honour of visiting its ruling sovereign."

"It is very unlike England," said the Queen, slowly unfurling her fan of soft white plumage and waving it to and fro.

"Very unlike, indeed!" he agreed, and a musing tenderness darkened his fine hazel eyes as he gazed out on the sparkling sea.

"You like England best?" resumed the Queen.

"Madam, I am an Englishman! To me there is no land so fair, or so much worth living and dying for, as England!"

"Yet—I suppose, like all your countrymen, you are fond of change?"

"Yes—and no, Madam!" replied Langton.—"In truth, if I am to speak frankly, it is only during the last thirty or forty years that my countrymen have blotted their historical scutcheons by this fondness for change. Where travelling is necessary for the attainment of some worthy object, then it is wise and excellent,—but where it is only for the purpose of distracting a self-satiated mind, it is of no avail, and indeed frequently does more harm than good."

"Self-satiated!" repeated the Queen,—"Is not that a strange word?"

"It is the only compound expression I can use to describe the discontented humour in which the upper classes of English society exist to-day," replied Sir Walter. "For many years the soul of England has been held in chains by men whose thoughts are all of Self,—the honour of England has been attainted by women whose lives are moulded from first to last on Self. To me, personally, England is everything,—I have no thought outside it—no wish beyond it. Yet I am as ashamed of some of its leaders of opinion to-day, as if I saw my own mother dragged in the dust and branded with infamy!"

"You speak of your Government?" began the Queen.

"No, Madam,—I have no more quarrel with my country's present Government than I could have with a child who is led into a ditch by its nurse. It is a weak and corrupted Government; and its actual rulers are vile and abandoned women."

The Queen's eyes opened in a beautiful, startled wonderment;—this man's clear, incisive manner of speech interested her.

"Women!" she echoed, then smiled; "You speak strongly, Sir Walter! I have certainly heard of the 'advanced' women who push themselves so much forward in your country, but I had no idea they were so mischievous! Are they to be admired? Or pitied?"

"Pitied, Madam,—most sincerely pitied!" returned Sir Walter;—"But such misguided simpletons as these are not the creatures who rule, or play with, or poison

the minds of the various members who compose our Government. The 'advanced'
women, poor souls, do nothing but talk platitudes. They are perfectly harmless.
They have no power to persuade men, because in nine cases out of ten, they have
neither wit nor beauty. And without either of these two charms, Madam, it is difficult to put even a clever cobbler, much less a Prime Minister, into leading strings!
No,—it is the spendthrift women of a corrupt society that I mean,—the women
who possess beauty, and are conscious of it,—the women who have a mordant wit
and use it for dangerous purposes—the women who give up their homes, their husbands, their children and their reputations for the sake of villainous intrigue, and
the feverish excitement of speculative money-making;—with these—and with the
stealthy spread of Romanism,—will come the ruin of my country!"

"So grave as all that!" said the Queen lightly;—"But, surely, Sir Walter, if you
see ruin and disaster threatening so great an Empire in the far distance, you and
other wise men of your land are able to stave it off?"

"Madam, I have no power!" he returned bitterly. "Those who have thought
and worked,—those who are able to see what is coming by the light of past experience, are seldom listened to, or if they get a hearing, they are not seldom ridiculed
and 'laughed down.' Till a strong man speaks, we must all remain dumb. There
is no real Government in England at present, just as there is no real Church. The
Government is made up of directly self-interested speculators and financiers rather
than diplomatists,—the Church, for which our forefathers fought, is yielding to the
bribery of Rome. It is a time of Sham,—sham politics, and sham religion! We have
fallen upon evil days,—and unless the people rise, as it is to be hoped to God they
will, serious danger threatens the glory and the honour of England!"

"Would you desire revolution and bloodshed, then?" enquired the Queen, becoming more and more interested as she saw that this Englishman did not, like most
of his sex, pass the moments in gazing at her in speechless admiration,—"Surely
not!"

"I would have revolution, Madam, but not bloodshed," he replied;—"I think
my countrymen are too well grounded in common-sense to care for any movement which could bring about internal dissension or riot,— but, at the same time,
I believe their native sense of justice is great enough to resist tyranny and wrong
and falsehood, even to the death. I would have a revolution—yes—but a silent and

bloodless one!"

"And how would you begin?" asked the Queen.

"The People must begin, Madam!" he answered;—"All reforms must begin and end with the People only! For example, if the People would decline to attend any church where the incumbent is known to encourage practices which are disloyal to the faith of the land, such disloyalty would soon cease. If the majority of women would refuse to know, or to receive, any woman of high position who had voluntarily disgraced herself, they would soon put a stop to the lax morality of the upper classes. If our builders, artisans and mechanics would club together, and refuse to make guns or ships for our enemies in foreign countries, we should not run the risk of being one day hoisted with our own petard. In any case, the work of Revolution rests with the people, though it is quite true they need teachers to show them how to begin."

"And are these teachers forthcoming?"

"I think so!" said Sir Walter meditatively. "Throughout all history, as far back as we can trace it, whenever a serious reform has been needed in either society or government, there has always been found a leader to head the movement."

The Queen's beautiful eyes rested upon him with a certain curiosity.

"What of your King?" she said.

"Madam, he is my King!" he replied,—"And I serve him faithfully!"

She was silent. She began to wonder whether he had any private motive to gain, any place he sought to fill, that he should assume such a touch-me-not air at this stray allusion to his Sovereign.

"Lese-majeste is so common nowadays!" she mused;—"It is such an ordinary thing to hear vulgar *parvenus* talk of their king as if he were a public-house companion of theirs, that it is somewhat remarkable to find one who speaks of his monarch with loyalty and respect. I suppose, however, like everyone else, he has his own ends to serve!—Kings are the last persons in the world who can command absolute fidelity!"

She glanced dreamily over the sea, and perceiving a slight shade of weariness on her face, Sir Walter discreetly rose, craving her permission to retire to the saloon, where he had promised to join the King. When he had left her, she turned to one of her ladies, the Countess Amabil, and remarked:

"A very personable gentleman, is he not?"

"Madam," rejoined the Countess, who was very lovely in herself, and of a bright and sociable disposition;—"I have often thought it would be more pleasant and profitable for all of us if we had many such personable gentlemen with us oftener!"

A slight frown of annoyance crossed the Queen's face. The Countess was a very charming lady; very fascinating in her own way, but her decided predilection for the sterner sex often led her to touch on dangerous ground with her Royal mistress. This time, however, she escaped the chilling retort her remark might possibly, on another occasion, have called down upon her. The Queen said nothing. She sat watching the sea,—and now and again took up her field-glass to study the picturesque coast of The Islands, which was rapidly coming into view. Teresa de Launay, the second lady in attendance on her, was reading, and, seeing her quite absorbed in her book, the Queen presently asked her what it contained.

"You have smiled twice over that book, Teresa," she said kindly;—"What is it about?"

"Madam, it speaks of love!" replied Teresa, still smiling.

"And love makes you smile?"

"I would rather smile than weep over it, Madam!" replied Teresa, with a slight colour warming her fair face;—"But as concerns this book, I smile, because it is full of such foolish verses,—as light and sweet— and almost as cloying,—as French *fondants*!"

"Let me hear!" said the Queen; "Read me a few lines."

"This one, called 'A Canzonet' is brief enough for your Majesty's immediate consideration," replied Teresa;—"It is just such a thing as a man might scribble in his note-book after a bout of champagne, when he is in love for ten minutes! He would not mean a word of it,—but it might sound pretty by moonlight!" Whereupon she read aloud:—

> My Lady is pleased to smile,
>   And the world is glad and gay;
> My Lady is pleased to weep;—
>   And it rains the livelong day!

My Lady is pleased to hate,
  And I lose my life and my breath;
My Lady is pleased to love,—
  And I am the master of Death!

I know that my Lady is Love,
  By the magical light about her;
I know that my Lady is Life,
  For I cannot live without her!

"And you do not think any man would truly mean as much love as this?" queried the Queen.

"Oh, Madam, you know he would not! If he had written such lines about the joys of dining, or the flavour of an excellent cigar, they might then indeed be taken as an expression of his truest and deepest feeling! But his 'Lady'! Bah! She is a mere myth,—a temporary peg to hang a stray emotion on!"

She laughed, and her laughter rippled merrily on the air.

"I do not think the men who write so easily about love can ever truly feel it," she went on;—"Those who really love must surely be quite unable to express themselves. This man who sings about his 'Lady' being pleased to do this or do that, was probably trying to obtain the good graces of some pretty housemaid or chorus girl!"

A slight contemptuous smile crossed the Queen's face; from her expression it was evident that she agreed in the main with the opinion of her vivacious lady-in-waiting. Just at that moment the King and his suite, with Sir Walter Langton and one or two other gentlemen, who had been invited to join the party, came up from the saloon, and the conversation became general.

"Have you seen Humphry at all to-day?" enquired the King aside of De Launay. "I sent him an early message asking him to join us, and was told he had gone out riding. Is that true?"

"I have not seen his Royal Highness since the morning, Sir," replied the equerry; "He then met me,—and Professor von Glauben also—in the gardens. He gave me no hint as to whether he knew of your intention to sail to The Islands this afternoon or not; he was reading, and with some slight discussion on the subject of the book he was interested in, he and the Professor strolled away together."

"But where is Von Glauben?" pursued the King; "I sent for him likewise, but he was absent."

"I understood him to say that you had not commanded his attendance again to-day, Sir," replied Sir Roger;—"He told me he had already waited upon you."

"Certainly I did not command his attendance when I saw him the first thing this morning," replied the King; "I summoned him then merely to satisfy his scruples concerning my health and safety, as he seemed last night to have doubts of both!" He smiled, and his eyes twinkled humourously. "Later on, I requested him to join us in this excursion, but his servant said he had gone out, leaving no word as to when he would return. An eccentricity! I suppose he must be humoured!"

Sir Roger was silent. The King looked at him narrowly, and saw that there was something in his thoughts which he was not inclined to utter, and with wise tact and discretion forbore to press any more questions upon him. It was not a suitable time for cross-examination, even of the most friendly kind; there were too many persons near at hand who might be disposed to listen and to form conjectures; moreover the favouring wind had so aided the Royal yacht in her swift course that The Islands were now close at hand, and the harbour visible, the run across from the mainland having been accomplished under the usual two hours.

The King scanned the coast through his glass with some interest.

"We shall obtain amusement from this unprepared trip," he said, addressing the friends who were gathered round him; "We have forbidden any announcement of our visit here, and, therefore, we shall receive no recognition, or welcome. We shall have to take the people as we find them!"

"Let us hope they will prove themselves agreeable, Sir," said one of the suite, the Marquis Montala, a somewhat effeminate elegant-looking man, with small delicate features and lazily amorous eyes,—"And that the women of the place will not be too alarmingly hideous."

"Women are always women." said the King gaily; "And you, Montala, if you cannot find a pretty one, will put up with an ugly one for the moment rather than have none at all! But beauty exists everywhere, and I daresay we shall find it in as good evidence here as in other parts of the kingdom. Our land is famous for its lovely women,"—and turning to Sir Walter Langton he added—"I think, Sir Walter, we can almost beat your England in that one particular!"

"Some years ago, Sir, I should have accepted that challenge," returned Sir Walter, "And with the deepest respect for your Majesty, I should have ventured to deny the assertion that any country in the world could surpass England for the beauty of its women. But since the rage for masculine sports and masculine manners has taken hold of English girls, I am not at all disposed to defend them. They have, unhappily, lost all the soft grace and modesty for which their grandmothers were renowned, and one begins to remark that their very shapes are no longer feminine. The beautiful full bosoms, admired by Gainsborough and Romney, are replaced by an unbecoming flatness—the feet and hands are growing large and awkward, instead of being well-shaped, white and delicate— the skin is becoming coarse and rough of texture, and there is very little complexion to boast of, if we except the artificial make-up of the women of the town. Some few pretty and natural women remain in the heart of the forest and the country, but the contamination is spreading, and English women are no longer the models of womanhood for all the world."

"Are you married, Sir Walter?" asked the King with a smile.

"To no woman, Sir! I have married England—I love her and work for her only!"

"You find that love sufficient to fill your heart?"

"Perhaps," returned Sir Walter musingly—"perhaps if I speak personally and selfishly—no! But when I argue the point logically, I find this— that if I had a wife she might probably occupy too much of my time,— certes, if I had children, I should be working for them and their future welfare;—as it is, I give all my life and all my work to my country, and my King!"

"I hope you will meet with the reward you merit," said the Queen gently; "Kings are not always well served!"

"I seek no reward," said Sir Walter simply; "The joy of work is always its own guerdon."

As he spoke the yacht ran into harbour, and with a loud warning cry the sailors flung out the first rope to a man on the pier, who stood gazing in open-mouthed wonder at their arrival. He seemed too stricken with amazement to move, for he failed to seize the rope, whereat, with an angry exclamation as the rope slipped back into the water, and the yacht bumped against the pier, a sailor sprang to land, and as it was thrown a second time, seized it and made it fast to the capstan. A few more moments and the yacht was safely alongside, the native islander remaining still motionless and staring. The captain of the Royal vessel stepped on shore and spoke to him.

"Are there any men about here?"

The individual thus addressed shook his head in the negative.

"Are you alone to keep the pier?"

The head nodded in the affirmative. A voice, emanating from a thickly bearded mouth was understood to growl forth something about 'no strange boats being permitted to harbour there.' Whereupon the Captain walked up to the uncouth-looking figure, and said briefly.

"We are here by the King's order! That vessel is the Royal yacht, and their Majesties are on board."

For one instant the islander stared more wildly than ever, then with a cry of amazement and evident alarm, ran away as fast as his legs could carry him and disappeared. The captain returned to the yacht and related his experience to Sir Roger de Launay. The King heard and was amused.

"It seems, Madam," he said, turning to the Queen, "That we shall have The Islands to ourselves; but as our visit will be but brief, we shall no doubt find enough to interest us in the mere contemplation of the scenery without other human company than our own. Will you come?"

He extended his hand courteously to assist her across the gangway of the vessel, and in a few minutes the Royal party were landed, and the yacht was left to the stewards and servants, who soon had all hands at work preparing the dinner which was to be served during the return sail.

CHAPTER XI
"GLORIA—IN EXCELSIS!"

THE King and Queen, followed by their suite and their guests, walked leisurely off the pier, and down a well-made road, sparkling with crushed sea-shells and powdered coral, towards a group of tall trees and green grass which they perceived a little way ahead of them. There was a soothing quietness everywhere,—save for the singing of birds and the soft ripple of the waves on the sandy shore, it was a silent land:

> "In which it seemed always afternoon—
> All round the coast the languid air did swoon—
> Breathing like one that hath a weary dream."

The Queen paused once or twice to look around her; she was vaguely touched and charmed by the still beauty of the scene.

"It is very lovely!" she said, more to herself than to any of her companions; "The world must have looked something like this in the first days of creation,—so unspoilt and fresh and simple!"

The Countess Amabil, walking with Sir Walter Langton, glanced coquettishly at her cavalier and smiled.

"It is idyllic!" she said;—"A sort of Arcadia without Corydon or Phyllis! Do all the inhabitants go to sleep or disappear in the daytime, I wonder?"

"Not all, I imagine," replied Sir Walter; "For here comes one, though, judging from the slowness of his walk, he is in no haste to welcome his King!"

The personage he spoke of was indeed approaching, and all the members of the Royal party watched his advance with considerable curiosity. He was tall and upright in bearing, but as he came nearer he was seen to be a man of great age, with a countenance on which sorrow and suffering had left their indelible traces. There were furrows on that face which tears had hollowed out for their swifter flowing, and the high intellectual brow bore lines and wrinkles of anxiety and pain, which were the soul's pen-marks of a tragic history. He was attired in simple fisherman's garb of rough blue homespun, and when he was within a few paces of the King, he raised his cap from his curly silver hair with an old-world grace and deferential courtesy. Sir Roger de Launay went forward to meet him and to explain the situation.

"His Majesty the King," he said, "has wished to make a surprise visit to his people of The Islands,—and he is here in person with the Queen. Can you oblige him with an escort to the principal places of interest?"

The old man looked at him with a touch of amusement and derision.

"There are no places here of interest to a King," he said; "Unless a poor man's house may serve for his curious comment! I am not his Majesty's subject—but I live under his protection and his laws,—and I am willing to offer him a welcome, since there is no one else to do so!"

He spoke with a refined and cultured accent, and in his look and bearing evinced the breeding of a gentleman.

"And your name?" asked Sir Roger courteously.

"My name is Rene Ronsard," he replied. "I was shipwrecked on this coast years ago. Finding myself cast here by the will of God, here I have remained!"

As he said this, Sir Roger remembered what he had casually heard at times about the 'life-philosopher' who had built for himself a dwelling on The Islands out of the timbers of wrecked vessels. This must surely be the man! Delighted at having thus come upon the very person most likely to provide some sort of diversion for their Majesties, and requesting Ronsard to wait at a distance for a moment, he hastened back to the King and explained the position. Whereupon the monarch at once advanced with alacrity, and as he approached the venerable personage who had offered him the only hospitality he was likely to receive in this part of his realm, he extended his hand with a frank and kindly cordiality. Rene Ronsard accepted it with a slight but not over- obsequious salutation.

"We owe you our thanks," said the King, "for receiving us thus readily, and without notice; which is surely the truest form of hospitable kindness! That we are strangers here is entirely our own fault, due to our own neglect of our Island subjects; and it is for this that we have sought to know something of the place privately, before visiting it with such public ceremonial and state as it deserves. We shall be indebted to you greatly if you will lend us your aid in this intention."

"Your Majesty is welcome to my service in whatever way it can be of use to you," replied Ronsard slowly; "As you see, I am an old man and poor —I have lived here for well-nigh thirty years, making as little demand as possible upon the resources of either rough Nature or smooth civilization to provide me with sustenance. There is poor attraction for a king in such a simple home as mine!"

"More than all men living, a king has cause to love simplicity," returned the monarch, as with his swift and keen glance he noted the old man's proud figure, fine worn features, and clear, though deeply- sunken eyes;—"for the glittering shows of ceremony are chiefly irksome to those who have to suffer their daily monotony. Let me present you to the Queen—she will thank you as I do, for your kindly consent to play the part of host to us to-day."

"Nay,"—murmured Ronsard—"No thanks—no thanks!" Then, as the King said a few words to his fair Consort, and she received the old man's respectful salutation in the cold, grave way which was her custom, he raised his eyes to her face, and started back with an involuntary exclamation.

"By Heaven!" he said suddenly and bluntly, "I never thought to see any woman's beauty that could compare with that of my Gloria!"

He spoke more to himself than to any listener, but the King hearing his words, was immediately on the alert, and when the whole Royal party moved on again, he, walking in a gracious and kindly way by the old man's side, and skilfully keeping up the conversation at first on mere generalities, said presently:—

"And that name of Gloria;—may I ask you who it is that bears so strange an appellation?"

Ronsard looked at him somewhat doubtingly.

"Your Majesty considers it strange? Had you ever seen her, you would think it the only fitting name for her," he answered,—"For she is surely the most glorious thing God ever made!"

"Your wife—or daughter?" gently hinted the King.

The old man smiled bitterly.

"Sir, I have never owned wife or child! For aught I know Gloria may have been born like the goddess Aphrodite, of the sunlight and the sea! No other parents have ever claimed her."

He checked himself, and appeared disposed to change the subject. The King looked at him encouragingly.

"May I not hear more of her?" he asked.

Ronsard hesitated—then with a certain abruptness replied—

"Nay—I am sorry I spoke of her! There is nothing to tell. I have said she is beautiful—and beauty is always stimulating—even to Kings! But your Majesty will have no chance of seeing her, as she is absent from home to-day."

The King smiled;—had the rumours of his many gallantries reached The Islands then?—and was this 'life-philosopher' afraid that 'Gloria '— whoever she was— might succumb to his royal fascinations? The thought was subtly flattering, but he disguised the touch of amusement he felt, and spoke his next words with a kindly and indulgent air.

"Then, as I shall not see her, you may surely tell me of her? I am no betrayer of confidence!"

A pale red tinged Ronsard's worn features—anon he said:—

"It is no question of confidence, Sir,—and there is no secret or mystery associated with the matter. Gloria was, like myself, cast up from the sea. I found her half-drowned, a helpless infant tied to a floating spar. It was on the other side of these Islands—among the rocks where there is no landing-place. There is a little church on the heights up there, and every evening the men and boys practise their sacred singing. It was sunset, and I was wandering by myself upon the shore, and in the church above me I heard them chant 'Gloria! Gloria! Gloria in excelsis Deo!' And while they were yet practising this line I came upon the child,—lying like a strange lily, in a salt pool,— between two shafts of rock like fangs on either side of her, bound fast with rope to a bit of ship's timber. I untied her little limbs, and restored her to life; and all the time I was busy bringing her back to breath and motion, the singing in the church above me was 'Gloria!' and ever again 'Gloria!' So I gave her that name. That was nineteen years ago. She is married now."

"Married!" exclaimed the King, with a curious sense of mingled relief and dis-appointment. "Then she has left you?"

"Oh, no, she has not left me!" replied Ronsard; "She stays with me till her husband is ready to give her a home. He is very poor, and lives in hope of better days. Meanwhile poverty so far smiles upon them that they are happy;—and happiness, youth and beauty rarely go together. For once they have all met in the joyous life of my Gloria!"

"I should like to see her!" said the King, musingly; "You have interested me greatly in her history!"

The old man did not reply, but quickening his pace, moved on a little in advance of the King and his suite, to open a gate in front of them, which guarded the approach to a long low house with carved gables and lattice windows, over which a wealth of roses and jasmine clambered in long tresses of pink and white bloom. Smooth grass surrounded the place, and tall pine trees towered in the background; and round the pillars of the broad verandah, which extended to the full length of the house front, clematis and honeysuckle twined in thick clusters, filling the air with delicate perfume. The Royal party murmured their admiration of this picturesque abode, while Ronsard, with a nimbleness remarkable for a man of his age, set chairs on the verandah and lawn for his distinguished guests. Sir Walter Langton and the Marquis Montala strolled about the garden with some of the ladies, commenting on the simple yet exquisite taste displayed in its planting and arrangement; while the King and Queen listened with considerable interest to the conversation of their venerable host. He was a man of evident culture, and his description of the coral-fishing community, their habits and traditions, was both graphic and picturesque.

"Are they all away to-day?" asked the King.

"All the men on this side of The Islands—yes, Sir," replied Ronsard; "And the women have enough to do inside their houses till their husbands return. With the evening and the moonlight, they will all be out in their fields and gardens, making merry with innocent dance and song, for they are very happy folk—much happier than their neighbours on the mainland."

"Are you acquainted with the people of the mainland, then?" enquired the King.

"Sufficiently to know that they are dissatisfied;" returned Ronsard quietly,—

"And that, deep down among the tangled grass and flowers of that brilliant plea-sure-ground called Society, there is a fierce and starving lion called the People, waiting for prey!"

His voice sank to a low and impressive tone, and for a moment his hearers looked astonished and disconcerted. He went on as though he had not seen the expression of their faces.

"Here in The Islands there was the same discontent when I first came. Every man was in heart a Socialist,—every young boy was a budding Anarchist. Wild ideas fired their brains. They sought Equality. No man should be richer than an-other, they said. Equal lots,—equal lives. They had their own secret Society, con-nected with another similar one across the sea yonder. They were brave, clever and desperate,—moved by a burning sense of wrong,—wrong which they had not the skill to explain, but which they felt. It was difficult to persuade or soothe such men, for they were men of Nature,—not of Shams. But fierce and obstinate as they were, they were good to me when I was cast up for dead on their seashore. And I, in turn, have tried to be good to them. That is, I have tried to make them happy. For happiness is what we all work for and seek for,—from the beginning to the end of life. We go far afield for it, when it oftener lies at our very doors. Well!—they are a peaceful community now, and have no evil intentions towards anyone. They grudge no one his wealth—I think if the truth were known, they rather pity the rich man than envy him. So, at any rate, I have taught them to do. But, formerly, they were, to say the least of it, dangerous!"

The King heard in silence, although the slightest quizzical lifting of his eye-brows appeared to imply that 'dangerous' was perhaps too strong a term by which to designate a handful of Socialistic coral-fishers.

"It is curious," went on Ronsard slowly, "how soon the sense of wrong and injustice infects a whole community. One malcontent makes a host of malcon-tents. This is a fact which many governments lose sight of. If I were the ruler of a country—"

Here he suddenly paused—then added with a touch of brusqueness—

"Pardon me, Sir; I have never known the formalities which apply to conversa-tion with a king, and I am too old to learn now. No doubt I speak too boldly! To me you are no more than man; you should be more by etiquette—but by simple humanity you are not!"

The King smiled, well pleased. This independent commoner, with his rough garb and rougher simplicity of speech, was a refreshing contrast to the obsequious personages by whom he was generally surrounded; and he felt an irresistible desire to know more of the life and surroundings of one who had gained a position of evident authority among the people of his own class.

"Go on, my friend!" he said. "Honest expression of thought can offend none but knaves and fools; and though there are some who say I have a smack of both, yet I flatter myself I am wholly neither of the twain! Continue what you were saying—if you were ruler of a country, what would you do?"

Rene Ronsard considered for a moment, and his furrowed brows set in a puzzled line.

"I think," he said slowly, at last, "I should choose my friends and confidants among the leaders of the people."

"And is not that precisely what we all do?" queried the King lightly; "Surely every monarch must count his friends among the members of the Government?"

"But the Government does not represent the actual people, Sir!" said Ronsard quietly.

"No? Then what does it represent?" enquired the King, becoming amused and interested in the discussion, and holding up his hand to warn back De Launay, and the other members of his suite who were just coming towards him from their tour of inspection through the garden—"Every member of the Government is elected by the people, and returned by the popular vote. What else would you have?"

"Ministers have not always the popular vote," said Ronsard; "They are selected by the Premier. And if the Premier should happen to be shifty, treacherous or self-interested, he chooses such men as are most likely to serve his own ends. And it can hardly be said, Sir, that the People truly return the members of Government. For when the time comes for one such man to be elected, each candidate secures his own agent to bribe the people, and to work upon them as though they were so much soft dough, to be kneaded into a political loaf for his private and particular eating. Poor People! Poor hard-working millions! In the main they are all too busy earning the wherewithal to Live, to have any time left to Think—they are the easy prey of the party agent, except— except when they gather to the voice of a real leader, one who though not in Government, governs!"

"And is there such an one?" enquired the King, while as he spoke his glance fell suddenly, and with an unpleasant memory, on the flashing blue of the sapphire in the Premier's signet he wore; "Here, or anywhere?"

"Over there!" said Ronsard impressively, pointing across the landscape sea-wards; "On the mainland there is not only one, but many! Women,—as well as men. Writers,—as well as speakers. These are they whom Courts neglect or ignore,—these are the consuming fire of thrones!" His old eyes flashed, and as he turned them on the statuesque beauty of the Queen, she started, for they seemed to pierce into the very recesses of her soul. "When Court and Fashion played their pranks once upon a time in France, there was a pen at work on the '*Contrat Social*'—the pen of one Rousseau! Who among the idle pleasure-loving aristocrats ever thought that a mere Book would have helped to send them to the scaffold!" He clenched his hand almost unconsciously—then he spoke more quietly. "That is what I mean, when I say that if I were ruler of a country, I should take special care to make friends with the people's chosen thinkers. Someone in authority"—and here he smiled quizzi-cally —"should have given Rousseau an estate, and made him a marquis—*in time*! The leaders of an advancing Thought,—and not the leaders of a fixed Government are the real representatives of the People!"

Something in this last sentence appeared to strike the King very forcibly.

"You are a philosopher, Rene Ronsard," he said rising from his chair, and laying a hand kindly on his shoulder. "And so, in another way am I! If I understand you rightly, you would maintain that in many cases discontent and disorder are the fer-mentation in the mind of one man, who for some hidden personal motive works his thought through a whole kingdom; and you suggest that if that man once obtained what he wanted there would be an end of trouble—at any rate for a time till the next malcontent turned up! Is not that so?"

"It is so, Sir," replied Ronsard; "and I think it has always been so. In every era of strife and revolution, we shall find one dissatisfied Soul—often a soul of genius and ambition—at the centre of the trouble."

"Probably you are right," said the monarch indulgently; "But evidently the dissatisfied soul is not in *your* body! You are no Don Quixote fighting a windmill of imaginary wrongs, are you?"

A dark red flush mounted to the old man's brow, and as it passed away, left him pale as death.

"Sir, I have fought against wrongs in my time; but they were not imaginary. I might have still continued the combat but for Gloria!"

"Ah! She is your peace-offering to an unjust world?"

"No Sir; she is God's gift to a broken heart," replied Ronsard gently. "The sea cast her up like a pearl into my life; and so for her sake I resolved to live. For her only I made this little home—for her I managed to gain some control over the rough inhabitants of these Islands, and encouraged in them the spirit of peace, mirth and gladness. I soothed their discontent, and tried to instil into them something of the Greek love of beauty and pleasure. But after all, my work sprang from a personal, I may as well say a selfish motive—merely to make the child I loved, happy!"

"Then do you not regret that she is married, and no longer yours to cherish entirely?"

"No, I regret nothing!" answered Ronsard; "For I am old and must soon die. I shall leave her in good and safe hands."

The King looked at him thoughtfully, and seemed about to ask another question, then suddenly changing his mind, he turned to his Consort and said a few words to her in a low tone, whereupon as if in obedience to a command, she rose, and with all the gracious charm which she could always exert if she so pleased, she enquired of Ronsard if he would permit them to see something of the interior of his house.

"Madam," replied Ronsard, with some embarrassment; "All I have is at your service, but it is only a poor place."

"No place is poor that has peace in it," returned the Queen, with one of those rare smiles of hers, which so swiftly subjugated the hearts of men. "Will you lead the way?"

Thus persuaded, Rene Ronsard could only bow a respectful assent, and obey the request, which from Royalty was tantamount to a command. Signing to the other members of the party, who had stood till now at a little distance, the Queen bade them all accompany her.

"The King will stay here till we return," she said, "And Sir Roger will stay with him!"

With these words, and a flashing glance at De Launay, she stepped across the lawn, followed by her ladies-in-waiting, with Sir Walter Langton and the other gentlemen; and in another moment the brilliant little group had disappeared behind the trailing roses and clematis, which hung in profusion from the oaken projections of the wide verandah round Ronsard's picturesque dwelling. Standing still for a moment, with Sir Roger a pace behind him, the King watched them enter the house— then quickly turning round on his heel, faced his equerry with a broad smile.

"Now, De Launay," he said, "let us find Von Glauben!"

Sir Roger started with surprise, and not a little apprehension.

"Von Glauben, Sir?"

"Yes—Von Glauben! He is here! I saw his face two minutes ago, peering through those trees!" And he pointed down a shadowy path, dark with the intertwisted gloom of untrained pine-boughs. "I am not dreaming, nor am I accustomed to imagine spectres! I am on the track of a mystery, Roger! There is a beautiful girl here named Gloria. The beautiful girl is married—possibly to a jealous husband, for she is apparently hidden away from all likely admirers, including myself! Now suppose Von Glauben is that husband!"

He broke off and laughed. Sir Roger de Launay laughed with him; the idea was too irresistibly droll. But the King was bent on mischief, and determined to lose no time in compassing it.

"Come along!" he said. "If this tangled path holds a secret, it shall be discovered before we are many minutes older! I am confident I saw Von Glauben; and what he can be doing here passes my comprehension! Follow me, Roger! If our worthy Professor has a wife, and his wife is beautiful, we will pardon him for keeping her existence a secret from us so long!"

He laughed again; and turning into the path he had previously indicated, began walking down it rapidly, Sir Roger following closely, and revolving in his own perplexed mind the scene of the morning, when Von Glauben had expressed such a strong desire to get away to The Islands, and had admitted that there was "a lady in the case."

"Really, it is most extraordinary!" he thought. "The King no sooner decides to break through conventional forms, than all things seem loosened from their moorings! A week ago, we were all apparently fixed in our orbits of exact routine and work—the King most fixed of all— but now, who can say what may happen next!"

At that moment the monarch turned round.

"This path seems interminable, Roger," he said; "It gets darker, closer and narrower. It thickens, in fact, like, the mystery we are probing!"

Sir Roger glanced about him. A straight band of trees hemmed them in on either side, and the daylight filtered through their stems pallidly, while, as the King had said, there seemed to be no end to the path they were following. They walked on swiftly, however, exchanging no further word, when suddenly an unexpected sound came sweeping up through the heavy branches. It was the rush and roar of the sea,—a surging, natural psalmody that filled the air, and quivered through the trees with the measured beat of an almost human chorus.

"This must be another way to the shore," said the King, coming to a standstill; "And there must be rocks or caverns near. Hark how the waves thunder and reverberate through some deep hollow!"

Sir Roger listened, and heard the boom of water rolling in and rolling out again, with the regularity and rhythm of an organ swell, but he caught an echo of something else besides, which piqued his curiosity and provoked him to a touch of unusual excitement,—it was the sweet and apparently quickly suppressed sound of a woman's laughter. He glanced at his Royal master, and saw at once that he, too, had sharp ears for that silvery cadence of mirth, for his eyes flashed into a smile.

"On, Roger," he said softly; "We are close on the heels of the problem!"

But they had only pressed forward a few steps when they were again brought to a sudden pause. A voice, whose gruffly mellow accents were familiar to both of them, was speaking within evidently close range, and the King, with a warning look, motioned De Launay back a pace or two, himself withdrawing a little into the shadow of the trees.

"Ach! Do not sing, my princess!" said the voice; "For if you open your rosy mouth of music, all the birds of the air, and all the little fishes of the sea will come to listen! And, who knows! Someone more dangerous than either a bird or a fish may listen also!"

The King grasped De Launay by the arm.

"Was I not right?" he whispered. "There is no mistaking Von Glauben's accent!"

Sir Roger looked, as he felt, utterly bewildered. In his own mind he felt it very difficult to associate the Professor with a love affair. Yet things certainly seemed pointing to some entanglement of the sort. Suddenly the King held up an admonitory finger.

"Listen!" he said.

Another voice spoke, rich and clear, and sweet as honey.

"Why should I not sing?" and there was a thrill of merriment in the delicious accents. "You are so afraid of everything to-day! Why? Why should I stay here with nothing to do? Because you tell me the King is visiting The Islands. What does that matter? What do I care for the King? He is nothing to me!"

"You would be something, perhaps, to him if he saw you," replied the guttural voice of Von Glauben. "It is safer to be out of his way. You are a very wilful princess this afternoon! You must remember your husband is jealous!"

The King started.

"Her husband! What the devil does Von Glauben know about her husband!"

De Launay was dumb. A nameless fear and dismay began to possess him.

"My husband!" And the sweet voice laughed out again. "It would be strange indeed for a poor sailor to be jealous of a king!"

"If the poor sailor had a beautiful wife he worshipped, and the King should admire the wife, he might have cause to be jealous!" replied Von Glauben; "And with some ladies, a poor sailor would stand no chance against a king! Why are you so rebellious, my princess, to-day? Have I not brought a letter from your beloved which plainly asks you to keep out of the sight of the King? Have I not been an hour with you here, reading the most beautiful poetry of Heine?"

"That is why I want to sing," said the sweet voice, with a touch of wilfulness in its tone. "Listen! I will give you a reading of Heine in music!" And suddenly, rich and clear as a bell, a golden cadence of notes rang out with the words:

"Ah, Hast thou forgotten, That I possessed thy heart?"

The King sprang lightly out of his hiding-place, and with De Launay moved on slowly and cautiously through the trees.

"Ach, mein Gott!" they heard Von Glauben exclaim—"That is a bird-call which will float on wings to the ears of the King!"

A soft laugh rippled on the air.

"Dear friend and master, why are you so afraid?" asked the caressing woman's voice again;—"We are quite hidden away from the Royal visitors,—and though you have been peeping at the King through the trees, and though you know he is actually in our garden, he will never find his way here! This is quite a secret little study and schoolroom, where you have taught me so much!—yes—so much!—and I am very grateful! And whenever you come to see me you teach me something more— you are always good and kind!—and I would not anger you for the world! But what is the good of knowing and feeling beautiful things, if I may not express them?"

"You do express them,—in yourself,—in your own existence and appearance!" said the Professor gruffly; "but that is a physiological accident which I do not expect you to understand!"

There was a moment's silence. Then came a slight movement, as of quick feet clambering among loose pebbles, and the voice rang out again.

"There! Now I am in my rocky throne! Do you remember—Ah, no!—you know nothing about it,—but I will tell you the story! It was here, in this very place, that my husband first saw me!"

"Ach so!" murmured Von Glauben. "It is an excellent place to make a first appearance! Eve herself could not have chosen more picturesque surroundings to make a conquest of Adam!"

Apparently his mild sarcasm fell on unheeding ears.

"He was walking slowly all alone on the shore," went on the voice, dropping into a more plaintive and tender tone; "The sun had sunk, and one little star was sparkling in the sky. He looked up at the star— and—"

"Then he saw a woman's eye," interpolated Von Glauben; "Which is always more attractive to weak man than an impossible-to-visit planet! What does Shakespeare say of women's eyes?

'Two of the fairest stars in all the heaven,
Having some business, do entreat her eyes
To twinkle in their spheres till they return.
What if her eyes were there, they in her head?
The brightness of her cheek would shame those stars,
As daylight doth a lamp; her eye in heaven

Would through the airy regions stream so bright,
That birds would sing and think it were not night!'Ach! That is so!"

As the final words left his lips, a rich note of melody stirred the air, and a song in which words and music seemed thoroughly welded together, rose vibratingly up to the quiet sky:

"Here by the sea,
My Love found me!
Seagulls over the waves were swinging;
Mermaids down in their caves were singing,—
And one little star in the rosy sky
Sparkled above like an angel's eye!
My Love found me,
And I and he
Plighted our troth eternally!
Oh day of splendour,
And self-surrender!
The day when my Love found me!

Here, by the sea,
My King crown'd me!
Wild ocean sang for my Coronation,
With the jubilant voice of a mighty nation!—
'Mid the towering rocks he set my throne,
And made me forever and ever his own!
My King crown'd me,
And I and he
Are one till the world shall cease to be!
Oh sweet love story!
Oh night of glory!
The night when my King crown'd me!"

No language could ever describe the marvellous sweetness of the voice that sung these lines; it was so full of exquisite triumph, tenderness and passion, that it seemed more supernatural than human. When the song ceased, a great wave dashed on the shore, like a closing organ chord, and Von Glauben spoke.

"There! You wanted your own way, my princess, and you have had it! You have sung like one of the seraphim;—do not be surprised if mortals are drawn to listen. Sst! What is that?"

There was a pause. The King had inadvertently cracked a twig on one of the pine-boughs he was holding back in an endeavour to see the speakers. But he now boldly pushed on, beckoning De Launay to follow close, and in another minute had emerged on a small sandy plateau, which led, by means of an ascending path, to a rocky eminence, encircled by huge boulders and rocky pinnacles, which somewhat resembled peaks of white coral,—and here, on a height above him,—with the afternoon sun-glow bathing her in its full mellow radiance, sat a visibly enthroned goddess of the landscape,—a girl, or rather a perfect woman, more beautiful than any he had ever seen, or even imagined. He stared up at her in dazzled wonder, half blinded by the brightness of the sun and her almost equally blinding loveliness.

"Gloria!" he exclaimed breathlessly, hardly conscious of his own utterance; "You are Gloria!"

The fair vision rose, and came swiftly forward with an astonished look in her bright deep eyes.

"Yes!" she said, "I am Gloria!"

CHAPTER XII
A SEA PRINCESS

SCARCELY had she thus declared herself, when the Bismarckian head and shoulders of Von Glauben appeared above the protecting boulders; and moving with deliberate caution, the rest of his body came slowly after, till he stood fully declared in an attitude of military 'attention.' He showed neither alarm nor confusion at seeing the King; on the contrary, the fixed, wooden expression of his countenance betokened some deeply- seated mental obstinacy, and he faced his Royal master with the utmost composure, lifting the slouched hat he wore with his usual stiff and soldierly dignity, though carefully avoiding the amazed stare of his friend, Sir Roger de Launay.

The King glanced him up and down with a smiling air of amused curiosity.

"So this is how you pursue your scientific studies, Professor!" he said lightly; "Well!"—and he turned his eyes, full of admiration, on the beautiful creature who stood silently confronting him with all that perfect ease which expresses a well-balanced mind,—"Wisdom is often symbolised to us as a marble goddess,—but when Pallas Athene takes so fair a shape of flesh and blood as this, who shall blame even a veteran philosopher for sitting at her feet in worship!"

"Pardon me, Sir," returned Von Glauben calmly; "There is no goddess of Wisdom here, so please you, but only a very simple and unworldly young woman. She is—" Here he hesitated a moment, then went on—"She is merely the adopted child of a fisherman living on these Islands."

"I am aware of that!" said the King still smiling. "Rene Ronsard is his name. He is my host to-day; and he has told me something of her. But, certes, he did not mention that you had adopted her also!"

Von Glauben flushed vexedly.

"Sir," he stammered, "I could explain—"

"Another time!" interrupted the King, with a touch of asperity. "Meanwhile, present your—your pupil in the poesy of Heine,—to me!"

Thus commanded, the Professor, casting a vexed glance at De Launay, who did not in the least comprehend his distress, went to the girl, who during their brief conversation had stood quietly looking from one to the other with an expression of half-amused disdain on her lovely features.

"Gloria," he began reluctantly—then whispering in her ear, he muttered—"I told you your voice would do mischief, and it has done it!" Then aloud—"Gloria,—this—this is the King!"

She smiled, but did not change her erect and easy attitude.

"The King is welcome!" she said simply.

She had evidently no intention of saluting the monarch; and Sir Roger de Launay gazed at her in mingled surprise and admiration. She was certainly wonderfully beautiful. Her complexion had the soft clear transparency of a pink sea-shell—her eyes, large and lustrous, were as densely blue as the dark azure in the depths of a wave,—and her hair, of a warm bronze chestnut, caught back with a single band of red coral, seemed to have gathered in its rich curling clusters all the deepest tints of autumn leaves flecked with a golden touch of the sun. Her figure, clad in a straight garment of rough white homespun, was the model of perfect womanhood. She stood a little above the medium height, her fair head poised proudly on regal shoulders, while the curve of the full bosom would have baffled the sculptural genius of a Phidias. The whole exquisite outline of her person was the expressed essence of beauty, from the lightest wave of her hair, down to her slender ankles and small feet; and the look that irradiated her noble features was that of child-like happiness and repose,—the untired expression of one who had never known any other life than the innocent enjoyment bestowed upon her by God and divine Nature. Beautiful as his Queen-Consort was and always had been, the King was forced to admit to himself that here was a woman far more beautiful,—and as he looked upon her critically, he saw that there was a light and splendour about her which only the happiness of Love can give. Her whole aspect was as of one uplifted into a finer atmosphere than that of earth,—she seemed to exhale purity from herself, as a rose exhales perfume, and her undisturbed serenity and dignity, when made aware of the Royal presence, were evidently not the outcome of ill-breeding or discourtesy, but of mere self-respect and independence. He approached her with a strange hesitation, which for him was quite a new experience.

"I am glad I have been fortunate enough to meet you!" he said gently;— "Some kindly fate guided my steps down the path which brought me to this part of the shore, else I might have gone away without seeing you!"

"That would have been no loss to your Majesty," answered Gloria calmly;— "For to see me, is of no use to anyone!"

"Would your husband say so?" hazarded the King with a smile.

Her eyes flashed.

"My husband would say what is right," she replied. "He would know better how to talk to you than I do!"

He had insensibly drawn nearer to her as he spoke; meanwhile Von Glauben, with a disconsolate air, had joined Sir Roger de Launay, who, by an enquiring look and anxious uplifting of his eyebrows, dumbly asked what was to be the upshot of this affair,—only to receive a dismal shake of the head in reply.

"Possibly I know your husband," went on the King, anxious to continue conversation with so beautiful a creature. "If I do, and he is in my personal service, he shall not lack promotion! Will you tell me his name?"

A startled look came into the girl's eyes, and a deep blush swept over her fair cheeks.

"I dare not!" she said;—"He has forbidden me!"

"Forbidden you!" The King recoiled a step—a vague suspicion rankled in his mind. "Then, though your King asks you a friendly question, you refuse to answer it?"

Von Glauben here gripped Sir Roger so fiercely by the arm, that the latter nearly cried out with pain.

"She must not tell," he muttered—"She must not—she will not!"

But Gloria was looking straight at her Royal questioner.

"I have no King but my husband!" she said firmly. "I have sworn before God to obey him in all things, and I will not break my vow!"

"Good girl! Wise girl!" exclaimed Von Glauben. "Ach, if all the beautiful women so guarded their tongues and obeyed their husbands, what a happy world it would be!"

The King turned upon him.

"True! But you are not bound by the confidences of marriage, Professor,—so that while in our service our will must be your law! You, therefore, can perhaps tell me the name of the fortunate man who has wedded this fair lady?"

The Professor's countenance visibly reddened.

"Sir," he stammered—"With every respect for your Majesty, I would rather lose my much-to-be-appreciated post with you than betray my friends!"

The King suddenly lost patience.

"By Heaven!" he exclaimed, "Is my command to be slighted and set aside as if it were naught? Not while I am king of this country! What mystery is here that I am not to know?"

Gloria laughed outright, and the pretty ripple of mirth, so unforced and natural, diverted the monarch's irritation.

"Oh, you are angry!" she said, her lovely eyes twinkling and sparkling like diamonds:—"So! Then your Majesty is no more than a very common man who loses temper when he cannot have his own way!" She laughed again, and the King stared at her unoffended,—being spellbound, both by her regal beauty, and her complete indifference to himself. "I will speak like the prophets do in the Bible and say, 'Lo! there is no mystery, O King!' I am only poor Gloria, a sailor's wife,—and the sailor has a place on board your son the Crown Prince's yacht, and he does not want his master to know that he is married lest he lose that place! Is not that plain and clear, O King? And why should I disobey my beloved in such a simple matter?"

The King was still in something of a fume.

"There is no reason why you should disobey," he said more quietly, but still with vexation;—"But, equally, there is no reason why your husband should be dismissed from the Crown Prince's service, because he has chosen to marry. If you tell me his name, I will make all things easy for him, for you, and your future. Can you not trust me?"

With wonderful grace and quickness Gloria suddenly sprang forward, caught the King's hand, kissed it, and then threw it lightly away from her.

"No!" she said, with a pretty defiance; "I kiss the hand of the country's King—but I have my own King to serve!"

And pausing for no more words, she turned away, sprang lightly up the rocks as swiftly as a roe-deer, and disappeared. And from some hidden corner, clear and full and sweet, her voice rang out above the peaceful plashing of the waves:

"My King crown'd me!
And I and he
Are one till the world shall cease to be!"

Stricken dumb and confused by the suddenness of her action, and the swiftness of her departure, the King stood for a moment inert, gazing up the rocky height with the air of one who has seen a vision of heaven withdrawn again into its native element. Some darkening doubt troubled his mind, and it was with an altogether changed and stern countenance that he confronted Von Glauben.

"Last night, Professor, you were somewhat anxious for our health and safety," he said severely; "It is our turn now to be equally anxious for yours! We are of opinion that you, like ourselves, run some risk of danger by meddling in affairs which do not concern you! Silence!" This, as the Professor, deeply moved by his Royal master's evident displeasure, made an attempt to speak. "We will hear all you have to say to-morrow. Meanwhile—follow your fair charge!" And he pointed up in the direction whither Gloria had vanished. "Her husband"—and he emphasized the word,—"whoever he is, appears to have entrusted her safety to you;—see that you do not betray his trust, even though you have betrayed mine!"

At this remark Von Glauben was visibly overcome.

"Sir, you have never had reason to complain of any lack of loyalty in me to you and to your service," he said with an earnest dignity which became him well;—"In the matter of the poor child yonder, whose beauty would surely be a fatal snare to any man, there is much to be told,— which if told truly, will prove that I am merely the slave of circumstances which were not created by me,—and which it is possible for a faithful servant of your Majesty to regret! But a betrayer of trust I have never been, and I beseech your Majesty to believe me when I say that the acuteness of that undeserved reproach cuts me to the heart! I yield to no man in the respect and affection I entertain for your Royal person, not even to De Launay here—who knows—who knows—"

He broke off, unable through strong emotion to proceed.

"'Who knows'—What?" enquired the King, turning his steadfast eyes on Sir Roger.

"Nothing, Sir! Absolutely nothing!" replied the equerry, opening his eyes as widely as their habitual langour would permit; "I am absolutely ignorant of everything concerning Von Glauben except that he is an honest man! That I certainly do know!"

A slight smile cleared away something of the doubt and displeasure on the King's face. Approaching the disconsolate Professor, he laid one hand on his shoulder and looked him steadily in the eyes.

"By my faith, Von Glauben, if I thought positively that you could play me false in any matter, I would never believe a man again! Come! Forgive my hasty speech, and do not look so downcast! Honest I have always known you to be,—and that you will prove your honesty, I do not doubt! But—there is something in this affair which awakens grave suspicion in my mind. For to-day I press no questions—but to-morrow I must know all! You understand? *All*! Say this to the girl, Gloria,—say it to her husband also—as, of course, you know who her husband is. If he serves on Prince Humphry's yacht, that is enough to say that Humphry himself has probably seen her. Under all the circumstances, I confess, my dear Von Glauben, that your presence here is a riddle which needs explanation!"

"It shall be explained, Sir—" murmured the Professor.

"Naturally! It must, of course be explained. But I hope you give me credit for not being altogether a fool; and I have an idea that my son's frequent mysterious visits to The Islands have something to do with this fair Gloria of Glorias!" Von Glauben started involuntarily. "You perhaps think it too? Or know it? Well, if it is so, I can hardly blame him overmuch,—though I am sorry he should have selected a poor sailor's wife as a subject for his secret amours! I should have thought him possessed of more honour. However—to-morrow I shall look to you for a full account of the matter. For the present, I excuse your attendance, and permit you to remain with her whom you call 'princess'!"

He stepped back, and, taking De Launay's arm, turned round at once, and walked away back to Ronsard's house by the path he had followed with such eagerness and care.

Von Glauben watched the two tall figures disappear, and then with a troubled look, began to climb slowly up the rocks in the direction where Gloria had gone. His reflections were not altogether as philosophical as usual, because as he said to himself—"One can never tell how a woman is going to meet misfortune! Sometimes she takes it well; and then the men who have ruthlessly destroyed her happiness go on their way rejoicing; but more often she takes it ill, and there is the devil to pay! Yet—Gloria is not like any ordinary woman—she is a carefully selected specimen of her sex, which a kindly Nature has produced as an example of what women were intended to be when they were first created. I wonder where she has hidden herself?"

Arriving at the summit of the ascent, he peered down towards the sea. Slopes of rank grass and sea-daisies tufted the rocks on this side, divided by certain deep hollows which the action of the waves had honeycombed here and there; and below the grass was the shore, powdered thickly with sand, of a fine, light, and sparkling colour, like gold dust. Here in the full light of the sinking sun lay Gloria, her head pillowed against a rough stone, on the top of which a tall cluster of daisies, sometimes called moon-flowers, waved like white plumes.

"Gloria!" called Von Glauben.

She looked up, smiling.

"Has Majesty gone?" she asked.

"Gone for the present," replied the Professor, beginning to put one foot cautiously before the other down a roughly hewn stairway in the otherwise almost inaccessible cliff. "But, like the sun which is setting to-night, he will rise again to-morrow!"

"Shall I come and help you down?" enquired the girl, turning on her elbow as she lay, and lifting her lovely face, radiant as a flower, towards him.

"Whether down or up, you shall never help me, my princess!" he replied. "When I can neither climb nor fall without the assistance of a woman's hand, I shall take a pistol and tell it to whisper in my ear—'Good- bye, Heinrich Von Glauben! You are all up—finish—gone!'"

Here, with a somewhat elephantine jump, he alighted beside her and threw himself on the warm sand with a deep sigh of mingled exhaustion and relief.

"You would be very wicked to put a pistol to your ear," said Gloria severely;—"It is only a coward who shoots himself!"

"Ach so! And it is a brave man who shoots others! That is curious, is it not, princess? It is a little bit of man's morality; but we have no time to discuss it now. We have something more serious to consider,— your husband!"

She looked at him wonderingly.

"My husband? Do you really think he will be very angry that the King saw me?"

The Professor appeared to be considering the question; but in reality he was studying the exquisite delicacy of the face turned so wistfully upon him, and the lovely lines of the slim throat and rounded chin—"So beautiful a creature"—he was saying within himself—"And must she also suffer pain and disillusion like all the rest of her unfortunate sex!" Aloud he replied.

"My princess, it is not for me to say he will be 'angry,'—for how could he be angry with the one he loves to such adoration! He will be sorry and troubled—it will put him into a great difficulty! Ach!—a whole nest of difficulties!"

"Why?" And Gloria's eyes filled with sudden tears. "I would not grieve him for the world! I cannot understand why it should matter at all, even if the King does find out that he is married. Are the rules so strict for all the men who serve on board the Royal vessels?"

Von Glauben bit his lips to hide an involuntary smile. But he answered her with quite a martinet air.

"Yes, they are strict—very strict! Particularly so in the case of your husband. You see, my child—you do not perhaps quite understand—but he is a sort of superior officer on board; and in close personal attendance on the Crown Prince."

"He did not tell me that!" said the girl a little anxiously; "Yet surely it would not matter if he loses one place; can he not easily get another?"

Von Glauben was looking at her with a grave, almost melancholy intentness.

"Listen, my princess,—listen to your poor old friend, who means you so much good, and no harm at all! Your husband—and I too, for that matter,—wished much to prevent the King from seeing you—for—for many reasons. When I heard he was coming to The Islands, I resolved to arrive here before him, and so I did. I said nothing to Ronsard, not even to warn him of the King's impending visit. I took you just quietly, as I have often done, for a walk, with a book to read and to explain to you, because you tell me you want to study; though in my opinion you know quite enough—for a woman. I gave you a letter from your husband, and you know he asked you in that letter to avoid all possibility of meeting with the King. Good! Well, now, what happens? You sing—and lo! his Majesty, like a fish on a hook, is drawn up open- mouthed to your feet! Now, who is to blame? You or I?"

A little perplexed line appeared on the girl's fair brows. "I am, I suppose!" she said somewhat plaintively,—"But yet, even now, I do not understand. What is the King? He is nothing! He does nothing for anybody! People make petitions to him, and he never answers them—they try to point out errors and abuses, and he takes no trouble to remedy them—he is no better than a wooden idol! He is not a real man, though he looks like one."

"Oh, you think he looks like one?" murmured Von Glauben; "That is to say you are not altogether displeased with his appearance?"

Gloria's eyes darkened a moment with thought,—then flashed with laughter.

"No," she said frankly—"He is more kingly than I thought a king could be. But he should not lose temper. That spoils all dignity!"

Von Glauben smiled.

"Kings are but mortal," he said, "and never to lose temper would be impossible to any man."

"It is such a waste of time!" declared Gloria—"Why should anyone lose self-control? It is like giving up a sword to an enemy."

"That is one of Rene Ronsard's teachings,"—said the Professor—"It is excellent in theory! But in practice I have seen Rene give way to temper himself, with considerable enjoyment of his own mental thunderstorm. As for the King, he is generally a very equable personage; and he has one great virtue—that is courage. He is brave as a lion—perhaps braver than many lions!"

She raised her eyes enquiringly.

"Has he proved it?"

Rather taken aback by the question, he stared at her solemnly.

"Proved it? Well! He has had no chance. The country has been at peace for many years—but if there should ever be a war——"

"Would he go and fight for the country?" enquired Gloria.

"In person? No. He would not be allowed to do that. His life would be endangered——"

"Of course!" interrupted the girl with a touch of contempt; "But if he would allow himself to be ruled by others in such a matter, I do not call him brave!"

The Professor drew out his spectacles, and fixing them on his nose with much care, regarded her through them with bland and kindly interest.

"Very simple and primitive reasoning, my princess!" he said; "And from an early historic point of view, your idea is correct. In the olden times kings went themselves to battle, and led their soldiers on to victory in person. It was very fine; much finer than our modern ways of warfare. But it has perhaps never occurred to you that a king's life nowadays is always in danger? He can do nothing more completely courageous than to show himself in public!"

"Are kings then so hated?" she asked.

"They are not loved, it must be confessed," returned Von Glauben, taking off his spectacles again; "But that is quite their own fault. They seldom do anything to deserve the respect,—much less the affection of their subjects. But this king—this man you have just seen—certainly deserves both."

"Why, what has he done?" asked Gloria wonderingly. "I have heard people say he is very wicked—that he takes other men's wives away from them—"

The Professor coughed discreetly.

"My princess, let me suggest to you that he could scarcely take other men's wives away from them, unless those wives were perfectly willing to go!"

She gave an impatient gesture.

"Oh, there are weak women, no doubt; but then a king should know better than to put temptation in their way. If a man undertakes to be strong, he should also be honourable. Then,—what of the taxes the King imposes on the people? The sufferings of the poor over there on the mainland are terrible!—I know all about them! I have heard Sergius Thord!"

The Professor gave an uncomfortable start.

"You have heard Sergius Thord? Where?"

"Here!" And Gloria smiled at his expression of wonderment. "He has spoken often to our people, and he is father Rene's friend."

"And what does he talk about when he speaks here?" enquired Von Glauben.

"When does he come, and how does he go?"

"Always at night," answered Gloria; "He has a sailing skiff of his own, and on many an evening when the wind sets in our quarter, he arrives quite suddenly, all alone, and in a moment, as if by magic, the Islanders all seem to know he is here. On the shore, or in the fields he assembles them round him, and tells them many things that are plain and true. I have heard him speak often of the shortness of life and its many sorrows, and he says we could all make each other happy for the little time we have to live, if we would. And I think he is right; it is only wicked and selfish people who make others unhappy!"

The Professor was silent. Gloria, watching him, wondered at his somewhat perturbed expression.

"Do you know the King very well?" she asked suddenly. "He seemed very cross with you!"

Von Glauben roused himself from a fit of momentary abstraction.

"Yes,—he was cross!" he rejoined. "I, like your husband, am in his service—and I ought to have been on duty to-day. It will be all right, however—all right! But—" He paused for a moment, then went on—"You say that only wicked and selfish people make others unhappy. Now suppose your husband were wicked and selfish enough to make *you* unhappy; what would you say?"

A sweet smile shone in her eyes.

"He could not make me unhappy!" she said. "He would not try! He loves me, and he will always love me!"

"But, suppose," persisted the Professor—"Just for the sake of argument —suppose he had deceived you?"

With a low cry she sprang up.

"Impossible!" she exclaimed; "He is truth itself! He could not deceive anyone!"

"Come and sit down again," said Von Glauben tranquilly; "It is disturbing to my mind to see you standing there pronouncing your faith in the integrity of man! No male creature deserves such implicit trust, and whenever a woman gives it, she invariably finds out her mistake!"

But Gloria stood still, The rich colour had faded from her cheeks—her eyes were dilated with alarm, and her breath came and went quickly.

"You must explain," she said hurriedly; "You must tell me what you mean by suggesting such a wicked thought to me as that my husband could deceive me! It is not right or kind of you,—it is cruel!"

The Professor scrambled up hastily out of his sandy nook, and approaching her, took her hand very gently and respectfully in his own and kissed it.

"My dear—my princess—I was wrong! Forgive me!" he murmured, and there was a little tremor in his voice; "But can you not understand the possibility of a man loving a woman very much, and yet deceiving her for her good?"

"It could never be for her good," said Gloria firmly; "It would not be for mine! No lie ever lasts!"

Von Glauben looked at her with a sense of reverence and something like awe. The after-glow of the sinking sun was burning low down upon the sea, and turning it to fiery crimson, and as she stood bathed in its splendour, the white rocks towering above her, and the golden sands sparkling at her feet, she appeared like some newly descended angel expressing the very truth of Heaven itself in her own presence on earth. As they stood thus, the sudden boom of a single cannon echoed clear across the waves.

"There goes the King!" said Von Glauben; "Majesty departs for the present, having so far satisfied his curiosity! That gun is the signal. Child!"—and turning towards her again, he took both her hands in his, and spoke with emphatic gravity and kindness—"Remember that I am your friend always! Whatever chances to you, do not forget that you may command my service and devotion till death! In this strange life, we never know from day to day what may happen to us, for constant change is the law of Nature and the universe,—but after all, there is something in the soul of a true man which does not change with the elements,—and that is— loyalty to a sworn faith! In my heart, I have sworn an oath of fealty to you, my beautiful little princess of the sea!—and it is a vow that shall never be broken! Do you understand? And will you remember?"

Her large dark blue eyes looked trustingly into his.

"Indeed, I will never forget!" she said, with a touch of wistfulness in her accents; "But I do not know why you should be anxious for me—there is nothing to fear for my happiness. I have all the love I care for in the world!"

"And long may you keep it!" said the Professor earnestly; "Come! It will soon be time for me to leave you, and I must see Rene before I go. If you follow my advice, you will say nothing to him of having met the King—not for the present, at any rate."

She agreed to this, though with some little hesitation,—then they ascended the cliff, and walking by way of the pine-wood through which the King had come, arrived at Ronsard's house, to find the old man quite alone, and peacefully engaged in tying up the roses and jessamine on the pillars of his verandah. His worn face lighted up with animation and tenderness as Gloria approached him and threw her arms around his neck, and to her he related the incident of the King and Queen's unexpected visit, as a sort of accidental, uninteresting, and wholly unimportant occurrence. The Queen, he said, was very beautiful; but too cold in her manner, though she had certainly taken much interest in seeing the house and garden.

"It was just as well you were absent, child," he added—"Royalty brings an atmosphere with it which is not wholesome. A king never knows what it is to be an honest man!"

"Those are your old, discarded theories, Ronsard!" said Von Glauben, shaking his head;—"You said you would never return to them!"

"Aye!" rejoined Ronsard;—"I have tried to put away all my old thoughts and dreams for her sake"—and his gaze rested lovingly on Gloria as, standing on tip-toe to reach a down-drooping rose, she gathered it and fastened it in her bosom. "There should only be peace and contentment where *she* dwells! But sometimes my life's long rebellion against sham and injustice stirs in my blood, and I long to pull down the ignorant people's idols of wood and straw, and set up men in place of dummies!"

"A Mumbo-Jumbo of some kind has always been necessary in the world, my friend," said the Professor calmly; "Either in the shape of a deity or a king. A wood and straw Nonentity is better than an incarnated fleshly Selfishness. Will you give me supper before I leave?"

Ronsard smiled a cheery assent, and Gloria preceding them, and singing in a low tone to herself as she went, they all entered the house together.

Meanwhile, the Royal yacht was scudding back to the mainland over crisp waters on the wings of a soft breeze, with a bright moon flying through fleecy clouds above, and silvering the foam-crests of the waves below. There was music on board,—the King and Queen dined with their guests, —and laughter and gay converse intermingled with the sound of song. They talked of their day's experience—of the beauty of The Islands—of Ronsard,—his quaint house and quainter self,—so different to the persons with whom they associated in their own exclusive and brilliant Court 'set,' and the pretty Countess Amabil flirting harmlessly with Sir Walter Langton, suggested that a 'Flower Feast' or Carnival should be held during the summer, for the surprise and benefit of the Islanders, who had never yet seen a Royal pageant of pleasure on their shores.

But Sir Roger de Launay, ever watching the Queen, saw that she was very pale, and more silent even than was her usual habit, and that her eyes every now and again rested on the King, with something of wonder, as well as fear.

CHAPTER XIII
SECRET SERVICE

IN one of the ultra-fashionable quarters of the brilliant and overcrowded metropolis which formed the nucleus and centre of everything notable or progressive in the King's dominions, there stood a large and aggressively-handsome house, over-decorated both outside and in, and implying in its general appearance vulgarity, no less than wealth. These two things go together very much nowadays; in fact one scarcely ever sees them apart. The fair, southern city of the sea was not behind other modern cities in luxury and self-aggrandisement, and there were certain members of the population who made it their business to show all they were worth in their domestic and home surroundings. One of the most flagrant money-exhibitors of this kind was a certain Jew named David Jost. Jost was the sole proprietor of the most influential newspaper in the kingdom, and the largest shareholder in three other newspaper companies, all apparently differing in party views, but all in reality working into the same hands, and for the same ends. Jost and his companies virtually governed the Press; and what was euphoniously termed 'public opinion' was the opinion of Jost. Should anything by chance happen to get into his own special journal, or into any of the other journals connected with Jost, which Jost did not approve of, or which might be damaging to Jost's social or financial interests, the editor in charge was severely censured; if the fault occurred again he was promptly dismissed. 'Public opinion' had to be formed on Jost's humour; otherwise it was no opinion at all. A few other newspapers led a precarious existence in offering a daily feeble opposition to Jost; but they had not cash enough to carry on the quarrel. Jost secured all the advertisers, and as a natural consequence of this, could well afford to be the 'voice of the people' ad libitum. He was immensely wealthy, openly vicious, and utterly unscrupulous; and made brilliant speculative 'deals' in the unsuspecting natures of those who were led, by that bland and cheery demeanour which is generally associated with a large paunch, to consider him a 'good fellow' with his 'heart in the right place.' With regard to this last assertion, it may be doubted whether he had a heart at all, in any place, right or wrong. He was certainly not given to sentiment. He had married for money, and his wife had died in a mad-house. He was now anxious to marry again for position; and while looking round the market for a sufficiently perfect person of high-breeding, he patronized the theatre largely, and 'protected' several ballet-girls and actresses. Everyone knew that his life was black with villainy and intrigue of the most shameless kind, yet everyone swore that he was a good man. Such is the value of a limitless money-bag!

It was very late in the evening of the day following that on which the King had paid his unexpected visit to The Islands,—and David Jost had just returned from a comic opera-house, where he had supped in private with two or three painted heroines of the footlights. He was in an excellent humour with himself. He had sprung a mine on the public; and a carefully-concocted rumour of war with a foreign power had sent up certain stocks and shares in which he had considerable interest. He smiled, as he thought of the general uneasiness he was creating by a few headlines in his newspaper; and he enjoyed to the full the tranquil sense of having flung a bone of discord between two nations, in order to watch them from his arm-chair fighting like dogs for it tooth and claw, till one or the other gave in.

"Lutera will have to thank me for this," he said to himself; "And he will owe me both a place and a title!"

He sat down at his desk in his warm and luxuriously-furnished study,— turned over a few letters, and then glanced up at the clock. Its hands pointed to within a few minutes of midnight. Taking up a copy of his own newspaper, he frowned slightly, as he saw that a certain leading article in favour of the Jesuit settlement in the country had not appeared.

"Crowded out, I suppose, for want of space," he said; "I must see that it goes in to-morrow. These Jesuits know a thing or two; and they are not going to plank down a thousand pounds for nothing. They have paid for their advertisement, and they must have it. They ought to have had it to-day. Lutera must warn the King that it will not do to offend the Church. There's a lot of loose cash lying idle in the Vatican,—we may as well have some of it! His Majesty has acted most unwisely in refusing to grant the religious Orders the land they want. He must be persuaded to yield it to them by degrees,—in exchange of course for plenty of cash down, without loss of dignity!"

At that moment the door-bell rang softly, as if it were pulled with extreme caution. A servant answered it, and at once came to his master's room.

"A gentleman to see you, sir, on business," he said.

Jost looked up.

"On business? At this time of night? Say I cannot see him—tell him to come again to-morrow!"

The servant withdrew, only to return again with a more urgent statement.

"The gentleman says he must see you, sir; he comes from the Premier."

"From the Premier?"

"Yes, sir; his business is urgent, he says, and private. He sent in his card, sir."

Here he handed over the card in question, a small, unobtrusive bit of pasteboard, laid in solitary grandeur on a very large silver salver.

David Jost took it up, and scanned it with some curiosity. "'Pasquin Leroy'! H'm! Don't know the name at all. 'Urgent business; bear private credentials from the Marquis de Lutera'!" He paused again, considering, —then turned to the waiting attendant. "Show him in.".

"Yes, sir!"

Another moment and Pasquin Leroy entered,—but it was an altogether different Pasquin Leroy to the one that had recently enrolled himself as an associate of Sergius Thord's Revolutionary Committee. *That* particular Pasquin had seemed somewhat of a dreamer and a visionary, with a peculiar and striking resemblance to the King; *this* Pasquin Leroy had all the alertness and sharpness common to a practised journalist, press-reporter or commercial traveller. Moreover, his countenance, adorned with a black mustache, and small pointed beard, wore a cold and concentrated air of business—and he confronted the Jew millionaire without the slightest embarrassment or apology for having broken in upon his seclusion at so unseasonable an hour. He used a pince-nez, and was constantly putting it to his eyes, as though troubled with short-sightedness.

"I presume your matter cannot wait, sir," said Jost, surveying him coolly, with-out rising from his seat,—"but if it can—"

"It cannot!" returned Leroy, bluntly.

Jost stared.

"So! You come from the Marquis de Lutera?"

"I do."

"Your credentials?"

Leroy stepped close up to him, and with a sudden movement, which was some-what startling, held up his right hand.

"This signet is, I believe, familiar to you,—and it will be enough to prove that I come on confidential business which cannot be trusted to writing!"

Jost gazed at the flashing sapphire on the stranger's hand with a sense of deadly apprehension. He recognised the Premier's ring well enough; and he also knew that it would never have been sent to him in this mysterious way unless the matter in question was almost too desperate for whispering within four walls. An uneasy sensation affected him; he pulled at his collar, looked round the room as though in search of inspiration, and then finally bringing his small, swine-like eyes to bear on the neat soldierly figure before him, he said with a careless air:

"You probably bring news for the Press affecting the present policy?"

"That remains to be seen!" replied Leroy imperturbably; "From a perfectly impartial standpoint, I should imagine that the present policy may have to alter considerably!"

Jost recoiled.

"Impossible! It cannot be altered!" he said roughly,—then suddenly recollect-ing himself, he assumed his usual indolent equanimity, and rising slowly, went to a side door in the room and threw it open.

"Step in here," he said; "We can talk without fear of interruption. Will you smoke?"

"With pleasure!" replied Leroy, accepting a cigar from the case Jost extended—then glancing with a slight smile at the broad, squat Jewish countenance which had, in the last couple of minutes, lost something of its habitual redness, he added—"I am glad you are disposed to discuss matters with me in a friendly, as well as in a confidential way. It is possible my news may not be altogether agreeable to you;—but of course you would be more willing to suffer personally, than to jeopardise the honour of Ministers."

He uttered the last sentence more as a question than a statement.

Jost shifted one foot against the other uneasily.

"I am not so sure of that," he said after a pause, during which he had drawn himself up, and had endeavoured to look conscientious; "You see I have the public to consider! Ministers may fall; statesmen may be thrown out of office; but the Press is the same yesterday, to-day, and for ever!"

"Except when a great Editor changes his opinions," said Leroy tranquilly,—"Which is, of course, always a point of reason and conscience, as well as of—advantage! In the present case I think—but —shall we not enter the sanctum of which you have so obligingly opened the door? We can scarcely be too private when the King's name is in question!"

Jost opened his furtive eyes in amazement.

"The King? What the devil has he to do with anything but his women and his amusements?"

A very close observer might have seen a curious expression flicker over Pasquin Leroy's face at these words,—an expression half of laughter, half of scorn,—but it was slight and evanescent, and his reply was frigidly courteous.

"I really cannot inform you; but I am afraid his Majesty is departing somewhat from his customary routine! He is, in fact, taking an active, instead of a passive part in national affairs."

"Then he must be warned off the ground!" said Jost irritably; "He is a Constitutional monarch, and must obey the laws of the Constitution."

"Precisely!" And Leroy looked carefully at the end of his cigar; "But at present he appears to have an idea that the laws of the Constitution are being tampered with by certain other kings;—for example,—the kings of finance!"

Jost muttered a half-inaudible oath.

"Come this way," he said impatiently;—"Bad news is best soon over!"

Leroy gave a careless nod of acquiescence,—then glancing round the room, up at the clock, and down again to Jost's desk, strewn with letters and documents of every description, he smiled a little to himself, and followed the all-powerful editor into the smaller adjoining apartment. The door closed behind them both, and Jost turned the key in the lock from within.

For a long time all was very silent. Jost's valet and confidential servant, sleepy and tired, waited in the hall to let his master's visitor out,—and hearing no sound, ventured to look into the study now and then,—but to no purpose. He knew the sanctity of that inner chamber beyond; he knew that when the Premier came to see the great Jost,—as he often did,—it was in that mysterious further room that business was transacted, and that it was as much as his place was worth to venture even to knock at the door. So, yawning heavily, he dozed on his bench in the hall,—woke with a start and dozed again,—while the clock slowly ticked away the minutes till with a dull clang the hour struck One. Then on again went the steady and wearisome tick-tick of the pendulum, for a quarter of an hour, half an hour,— and three- quarters,—till the utterly fatigued valet was about to knock down a few walking-sticks and umbrellas, and make a general noise of reminder to his master as to how the time was going, when, to his great relief, he heard the inner door open at last, and the voice of the mysterious visitor ring out in clear, precise accents.

"Nothing will be done publicly, of course,—unless Parliament insists on an enquiry!" The speaker came towards the hall, and the valet sprang up from his bench, and stood ready to show the stranger out.

Jost replied, and his accents were thick and unsteady.

"Enquiry cannot be forced! The Marquis himself can burk any such attempt."

"But—if the King should insist?"

"He would be breaking all the rules of custom and precedent," said Jost,—"And he would deserve to be dethroned!"

Pasquin Leroy laughed.

"True! Good-night, Mr. Jost! Can I do anything for you in Moscow?" The two men now came into the full light shed by the great lamp in the hall. Jost looked darkly red in the face—almost apoplectic; Leroy was as cool, imperturbable and easy of manner as a practised detective or professional spy.

"In Moscow," Jost repeated—"You are going straight to Russia?"

"I think so."

"I suppose you are in the secret service?"

"Exactly! A curious line of business, too, which the outside world knows very little of. Ah!—if the excellent people—the masses as we call them—knew what rogues had the ruling of their affairs in some countries—not in this country, of course!" he added with a quizzical smile,—"but in some others, not very far away, I wonder how many revolutions would break out within six months! Good-night, Mr. Jost!"

"Good-night!" responded Jost briefly. "You will let me know any further developments?"

"Most assuredly!"

The servant opened the door, and Pasquin Leroy slipped a gold coin worth a sovereign into his hand, whereupon, of course, the worthy domestic considered him to be a 'real gentleman.' As soon as he had passed into the street, and the door was shut and barred for the night, Jost bade his man go to bed, a command which was gladly obeyed; and re- entering his study, passed all the time till the breaking of dawn in rummaging out letters and documents from various desks, drawers and despatch-boxes, and burning them carefully one by one in the open grate. While thus employed, he had a truly villainous aspect,—each flame he kindled with each paper seemed to show up a more unpleasing expression on his countenance, till at last,—when such matter was destroyed as he had at present determined on,—he drew himself up and stood for a moment surveying the pile of light black ashes, which was all that was left of about a hundred or more incriminating paper witnesses to certain matters in which he had more than a lawful interest.

"It will be difficult now to trace my hand in the scheme!" he said to himself, frowning heavily, as he considered various uncomfortable contingencies arising out of his conversation with his late visitor. "If the thunderbolt falls, it will crush Carl Perousse—not me. Yes! It means ruin for him—ruin and disgrace—but for me— well! I shall find it as easy to damn Perousse as it has been to support him, for he cannot involve me without adding tenfold to his own disaster! I think it will be safe enough for me—possibly not so safe for the Premier. However, I will write to him to-morrow, just to let him know I received his messenger."

In the meantime, while David Jost was thus cogitating unpleasant and even dangerous possibilities, which were perhaps on the eve of occurring to himself and certain of his associates in politics and journalism, Pasquin Leroy was hurrying along the city streets under the light of a clear, though pallid and waning moon. Few wanderers were abroad; the police walked their various rounds, and one or two miserable women passed him, like flying ghosts in the thin air of night. His mind was in a turmoil of agitation; and the thoughts that were tossing rapidly through his brain one upon the other, were such as he had never known before. He had fathomed a depth of rascality and deception, which but a short month ago, he could scarcely have believed capable of existence. The cruel injury and loss preparing for thousands of innocent persons through the self-interested plotting of a few men, was almost incalculable,—and his blood burned with passionate indignation as he realized on what a verge of misery, bloodshed, disaster and crime the unthinking people of the country stood, pushed to the very edge of a fall by the shameless and unscrupulous designs of a few financiers, playing their gambling game with the public confidence,—and cheating nations as callously as they would have cheated their partners at cards.

"Thank God, it is not too late!" he murmured; "Not quite too late to save the situation!—to rescue the people from long years of undeserved taxation, loss of trade and general distress! It is a supreme task that has been given me to accomplish!—but if there is any truth and right in the laws of the Universe, I shall surely not be misjudged while accomplishing it!"

He quickened his pace;—and to avoid going up one of the longer thoroughfares which led to the citadel and palace, he decided to cross one of the many picturesque bridges, arched over certain inlets from the sea, and forming canals, where barges and other vessels might be towed up to the very doors of the warehouses which received their cargoes. But just as he was about to turn in the necessary direction, he halted abruptly at sight of two men, standing at the first corner in the way of his advance, talking earnestly. He recognized them at once as Sergius Thord and the half-inebriated poet, Paul Zouche. With noiseless step he moved cautiously into the broad stretch of black shadow cast by the great facade of a block of buildings which occupied half the length of the street in which he stood, and so managing to slip into the denser darkness of a doorway, was able to hear what they were saying. The full, mellow, and persuasive tone of Thord's voice had something in it of reproach.

"You shame yourself, Zouche!" he said; "You shame me; you shame us all! Man, did God put a light of Genius in your soul merely to be quenched by the cravings of a bestial body? What associate are you for us? How can you help us in the fulfilment of our ideal dream? By day you mingle with litterateurs, scientists, and philosophers,—report has it that you have even managed to stumble your way into my lady's boudoir;—but by night you wander like this,—insensate, furious, warped in soul, muddled in brain, and only the heart of you alive,—the poor unsatisfied heart—hungering and crying for what itself makes impossible!"

Zouche broke into a harsh laugh. Turning up his head to the sky, he thrust back his wild hair, and showed his thin eager face and glittering eyes, outlined cameo-like by the paling radiance of the moon.

"Well spoken, my Sergius!" he exclaimed. "You always speak well! Your thoughts are of flame—your speech is of gold; the fire melts the ore! And then again you have a conscience! That is a strange possession!— quite useless in these days, like the remains of the tail we had when we were all happy apes in the primeval forest, pelting the Megatherium or other such remarkable beasts with cocoanuts! It was a much better life, Sergius, believe me! A Conscience is merely a mental Appendicitis! There should be a psychical surgeon with an airy lancet to cut it out. Not for me!—I was born perfect—without it!"

He laughed again, then with an abrupt change of manner he caught Thord violently by the arm.

"How can you speak of shame?" he said—"What shame is left in either man or woman nowadays? Naked to the very skin of foulness, they flaunt a nudity of vice in every public thoroughfare! Your sentiments, my grand Sergius, are those of an old world long passed away! You are a reformer, a lover of truth—a hater of shams—and in the days when the people loved truth,—and wanted justice,—and fought for both, you would have been great! But greatness is nowadays judged as 'madness'—truth as 'want of tact'—desire for justice is 'clamour for notoriety.' Shame? There is no shame in anything, Sergius, but honesty! That is a disgrace to the century; for an honest man is always poor, and poverty is the worst of crimes." He threw up his arms with a wild gesture,— "The worst of crimes! Do I not know it!"

Thord took him gently by the shoulder.

"You talk, Zouche, as you always talk, at random, scarcely knowing, and certainly not half meaning what you say. There is no real reason in your rages against fate and fortune. Leave the accursed drink, and you may still win the prize you covet—Fame."

"Not I!" said Zouche scornfully,—"Fame in its original sense belonged also to the growing-time of the world—when, proud of youth and the glow of life, the full-fledged man judged himself immortal. Fame now is adjudged to the biped-machine who drives a motor-car best,—or to the fortunate soap-boiler who dines with a king! Poetry is understood to be the useful rhyme which announces the virtues of pills and boot- blacking! Mark you, Sergius!—my latest volume was 'graciously accepted by the King'! Do you know what that means?"

"No," replied Thord, a trifle coldly; "And if it were not that I know your strange vagaries, I should say you wronged your election as one of us, to send any of your work to a crowned fool!"

Zouche laughed discordantly.

"You would? No, you would not, my Sergius, if you knew the spirit in which I sent it! A spirit as wild, as reckless, as ranting, as defiant as ever devil indulged in! The humility of my presentation letter to his Majesty was beautiful! The reply of the flunkey-secretary was equally beautiful in smug courtesy: 'Sir, I am commanded by the King to thank you for the book of poems you have kindly sent for his acceptance!' I say again, Thord, do you know what it means?"

"No; I only wish that instead of talking here, you would let me see you safely home."

"Home! I have no home! Since *she* died—" He paused, and a grey shadow crossed his face like the hue of approaching sickness or death. "I killed her, poor child! Of course you know that! I neglected her,— deserted her—left her to die! Well! She is only one more added to the list of countless women martyrs who have been tortured out of an unjust world—and now—now I write verses to her memory!" He shivered as with cold, still clinging to Thord's arm. "But I did not tell you what great good comes of sending a book to the King! It means less to a writer than to a boot-maker. For the boot-maker can put up a sign: 'Special Fitter for the ease of His Majesty's Corns'—but if a poet should say his verse is 'accepted' by a monarch, the shrewd public take it at once to be bad verse, and will have none of it! That is the case with my book to-day!"

"Why did you send it?" asked Thord, with grave patience. "Your business with kings is to warn, not to flatter!"

"Just so!" cried Zouche; "And if His Most Gracious and Glorious had been pleased to look inside the volume, he would have seen enough to startle him! It was sent in hate, my Sergius,—not in humility,—just as the flunkey-secretary's answer was penned in derision, aping courtesy! How you look, under this wan sky of night! Reproachful, yet pitying, as the eyes of Buddha are your eyes, my Sergius! You are a fine fellow—your brain is a dome decorated with glorious ideals!—and yet you are like all of us, weak in one point, as Achilles in the heel. One thing could turn you from man into beast—and that would be if Lotys loved—not you—she never will love you—but another!"—Thord started back as though suddenly stabbed, and angrily shook off his companion, who only laughed again,—a shrill, echoing laugh in which there was a note of madness and desolation. "Bah!" he exclaimed; "You are a fool after all! You work for a woman as I did—once! But mark you!—do not kill her—as I did—once! Be patient! Watch the light shine, even though it does not illumine your path; be glad that the rose blooms for itself, if not for you! It will be difficult!— meanwhile you can live on hope—a bitter fruit to eat; but gnaw it to the last rind, my Sergius! Hope that Lotys may melt in your fire, as a snowflake in the sun! Come! Now take the poor poet home,—the drunken child of inspiration—take him home to his garret in the slums—the poet whose book has been accepted by the King!"

Pulling himself up from his semi-crouching position, he seized Thord's arm again more tightly, and began to walk along unsteadily. Presently he paused, smiling vacantly up at the gradually vanishing stars.

"Lotys speaks to our followers on Saturday," he said; "You know that?"

Thord bent his head in acquiescence.

"You will be there, of course. I shall be there! What a voice she has! Whether we believe what she says or not, we must hear,—and hearing, we must follow. Where shall we drink in the sweet Oracle this time?"

"At the People's Assembly Rooms," responded Thord; "But remember, Zouche, she does not speak till nine o'clock. That means that you will be unfit to listen!"

"You think so?" responded Zouche airily, and leaning on Thord he stumbled onward, the two passing close in front of the doorway where Pasquin Leroy stood concealed. "But I am more ready to understand wisdom when drunk, than when sober, my Sergius! You do not understand. I am a human eccentricity—the result of an *amour* between a fiend and an angel! Believe me! I will listen to Lotys with all my devil-saintly soul,—you will listen to her with all your loving, longing heart—and with us two thus attentive, the opinions of the rest of the audience will scarcely matter! How the street reels! How the old moon dances! So did she whirl pallidly when Antony clasped his Egyptian Queen, and lost Actium! Remember the fate of Antony, Sergius! Kingdoms would have been seized and controlled by men such as you are, long before now—if there had not always been a woman in the case—a Cleopatra—or a Lotys!"

Still laughing foolishly, he reeled onwards, Sergius Thord half- supporting, half-leading him, with grave carefulness and brotherly compassion. They were soon out of sight; and Pasquin Leroy, leaving his dark hiding-place, crossed the bridge with an alert step, and mounted a steep street leading to the citadel. From gaps between the tall leaning houses a glimpse of the sea, silvered by the dying moonlight, flashed now and again; and in the silence of the night the low ripple of small waves against the breakwater could be distinctly heard. A sense of holy calm impressed him as he paused a moment; and the words of an old monkish verse came back to him from some far-off depth of memory:

> Lord Christ, I would my soul were clear as air,
> With only Thy pure radiance falling through!

He caught his breath hard—there was a smarting sense as of tears in his eyes.

"So proudly throned, and so unloved!" he muttered. "Yet,—has not the misprisal and miscomprehension been merited? Whose is the blame? Not with the People, who, despite the prophet's warning, 'still put their trust in princes'—but with the falsity and hollowness of the system! Sovereignty is like an old ship stuck fast in the docks, and unfit for sailing the wide seas—crusted with barnacles of custom and prejudice, —and in every gale of wind pulling and straining at a rusty chain anchor. But the spirit of Change is in the world; a hurrying movement that has wings of fire, and might possibly be called Revolution! It is better that the torch should be lighted from the Throne than from the slums!"

He went on his way quickly,—till reaching the outer wall of the citadel, he was challenged by a sentinel, to whom he gave the password in a low tone. The man drew back, satisfied, and Leroy went on, mounting from point to point of the cliff, till he reached a private gate leading into the wide park-lands which skirted the

King's palace. Here stood a muffled and cloaked figure evidently watching for him; for as soon as he appeared the gate was noiselessly opened for his admittance, and he passed in at once. Then he and the person who had awaited his coming, walked together through the scented woods of pine and rhododendrons, and talking in low and confidential voices, slowly disappeared.

CHAPTER XIV
THE KING'S VETO

THE Marquis de Lutera was a heavy sleeper, and for some time had been growing stouter than was advisable for the dignity of a Prime Minister. He had been defeated of late years in one or two important measures; and his colleague, Carl Perousse, had by gradual degrees succeeded in worming himself into such close connection with the rest of the members of the Cabinet, that he, Lutera, felt himself being edged out, not only from political 'deals,' but from the profits appertaining thereto. So, growing somewhat indifferent, as well as disgusted at the course affairs were taking, he had made up his mind to retire from office, as soon as he had carried through a certain Bill which, in its results, would have the effect of crippling the people of the country, while helping on his own interests to a considerable degree. At the immediate moment he had a chance of looming large on the political horizon. Carl Perousse could not do anything of very great importance without him; they were both too deeply involved together in the same schemes. In point of fact, if Perousse could bring the Premier to a fall, the Premier could do the same by Perousse. The two depended on each other; and Lutera, conscious that if Perousse gained any fresh accession of power, it would be to his, Lutera's, advantage, was gradually preparing to gracefully resign his position in the younger and more ambitious man's favour. But he was not altogether comfortable in his mind since his last interview with the King. The King had shown unusual signs of self-will and obstinacy. He had presumed to give a command affecting the national policy; and, moreover, he had threatened, if his command were not obeyed, to address Parliament himself on the subject in hand, from the Throne.

Such an unaccustomed, unconstitutional idea was very upsetting to the Premier's mind. It had cost him a sleepless night; and when he woke to a new day's work, he was in an extremely irritable humour. He was doubtful how to act;—for to complain of the King would not do; and to enlighten the members of the Cabinet as to his Majesty's declared determination to dispose amicably of certain difficulties with a foreign power, which the Ministry had fully purposed fanning up into a flame of war, might possibly awaken a storm of dissension and discussion.

"We all want money!" said the Marquis gloomily, as he rose from his tumbled bed to take his first breakfast, and read his early morning letters—"And to crush a small and insolent race, whose country is rich in mineral product, is simply the act of squeezing an orange for the necessary juice. Life would be lost, of course, but we are over- populated; and a good war would rid the country of many scamps and vagabonds. Widows and orphans could be provided for by national subscriptions, invested as the Ministry think fit, and paid to applicants after about twenty years' waiting!" He smiled sardonically. "The gain to ourselves would be incalculable; new wealth, new schemes, new openings for commerce and speculation in every way! And now the King sets himself up as an obstacle to progress! If he were fond of money, we could explain the whole big combine, and offer him a share;— but with a character such as he possesses, I doubt if it would work! With some monarchs whom I could name, it would be perfectly easy. And yet,—for the three years he has been on the throne, he has been passive enough,—asking no questions,—signing such documents as he has been told to sign,—uttering such speeches as have been written for him,—and I was never more shocked and taken aback in my life than yesterday morning, when he declared he had decided to think and act for himself! Simply preposterous! An ordinary man who presumes to think and act for himself is always a danger to the community—but a king! Good Heavens! We should have the old feudal system back again."

He sipped his coffee leisurely, and opened a few letters; there were none of very pressing importance. He was just about to glance through the morning's newspaper, when his man-servant entered bearing a note marked 'Private and Immediate.' He recognized the handwriting of David Jost.

"Anyone waiting for an answer?" he enquired.

"No, Excellency."

The man retired. The Marquis broke the large splotchy seal bearing the coat-of-arms which Jost affected, but to which he had no more right than the man in the moon, and read what seemed to him more inexplicable than the most confusing conundrum ever invented.

"MY DEAR MARQUIS,—I received your confidential messenger last night, and explained the entire situation. He left for Moscow this morning, but will warn us of any further developments. Sorry matters look so grave for you. Should like a few minutes private chat when you can spare the time.—

"Yours truly, DAVID JOST."

Over and over again the Marquis read this brief note, staring at its every word and utterly unable to understand its meaning.

"What in the world is the fellow driving at!" he exclaimed angrily— "'My messenger'! 'Explained the entire situation'! The devil! 'Left for Moscow'! Upon my soul, this is maddening!" And he rang the bell sharply.

"Who brought this note?" he asked, as his servant entered.

"Mr. Jost's own man, Excellency."

"Has he gone?"

"Yes, Excellency."

"Wait!" And sitting down he wrote hastily the following lines:

"DEAR SIR,—Your letter is inexplicable. I sent no messenger to you last night. If you have any explanation to offer, I shall be disengaged and alone till 11.30 this morning.

"Yours truly,—DE LUTERA."

Folding, sealing, and addressing this, he marked it 'Private' and gave it to his man.

"Take this yourself," he said, "and put it into Mr. Jost's own hands. Trust no one to deliver it. Ask to see him personally, and then give it to him. You understand?"

"Yes, Excellency."

His note thus despatched, the Marquis threw himself down in his arm-chair, and again read Jost's mysterious communication.

"Whatever messenger has passed himself off as coming from me, Jost must have been crazy to receive him without credentials," he said. "There must be a mistake somewhere!"

A vague alarm troubled him; he was not moved by conscientious scruples, but the idea that any of his secret moves should be 'explained' to a stranger was, to say the least of it, annoying, and not conducive to the tranquillity of his mind. A thousand awkward possibilities suggested themselves at once to his brain, and as he carried a somewhat excitable disposition under his heavy and phlegmatic exterior, he fumed and fretted himself for the next half hour into an impatience which only found vent in the prosaic and everyday performance of dressing himself. Ah!—if those who consider a Prime Minister great and exalted, could only see him as he pulls on his trousers, and fastens his shirt collar, what a disillusion would be promptly effected! Especially if, like the Marquis de Lutera, he happened to be over-stout, and difficult to clothe! This particular example of Premiership was an ungainly man; his proud position could not make him handsome, nor lend true dignity to his deportment. Old Mother Nature has a way of marking her specimens, if we will learn to recognize the signs she sets on certain particular 'makes' of man. The Marquis de Lutera was 'made' to be a stock-jobber, not a statesman. His bent was towards the material gain and good of himself, more than the advantage of his country. His reasoning was a slight variation of Falstaff's logical misprisal of honour. He argued; "If I am poor, then what is it to me that others are rich? If I am neglected, what do I care that the people are prosperous? Let me but secure and keep those certain millions of money which shall ensure to me and my heritage a handsome endowment, not only for my life, but for all lives connected with mine which come after me,—and my 'patriotism' is satisfied!"

He had just finished insinuating himself by degrees into his morning coat, when his servant entered.

"Well!" he asked impatiently.

"Mr. Jost is coming round at once, Excellency. He ordered his carriage directly he read your note."

"He sent no answer?"

"None, Excellency."

"When he arrives, show him into the library."

"Yes, Excellency."

The Marquis thereupon left his sleeping apartment, and descended to the library himself. The sun was streaming brilliantly into the room, and the windows, thrown wide open, showed a cheerful display of lawn and flower-garden, filled with palms and other semi-tropical shrubs, for though the Premier's house was in the centre of the fashionable quarter of the city, it had the advantage of extensive and well-shaded grounds. A law had been passed in the late King's time against the felling of trees, it having been scientifically proved that trees in a certain quantity, not only purify the air from disease germs affecting the human organization, but also save the crops from many noxious insect- pests and poisonous fungi. Having learned the lesson at last, that the Almighty may be trusted to know His own business, and that trees are intended for wider purposes than mere timber, the regulations were strict concerning them. No one could fell a tree on his own ground without, first of all, making a statement at the National Office of Aboriculture as to the causes for its removal; and only if these causes were found satisfactory, could a stamped permission be obtained for cutting it down or 'lifting' it to other ground. The result of this sensible regulation was that in the hottest days of summer the city was kept cool and shady by the rich foliage branching out everywhere, and in some parts running into broad avenues and groves of great thickness and beauty. The Marquis de Lutera's garden had an additional charm in a beautiful alley of orange trees, and the fragrance wafted into his room from the delicious blossoms would have refreshed and charmed anyone less troubled, worried and feverish, than he was at the time. But this morning the very sunshine annoyed him;—never a great lover of Nature, the trees and flowers forming the outlook on which his heavy eyes rested were almost an affront. The tranquil beauty of an ever renewed and renewing Nature is always particularly offensive to an uneasy conscience and an exhausted mind.

The sound of wheels grinding along the outer drive brought a faint gleam of satisfaction on his brooding features, and he turned sharply round, as the door of the library was thrown open to admit Jost, whose appearance, despite his jaunty manner, betokened evident confusion and alarm.

"Good-morning, Mr. Jost!" said the Marquis stiffly, as his confidential man ushered in the visitor,—then when the servant had retired and closed the door, he added quickly—"Now what does this mean?"

Jost dropped into a chair, and pulling out a handkerchief wiped the perspiration from his brow.

"I don't know!" he said helplessly; "I don't know what it means! I have told you the truth! A man came to see me late last night, saying he was sent by you on urgent business. He said you wished me to explain the position we held, and the amount of the interests we had at stake, as there were grave discoveries pending, and complexities likely to ensue. He gave his name—there is his card!"

And with a semi-groan, he threw down the bit of pasteboard in question.

The Marquis snatched it up.

"'Pasquin Leroy'! I never heard the name in my life," he said fiercely. "Jost, you have been done! You mean to tell me you were such a fool as to trust an entire stranger with the whole financial plan of campaign, and that you were credulous enough to believe that he came from me—me —De Lutera,—without any credentials?"

"Credentials!" exclaimed Jost; "Do you suppose I would have received him at all had credentials been lacking? Not I! He brought me the most sure and confidential sign of your trust that could be produced—your own signet-ring!"

The Marquis staggered back, as though Jost's words had been so many direct blows on the chest,—his countenance turned a livid white.

"My signet-ring!" he repeated,—and almost unconsciously he looked at the hand from which the great jewel was missing; "My signet!"—Then he forced a smile—"Jost, I repeat, you have been done!—doubly fooled!— no one could possibly have obtained my signet,—for at this very moment it is on the hand of the King!"

Jost rose slowly out of his chair, his eyes protruding out of his head, his jaw almost dropping in the extremity of his amazement.

"The King!"—he gasped—"The King!"

"Yes, man, the King!" repeated De Lutera impatiently,—"Only yesterday morning his Majesty, having mislaid his own ring for the moment, borrowed mine just before starting on his yachting cruise. How you stare! You have been fooled!—that is perfectly plain and evident!"

"The King!" repeated Jost stupidly—"Then the man who came to me last night—" He broke off, unable to find any words for the expression of the thoughts which began to terrify him.

"Well!—the man who came to you last night," echoed the Marquis,—"He was not the King, I suppose, was he?" And he laughed derisively.

"No—he was not the King," said Jost slowly; "I know *him* well enough! But it might have been someone in the King's service! For he knew, or said he knew, the King's intentions in a certain matter affecting both you and Carl Perousse,—and in a more distant way, myself—and warned me of a coming change in the policy. Ah!—it is now your turn to stare, Marquis! You had best be on your guard, for if the person who came to me last night was not your messenger, he was the King's spy! And, in that case, we are lost!"

The Marquis paced the room with long uneven strides,—his mind was greatly agitated, but he had no wish to show his perturbation too openly to one whom he considered as a mere tool in his service.

"I know," went on Jost emphatically, "that the ring he wore was yours! I noticed it particularly while I was talking to him. It would take a long time and exceptional skill to make any imitation of that sapphire. There is no doubt that it was your signet!"

The Premier halted suddenly in his nervous walk.

"You told him the whole scheme, you say?"

"I did."

"And his reply?"

"Was, that the King had discovered it, and proposed insisting on an enquiry."

"And then?"

"Well! Then he warned me to look out for myself,—as anyone connected with Carl Perousse's financial deal would inevitably be ruined during the next few weeks."

"Who is going to work the ruin?" asked the Marquis with a sneer; "Do you not know that if the King dared to give an opinion on a national crisis, he would be dethroned?"

"There are the People—" began Jost.

"The People! Human emmets—born for crushing under the heel of power! A couple of 'leaders' in your paper, Jost, can guide the fool-mob any way!"

"That depends!" said Jost hesitatingly; "If what the fellow said last night be true—"

"It is not true!" said the Premier authoritatively. "We are going on in precisely the same course as originally arranged. Neither King nor People can interfere! Go home, and write an article about love of country, Jost! You look in the humour for it!"

The Jew's expression was anything but amiable.

"What is to be done about last night?" he asked sullenly.

"Nothing at present. I am going to the palace at two o'clock—I shall see the King, and find out whether my signet is lost, stolen or strayed. Meanwhile, keep your own counsel! If you have been betrayed into giving your confidence to a spy in the foreign service, as I imagine—(for the King has never employed a spy, and is not likely to do so), and he makes known his information, it can be officially denied. The official denial of a Government, Jost, like charity, has before now covered a multitude of sins!"

An instinctive disinclination for further conversation brought the interview between them abruptly to a close, and Jost, full of a suspicious alarm, which he was ashamed to confess, drove off to his newspaper offices. The Premier, meantime, though harassed by secret anxiety, managed to display his usual frigid equanimity, when, after Jost's departure, his private secretary arrived at the customary time, to transact under his orders the correspondence and business of the day. This secretary, Eugene Silvano by name, was a quiet self-contained young man, highly ambitious, and keenly interested in the political situation, and, though in the Premier's service, not altogether of his way of thinking. He called the Marquis's attention now to a letter that had missed careful reading on the previous day. It was from the Vicar- General of the Society of Jesus, expressing surprise and indignation that the King should have refused the Society's request for such land as was required to be devoted to religious and educational purposes, and begging that the Premier would exert his influence with the monarch to persuade him to withdraw or mitigate his refusal.

"I can do nothing;" said the Marquis irritably,—"the lands they want belong to the Crown. The King can dispose of them as he thinks best."

The secretary set the letter aside.

"Shall I reply to that effect?" he enquired.

The Marquis nodded.

"I know," said Silvano presently with a slight hesitation, "that you never pay any attention to anonymous communications. Otherwise, there is one here which might merit consideration."

"What does it concern?"

"A revolutionary meeting," replied Silvano, "where it appears the woman, Lotys, is to speak."

The Premier shrugged his shoulders and smiled. "You must enlighten me! Who is the woman Lotys?"

"Ah, that no one exactly knows!" replied the secretary. "A strange character, without doubt, but—" He paused and spoke more emphatically—"She has power!"

Lutera gave a gesture of irritation.

"Bah! Over whom does she exercise it. Over one man or many?"

"Over one half the population at least," responded Silvano, quietly, turning over a few papers without looking up.

The Marquis stared at him, slightly amused.

"Have you taken statistics of the lady's followers," he asked; "Are you one of them yourself?"

Silvano raised his eyes,—clear dark eyes, deep-set and steady in their glance.

"Were I so, I should not be here;" he replied—"But I know how she speaks; I know what she does! and from a purely political point of view I think it unwise to ignore her."

"What is this anonymous communication you speak of?" asked the Premier, after a pause.

"Oh, it is brief enough," answered Silvano unfolding a paper, and he read aloud:

"To the Marquis de Lutera, Premier.

"Satisfy yourself that those who meet on Saturday night where Lotys speaks, have already decided on your downfall!"

"Oracular!" said the Marquis carelessly;—"To decide is one thing—to fulfil the decision is another! Lotys, whoever she may be, can preach to her heart's content, for all I care! I am rather surprised, Silvano, that a man of your penetration and intelligence should attach any importance to revolutionary meetings, which are always going on more or less in every city under the sun. Why, it was but the other day, the police were sent to disperse a crowd which had gathered round the fanatic, Sergius Thord; only the people had sufficient sense to disperse themselves. A street-

preacher or woman ranter is like a cheap- jack or a dispenser of quack medicines;—
the mob gathers to such persons out of curiosity, not conviction."

The secretary made no reply, and went on with other matters awaiting his
attention.

At a few minutes before two o'clock the Marquis entered his carriage, and was
driven to the palace. There he learned that the King was receiving, more or less un-
officially, certain foreign ambassadors and noblemen of repute in the Throne-room.
A fine band was playing military music in the great open quadrangle in front of
the palace, where pillars of rose-marble, straight as the stems of pine-trees, held up
fabulous heraldic griffins, clasping between their paws the country's shield. Flags
were flying,—fountains flashing,—gay costumes gleamed here and there,—and the
atmosphere was full of brilliancy and gaiety, —yet the Marquis, on his way to the
audience-chamber, was rendered uncomfortably aware of one of those mysterious
impressions which are sometimes conveyed to us, we know not how, but which
tend to prepare us for surprise and disappointment. Some extra fibre of sensitive-
ness in his nervous organization was acutely touched, for he actually fancied he saw
slighting and indifferent looks on the faces of the various flunkeys and retainers
who bowed him along the different passages, or ushered him up the state stairway,
when—as a matter of fact,—all was precisely the same as usual, and it was only his
own conscience that gave imaginary hints of change. Arrived at the ante-chamber
to the Throne-room, he was surprised to find Prince Humphry there, talking ani-
matedly to the King's physician, Professor Von Glauben. The Prince seemed unusually excited; his face was flushed, and his eyes extraordinarily brilliant, and as
he saw the Premier, he came forward, extending his hand, and almost preventing
Lutera's profound bow and deferential salutation.

"Have you business with the King, Marquis?" enquired the young man with a
light laugh. "If you have, you must do as I am doing,—wait his Majesty's pleasure!"

The Premier lifted his eyebrows, smiled deprecatingly, and murmuring something about pressure of State affairs, shook hands with Von Glauben, whose countenance, as usual, presented an impenetrable mask to his thoughts.

"It is rather a new experience for me," continued the Prince, "to be treated as a
kind of petitioner on the King's favour, and kept in attendance,—but no matter!—
novelty is always pleasing! I have been cooling my heels here for more than an

hour. Von Glauben, too, has been waiting;—contrary to custom, he has not even been permitted to enquire after his Majesty's health this morning!"

Lutera maintained his former expression of polite surprise, but said nothing. Instinct warned him to be sparing of words lest he should betray his own private anxiety.

The Prince went on carelessly.

"Majesty takes humours like other men, and must, more than other men, I suppose, be humoured! Yet there is to my mind something unnatural in a system which causes several human beings to be dependent on another's caprice!"

"You will not say so, Sir, when you yourself are King," observed the Marquis.

"Long distant be the day!" returned the Prince. "Indeed, I hope it may never be! I would rather be the simplest peasant ploughing the fields, and happy in my own way, than suffer the penalties and pains surrounding the possession of a Throne!"

"Only," put in Von Glauben sententiously, "you would have to take into consideration, Sir, whether the peasant ploughing the fields is happy in his own way. I have made 'the peasant ploughing the fields' a special form of study,—and I have always found him a remarkably discontented, often ill-fed—and therefore unhealthy individual."

"We are all discontented, if it comes to that!" said Prince Humphry with a light laugh,—"Except myself! I am perfectly contented!"

"You have reason to be, Sir," said Lutera, bowing low.

"You are quite right, Marquis!—I have! More reason than perhaps you are aware of!"

His eyes lightened and flashed; he looked unusually handsome, and the Premier's shifty glance rested on him for a moment with a certain curiosity. But he had not been accustomed to pay very much attention to the words or actions of the Heir-Apparent, considering him to be a very 'ordinary' young man, without either the brilliancy or the ambition which should mark him out as worthy of his exalted station. And before any further conversation could take place, Sir Roger de Launay entered the room and announced to the Marquis that the King was ready to receive him. Prince Humphry turning sharply round, faced the equerry.

"I am still to wait?" he enquired, with a slight touch of hauteur.

Sir Roger bowed respectfully.

"Your instant desire to see the King, your father, Sir, was communicated to his Majesty at once," he replied. "The present delay is by his Majesty's own orders. I much regret——"

"Regret nothing, my dear Sir Roger," he said. "My patience does not easily tire! Marquis, I trust your business will not take long?"

"I shall endeavour to make it as brief as possible, Sir," replied the Premier deferentially as he withdrew.

It was with a certain uneasiness, however, in his mind that he followed Sir Roger to the Throne-room. There was no possibility of exchanging so much as a word with the equerry; besides, De Launay was not a talking man. Passing between the lines of attendants, pages, lords-in-waiting and others, he was conscious of a certain loss of his usual self- possession as he found himself at last in the presence of the King,— who, attired in brilliant uniform, was conversing graciously and familiarly with a select group of distinguished individuals whose costume betokened them as envoys or visitors from foreign courts in the diplomatic service. Perceiving the Premier, however, he paused in his conversation, and standing quite still awaited his approach. Then he extended his hand, with his usual kindly condescension. Instinctively Lutera's eyes searched that hand, with the expression of a guilty soul searching for a witness to its innocence. There shone the great sapphire—his own signet—and to his excited fancy its blue glimmer emitted a witch-like glow of menace. Meanwhile the King was speaking.

"You are just a few minutes late, Marquis!" he said; "Had you come a little earlier, you would have met M. Perousse, who has matters of import to discuss with you." Here he moved aside from those immediately in hearing. "It is perhaps as well you should know I have 'vetoed' his war propositions. It will rest now with you, to call a Council to- morrow,—the next day,—or,—when you please!"

Completely taken aback, the Premier was silent for a moment, biting his lips to keep down the torrent of rage and disappointment that threatened to break out in violent and unguarded speech.

"Sir!—Your Majesty! Pardon me, but surely you cannot fail to understand that in a Constitution like ours, the course decided upon by Ministers *cannot* be vetoed by the King?"

The monarch smiled gravely.

"'Cannot' is a weak word, Marquis! I do not include it in my vocabulary! I fully grant you that a plan of campaign decided upon by Ministers as you say, has *not* been 'vetoed' by a reigning sovereign for at least a couple of centuries,—and the custom has naturally fallen into desuetude,—but if it should be found at any time,—(I do not say it *has* been found) that Ministers are engaged in a seriously mistaken policy, and are being misled by the doubtful propositions of private financial speculators, so much as to consider their own advantage more important and valuable than the prosperity of a country or the good of a people,—then a king who does *not* veto the same is a worse criminal than those he tacitly supports and encourages!"

Lutera turned a deadly white,—his eyes fell before the clear, straight gaze of his Sovereign,—but he said not a word.

"A king's 'veto' has before now brought about a king's dethronement," went on the monarch; "Should it do so in my case, I shall not greatly care,—but if things trend that way, I shall lay my thoughts openly before the People for their judgment. They seldom or never hear the Sovereign whom they pay to keep, speak to them on a matter gravely affecting their national destinies,—but they shall hear *me*,—if necessary!"

The Marquis moistened his dry lips, and essayed to pronounce a few words.

"Your Majesty will run considerable risk——"

"Of being judged as something more than a mere dummy," said the King— "Or a fool set on a throne to be fooled! True! But the risk can only involve life,—and life is immaterial when weighed in the balance against Honour. By the way, Marquis, permit me to return to you this valuable gem";—Here drawing off the Premier's sapphire signet, he handed it to him—"Almost I envy it! It is a fine stone!—and worthy of its high service!"

"Your Majesty has increased its value by wearing it," said Lutera, recovering a little of his strayed equanimity in his determination to probe to the bottom of the mystery which perplexed his mind. "May I ask——"

"Anything in reason, my dear Marquis," returned the King lightly, and smiling as he spoke. "A thousand questions if you like!"

"One will suffice," answered the Premier. "I had an unpleasant dream last night about this very ring——"

"Ah!" ejaculated the King; "Did you dream that I had dropped it in the sea on my way to The Islands yesterday?"

He spoke jestingly, yet with a kindly air, and Lutera gained courage to look boldly up and straight into his eyes.

"I did not dream that you had lost it, Sir," he answered—"but that it had been stolen from your hand, and used by a spy for unlawful purposes!"

A strange expression crossed the King's face,—a look of inward illumination; he smiled, but there was a quiver of strong feeling under the smile. Advancing a step, he laid his hand with a light, half- warning pressure on the Premier's shoulder.

"Dreams always go by contraries, Marquis!" he said;—"I assure you, on my honour as a king and a gentleman, that from the moment you lent it to me, till now,—when I return it to you,— *that ring has never left my finger!*"

CHAPTER XV
"MORGANATIC" OR—?

THE Royal 'at home' was soon over. Many of those who had the felicity of breathing in the King's presence that afternoon remarked upon his Majesty's evident good health and high spirits, while others as freely commented on the unapproachableness and irritability of the Marquis de Lutera. Sir Walter Langton, the great English traveller, who was taking his leave of the Sovereign that day, being bound on an expedition to the innermost recesses of Africa, was not altogether agreeably impressed by the Premier, whom he met on this occasion for the first and only time. They had begun their acquaintance by talking generalities,—but drifted by degrees into the dangerous circle of politics, and were skirting round the edge of various critical questions of the day, when the Marquis said abruptly:

"An autocracy would not flourish in your country, I presume, Sir Walter? The British people have been too long accustomed to sing that they 'never, never will be slaves.' Your Government is really more or less of a Republic."

"All Governments are so in these days, I imagine," replied Langton. "Autocracy on the part of a monarch is nowhere endured, save in Russia,—and what is Russia? A huge volcano, smouldering with fire, and ever threatening to break out in flame and engulf the Throne! Monarchs were not always wisdom personified in olden times,—and I venture to consider them nowadays less wise and more careless than ever. Only a return to almost barbaric ignorance and superstition would tolerate any complete monarchical authority in these present times of progress. It is only the long serfdom of Russia that hinders the triumph of Liberty there, as elsewhere."

The Marquis listened eagerly, and with evident satisfaction.

"I agree with you!" he said. "You consider, then, that in no country, under any circumstances, could the people be expected to obey their monarch blindly?"

"Certainly not! Even Rome, with its visible spiritual Head and Sovereign, has no real power. It imagines it has; but let it make any decided step to ensnare the liberties of the people at large, and the result would be somewhat astonishing! Personally—" and he smiled gravely—"I have often thought that my own country would be very much benefited by a couple of years existence under an autocrat—an autocrat like Cromwell, for example. A man strong and fierce, intelligent and candid,—who would expose shams and destroy abuses,—who would have no mercy on either religious, social, or political fraud, and who would perform the part of the necessary hard broom for sweeping the National house. But, unfortunately, we have no such man. You have,—in your Sergius Thord!"

The Premier heard this name with unconcealed amazement.

"Sergius Thord! Why he is a mere fanatic——"

"Pardon me!" interrupted Sir Walter,—"so was Cromwell!"

"But, my dear sir!" remonstrated the Marquis smilingly,—"Is it possible that you really consider Sergius Thord any sort of an influence in this country? If you do, I assure you you are greatly mistaken!"

"I think not," responded Sir Walter quietly; "With every respect for you, Marquis, I believe I am not mistaken! Books written by Sergius Thord are circulating in their thousands all over the world—his speeches are reported not only here, but in journals which probably you never hear of, in far-off countries,—in short, his propaganda is simply enormous. He is a kind of new Rousseau, without,—so far as I can learn,—Rousseau's private vices. He is a man I much wished to see during my stay here, but I have not had the opportunity of finding him out. He is an undoubted genius,—but I need not remind you, Marquis, that a man is never a prophet in his own country! The world's 'celebrity' is always eyed with more or less suspicion as a strange sort of rogue or vagabond in his own native town or village!"

At that moment, the King, having concluded a conversation with certain of his guests, who were thereupon leaving the Throne-room, approached them. He had not spoken a word to the Premier since returning him his signet-ring, but now he said:

"Marquis, I was almost forgetting a special request I have to make of you!"

"A request from you is a command, Sir!" replied Lutera with hypocritical deference and something of a covert sneer, which did not escape the quick observation of Sir Walter Langton.

"In certain cases it should be so," returned the King tranquilly; "And in this you will probably make it so! I have received a volume of poems by one Paul Zouche. His genius appears to me deserving of encouragement. A grant of a hundred golden pieces a year will not be too much for his hundred best poems. Will you see to this?"

The Marquis bowed.

"I have never heard of the man in question," he replied hesitatingly.

"Probably not," returned the King smiling;—"How often do Premiers read poetry, or notice poets? Scarcely ever, if we may credit history! But in this case——"

"I will make myself immediately acquainted with Paul Zouche, and inform him of your Majesty's gracious intention," the Marquis hastened to say.

"It is quite possible he may refuse the grant," continued the King; "Sometimes—though seldom—poets are prouder than Prime Ministers!"

With a brief nod of dismissal he turned away, inviting Sir Walter Langton to accompany him, and there was nothing more for the Marquis to do, save to return even as he had come, with two pieces of information puzzling his brain,—one, that the King's 'veto' had stopped a declaration of war,—unless,—which was a very remote contingency,—he and his party could persuade the people to go against the King,—the other, that some clever spy, with the assistance of a fraudulent imitation of his signet-ring, had become aware of the financial interests involved in a private speculation depending on the intended war, which included himself, Carl Perousse, and two or three other members of the Ministry. And, out of these two facts might possibly arise a whole train of misfortune, ruin and disgrace to those concerned.

It was considerably past three o'clock in the afternoon when the King, retiring to his own private cabinet, desired Sir Roger de Launay to inform Prince Humphry that he was now prepared to receive him. Sir Roger hesitated a moment before going to fulfil the command. The King looked at him with an indulgent smile.

"Things are moving too quickly, you think, Roger?" he queried. "Upon my soul, I am beginning to find a new zest in life! I feel some twenty years younger since

I saw the face of the beautiful Gloria yesterday! We must promote her sailor husband, and bring his pearl of the sea to our Court!"

"It was on this very subject, Sir, that Von Glauben wished to see your Majesty
the first thing this morning," said Sir Roger;—"But you refused him so early an audience. Yet you will remember that yesterday you told him you wished for an explanation of his acquaintance with this girl. He was ready and prepared to give it, but
was prevented,— not only by your refusal to see him,—but also by the Prince."

Drawing up a chair to the open window, the King seated himself deliberately,
and lit a cigar.

"Presumably the Prince knows more than the Professor!" he said calmly; "We
will hear both, and give Royalty the precedence! Tell Prince Humphry I am waiting
for him."

Sir Roger withdrew, and in another two or three minutes returned, throwing
open the door and ushering in the Prince, who entered with a quick step, and brief,
somewhat haughty salutation. Puffing leisurely at his cigar, the King glanced his
son up and down smilingly, but said not a word. The Prince stood waiting for his
father to speak, till at last, growing impatient and waiving ceremony, he began.

"I came, Sir, to spare Von Glauben your reproaches,—which he does not merit.
You accused him yesterday, he tells me, of betraying your trust; he has neither betrayed your trust nor mine! I alone am to blame in this matter!"

"In what matter?" enquired the King quietly.

Prince Humphry coloured deeply, and then grew pale. There was a ray of defiance in the light of his fine eyes, but the tumult within his soul showed itself only
in an added composure of his features.

"You wish me to speak plainly, I suppose," he said;—"though you know already what I mean. I repeat,—I, and I alone, am to blame,—for—for anything that
seemed strange to you yesterday, when you met Von Glauben at The Islands."

The King's serious face lightened with a gleam of laughter.

"Nothing seemed very strange to me, Humphry," he said, "except the one fact
that I found Von Glauben,—whom I supposed to be studying scientific problems,—
engaged in studying a woman instead! A very beautiful woman, too, who ought to
be something better than a sailor's wife. And I do not understand, as yet, what he
has to do with her, unless—" Here he paused and went on more slowly—"Unless

he is, as I suspect, acting for you in some way, and trying to tempt the fair creature with the prospect of a prince's admiration while the sailor husband is out of the way! Remember, I know nothing—I merely hazard a guess. You are an habitue of The Islands;—though I learned, on enquiry of the interesting old gentleman who was good enough to be my host, Rene Ronsard, that nobody had ever seen you there. They had only seen your yacht constantly cruising about the bay. This struck me as curious, I must confess. Some of your men were well known,— particularly one,—the husband of the pretty girl I saw. Her name, it seems, is Gloria,—and I must admit that it entirely suits her. I can hardly imagine that if you have visited The Islands as often as you seem to have done, you can have escaped seeing her. She is too beautiful to remain unknown to you—particularly if her husband is, as they tell me, in your service. I asked her to give me his name, but she refused it point-blank. I do not wish to accuse you of an amour, which you are perhaps quite innocent of—but certain things taken in their conjunction look suspicious,—and I would remind you that honour in princes,—as in all men,—should come before self-indulgence."

"I entirely agree with you, Sir!" said the Prince, composedly; "And in the present case honour has been my first thought, as it will be my last. Gloria is my wife!"

"Your wife!" The King rose, his tall figure looking taller, his eyes sparkling with anger from under their deep-set brows. "Your wife! Are you mad, Humphry! You!——the Heir-Apparent to the Throne! You have married her!"

"I have!" replied the Prince, and the words now came coursing rapidly from his lips in his excitement—"I love her! I love her with all my heart and soul!—and I have given her the only shield and safeguard love in this world can give! I have married her in my own name—the name of our family,—which neither she nor any of the humble folk out yonder have ever heard—but she is wedded to me as fast as Church and Law can make it,—and there is only one wrong connected with my vows to her—she does not know who I am. I have deceived her there,—but in nothing else. Had I told her of my rank, she would never have married me. But now she is mine,—and for her sake I am willing to resign all pretension to the Throne in favour of my brother Rupert. Let it be so, I implore you! Let me live my own life of love and liberty in my own way!"

Rigid as a statue the King stood,—his lips were set hard and his eyes lowered.

Long buried thoughts rose up from the innermost recesses of his being, and rushed upon his brain in a deluge of remembrance and regret. What!—after all these years, had the ghost of his first love, the little self-slain maiden of his boyhood's dream, risen to avenge herself in the life of his son? The strangeness of the comparison between himself as he was now, and the eager passionate youth he was then, smote him with a sense of sharp pain. Away in those far-off days he had believed in love as the chief glory of existence; he had considered it as the poets would have us consider it,—a saving, binding, holding and immortal influence, which leads to all pure and holy things, even unto God Himself, the Highest and Holiest of all. When he lost that belief, how great was his loss!—when he ceased to experience that pure idealistic emotion, how bitter became the monotony of living! Rapidly the stream of memory swept over his innermost soul and shook his nerves, and it was only through a strong effort of self- repression that at last, lifting up his eyes he fixed them on the flushed face of his son, and said in measured tones.

"This is a very unexpected and very unhappy confession of yours, Humphry! You have acted most unwisely!—you have been disloyal to me, who am not only your father, but your King! You have proved yourself unworthy of the nation's trust,—and you have deceived, more cruelly than you think, an innocent and too-confiding girl. I shall not dispute the legality of your marriage;—that would not be worth my while. You have no doubt taken every step to make it as binding as possible;— however, that is but a trifling matter in your case. You know that such a marriage is, and can only be morganatic;—and as the immediate consequence of your amazing folly, a suitable Royal alliance must be arranged for you at once. The nuptials can be celebrated with the attainment of your majority next year."

He spoke coldly and calmly, but his heart was beating with mingled wrath and pain, and even while he thus pronounced her doom, the exquisite face of Gloria floated before him like the vision of a perfect innocence ruined and betrayed. He realised that he possibly had an unusual character to reckon with in her,—and he had lately become fully aware that there was as much determination and latent force in the disposition of his son, as in the mother who had given him birth. Pale and composed, the young Prince heard him in absolute silence, and when he had finished, still waited a moment, lest any further word should fall from the lips of his parent and Sovereign. Then he spoke in quite as measured, cold and tranquil a manner as the King had done.

"I need not remind you, Sir, that the days of tyranny are over. You cannot force me into bigamy against my will!"

His father uttered a quick oath.

"Bigamy! Who talks of bigamy?"

"You do, Sir! I have married a beautiful and innocent woman,—she is my lawful wife in the sight of God and man; yet you coolly propose to give me a second wife under the 'morganatic' law, which, as I view it, is merely a Royal excuse for bigamy! Now I have no wish to excuse myself for marrying Gloria,—I consider she has honoured me far more than I have honoured her. She has given me all her youth, her life, her love, her beauty and her trust, and whatever I am worth in this world shall be hers and hers only. I am quite prepared"—and he smiled somewhat sarcastically,—"to make it a test case, and appeal to the law of the realm. If that law tolerates a crime in princes, which it would punish in commoners, then I shall ask the People to judge me!"

"Indeed!" And the King surveyed him with a touch of ironical amusement and vague admiration for his audacity. "And suppose the people fail to appreciate the romance of the situation?"

"Then I shall resign my nationality;" said the young man coolly; "Because a country that legalises a wrong done to the innocent, is not worth belonging to! Concerning the Throne,—as I told you before—I am ready to abandon it at once. I would rather lose all the kingdoms of the world than lose Gloria!"

There was a pause, during which the King took two or three slow paces up and down the room. At last he turned and faced his son; his eyes were softer—his look more kindly.

"You are very much in love just now, Humphry!" he said; "And I do not wish to be too hard on you in this matter, for there can be no question as to the extraordinary beauty of the girl you call your wife——"

"The girl who *is* my wife," interrupted the Prince decisively.

"Very well; so let it be!" said his father calmly; "The girl who *is* your wife—for the present! I will give you time—plenty of time—to consider the position reasonably!"

"I have already considered it," he declared.

"No doubt! You think you have considered it. But if *you* do not want to medi-tate any further upon your marriage problem, you must allow me the leisure to do so, as one who has seen more of life than you,—as one who takes things philosoph-ically—and also—as one who was young— once;—who loved—once;—and who had his own private dreams of happiness—once!" He rested a hand on his son's shoulder, and looked him full and fairly in the eyes. "Let me advise you, Humphry, to go abroad! Travel round the world for a year!"

The Prince was silent,—but his eyes did not flinch from his father's steady gaze. He seemed to be thinking rapidly; but his thoughts were not betrayed by any movement or expression that could denote anxiety. He was alert, calm, and per-fectly self-possessed.

"I have no objection," he said at last; "A year is soon past!"

"It is," agreed the King, with a sense of relief at his ready assent; "But by the end of that time——"

"Things will be precisely as they are now," said the Prince tranquilly; "Gloria will still be my wife, and I shall still be her husband!"

The King gave a gesture of annoyance.

"Whatever the result," he said, "she cannot, and will not be Crown Princess!"

"She will not envy that destiny in my brother Rupert's wife," said Prince Humphry quietly; "Nor shall I envy my brother Rupert!"

"You talk like a fool, Humphry!" said the King impatiently; "You cannot re-sign your Heir-Apparency to the Throne, without giving a reason;—and so making known your marriage."

"That is precisely what I wish to do," returned the young man. "I have no intention of keeping my marriage secret. I am proud of it! Gloria is mine—the joy of my soul—the very pulse of my life! Why should I hide my heart's light under a cloud?"

His voice vibrated with tender feeling,—his handsome features were softened into finer beauty by the passion which invigorated him, and his father looking at him, thought for a moment that so might the young gods of the fabled Parnassus have appeared in the height of their symbolic power and charm. His own eyes grew melancholy, as he studied this vigorous incarnation of ardent love and passionate resolve; and a slight sigh escaped him unconsciously.

"You forget!" he said slowly, "you have, up to the present deceived the girl. She does not know who you are. When she hears that you have played a part,—that you are no sailor in the service of the Crown Prince, as you have apparently represented yourself to be, but the Crown Prince himself, what will she say to you? Perhaps she will hate you for the deception, as much as she now loves you!"

A shadow darkened the young Prince's open countenance, but it soon passed away.

"She will never hate me!" he said,—"For when I do tell her the truth, it will be when I have resigned all the ridiculous pomp and circumstance of my position for her sake——"

"Perhaps she will not let you resign it!" said the King; "She may be as unselfish as she is beautiful!"

There was a slight, very slight note of derision in his voice, and the Prince caught it up at once.

"You wrong yourself, Sir, more than you wrong my wife by any lurking mis-judgment of her," he said, with singularly masterful and expressive dignity. "As her husband, and the guardian of her honour, I also claim her obedience. What I desire is her law!"

The King laughed a little forcedly.

"Evidently you have found the miracle of the ages, Humphry!" he said; "A woman who obeys her master! Well! Let us talk no more of it. You have been guilty of an egregious folly,—but nothing can make your marriage otherwise than morga-natic. And when the State considers a Royal alliance for you advisable, you will be compelled to obey the country's wish,—or else resign the Throne."

"I shall obey the country's wish most decidedly," said the Prince, "unless it asks me to commit bigamy,—as you suggest,—in which case I shall decline! Three or four Royal sinners of this class I know of, who for all their pains have not suc-ceeded in winning the attachment of their people, either for themselves or their heirs. Their people know what they are, well enough, and despise their fraudulent position as heartily as I do! I am perfectly convinced that if it were put to the vote of the country, no people in the world would wish their future monarch to be a bigamist!"

"How you stick to a word and a phrase!" exclaimed the King irritably; "The morganatic rule does away with the very idea of bigamy!"

"How do you prove it, Sir?" queried the Prince. "Bigamy is the act of contract-ing a second marriage while the first partner is alive. It is punished severely in commoners;—why should Royalty escape?"

The King began to laugh. This boy was developing 'discursive philosophies' such as his own old tutor had abhorred.

"Upon my life, I do not know, Humphry!" he declared; "You must ask the de-parted shades of those who made themselves responsible for kingship in the first place. Personally, I do not come under the law. I have only married once myself!"

His son looked full at him;—and the intensity of that look affected and unstead-ied his usual calm nerves. But he was not one to shirk an unpleasant suggestion.

"You would say, Humphry, if your filial respect permitted you, that my one marriage has been amplified in various other ways. Perfectly true! When women lie down and ask you to walk over them, you do it if you are a man and a king! When, on the contrary, women show you that they do not care whether you are royal or the reverse, and despise you more than admire you, you run after them for all you are worth! At least I do! I always have done so. And, to a certain extent, it has been amusing. But the limit is reached. I am growing old!" Here he took up the cigar he had thrown aside when his son had first startled him by the announcement of his marriage, and relighting it, began to smoke peaceably. "I am, as I say, growing old. I have never found what is called love. You have—or think you have! Enjoy your dream, Humphry— but—take my advice and go abroad! See whether travel does not work a change in you or,—in her!" He paused a moment, and while the Prince still regarded him fixedly, added; "Will you tell the Queen?"

"I will leave you to tell her, Sir, with your permission;" replied the Prince; "I cannot expect her sympathy."

"Von Glauben, then, is the only person you have trusted with your confidence?"

"Von Glauben was no party to my marriage, Sir. I was married fully three months before I told him. He was greatly vexed and troubled,— but when he saw Gloria, he was glad."

"Glad!" echoed the King; "For what reason, pray?"

"I am afraid, Sir," said the young man with a smile, "his gladness was but a part of his science! He said it was better for a prince to wed a healthy and beautiful commoner, than the daughter of a hundred scrofulous kings!"

With a movement of intense indignation, the monarch sprang up from the chair in which he had just seated himself.

"Now, by Heaven!" he exclaimed; "Von Glauben goes too far! He shall suffer for this!"

"Why?" queried the Prince calmly; "You know that what he says is perfectly true. True? Why, there is scarcely a Royal house in the world save our own, without its hereditary curse of disease or insanity. We pay more attention to the breeding of horses than the breeding of kings!"

The plain candour and veracity of the statement, left no room for denial.

"You have seen Gloria," went on the Prince; "You know she is the most beautiful creature your eyes ever rested upon! Von Glauben told me you were stricken dumb, and almost stupefied at sight of her——"

"Damn Von Glauben!" said the King.

His son smiled ever so slightly, but continued.

"You have made yourself acquainted with her history——"

"Yes!" said the King; "That she is a foundling picked up from the sea— a castaway from a wreck!—no one knows who her father and mother were, and yet you, in your raving madness and folly of love, would make her Crown Princess and future Queen!"

The Prince went on unheedingly.

"She is beautiful—and the simple method of her bringing up has left her unspoilt and innocent. She is ignorant of the world's ways—because —" and his voice sank to a reverential tenderness—"God's ways are more familiar to her!" He paused, but his father was silent; he therefore went on. "She is healthy, strong, simple and true,—more fit for a throne, if such were her destiny, than any daughter of any Royal house I know of. Happy the nation that could call such a woman their Queen!"

"As I have already told you, Humphry," returned the King, "you are in love!— with the love of a headstrong, passionate boy for a beautiful and credulous girl. I do not propose to discuss the subject further. You are willing to go abroad, you tell me,—then make your preparations at once. I will select one or two necessary companions for you, and you can start when you please. I would let Von Glauben accompany you, but— for the present—I cannot well spare him. Your intended voyage must be made public, and in this way nothing will be known of the manner in which you have privately chosen to make a fool of yourself. I will explain the situation to the Queen;—but beyond that I shall say nothing. Let me know by to-morrow how soon you can arrange your departure."

The Prince bowed composedly, and was about to retire, when the King called him back.

"You do not ask my pardon, Humphry, for the offence you have committed?"

The young man flushed, and bit his lip.

"Sir, I cannot ask pardon for what I do not consider is wrong! I have married the woman I love; and I intend to be faithful to her. You married a woman you did not love—and the result, according to my views, and also according to my experience of my mother and yourself, is more or less regrettable. If I have offended you, I sincerely beg your forgiveness, but you must first point out the nature of the offence. Surely, it must be more gratifying to you to know that I prefer to be a man of honour than a common seducer?"

The King looked at him, and his own eyes fell under his son's clear candid gaze.

"Enough! You may go!" he said briefly.

The door opened and closed again;—he was gone.

The King, left alone, fixed his eyes on the sparkling line of the sea, brightly blue, and the flower-bordered terrace in front of him. Life was becoming interesting;—the long burdensome monotony of years had changed into a variety of contrasting scenes and colours,—and in taking up the problem of human life as lived by others, more than as lived by himself, he had entered on a new path, untrodden by conventionalities, and leading, he knew not whither. But, having begun to walk in it, he was determined to go on—and to use each new experience as a guide for the rest of his actions. His son's marriage with a commoner—one who indeed was not only a commoner but a foundling—might after all lead to good, if properly taken in hand,— and he resolved not to make the worst of it, but rather to let things take their own natural course.

"For love," he said to himself somewhat bitterly, "in nine cases out of ten ends in satiety,—marriage, in separation by mutual consent! Let the boy travel for a year, and forget, if he can, the fair face which captivates him,—for it is a fair face,—and more than that,—I honestly believe it is the reflex of a fair soul!"

His eyes grew dreamy and absorbed; away on the horizon a little white cloud, shaped like the outspread wings of a dove, hovered over the sea just where The Islands lay.

"Yes! Let him see new scenes—strange lands, and varying customs; let him hear modern opinions of life, instead of reading the philosophies of Aurelius and Epictetus, and the poetry written ages ago by the dead wild souls of the past;—and so he will forget—and all will be well! While for Gloria herself,—and the old revolutionist Ronsard—we shall doubtless find ways and means of consolation for them both!"

Thus he mused,—yet in the very midst of his thoughts the echoing memory of a golden voice, round and rich with delight and triumph rang in his ears:

> "My King crown'd me!
>   And I and he
> Are one till the world shall cease to be!"

CHAPTER XVI
THE PROFESSOR ADVISES

I HAVE discovered the secret of successful living, Professor," said the King, a couple of hours later as, walking in one of the many thickly wooded alleys of the palace grounds, he greeted Von Glauben, who had been told to meet him there, and who had been waiting the Royal approach with some little trepidation,—"It is this,—to draw a straight line of conduct, and walk in it, regardless of other people's crooked curves!"

The Professor looked at him, and saw nothing but kindliness expressed in his eyes and smile,—therefore, taking courage he replied without embarrassment,—

"Truly, Sir, if a man is brave enough to do this, he may conquer everything but death, and even face this last enemy without much alarm."

"I agree with you!" replied the monarch; "And Humphry's line has certainly been straight enough, taken from the point of his own perspective! Do you not think so?"

Von Glauben hesitated a moment—then spoke out boldly.

"Sir, as you now know all, I will frankly assure you that I think his Royal Highness has behaved honourably, and as a true man! Society pardons a prince for seducing innocence—but whether it will pardon him for marrying it, is quite another question! And that is why I repeat, he has behaved well. Though when he first told me he was married, I suffered a not-to-be-explained misery and horror; 'For,' said he—'I have married an angel!' Which naturally I thought (deducting a certain quantity of the enthusiasm of youth for the statement) meant that he had married a bouncing housemaid with large hands and feet. 'That is well,' I told him—'For divorce is now made easy in this country, and you can easily return the celestial creature to her native element!' At which I resigned myself to hear some oaths, for violent expletives are always refreshing to the masculine brain-matter. But his Royal Highness maintained the good breeding which always distinguishes him, and merely proceeded with his strange confession of romance,—which, as you, Sir, are now happily aware of it, I need not recapitulate. Your knowledge of the matter has lifted an enormous burden from my mind; Ach! Enormous!"

He gave a deep breath, and drew himself up to his full height—squared his shoulders, and then, as it were stood firm, as though waiting attack.

The King laughed good-naturedly, and took him by the arm.

"Tell me all you know, Von Glauben!" he said; "I am acquainted with the gist and upshot of the matter,—namely, Humphry's marriage; but I am wholly ignorant of the details."

"There is little to tell, Sir," said Von Glauben;—"Of the Prince's constant journeyings to The Islands we were all aware long ago; but the cause of those little voyages was not so apparent. To avoid the suspicion with which a Royal visitor would be viewed, the Prince, it appears, assumed to be merely one of the junior officers on his own yacht,—and under this disguise became known and much liked by the Islanders generally. He fell in love at first sight with the beautiful girl your Majesty saw yesterday—Gloria; 'Glory-of-the-Sea'—as I sometimes call her, and they were married by the old parish priest in the little church among the rocks—the very church where, as her adopted father, Ronsard, tells me, he heard the choristers singing a 'Gloria in Excelsis' on the day he found her cast up on the shore."

"Well!" said the King, seeing that he paused; "And is the marriage legal, think you?"

"Perfectly so, Sir!" replied Von Glauben; "Registered by law, as well as sanctified by church. The Prince tells me he married her in his own name,—but no one,—not even the poor little priest who married them,— knew the surname of your Majesty's distinguished house, and I believe, —nay I am sure—" here he heaved an unconscious sigh, "it will bring a tragedy to the girl when she knows the true rank and title of her husband!"

"How came *you* to make her acquaintance? Tell me everything!—you know I will not misjudge you!"

"Indeed, Sir, I hope you will not!" returned the Professor earnestly;— "For there was never a man more hopelessly involved than myself in the net prepared for me by this romantic lover, who has the honour to be your son. In the first place, directly I heard this confession of marriage, I was for telling you at once; but as he had bound me by my word of honour before he began the story, to keep his confidence sacred, I was unable to disburden myself of it. He said he wanted to secure me as a friend for his wife. 'That,' said I firmly, 'I will never be! For there will be difficulty when all is known; and if it comes to a struggle between a pretty fishwife and the good of a king— ach!—mein Gott!—I am not for the fishwife!'"

The King smiled; and Von Glauben went on.

"Well, he assured me she was not a fishwife. I said 'What is she then?' 'I tell you,' he replied, 'she is an angel! You will come and see her; you will pass as an old friend of her sailor husband; and when you have seen her you will understand!' I was angry, and said I would not go with him; but afterwards I thought perhaps it would be best if I did, as I might be able to advise him to some wise course. So I accompanied him one afternoon in the past autumn to The Islands (he was married last summer) and saw the girl,—the 'Glory-of-the-Sea.' And I must confess to your Majesty, my heart went down before her beauty and innocence in absolute worship! And if you were to kill me for it, I cannot help it—I am now as devoted to her service as I am to yours!"

"Good!" said the King gently;—"Then you must help me to console her in Humphry's absence!"

Professor Von Glauben's eyes opened widely, with a vague look of alarm.

"In his absence, Sir?"

"Yes! I am sending him abroad. He is quite willing to go, he tells me. His departure will make all things perfectly easy for us. The girl must remain in her present ignorance as to the position of the man she has really married. The sailor she supposes him to be will accompany the Prince on his yacht,—and it must be arranged that he never returns! She is young, and will easily be consoled!"

Von Glauben was silent.

"*You* will not betray the Prince's identity with her lover," went on the King, "and no one else knows it. In fact, you will be the very person best qualified to tell her of his departure, and—in due time, of his fictitious death!"

They were walking slowly under the heavy shadow of crossed ilex boughs,—and Von Glauben came to a dead halt.

"Sir," he said, in rather unsteady accents; "With every respect for your Majesty, I must altogether decline the task of breaking a pure heart, and ruining a young life! Moreover, if your Majesty, after all your recent experiences,"—and he laid great emphasis on these last words, "thinks there is any ultimate good to be obtained by keeping up a lie, and practising a fraud, the lessons we have learned in these latter days are wholly unavailing! You began this conversation with me by speaking of a straight line of conduct, which should avoid other people's crooked curves. Is this your Majesty's idea of a straight line?"

He spoke with unguarded vehemence, but the King was not offended. On the contrary, he looked whimsically interested and amused.

"My dear Von Glauben, you are not usually so inconsistent! Humphry himself has kept up a lie, and practised a fraud on the girl——"

"Only for a time!" interrupted the Professor hastily.

"Oh, we all do it 'only for a time.' Everything—life itself—is 'only for a time!' You know as well as I do that this absurd marriage can never be acknowledged. I explained as much to Humphry; I told him he could guard himself by the morganatic law, provided he would consent to a Royal alliance immediately—but the young fool swore it would be bigamy, and took himself off in a huff."

"He was right! It would be bigamy;—it *is* bigamy!", said the Professor; "Call it by what name you like in Court parlance, the act of having two wives is forbidden in this country. The wisest men have come to the conclusion that one wife is enough!"

"Humphry's ideas being so absolutely childish," went on the King, "it is necessary for him to expand them somewhat. That is why I shall send him abroad. You have a strong flavour of romance in your Teutonic composition, Von Glauben,—and I can quite sympathise with your admiration for the 'Glory-of-the-Sea' as you call her. From a man's point of view, I admire her myself. But I know nothing of her moral or mental qualities; though from her flat refusal to give me her husband's name yesterday, I judge her as wilful,—but most pretty women are that. And as for my line of conduct, it will, I assure you, be perfectly 'straight,'—in the direction of my duty as a King,—apart altogether from sentimental considerations! And in this, as in other things,—" he paused and emphasised his words—"I rely on your honour and faithful service!"

The Professor made no reply. He was, thinking deeply. With a kind of grim scorn, he pointed out to himself that his imagination was held captive by the mental image of a woman, whose eyes had expressed trust in him; and almost as tenderly as the lover in Tennyson's 'Maud' he could have said that he 'would die, To save from some slight shame one simple girl.' Presently he braced himself up, and confronted his Royal master.

"Sir," he said very quietly, yet with perfect frankness; "Your Majesty must have the goodness to pardon me if I say you must not rely upon me at all in this matter! I will promise nothing, except to be true to myself and my own sense of justice. I have given up my own country for conscience' sake—I can easily give up another which is not my own, for the same reason. In the matter of this marriage or 'mesalliance' as the worldly would call it,—I have nothing whatever to do. While the Prince asked me to keep his secret, I kept it. Now that he has confided it to your Majesty, I am relieved and satisfied; and shall not in any way, by word or suggestion, interfere with your Majesty's intentions. But, at the same time, I shall not assist them! For as regards the trusting girl who has been persuaded that she has won a great love and complete happiness for all her life,—I have sworn to be her friend;—and I must respectfully decline to be a party to any further deception in her case. Knowing what I know of her character, which is a pure and grand one, I think it would be far better to tell her the whole truth, and let her be the arbiter of her own destiny. She will decide well and truly, I am sure!"

He ceased; the King was silent. Von Glauben studied his face attentively.

"You are a thinker, Sir,—a student and a philosopher. You are not one of those kings who treat their kingship as a license for the free exercise of intolerant humours and vicious practices. Were you no monarch at all, you would still be a sane and thoughtful man. Take my humble advice, Sir—for once put the unspoilt nature of a pure woman to the test, and find out what a grand creature God intended woman to be, in her pristine simplicity and virtue! Send for Gloria to this Court;— tell her the truth!—and await the result with confidence!"

There was a pause. The King walked slowly up and down; at last he spoke.

"You may be right! I do not say you are wrong. I will consider your suggestion.

Certainly it would be the straightest course. But first a complete explanation is due to the Queen. She must know all,—and if her interest can be awakened by such a triviality as her son's love- affair—" and he smiled somewhat bitterly,—"perhaps she may agree to your plan as the best way out of the difficulty. In any case"— here he extended his hand which the Professor deferentially bowed over—"I respect your honesty and plain speaking, Professor! I have reason to approve highly of sincerity,—wherever and however I find it,—at the present crisis of affairs. For the moment, I will only ask you to be on your guard with Humphry;—and say as little as possible to him on the subject of his marriage or intended departure from this country. Keep everything as quiet as may be;—till—till we find a clear and satisfactory course to follow, which shall inflict as little pain as possible on all concerned. And now, a word with you on other matters."

They walked on side by side, through the garden walks and ways, conversing earnestly,—and by and by penetrating into the deeper recesses of the outlying woodlands, were soon hidden among the crossing and recrossing of the trees. Had they kept to the open ground, from whence the wide expanse of the sea could be viewed from end to end, their discussions might perhaps have been interrupted, and themselves somewhat startled,—for they would have seen Prince Humphry's yacht, with every inch of canvas stretched to the utmost, flying rapidly before the wind like a wild white bird, winging its swift, straight way to the west where the sun shot down Apollo-like shafts of gold on the gleaming purple coast-line of The Islands.

CHAPTER XVII
AN "HONOURABLE" STATESMAN

IT is not easy to trace the causes why it so often happens that semi- educated, and more or less shallow men rise suddenly to a height of brilliant power and influence in the working of a country's policy. Sometimes it is wealth that brings them to the front; sometimes the strong support secretly given to them by others in the background, who have their own motives to serve, and who require a public representative; but more often still it is sheer unscrupulousness,—or what may be described as 'walking over' all humane and honest considerations,— that places them in triumph at the helm of affairs. To rise from a statesman to be a Secretary of State augurs a certain amount of brain, though not necessarily of the highest quality; while it certainly betokens a good deal of dash and impudence. Carl Perousse, one of the most prominent among the political notabilities of Europe, had begun his career by small peddling transactions in iron and timber manufactures; he came of a very plebeian stock, and had received only a desultory sort of education, picked up here and there in cheap provincial schools. But he had a restless, domineering spirit of ambition. Ashamed of his plebeian origin, and embittered from his earliest years by a sense of grudge against those who moved in the highest and most influential circles of the time, the idea was always in his mind that he would one day make himself an authority over the very persons, who, in the rough and tumble working-days of his younger manhood, would not so much as cast him a word or a look. He knew that the first thing necessary to attain for this purpose was money; and he had, by steady and constant plod, managed to enlarge and expand all his business concerns into various, important companies, which he set afloat in all quarters of the world,—with the satisfactory result that by the time his years had run well into the forties, he was one of the wealthiest men in the country. He had from the first taken every opportunity to insinuate himself into politics; and in exact proportion to the money he made, so was his success in acquiring such coveted positions in life as brought with them the masterful control of various conflicting aims and interests. His individual influence had extended by leaps and bounds till he had become only secondary in importance to the Prime Minister himself; and he possessed a conveniently elastic conscience, which could be stretched at will to suit any party or any set of principles. In personal appearance he was not prepossessing. Nature had branded him in her own special way 'Trickster,' for those who cared to search for her trademark. He was tall and thin, with a narrow head and a deeply-lined, clean-shaven countenance, the cold immovability of which was sometimes broken up by an unpleasant smile, that merely widened the pale set lips without softening them, and disclosed a crooked row of smoke-coloured teeth, much decayed. He had small eyes, furtively hidden under a somewhat restricted frontal development,— his brows were narrow,—his forehead ignoble and retreating. But despite a general badness, or what may be called a 'smirchiness' of feature, he had learned to assume an air of superiority, which by its sheer audacity prevented a casual observer from setting him down as the vulgarian he undoubtedly was; and his amazing pluck, boldness and originality in devising ways and means of smothering popular discontent under various 'shows' of apparent public prosperity, was immensely useful to all such 'statesmen,' whose statesmanship consisted in making as much money as possible for themselves out of the pockets of their credulous countrymen. He was seldom disturbed by opposing influences; and even now when he had just returned from the palace with the full knowledge that the King was absolutely resolved on vetoing certain propositions he had set down in council for the somewhat arbitrary treatment of a certain half- tributary power which had latterly turned rebellious, he was more amused than irritated.

"I suppose his Majesty wants to distinguish himself by a melodramatic *coup d'etat*" he said, leaning easily back in his chair, and studying the tips of his carefully pared and polished finger-nails;— "Poor fool! I don't blame him for trying to do something more than walk about his palace in different costumes at stated intervals,—but he will find his 'veto' out of date. We shall put it to the country;—

and I think I can answer for that!"

He smiled, as one who knows where and how to secure a triumph, and his equanimity was not disturbed in the least by the unexpected arrival of the Premier, who was just then announced, and who, coming in his turn from the King's diplomatic reception, had taken the opportunity to call and see his colleague on his way home.

"You seem fatigued, Marquis!" he said, as, rising to receive his distinguished guest, he placed a chair for him opposite his own. "Was his Majesty's conversazione more tedious than usual?"

Lutera looked at him with a dubious air.

"No!—it was brief enough so far as I was immediately concerned," he replied;— "I do not suppose I stayed more than twenty minutes in the Throne-room altogether. I understand you have been told that our proposed negotiations are to be vetoed?"

Perousse smiled.

"I have been told—yes!—but I have been told many things which I do not believe! The King certainly has the right of veto; but he dare not exercise it."

"Dare not?" echoed the Marquis—"From his present unconstitutional attitude it seems to me he dare do anything!"

"I tell you he dare not!" repeated Perousse quietly;—"Unless he wishes to lose the Throne. I daresay if it came to that, we should get on quite as well—if not better—with a Republic!"

Lutera looked at him with an amazed and reluctant admiration.

"*You* talk of a Republic? You,—who are for ever making the most loyal speeches in favour of the monarchy?"

"Why not?" queried Perousse lightly;—"If the monarchy does not do as it is told, whip it like a naughty child and send it to bed. That has been easily arranged before now in history!"

The Marquis sat silent,—thinking, or rather brooding heavily. Should he, or should he not unburden himself of certain fears that oppressed his mind? He cleared his throat of a troublesome huskiness and began,—

"If the purely business transactions in which you are engaged——"

"And you also," put in Perousse placidly.

The Premier shifted his position uneasily and went on.

"I say, if the purely business transactions of this affair were publicly known——"

"As well expect Cabinet secrets to be posted on a hoarding in the open thoroughfare!" said Perousse. "What afflicts you with these sudden pangs of distrust at your position? You have taken care to provide for all your own people! What more can you desire?"

Lutera hesitated; then he said slowly:—

"I think there is only one thing for me to do,—and that is to send in my resignation at once!"

Carl Perousse raised himself a little out of his chair, and opened his narrow eyes.

"Send in your resignation!" he echoed; "On what grounds? Do me the kindness to remember, Marquis, that I am not yet quite ready to take your place!"

He smiled his disagreeable smile,—and the Marquis began to feel irritated.

"Do not be too sure that you will ever have it to take," he said with some acerbity; "If the King should by any means come to know of your financial deal——"

"You seem to be very suddenly afraid of the King!" interrupted Perousse; "Or else strange touches of those catch-word ideals 'Loyalty' and 'Patriotism' are troubling your mind! You speak of *my* financial deal,—is not yours as important? Review the position;—it is simply this;—for years and years the Ministry have been speculating in office matters,—it is no new thing. Sometimes they have lost, and sometimes they have won; their losses have been replaced by the imposition of taxes on the people,—their gains they have very wisely said nothing about. In these latter days, however, the loss has been considerably more than the gain. 'Patriotism,' as stocks, has gone down. 'Honour' will not pay the piper. We cannot increase taxation just at present; but by a war, we can clear out some of the useless population, and invest in contracts for supplies. The mob love fighting,—and every small victory won, can be celebrated in beer and illuminations, to expand what is called 'the heart of the People.' It is a great 'heart,' and always leaps to strong drink,—which is cheap enough, being so largely adulterated. The country we propose to subdue is rich,—and both you and I have large investments of land there. With the success which our arms are sure to obtain, we shall fill not only the State coffers (which have been somewhat emptied by our predecessors' peculations), but our own coffers as well.

The King 'vetoes' the war; then let us hear what the People say! Of course we must work them up first; and then get their verdict while they are red- hot with patriotic excitement. The Press, ordered by Jost, can manage that! Put it to the country; (through Jost);—but do not talk of resigning when we are on the brink of success! *I* will carry this thing through, despite the King's 'veto'!"

"Wait!" said the Marquis, drawing his chair closer to Perousse, and speaking in a low uneasy tone; "You do not know all! There is some secret agency at work against us; and, among other things, I fear that a foreign spy has been inadvertently allowed to learn the mainspring of our principal moves. Listen, and judge for yourself!"

And he related the story of David Jost's midnight experience, carefully emphasising every point connected with his own signet-ring. As he proceeded with the narration, Perousse's face grew livid,—once or twice he clenched his hand nervously, but he said nothing till he had heard all.

"Your ring, you say, had never left the King's possession?"

"So the King himself assured me, this very afternoon."

"Then someone must have passed off an imitation signet on David Jost," continued Perousse meditatively. "What name did the spy give?"

"Pasquin Leroy."

Carl Perousse opened a small memorandum book, and carefully wrote the name down within it.

"Whatever David Jost has said, David Jost alone is answerable for!" he then said calmly—"A Jew may be called a liar with impunity, and whatever a Jew has asserted can be flatly denied. Remember, he is in our pay!"

"I doubt if he will consent to be made the scapegoat in this affair," said Lutera; "Unless we can make it exceptionally to his advantage;—he has the press at his command."

"Give him a title!" returned Perousse contemptuously; "These Jew press- men love nothing better!"

The Marquis smiled somewhat sardonically.

"Jost, with a patent of nobility would cut rather an extraordinary figure!" he said; "Still he would probably make good use of it,— especially if he were to start a newspaper in London! They would accept him as a great man there!"

Perousse gave a careless nod; his thoughts were otherwise occupied.

"This Pasquin Leroy has gone to Moscow?"

"According to his own words, he was leaving this morning."

"I daresay that statement is a blind. I should not at all wonder if he is still in the city. I will get an exact description of him from Jost, and set Bernhoff on his track."

"Do not forget," said the Marquis impressively, "that he told Jost in apparently the most friendly and well-meaning manner possible, that the King had discovered the whole plan of our financial campaign. He even reported *me* as being ready to resign in consequence——"

"Which apparently you are!" interpolated Perousse with some sarcasm.

"I certainly have my resignation in prospect," returned Lutera coldly— "And, so far, this mysterious spy has seemingly probed my thoughts. If he is as correct in his report concerning the King, it is impossible to say what may be the consequence."

"Why, what can the King do?" demanded Perousse impatiently, and with scorn for the vacillating humour of his companion; "Granted that he knew everything from the beginning——"

"Including your large land purchases and contract concessions in the very country you propose war with," put in the Marquis,—"Say that he knew you had resolved on war, and had already started a company for the fabrication of the guns and other armaments, out of which you get the principal pickings—what then?"

"What then?" echoed Perousse defiantly—"Why nothing! The King is as powerless as a target in a field, set up for arrows to be aimed at! He dare not divulge a State secret; he has no privilege of interference with politics; all he can do is to 'lead' fashionable society—a poor business at best—and at present his lead is not particularly apparent. The King must do as We command!"

He rose and paced up and down with agitated steps.

"To-day, when he told me he had resolved to 'veto' my propositions, I accepted his information without any manifestation of surprise. I merely said it would have to be stated in the Senate, and that reasons would have to be given. He agreed, and said that he himself would proclaim those reasons. I told him it was impossible!"

"And what was his reply?" asked the Marquis.

"His reply was as absurd as his avowed intention. 'Hitherto it has been impossible,' he said; 'But in Our reign we shall make it possible!' He declined any further conversation with me, referring me to you and our chief colleagues in the Cabinet."

"Well?"

"Well! I pay no more attention to a King's sudden caprice than I do to the veering of the wind! He will alter his mind in a few days, when the exigency of the matters in hand becomes apparent to him. In the same way, he will revoke his decision about that grant of land to the Jesuits. He must let them have their way."

"What benefit do we get by favouring the Jesuits?" asked Lutera.

"Jost gets a thousand a year for putting flattering notices of the schools, processions, festivals and such nonsense in his various newspapers; and our party secures the political support of the Vatican in Europe,—which just now is very necessary. The Pope must give his Christian benediction not only to our Educational system, but also to the war!"

"Then the King has set himself in our way already, even in this matter?"

"He has! Quite unaccountably and very foolishly. But we shall persuade him still to be of our opinion. The ass that will not walk must be beaten till he gallops! I have no anxiety whatever on any point; even the advent of Jost's spy, with an imitation of your signet on his finger appears to me quite melodramatic, and only helps to make the general situation more interesting,—to me at least;—I am only sorry to see that you allow yourself to be so much concerned over these trifles!"

"I have my family to think of," said the Marquis slowly; "My reputation as a statesman, and my honour as a minister are both at stake." Perousse smiled oddly, but said nothing. "If in any way my name became a subject of popular animadversion, it would entirely ruin the position I believe I have attained in history. I have always wished,—" and there was a tinge of pathos in his voice—"my descendants to hold a certain pride in my career!"

Perousse looked at him with grim amusement.

"It is a curious and unpleasant fact that the 'descendants' of these days do not care a button for their ancestors," he said; "They generally try to forget them as fast as possible. What do the descendants of Robespierre, (if there are any), care about him? The descendants of Wellington? The descendants of Beethoven or Lord Byron? Among the many numerous advantages attending the world-wide fame of Shakespeare is that he has left no descendants. If he had, his memory would have been more vulgarised by *them,* than by any Yankee kicker at his grave! One of the most remarkable features of this progressive age is the cheerful ease with which sons forget they ever had fathers! I am afraid, Marquis, you are not likely to escape the common doom!"

Lutera rose slowly, and prepared to take his departure.

"I shall call a Cabinet Council for Monday," he said; "This is Friday. You will find it convenient to attend?"

Perousse, rising at the same time, assented smilingly.

"You will see things in a better and clearer light by then," he said. "Rely on me! I have not involved you thus far with any intention of bringing you to loss or disaster. Whatever befalls you in this affair must equally befall me; we are both in the same boat. We must carry things through with a firm hand, and show no hesitation. As for the King, his business is to be a Dummy; and as Dummy he must remain."

Lutera made no reply. They shook hands,—not over cordially,—and parted; and as soon as Perousse heard the wheels of the Premier's carriage grinding away from his outer gate, he applied himself vigorously to the handle of one of the numerous telephone wires fitted up near his desk, and after getting into communication with the quarter he desired, requested General Bernhoff, Chief of the Police, to attend upon him instantly. Bernhoff's headquarters were close by, so that he had but to wait barely a quarter of an hour before that personage,—the same who had before been summoned to the presence of the King,— appeared.

To him Perousse handed a slip of paper, on which he had written the words 'Pasquin Leroy.'

"Do you know that name?" he asked.

General Bernhoff looked at it attentively. Only the keenest and closest observer could have possibly detected the slight flicker of a smile under the stiff waxed points of his military moustache, as he read it. He returned it carefully folded.

"I fancy I have heard it!" he said cautiously; "In any case, I shall remember it."

"Good! There is a man of that name in this city; trace him if you can! Take this note to Mr. David Jost"—and while he spoke he hastily scrawled a few lines and addressed them—"and he will give you an exact personal description of him. He is reported to have left for Moscow,— but I discredit that statement. He is a foreign spy, engaged, we believe, in the work of taking plans of our military defences,—he must be arrested, and dealt with rigorously at once. You understand?"

"Perfectly," replied Bernhoff, accepting the note handed to him; "If he is to be discovered, I shall not fail to discover him!"

"And when you think you are on the track, let me have information at once," went on Perousse; "But be well on your guard, and let no one learn the object of your pursuit. Keep your own counsel!"

"I always do!" returned Bernhoff bluntly. "If I did not there might be trouble!"

Perousse looked at him sharply, but seeing the wooden-like impassiveness of his countenance, forced a smile.

"There might indeed!" he said; "Your tact and discretion, General, do much to keep the city quiet. But this affair of Pasquin Leroy is a private matter."

"Distinctly so!" agreed Bernhoff quietly; "I hold the position entirely!"

He shortly afterwards withdrew, and Carl Perousse, satisfied that he had at any rate taken precautions to make known the existence of a spy in the city, if not to secure his arrest, turned to the crowding business on his hands with a sense of ease and refreshment. He might not have felt quite so self-assured and complacent, had he seen the worthy Bernhoff smiling broadly to himself as he strolled along the street, with the air of one enjoying a joke, the while he murmured,—

"Pasquin Leroy,—engaged in taking plans of the military defences—is he? Ah!—a very dangerous amusement to indulge in! Engaged in taking plans!—Ah!—Yes!—Very good,—very good; excellent! Do I know the name? Yes! I fancy I might have heard it! Oh, yes, very good indeed— excellent! And this spy is probably still in the city? Yes!—Probably! Yes—I should imagine it quite likely!"

Still smiling, and apparently in the best of humours with himself and the world at large, the General continued his easy stroll by the sea- fronted ways of the city, along the many picturesque terraces, and up flights of marble steps built somewhat in the fashion of the prettiest corners of Monaco, till he reached the chief prom- enade and resort of fashion, which being a broad avenue running immediately un- der and in front of the King's palace facing the sea, was in the late sunshine of the afternoon crowded with carriages and pedestrians. Here he took his place with the rest, saluting a fellow officer here, or a friend there,—and stood bareheaded with the rest of the crowd, when a light gracefully-shaped landau, drawn by four greys, and escorted by postillions in the Royal liveries, passed like a triumphal car, enshrining the cold, changeless and statuesque beauty of the Queen, upon whom the public were never weary of gazing. She was a curiosity to them—a living miracle in her unwithering loveliness; for, apparently unmoved by emotion herself, she roused all sorts of emotions in others. Bernhoff had seen her a thousand times, but never without a sense of new dazzlement.

"Always the same Sphinx!" he thought now, with a slight frown shading the bluff good-nature of his usual expression; "She is a woman who will face Death as she faces Time,—with that cold smile of hers which expresses nothing but scorn of all life's little business!"

He proceeded meditatively on his way to the palace itself, where, on demand, he was at once admitted to the private apartments of the King.

CHAPTER XVIII
ROYAL LOVERS

SILVER-WHITE glamour of the moon, and velvet darkness of deep branching foliage held the quiet breadth of The Islands between them. Low on the shore the fantastic shapes of one or two tall cliffs were outlined black on the fine sparkling sand,—tiny waves rose from the bosom of the calm sea, and cuddling together in baby ripples made bubbles of their crests, and broke here and there among the pebbles with low gurgles of laughter, and in the warm silence of the southern night the nightingales began to tune up their delicate fluty voices with delicious tremors and pauses in the trying of their song. The under- scent of hidden violets among moss flowed potently upon the quiet air, mingled with strong pine-odours and the salt breath of the gently heaving sea,—and all the land seemed as lonely and as fair as the fabled Eden might have been, when the first two human mated creatures knew it as their own. To every soul that loves for the first time, the vision of that Lost Paradise is granted; to every man and woman who know and feel the truth of the divine passion is vouchsafed a flashing gleam of glory from that Heaven which gives them to each other. For the voluptuary—for the animal man,—who like his four-footed kindred is only conscious of instinctive desire, this pure expansion of the heart and ennobling of the thought is as a sealed book,—a never-to-be- divulged mystery of joy, which, because he cannot experience it, he is unable to believe in. It is a glory-cloud in which the privileged ones are 'caught up and received out of sight.' It transfuses the roughest elements into immortal influences,—it colours the earth with fairer hues, and fills the days with beauty; every hour is a gem of sweet thought set in the dreaming soul, and the lover, at certain times of rapt ecstasy, would smile incredulously were he told that anyone living could be unhappy. For love goes back to the beginning of things,—to the time when the world was new. It has its birth in that primeval light when 'the morning stars sang together, and all the sons of God shouted for joy.' If it is real, deep, passionate and disinterested love, it sees no difficulties and knows no disillusions. It is a sufficient assurance of God to make life beautiful. But in these days of the eld-time of nations, when all things are being mixed and prepared for casting into a new mould of world-formation, where we and our civilizations are not, and shall not be,—any more than the Egyptian Rameses is part of us now,—love in its pristine purity, faith and simplicity, is rare. Very little romance is left to hallow it; and it is doubtful whether the white moon, swinging like a silver lamp in heaven above the peaceful Islands, shed her glory anywhere on any such lovers in the world, as the two who on this fair night of the southern springtime, with arms entwined round each other, moved slowly up and down on the velvet greensward outside Ronsard's cottage,— Gloria and her 'sailor' husband.

Gloria was happy,—and her happiness made her doubly beautiful. Clad in her usual attire of white homespun, with her rich hair falling unbound over her shoulders in girl-fashion, and just kept back by a band of white coral, she looked like a young goddess of the sea; her lustrous, starlike eyes gazed up into the tender responsive ones of the handsome stripling she had so trustfully wedded, and not a shadow of doubt or fear darkened the heaven of her confidence. She did not know how beautiful she was,—she did not realise that her body was like one of the unfettered, graceful and perfectly-proportioned figures of women left to our wondering reverence by the Greek sculptors,—she had never thought about herself at all, not even to compare her fair brilliancy of skin with the bronzed, weather-beaten faces of the fisher-folk among whom she dwelt. Resting her delicate classic head against the encircling arm of her lover and lord, her beauty seemed almost unearthly in its pure transparency of feature, outlined by the silver glimmer of the moonbeams; and the young man by her side, with his handsome dark head, tall figure and distinguished bearing, looked the fitting mate for her fair, blossoming womanhood. No two lovers were ever more ideally matched in physical perfection; and as they moved slowly to and fro on the soft dark grass, brushing the dewy scent from hanging rose-boughs that pushed out inviting tufts of white and pink bloom here and there from the surrounding foliage, they would have served many a poet for some sweet idyll, or romance in rhyme, which should hold in its stanzas the magic of immortality. Yet there was a shade of uneasiness in the minds of both,—Prince Humphry was more silent than usual, and seemed absorbed in thought; and Gloria, looking timidly up from time to time at the dark poetic face of her 'sailor' lover, felt with a woman's quick instinct that something was troubling him, and remorsefully concluded that she was to blame,—that he had heard of her having been seen by the King, and that he was evidently vexed by it. He had arrived that evening suddenly and unexpectedly; for she and her 'little father,' as she called Rene Ronsard, had just begun their frugal supper, when the Crown Prince's yacht swept into the bay and dropped anchor. Half an hour later he, the much-beloved 'junior officer' in the Crown Prince's service had appeared at the cottage door, greatly to their delight, for they did not expect to see him so soon. They had supped together, and then Ronsard himself had gone to superintend a meeting at a small social club he had started for the amusement of the fisher-folk, wisely leaving the young wedded lovers to themselves. And they had for a long time been very quiet, save for such little words of love as came into tune with the interchange of caresses,—and after a pause of anxious inward thought, Gloria ventured on a timid query.

"Dearest,—are you *very* angry with me?"

He started,—and stopping in his walk, turned the fair face up between his two hands, as one might lift a rose on its stem, and kissed it tenderly.

"Angry? How can I ever be angry with you, Sweet? Besides what cause have I for anger?"

"I thought, perhaps—" murmured Gloria, "that if the Professor told you what I did yesterday,—when the King came—"

"He did tell me;" and the Prince still gazed down on that heavenly beauty which was the light of the world to him. "He told me that you sang;—and that your golden voice was a musical magnet which drew his Majesty to your feet! I am not surprised,—it was only natural! But I could have wished it had not happened just yet; however, it has happened, and we must make the best of it!"

"It was my fault," said the girl penitently;—"I had the fancy to sing; and I *would* sing, though the good Professor told me not to do so!"

The Prince was silent. He was bracing his mind to the inevitable. He had determined that on this very night Gloria should know the truth. For he was instinctively certain that if he went abroad, as his father wished him to do, some means would be taken to remove her altogether from the country before his return; and his idea was to tell her all, and make her accompany him on his travels. As his wife, she was bound to obey him, he argued within himself; she should, she must go with him! Unconsciously Gloria's next words supplied him with an opening to the subject.

"Why did you never tell me that the Professor was in the King's service?" she asked. "He seemed to know him quite well,—indeed, almost as a friend!"

"He is the King's physician," answered the Prince abruptly; "And, therefore, he is very greatly in the King's confidence."

He walked on, still keeping his arm round her, and seemed not to see the half-frightened glance she gave him.

"The King's physician!" she echoed;—"He does not seem a great person at all,— he is quite a simple old German man!"

Her lover smiled.

"To be physician to the King, my Gloria, is not a very wonderful honour! It merely implies that the man so chosen is perhaps the ablest fencer with sickness and death; the greatness is in the simple old German himself, not in the King's preference. Von Glauben is a good man."

"I know it;" said Gloria gently; "He is good,—and very kind. He said he would always be my friend,—but he was very strange in his manner yesterday, and almost I was vexed with him. Do you know what he said? He asked me what I should do if you—my husband, had deceived me? Can you imagine such a thing?"

Now was the supreme moment. With a violently beating heart the Prince halted, and putting both arms round her waist, drew her up to him in such a way that their eyes looked close into each other's, and their lips were within kissing touch.

"Yes, my sweetest one! I can imagine such a thing! Such a thing is possible! Consider it to be true! Consider that I *have* deceived you!"

She did not move from his clasp, but into her large, lovely trusting eyes came a look of grief and terror, and her face grew ashy pale.

"In what way?" she whispered faintly; "Tell me! I—I—cannot believe it!"

"Gloria,—Gloria! My love, my darling! Do not tremble so! Do not fear! I have not deceived you in any evil way,—what I have done was for your good and mine;

but now—now there is no longer any need of deception,— you may, and *shall* know all the truth, my wife, my dearest in the world! You shall know me as I truly am at last!"

She moved restlessly in his strong clasp,—she was trembling from head to foot, as if her blood was suddenly chilled.

"As you truly are!" she echoed, with pale lips—"Are you not then what I have believed you to be?"

And she made an effort to withdraw herself entirely from his embrace. But he held her fast.

"I am your husband, Gloria!" he said, "and you are my wife! Nothing can alter that; nothing can change our love or disunite our lives. But I am not the poor naval officer I have represented myself to be!—though I am glad I adopted such a disguise, because by its aid I wooed and won your love! I am not in the service of the Crown Prince,—except in so far as I serve my own needs! Why, how you tremble!"—and he held her closer—"Do not be afraid, my darling! Lift up your eyes and look at me with your own sweet trusting look,—do not turn away from me, because instead of being the Prince's servant, I am the Prince himself!"

"The Prince!" And with a cry of utter desolation, Gloria wrenched herself out of his arms, and stood apart, looking at him in wild alarm and bewilderment. "The Prince! You—you!—my husband! You,—the King's son! And you have married *me*!—oh, how cruel of you!—how cruel! —how cruel!"

Covering her face with her hands, she broke into a low sobbing,—and the Prince, cut to the heart by her distress, caught her again in his arms.

"Hush, Gloria!" he said, with an accent of authority, though his own voice was tremulous; "You must not grieve like this! You will break my heart! Do you not understand? Do you not see that all my life is bound up in you?—that I give it to you to do what you will with?—that I care nothing for rank, state or throne without you?—that I will let all the world go rather than lose you? Gloria, do not weep so!—do not weep! Every tear of yours is a pang to me! What does it matter whether I am prince or commoner? I love you!—we love each other!—we are one in the sight of Heaven!"

He held her passionately in his arms, kissing the soft clusters of hair that fell against his breast, and whispering all the tenderest words of endearment he could think of to console and soothe her anguish. By degrees she grew calmer, and her sobs gradually ceased. Dashing the tears from her eyes, she looked up,—her face white as marble.

"You must not tell Ronsard!" she said in faint tones that shook with fear; "He would kill you!"

The Prince smiled indulgently; his only thought was for her, and so long as he could dry her tears, Ronsard's rage or pleasure was nothing to him.

"He would kill you!" repeated Gloria, with wide open tear-wet eyes; "He hates all kings, in his heart!—and if he knew that you—*you*—my husband,—were what you say you are;—if he thought you had married me under a disguise, only to leave me and never to want me any more——"

"Gloria, Gloria!" cried the Prince, in despair; "Why will you say such things! Never to want you any more! I want you all my life, and every moment of that life! Gloria, you must listen to me—you must not turn from me at the very time I need you most! Are you not brave? Are you not true? Do you not love me?"

With a pathetic gesture she stretched out her hands to him.

"Oh, yes, I love you!" she said; "I love you with all my heart! But you have deceived me!—my dearest, you have deceived me! And if you had only told me the truth, I would never,—for your own sake,—have married you!"

"I know that!" said the Prince; "And that is why I determined to win you under the mask of poverty! Now listen, my Princess and my Queen!— for you are both! I want all your help—all your love—all your trust! Do not be afraid of Ronsard; he will, he can do nothing to harm me! You are my wife, Gloria,—you have promised before God to obey me! I claim your obedience!"

She stood silent, looking at him,—pale and fair as an ivory statue of Psyche, seen against the dark background of the heavily-branched trees. Her mind was stunned and confused; she had not yet grasped the full consciousness of her position,—but as he spoke, the old primitive lessons of faith, steadfastness of purpose, and unwavering love and trust in God, which her adopted father had instilled into her from childhood, rose and asserted their sway over her startled, but unspoilt soul.

"You need not claim it!" she said, slowly; "It is yours always! I shall do whatever you tell me, even if you command me to die for your sake!"

With a swift impulsive action, full of grace and spirit, he dropped on one knee and kissed her hand.

"And so I pledge my faith to my Queen!" he said joyously. "Gloria! my 'Glory-of-the-Sea'!—you will forgive me for having in this one thing misled you? Think of me as your sailor lover still!—it is a much harder thing to be a king's son than a simple, independent seafarer! Pity me for my position, and help me to make it endurable! Come now with me down to that rocky nook on the shore where I first saw you,— and I will tell you exactly how everything stands,—and how I trust to your love for me and your courage, to clear away all the difficulties before us. You do not love me less?"

"I could not love you less!" she replied slowly; "but I cannot think of you as quite the same!"

A shadow of pain darkened his face.

"Gloria," he said sadly; "If your love was as great as mine you would forgive!"

She stood a moment wavering and uncertain; their eyes were riveted on each other in a strange spiritual attraction—her soft lips were a little relaxed from their gravity as she steadfastly regarded him. She was embarrassed, conscious, and very pale; but he drank in gratefully the wonder and shy worship of those pure eyes,—and waited. Suddenly she sprang to him and closed her arms about his neck, kissing him with simple and loving tenderness.

"I do forgive! Oh, I do forgive!" she murmured; "Because I love you, my darling—because I love you! Whatever you wish I will do for your love's sake—believe me!—but I am frightened just now!—it is as if I did not know you—as if someone had taken you suddenly a long way off! Give me a little time to recover my courage!—and to know"—here a faint smile trembled on her beautiful curved mouth—"to know,—and to *feel*,—that you are still my own!—even though the world may try to part you from me!—still my very own!"

The warmth of passionate feeling in her face flushed it into a rose- glow that spread from chin to brow,—and clasping her to his breast, he gave her the speech-less answer that love inscribes on eyes and lips,— then, keeping his arm tenderly about her, he led her gently into the path through the pinewood, which wound down to their favourite haunt by the sea.

The moonlight had now increased in brilliancy, and illumined the landscape with all the opulence, splendour and superabundance of radiance common to the south,—the air was soft and balmy, and one great white cloud floating lazily under the silver orb, moved slowly to the centre of the heavens,—the violet-blue of night falling around it like an imperial robe of state. The two youthful figures passed under the pine-boughs, which closed over them odorously in dark arches of shadow, and wended their slow way down to the seashore, from whence they could see the Royal yacht lying at anchor, every tapering line of her fair proportions distinctly outlined against the sky, and all her masts shining as if they had been washed with silver dew; and the Heir- Apparent to a throne was,—for once in the history of Heir-Apparents,— happy—happy in knowing that he was loved as princes seldom or never are loved,—not for his power, not for his rank, but simply for himself alone, by one of the most beautiful women in the world, who,—if she knew neither the ways of a Court, nor the wiles of fashion,—had something better than either of these,—the sanctity of truth and the strength of innocence.

Rene Ronsard, coming back from his pleasurable duties as host and chairman to his fishermen-friends, found the cottage deserted, and smiled, as he sat himself down in the porch to smoke, and to wait for the lover's return.

"What a thing it is to be young!" he sighed, as he gazed meditatively at the still beauty of the night around him;—"To be young,—and in love with the right person! Hours go like moments—the grass is never damp—the air is never cold—there is never time enough to give all the kisses that are waiting to be given; and life is so beautiful, that we are almost able to understand why God created the universe! The rapture passes very quickly, unfortunately—with some people;—but if I ever prayed for anything—which I do not—I should pray that it might remain with Gloria! It surely cannot offend the Supreme Being who is responsible for our existence, to see one woman happy out of all the tortured millions of them! One exception to the universal rule would not make much difference! The law that the strong should prey on the weak, nearly always prevails,—but it is possible to hope and believe that on rare occasions the strong may be magnanimous!"

He smoked on placidly, considering various points of philosophic meditation, and by and by fell into a gentle doze. The doze deepened into a dream which grew sombre and terrible,—and in it he thought he saw himself standing bareheaded on a raised platform above surging millions of people who all shouted with one terrific uproar of unison— "Regicide! Regicide!" He looked down upon his hands, and saw

them red with blood!—he looked up to the heavens, and they were flushed with the
same ominous hue. Blood!—blood!—the blood of kings,—the dust of thrones!—and
he, the cause! Choked and tormented with a parching thirst, it seemed in the dream
that he tried to speak,—and with all his force he cried out—"For her sake I did it!
For her sake!" But the clamour of the crowd drowned his voice,—and then it was
as if the coldness of death crept slowly over him,—slowly and cruelly, as though
his whole body were being enclosed within an iceberg,—and he saw Gloria, the
child of his love and care, laid out before him dead,—but robed and crowned like
a queen, and placed on a great golden bier of state, with purple velvet falling about
her, and tall candles blazing at her head and feet. And voices sang in his ears—
"Gloria! Gloria in excelsis Deo!"—mingling with the muffled chanting of priests at
some distant altar; and he thought he made an attempt to touch the royal velvet pall
that draped her beautiful lifeless body, when he was roughly thrust back by armed
men with swords and bayonets who asked him "What do you here? Are you not her
murderer?"—and he cried out wildly "No, no! Never could I have harmed the child
of my love! Never could I hurt a hair of her head, or cause her an hour's sorrow!
She is all I had in the world!—I loved her!—I loved her! Let me see her!—let me
touch her!—let me kiss her once again!" And then the scene suddenly changed,—
and it was found that Gloria was not dead at all, but walking peacefully alone in a
garden of flowers, with lilies crowning her, and all the sunshine about her; and that
the golden bier of state had changed into a ship at sea which was floating, floating
westward bearing some great message to a far country, and that all was well for
him and his darling. The troubled vision cleared from his brain, and his sleep grew
calmer; he breathed more easily, and flitting glimpses of fair scenes passed before
his dreaming eyes,—scenes in some peaceful and beautiful world, where never a
shadow of sorrow or trouble darkened the quiet contentment of happy and innocent lives. He smiled in his sleep, and heaved a deep sigh of pleasure,—and so,
gently awoke, to feel a light touch on his shoulder, and to see Gloria standing before
him. A smile was on her face,—the fragrance of the woodlands and the sea clung
about her garments,—she held a few roses in her hand, and there was something
in her whole appearance that struck him as new, commanding, and more than ever
beautiful.

"You have returned alone?" he said wonderingly.

"Yes. I have returned alone! I have much to tell you, dear! Let us go in!"

CHAPTER XIX
OF THE CORRUPTION OF THE STATE

THE large gaunt building, which was dignified by the name of the 'People's Assembly Rooms,' stood in a dim unfashionable square of the city which had once been entirely devoted to warehouses and storage cellars. It had originally served a useful purpose in providing temporary shelter for foreign-made furniture, which was badly constructed and intrinsically worthless,— but which, being cheaply imported and showy in appearance, was patronized by some of the upper middle-classes in preference to goods of their own home workmanship. Lately, however, the foreign import had fallen to almost less than nothing; and whether or no this was due to the secret machinations of Sergius Thord and his Revolutionary Committee, no one would have had the hardihood to assert. Foreign tradesmen, however, and foreign workmen generally had certainly experienced a check in their inroads upon home manufactures, and some of the larger business firms had been so successfully intimidated as to set up prominent announcements outside their warehouses to the effect that "Only native workmen need apply." Partly in consequence of the "slump" in foreign goods, the "Assembly Rooms," as a mere building had for some time been shut up, and given over to dust and decay, till the owners of the property decided to let it out for popular concerts, meetings and dances, and so make some little money out of its bare whitewashed walls and comfortless ugliness. The plan had succeeded fairly well, and the place was beginning to be known as a convenient centre where thousands were wont to congregate, to enjoy cheap music and cheap entertainment generally. It was a favourite vantage ground for the disaffected and radical classes of the metropolis to hold forth on their wrongs, real or imaginary,—and the capacities of the largest room or hall in the building were put to their utmost extent to hold the enormous audiences that always assembled to hear the picturesque, passionate and striking oratory of Sergius Thord.

But there were one or two rare occasions when even Sergius Thord's attractions as a speaker were thrown into the background, by the appearance of that mysterious personality known as Lotys,—concerning whom a thousand extravagant stories were rife, none of which were true. It was rumoured among other things as wild and strange, that she was the illegitimate child of a certain great prince, whose amours were legion—that she had been thrown out into the street to perish, deserted as an infant, and that Sergius Thord had rescued her from that impending fate of starvation and death,—and that it was by way of vengeance for the treatment of her mother by the Exalted Personage involved, that she had thrown in her lot with the Revolutionary party, to aid their propaganda by her intellectual gifts, which were many. She was known to be very poor,—she lived in cheap rooms in a low quarter of the city; she was seldom or never seen in the public thoroughfares, —she appeared to have no women friends, and she certainly mixed in no form of social intercourse or entertainment. Yet her name was on the lips of the million, and her influence was felt far beyond the city's radius. Even among some of the highest and wealthiest classes of society this peculiar appellation of "Lotys," carrying no surname with it, and spoken at haphazard had the effect of causing a sudden silence, and the interchange of questioning looks among those who heard it, and who, without knowing who she was, or what her aims in life really were, voted her "dangerous." Those among the superior classes who had by rare chance seen her, were unanimous in their verdict that she was not beautiful,—"but!"—and the "but" spoke volumes. She was known to possess something much less common, and far more potent than beauty,— and that was a fascinating, compelling spiritual force, which magnetised into strange submission all who came within its influence,— and many there were who admitted, though with bated breath that 'An' if she chose' she could easily become a very great personage indeed.

She herself was, or seemed to be, perfectly unconscious of the many discussions concerning her and her origin. She had her own secret sorrows,—her sad private history, which she shut close within her own breast,—but out of many griefs and poverty-stricken days of struggle and cruel environment, she had educated herself to a wonderful height of moral self-control and almost stoical rectitude. Her nature was a broad and grand one, absolutely devoid of pettiness, and full of a strong, almost passionate sympathy with the wrongs of others,—and she had formed herself on such firm, heroic lines of courage and truth and self-respect, that the meaner vices of her sex were absolutely unknown to her. Neither vanity, nor envy, nor malice, nor spleen disturbed the calmly-flowing current of her blood,—her soul was absorbed in pity for human kind, and contemplation of its many woes,—and so living alone, and studiously apart from the more frivolous world, she had attained a finely tempered and deeply thoughtful disposition which gave her equally the courage of the hero and the resignation of the martyr. She had long put away out of her life all possibility of happiness for herself. She had, by her unwearying study of the masses of working, suffering men and women, come to the sorrowful conclusion that real happiness could only be enjoyed by the extremely young, and the extremely thoughtless,—and that love was only another name for the selfish and often cruel and destructive instincts of animal desire. She did not resent these ugly facts, or passionately proclaim against the gloomy results of life such as were daily displayed to her,—she was only filled with a profound and ceaseless compassion for the evils which were impossible to cure. Her tireless love for the sick, the feeble, the despairing, the broken-hearted and the dying, had raised her to the height of an angel's quality among the very desperately poor and criminal classes;—the fiercest ruffians of the slums were docile in her presence and obedient to her command;—and many a bold plan of robbery,—many a wicked scheme of murder had been altogether foregone and abandoned through the intervention of Lotys, whose intellectual acumen, swift to perceive the savage instinct, or motive for crime, was equally swift to point out its uselessness as a means of satisfying vengeance. No preacher could persuade a thief of the practical ingloriousness of thieving, as Lotys could,—and a prison chaplain, remonstrating with an assassin after his crime, was not half as much use to the State as Lotys, who could induce such an one to resign his murderous intent altogether, before he had so much as possessed himself of the necessary weapon. Thousands of people were absolutely under her moral dominion,—and the power she exercised over them was so great, and yet so unobtrusive, that had she bidden the whole city rise in revolt, she would most surely have been obeyed by the larger and fiercer half of its population.

With the moneyed classes she had nothing in common, though she viewed them with perhaps more pity than she did the very poor. An overplus of cash in any one person's possession that had not been rightfully earned by the work of brain or body, was to her an incongruity, and a defection from the laws of the universe;— show and ostentation she despised,—and though she loved beautiful things, she found them,—as she herself said,—much more in the everyday provisions of nature, than in the elaborate designs of art. When she passed the gay shops in the principal thoroughfares she never paused to look in at the jewellers' windows,—but she would linger for many minutes studying the beauty of the sprays of orchids and other delicate blossoms, arranged in baskets and vases by the leading florists; while,—best delight of all to her, was a solitary walk inland among the woods, where she could gather violets and narcissi, and, as she expressed it 'feel them growing about her feet.' She would have been an extraordinary personality as a man,—as a woman she was doubly remarkable, for to a woman's gentleness she added a force of will and brain which are not often found even in the stronger sex.

Mysterious as she was in her life and surroundings, enough was known of her by the people at large, to bring a goodly concourse of them to the Assembly Rooms on the night when she was announced to speak on a subject of which the very title seemed questionable, namely, "On the Corruption of the State." The police had been notified of the impending meeting, and a few stalwart emissaries of the law in plain clothes mixed with the in-pouring throng. The crowd, however, was very orderly;—there was no pushing, no roughness, and no coarse language. All the members of Sergius Thord's Revolutionary Committee were present, but they came as stragglers, several and apart,—and among them Paul Zouche the poet, was perhaps the most noticeable. He had affected the picturesque in his appearance;—his hat was of the Rembrandt character, and he had donned a very much worn, short velveteen jacket, whose dusty brown was relieved by the vivid touch of a bright red tie. His hair was wild and bushy, and his eyes sparkled with unwonted brilliancy, as he nodded to one or two of his associates, and gave a careless wave of the hand to Sergius Thord, who, entering slowly, and as if with reluctance, took a seat at the very furthest end of the hall, where his massive figure showed least conspicuous among the surging throng. Keeping his head down in a pensive attitude of thought, his eyes were, nevertheless, sharp to see every person entering who belonged to his own particular following,—and a ray of satisfaction lighted up his face, as he perceived his latest new associate, Pasquin Leroy, quietly edge his way through the crowd, and secure a seat in one of the obscurest and darkest corners of the badly lighted hall. He was followed by his comrades, Max Graub and Axel Regor,—and Thord felt a warm glow of contentment in the consciousness that these lately enrolled members of the Revolutionary Committee were so far faithful to their bond. Signed and sealed in the blood of Lotys, they had responded to the magnetism of her name with the prompt obedience of waves rising to the influence of the moon,—and Sergius, full of a thousand wild schemes for the regeneration of the People, was more happy to know them as subjects to her power, than as adherents to his own cause. He was calmly cognisant of the presence of General Bernhoff, the well-known Chief of Police;—though he was rendered a trifle uneasy by observing that personage had seated himself as closely as possible to the bench occupied by Leroy and his companions. A faint wonder crossed his mind as to whether the three, in their zeal for the new Cause they had taken up, had by any means laid themselves open to suspicion; but he was not a man given to fears; and he felt convinced in his own mind, from the close personal observation he had taken of Leroy, and from the boldness of his speech on his enrolment as a member of the Revolutionary Committee, that, whatever else he might prove to be, he was certainly no coward.

The hall filled quickly, till by and by it would have been impossible to find standing room for a child. A student of human nature is never long in finding out the dominant characteristic of an audience,— whether its attitude be profane or reverent, rowdy or attentive, and the bearing of the four or five thousand here assembled was remarkable chiefly for its seriousness and evident intensity of purpose. The extreme orderliness of the manner in which the people found and took their seats,—the entire absence of all fussy movement, fidgeting, staring, querulous changing of places, whispering or laughter, showed that the crowd were there for a deeper purpose than mere curiosity. The bulk of the assemblage was composed of men; very few women were present, and these few were all of the poor and hard-working classes. No female of even the lower middle ranks of life, with any faint pretence to 'fashion,' would have been seen listening to "that dreadful woman,"—as Lotys was very often called by her own sex,—simply because of the extraordinary fascination she secretly exercised over men. Pasquin Leroy and his companions spoke now and then, guardedly, and in low whispers, concerning the appearance and demeanour of the crowd, Max Graub being particularly struck by the general physiognomy and type of the people present.

"Plenty of good heads!" he said cautiously. "There are thinkers here— and thinkers are a very dangerous class!"

"There are many people who 'think' all their lives and 'do' nothing!" said Axel Regor languidly.

"True, my friend! But their thought may lead, while, they themselves remain passive," joined in Pasquin Leroy sotto-voce;—"It is not at all impossible that if Lotys bade these five thousand here assembled burn down the citadel, it would be done before daybreak!"

"I have no doubt at all of that," said Graub. "One cannot forget that the Bastille was taken while the poor King Louis XVI. was enjoying a supper-party and 'a little orange-flower-water refreshment' at Versailles!"

Leroy made an imperative sign of silence, for there was a faint stir and subdued hum of expectation in the crowd. Another moment,—and Lotys stepped quietly and alone on the bare platform. As she confronted her audience, a low passionate sound, like the murmur of a rising storm, greeted her,—a sound that was not anything like the customary applause or encouragement offered to a public speaker, but that suggested extraordinary satisfaction and expectancy, which almost bordered on exultation. Pasquin Leroy, raising his eyes as she entered, was startled by an altogether new impression of her to that which he had received on the night he first saw her. Her personality was somehow different—her appearance more striking, brilliant and commanding. Attired in the same plain garment of dead white serge in which he had previously seen her, with the same deep blood-red scarf crossing her left shoulder and breast,—there was something to-night in this mere costume that seemed emblematic of a far deeper power than he had been at first inclined to give her. A curious sensation began to affect his nerves,—a sudden and overwhelming attraction, as though his very soul were being drawn out of him by the calm irresistible dominance of those slumbrous dark-blue iris-coloured eyes, which had the merit of appearing neither brilliant nor remarkable as eyes merely, but which held in their luminous depths that intellectual command which represents the active and passionate life of the brain, beside which all other life is poor and colourless. These eyes appeared to rest upon him now from under their drooping sleepy white eyelids with an inexpressible tenderness and fascination, and he was suddenly reminded of Heinrich Heine's quaint love-fancy; "Behind her dreaming eyelids the sun has gone to rest; when she opens her eyes it will be day, and the birds will be heard singing!" He began to realise depths in his own nature which he had till now been almost unconscious of; he knew himself to a certain extent, but by no means thoroughly; and awakening as he was to the fact that other lives around him presented strange riddles for consideration, he wondered whether after all, his own life might not perhaps prove one of the most complex among human conundrums? He had often meditated on the inaccessibility of ideal virtues, the uselessness of persuasion, the commonplace absurdity, as he had thought, of trying to embody any lofty spiritual dream,—yet he was himself a man in whom spiritual forces were so strong that he was personally unaware of their overflow, because they were as much a part of him as his breathing capacity. True, he had never consciously tested them, but they were existent in him nevertheless.

He watched Lotys now, with an irritable, restless attention,—there was a thrill of vague expectation in his soul as of new things to be done,—changes to be made in the complex machinery of human nature,— and a great wonder, as well as a great calm, fell upon him as the first clear steady tones of her voice chimed through the deep hush which had prepared the way for her first words. Her voice was a remarkable one, vibrant, yet gentle,—ringing out forcefully, yet perfectly sweet. She began very simply,—without any attempt at a majestic choice of words, or an impressive flow of oratory. She faced her audience quietly,—one bare rounded arm resting easily on a small uncovered deal table in front of her;—she had no 'notes' but her words were plainly the result of deliberate and careful thinking-out of certain problems needful to be brought before the notice of the people. Her face was colourless,—the dead gold hair rippling thickly away in loose clusters from the white brows, fell into their accustomed serpentine twisted knot at the nape of her neck; and the scarlet sash she wore, alone relieved the statuesque white folds of her draperies; but as she spoke, something altogether superphysical seemed to exhale from her as heat exhales from fire—a strange essence of overpowering and compelling sweetness stole into the heavy heated air, and gave to the commonplace surroundings and the poorly clothed crowd of people an atmosphere of sacredness and beauty. This influence deepened steadily under the rhythmic cadence of her voice, till every agitated soul, every resentful and troubled heart in the throng was conscious of a sudden ingathering of force and calm, of self-respect and self-reliance. The gist of her intention was plainly to set people thinking for themselves, and in this there could be no manner of doubt but that she succeeded. Of the 'Corruption of the State' she spoke as a thing thoroughly recognised by the masses.

"We know,—all of us,"—she said, in the concluding portion of her address, "that we have Ministers who personally care nothing for the prosperity or welfare of the country. We know—all of us,—that we have a bribed Press; whose business it is to say nothing that shall run counter to Ministerial views. We know,—all of us,—that it is this bribed Ministerial press which leads the ignorant, (who are not behind the scenes,) to wrong and false conclusions;—and that it is solely upon these wrong and false conclusions of the wilfully misled million, that the Ministry itself rests for support. On one side the Press is manipulated by the Jews; on the other by the Jesuits. There is no journal in this country that will, or dare, publish the true reflex of popular opinion. Therefore the word 'free' cannot be applied to that recording-force of nations which we call Journalism; inasmuch as it is now a merely purchased Chattle. We should remember, when we read 'opinions of the Press,'—on any great movement or important change in policy, that we are merely accepting the opinions of the bound and paid Slave of Capitalists;—and we should take care to form our judgment for ourselves, rather than from the Capitalist point of view. Were there a strong man to lead,—the shiftiness, treachery, and deliberate neglect practised on the million by those who are now in office, could not possibly last;—but where there is no strength, there must be weakness,—and where a long career of deceit has been followed, instead of a course of plain dealing, failure in the end is inevitable. With failure comes disaster; and often something which augments disaster— Revolt. The people, weary of constant imposition,—of incessant delays of the justice due to them,—as well as the unscrupulous breaking of promises solemnly pledged,—will—in the long run, take their own way, as they have done before in history, of securing instant amelioration of those wrongs which their paid rulers fail to redress. Who will dare to say that, under such circumstances, it is ill for the people to act? Sometimes it is a greater Consciousness than their own that moves them; and the wronged and half-forgotten Cause of all worlds makes His command known through His creatures, who obey His impulse,—even as the atoms gathering in space cluster at His will into solar systems, and bring forth their burden of life!"

She paused, and leaning forward a little, her eyes poured out their flashing searchlight as it seemed into the very souls of her hearers.

"Dear friends!—dear children!" she said, and in her tone there was the tenderness of a great compassion, almost bordering on tears,—"What is it, think you all, that makes the age in which we live so sad, so colourless, so restless and devoid of hope and peace? It is not that we are the inhabitants of a less wonderful or less beautiful world,—it is not as if the sun had ceased to shine, or the birds had forgotten how to sing! Triumphs of science,—triumphs of learning and discovery, these are all on the increase for our help and furtherance. With so much gain in evident advancement, what is it we have lost?—what is it we miss?—whence come the dreariness and emptiness and satiety,—the intolerable sense of the futility of life, even when life has most to offer? Dear children, you are all so sad!—many of you so broken- hearted!—why is it?—how is it? Poverty alone is not the cause,—for it is quite possible to be poor, yet happy! True enough it is that in these days you are ground down by the imposition of taxes, which try all the strength of your earnings to pay; but even this is an evil you could mitigate for yourselves, by strong and united public protest. How is it that you do not realise your own strength? You are not like the poor brutes of the field and forest, who lack the reason which would show them how superior in physical force alone they are to the insignificant biped who commands them. Could the ox understand his own strength, he would never be led to the slaughter-house;—he and his kind would become a terror instead of a provision. You are not oxen,— yet often you are as patient, as dull, as blind and reasonless as they! You form clubs, societies, and trades-unions;—but in how many cases do you not enter upon small and querulous differences which so weaken your unity that presently it falls to pieces and has no more power in it? This is what your tyrants in trade rely on and hope for; the constant recurrence of quarrels and dissensions among yourselves. No Society lasts which tolerates conflicting argument or differing sentiments in itself. Why is it that the Jesuits,—whom you are all unanimous in hating,—are still the strongest political Brotherhood on the face of the earth? Because they are bound to maintain in every particular the tenets of their Order. No matter how vile, or how reprehensibly false their theories, they are compelled to carry on the work and propaganda of their Union, despite all loss and sacrifice to themselves. This is the secret of their force. Expelled from one land, they take root in another. Suppressed entirely by Pope Clement XIV., in 1773, they virtually ignored suppression, and took up their headquarters in Russia. The influence they exerted there still lies on the serf population, like one of the many chains fastened to a Siberian exile's body. Yet they were driven from Russia in 1820,—from Holland in 1816,—from Switzerland in 1847, and from Germany in 1872. Latterly they have been expelled from France. Nevertheless, in spite of these numerous expulsions, and the universal odium in which they are held,— they still flourish; still are they able to maintain their twenty-two generals and their four Vicars;—and still all countries have, in their turn, to deal with their impending or fulfilled invasion. Why is it that a Society so criminal in historic annals, should yet remain as a force in our advanced era of civilization? Simply, because it is of One Mind! Bent on evil, or good,—self-renunciation or self- aggrandisement,—it is still of One Mind! Friends,—were you like them, also of One Mind, your injuries, your oppressions, your taxations would not last long! The remedy for all is easy, and rests with yourselves,— only yourselves! But some of you have lost heart—and other some have lost patience. You look round upon the squalid corners of this great city—you shudder at the cruelty of the daily life with which you have to contend,—you enter poor rooms, which you are compelled to call 'home,' where the sick and dying, the newly-born and the dead are huddled all together,—ten, and sometimes fifteen in one small den of four whitewashed walls;—and sickened and tired, you cry out 'Is life worth no more than this? Is God's scheme for the human race no more than this? Then why were we born at all? Or, being born, why may we not die at once, self-slain?' Ah, yes, dear friends!—you often feel like this; we all of us often feel like this! But—it is not God who has made life thus hard for you,—it is yourselves! It is you who consent to be down-trodden,—it is you who resign your freewill, your thought, your originality of character, into the dominating power of others. True,—wealth controls affairs to a vast extent nowadays,—but there is a stronger power than wealth, and that is Soul! It is not the possession of gold that has given the greatest men their position. This is a commercial age, we own,—and certainly,—because of the base and degrading love of accumulation,—

Intellectuality is for the moment often set aside as something valueless—but whenever Intellectuality truly asserts itself, there is at once made visible an acting force
of the Divine, which is practically limitless and irresistible. Think for yourselves,
friends!—do not let a hired Press think for you! Think for yourselves—judge for
yourselves, and act for yourselves! By your observation of a statesman's life, you
shall know his capabilities. If he has once been a turncoat, he will be a turncoat
again. If he has been known to speculate privately in a forthcoming political crisis,
which he alone knows of in advance——"

Here the speaker was interrupted by what sounded more like a snarl than a
shout. "Perousse! Perousse!"

The name was hissed out, and tossed from one rank to another of the audience,
and one or two of the police present glanced enquiringly towards Bernhoff their
chief,—but he sat with folded arms and inscrutable demeanour, making no sign.
Lotys raised her small, beautifully-shaped white hand to enjoin silence. She was
obeyed instantly.

"I speak of no one man," she said with deliberate emphasis; "I accuse no one
man,—or any man! I say 'if' any man gambles with State policy, he is a traitor to
the country! But such gambling is not a novelty in the history of nations. It has
been practised over and over again. Only mark you all this one God's truth!—that
whenever it *has* occurred—whenever the rulers of a State *are* corrupt,—whenever
society sinks into such moral defilement that it sees nothing better, nothing higher
than the love of money,—then comes the downfall!—then Ruin and Anarchy set
up their dominion,—and Heaven's rage rolls out upon the offenders, till their offence be cleansed away in rivers of blood and tears!"

She waited a moment,—and changing her attitude, seemed as it were, to project her thought into her audience, by the sudden passion of her commanding gesture, and the flash of her deep luminous eyes.

"We have heard of the Great Renunciation!" she said; "How God Himself took
human form, and came to this low little earth to prove how nobly we should live
and die! But in our day,—we with our preachers and teachers, our press and our
parliamentary orators,—our atheistical statesmen on all hands, have come upon the
Great Obliteration!—the Obliteration of God altogether in our ways of life! We push
Him out, as if He were not. He is not in our Churches—He is not in our Laws—He

is not in our Commerce. Only when we are brought low by pain and sickness—when we are confronted by death itself—then we call out 'God! God!' like cowards, praying for help from the Power we have negatived all our lives! Here is the evil, O children all!—we have forgotten Our Father! We arrange all our affairs in life without giving Him a thought! Our pleasures, our gains, our advantages,—are calculated without consulting His good pleasure. He is last, or not at all,—when He should be first, and in everything! The end of this is misery;—it must be so; it cannot by law be anything else. For what is God? Who is God? God is a name merely,—but we give it to that Unseen, but ever working Force which rules the Universe! The coldest atheist that ever breathed must own that somehow,—by some means or other,— the Universe *is* ruled,—for if it were not, we should know nothing of it. Therefore, when we set aside, or leave out the consciousness and acknowledgment of the Ruler, the ruling of our affairs must, of necessity, go wrong!

"I cannot preach to you—I cannot out of my own conscience recommend to you one or the other form of faith as the way to peace and wisdom;—but I can and do Beseech you to remember the Note Dominant of this great Universe—the Note that sounds through high and low,—through small and great alike!—and that must and will in due course absorb all our discords into Everlasting Harmony! Try not to put this fact out of your lives,—that Justice and Order are the rule of the spheres; and that whenever we depart from these, even in the smallest contingency, confusion reigns. How hard it is to believe in Justice and Order, you will tell me,—when the poor are not treated with the same consideration as the rich,—and when money will buy place and position! True! It is hard to believe,—but it is believable nevertheless. As the lungs and the heart are the life of the human body, so are Justice and Order the life of the Universe,—and when these are pushed out of place, or become diseased in the composition of a human state or community, then the life of that state or community is threatened;—and unless remedies are quickly to hand, it must end. You all know the position of things among yourselves to-day;—you all know that there is no trust to be placed in Churches, Kings or Parliaments;—that the world is in a state of ferment and unrest,—moving towards Change;— change imminent—change, possibly, disastrous! And if it is You who know, it is likewise You who must seize the hour as it approaches!— seize it as you would seize a robber by the throat, and demand its business;—search its heart;—deprive it of its weapons;—and learn from it its message! A message it may be of wild alarm—of tearing up old conventions;—of thrusting forth old abuses; a message full of clamour and outcry—but whatever the uproar, doubt not that we shall hear the voice of the Forgotten God thundering in our ears at the close! We shall have found our way closer to Him—and with penitence and prayer, we shall ask to be forgiven for having wandered away from Him so long!

"And will He not pardon? Yes,—He will, because He must! To Him we owe our existence;—He alone is responsible for our life, our probation, our progress, our striving through many errors towards Perfection! He, who sees all, must needs have pity for His creature Man! Out of the evolutions of a blind Time, He has made the poor weak human being, who in the first days of his sojourn on earth had neither covering nor home. Less protected than the beasts of the forest, he found himself compelled to Think!—to think out his own means of shelter,—to contrive his own weapons of defence. Slowly, and by painful degrees, from Savagery he has emerged to Civilization;—wherefore it is evident that his Maker meant Thought to be his first principle, and Action his second. He who does not work, shall not eat;—he who does not use all his faculties for improvement, shall by and by have none to use. Injustice and corruption are amongst us, merely because we ourselves have failed to resist their first inroads. Who is it that complains of wrong? Let him hasten to his own amending,—and he will find a thousand hands, a thousand hearts ready to work with him! All Nature is on the side of health in the body, as of health in the State. All Nature fights against disease,—physical and moral. Therefore do not,—dear friends and children!—sit idle and passive, submitting yourselves to be deceived, as if you had no force to withstand deception! Show that you hate lies, and will have none of them,—show that you will not be imposed upon—and decline to be led or governed by party agents, who persuade you to your own and your country's destruction! The voice of the People can no longer be heard in a purchased Press;—let it echo forth then, in stronger form than ephemeral print, which to-day is glanced at, and to-morrow is forgotten;—wherever and whenever you are given the chance to meet, and to speak, let your authority as the workers, the ratepayers, and supporters of the State be heard; and do not You, without whom even the King could not keep his throne, consent to be set aside as the Unvalued Majority! Prove, by your own firm attitude that without You, nothing can be done!

It is time, oh people of my heart!—it is time you spoke clearly! God is moving His thought through your souls—God stirs in you the fear, the discontent, the suspicion that all is not well with your country;—and it is the Spirit of God which breathes in the warning note of the time—

> "'Hark to the voice of the time!
>   The multitude think for
> themselves,
>   And weigh their condition each one;
>   The drudge has
> a spirit sublime,
>   And whether he hammers or delves,
>   He reads
> when his labour is done;
>   And learns, though he groan under poverty's ban,
>   That freedom to Think, is the birthright of man!'

"Learn," she continued,—as a low deep murmur of agreement ran through the room; "Learn to what strange uses God puts even such men of this world, whose sole existence has been for the cause of amassing money! They have acted as the merest machines, gathering in the millions;— gathering, gathering them in! For what purpose? Lo, they are smitten down in the prime of their lives, and the gold they have piled up is at once scattered! Much of it becomes used for educational purposes;— and some of these dead millionaires have, as it were thrown Education at the heads of the people, and almost pauperised it. Far away in Great Britain, a millionaire has recently made the Scottish University education 'free' to all students,—instead of, as it used to be, hard to get, and well worth working to win. Now,—through the wealth of one man, it is turned into a pauper's allowance;—like offering the smallest silver coin to a reduced gentleman. The pride,—the skill,— the self-renunciation,— the strong determination to succeed, which form fine character, and which taught the struggling student to win his own University education, are all wiped out;— there is no longer any necessity for the practice of these manly and self-sustaining virtues. The harm that will be done is probably not yet perceivable; but it will be incalculable. Education, turned into a kind of pauper's monopoly, will have widely different results to those just now imagined! But with all the contemptuous throwing out of the unneeded kitchen-waste of millionaires,—still Education is the thing to take at any price, and under any circumstances;—because it alone is capable of giving power! It alone will 'put down the mighty from their seats, and exalt the humble and the meek.' It alone will give us the force to fight our taskmasters with their own weapons, and to place them where they should be, coequal with us, but not superior,—considerate of us, but not commanding us,—and above all things, bound to make their records of such work as they do for the State—clean!"

A hurricane of applause interrupted her,—she waited till it subsided, then went on quietly.

"There should be no scheming in the dark; no secret contracts for which we have to pay blindly;—no refusal to explain the way in which the people's hard-earned money is spent; and before foreign urbanities and diplomacies and concessions are allowed to take up time in the Senate, it is necessary that the frightful and abounding evils of our own land,—our own homes,—be considered. For this we purpose to demand redress,—and not only to demand it, but to obtain it! Ministers may refuse to hear us; but the Country's claims are greater than any Ministry! A King's displeasure may cause court-parasites to tremble— but a People's Honour is more to be guarded than a thousand thrones!"

As she concluded with these words, she seemed to grow taller, nobler, more inspired and commanding,—and while the applause was yet shaking the rafters of the hall, she left the platform. Shouts of "Lotys! Lotys!" rang out again and again with passionate bursts of cheering,— and in response to it she came back, and by a slight gesture commanded silence.

"Dear friends, I thank you all for listening to me!" she said simply, her rich voice trembling a little; "I speak only with a woman's impulse and unwisdom—just as I think and feel—and always out of my great love for you! As you all know, I have no interests to serve;—I am only Lotys, your own poor friend,—one who works with you, and dwells among you, seeing and sharing your hard lives, and wishing with all my heart that I could help you to be happier and freer! My life is at your service,—my love for you is all too great for any words to express,— and my gratitude for your faith and trust in me forms my daily thanksgiving! Now, dear children all,—for you are truly as children in your patience, submission and obedience to bitter destiny!—I will ask you to disperse quietly without noise or confusion, or any trouble that may give to the paid men of law ungrateful work to do;—and in your homes, think of me!—remember my words!—and while you maintain order by the steadiness and reasonableness of your difficult lives, still avoid and resent that slavish obedience to the yoke fastened upon you by capitalists,—who have no other comfort to offer you in poverty than the workhouse; and no other remedy for the sins into which you are thrust by their neglect, than the prison! Take, and keep the rights of your humanity!—the right to think,—the right to speak,—the right to know what is being done with the money you patiently earn for others;— and work, all together in unity. Put aside all petty differences,—all small rancours and jealousies; and even as a Ministry may unite to defraud and deceive you, so do you, the People, unite to expose the fraud, and reject the deception! There is no voice so resonant and convincing as the voice of the public; there is no power on earth more strong or more irresistible than the power of the People!"

She stood for one moment more,—silent; her eyes brilliant, her face beautiful with inspired thought,—then with a quiet, half-deprecatory gesture, in response to the fresh outbreak of passionate cheering, she retired from the platform. Pasquin Leroy, whose eyes had been riveted on her from the first to the last word of her oration, now started as from a dream, and rose up half-unconsciously, passing his hand across his brow, as though to exorcise some magnetic spell that had crept over his brain. His face was flushed, his pulses were throbbing quickly. His companions, Max Graub and Axel Regor, looked at him inquisitively. The audience was beginning to file out of the hall in orderly groups.

"What next?" said Graub; "Shall ye go?"

"I suppose so," said Leroy, with a quick sigh, and forcing a smile; "But—I should have liked to speak with her——"

At that moment his shoulder was touched by a man he recognised as Johan Zegota. He gave the sign of the Revolutionary Committee bond, to which Leroy and his comrades responded.

"Will you all three come over the way?" whispered Zegota cautiously; "We are entertaining Lotys to supper at the inn opposite,—the landlord is one of us. Thord saw you sitting here, and sent me to ask you to join us."

"With pleasure," assented Leroy; "We will come at once!"

Zegota nodded and disappeared.

"So you will see the end of this escapade!" said Max Graub, a trifle crossly. "It would have been much better to go home!"

"You have enjoyed escapades in your time, have you not, my friend? Some even quite recently?" returned Leroy gaily. "One or two more will not hurt you!"

They edged their way out among the quietly moving crowd, and happening to push past General Bernhoff, that personage gave an almost imperceptible salute, which Leroy as imperceptibly returned. It was clear that the Chief of Police was acquainted with Pasquin Leroy, the 'spy' on whose track he had been sent by Carl Perousse, and moreover, that he was evidently in no hurry to arrest him. At any rate he allowed him to pass with his friends unmolested, out of the People's Assembly Rooms, and though he followed him across the road, 'shadowing him,' as it were, into a large tavern, whose lighted windows betokened some entertainment within, he did not enter the hostelry himself, but contented his immediate humour by walking past it to a considerable distance off, and then slowly back again. By and by Max Graub came out and beckoned to him, and after a little earnest conversation Bernhoff walked off altogether, the ring of his martial heels echoing for some time along the pavement, even after he had disappeared. And from within the lighted tavern came the sound of a deep, harmonious, swinging chorus—

"Way, make way!—for our banner is unfurled,
    Let each man
  stand by his neighbour!
    The thunder of our footsteps shall roll
  through the world,
      In the March of the Men of Labour!"

"Yes!" said Max Graub, pausing to listen ere re-entering the tavern— "If—and it is a great 'if'—if every man will stand by his neighbour, the thunder will be very loud,—and by all the deities that ever lived in the Heaven blue, it is a thunder that is likely to last some time! The possibility of standing by one's neighbour is the only doubtful point!"

CHAPTER XX
THE SCORN OF KINGS

I NSIDE the tavern, from whence the singing proceeded, there was a strange scene,—somewhat disorderly yet picturesque. Lotys, seated at the head of a long supper-table, had been crowned by her admirers with a wreath of laurels,—and as she sat more or less silent, with a rather weary expression on her face, she looked like the impersonation of a Daphne, exhausted by the speed of her flight from pursuing Apollo. Beside her, nestling close against her caressingly, was a little girl with great black Spanish eyes,—eyes full of an appealing, half-frightened wistfulness, like those of a hunted animal. Lotys kept one arm round the child, and every now and again spoke to her some little caressing word. All the rest of the guests at the supper-board were men,—and all of them members of the Revolutionary Committee. When Pasquin Leroy and his friends entered, there was a general clapping of hands, and the pale countenance of Lotys flushed a delicate rose-red, as she extended her hand to each.

"You begin your career with us very well!" she said gently, her eyes resting musingly on Leroy; "I had not expected to see you to-night!"

"Madame, I had never heard you speak," he answered; and as he addressed her, he pressed her hand with unconscious fervour, while his eloquent eyes dilated and darkened, as, moved by some complex emotion, she quickly withdrew her slender fingers from his clasp. "And I felt I should never know you truly as you are, till I saw you face the people. Now——"

He paused. She looked at him wonderingly, and her heart began to beat with a strange quick thrill. It is not always easy to see the outlines of a soul's development, or the inchoate formation of a great love,— and though everything in a certain sense moved her and appealed to her that was outside herself, it was difficult to her to believe or to admit that she, in her own person, might be the cause of an entirely new set of thoughts and emotions in the mind of one man. Seeing he was silent, she repeated softly and with a half smile.

"'Now'?"

"Now," continued Leroy quickly, and in a half-whisper; "I do know you partly,—but I must know you more! You will give me the chance to do that?"

His look said more than his words, and her face grew paler than before. She turned from him to the child at her side—

"Pequita, are you very tired?"

"No!" was the reply, given brightly, and with an upward glance of the dark eyes.

"That is right! Pasquin Leroy my friend! this is Pequita,—the child we told you of the other night, the only daughter of Sholto. She will dance for us presently, will you not, my little one?"

"Yes, indeed!" and the young face lighted up swiftly at the suggestion; while Leroy, taking the seat indicated to him at the supper-table, experienced a tumult of extraordinary sensations,—the chief one of which was, that he felt himself to have been 'snubbed,' very quietly but effectually, by a woman who had succeeded, though he knew not how, in suddenly awakening in him a violent fever of excitement, to which he was at present unable to give a name. Rallying himself, however, he glanced up and down the board smilingly, lifting his glass to salute Sergius Thord, who responded from his place at the bottom of the table,—and very soon he regained his usual placidity, for he had enormous strength of will, and kept an almost despotic tyranny over his feelings. His companions, Max Graub and Axel Regor, were separated from him, and from each other, at different sides of the table, and Paul Zouche the poet, was almost immediately opposite to him. He was glad to see that he was next but one to Lotys—the man between them being a desperado-looking fellow with a fierce moustache, and exceedingly gentle eyes,— who, as he afterwards discovered, was one of the greatest violinists in the world,— the favourite of kings and Courts,—and yet for all that, a prominent member of the Revolutionary Committee. The supper, which was of a simple, almost frugal character, was soon served, and the landlord, in setting the first plate before Lotys, laid beside it a knot of deep crimson roses, as an offering of homage and obedience from himself. She thanked him with a smile and glance, and taking up the flowers, fastened them at her breast. Conversation now became animated and general; and one of the men present, a delicate- looking young fellow, with a head resembling somewhat that of Keats, started a discussion by saying suddenly—

"Jost has sold out all his shares in that new mine that was started the other day. It looks as if he did not think, after all his newspaper puffs, that the thing was going to work."

"If Jost has sold, Perousse will," said his neighbour; "The two are concerned together in the floating of the whole business."

"And yet another piece of news!" put in Paul Zouche suddenly; "For if we talk of stocks and shares, we talk of money! What think you, my friends! I, Paul Zouche, have been offered payment for my poems! This very afternoon! Imagine! Will not the spheres fall? A poet to be paid for his poems is as though one should offer the Creator a pecuniary consideration for creating the flowers!"

His face was flushed, and his eyes deliriously bright.

"Listen, my Sergius!" he said; "Wonders never cease in this world; but this is the most wonderful of all wonders! Out of the merest mischief and monkeyish malice, the other day I sent my latest book of poems to the King—"

"Shame! shame!" interrupted a dozen voices. "Against the rules, Paul! You have broken the bond!"

Paul Zouche laughed loudly.

"How you yell, my baboons!" he cried; "How you screech about the rules of your lair! Wait till you hear! You surely do not suppose I sent the book out of any humility or loyalty, or desire for notice, do you? I sent it out of pure hate and scorn, to show him as a fool-Majesty, that there was something he could not do—something that should last when *he* was forgotten!—a few burning lines that should, like vitriol, eat into his Throne and outlast it! I sent it some days ago, and got an acknowledgment from the flunkey who writes Majesty's letters. But this afternoon I received a much more important document, —a letter from Eugene Silvano, secretary to our very honourable and trustworthy Premier! He informs me in set terms, that his Majesty the King has been pleased to appreciate my work as a poet, to the extent of offering me a hundred golden pieces a year for the term of my natural life! Ha-ha! A hundred golden pieces a year! And thus they would fasten this wild bird of Revolutionary song to a Royal cage, for a bit of sugar! A hundred golden pieces a year! It means food and lodging—warm blankets to sleep in—but it means something else,—loss of independence!"

"Then you will not accept it?" said Pasquin Leroy, looking at him with interest over the rim of the glass from which he was just sipping his wine.

"Accept it! I have already refused it! By swift return of post!"

Shouts of "Bravo! bravo!" echoed around him on all sides; men sprang up and shook hands with him and patted him on the back, and even over the dark face of Sergius Thord there passed a bright illumining smile.

"Zouche, with all thy faults, thou art a brave man!" said the young man with the Keats-like head, who was in reality confidential clerk to one of the largest stock-brokers in the metropolis; "A thousand times better to starve, than to accept Royal alms!"

"To your health, Zouche!" said Lotys, leaning forward, glass in hand. "Your refusal of the King's offered bounty is a greater tragedy than any you have ever tried to write!"

"Hear her!" cried Zouche, exultant; "She knows exactly how to put it! For look you, there are the true elements of tragedy in a worn coat and scant food, while the thoughts that help nations to live or die are burning in one's brain! Then comes a King with a handful of gold—and gold would be useful—it always is! But—by Heaven! to pay a poet for his poems is, as I said before, as if one were to meet the Deity on His way through space, scattering planets and solar systems at a touch, and then to say—'Well done, God! We shall remunerate You for your creative power as long as You shall last—so much per aeon!'"

Leroy laughed.

"You wild soul!" he said; "Would you starve then, rather than accept a king's bounty?"

"I would!" answered Paul. "Look you, my brave Pasquin! Read back over all the centuries, and see the way in which these puppets we call kings have rewarded the greatest thinkers of their times! Is it anywhere recorded that the antique virgin, Elizabeth of England, ever did anything for Shakespeare? True—he might have been 'graciously permitted' to act one of his sublime tragedies before her—by Heaven!— she was only fit to be his scrubbing woman, by intellectual comparison! Kings and Queens have always trembled in their shoes, and on their thrones, before the might of the pen!—and it is natural therefore that they should ignore it as much as conveniently possible. A general, whose military tactics succeed in killing a hundred thousand innocent men receives a peerage and a hundred thousand a year,—a speculator who snatches territory and turns it into stock-jobbing material, is called an 'Empire Builder'; but the man whose Thought destroys or moulds a new World, and raises up a new Civilization, is considered beneath a crowned Majesty's consideration! 'Beneath,' by Heaven!—I, Paul Zouche, may yet mount behind Majesty's chair, and with a single rhyme send his crown spinning into space! Meanwhile, I have flung back his hundred golden pieces, with as much force in the edge of my pen as there would be in my hand if *you* were his Majesty sitting there, and I flung them across the table now!"

Again Leroy laughed. His eyes flashed, but there was a certain regret and wistfulness in them.

"You approve, of course?" he said, turning to Sergius Thord.

Sergius looked for a moment at Zouche with an infinitely grave and kindly compassion.

"I think Paul has acted bravely;" he then said slowly; "He has been true to the principles of our Order. And under the circumstances, it must have been difficult for him to refuse what would have been a certain competence,—"

"Not difficult, Sergius!" exclaimed Zouche, "But purely triumphant!"

Thord smiled,—then went on—"You see, my friend," and he addressed himself now to Leroy; "Kings have scorned the power of the pen too long! Those who possess that power are now taking vengeance for neglect. Thousands of pens all over the world to-day are digging the grave of Royalty, and building up the throne of Democracy. Who is to blame? Royalty itself is to blame, for deliberately passing over the claims of art and intellect, and giving preference to the claims of money. The moneyed man is ever the friend of Majesty,—but the brilliant man of letters is left out in the cold. Yet it is the man of letters who chronicles the age, and who will do so, we may be sure, according to his own experience. As the King treats the essayist, the romancist or the historian, so will these recording scribes treat the

King!"

"It is possible, though," suggested Leroy, "that the King meant well in his offer to our friend Zouche?"

"Quite possible!" agreed Thord; "Only his offer of one hundred gold pieces a year to a man of intellect, is out of all proportion to the salary he pays his cook!"

A slight flush reddened Leroy's bronzed cheek. Thord observed him attentively, and saw that his soul was absorbed by some deep-seated intellectual irritation. He began to feel strangely drawn towards him; his eyes questioned the secret which he appeared to hold in his mind, but the quiet composure of the man's handsome face baffled enquiry. Meanwhile around the table the conversation grew louder and less restrained. The young stockbroker's clerk was holding forth eloquently concerning the many occasions on which he had seen Carl Perousse at his employer's office, carefully going into the closest questions of financial losses or gains likely to result from certain political moves,—and he remembered one day in particular, when, after purchasing a hundred thousand shares in a certain company, Perousse had turned suddenly round on his broker with the cool remark—"If ever you breathe a whisper about this transaction, I will shoot you dead!"

Whereat the broker had replied that it was not his custom to give away his clients' business, and that threats were unworthy of a statesman. Then Perousse had become as friendly as he had been before menacing; and the two had gone out of the office and lunched together. And the confidential clerk thus chattering his news, declared that his employer was now evidently uneasy; and that from that un-easiness he augured a sudden fluctuation or fall in what had lately seemed the most valuable stock in the market.

"And you? Your news, Valdor," cried one or two eager voices, while several heads leaned forward in the direction of the fiercely- moustached man who sat next to Lotys. "Where have you been with your fiddle? Do you arrive among us to-night infected by the pay, or the purple of Royalty?"

Louis Valdor, by birth a Norseman, and by sympathies a cosmopolitan, looked up with a satiric smile in his dark eyes.

"There is no purple left to infect a man with, in the modern slum of Royalty!" he said; "Tobacco-smoke, not incense, perfumes the palaces of the great nowadays— and card-playing is more appreciated than music! Yet I and my fiddle have made many long journeys lately,—and we have sent our messages of Heaven thrilling through the callous horrors of Hell! A few nights since, I played at the Russian Court—before the beautiful Empress—cold as a stone—with her great diamonds flashing on her unhappy breast,—before the Emperor, whose furtive eyes gazed unseeingly before him, as though black Fate hovered in the air—before women, whose lives are steeped in the lowest intrigue—before men, whose faces are as bearded masks, covering the wolf's snarl,—yes!—I played before these,—played with all the chords of my heart vibrating to the violin, till at last a human sigh quivered from the lips of the statuesque Empress,—till a frown crossed the brooding brow of her spouse—till the intriguing women shook off the spell with a laugh, and the men did the same with an oath—and I was satisfied! I received neither 'pay,' nor jewel of recognition,—I had played 'for the honour' of appearing before their Majesties!—but my bow was a wand to wake the little poisoned asp of despair that stings its way into the heart under every Royal mantle of ermine, and that sufficed me!"

"Sometimes," said Leroy, turning towards him; "I pity kings!"

"I' faith, so do I!" returned Valdor. "But only sometimes! And if you had seen as much of them as I have, the 'sometimes' would be rare!"

"Yet you play before them?" put in Max Graub.

"Because I must do so to satisfy the impresarios who advertise me to the public," said Valdor. "Alas!—why will the public be so foolish as to wish their favourite artist to play before kings and queens? Seldom, if ever, do these Royal people understand music,—still less do they understand the musician! Believe me, I have been treated as the veriest scullion by these jacks-in-office; and that I still permit myself to play before them is a duty I owe to this Brotherhood,—because it deepens and sustains my bond with you all. There is no king on the face of the earth who has dignity and nobleness of character enough to command my respect,—much less my reverence! I take nothing from kings, remember!—they dare not offer me money—they dare not insult me with a jewelled pin, such as they would give to a station-master who sees a Royal train off. Only the other day, when I was summoned to play before a certain Majesty, a lord-in-waiting addressed me when I arrived with the insolent words—'You are late, Monsieur Valdor!—You have kept the King waiting!' I replied—'Is that so? I regret it! But having kept his Majesty waiting, I will no longer detain him; au revoir!' And I returned straightway to the carriage in which I had come. Majesty did without his music that evening, owing to the insolence of his flunkey- man! Whether I ever play before him again or not, is absolutely immaterial to me!"

"Tell me," said Pasquin Leroy, pushing the flask of wine over to him as he spoke; "What is it that makes kings so unloved? I hate them myself! —but let us analyse the reasons why."

"Discuss—discuss!" cried Paul Zouche; "Why are kings hated? Let Thord answer first!"

"Yes—yes! Let Thord answer first!" was echoed a dozen times.

Thord, thus appealed to, looked up. His melancholy deep eyes were sombre, yet full of fire,—lonely eyes they were, yearning for love.

"Why are kings hated?" he repeated; "Because today they are the effete representatives of an effete system. I can quite imagine that if, as in olden times, kings had maintained a position of personal bravery, and personal influence on their subjects, they would have been as much beloved as they are now despised. But what we have to see and to recognise is this: in one land we hear of a sovereign who speculates hand-and-glove with low-born Jew contractors and tradesmen,—another monarch makes no secret of his desire to profit financially out of a gambling hell started in his dominions,—another makes his domestic affairs the subject of newspaper comment,—another is always apostrophising the Almighty in public;—another is insane or stupid,— and so on through the whole gamut. Is it not natural that an intelligent People should resent the fact that their visibly governing head is a gambler, or a voluptuary? Myself, I think the growing unpopularity of kings is the result of their incapability for kingship."

"Now let me speak!" cried Paul Zouche excitedly; "There is another root to the matter,—a root like that of a certain tropical orchid, which according to superstition, is shaped like a man, and utters a shriek when it is pulled out of the earth! Pull out this screaming mystery,— hatred of kings! In the first place it is because they are hateful in themselves,—because they have been brought up and educated to take an immeasurable and all-absorbing interest in their own identity, rather than in the lives, hopes and aims of their subjects. In the second—as soon as they occupy thrones, they become overbearing to their best friends. It is a well-known fact that the more loyal and faithful you are to a king, the more completely is he neglectful of you! 'Put not your trust in princes,' sang old David. He knew how untrustworthy they were, being a king himself, and a pious one to boot! Thirdly and lastly,—they only give their own personal attention to their concubines, and leave all their honest and respectable subjects to be dealt with by servants and secretaries. Our King, for example, never smiles so graciously as on Madame Vantine, the wife of Vantine the wine-grower;—and he buys Vantine's wines as well as his wife, which brings in a double profit to the firm!"

Leroy looked up.

"Are you sure of that?"

Zouche met his eyes with a stare and a laugh.

"Sure? Of course I am sure! By my faith, your resemblance to his Majesty is somewhat striking to-night, my bold Leroy! The same straight brows—the same inscrutable, woman-conquering smile! I studied his portrait after the offer of the hundred golden pieces—and I swear you might be his twin brother!"

"I told you so!" replied Leroy imperturbably;—"It is a hateful resemblance! I wish I could rid myself of it. Still after all, there is something unique in being countenanced like a King, and minded as a Socialist!"

"True!" put in Thord gently;—"I am satisfied, Pasquin Leroy, that you are an honest comrade!"

Leroy met his eyes with a grave smile, and touched his glass by way of acknowledgement.

"You do not ask me," he said then, "whether I have been able to serve your Cause in any way since last we met?"

"This is not our regular meeting," said Johan Zegota; "We ask no questions till the general monthly assembly."

"I see!" And Leroy looked whimsically meditative—"Still, as we are all friends and brothers here, there is no harm in conveying to you the fact that I have so far moved, in the appointed way, that Carl Perousse has ordered the discovery and arrest of one Pasquin Leroy, supposed to be a spy on the military defences of the city!"

Lotys gave a little cry.

"Not possible! So soon!"

"Quite possible, Madame," said Leroy inclining his head towards her deferentially. "I have lost no time in doing my duty!" And his eyes flashed upon her with a passionate, half-eager questioning. "I must carry out my Chief's commands!"

"But you are in danger, then?" said Sergius Thord, bending an anxious look of enquiry upon him.

"Not more so than you, or any of my comrades are," replied Leroy; "I have commenced my campaign—and I have no doubt you will hear some results of it ere long!"

He spoke so quietly and firmly, yet with such an air of assurance and authority, that something of an electric thrill passed through the entire company, and all eyes were fixed on him in mingled admiration and wonderment.

"Of the 'Corruption of the State,' concerning which our fair teacher has spoken to-night," he continued, with another quick glance at Lotys —"there can be no manner of doubt. But we should, I think, say the 'Corruption of the Ministry' rather than of the State. It is not because a few stock-jobbers rule the Press and the Cabinet, that the State is necessarily corrupt. Remove the corruptors,—sweep the dirt from the house—and the State will be clean."

"It will require a very long broom!" said Paul Zouche. "Take David Jost, for example,—he is the fat Jew-spider of several newspaper webs,—and to sweep him out is not so easy. His printed sheets are read by the million; and the million are deluded into believing him a reliable authority!"

"Nothing so easy as to prove him unreliable," said Leroy composedly; "And then——"

"Then the million will continue to read his journals out of sheer curiosity, to see how long a liar can go on lying!" said Zouche;— "Besides a Jew can turn his coat a dozen times a day; he has inherited Joseph's 'coat of many colours' to suit many opinions. At present Jost supports Perousse, and calls him the greatest statesman living; but if Perousse were once proved a fraud, Jost would pen a sublimely- conscientious leading article, beginning in this strain;—' We are now at liberty to confess that we always had our doubts of M. Perousse!'"

A murmur of angry laughter went round the board.

"There was an article this evening in one of Jost's off-shoot journals," went on Zouche, "which must have been paid for at a considerable cost. It chanted the praises of one Monsignor Del Fortis, —who, it appears, preached a sermon on 'National Education' the other day, and told all the sleepy, yawning people how necessary it was to have Roman Catholic schools in every town and village, in order that souls might be saved. The article ended by saying—'We hear on good authority that his Majesty the King has been pleased to grant a considerable portion of certain Crown lands to the Jesuit Order, for the necessary building of a monastery and schools'——"

"That is a lie!" broke in Pasquin Leroy, with sudden vehemence. "The King is in many respects a scoundrel, but he does not go back on his word!"

Axel Regor looked fixedly across at him, with a warning flash in the light of his cold languid eyes.

"But how do you know that the King has given his word?"

"It was in the paper," said Leroy, more guardedly; "I was reading about it, as you know, on the very night I encountered Thord."

"Ah! But you must recollect, my friend, that a statement in the papers is never true nowadays!" said Max Graub, with a laugh; "Whenever I read anything in the newspaper, unless it is an official telegram, I know it is a lie; and even official telegrams have been known to emanate from unofficial sources!"

By this time supper was nearly over, and the landlord, clearing the remains of the heavier fare, set fruit and wine on the board. Sergius Thord filled his glass, and made a sign to his companions to do the same. Then he stood up.

"To Lotys!" he said, his fine eyes darkening with the passion of his thought. "To Lotys, who inspires our best work, and helps us to retain our noblest ideals!"

All present sprang to their feet.

"To Lotys!"

Pasquin Leroy fixed a straight glance on the subject of the toast, sitting quietly at the head of the table.

"To Lotys!" he repeated; "And may she always be as merciful as she is strong!"

She lifted her dark-blue slumbrous eyes, and met his keen scrutinizing look. A very slight tremulous smile flickered across her lips. She inclined her head gently, and in the same mute fashion thanked them all.

"Play to us, Valdor!" she then said; "And so make answer for me to our friends' good wishes!"

Valdor dived under the table, and brought up his violin case, which he un-locked with jealous tenderness, lifting his instrument as carefully as though it were a sleeping child whom he feared to wake. Drawing the bow across the strings, he invoked a sweet plaintive sound, like the first sigh of the wind among the trees; then, without further preliminary wandered off into a strange labyrinth of melody, wherein it seemed that the voices of women and angels clamoured one against the other,—the appeals of earth with the refusals of Heaven,—the loneliness of life with the fulness of immortality,—so, rising, falling, sobbing, praying, alternately, the music expostulated with humanity in its throbbing chords, till it seemed as if some Divine interposition could alone end the heart-searching argument. Every man sat motionless and mute, listening; Paul Zouche, with his head thrown back and eyes closed as in a dream,—Johan Zegota's hard, plain and careworn face growing softer and quieter in its expression,—while Sergius Thord, leaning on one elbow, covered his brow with one hand to shade the lines of sorrow there.

When Valdor ceased playing, there was a burst of applause.

"You play before kings,—kings should be proud to hear you!" said Leroy.

"Ah! So they should," responded Valdor promptly; "Only it happens that they are not! They treat me merely as a *laquais de place*,—just as they would treat Zouche, had he accepted his Sovereign's offer. But this I will admit,—that mediocre musi-cians always get on very well with Royal persons! I have heard a very great Majesty indeed praise a common little American woman's abominable singing, as though she were a prima-donna, and saw him give a jewelled cigar-case to an amateur pia-nist, whose fingers rattled on the keyboard like bones on a tom-tom. But then the common little American woman invited his Majesty's 'cheres amies' to her house; and the amateur pianist was content to lose money to him at cards! Wheels within wheels, my friend! In a lesser degree the stock-jobber who sets a little extra cash rolling on the Exchange is called an 'Empire Builder.' It is a curious world! But kings were never known to be 'proud' of any really 'great' men in either art or literature; on the contrary, they were always afraid of them, and always will be! Among mu-sicians, the only one who ever got decently honoured by a monarch was Richard Wagner,—and the world swears that *his* Royal patron was mad!"

Paul Zouche opened his eyes, filled his glass afresh, and tossed down the liquor it contained at a gulp.

"Before we have any more music," he said, "and before the little Pequita gives us the dance which she has promised,—not to us, but to Lotys—we ought to have prayers!"

A loud laugh answered this strange proposition.

"I say we ought to have prayers!" repeated Zouche with semi-solemn earnestness,—"You talk of news,—news in telegram,—news in brief,— official scratchings for the day and hour,—and do you take no thought for the fact that his Holiness the Pope is ill—perhaps dying?"

He stared wildly round upon them all; and a tolerant smile passed over the face of the company.

"Well, if that be so, Paul," said a man next to him, "it is not to be wondered at. The Pope has arrived at a great age!"

"No age at all!—no age at all!" declared Zouche. "A saint of God should live longer than a pauper! What of the good old lady admitted to hospital the other day whose birth certificate proved her beyond doubt to be one hundred and twenty-one years old? The dear creature had not married;—nor has his Holiness the Pope,—the real cause of death is in neither of them! Why should he not live as long as his aged sister, possessing, as he does the keys of Heaven? He need not unlock the little golden door, even for himself, unless he likes. That is true orthodoxy! Pasquin Leroy, you bold imitation of a king, more wine!"

Leroy filled the glass he held out to him. The glances of the company told him Zouche was 'on,' and that it was no good trying to stem the flow of his ideas, or check the inconsequential nature of his speech. Lotys had moved her chair a little back from the table, and with both arms encircling the child, Pequita, was talking to her in low and tender tones.

"Brethren, let us pray!" cried Zouche; "For all we know, while we sit here carousing and drinking to the health of our incomparable Lotys, the soul of St. Peter's successor may be careering through Sphere- Forests, and over Planet-Oceans, up to its own specially built and particularly furnished Heaven! There is only one Heaven, as we all know,—and the space is limited, as it only holds the followers of St. Peter, the good disciple who denied Christ!"

"That is an exploded creed, Zouche," said Thord quietly; "No man of any sense or reason believes such childish nonsense nowadays! The most casual student of astronomy knows better."

"Astronomy! Fie, for shame!" And Zouche gave a mock-solemn shake of the head; "A wicked science! A great heresy! What are God's Facts to the Church Fallacies? Science proves that there are millions and millions of solar systems,— millions and millions of worlds, no doubt inhabited;—yet the Church teaches that there is only one Heaven, specially reserved for good Roman Catholics; and that St. Peter and his successors keep the keys of it. God,—the Deity—the Creator,—the Supreme Being, has evidently nothing at all to do with it. In fact, He is probably outside it! And of a surety Christ, with His ideas of honesty and equality, could never possibly get into it!"

"There you are right!" said Valdor; "Your words remind me of a conversation I overheard once between a great writer of books and a certain Prince of the blood Royal. 'Life is a difficult problem!' said the Prince, smoking a fat cigar. 'To the student, it is, Sir,' replied the author; 'But to the sensualist, it is no more than the mud-stye of the swine,—he noses the refuse and is happy! He has no need of the Higher life, and plainly the Higher life has no need of him. Of course,' he added with covert satire, 'your Highness believes in a Higher life?' 'Of course, of course!' responded the Royal creature, unconscious of any veiled sarcasm; 'We must be Christians before anything!' And that same evening this hypocritical Highness 'rooked' a foolish young fellow of over one thousand English pounds!"

"Perfectly natural!" said Zouche. "The fashionable estimate of Christianity is to go to church o' Sundays, and say 'I believe in God,' and to cheat at cards on all the other days of the week, as active testimony to a stronger faith in the devil!"

"And with it all, Zouche," said Lotys suddenly; "There is more good in humanity than is apparent."

"And more bad, beloved Lotys," returned Paul. "Tout le deux se disent! But let us think of the Holy Father!—he who, after long years of patient and sublime credulity, is now, for all we know, bracing himself to take the inevitable plunge into the dark waters of Eternity! Poor frail old man! Who would not pity him! His earthly home has been so small and cosy and restricted,—he has been taken such tender care of— the faithful have fallen at his feet in such adoring thousands,—and now—away from all this warmth and light and incense, and colour of pictures and stained-glass windows, and white statuary and purple velvets, and golden-fringed palanquins,—now—out into the cold he must go!—out into the darkness and mystery and silence!—where all the former generations of the world, immense and endless, and all the old religions, are huddled away in the mist of the mouldered past!—out into the thick blackness, where maybe the fiery heads of Bel and the Dragon may lift themselves upward and leer at him!—or he may meet the frightful menace of some monstrous Mexican deity, once worshipped with the rites of blood!—out—out into the unknown, unimaginable Amazement must the poor naked Soul go shuddering on the blast of death, to face he truly knows not what!—but possibly he has such a pitiful blind trust in good, that he may be re-transformed into some pleasant living consciousness that shall be more agreeable even than that of Pope of Rome! 'Mourir c'est rien,—mais souffrir!' That is the hard part of it! Let us all pray for the Pope, my friends!—he is an old man!"

"When you are silent, Zouche," said Thord with a half smile; "We may perhaps meditate upon him in our thoughts,—but not while you talk thus volubly! You take up time—and Pequita is getting tired."

"Yes," said Lotys; "Pequita and I will go home, and there will be no dancing to-night."

"No, Lotys! You will not be so cruel!" said Zouche, pushing his grey hair back from his brows, while his wild eyes glittered under the tangle, like the eyes of a beast in its lair; "Think for a moment! I do not come here and bore you with my poems, though I might very well do so! Some of them are worth hearing, I assure you;—even the King— curse him!—has condescended to think so, or else why should he offer me pay for them? Kings are not so ready to part with money, even when it is Government money! In England once a Premier named Gladstone, gave two hundred and fifty pounds a year pension to the French Prince, Lucien Buonaparte, 'for his researches into Celtic literature'! Bah! There were many worthier native-born men who had worked harder on the same subject, to choose from,—without giving good English money to a Frenchman! There is a case of your Order and Justice, Lotys! You spoke to-night of these two impossible things. Why will you touch on such subjects? You know there is no Order and no Justice anywhere! The Universe is a chance whirl of gas and atoms; though where the two mischiefs come from nobody knows! And why the devil we should be made the prey of gas and atoms is a mystery which no Church can solve!"

As he said this, there was a slight movement of every head towards Lotys, and enquiring eyes looked suggestively at her. She saw the look, and responded to it.

"You are wrong, Zouche!—I have always told you you are wrong," she said emphatically, "It is in your own disordered thoughts that you see no justice and no order,—but Order there is, and Justice there is,— and Compensation for all that seems to go wrong. There is an Intelligence at the core of Creation! It is not for us to measure that Intelligence, or to set any limits to it. Our duty is to recognize it, and to set ourselves as much as possible in harmony with it. Do you never, in sane moments, study the progress of humanity? Do you not see that while the brute creation remains stationary, (some specimens of it even becoming extinct), man goes step by step to higher results? This is, or should be, sufficient proof that death is not the end for us. This world is only one link in our chain of intended experience. I think it depends on ourselves as to what we make of it. Thought is a great power by which we mould ourselves and others; and we have no right to subvert that power to base uses, or to poison it by distrust of good, or disbelief in the Supreme Guidance. You would be a thousand times better as a man, Zouche, and far greater as a poet, if you could believe in God!"

She spoke with eloquence and affectionate earnestness, and among all the men there was a moment's silence.

"Well, *you* believe in Him;" said Zouche at last, "and I will catch hold of your angel's robe as you pass into His Presence and say to Him;—' Here comes poor Zouche, who wrote of beautiful things among ugly surroundings, and who, in order to be true to his friends, chose poverty rather than the gold of a king!'"

Lotys smiled, very sweetly and indulgently.

"Such a plea would stand you in good stead, Zouche! To be always true to one's friends, and to persistently believe in beauty, is a very long step towards Heaven!"

"I did not say I *believed* in beauty," said Zouche suddenly and obstinately;—"I dream it—I think it—but I do not see it! To me the world is one Horror—nothing but a Grave into which we all must fall! The fairest face has a hideous skull behind it,—the dazzling blue of the sea covers devouring monsters in its depths—the green fields, the lovely woodlands, are full of vile worms and noxious beetles,—and space itself swarms with thick-strewn worlds,—flaming comets,—blazing nebulae,— among which our earth is but a gnat's wing in a huge flame! Horrible!—horrible!"

And he spoke with a kind of vehement fury. "Let us not think of it! Why should we insist on Truth? Let us have lies!— dear, sweet lies and fond delusions! Let us believe that men are all honest, and women all loving!—that there are virgins and saints and angels, as well as bishops and curates, looking after us in this wild world of terror,—oh, yes!—let us believe!—better the Pope's little private snuggery of a Heaven, than the crushing truth which says 'Our God is a consuming fire'! Knowledge deepens sorrow,—truth kills!—we must—we must have a little love, and a few lies to lean upon!"

His voice faltered,—and a sudden ashy paleness overspread his features,—his head fell back helplessly, and he seemed transfixed and insensible. Leroy and one or two of the others rose in alarm, thinking he had swooned, but Sergius Thord warned them back by a sign. The little Pequita, slipping from the arms of Lotys, went softly up to him.

"Paul! Dear Paul!" she said in her soft childish tones.

Zouche stirred, and stretching out one hand, groped with it blindly in the air. Pequita took it, warming it between her own little palms.

"Paul!" she said; "Do wake up! You have been asleep such a long time!"

He opened his eyes. The grey pallor passed from his face; he lifted his head and smiled.

"So! There you are, Pequita!" he said gently; "Dear little one! So brave and cheerful in your hard life!"

He lifted her small brown hand, and kissed it. The feverish tension of his brain relaxed,—and two large tears welled up in his eyes, and rolled down his cheeks. "Poor little girl!" he murmured weakly; "Poor little hard-working girl!"

All the men sat silent, watching the gradual softening of Zouche's drunken delirium by the mere gentle caress of the child; and Pasquin Leroy was conscious of a curious tightening of the muscles of his throat, and a straining compassion at his heart, which was more like acute sympathy with the griefs and sins of humanity than any emotion he had ever known. He saw that the thoughtful, pitiful eyes of Lotys were full of tears, and he longed, in quite a foolish, almost boyish fashion, to take her in his arms and by a whispered word of tenderness, persuade those tears away. Yet he was a man of the world, and had seen and known enough. But had he known them humanly? Or only from the usual standpoint of masculine egotism? As he thought this, a strain of sweet and solemn music stole through the room,—Louis Valdor had risen to his feet, and holding the violin tenderly against his heart, was coaxing out of its wooden cavity a plaintive request for sympathy and attention. Such delicious music thrilled upon the dead silence as might have fitted Shelley's exquisite lines.

> "There the voluptuous nightingales,
>   Are awake through all the broad noon-day,
> When one with bliss or sadness fails,
>   And through the windless ivy-boughs
> Sick with sweet love, droops dying away
>   On its mate's music-panting bosom;
>   Another from the swinging blossom,
> Watching to catch the languid close
>   Of the last strain; then lifts on high
>   The wings of the weak melody,
> Till some new strain of feeling bear
>   The song, and all the woods are mute;
> When there is heard through the dim air
> The rush of wings, and rising there
>   Like many a lake-surrounded flute
> Sounds overflow the listener's brain,
> So sweet that joy is almost pain."

"Thank God for music!" said Sergius Thord, as Valdor laid aside his bow; "It exorcises the evil spirit from every modern Saul!"

"Sometimes!" responded Valdor; "But I have known cases where the evil spirit has been roused by music instead of suppressed. Art, like virtue, has two sides!"

Zouche was still holding Pequita's hand. He looked ill and exhausted, like a man who had passed through a violent paroxysm of fever.

"You are a good child, Pequita!" he was saying softly; "Try to be always so!—it is difficult—but it is easier to a woman than to a man! Women have more of good in them than men!"

"How about the dance?" suggested Thord; "The hour is late,—close on midnight—and Lotys must be tired.”

“Shall I dance now?” enquired Pequita.

Lotys smiled and nodded. Four or five of the company at once got up, and helped to push aside the table.

“Will you play for me, Monsieur Valdor?” asked the little girl, still standing by the side of Zouche.

“Of course, my child! What shall it be? Something to suggest a fairy hopping over mushrooms in the moonlight?—or Shakespeare’s Ariel swinging on a cobweb from a bunch of may?”

Pequita considered, and for a moment did not reply, while Zouche, still holding her little brown hand, kissed it again.

“You are very fond of dancing?” asked Pasquin Leroy, looking at her dark face and big black eyes with increasing interest.

She smiled frankly at him.

“Yes! I would like to dance before the King!”

“Fie, fie, Pequita!” cried Johan Zegota, while murmurs of laughter and playful cries of ‘Shame, Shame’ echoed through the room.

“Why not?” said Pequita; “It would do me good, and my father too! Such poor, sad people come to the theatre where I dance,—they love to see me, and I love to dance for them—but then—they too would be pleased if I could dance at the Royal Opera, because they would know I could then earn enough money to make my father comfortable.”

“What a very matter-of-fact statement in favour of kings!” exclaimed Max Graub;—”Here is a child who does not care a button for a king as king; but she thinks he would be useful as a figure-head to dance to,— for idiotic Fashion, grouping itself idiotically around the figure- head, would want to see her dance also—and then—oh simple conclusion!—she would be able to support her father! Truly, a king has often been put to worse uses!”

“I think,” said Pasquin Leroy, “I could manage to get you a trial at the Royal Opera, Pequita! I know the manager.”

She looked up with a sudden blaze of light in her eyes, sprang towards him, dropped on one knee with an exquisite grace, and kissed his hand.

“Oh!—you will be goodness itself!” she cried;—”And I will be grateful—indeed

I will!—so grateful!"

He was startled and amazed at her impulsive action, and taking her little hand, gently pressed it.

"Poor child!" he said;—"You must not thank me till I succeed. It is very little to do—but I will do all I can."

"Someone else will be grateful too!" said Lotys in her rich thrilling voice; and her eyes rested on him with that wonderful magnetic sweetness which drew his soul out of him as by a spell; while Zouche, only partially understanding the conversation said slowly:—

"Pequita deserves all the good she can get; more than any of us. We do nothing but try to support ourselves; and we talk a vast amount about supporting others,—but Pequita works all the time and says nothing. And she is a genius—she does not know it, but she is. Give us the Dagger Dance, Pequita! Then our friend Leroy can judge of you at your best, and make good report of you."

Pequita looked at Lotys and received a sign of assent. She then nodded to Valdor.

"You know what to play?"

Valdor nodded in return, and took up his violin. The company drew back their seats, and sat, or stood aside, from the centre of the room. Pequita disappeared for a moment, and returned divested of the plain rusty black frock she had worn, and merely clad in a short scarlet petticoat, with a low white calico bodice—her dark curls tumbling in disorder, and grasping in her right hand a brightly polished, unsheathed dagger. Valdor began to play, and with the first wild chords the childish figure swayed, circled, and leaped forward like a young Amazon, the dagger brandished aloft, and gleaming here and there as though it were a snaky twist of lightning. Very soon Pasquin Leroy found himself watching the evolutions of the girl dancer with fascinated interest. Nothing so light, so delicate or so graceful had he ever seen as this little slight form bending to and fro, now gliding with the grace of a swan on water—now leaping swiftly as a fawn,— while the attitudes she threw herself into, sometimes threatening, sometimes defiant, and often commanding, with the glittering steel weapon held firmly in her tiny hand, were each and all pictures of youthful pliancy and animation. As she swung and whirled,—sometimes pirouetting so swiftly that her scarlet skirt looked like a mere red flower in the wind,—

her bright eyes flashed, her dark hair tangled itself in still richer masses, and her lips, crimson as the pomegranate, were half parted with her panting breath.

"Brava! Brava!" shouted the men, becoming more and more excited as their eyes followed the flash of the dagger she held, now directed towards them, now shaken aloft, and again waved threateningly from side to side, or pointed at her own bosom, while her little feet twinkled over the floor in a maze of intricate and perfectly performed steps;— and "Brava!" cried Pasquin Leroy, as breathless, but still glowing and bright with her exertions, she suddenly out of her own impulse, dropped on one knee before him with the glittering dagger pointed straight at his heart!

"Would that please the King?" she asked, her pearly teeth gleaming into a mischievous smile between the red lips.

"If it did not, he would be a worse fool than even I take him for!" replied Leroy, as she sprang up again, and confronted him. "Here is a little souvenir from me, child!—and if ever you do dance before his Majesty, wear it for my sake!"

He took from his pocket a ring, in which was set a fine brilliant of unusual size and lustre.

She looked at it a moment as he held it out to her.

"Oh, no," she faltered, "I cannot take it—I cannot! Lotys dear, you know I cannot!"

Lotys, thus appealed to, left her seat and came forward. Taking the ring from Leroy's hand, she examined it a moment, then gently returned it.

"This is too great a temptation for Pequita, my friend," she said quietly, but firmly. "In duty bound, she would have to sell it in order to help her poor father. She could not justly keep it. Let me be the arbiter in this matter. If you can carry out your suggestion, and obtain for her an engagement at the Royal Opera, then give it to her, but not till then! Do you not think I am right?"

She spoke so sweetly and persuasively, that Leroy was profoundly touched. What he would have liked would have been to give the child a roll of gold pieces,— but he was playing a strange part, and the time to act openly was not yet.

"It shall be as you wish, Madame!" he said with courteous deference. "Pequita, the first time you dance before the King, this shall be yours!"

He put aside the jewel, and Pequita kissed his hand impulsively,—as impulsively she kissed the lips of her friend Lotys—and then came the general dispersal and break-up of the assembly.

"Tell me;" said Sergius Thord, catching Leroy's hand in a close and friendly grasp ere bidding him farewell; "Are you in very truth in personal danger on account of serving our Cause?"

"No!" replied Leroy frankly, returning the warm pressure; "And rest assured that if I were, I would find means to elude it! I have managed to frighten Carl Perousse, that is all—and Jost!"

"Jost!" echoed Sergius; "The Colossus of the Press? Surely it would take more than one man to frighten him!"

Leroy laughed.

"I grant you the Jewish centres of journalism are difficult to shake! But they all depend on stocks and shares!"

A touch on his arm caused him to turn round,—Paul Zouche confronted both him and Thord, with a solemn worn face, and lack-lustre eyes.

"Good-night, friends!" he said; "I have not kicked at a king with my boot, but I have with my brain!—and the effort is exhausting! I am going home to bed."

"Where is your home?" asked Leroy suddenly.

Zouche looked mysterious.

"In a palace, dear sir! A palace of golden air, peopled with winged dreams! No money could purchase it;—no 'Empire Builder' could build it!—it is mine and mine alone! And I pay no taxes!"

"Will you put this to some use for me?" said Leroy, holding out a gold piece; "Simply as comrade and friend?"

Zouche stared at him.

"You mean it?"

"Of course I mean it! Zouche, believe me, you are going to be the fashion! You will be able to do *me* a good turn before long!"

Zouche took the gold piece, and as he took it, pressed the giver's hand.

"You mean well!" he said tremulously; "You know—as Sergius does, that I am poor,—often starving—often drunk—but you know also that there is something *here*!"—and he touched his forehead meaningly. "But to be the 'fashion'! Bah! I do not belong to the Trade-ocracy! Nobody becomes the 'fashion' nowadays unless they have cheated their neighbours by short weight and falsified accounts! Good-night! You might be the King from your looks;—but you have something better than kingship—Heart! Good-night, Pequita! You danced well! Good-night, Lotys! You spoke well! Everyone does everything well, except poor Zouche!"

Pequita ran up to him.

"Good-night, dear Paul!"

He stooped and kissed her gently.

"Good-night, little one! If ever you show your twinkling feet at the Opera, *you* will be the 'fashion'—and will you remember Paul then?"

"Always—always!" said Pequita tenderly; "Father and Lotys and I will always love you!"

Zouche gave a short laugh.

"Always love me! Me! Well!—what strange things children will say, not knowing in the least what they mean!"

He gave a vague salute to the entire company, and walked out of the tavern with drooping head. Others followed him,—every man in going, shook hands with Lotys and Sergius Thord,—the lamps were extinguished, and the landlord standing in the porch of his tavern watched them all file out, and bade them all a cordial fare-well. Pequita's home was with her father in the house where Sergius Thord dwelt, and Lotys kissing her tenderly good-night, left her to Thord's care.

"And who will see you home, Lotys?" enquired Thord.

"May I for once have that honour?" asked Pasquin Leroy. His two companions stared in undisguised amazement, and there was a moment's silence.

Then Lotys spoke.

"You may!" she said simply.

There was another silence while she put on her hat, and wrapped herself in her long dark cloak. Then Thord took Pequita by the hand.

"Good-night, Lotys!"

"Good-night, Sergius!"

Leroy turned to his two friends and spoke to them in a low tone.

"Go your ways!" he said peremptorily; "I will join you later!"

Vain were their alarmed looks of remonstrance; and in another moment all the party had separated, and only Max Graub and Axel Regor remained on the pavement outside the tavern, disconsolately watching two figures disappearing in the semi-shadowed moonlight—Pasquin Leroy and Lotys— walking closely side by side.

"Was there ever such a drama as this?" muttered Graub, "He may lose his life at any moment!"

"If he does," responded Regor, "It will not be our fault. We do our best to guard him from the consequence of one folly,—and he straightway runs into another! There is no help for it; we have sworn to obey him, and we must keep our oath!"

They passed slowly along the street, too absorbed in their own uncomfortable reflections for the interchange of many words. By the rules of the Revolutionary Committee, they were not allowed 'to follow or track any other member' so they were careful to walk in a reverse direction to that taken by their late comrades. The great bell of the Cathedral boomed midnight as they climbed towards the citadel, and the pale moon peeping whitely through piled-up fleecy clouds, shed a silver glare upon the quiet sea. And down into the 'slums,' down, and ever deeper, into the sad and cheerless 'Quarter of the Poor' Pasquin Leroy walked as though he trod lightly on a path of flowers,—his heart beating high, and his soul fully awakened within him, thrilled, he knew not why, to the heart's core by the soft low voice of Lotys,—and glad that in the glimpses of the moonlight her eyes were occasionally lifted to his face, with something of a child's trust, if not of a woman's tenderness.

CHAPTER XXI
AN INVITATION TO COURT

THE spring was now advancing into full summer, and some time had passed since the Socialist party had gathered under their leaders to the voice of Lotys. Troublous days appeared to be impending for the Senate, and rumours of War,—war sometimes apparently imminent, and again suddenly averted,—had from time to time worried the public through the Press. But what was even more disturbing to the country, was the proposed infliction of new, heavy and irritating taxes, which had begun to affect the popular mind to the verge of revolt. Twice since Lotys had spoken at the People's Assembly Rooms had Sergius Thord addressed huge mass meetings, which apparently the police had no orders to disperse, and his power over the multitude was increasing by leaps and bounds. Whenever he spoke, wherever he worked, the indefatigable Pasquin Leroy was constantly at his side, and he, in his turn began to be recognized by the Revolutionary Committee as one of their most energetic members, —able, resolute, and above all, of an invaluably inscrutable and self- contained demeanour. His two comrades were not so effectual in their assistance, and appeared to act merely in obedience to his instructions. Their attitude, however, suited everyone concerned as well as, if not better than, if they had been overzealous. Owing to what Leroy had stated concerning the possibility of his arrest as a spy, his name was never mentioned in public by one single member of the Brotherhood; and to the outside Socialist following, he therefore appeared simply as one of the many who worked under Sergius Thord's command. Meanwhile, there were not lacking many other subjects for popular concern and comment; all of which in their turn gave rise to anxious discussion and vague conjecture. A Cabinet Council had been held by the Premier, at which, without warning, the King had attended personally, but the results were not made known to the public. Yet the general impression was that his Majesty seemed to be perfectly indifferent to the feelings or the well-being of his subjects; in fact, as some of them said with dismal shakings of the head, "It was all a part of the system; kings were not allowed to do anything even for the benefit of their people." And rising Socialism, ever growing stronger, and amassing in its ranks all the youthful and ambitious intellects of the time, agreed and swore that it was time for a Republic. Only by a complete change of Government could the cruelly-increasing taxation be put down; and if Government was to be changed, why not the dummy figure-head of Government as well?

Thus Rumour talked, sometimes in whispers—sometimes in shouts;—but through it all the life of the Court and fashion went on in the same way,—the King continued to receive with apparent favour the most successful and most moneyed men from all parts of the world; the Queen drove or walked, or rode;—and the only prospective change in the social routine was the report that the Crown Prince was about to leave the country for a tour round the world, and that he would start on his journey in his own yacht about the end of the month. The newspapers made a great fuss in print over this projected tour; but the actual people were wholly indifferent to it. They had seen very little of the Crown Prince,—certainly not enough to give him their affection; and whether he left the kingdom or stayed in it concerned them not at all. He had done nothing marked or decisive in his life to show either talent, originality of character, or resolution; and the many 'puffs' in the press concerning him, were scarcely read at all by the public, or if they were, they were not credited. The expression of an ordinary working-man with regard to his position was entirely typical of the general popular sentiment;—"If he would only do something to prove he had a will of his own, and a mind, he would perhaps be able to set the Throne more firmly on its legs than it is at present."

How thoroughly the young man *had* proved that he indeed possessed 'a will of his own,' was not yet disclosed to the outside critics of his life and conduct. Only the King and Queen, and Professor von Glauben knew it;—for even Sir Roger de Launay had not been entrusted with the story of his secret marriage. The Queen had received the news with her usual characteristic immobility. A faint cold smile had parted her lips as she listened to the story of her son's romance,—and her reply to the King's brief explanation was almost as brief:—

"Nearly all the aristocracy marry music-hall women!" she said; "One should therefore be grateful that a Crown Prince does not go lower in his matrimonial choice than an innocent little peasant!"

"The marriage is useless, of course," said the King; "It has satisfied Humphry's exalted notions of honour; but it can never be acknowledged or admitted."

"Of course not!" she agreed languidly; "It certainly clears up the mystery of The Islands, which you were so anxious to visit;—and I suppose the next thing you will do is to marry him again to some daughter of a Royal house?"

"Most assuredly!"

"As *you* were married to me?" she said, raising her eyes to his face with that strange deep look which spoke eloquently of some mystery hidden in her soul.

His cheeks burned with an involuntary flush. He bowed.

"Precisely! As I married you!" he replied.

"The experiment was hardly successful!" she said with her little cold smile. "I fear you have often regretted it!"

He looked at her, studying her beauty intently,—and the remembrance of another face, far less fair of feature, but warm and impassioned by the lovely light of sympathy and tenderness, came between his eyes and hers, like a heavenly vision.

"Had you loved me," he said slowly, "I might never have known what it was to need love!"

A slight tremor ran through her veins. There was a strange tone in his voice,—a soft cadence to which she was unaccustomed,—something that suggested a new emotion in his life, and a deeper experience.

"I never loved anyone in my life!" she answered calmly—"And now the days are past for loving. Humphry, however, has made up for my lack of the tender passion!"

She turned away indifferently, and appeared to dismiss the matter altogether from her mind. The first time she saw her son, however, after hearing of his marriage, she looked at him curiously.

"And so your wife is very lovely, Humphry!" she said with a slightly derisive smile.

He was not startled by the suddenness of her observation nor put out by it.

"She is the loveliest woman I have ever seen,—not excepting yourself," he replied.

"It is a very foolish affair!" she continued composedly; "But fortunately in our line of life such things are easily arranged;—and your future will not be spoiled by it. I am glad you are going abroad, as you will very soon forget!"

The Prince regarded her steadfastly with something of grave wonderment as well as compassion,—but he made no reply, and with the briefest excuse left her presence as soon as possible, in order to avoid further conversation on the subject. She, herself, however, found her mind curiously perturbed and full of conjectures concerning her son's idyllic love-story, in which all considerations for her as Queen and mother seemed omitted,—and where she, as it were, appeared to be shut outside a lover's paradise, the delights of which she had never experienced. The King held many private conferences with her on the matter, in which sometimes Professor von Glauben was permitted to share;—and the upshot of these numerous discussions resulted in a scheme which was as astonishing in its climax as it was unexpected. Over and over again it has been proved to nations as well as to individuals, that the whole course of events may be changed by the fixed determination of one resolute mind; but it is not often that the moral force of a mere girl succeeds in competing with the authority of kings and parliaments. But so it chanced on this occasion, and in the following manner.

One glorious early morning, the sun having risen without a cloud in the deep blue of the sky, and the sea being as calm as an inland lake, the King's yacht was seen to weigh anchor and steam away at her fullest speed towards The Islands. Little or no preparation had been made for her short voyage; there was no Royal party on board, and the only passenger was Professor von Glauben. He sat solitary on deck in a luxurious chair, smoking his meerschaum pipe, and dubiously considering the difficult and peculiar situation in which he was placed. He made no attempt to calculate the possible success or failure of his mission— 'for,' said he very sagely, 'it all depends on a woman, and God alone knows what a woman will do! Her ways are dark and wonderful, and altogether beyond the limit of the comprehension of man!'

His journey was undertaken at the King's command; and equally by the King's command he had been compelled to keep it a secret from Prince Humphry. He had never been to The Islands since the King's 'surprise visit' there, and he was of course not aware that Gloria now knew the real rank and position of her supposed 'sailor' husband. He was at present charged to break the news to her, and bring her straightway to the palace, there to confront both the King and Queen, and learn from them the true state of affairs.

"It is a cruel ordeal," he said, shaking his head sorrowfully; "Yet I myself am a party to its being tried. For once in my life I have pinned my faith on the unspoilt soul of an unworldly woman. I wonder what will come of it? It rests entirely with Gloria herself, and with no one else in the world!"

As the yacht arrived at its destination and dropped anchor at some distance from the pier, owing to the shallowness of the tide at that hour of the day, The Islands presented a fair aspect in the dancing beams of the summer sunlight. Numbers of fruit trees were bursting into blossom,—the apple, the cherry, the pink almond and the orange blossom all waved together and whispered sweetness to one another in the pure air, and the full-flowering mimosa perfumed every breath of wind. Fishermen were grouped here and there on the shore, mending or drying their nets; and in the fields beyond could be perceived many workers pruning the hedges or guiding the plough. The vision of a perfect Arcadia was presented to the eye; and so the Professor thought, as getting into the boat lowered for him, he was rowed from the yacht to the landing-place, and there dismissed the sailors, warning them that at the first sound of his whistle they should swiftly come for him again.

"What a pity to spoil her peace of mind—her simplicity of life!" he thought, as he walked at a slow and reluctant pace towards Ronsard's cottage; "And I fear we shall have trouble with the old man! I wonder if his philosophy will stand hard wear and tear!"

The pretty, low timber-raftered house confronted him at the next bend in the road, and presented a charming aspect of tranquillity. The grass in front of it was smooth as velvet and emerald-green, and in one of the flower borders Ronsard himself was digging and planting. He looked up as he heard the gate open, but did not attempt to interrupt his work;—and Von Glauben advanced towards him with a considerable sense of anxiety and insecurity in his mind. Anon he paused in the very act of greeting, as the old man turned his strong, deeply-furrowed countenance upon him with a look of fierce indignation and scorn.

"So! You are here!" he said; "Have you come to look upon the evil your Royal master has worked? Or to make dutiful obeisance to Gloria as Crown-Princess?"

Von Glauben was altogether taken aback.

"Then—you know—?" he stammered.

"Oh yes, I know!" responded Ronsard sternly and bitterly; "I know everything! There has been full confession! If the husband of my Gloria were more prince than man, my knife would have slit his throat! But he is more man than prince!—and I have let him live—for her sake!"

"Well—that is so far good!" said Von Glauben, wiping the perspiration from his brow, and heaving a deep sigh of relief; "And as you fully comprehend the situation, it saves me the trouble of explaining it! You are a philosopher, Ronsard! Permit me to remind you of that fact! You know, like myself, that what is done, even if it is done foolishly, cannot be undone!"

"I know it! Who should know it so well as I!" and Ronsard set a delicate rose-tree roughly in the hole he had dug for it, and began to fiercely pile in the earth around it;—"Fate is fate, and there is no gainsaying it! The law of Compensation will always have its way! Look you, man!—and listen! I, Rene Ronsard, once killed a king!—and now in my old age, the only creature I ever loved is tricked by the son of a king! It is just! So be it!"

He bent his white head over his digging again, and Von Glauben was for a moment silent, vaguely amazed and stupefied by this sudden declaration of a past crime.

"You should not say 'tricked,' my friend!" he at last ventured to remark; "Prince Humphry is an honest lad;—he means to keep his word!"

Ronsard looked up, his eyes gleaming with fury.

"Keep his word? Bah! How can he? Who in this wide realm will give him the honourable liberty to keep his word? Will he acknowledge Gloria as his wife before the nation?—she a foundling and a castaway? Will he make her his future queen? Not he! He will forsake her, and live with another woman, in sin which the law will sanctify!"

He went on planting the rose-tree, then,—dropping his spade,—tossed up his head and hands with a wild gesture.

"What, and who is this God who so ordains our destiny!" he exclaimed; "For surely this is His work,—not mine! Hidden away from all the world with my life's secret buried in my soul, I, without wife, or children or friends, or any soul on earth to care whether I lived or died, was sent an angel comforter;—the child I rescued from the sea! 'Gloria, Gloria in excelsis Deo!' the choristers sang in the church when I found her! I thought it true! With her,—in every action, in every thought and word, I strove,—and have faithfully striven,—to atone for my past crime;—for I was forced through others to kill that king! When proved guilty of the deed, I was told by my associates to assume madness,—a mere matter of acting,—and, being adjudged as insane, I was sent with other criminals on a convict ship, bound for a certain coast-prison, where we were all to be kept for life. The ship was wrecked off the rocks yonder, and it was reported that every soul on board went down, but I escaped—only I,—for what inscrutable reason God alone knows! Finding myself saved and free, I devoted my life to hard work, and to doing all the good I could think of to atone—to atone—always to atone! Then the child was sent to me; and I thought it was a sign that my penance was accepted; but no!—no!—the compensating curse falls,— not on me,—not on me, for if only so, I would welcome it—but on Her! —the child of my love—the heart of my heart!—on Her!"

He turned away his face, and a hard sob broke from his labouring chest. Von Glauben laid a gentle, protective hand on his shoulder.

"Ronsard, be a man!" he said in a kind, firm voice; "This is the first time you have told me your true history—and—I shall respect your confidence! You have suffered much—equally you have loved much! Doubt not that you are forgiven much. But why should you assume, or foresee unhappiness for Gloria? Why talk of a curse where perhaps there is only an intended blessing? Is she unhappy, that you are thus moved?"

Ronsard furtively dashed away the tears from his eyes.

"She? Gloria unhappy? No,—not yet! The delights of spring and summer have met in her smile,—her eyes, her movements! It was she herself who told me all! If he had told me, I would have killed him!"

"Eminently sensible!" said Von Glauben, recovering his usual phlegmatic calm; "You would have killed the man she loves best in the world. And so with perfect certainty you would have killed her as well,—and probably yourself afterwards. A perfect slaughterhouse, like the last scene in Hamlet, by the so admirable Shakespeare! It is better as it is. Life is really very pleasant!"

He sniffed the perfumed air,—listened with appreciation to the trilling of a bird swinging on a bough of apple-blossom above him, and began to feel quite easy in his mind. Half his mission was done for him, Prince Humphry having declared himself in his true colours. "I always said," mused the Professor, "that he was a very honest young man! And I think he will be honest to the end." Aloud he asked:

"When did you know the truth?"

"Some days since," replied Ronsard. "He—Gloria's husband—I can as yet call him by no other name—came suddenly one evening;—the two went out together as usual, and then—then my child returned alone. She told me all,—of the disguise he had assumed—and of his real identity—and I— well! I think I was mad! I know I spoke and acted like a madman!"

"Nay, rather say like a philosopher!" murmured Von Glauben with a humorous smile; "Remember, my good fellow, that there is no human being who loses self-control more easily and rapidly than he who proclaims the advantage of keeping it! And what did Gloria say to you?"

Ronsard looked up at the tranquil skies, and was for a moment silent. Then he answered.

"Gloria is—just Gloria! There is no woman like her,—there never will be any woman like her! She said nothing at all while I raged and swore;—she stood before me white and silent,—grand and calm, like some great angel. Then when I cursed *him*,—she raised her hand, and like a queen she said: 'I forbid you to utter one word against him!' I stood before her mute and foolish. 'I forbid you!' She,—the child I reared and nurtured—menaced me with her 'command' as though I were her slave and servant! You see I have lost her!—she is not mine any more—she is *his*—to be treated as he wills, and made the toy of his pleasure! She does not know the world, but I know it! I know the misery that is in store for her! But there is yet time—and I will live to avenge her wrong!"

"Possibly there will be no wrong to avenge," said Von Glauben composedly; "But if there is, I have no doubt you would kill another king!" Ronsard turned pale and shuddered. "It is stupid work, killing kings," went on the Professor; "It never does any good; and often increases the evil it was intended to cure. Your studies in

philosophy must have taught you that much at least! As for your losing Gloria,—
you lost her in a sense when you gave her to her husband. It is no use complaining
now, because you find he is not the man you took him for. The mischief is done. At
any rate you are bound to admit that Gloria has, so far, been perfectly happy; she
will be happy still, I truly believe, for she has the secret of happiness in her own
beautiful nature. And you, Ronsard, must make the best of things, and meet fate
with calmness. To-day, for instance, I am here by the King's command,— I bear his
orders,—and I have come for Gloria. They want her at the Palace."

Ronsard stepped out of his flower-border, and stood on the greensward amazed,
and indignantly suspicious.

"They want her at the Palace!" he repeated; "Why? What for? To do her harm?
To make her miserable? To insult and threaten her? No, she shall not go!"

"Look here, my friend," said the Professor with mild patience; "You have—for
a philosopher—a most unpleasant habit of jumping to wrong conclusions! Please
endeavour to compose the tumult in your soul, and listen to me! The King has sent
for Gloria, and I am instructed to take charge of her, and escort her to the presence
of their Majesties. No insult, no threat, no wrong is intended. I will bring her back
again safe to you immediately the audience is concluded. Be satisfied, Ronsard! For
once 'put your trust in princes,' for her husband will be there,—and do you think
he would suffer her to be insulted or wronged?"

Ronsard's sunken eyes looked wild,—his aged frame trembled violently, and
he gave a hopeless gesture.

"I do not know—I do not know!" he said incoherently; "I am an old man, and I
have always found it a wicked world! But—if you give me your word that she shall
come to no harm, I will trust *you*!"

Silently Von Glauben took his hand and pressed it. Two or three minutes
passed, weighted with unuttered and unutterable thoughts in the minds of both
men; and then, in a somewhat hushed voice, the Professor said:

"Ronsard, I am just now reminded of the tragic story of Rudolf of Austria, who
killed himself through the maddening sorrow of an ill- fated love! We, in our different lines of life should remember that,— and let no young innocent heart suffer
through our follies—our rages against fate—our conventions—our more or less idiotic laws of restraint and hypocrisy. The tragedy of Prince Rudolf and the unhappy

Marie Vetsera whom he worshipped, was caused by the sin and the falsehood of others,—not by the victims of the cruel catastrophe. Therefore, I say to you, my friend, be wise in time!—and control the natural stormy tendency of your passions in this present affair. I assure you, on my faith and honour as a man, that the King has a kindly heart and a brave one,—together with a strong sense of justice. He is not truly known to his people;—they only see him through the pens of press reporters, or the slavish descriptions of toadies and parasites. Then again, the Crown Prince is an honourable lad; and from what I know of him, he is not likely to submit to conventional usages in matters which are close to his life and heart. Gloria herself is of such an exceptional character and disposition, that I think she may be safely left to arbitrate her own destiny——"

"And the Queen?" interrupted Ronsard suddenly;—"She, at any rate, as a woman, wife and mother, will be gentle?"

"Gentle, she certainly is," said Von Glauben, with a slight sigh; "But only because she does not consider it worth while to be otherwise! God has put a stone in the place where her heart should be! However,—she will have little to say, and still less to do with to-day's business. You tell me you will trust me; I promise you, you shall not repent your trust! But I must see Gloria herself. Where is she?"

Ronsard pointed towards the cottage.

"She is in there, studying," he said; "Books of the old time;—books that few read. She gets them all from Sergius Thord. How would it be, think you, if he knew?"

The pleasantly rubicund countenance of the Professor grew a shade paler.

"Sergius Thord—Sergius Thord?—H'm—h'm—let me see!—who is he? Ah! I remember,—he is the Socialist lion, for ever roaring through the streets and seeking whom he may devour! I daresay he is not without cleverness!"

"Cleverness!" echoed Ronsard; "That is a tame word! He has genius, and the people swear by him. Since the proposed new taxation, and other injustices of the Government, he has gained adherents by many thousands. You,—whom I once took to be a mere German schoolmaster, a friend of the young 'sailor' whom my child so innocently wedded,—you whom I now know to be the King's physician— surely you cannot live on the mainland, and in the metropolis, without knowing of the power of Sergius Thord?"

"I know something—not much;" replied the Professor guardedly; "But come, my friend, *I* have not deceived you! I was in very truth a poor 'German schoolmaster,' once,—before I became a student of medicine and surgery. And that I am the King's physician, is merely one of those accidental circumstances which occur in a world of chance. But schoolmaster as I have been, I doubt if I would set our 'Glory-of-the- Sea' to study books recommended to her by Sergius Thord. The poetry of Heine is more suitable to her age and sex. Let us break in upon her meditations." And he walked across the grass with one arm thrust through that of Ronsard; "For she must prepare herself. We ought to be gone within an hour."

They passed under the low, rose-covered porch into a wide square room, with raftered ceiling and deep carved oak ingle nook,—and here at the table, with a quarto volume opened out before her, sat Gloria, resting her head on one fair hand, her rich hair falling about her in loose shining tresses, and her whole attitude expressive of the deepest absorption in study. As they entered, she looked up and smiled,—then rose, her hand still resting on the open book.

"At last you have come again, dear Professor!" she said; "I began to think you had grown weary in well-doing!"

Von Glauben stared at her, stricken speechless for a moment. What mysterious change had passed over the girl, investing her with such an air of regal authority? It was impossible to say. To all appearance she was the same beautiful creature, clad in the same simple white homespun gown,—yet were she Empress of half the habitable globe, she could not have looked more environed with dignity, sweetness and delicately gracious manner. He understood the desolating expression of Ronsard,— 'You see I have lost her!—she is not mine any more—she is his!' He recognised and was suddenly impressed by that fact;—she was 'his'—the wife of the Crown Prince and Heir-Apparent to the Throne;—and evidently with the knowledge of her position had arisen the pride of love and the spirit of grace to support her honours worthily. And so, as Von Glauben met her eyes, which expressed their gentle wonder at his silence, and as she extended her hand to him, he came slowly forward and bowing low, respectfully kissed that hand.

"Princess," he said, in a voice that trembled ever so slightly; "I shall never be weary in well-doing,—if you are good enough to call my service and friendship for you by that name! I hesitated to come before,—because I thought—I feared—I did not know!—"

"I understand!" said Gloria tranquilly; "You did not think the Prince, my husband, would tell me the truth so soon! But I know all, and now—I am glad to know it! Dearest," and she moved swiftly to Ronsard who was standing silent in the doorway—"come in and sit down! You make yourself so tired sometimes in the garden;" and she threw a loving arm about him. "You must rest; you look so pale!"

For all answer, he lifted the hand that hung about his neck, to his lips and kissed it tenderly.

"They want you, Gloria!" he said tremulously; "They want you at the Palace. You must go to-day!"

She lifted her brilliant eyes enquiringly to Von Glauben, who responded to the look by at once explaining his mission. He was there, he said, by the King's special command;—their Majesties had been informed of their son's marriage by their son himself; and they desired at once to see and speak with their unknown daughter-in-law. The interview would be private; his Royal Highness the Crown Prince would be present;—it might last an hour, perhaps longer,—and he, Von Glauben, was entrusted to bring Gloria to the Palace, and escort her back to The Islands again when all was over. Thus, with elaborate and detailed courtesy, the Professor unfolded the nature of his enterprise, while Gloria, still keeping one arm round Ronsard, heard and smiled.

"I shall obey the King's command!" she said composedly; "Though,— having no word from the Prince, my husband, concerning this mandate,—I might very well refuse to do so! But it may be as well that their Majesties and their son's wife should plainly, and once for all, understand each other. Dear Professor, you look sadly troubled. Is there some little convention, some special ceremonial of so-called 'good manners,' which you are commissioned to teach me, before I make my appearance at Court under your escort?"

Her lovely lips smiled,—her eyes laughed,—she looked the very incarnation of Beauty triumphant. Von Glauben's brain whirled,—he felt bewitched and dazzled.

"I?—to teach you anything? No, my princess!—and please think how loyally I have called you 'Princess' from the beginning!—I have always told you that you have a spiritual knowledge far surpassing all material wisdom. Conventions and ceremonials are not for you,—you will make fashion, not follow it! I am not troubled, save for your sake, dear child!—for you know nothing of the world, and the ways of the Court may at first offend you—"

"The ways of Hell must have seemed dark to Proserpine," said Ronsard in his harsh, strong voice; "But Love gave her light!"

"A very just reminder!" said Von Glauben, well pleased;—"Consider Gloria to be the new Proserpine to-day! And now she must forgive me for playing the part of a tyrannical friend, and urging her to hasten her preparations."

Gloria bent down and kissed Ronsard gently.

"Trust me, little father!" she whispered; "You have not taught me great lessons of truth in vain!"

Aloud she said.

"The King and Queen wish to see me and speak with me,—and I know the reason why! They desire to fully explain to me all that my husband has already told me,—which is that according to the rules made for monarchs, our marriage is inadmissible. Well!—I have my answer ready; and you, Professor, shall hear me give it! Wait but a few moments and I will come with you."

She left the room. The two men looked at each other in silence. At last Von Glauben said:—

"Ronsard, I think you will soon reap the reward of your 'life- philosophy' system! You have fed that girl from her childhood on strong intellectual food, and trained the mental muscles rather than the physical ones. Upon my word, I believe you will see a good result!"

Ronsard, who had grown much calmer and quieter during the last few minutes, raised himself a little from the chair into which he had sunk with an air of fatigue, and looked dreamily towards the open lattice window, where the roses hung in a curtain of crimson blossom.

"If it be so, I shall praise God!" he said; "But the years have come and gone with me so peacefully since I made my home on these quiet shores, that the exercise of what I have presumed to call 'philosophy' has had no chance. Philosophy! It is well to preach it,—but when the blow of misfortune falls, who can practise it?"

"You can," replied the Professor;—"I can! Gloria can! I think we all three have clear brains. There is a tendency in the present age to overlook and neglect the greatest power in the whole human composition,—the mental and psychical part of it. Now, in the present curious drama of events, we have a chance given to exercise it; and it will be our own faults if we do not make our wills rule our destinies!"

"But the position is intolerable—impossible!" said Ronsard, rising and pacing the room with a fresh touch of agitation. "Nothing can do away with the fact that we—my child and I—have been cruelly deceived! And now there can be only one of two contingencies; Gloria must be acknowledged as the Prince's wife,—in which case he will be forced to resign all claim to the Throne;—or he must marry again, which makes her no wife at all. That is a disgrace which her pride would never submit to, nor mine;—for did I not kill a king?"

"Let me advise you for the future not to allude to that disagreeable incident!" said Von Glauben persuasively: "Exercise discretion,—as I do! Observe that I do not ask you what king you killed;—I am as careful on that matter as I am concerning the reasons for which I myself left my native Fatherland! I make it a rule never to converse on painful subjects. You tell me you have tried to atone; then believe that the atonement is made, and that Gloria is the sign of its acceptance, and—happy augury!—here she comes."

They both instinctively turned to confront the girl as she entered. She had changed her ordinary white homespun gown for another of the same kind, equally simple, but fresh and unworn; her glorious bronze- chestnut hair was unbound to its full rippling length, and was held back by a band or fillet of curiously carved white coral, which surmounted the rich tresses somewhat in the fashion of a small crown, and she carried, thrown over one arm, the only kind of cloak she ever wore,—a burnous-like wrap of the same white homespun as her dress, with a hood, which, as the Professor slowly took out his glasses and fixed them on his nose out of mere mechanical habit, to look at her more closely, she drew over her head and shoulders, the soft folds about her exquisite face completing a classic picture of such radiant beauty as is seldom seen nowadays among the increasingly imperfect and repulsive specimens of female humanity which 'progress' combined with sensuality, produce for the 'advancement' of the race.

"I have no Court dress," she said smiling; "And if I had I should not wear it! The King and Queen shall see me as my husband sees me,—what pleases him, must suffice to please them! I am quite ready!"

Von Glauben removed the spectacles he had needlessly put on. They were dim with a moisture which he furtively polished off, blinking his eyes meanwhile as if the light hurt him. He was profoundly moved—thrilled to the very core of his soul by the simplicity, frankness and courage of this girl whose education was chiefly out of wild Nature's lesson- book, and who knew nothing of the artificial world of fashion.

"And I, my princess, am at your service!" he said; "Ronsard, it is but a few hours that we shall be absent. To-night with the rising of the moon we shall return, and I doubt not with the Prince himself as chief escort! Keep a good heart and have faith! All will be well!"

"All *shall* be well if Love can make it so!" said Ronsard;— "Gloria—my child—!" He held out his wrinkled hands pathetically, unable to say more. She sank on her knees before him, and tenderly drawing down those hands upon her head, pressed them closely there.

"Your blessing, dearest!" she said; "Not in speech—but in thought!"

There was a moment's sacred silence;—then Gloria rose, and throwing her arms round the old man, the faithful protector of her infancy and girlhood, kissed him tenderly. After that, she seemed to throw all seriousness to the winds, and running out under the roses of the porch made two or three light dancing steps across the lawn.

"Come!" she cried, her eyes sparkling, her face radiant with the gaiety of her inward spirit; "Come, Professor! This is not what we call a poet's day of dreams,—it is a Royal day of nonsense! Come!" and here she drew herself up with a stately air— "WE are prepared to confront the King!"

The Professor caught the infection of her mirth, and quickly followed her; and within the next half-hour Rene Ronsard, climbing slowly to the summit of one of the nearest rocks on the shore adjacent to his dwelling, shaded his eyes from the dazzling sunlight on the sea, and strained them to watch the magnificent Royal yacht steaming swiftly over the tranquil blue water, with one slight figure clad in white leaning against the mast, a figure that waved its hand fondly towards The Islands, and of whom it might have been said:

> "Her gaze was glad past love's own singing of,
> And her face lovely past desire of love!"

CHAPTER XXII
A FAIR DEBUTANTE

THAT same afternoon there was a mysterious commotion at the Palace,— whispers ran from lip to lip among the few who had seen her, that a beautiful woman,—lovelier than the Queen herself,—had, under the escort of the uncommunicative Professor von Glauben, passed into the presence of the King and Queen, to receive the honour of a private audience. Who was she? What was she? Where did she come from? How was she dressed? This last question was answered first, being easiest to deal with. She was attired all in white,—'like a picture' said some— 'like a statue' said others. No one, however, dared ask any direct question concerning her,—her reception, whoever she was, being of a strictly guarded nature, and peremptory orders having been given to admit no one to the Queen's presence-chamber, to which apartment she had been taken by the King's physician. But such dazzling beauty as hers could not go altogether unnoticed by the most casual attendant, sentinel, or lord-in-waiting, and the very fact that special commands had been issued to guard all the doors of entrance to the Royal apartments on either hand, during her visit, only served to pique and inflame the general curiosity.

Meantime,—while lesser and inferior personages were commenting on the possibility of the unknown fair one being concerned with some dramatic incident that might have to be included among the King's numerous gallantries,—the unconscious subject of their discussion was quietly seated alone in an ante-room adjoining the Queen's apartments, waiting till Professor von Glauben should announce that their Majesties were ready to receive her. She was not troubled or anxious, or in any way ill at ease. She looked curiously upon the splendid evidences of Royal state, wealth and luxury which surrounded her, with artistic appreciation but no envy. She caught sight of her own face and figure in a tall mirror opposite to her, set in a silver frame; and she studied herself quietly and critically with the calm knowledge that there was nothing to deplore or to regret in the way God and Nature had been pleased to make her. She was not in the slightest degree vain,— but she knew that a healthy and quiet mind in a healthy and unspoilt body, together form what is understood as the highest beauty,—and that these two elements were not lacking in her. Moreover, she was conscious of a great love warming her heart and strengthening her soul,—and with this great motive-force to brace her nerves and add extra charm to her natural loveliness, she had no fear. She had enjoyed the swift voyage across the sparkling sea, and the fresh air had made her eyes doubly lustrous, her complexion even more than usually fair and brilliant. She did not permit herself to be rendered unhappy or anxious as to the possible attitude of the King and Queen towards her, —she was prepared for all contingencies, and had fully made up her mind what to say. Therefore, there was no need to fret over the position, or to be timorously concerned because she was called upon to confront those who by human law alone were made superior in rank to the rest of mankind.

"In God's sight all men are equal!" she said to herself: "The King is a mere helpless babe at birth, dependant on others,—as he is a mere helpless corpse at death. It is only men's own foolish ideas and conventions of usage in life that make any difference!"

At that moment the Professor entered hurriedly, and impulsively seizing her hands in his own, kissed them and pressed them tenderly. His face was flushed—he was evidently strongly excited.

"Go in there now, Princess!" he whispered, pointing to the adjacent room, of which the door stood ajar; "And may God be on your side!"

She rose up, and releasing her hands gently from his nervous grasp, smiled.

"Do not be afraid!" she said; "You, too, are coming?"

"I follow you!" he replied.

And to himself he said: "Ach, Gott in Himmel! Will she keep her so beautiful calm? If she will—if she can—a throne would be well lost for such a woman!"

And he watched her with an admiration amounting almost to fear, as she passed before him and entered the Royal presence-chamber with a proud light step, a grace

of bearing and a supreme distinction, which, had she been there on a day of diplomatic receptions, would have made half the women accustomed to attend Court,
look like the merest vulgar plebeians.

The room she entered was very large and lofty. A dazzle of gold ceiling, painted walls and mirrors flashed upon her eyes, with the hue of silken curtains and
embroidered hangings,—the heavy perfume of hundreds of flowers in tall crystal
vases and wide gilded stands made the air drowsy and odorous, and for a moment,
Gloria, just fresh from the sweet breath of the sea, felt sickened and giddy,—but
she recovered quickly, and raised her eyes fearlessly to the two motionless figures,
which, like idols set in a temple for worship, waited her approach. The King, stiffly
upright, and arrayed in military uniform, stood near the Queen, who was seated
in a throne-like chair over- canopied with gold,—her trailing robes were of a pale
azure hue bordered with ermine, and touched here and there with silver, giving out
reflexes of light, stolen as it seemed from the sea and sky,—and her beautiful face,
with its clear-cut features and cold pallor, might have been carved out of ivory, for
all the interest or emotion expressed upon it. Gloria came straight towards her, then
stopped. With her erect supple form, proud head and fair features, she looked the
living embodiment of sovereign womanhood,—and the Queen, meeting the full
starry glance of her eyes, stirred among her Royal draperies, and raised herself with
a slow graceful air of critical observation, in which there was a touch of languid
wonder mingled with contempt. Still Gloria stood motionless,—neither abashed
nor intimidated,—she made no curtsey or reverential salutation of any kind, and
presently removing her gaze from the Queen, she turned to the King.

"You sent for me," she said; "And I have come. What do you want with me?"

The King smiled. What a dazzling Perfection was here, he thought! A second
Una unarmed, and strong in the courage of innocence! But he was acting a special
part, and he determined to play it well and thoroughly. So he gave her no reply, but
turned with a stiff air to Von Glauben.

"Tell the girl to make her obeisance to the Queen!" he said.

The Professor very reluctantly approached the 'Glory-of-the-Sea' with this
suggestion, cautiously whispered. Gloria obeyed at once. Moving swiftly to the
Queen's chair, she bent low before her.

"Madam!" she said, "I am told to kneel to you, because you are the Queen,—but it is not for that I do so. I kneel, because you are my husband's mother!"

And raising the cold impassive hand covered with great gems, that rested idly on the rich velvets so near to her touch, she gently kissed it,—then rose up to her full height again.

"Is it always like this here?" she asked, gazing around her. "Do you always sit thus in a chair, dressed grandly and quite silent?"

The smile deepened on the King's face; the Queen, perforce moved at last from her inertia, half rose with an air of amazement and indignation, and Von Glauben barely saved himself from laughing outright.

"You," continued Gloria, fixing her bright glance on the King; "You have seen me before! You have spoken to me. Then why do you pretend not to know me now? Is that Court manners? If so, they are not good or kind!"

The King relaxed his formal attitude, and addressed his Consort in a low tone.

"It is no use dealing with this girl in the conventional way," he said; "She is a mere child at heart, simple and uneducated;—we must treat her as such. Perhaps you will speak to her first?"

"No, Sir, I much prefer that you should do so," she replied. "When I have heard her answers to you, it will be perhaps my turn!"

Thereupon the King advanced a step or two, and Gloria regarded him steadfastly. Meeting the pure light of those lovely eyes, he lost something of his ordinary self-possession,—he was conscious of a certain sense of embarrassment and foolishness;—his very uniform, ablaze with gold and jewelled orders, seemed a clown's costume compared with the classic simplicity of Gloria's homespun garb, which might have fitly clothed a Greek goddess. Sensible of his nervous irritation, he however overcame it by an effort, and summoning all his dignity, he 'graciously,' as the newspaper parasites put it, extended his hand. Gloria smiled archly.

"I kissed your hand the other day when you were cross!" she said; "You would like it kissed again? There!"

And with easy grace of gesture she pressed her lips lightly upon it. It would have needed something stronger than mere flesh and blood to resist the natural playfulness and charm of her action, combined with her unparalleled beauty, and the King, who was daily and hourly proving for himself the power and intensity of that Spirit of Man which makes clamour for higher things than Man's conventionalities, became for the moment as helplessly overwhelmed and defeated by a woman's smile, a woman's eyes, as any hero of old times, whose conquests have been reported to us in history as achieved for the sake of love and beauty. But he was compelled to disguise his thoughts, and to maintain an outward expression of formality, particularly in the presence of his Queen-Consort,—and he withdrew the hand that bore her soft kiss upon it with a well-simulated air of chill tolerance. Then he spoke gravely, in measured precise accents.

"Gloria Ronsard, we have sent for you in all kindness," he said; "out of a sincere wish to remedy any wrong which our son, the Crown Prince has, in the light folly and hot impulse of his youth, done to you in your life. We are given to understand that there is a boy-and-girl attachment between you; that he won your attachment under a disguised identity, and that you were thus innocently deceived,—and that, in order to satisfy his own honourable scruples, as well as your sense of maidenly virtue, he has, still under a disguise, gone through the ceremony of marriage with you. Therefore, it seems that you now imagine yourself to be his lawful wife. This is a very natural mistake for a girl to make who is as young and inexperienced as you are, and I am sorry,—very sorry for the false position in which my son the Crown Prince has so thoughtlessly placed you. But, after very earnest consideration, I,—and the Queen also,—think it much better for you to know the truth at once, so that you may fully realize the situation, and then, by the exercise of a little common sense, spare yourself any further delusion and pain. All we can do to repair the evil, you may rest assured shall be done. But you must thoroughly understand that the Crown Prince, as heir to the Throne, cannot marry out of his own station. If he should presume to do so, through some mad and hot-headed impulse, such a marriage is not admitted or agreed to by the nation. Thus you will see plainly that, though you have gone through the marriage ceremony with him, that counts as nothing in your case,—for, according to the law of the realm, and in the sight of the world, you are not, and cannot be his wife!"

Gloria raised her deep bright eyes and smiled.

"No?" she said, and then was silent.

The King regarded her with surprise, and a touch of anger. He had expected tears, passionate declamations, and reiterated assurances of the unalterable and indissoluble tie between herself and her lover, but this little indifferently-queried

"No?" upset all his calculations.

"Have you nothing to say?" he asked, somewhat sternly.

"What should I say?" she responded, still smiling; "You are the King; it is for you to speak!"

"She does not understand you, Sir," interrupted the Queen coldly; "Your words are possibly too elaborate for her simple comprehension!"

Gloria turned a fearless beautiful glance upon her.

"Pardon me, Madam, but I do understand!" she said; "I understand that by the law of God I am your son's wife, and that by the law of the world I am no wife! I abide by the law of God!"

There was a moment's dead silence. Professor von Glauben gave a discreet cough to break it, and the King, reminded of his presence turned towards him.

"Has she no sense of the position?" he demanded.

"Sir, I have every reason to believe that she grasps it thoroughly!" replied Von Glauben with a deferential bow.

"Then why——"

But here he was again interrupted by the Queen. She, raising herself in her chair, her beautiful head and shoulders lifted statue-like from her enshrining draperies of azure and white, stretched forth a hand and beckoned Gloria towards her.

"Come here, child!" she said; then as Gloria advanced with evident reluctance, she added; "Come closer—you must not be afraid of me!"

Gloria smiled.

"Nay, Madam, trouble not yourself at all in that regard! I never was afraid of anyone!"

A shadow of annoyance darkened the Queen's fair brows.

"Since you have no fear, you may equally have no shame!" she said in icy-cold accents; "Therefore it is easy to understand why you deliberately refuse to see the harm and cruelty done to our son, the Crown Prince, by his marriage with you, if such marriage were in the least admissible, which fortunately for all concerned, it is not. He is destined to occupy the Throne, and he must wed someone who is fit to share it. Kings and princes may love where they choose,—but they can only marry where they must! You are my son's first love;—the thought and memory of that may perhaps be a consolation to you,—but do not assume that you will be his last!"

Gloria drew back from her; her face had paled a little.

"You can speak so!" she said sorrowfully; "You,—his mother! Poor Queen— poor woman! I am sorry for you!"

Without pausing to notice the crimson flush of vexation that flew over the Queen's delicate face at her words, she turned, now with some haughtiness, to the King.

"Speak plainly!" she said; "What is it you want of me?"

Her flashing eyes, her proud look startled him—he moved back a step or two. Then he replied with as much firmness and dignity as he could assume.

"Nothing is wanted of you, my child, but obedience and loyalty! Resign all claim upon the Crown Prince as his wife; promise never to see him again, or cor- respond with him,—and—you shall lose nothing by the sacrifice you make of your little love affair to the good of the country."

"The good of the country!" echoed Gloria in thrilling tones. "Do *you* know any- thing about it? You—who never go among your people except to hunt and shoot and amuse yourself generally? You, who permit wicked liars and spendthrifts to gamble with the people's money! The good of the country! If my life could only lift the burden of taxation from the country, I would lay it down gladly and freely! If I were Queen, do you think I could be like her?" and she stretched forth her white arm to where the Queen, amazed, had risen from her seat, and now stood erect, her rich robes trailing yards on the ground, and flashing at every point with jewels. "Do you think I could sit unmoved, clad in rich velvet and gems, while one single starving creature sought bread within my kingdom? Nay, I would sell everything I possessed and go barefoot rather! I would be a sister, not a mere 'patroness' to the poor;—I would never wear a single garment that had not been made for me by the workers of my own land;—and the 'good of the country' should be 'good' indeed, not 'bad,' as it is now!"

Breathless with the sudden rush of her thoughts into words, she stood with heaving bosom and sparkling eyes, the incarnation of eloquence and inspiration, and before the astonished monarch could speak, she went on.

"I am your son's wife! He loves me—he has wedded me honourably and law- fully. You wish me to disclaim that. I will not! From him and him alone, must come my dismissal from his heart, his life and his soul. If he desires his marriage with me dissolved, let him tell me so himself face to face, and before you and his mother! Then I shall be content to be no more his wife. But not till then! I will promise nothing without his consent. He is my husband,—and to him I owe my first obedience. I seek no honour, no rank, no wealth,—but I have won the greatest treasure in this world, his love!—and that I will keep!"

A door opened at the further end of the room—a curtain was quietly pushed aside, and the Crown Prince entered. With a composed, almost formal demeanour, he saluted the King and Queen, and then going up to Gloria, passed his arm around her waist, and held her fast.

"When you have concluded your interview with my wife, Sir,—an interview of which I had no previous knowledge," he said quietly, addressing the King; "I shall be glad to have one of my own with her!"

The King answered him calmly enough.

"Your wife,—as you call her,—is a very incorrigible young person," he said. "The sooner she returns to her companions, the fisher-folk on The Islands, the better! From her looks I imagined she might have sense; but I fear that is lacking to her composition! However, she is perfectly willing to consider her marriage with you dissolved, if you desire it. I trust you *will* desire it;—here, now, and at once, in my presence and that of the Queen, your mother;—and thus a very unpleasant and unfortunate incident in your career will be satisfactorily closed!"

Prince Humphry smiled.

"Dissolve the heavens and its stars into a cup of wine, and drink them all down at one gulp!" he said; "And then, perhaps, you may dissolve my marriage with this lady! If you consider it illegal, put the question to the Courts of Law;—to the Pope, who most strenuously supports the sanctity of the marriage-tie;—ask all who know anything of the sacrament, whether, when two people love each other, and are bound by holy matrimony to be as one, and are mutually resolved to so remain, any earthly power can part them! 'Those whom God hath joined together, let no man put asunder.' Is that mere lip mockery, or is it a holy bond?"

The King gave an impatient gesture.

"There is no use in argument," he said, "when argument has to be carried on with such children as yourselves. What cannot be done by persuasion, must be done by force. I wished to act kindly and reasonably by both of you—and I had hoped better things from this interview,—but as matters have turned out, it may as well be concluded."

"Wait!" said Gloria, disengaging herself gently from her husband's embrace; "I have something to say which ought to meet your wishes, even though it may not be all you desire. I will not promise to give up my husband;—I will not promise never to see him, and never to write to him—but I will swear to you one thing that should completely put your fears and doubts of me at rest!"

Both the King and Queen looked at her wonderingly;—a brighter, more delicate beauty seemed to invest her,—she stood very proudly upright, her small head lifted,—her rich hair glistening in the soft sunshine that streamed in subdued tints through the high stained-glass windows of the room,—her figure, slight and tall, was like that of the goddess dreamt of by Endymion.

"You are so unhappy already," she continued, turning to the Queen; "You have lost so much, and you need so much, that I should be sorry to add to your burden of grief! If I thought I could make you glad,—if I thought I could make you see the world through my eyes, with all the patient, loving human hearts about you, waiting for the sympathy you never give; I would come to you often, and try to find the warm pulse of you somewhere under all that splendour which you clothe yourself in, and which is as valueless to me as the dust on the common road! And if I could show *you*" and here she fixed her steadfast glance upon the King,—"where you might win friends instead of losing them,—if I could persuade you to look and see where the fires of Revolution are beginning to smoulder and kindle under your very Throne,—if I could bear messages from you of compassion and tenderness to all the disaffected and disloyal, I would ask you on my knees to let me be your daughter in affection, as I am by marriage; and I would unveil to you the secrets of your own kingdom, which is slowly but steadily rising against you! But you judge me wrongly—you estimate me falsely,—and where I might have given aid, your own misconception of me makes me useless! You consider me low-born and a mere peasant! How can you be sure of that?—for truly I do not know who I am, or where I came from. For aught I can tell, the storm was my father, and the sea my mother,— but my parents may as easily have been Royal! You judge me half-educated,—and wholly unworthy to be your son's wife. Will the ladies of your Court compete with me in learning? I am ready! What I hear of their attainments has not as yet commanded my respect or admiration,— and you yourself as King, do nothing to show that you care for either art or learning! I wonder, indeed, that you should even pause to consider whether your son's wife is educated or not!"

Absolutely silent, the King kept his eyes upon her. He was experiencing a novel sensation which was altogether delightful to him, and more instructive than any essay or sermon. He, the ostensible ruler of the country, was face to face with a woman who had no fear of him,—no awe for his position,—no respect for his rank, but who simply spoke to him as though he had been any ordinary person. He saw a scarcely perceptible smile on his son's handsome features,—he saw that Von Glauben's eyes twinkled, despite his carefully preserved seriousness of demeanour, and he realized the almost absurd powerlessness of his authority in such an embarrassing position. The assumption of a mute contempt, such as was vaguely expressed by the Queen, appeared to him to be the best policy;—he therefore adopted that attitude, without however producing the least visible effect. Gloria's face, softly flushed with suppressed emotion, looked earnest and impassioned, but neither abashed nor afraid.

"I have read many histories of kings," she continued slowly; "Of their treacheries and cruelties; of their neglect of their people! Seldom have they been truly great! The few who are reported as wise, lived and reigned so many ages ago, that we cannot tell whether their virtues were indeed as admirable as described,—or whether their vices were not condoned by a too-partial historian. A Throne has no attraction for me! The only sorrow I have ever known in my life, is the discovery that the man I love best in the world is a king's son! Would to God he were poor and unrenowned as I thought him to be, when I married him!—for so we should always have been happy. But now I have to think for him as well as for myself;—his position is as hard as mine,—and we accept our fate as a trial of our love. Love cannot be forced,—it must root itself, and grow where it will. It has made us two as one;—one in thought,—one in hope,—one in faith! No earthly power can part us. You would marry him to another woman, and force him to commit a great sin 'for the good of the country'? I tell you, if you do that,—if any king or prince does that,—God's curse will surely fall upon the Throne, and all that do inherit it!"

She did not raise her voice,—she spoke in low thrilling accents, without excitement, but with measured force and calm. Then she beckoned the Crown Prince to her side. He instantly obeyed her gesture. Taking him by the hand, she advanced a little, and with him confronted both the King and Queen.

"Hear me, your Majesties both!" she said in clear, firm accents; "And when you have heard, be satisfied as to 'the good of the country,' and let me depart to my own home in peace, away from all your crushing and miserable conventions. I take your son by the hand, and even as I swore my faith to him at the marriage altar, so I swear to you that he is free to follow his own inclination;—his law is mine,— his will my pleasure,—and in everything I shall obey him, save in this one decree, which I make for myself in your Majesties' sovereign presence—that never, so help me God, will I claim or share my husband's rank as Crown Prince, or set foot within this palace, which is his home, again, till a greater voice than that of any king,—the voice of the Nation itself, calls upon me to do so!"

This proud declaration was entirely unexpected; and both the King and Queen regarded the beautiful speaker in undisguised amazement. She, gently dropping the Prince's hand, met their eyes with a wistful pathos in her own.

"Will that satisfy you?" she asked, a slight tremor shaking her voice as she put the question.

The King at once advanced, and now spoke frankly, and without any ceremony.

"Assuredly! You are a brave girl! True to your love, and true to the country at one and the same time! But while I accept your vow, let me warn you not to indulge in any lurking hope or feeling that the Nation will ever recognize your marriage. Your own willingly-taken oath at this moment practically makes it null and void, so far as the State is concerned;—but perhaps it strengthens it as a bond of—youthful passion!"

An open admiration flashed in his bold fine eyes as he spoke,—and Gloria grew pale. With an involuntary movement she turned towards the Queen.

"You—Madam—you—Ah! No,—not you!—you are cruel!—you have not a woman's heart! My love—my husband!"

The Prince was at once beside her, and she clung to him trembling.

"Take me away!" she whispered; "Take me away altogether—this place stifles me!"

He caught her in his strong young arms, and was about to lead her to the door, when she suddenly appeared to remember something, and releasing herself from his clasp, put him away from her with a faint smile.

"No, dearest! You must stay here;—stay here and make your father and mother understand all that I have said. Tell them I mean to keep my vow. You know how thoroughly I mean it! The Professor will take me home!"

Then the Queen moved, and came towards her with her usual slow noiseless grace.

"Let me thank you!" she said, with an air of gracious condescension; "You are a very good girl, and I am sure you will keep your word! You are so beautiful that you are bound to do well; and I hope your future life will be a happy one!"

"I hope so, Madam!" replied Gloria slowly; "I think it will! If it is not happier than yours, I shall indeed be unfortunate!"

The Queen drew back, offended; but the King, who had been whispering aside to Von Glauben, now approached and said kindly.

"You must not go away, my child, without some token of our regard. Wear this for Our sake!"

He offered her a chain of gold bearing a simple yet exquisitely designed pendant of choice pearls. Her face crimsoned, and she pushed it disdainfully aside.

"Keep it, Sir, for those whose love and faith can be purchased with jewelled toys! Mine cannot! You mean kindly no doubt,—but a gift from you is an offence, not an honour! Fare-you-well!"

Another moment and she was gone. Von Glauben, at a sign from the King, hastily followed her. Prince Humphry, who had remained almost entirely mute during the scene, now stood with folded arms opposite his Royal parents, still silent and rigid. The King watched him for a minute or two—then laid a hand gently on his arm.

"We do not blame you over-much, Humphry!" he said; "She is a beautiful creature, and more intelligent than I had imagined. Moreover she has great calmness, as well as courage."

Still the Prince said nothing.

"You are satisfied, Madam, I presume?" went on the King addressing his Consort;—"The girl could hardly make a more earnest vow of abnegation than she has done. And when Humphry has travelled for a year and seen other lands, other manners, and other faces, we may look upon this boyish incident in his career as finally closed. I think both you and I can rest assured that there will be no further cause for anxiety?"

He put the question carelessly. The Queen bent her head in acquiescence, but her eyes were fixed upon her son, who still said nothing.

"We have not received any promise from Humphry himself," she said; "Apparently he is not disposed to take a similar oath of loyalty!"

"Truly, Madam, you judge me rightly for once!" said the Prince, quietly; "I am certainly not disposed to do anything but to be master of my own thoughts and actions."

"Remain so, Humphry, by all means!" said the King indulgently. "The present circumstances being so far favourable, we exact nothing more from you. Love will be love, and passion must have its way with boys of your age. I impose no further restriction upon you. The girl's own word is to me sufficient bond for the preservation of your high position. All young men have their little secret love-affairs; we shall not blame you for yours now, seeing, as we do, the satisfactory end of it in sight! But I fear we are detaining you!" This with elaborate politeness. "If you wish to follow your fair *inamorata*, the way is clear! You may retire!"

Without any haste, but with formal military stiffness the Prince saluted,—and turning slowly on his heel, left the presence-chamber. Alone, the King and his beautiful Queen-Consort looked questioningly at one another.

"What think you, Madam, of the heroine of this strange love-story?" he asked with a touch of bitterness in his voice. "Does it not strike you that even in this arid world of much deception, there may be after all such a thing as innocence?—such a treasure as true and trusting love? Were not the eyes of this girl Gloria, when lifted to your face, something like the eyes of a child who has just said its prayers to God,—who fears nothing and loves all? Yet I doubt whether you were moved!"

"Were you?" she asked indifferently, yet with a strange fluttering at her heart, which she could not herself comprehend.

"I was!" he answered. "I confess it! I was profoundly touched to see a girl of such beauty and innocence confront us here, with no other shield against our formal and ridiculous conventionalities, save the pure strength of her own love for Humphry, and her complete trust in him. It is easy to see that her life hangs on his will; it is not so much her with whom we have to deal, as with him. What he says, she will evidently obey. If he tells her he has ceased to love her, she will die quite uncomplainingly; but so long as he does love her, she will live, and expand in beauty and intelligence on that love alone; and you may be assured, Madam, that in that case, he will never wed another woman! Nor could I possibly blame him, for he is bound to find all—or most women inferior to her!"

She regarded him wonderingly.

"Your admiration of her is keen, Sir!" she said, amazed to find herself somewhat irritated. "Perhaps if she were not morganatically your daughter-in-law, you might be your son's rival?"

He turned upon her indignantly.

"Madam, the days were, when you, as my wife, had it in your power to admit no rivals to the kingdom of your own beauty! Since then, I confess, you have had many! But they have been worthless rivals all,— crazed with their own vanity and greed, and empty of truth and honour. A month or two before I came to the Throne, I was beginning to think that women were viler than vermin,—I had grown utterly weary of their beauty,—weary—ay, sick to death of their alluring eyes, sensual lips, and too freely-offered caresses; the uncomely, hard-worked woman, earning bread for her half-starved children, seemed the only kind of feminine creature for which I could have any respect—but now—I am learning that there *are* good women who are fair to see,—women who have hearts to love and suffer, and who are true—ay— true as the sun in heaven to the one man they worship!"

"A man who is generally quite unworthy of them!" said the Queen with a chill laugh; "Your eloquence, Sir, is very touching, and no doubt leads further than I care to penetrate! The girl Gloria is certainly beautiful, and no doubt very innocent and true at present,—but when Humphry tires of her, as he surely will, for all men quickly tire of those that love them best,—she will no doubt sink into the ordinary ways of obtaining consolation. I know little concerning these amazingly good women you speak of; and nothing concerning good men! But I quite agree with you that many women are to be admired for their hard work. You see when once they do begin to work, men generally keep them at it!" She gathered up her rich train on one arm, and prepared to leave the apartment. "If you think," she continued, "as you now say, that Humphry will never change his present sentiments, and never marry any other woman, the girl's oath is a mere farce and of no avail!"

"On the contrary, it is of much avail," said the King, "for she has sworn before us both never to claim any right to share in Humphry's position, till the nation itself asks her to do so. Now as the nation will never know of the marriage at all, the 'call' will not be forthcoming."

The Queen paused in the act of turning away.

"If you were to die," she said; "Humphry would be King. And as King, he is quite capable of making Gloria Queen!"

He looked at her very strangely.

"Madam, in the event of my death, all things are possible!" he said; "A dying Sovereignty may give birth to a Republic!"

The Queen smiled.

"Well, it is the most popular form of government nowadays," she responded, carelessly moving slowly towards the door; "And perhaps the most satisfactory. I think if I were not a Queen, I should be a republican!"

"And I, if I were not a King," he responded, "should be a Socialist! Such are the strange contradictions of human nature! Permit me!" He opened the door of the room for her to pass out,—and as she did so, she looked up full in his face.

"Are you still interested in your new form of amusement?" she said; "And do you still expose yourself to danger and death?"

He bowed assent.

"Still am I a fool in a new course of folly, Madam!" he answered with a smile, and a half sigh. "So many of my brother monarchs are wadded round like peaches in wool, with precautions for their safety, lest they bruise at a touch, that I assure you I take the chances of danger and death as exhilarating sport, compared to their guarded condition. But it is very good of you to assume such a gracious solicitude for my safety!"

"Assume?" she said. Her voice had a slight tremor in it,—her eyes looked soft and suffused with something like tears. Then, with her usual stately grace, she saluted him, and passed out.

Struck at the unwonted expression in her face, he stood for a moment amazed. Then he gave vent to a low bitter laugh.

"How strange it would be if she should love me now!" he murmured. "But —after all these years—too late! Too late!"

That night before the King retired to rest, Professor von Glauben reported himself and his duty to his Majesty in the privacy of his own apartments. He had, he stated, accompanied Gloria back to her home in The Islands; and, he added somewhat hesitatingly, the Crown Prince had returned with her, and had there remained. He, the Professor, had left them together, being commanded by the Prince so to do.

The King received this information with perfect equanimity.

"The boy must have his way for the present," he said. "His passion will soon exhaust itself. All passion exhausts itself sooner or—later!"

"That depends very much on the depth or shallowness of its source, Sir," replied the Professor.

"True! But a boy!—a mere infant in experience! What can he know of the depths in the heart and soul! Now a man of my age——"

He broke off abruptly, seeing Von Glauben's eyes fixed steadfastly upon him, and the colour deepened in his cheek. Then he gave a slight laugh.

"I tell you, Von Glauben, this little love-affair—this absurd toy- marriage is not worth thinking about. Humphry leaves the country at the end of this month,—he will remain absent a year,—and at the expiration of that time we shall marry him in good earnest to a royally-born bride. Meanwhile, let us not trouble ourselves about this sentimental episode, which is so rapidly drawing to its close."

The Professor bowed respectfully and retired. But not to sleep. He had a glowing picture before his eyes,—a picture he could not forget, of the Crown Prince and Gloria standing with arms entwined about each other under the rose-covered porch of Ronsard's cottage saying "Good- night" to him, while Ronsard himself, his tranquillity completely restored, and his former fears at rest, warmly shook his hand, and with a curious mingling of pride and deference thanked him for all his friendship—'all his goodness!'

"And no goodness at all is mine," said the meditative Professor, "save that of being as honest as I can to both sides! But there is some change in the situation which I do not quite understand. There is some new plan on foot I would swear! The Prince was too triumphant—Gloria too happy—Ronsard too satisfied! There is something in the wind!—but I cannot make out what it is!"

He pondered uneasily for a part of the night, reflecting that when he had returned from The Islands in the King's yacht, he had met the Prince's own private vessel on her way thither, gliding over the waves, a mere ghostly bunch of white sails in the glimmering moon. He had concluded that it was under orders to embark the Prince for home again in the morning; and yet, though this was a perfectly natural and probable surmise, he had been unable to rid himself altogether of a doubtful presentiment, to which he could give no name. By degrees, he fell into an uneasy slumber, in which he had many incompleted dreams,— one of which was that he found himself all alone on the wide ocean which stretched for thousands of miles beyond The Islands,—alone in a small boat, endeavouring to row it towards the great Southern Continent that lay afar off in the invisible distance,—where few but the most adventurous travellers ever cared to wander. And as he pulled with weak, ineffectual oars against the mighty weight of the rolling billows, he thought he heard the words of an old Irish song which he remembered having listened to, when as quite a young man he had paid his first and last visit to the misty and romantic shores of Britain.

> "Come o'er the sea
> *Cushla ma chree*!—
> Mine through sunshine, storm and snows!—
> Seasons may roll,
> But the true soul,
> Burns the same wherever it goes;
> Let fate frown on, so we love and part not,
> 'T is life where thou art, 't is death where thou art not!
> Then come o'er the sea,
> *Cushla ma chree*!
> Mine wherever the wild wind blows!"

Then waking with a violent start, he wondered what set of brain-cells had been stirred to reproduce rhymes that he had, or so he deemed, long ago forgotten. And still musing, he almost mechanically went on with the wild ditty.

> "Was not the sea
> Made for the free,

Land for Courts and chains alone!—
Here we are slaves,
But on the waves,
Love and liberty are our own!"

"This will never do!" he exclaimed, leaping from his bed; "I am becoming a mere driveller with advancing age!"

He went to the window and looked out. It was about six o'clock in the morning,—the sun was shining brightly into his room. Before him lay the sea, calm as a lake, and clear-sparkling as a diamond;—not a boat was in sight;—not a single white sail on the distant horizon. And in the freshness and stillness of the breaking day, the world looked but just newly created.

"How we fret and fume in our little span of life!" he murmured. "A few years hence, and for us all the troubles which we make for ourselves will be ended! But the sun and the sea will shine on just the same—and Love, the supremest power on earth, will still govern mankind, when thrones and kings and empires are no more!"

His thoughts were destined to bear quick fruition. The morning deepened into noon—and at that hour a sealed dispatch brought by a sailor, who gave no name and who departed as soon as he had delivered his packet, was handed to the King. It was from the Crown Prince, and ran briefly thus:—

"At your command, Sir, and by my own desire, I have left the country over which you hold your sovereign dominion. Whither I travel, and how, is my own affair. I shall return no more *till the Nation demands my service*,—whereof I shall doubtless hear should such a contingency ever arise. I leave you to deal with the situation as seems best to your good pleasure and that of the Government,—but the life God has given me can only be lived once, and to Him alone am I responsible for it. I am resolved therefore to live it to my own liking,—in honesty, faith and freedom. In accordance with this determination, Gloria, my wife, as in her sworn marriage-duty bound, goes with me."

For one moment the King stood transfixed and astounded; a cloud of anger darkened his brows. Crumpling up the document in his hand, he was about to fling it from him in a fury. What! This mere boy and girl had baffled the authority of a king! Anon, his anger cooled—his countenance cleared. Smoothing the paper out he read its contents again,—then smiled.

"Well! Humphry has something of me in him after all!" he said. "He is not entirely his mother! He has a heart,—a will, and a conscience,— all three generally lacking to sons of kings! Let me be honest with myself! If he had given way to me, I should have despised him!—'but for Love's sake he has opposed me; and by my soul!—I respect him!"

CHAPTER XXIII
THE KING'S DEFENDER

RUMOUR, we are told, has a million tongues, and they were soon all at work, wagging out the news of the Crown Prince's mysterious departure. Each tongue told a different story, and none of the stories tallied. No information was to be obtained at Court. There nothing was said, but that the Prince, disliking the formal ceremony of a public departure, had privately set sail in his own yacht for his projected tour round the world. Nobody believed this; and the general impression soon gained ground that the young man had fallen into disgrace with his Royal parents, and had been sent away for a time till he should recognize the enormity of his youthful indiscretions.

"Sent away—you understand!" said the society gossips; "To avoid further scandal!"

The Prince's younger brothers, Rupert and Cyprian, were often plied with questions by their intimates, but knowing nothing, and truly caring less, they could give no explanation. Neither King nor Queen spoke a word on the subject; and Sir Roger de Launay, astonished and perplexed beyond measure as he was at this turn in affairs, dared not put any questions even to his friend Professor von Glauben who, as soon as the news of the Prince's departure was known, resolutely declined to speak, so he said, "on what did not concern him." Gradually, however, this excitement partially subsided to give place to other forms of social commotion, which beginning in trifles, swiftly expanded to larger and more serious development. The first of these was the sudden rise of a newspaper which had for many years subsisted with the greatest difficulty in opposition to the many journals governed by David

Jost. It happened in this manner.

Several leading articles written in favour of a Jesuit settlement in the country, had appeared constantly in Jost's largest and most widely circulated newspaper, and the last of these 'leaders,' had concluded with the assertion that though his Majesty, the King, had at first refused the portion of Crown-lands needed by the Society for building, he had now 'graciously' re-considered the situation, and had been pleased to revoke his previous decision. Whereat, the very next morning the rival 'daily' had leaped into prominence by merely two headlines:

THE JESUIT SETTLEMENT STATEMENT BY HIS MAJESTY THE KING.

And there, plainly set forth, was the Royal and authoritative refusal to grant the lands required, 'Because of the earnest petition of our loving subjects against the said grant,'—and till 'our loving subjects" objections were removed, the lands would be withheld. This public announcement signed by the King in person, created the most extraordinary sensation throughout the whole country. It was the one topic at every social meeting; it was the one subject of every sermon. Preachers stormed and harangued in every pulpit, and Monsignor Del Fortis, lifting up his harsh raucous voice in the Cathedral itself, addressed an enormous congregation one Sunday morning on the matter, and denounced the King, the Queen, and the mysteriously-departed Crown Prince in the most orthodox Christian manner, commending them to the flames of hell, and the mercy of a loving God at one and the same moment.

Meanwhile, the newspaper that had been permitted to publish the King's statement got its circulation up by tens of thousands, the more so as certain brilliant and fiery articles on the political situation began to appear therein signed by one Pasquin Leroy, a stranger to the reading public, but in whom the spirit of a modern 'Junius' appeared to have entered for the purpose of warning, threatening and commanding. A scathing and audacious attack upon Carl Perousse, Secretary of State, in which the small darts of satire flew further than the sharpest arrows of assertion, was among the first of these, and Perousse himself, maddened like a bull at the first prick of the toreador, by the stinging truths the writer uttered, or rather suggested, lost no time in summoning General Bernhoff to a second interview.

"Did I not tell you," he said, pointing to the signature at the end of the offending article, "to 'shadow' that man, and arrest him as a common spy?"

Bernhoff bowed stiffly.

"You did! But it is difficult to arrest one who is not capable of being arrested. I must be provided first with proofs of his guilt; and I must also obtain the King's order."

"Proofs should be easy enough for you to obtain," said Perousse fiercely; "And the King will sign any warrant he is told. At least, you can surely find this rascal out?—where he lives, and what are his means of subsistence?"

"If he were here, I could," responded Bernhoff calmly; "I have made all the necessary preliminary enquiries. The man is a gentleman of considerable wealth. He writes for his own amusement, and—from a distance. I advise you—" and here the General held up an obstinate- looking finger of warning; "I advise you, I say, to let him alone! I can find no proof whatever that he is a spy."

"Proof! I can give you enough—" began Perousse hotly, then paused in confusion. For what could he truly say? If he told the Chief of Police that this Pasquin Leroy was believed to have counterfeited the Prime Minister's signet, in order to obtain an interview with David Jost, why then the Chief of Police would be informed once and for all that the Prime Minister was in confidential communication with the Jew- proprietor of a stock-jobbing newspaper! And that would never do! It would, at the least, be impolitic. Inwardly chafing with annoyance, he assumed an outward air of conscientious gravity.

"You will regret it, General, I think, if you do not follow out my suggestions respecting this man," he said coldly; "He is writing for the press in a strain which is plainly directed against the Government. Of course we statesmen pay little or no heed to modern journalism, but the King, having taken the unusual, and as I consider it, unwise step of proclaiming certain of his intentions in a newspaper which was, until his patronage, obscure and unsuccessful, the public attention has been suddenly turned towards this particular journal; and what is written therein may possibly influence the masses as it would not have done a few weeks ago."

"I quite believe that!" said Bernhoff tersely; "But I cannot arrest a man for writing clever things. Literary talent is no proof of dishonesty."

Perousse looked at him sharply. But there was no satire in Bernhoff's fixed and glassy eye, and no expression whatever in his woodenly- composed countenance.

"We entertain different opinions on the matter, it is evident!" he said; "You will at least grant that if he cannot be arrested, he can be carefully watched?"

"He *is* carefully watched!" replied Bernhoff; "That is to say, as far as *I* can watch him!"

"Good!" and Perousse smiled, somewhat relieved. "Then on the first suspicion of a treasonable act——"

"I shall arrest him—in the King's name, when the King signs the warrant," said Bernhoff; "But he is one of Sergius Thord's followers, and at the present juncture it might be unwise to touch any member of that particularly inflammable body."

Perousse frowned.

"Sergius Thord ought to have been hanged or shot years ago——"

"Then why did not you hang or shoot him?" enquired Bernhoff.

"I was not in office."

"Why do you not hang or shoot him now?"

"Why? Because——"

"Because," interrupted Bernhoff, again lifting his grim warning finger; "If you did, the city would be in a tumult and more than half the soldiery would be on the side of the mob! By way of warning, M. Perousse, I may as well tell you frankly, on the authority of my position as Head of the Police, that the Government are on the edge of a dangerous situation!"

Perousse looked contemptuous.

"Every Government in the world is on the edge of a dangerous situation nowa-days!" he retorted;—"But any Government that yields to the mob proves itself a mere ministry of cowardice."

"Yet the mob often wins,—not only by excess of numbers, but by sheer force of—honesty!"—said Bernhoff sententiously; "It has been known to sweep away, and re-make political constitutions before now."

"It has,"—agreed Perousse, drawing pens and paper towards him, and feigning to be busily occupied in the commencement of a letter—"But it will not indulge itself in such amusements during *my* time!"

"Ah! I wonder how long your time will last!" muttered Bernhoff to himself as he withdrew—"Six months or six days? I would not bet on the longer period!"

In good truth there was considerable reason for the General's dubious outlook on affairs. A political storm was brewing. A heavy tidal wave of discontent was sweeping the masses of the people stormily against the rocks of existing authority, and loud and bitter and incessant were the complaints on all sides against the increased taxation levied upon every rate-payer. Fiercest of all was the clamour made by the poor at the increasing price of bread, the chief necessity of life; for the imposition of a heavy duty upon wheat and other cereals had made the common loaf of the peasant's daily fare almost an article of luxury. Stormy meetings were held in every quarter of the city,—protests were drawn up and signed by thousands,—endless petitions were handed to the King,—but no practical result came from these. His Majesty was 'graciously pleased' to seem blind, deaf and wholly indifferent to the agitated condition of his subjects. Now and then a Government orator would mount the political rostrum and talk 'patriotism' for an hour or so, to a more or less sullen audience, informing them with much high- flown eloquence that, by responding to the Governmental demands and supporting the Governmental measures, they were strengthening the resources of the country and completing the efficiency of both Army and Navy; but somehow, his hydraulic efforts at rousing the popular enthusiasm failed of effect. Whereas, whenever Sergius Thord spoke, thousands of throats roared acclamation,—and the very sight of Lotys passing quietly down the poorer thoroughfares of the city was sufficient to bring out groups of men and women to their doors, waving their hands to her, sending her wild kisses,—and almost kneeling before her in an ecstasy of trust and adoration. Thord himself perceived that the situation was rapidly reaching a climax, and quietly prepared himself to meet and cope with it. Two of the monthly business meetings of the Revolutionary Committee had been held since that on which Pasquin Leroy and his two friends had been enrolled as members of the Brotherhood, and at the last of these, Thord took Leroy into his full confidence, and gave him all the secret clues of the Revolutionary organization which honeycombed the metropolis from end to end. He had trusted the man in many ways and found him honest. One trifling proof of this was perhaps the main reason of Thord's further reliance upon him; he had fulfilled his half-suggested promise to bring the sunshine of prosperity into the hard-working, and more or less sordid life of the little dancing-girl, Pequita. She had been sent for one morning by the manager of the Royal Opera, who having seen the ease, grace, and dexterity of her performance, forthwith engaged her for the entire season at a salary which when named to the amazed child, seemed like a veritable shower of gold tumbling by rare chance out of the lap of Dame Fortune. The manager was a curt, cold business man, and she was afraid to ask him any questions, for when the words—"I am sure a kind friend has spoken to you of me—" came timidly from her lips, he had shut up her confidence at once by the brief answer—

"No. You are mistaken. We accept no personal recommendations. We only employ proved talent!"

All the same Pequita felt sure that she owed the sudden lifting of her own and her father's daily burden of life, to the unforgetting care and intercession of Leroy. Lotys was equally convinced of the same, and both she and Sergius Thord highly appreciated their new associate's unobtrusive way of doing good, as it were, by stealth. Pequita's exquisite grace and agility had made her at once the fashion; the Opera was crowded nightly to see the 'wonderful child-dancer'; and valuable gifts and costly jewels were showered upon her, all of which she brought to Lotys, who advised her how to dispose of them best, and put by the money for the comfort and care of her father in the event of sickness, or the advance of age. Flattered and petted by the great world as she now was, Pequita never lost her head in the whirl of gay splendour, but remained the same child-like, loving little creature,— her one idol her father,—her only confidante, Lotys, whose gentle admonitions and constant watchfulness saved her from many a dangerous pitfall. As yet, she had not attained the wish she had expressed, to dance before the King,—but she was told that at any time his Majesty might visit the Opera, and that steps would be taken to induce him to do so for the special purpose of witnessing her performance. So with this half promise she was fain to be content, and to bear with the laughing taunts of her 'Revolutionary' friends, who constantly teased her and called her 'little traitor' because she sought the Royal favour.

Another event, which was correctly or incorrectly traced to Leroy's silently working influence, was the sudden meteoric blaze of Paul Zouche into fame. How it happened, no one knew;—and *why* it happened was still more of a mystery, because by all its own tenets and traditions the social world ought to have set itself dead against the 'Psalm of Revolution,'—the title of the book of poems which created such an amazing stir. But somehow, it got whispered about that the King had attempted to 'patronise' the poet, and that the poet had very indignantly resented the offered Royal condescension. Whereat, by degrees, there arose in society circles a murmur of wonder at the poet's 'pluck,' wonder that deepened into admiration, with incessant demand for his book,—and admiration soon expanded, with the aid of the book, into a complete "craze." Zouche's name was on every lip; invitations to great houses reached him every week;—his poems began to sell by thousands; yet with all this, the obstinacy of his erratic nature asserted itself as usual, undiminished, and Zouche withdrew from the shower of praise like a snail into its shell,—answered none of the flattering requests for 'the pleasure of his company,' and handed whatever money he made by his poems over to the funds of the Revolutionary Committee, only accepting as much out of it as would pay for his clothes, food, lodging, and—drink! But the more he turned his back on Fame, the more hotly it pursued him;—his very churlishness was talked about as something remarkable and admirable,—and when it was suggested that he was fonder of strong liquor than was altogether seemly, people smiled and nodded at each other pleasantly, tapped their foreheads meaningly and murmured: 'Genius! Genius!' as though that were a quality allied of divine necessity to alcoholism.

These two things,—the advent of a new dancer at the Opera, and the fame of Paul Zouche, were the chief topics of 'Society' outside its own tawdry personal concern; but under all the light froth and spume of the pleasure-seeking, pleasure-loving whirl of fashion, a fierce tempest was rising, and the first whistlings of the wind of revolt were already beginning to pierce through the keyholes and crannies of the stately building allotted to the business of Government;—so much so indeed that one terrible night, all unexpectedly, a huge mob, some twenty thousand strong, surrounded it, armed with every conceivable weapon from muskets to pickaxes, and shouted with horrid din for 'Bread and Justice!'—these being considered co-equal in the bewildered mind of the excited multitude. Likewise did they scream with protrusive energy: 'Give us back our lost Trades!' being fully aware, despite their delirium, that these said 'lost Trades' were being sold off into 'Trusts,' wherein Ministers themselves held considerable shares, A two- sided clamour was also made for 'The King! The King!' one side appealing, the other menacing,—the latter under the belief that his Majesty equally had 'shares' in the bartered Trades,—the former in the hope that the country's Honour might still be saved with the help of their visible Head.

Much difficulty was experienced in clearing this surging throng of indignant humanity, for though the soldiery were called out to effect the work, they were more than half-hearted in their business, having considerable grievances of their own to avenge,—and when ordered to fire on the people, flatly refused to do so. Two persons however succeeded at last in calming and quelling the tumult. One was Sergius Thord,—the other Lotys. Carl Perousse, seized with an access of 'nerves' within the cushioned luxury of his own private room in the recesses of the Government buildings, from whence he had watched the demonstration, peered from one of the windows, and saw one half of the huge mob melt swiftly away under the command of a tall, majestic- looking creature, whose massive form and leonine head appeared Ajax- like above the throng; and he watched the other half turn round in brisk order, like a well-drilled army, and march off, singing loudly and lustily, headed by a woman carried shoulder-high before them, whose white robes gleamed like a flag of truce in the glare of the torches blazing around her;—and to his utter amazement, fear and disgust, he heard the very soldiers shouting her name: "Lotys! Lotys!" with ever- increasing and thunderous plaudits of admiration and homage. Often and often had he heard that name,—often and often had he dismissed it from his thoughts with light masculine contempt. Often, too, had it come to the ears of his colleague the Premier, who as has been shown, even in intimate converse with his own private secretary, feigned complete ignorance of it. But it is well understood that politicians generally, and diplomatists always, assume to have no knowledge whatever concerning those persons of whom they are most afraid. Yet just now it was unpleasantly possible that "the stone which the builders rejected" might indirectly be the means of crushing the Ministry, and reorganizing the affairs of the country. His meditations on this occasion were interrupted by a touch on the shoulder from behind, and, looking up, he saw the Marquis de Lutera.

"Almost a riot!" he said, forcing a pale smile,—"But not quite!"

"Say, rather, almost a revolution!" retorted the Marquis brusquely;— "Jesting is out of place. We are on the brink of a very serious disaster! The people are roused. To-night they threatened to burn down these buildings over our heads,—to sack and destroy the King's Palace. The Socialist leader, Thord, alone saved the situation."

"With the aid of his mistress?" suggested Perousse with a sneer.

"You mean the woman they call Lotys? I am not aware that she is his mistress. I should rather doubt it. The people would not make such a saint of her if she were.

At any rate, whatever else she may be, she is certainly dangerous;—and in a country less free than ours would be placed under arrest. I must confess I never believed in her 'vogue' with the masses, until to-night."

Perousse was silent. The great square in front of the Government buildings was now deserted,—save for the police and soldiery on guard; but away in the distance could still be heard faint echoes of singing and cheering from the broken-up sections of the crowd that had lately disturbed the peace.

"Have you seen the King lately?" enquired Lutera presently.

"No."

"By his absolute 'veto' against our propositions at the last Cabinet Council, the impending war which would have been so useful to us, has been quashed in embryo," went on the Premier with a frown;—"This of course you know! And he has the right to exercise his veto if he likes. But I scarcely expected you after all you said, to take the matter so easily!"

Perousse smiled, and shrugged his shoulders deprecatingly.

"However," continued the Marquis with latent contempt in his tone;—"I now quite understand your complacent attitude! You have simply turned your 'Army Supplies Contract' into a 'Trust' Combine with other nations,—so you will not lose, but rather gain by the transaction!"

"I never intended to lose!" said Perousse calmly; "I am not troubled with scruples. One form of trade is as good as another. The prime object of life nowadays is to make money!"

Lutera looked at him, but said nothing.

"To amalgamate all the steel industries into one international Union, and get as many shares myself in the combine is not at all an unwise project," went on Perousse,—"For if our country is not to fight, other countries will;—and they will require guns and swords and all such accoutrements of war. Why should we not satisfy the demand and pocket the cash?"

Still the Marquis looked at him steadily.

"Are you aware,"—he asked at last, "that Jost, to save his 'press' prestige, has turned informer against you?"

Perousse sprang up, white with fury.

"By Heaven, if he has dared!—"

"There is no 'if' in the case"—said Lutera very coldly—"He has, as he himself says, 'done his duty.' You must be pretty well cognisant of what a Jew's notions of 'duty' are! They can be summed up in one sentence;—'to save his own pocket.' Jost is driven to fury and desperation by the sudden success of the rival newspaper, which has been so prominently favoured by the King. The shares in his own journalistic concerns are going down rapidly, and he is determined— naturally enough—to take care of himself before anyone else. He has sold out of every company with which you have been, or are associated— and has—so I understand,—sent a complete list of your proposed financial 'deals,' investments and other 'stock' to—"

He paused.

"Well!" exclaimed Perousse irascibly—"To whom?"

"To those whom it may concern,"—replied Lutera evasively—"I really can give you no exact information. I have said enough by way of warning!"

Perousse looked at him heedfully, and what he saw in that dark brooding face was not of a quieting or satisfactory nature.

"You are as deeply involved as I am—" he began.

"Pardon!" and the Marquis drew himself up with some dignity—"I *was* involved;—I am not now. I have also taken care of myself! I may have been misled, but I shall let no one suffer for my errors. I have sent in my resignation."

"Fool!" ejaculated Perousse, forgetting all courtesy in the sudden access of rage that took possession of him at these words;—"Fool, I say! At the very moment when you ought to stick to the ship, you desert it!"

"Are *you* not ready to run to the helm?" enquired Lutera with a satiric smile; "Surely you can have no doubt but that his Majesty will command you to take office!"

With this, he turned on his heel, and left his colleague to a space of very disagreeable meditation. For the first time in his bold and unscrupulous career, Perousse found himself in an awkward position. If it were indeed true that Jost and Lutera had thrown up the game, especially Jost, then he, Perousse, was lost. He had made of Jost, not only a tool, but a confidant. He had used him, and his great leading newspaper for his own political and financial purposes. He had entrusted him with State secrets, in order to speculate thereon in all the money-markets of the world. He had induced him to approach the Premier with crafty promises of support, and to inveigle him by insidious degrees into the same dishonourable financial 'deal.' So that if this one man,—this fat, unscrupulous turncoat of a Jew,—chose to speak out, he, Carl Perousse, Secretary of State, would be the most disgraced and ruined Minister that ever attempted to defraud a nation! His brows grew moist with fever-heat, and his tongue parched, with the dry thirst of fear, as the gravity of the situation was gradually borne in upon him. He began to calculate contingencies and possibilities of escape from the toils that seemed closing around him,—and much to his irritation and embarrassment, he found that most of the ways leading out of difficulty pointed first of all to,—the King.

The King! The very personage whom he had called a Dummy, only bound to do as he was told! And now, if he could only persuade the King that he,—the poor Secretary of State,—was a deeply-injured man, whose life's effort had been solely directed towards 'the good of the country,' yet who nevertheless was cruelly wronged and calumniated by his enemies, all might yet be well.

"Were he only like other monarchs whom I know," he reflected. "I could have easily involved him in the Trades deal! Then the press could have been silenced, and the public fooled. With five or six hundred thousand shares in the biggest concerns, he would have been compelled to work under me for the amalgamation of our Trades with the financial forces of other countries, regardless of the rubbish talked by 'patriots' on the loss of our position and prestige. But he is not fond of money,— he is not fond of money! Would that he were!—for so *I* should be virtually king of the King!"

Cogitating various problems on his return to his own house that evening, he remembered that despite numerous protests and petitions, the King had, up to the present, paid no attention to the appeals of his people against the increasing inroads of taxation. The only two measures he had carried with a high and imperative hand, were first,— the 'vetoing' of an intended declaration of war,—and the refusal of extensive lands to the Jesuits. The first was the more important action, as, while it had won the gratitude and friendship of a previously hostile State, it had lost several 'noble' gamblers in the griefs of nations, some millions of money. The check to the Jesuits was comparatively trivial, yet it had already produced far-reaching effects, and had offended the powers at the Vatican. But, beyond this, things remained apparently as they were; true, the Socialists were growing stronger;—but there was no evidence that the Government was growing weaker.

"After all," thought Perousse, as a result of his meditations; "there is no imme-diate cause for anxiety. If Lutera has sent in his resignation, it may not be accepted. That rests—like other things— with the King." And a vague surprise affected him at this fact. "Curious!" he muttered,—"Very curious that he, who was a Nothing, should now be a Something! The change has taken place very rapidly,— and very strangely! I wonder what—or who—is moving him?"

But to this inward query he received no satisfactory reply. The mysterious up-shot of the whole position was the same,—namely, that somehow, in the most un-accountable, inexplicable manner, the wind and weather of affairs had so veered round, that the security of Ministers and the stability of Government rested, not with themselves or the nature of their quarrels and discussions, but solely on one whom they were accustomed to consider as a mere ornamental figure-head,—the King.

Some few days after the unexpected turbulent rising of the mob, it was judged advisable to give the people something in the way of a 'gala,' or spectacle, in or-der to distract their attention from their own grievances, and to draw them away from their Socialistic clubs and conventions, to the contemplation of a parade of Royal state and splendour. The careful student of History cannot fail to note that whenever the rottenness and inadequacy of a Government are most apparent, great 'shows' and Royal ceremonials are always resorted to, in order to divert the minds of the people from the bitter consideration of a deficient Exchequer and a dimin-ishing National Honour. The authorities who organize these State masquerades are wise in their generation. They know that the working-classes very seldom have the leisure to think for themselves, and that they often lack the intelligent ability to foresee the difficulties and dangers menacing their country's welfare;—but that they are always ready, with the strangest fatuity, patience, and good-nature, to take their wives and families to see any new variation of a world's 'Punch and Judy' play, particularly if there is a savour of Royalty about it, accompanied by a brass band, well-equipped soldiers, and gilded coaches. Though they take no part in the pageant, beyond consenting to be hustled and rudely driven back by the police like intrusive sheep, out of the sacred way of a Royal progress, they nevertheless have an instinctive (and very correct) idea that somehow or other it is all part of the 'fun' for which they have paid their money. There is no more actual reverence or respect for the positive Person of Royalty in such a parade, than there is for the Wonderful Performing Pig who takes part in a circus- procession through a country town. The public impression is simple,— That having to pay for the up-keep of a Throne, its splendours should be occasionally 'trotted out' to see whether they are worth the nation's annual expenditure.

Moved entirely by this plain and practical sentiment, the popular breast was thrilled with some amount of interest and animation when it was announced that his Majesty the King would, on a certain afternoon, go in state to lay the foundation-stone of the Grand National Theatre, which was the very latest pet project of various cogitating Jews and cautious millionaires. The Grand National Theatre was intended to 'supply,' according to a stock newspaper phrase, 'a long-felt want.' It was to be a 'philanthropic' scheme, by which the 'Philanthropists' would receive excellent interest for their money. Ostensibly, it was to provide the 'masses' with the highest form of dramatic entertainment at the lowest cost;—but there were many intricate wheels within wheels in the elaborate piece of stock-jobbing mechanism, by which the public would be caught and fooled—as usual—and the speculators therein rendered triumphant. Sufficient funds were at hand to start the building of the necessary edifice, and the King's 'gracious' consent to lay the first stone, with full state and ceremony, was hailed by the promoters of the plan as of the happiest augury. For with such approval and support openly given, all the Snob-world would follow the Royal 'lead'—quite as infallibly as it did in the case of another monarch who, persuaded to drink of a certain mineral spring, and likewise to 'take shares' in its bottled waters, turned the said spring into a 'paying concern' at once, thereby causing much rejoicing among the Semites. The 'mob' might certainly decline to imitate the Snob-world,— but, considering the recent riotous outbreak, it might be as well that the overbold and unwashen populace should be awed by the panoply and glory of earthly Majesty passing by in earthly splendour.

Alas, poor Snob-world! How often has it thought the same thing! How often has it fancied that with show and glitter and brazen ostentation of mere purse-power, it can quell the rage for Justice, which, like a spark of God's own eternal Being, burns for ever in the soul of a People! Ah, that rage for Justice!—that divine fury and fever which with strong sweating and delirium shakes the body politic and cleanses it from accumulated sickly humours and pestilence! What would the nations be without its periodical and merciful visitations! Tearing down old hypocrisies,—rooting up weedy abuses,—rending asunder rotten conventions,—what wonder if thrones and sceptres, and even the heads of kings get sometimes mixed into the general swift clearance of long- accumulated dirt and disorder! And vainly at such times does the Snob- world anxiously proffer golden pieces for the price of its life! There shall not then be millions enough in all the earth, to purchase the safety of one proved Liar who has wilfully robbed his neighbour!

No hint of the underworkings of the people's thought, or the movement of the times was, however, apparent in the aspect of the gay multitudes that poured along the principal thoroughfares of the metropolis on the day appointed for the ceremony in which the King had consented to take the leading part. Poor and rich together, vied with one another to secure the various best points of view from whence the Royal pageant could be seen, winding down in glittering length from the Palace and Citadel, past the Cathedral, and so on to the great open square, where, surrounded by fluttering flags and streamers, a huge block of stone hung suspended by ropes from a crane, ready to be lowered at the Royal touch, and fixed in its place by the Royal trowel, as the visible and solid beginning of the stately fabric, which, according to pictorial models was to rise from this, its first foundation, into a temple of art and architecture, devoted to Melpomene and Thalia.

It was a glorious day,—the sun shone with vigorous heat and lustre from a cloudless sky,—the sea was calm as an inland pool—and people wore their lightest, brightest and most festive attire. Fair "society" dames, clad in the last capricious mode of ever-changing Fashion, and shading their delicate, and not always natural, complexions with airy parasols, filmy and finely-coloured as the petals of flowers, queened it over the flocking crowds of pedestrians, as they were driven past in their softly-cushioned carriages drawn by high-stepping horses;—all the boudoirs and drawing-rooms of the most exclusive houses seemed to have emptied their luxury-loving occupants into the streets,—and the whole town was, for a few hours at any rate, apparently given over to holiday. As the long line of soldiery preceding the King's carriage, wound down from the Citadel, groups of people cheered, and waved hats and handkerchiefs,—then, when his Majesty's own escort came into view, the cheering was redoubled,—and at last when the cumbrous, over- gilded, over-painted "Cinderella" State-coach appeared, and the familiar, but somewhat sternly-composed features of the King himself were perceived through the glass windows, a roar of acclamation, like the thundering of a long wave on an extensive stretch of rock-bound coast, echoed far and near, and again and again was repeated with increased and ever-increasing clamour. Who,—hearing such an enthusiastic greeting—would or could have imagined for one moment that the King, who was the object and centre of these tremendous plaudits, was at the same time judged as an enemy and an obstruction to justice by more than one half of the population! Yet it was so,—and so has often been. The populace will shout itself hoarse for any cause; whether it be a king going to be crowned, or a king going to be executed, the stimulus is the same, and the enthusiasm as passionate. It is merely the contagious hysteria of a moment that tickles their lungs to expansion in noise;—but the real sentiment of admiration for a fine character which might perhaps have moved the subjects of Richard Coeur de Lion to cries of exultation, is generally non-existent. And why? For no cause truly!—save that Lion-Hearts in kings no more pulsate through nations.

By the time the Royal procession reached its destination the crowd had largely increased, and the press of people round the scene of the forthcoming function was great enough to be seriously embarrassing to both the soldiery and the police. Slowly the gorgeous State-coach lumbered up to the entrance of the ground railed off for the ceremony, —and between a line of armed guards, the King alighted. Vociferous cheering again broke out on all sides, which his Majesty acknowledged in the usual formal manner by a monotonous military salute performed at regular intervals. Received with obsequious deference by all the persons concerned in the Grand National Theatre project, he conversed with one or two, shook hands with others, and was just on the point of addressing a few of his usual suave compliments to some pretty women who had been invited to adorn the scene, when David Jost advanced smilingly, evidently sure of a friendly recognition. For had not the King, when Crown Prince and Heir-Apparent, hunted game in his preserves?—yea, had he not even dined with him?—and had not he, Jost, written whole columns of vapid twaddle about the 'Royal smile' and the 'Royal favour' till the outside public had sickened at every stroke of his flunkey pen? How came it, then, that his Majesty seemed on this occasion to have no recollection of him, and looked over and beyond him in the airiest way, as though he were a far-off Jew in Jerusalem, instead of being the assumptive-Orthodox proprietor of several European newspapers published for the general misinformation and plunder of gullible Christians? Dismayed at the Royal coldness of eye, Jost stepped back with an uncomfortably crimson face; and one of the ladies present, personally knowing him, and seeing his discomfiture, ventured to call the King's attention to his presence and to make way for his approach, by murmuring gently, "Mr. Jost, Sir!"

"Ah, indeed!" said the monarch, with calm grey eyes still fixed on vacancy,—"I do not know anyone of that name! Permit me to admire that exquisite arrangement of flowers!" and, smiling affably on the astonished and embarrassed lady, he led her aside, altogether away from Jost's vicinity.

Stricken to the very dust of abasement by this direct "cut" so publicly administered, the crestfallen editor and proprietor of many journals stood aghast for a moment,—then as various unbidden thoughts began to chase one another through his bewildered head, he was seized with a violent trembling. He remembered every foolish, imprudent and disloyal remark he had made to the stranger named Pasquin Leroy who had called upon him bearing the Premier's signet,—and reflecting that this very Pasquin Leroy was now, by some odd chance, a contributor of political leaders and other articles to the rival daily newspaper which had published the King's official refusal of a grant of land to the Jesuits, he writhed inwardly with impotent fury. For might not this unknown man, Leroy,—if he were,—as he possibly was,—a friend of the King's—go to the full length of declaring all he knew and all he had learned from Jost's own lips, concerning certain 'financial secrets,' which if fully disclosed, would utterly dismember the Government and put the nation itself in peril? Might he not already even have informed the King? With his little, swine-like eyes retreating under the crinkling fat of his lowering brows, Jost, hot and cold by turns, wandered confusedly out of the 'exclusive' set of persons connected with the 'Grand National Theatre' scheme, who were now gathered round the suspended foundation-stone to which the King was approaching. He pretended not to see the curious eyes that stared at him, or the sneering mouths that smiled at the open slight he had received. Pushing his way through the crowd, he jostled against the thin black-garmented figure of a priest,—no other than Monsignor Del Fortis, who, with an affable word of recognition, drew aside to allow him passage. Affecting his usual 'company-manner' of tolerant good-nature, he forced himself to speak to this 'holy' man, who, at any rate, had paid him good money in round sums for so-called 'articles' or rather puff-advertisements in his paper concerning Church matters.

"Good-day, Monsignor!" he said—"You are not often seen at a Royal pageant! How comes it that you, of all persons in the world have brought yourself to witness the laying of the foundation-stone of a Theatre? Does not your calling forbid any patronage of the mimic Art?"

The priest's thin lips parted, showing a glimmer of wolfish teeth behind the pale stretched line of flesh.

"Not by any means!" he replied suavely—"In the present levelling and amalgamation of social interests, the Church and Stage are drawing very closely together."

"True!" said Jost, with a grin—"One might very well be taken for the other!"

Del Fortis looked at him meditatively.

"This," he said, waving his lean hand towards the centre of the brilliant crowd where now the King stood, "is a kind of drama in its way. And you, Mr. Jost, have just played one little scene in it!"

Jost reddened, and bit his lip.

"I am also another actor on the boards," continued Del Fortis smiling darkly;— "if only as a spectator in the 'super' crowd. And other comedians and tragedians are doubtless present, of whom we may hear anon!"

"The King has nasty humours sometimes," said Jost shortly, looking down at the flower in his buttonhole, and absently flicking off one of its petals with his fat forefinger—"He ought to be made to pay for them!"

"Ha, ha! Very good! Certainly!" and Del Fortis gave a piously- deprecating nod—"He ought to be made to pay! Especially when he hurts the feelings of his old friends! Are you going, Mr. Jost? Yes? What a pity! But you no doubt have your reporters present?"

"Oh, there are plenty of them about,"—said Jost carelessly, "But I shall condense all the account of these proceedings into a few lines."

"Ha,—ha!" laughed Del Fortis,—"I understand! Revenge—revenge! But— in certain cases—the briefest description is sometimes the most graphic—and startling! Good-day!"

Jost returned the salute curtly, and went,—not to leave the scene altogether, but merely to take up a position of vantage immediately above and behind the surging crowd, where from a distance he could watch all that was going on. He saw the King lift his hand towards the ropes and pulleys of the crane above him,—and as it was touched by the Royal finger, the foundation stone was slowly lowered into the deep socket prepared for it, where gold and silver coins of the year's currency had already been strewn. Then, with the aid of a silver trowel set in a handle of gold, and obsequiously presented by the managing director of the scheme, his Majesty dabbed in a little mortar, and declared in a loud voice that the stone was 'well and truly laid.' A burst of cheering greeted the announcement, and the band struck up the country's National Hymn, this being the usual sign that the ceremony was at an end. Whereupon the King, shaking hands again cordially with the various parties concerned, and again shedding the lustre of his smile upon the various ladies with whom he had been conversing, made his way very leisurely to his State equipage, which, with its six magnificently caparisoned horses, stood prepared for his departure, the door being already held open for him by one of the attendant powdered and gold-laced flunkeys. Sir Roger de Launay walked immediately behind his Sovereign, and Professor von Glauben was close at hand, companioned by two of the gentlemen of the Royal Household. All at once a young man pushed himself out of the crowd nearest to the enclosure,—paused a moment irresolute, and then, with a single determined bound reached the King's side.

"Thief of the People's money! Take that!" he shouted, wildly,—and, brandishing aloft a glittering stiletto, he aimed it straight at the monarch's heart!

But the blow never reached its destination, for a woman, closely veiled in black, suddenly threw herself swiftly and adroitly between the King's body and the descending blade, shielding his breast with both her outstretched arms. The dagger struck her violently, piercing her flesh through the upper part of her right shoulder, and under the sheer force of the blow, she fell senseless.

The whole incident took place in less time than it could be breathlessly told,—and even as she who had risked her life to save the King's, sank bleeding to the ground, the police seized the assassin red-handed in his mad and criminal act, and wrenched the murderous weapon from his hand. He was a mere lad of eighteen or twenty, and seemed dazed, submitting to be bound and handcuffed without a word. The King, perfectly tranquil and unhurt, bared his head to the wild cries and hysterical cheering of the excited spectators to whom his narrow escape from death appeared a kind of miracle, moving them to frantic paroxysms of passionate enthusiasm, and then bent anxiously down over the prostrate form of his rescuer, endeavouring himself to raise her from the ground. A hundred hands at once proffered assistance;—Sir Roger de Launay, pale to the lips with the shock of sick horror he had experienced at what might so easily have been a national catastrophe, assisted the police in forming a strong cordon round the person of his beloved Royal master, in order to guard him against any further possible attack,—and Professor von Glauben, obeying the King's signal, knelt down by the unconscious woman's side to examine the extent of her injury. Gently he turned back the close folds of her enveloping veil,— then gave a little start and cry:

"Gott in Himmel!" And he hastily drew down the veil again as the King approached with the question—

"Is she dangerously hurt?"

"No, Sir!—I think not—I hope not—but—!"

And the Professor's eyes looked volumes of suggestion. Catching his expression, the King drew still nearer.

"Uncover her face,—give her air!" he commanded.

With a perplexed side-glance at Sir Roger de Launay, the Professor obeyed,— and the sunshine fell full on the white calm features and closed eyelids of "the woman known as Lotys." Her black dress was darkly stained and soaked with oozing blood—and the deep dull gold of her hair was touched here and there with the same crimson hue;—but there was a smile on her lips, and her face was as fair and placid as though it had been smoothed out of all pain and trouble by the restful touch of Death. Silently, and with a perfectly inscrutable demeanour, the King surveyed her for a moment. Then, raising his plumed hat with grave grace and courtesy, he looked on all those who stood about him, soldiery, police and spectators.

"Does anyone here present know this lady?" he demanded.

A crowd of eager heads were pushed forward, and then a low murmur began, which deepened into a steady roar of delighted acclamation.

"Lotys! Lotys!"

The name was caught up quickly and repeated from mouth to mouth—till

away on the extreme outskirts of the crowd it was tossed back again with shouts—
"Lotys! Lotys!"

Swiftly the news ran like an electric current through the whole body of the populace, that it was Lotys, their own Lotys, their friend, their fellow-worker, the idol of the poorer classes, that had saved the life of the King! Half-incredulous, half-admiring, the mob listened to the growing rumour, and the general excitement increased in intensity among them. David Jost, from his point of observation, caught the infection, and realizing at once the value of the dramatic "copy" for his paper, to be obtained out of such a situation, jumped into the nearest vehicle and was driven straight to his offices, there to send electric messages of the news to every quarter of the world, and to endeavour by printed loyal outbursts of "gush" to turn the current of the King's displeasure against him into a more favourable direction. Meanwhile the King himself gave orders that his wounded rescuer should be conveyed in one of the Royal carriages straight to the Palace, and there attended by his own physician. Professor von Glauben was entrusted with the carrying-out of this command,—and the monarch, then entering his own State-equipage, started on his homeward progress.

Thundering cheers now greeted him at every step;—for an hour at least the populace went mad with rapture, shouting, singing and calling alternately for "The King!" and "Lotys!" with no respect of persons, or consideration as to their differing motives and opposite stations in life. Two facts only were clear to them,—first an attempt had been made to assassinate the King,—secondly, that Lotys had frustrated the attempt, and risked her own life to save that of the monarch. These were enough to set fire to the passionate sentiments of a warm-blooded, restless Southern people, and they gave full sway to their feelings accordingly. So, amid deafening plaudits, the Royal procession wended its way back to the Citadel, the State-coach moving at a snail's pace in order to allow the people to see the King for themselves, and make sure he was uninjured, as they cheered, and followed it in surging throngs to the very gates of the Palace,—while in another and reverse direction the wretched youth whose miserable effort to commit a dastard crime had so fortunately failed, was marched off, under the guard of a strong body of police to the State-Prison, there to await his trial and condemnation. A small crowd, hooting and cursing the criminal, pursued him as he went, and one personage, austere and dignified, also followed, at a distance, as though curious to see the last of the would-be murderer ere he was shut out from liberty,—and this was Monsignor Del Fortis.

CHAPTER XXIV
A WOMAN'S REASON

WHEN Lotys recovered from her death-like swoon, she found herself on a sofa among heaped-up soft cushions, in a small semi-darkened room hung with draperies of rose satin, which were here and there drawn aside to show exquisite groupings of Saxe china and rare miniatures on ivory;— the ceiling above her was a painted mirror, where Venus in her car of flowers, drawn by doves, was pictured floating across a crystal sea,— the floor was strewn with white bearskins,—the corners were filled with palms and flowers. As she regarded these unaccustomed surroundings wonderingly, a firm hand was laid on her wrist, and a brusque voice said in her ear:—

"Lie still, if you please! You have been seriously hurt! You must rest."

She turned feebly towards the speaker, and saw a big burly man with a bald head, seated at her side, who held a watch in one hand, and felt her pulse with the other. She could not discern his features plainly, for his back was set to the already shaded light, and her own eyes were weak and dim.

"You are very kind!" she murmured—"I do not quite remember—Ah, yes!" and a quick flash of animation passed over her face—"I know now! The King! Is—is all well?"

"All is well, thanks to you!" replied the gruff voice—"You have saved his life."

"Thank God!"—and she closed her eyes again wearily, while two slow tears trickled from under the shut white lids—"Thank God!"

Professor von Glauben, placed in charge of her by the King's command, gently relinquished the small white hand he held, and stepping noiselessly to a table near at hand, poured out from one of the various little flasks set thereon, a cordial the properties of which were alone known to himself, and held the glass to her lips.

"Drink this off at once!"—he said authoritatively, yet kindly.

She obeyed. He then, turning aside with the empty glass, sat down and watched her from a little distance. Soon a faint flush tinged her dead- white skin, and presently, with a deep sigh, she opened her eyes again. Then she became aware of a stiffness and smart in her right shoulder, and saw that it was tightly bandaged, and that the bodice of her dress was cut away from it. Lying perfectly still, she gradually brought her strong spirit of self-control to bear on the situation, and tried to collect her scattered thoughts. Very few minutes sufficed her to recollect all that had happened, and as she realised more and more vividly that she was in some strange and luxurious abode where she had no business or desire to be, she gathered all the forces of her mind to her aid, and with but a slight effort, sat upright. Professor von Glauben came towards her with an exclamation of warning—but she motioned him back with a very decided gesture.

"Please do not trouble!" she said—"I am quite able to move—to stand— see!" And she rose to her feet, trembling a little, and steadying herself by resting one hand on the edge of the sofa. "I do not know who you are, but I am sure you have been most kind to me! And if you would do me a still greater kindness, you will let me go away from here at once!"

"Impossible, Madame!" declared the Professor, firmly—"His Majesty, the King——"

"What of his Majesty, the King?" demanded Lotys with sudden hauteur— "Am I not mistress of my own actions?"

The Professor made an elaborate bow.

"Most unquestionably you are, Madame!" he replied—"But you are also for the moment, a guest in the King's Palace; and having saved his life, you will surely not withhold from him the courteous acceptance of his hospitality?"

"The King's Palace!" she echoed, and a little disdainful smile crossed her lips— "I,—Lotys,—in the King's Palace!" She moved a few steps, and drew herself proudly erect. "You, sir, are a servant of the King's?"

"I am his Majesty's resident physician, at your service!" he said, with another bow—"I have had the honour of attending to the wound you so heroically received in his defence,—and though it is not a dangerous wound, it is an exceedingly un-pleasant one I assure you,—and will give you a good deal of pain and trouble. Let me advise you very earnestly to stay where you are, and rest—do not think of leaving the Palace to-night."

She sighed restlessly. "I must not think of staying in it!" she replied. "But I do not wish to seem churlish—or ungrateful for your care and kindness;—will you tell the King—" Here she broke off abruptly, and fixed her eyes searchingly on his face. "Strange!" she murmured—"I seem to have seen you before,—or someone very like you!"

The Professor was troubled with a sudden fit of coughing which made him very red in the face, and obliged him to turn away for a moment in order to recover himself. Still struggling with that obstinate catch in his throat he said:

"You were saying, Madame, that you wished me to tell the King something?"

"Yes!" said Lotys eagerly—"if you will be so good! Tell him that I thank him for his courtesy;—but that I must go away from this Palace, —that I cannot—may not—stop in it an hour longer! He does not know who it is that saved his life,—if he did, he would not wish me to remain a moment under his roof! He would be as anxious and willing for me to leave as I am to go! Will you tell him this?"

"Madame, I will tell him," replied the Professor deferentially, yet with a slight smile—"But—if it will satisfy your scruples, or ease your mind at all,—I may as well inform you that his Majesty does know who you are! The populace itself declared your name to him, with shouts of acclamation." She flushed a vivid red, then grew very pale.

"If that be so, then he must also be aware that I am his sworn enemy!" she said,—"And, that in accordance with the principles I hold, I cannot possibly remain under his roof! Therefore I trust, sir, you will have the kindness to provide me with a way of quick exit before my presence here becomes too publicly reported."

The Professor was slightly nonplussed. He considered for a moment; then rapidly made up his mind.

"Madame, I will do so!" he said—"That is, if you will permit me first of all to announce your intention of leaving the Palace, to the King. Pardon me for suggesting that his Majesty can hardly regard as an enemy a lady who has saved his life at the risk of her own."

"I did not save it because he is the King," she said curtly, "And you are at liberty to tell him so. Please make haste to inform him at once of my desire to leave the Palace,—and say also, that if he considers he owes me any gratitude, he will show it by not detaining me."

The Professor bowed and retired. Lotys, left alone, sat down for a moment in one of the luxuriously cushioned chairs, and pressed her left hand hard over her eyes to try and still their throbbing ache. Her right arm was bound up and useless,— and the pain from the wound in her shoulder caused her acute agony,—but she had a will of iron, and she had trained her mental forces to control, if not entirely to master, her physical weaknesses. She thought, not of her own suffering, but of the exciting incident in which mere impulse had led her to take so marked a share. It was by pure accident that she had joined the crowd assembled to see the King lay the foundation-stone of the proposed new Theatre. She had been as it were, entangled in the press of the people, and had got pushed towards the centre of the scene almost against her own volition. And while she had stood,—a passive and unwilling spectator of the pageant,—her attention had been singularly attracted towards the uneasy and restless movements of the youth who had afterwards attempted the assassination of the monarch. She had watched him narrowly; though she could not have explained why she did so, even to herself. He was a complete stranger to her, and yet, with her quick intuition, she had discerned a curious expression of anxiety and fear in his face, as though of the impending horror of a crime,—a look which, because it was so strained and unnatural, had aroused her suspicion. When she had sprung forward to shield the King, only one idea had inspired her,—and that idea she would not now fully own even to herself, because it was so entirely, weakly feminine. Nevertheless, from woman's weakness has often sprung a hero's strength—and so it had proved in this case. She did not, however, allow herself to dwell on the instinctive impulse which had thrown her on the King's breast, ready to receive her own death-blow rather than that he should die; she preferred to elude that question, and to consider her action solely from the standpoint of those Socialistic theories with which she was indissolubly associated.

"Had I not frustrated the attempt, the crime would have been set down to us and our Brotherhood," she said to herself, "Sergius—or Paul Zouche—or I myself— or even Pasquin—yes, even he!—might, and doubtless would, have been accused of instigating it. As it is, I think I have saved the situation." She rose and walked slowly up and down the room. "I wonder who is behind the wretched boy concerned in this business? He is too young to have determined on such a deed himself,— unless he is mad;—he must be a tool in the hands of others."

Here spying her long black cloak hanging across a chair, she took it up and threw it round her,—her face was reflected back upon her from a mirror set in the wall, round which a cluster of ivory cupids clambered,—and she looked critically at her white drawn features, and the disordered masses of her hair. Loosening these abundant locks, she shook them down and gathered them into her one uncrippled hand, preparatory to twisting them into the usual knot at the back of her head, the while she looked at the little sculptured *amorini* set round the mirror, with a compassionate smile.

"Such a number of mimic Loves where there is no real love!" she said half aloud,—when the opening of a door, and the swaying movement of a curtain pushed aside, startled her; and still holding her rich hair up in her hand she turned quickly,—to find herself face to face with,— the King.

There was an instant's dead silence. Dropping the silken gold weight of her tresses to fall as they would, regardless of conventional appearances, she stood erect, making all unconsciously to herself, a picture of statuesque and beauteous tragedy. Her plain black garments, —the long cloak enveloping her slight form, and the glorious tangle of her unbound hair rippling loosely about her pale face, in which her eyes shone like blue flowers, made luminous by the sunlight of the inspired soul behind them, all gave her an almost supernatural air,— and made her seem as wholly unlike any other woman as a strange leaf from an unexplored country is unlike the foliage common to one's native land. The King looked steadfastly upon her; she, meeting his gaze with equal steadfastness, felt her heart beating violently, though, as she well knew, it was not with fear. She had no thought of Court etiquette,—nor had she any reason to consider it, his Majesty having himself deliberately trespassed upon its rules by visiting her thus alone and unattended. She offered no reverence,—no salutation;—she simply stood before him, quite silent, awaiting his pleasure,—though in her eyes there shone a dangerous brilliancy that was almost feverish, and nervous tremors shook her from head to foot. The strange dumb spell between them relaxed at last. With a kind of effort which expressed itself in the extra rigidity and pallor of his fine features, the King spoke:

"Madame, I have come to thank you! Your noble act of heroism this afternoon has saved my life. I do not say it is worth saving!—but the Nation appears to think it is,—and in the name of the Nation, whose servant I am, I offer you my personal gratitude—and service!"

He bowed low as he said these words gravely and courteously. Her eyes still searched his face wistfully, with the eager plaintive expression of a child looking for some precious treasure it has lost. She strove to calm her throbbing pulses,—to quiet the hurrying blood in her veins,—to brace herself up to her usual impervious height of composure and self-control.

"I need no thanks!" she answered briefly—"I have only done my duty!"

"Nay, Madame, is it quite consistent with your duty to shield from death one so hated by your disciples and followers?" he asked, with a tinge of melancholy in his accents—"You—as the famous Lotys—should have helped to kill, not to save!"

She regarded him fearlessly.

"You mistake!" she said—"As King, you should learn to know your subjects better! We are not murderers. We do not seek your life,—we seek to make you understand the need there is of honesty and justice. We live our lives among the poor; and we see those poor crushed down into the dust by the rich, without hope and without help,—and we endeavour to rouse them to a sense of this Wrong, so that they may, by persistence, obtain Right. We do not want the death of any man! Even to a traitor we give warning and time, ere we punish his treachery. The unhappy wretch who attempted your life to-day was not of our party, or our teaching, thank God!"

"I am sure of that!" he said very gently, his face brightening with a kind smile,— then, seeing her swerve, as though about to fall, he caught her on one arm—"You are faint! You must not stand too long. I fear you are suffering from the pain of that cruel wound inflicted on you for my sake!"

"A little—" she managed to say, with white lips—"But it is nothing— it will soon pass——"

She sank helplessly into the chair he placed for her, and mutely watched him as he walked to the window and threw it open, admitting the sweet, fresh, sea-scented air, and a flood of crimson radiance from the setting sun.

"I am informed that you wish to quit the Palace at once," he said, averting his gaze from hers for a moment;—"Need I say how much I regret this decision of yours? Both I and the Queen had hoped you would have remained with us, under the care of our own physician, till you were quite recovered. But I owe you too great a debt already to make any further claim upon you—and I will not command you to stay, if you desire to go."

She lifted her head;—the faint colour was returning to her cheeks.

"I thank you!" she said simply;—"I do indeed desire to go. Every moment spent here is a moment wasted!"

"You think so?"—and, turning from the window where he stood, he confronted her again;—"May I venture to suggest that you hardly do justice to me, or to the situation? You have placed me under very great obligations—surely you should endure my company long enough to tell me at least how I can in some measure show my personal recognition of your brave and self-sacrificing action!"

She looked at him in musing silence. A strange glow came into her eyes,—a deeper crimson flushed her cheek.

"You can do nothing for me!" she said, after a long pause, "You are a King—I, a poor commoner. I would not be indebted to you for all the world! I am prouder of my 'common' estate than you are of your royalty! What are 'royal' rewards? Jewels, money, place, title! All valueless to me! If you would serve anyone, serve the People;—do something to deserve their trust! If you would show *me* any personal recognition, as you say, for saving your life, make that life more noble!"

He heard her without offence, holding himself mute and motionless. She rose from her seat, and approached him more closely.

"Perhaps, after all, it is well that I was,—unconsciously and against my own volition,—brought here," she said; "Perhaps it is God's will that I should speak with you! For, as a rule none of your unknown subjects can, or may speak with you!—you are so much hemmed in and ringed round with slaves and parasites! In so far as this goes, you are to be pitied; though it rests with you to shake yourself free from the toils of vulgar adulation. Your flatterers tell you nothing. They are careful to keep you shut out of your own kingdom—to hide from you things that are true,—things that you ought to know; they fool you with false assurances of national tranquillity and content,—they persuade you to play, like an over-grown child, with the toys of luxury,—they lead you, a mere puppet, round and round in the clockwork routine of a foolish and licentious society,—when you might be a Man! —up and doing man's work that should help you to regenerate and revivify the whole country! I speak boldly—yes!—because I do not fear you!—because I have no favours to gain from you,—because to me,— Lotys,—you,—the King—are nothing!"

Her voice, perfectly tranquil, even, and coldly sweet, had not a single vibration of uncertainty or hesitation in it—and her words seemed to cut through the stillness of the room with clean incisiveness like the sweep of a sword-blade. Outside, the sea murmured and the leaves rustled,—the sun had sunk, leaving behind it a bright, pearly twilight sky, flecked with pink clouds like scattered rose-petals.

He looked straight at her,—his clear dark grey eyes were filled with the glowing fire of strongly suppressed feeling. Some hasty ejaculation sprang to his lips, but he checked it, and pacing once or twice up and down, suddenly wheeled round, and again confronted her.

"If, as a king, I fall so far short of kingliness, and am nothing to you,"—he said deliberately; "Why did you shield me from the assassin's dagger a while ago? Why not have let me perish?"

She shook back her gold hair, and regarded him almost defiantly.

"I did not save you because you are the King!" she replied—"Be assured of that!"

He was vaguely astonished.

"Merely a humane sentiment then?" he said—"Just as you would have saved a dog from drowning!"

A little smile crept reluctantly round the corners of her mouth.

"There was another reason," she began in a low tone,—then paused— "But— only a woman's reason!"

Something in her changing colour,—some delicate indefinable touch of tenderness and pathos, which softened her features and made them almost ethereal, sent a curious thrill through his blood.

"A woman's reason!" he echoed; "May I not hear it?"

Again she hesitated,—then, as if despising herself for her own irresolution she spoke out bravely.

"You may!"—she said—"There is nothing to conceal—nothing of which I am ashamed! Besides, it is the true motive of the action which you are pleased to call 'heroic.' I saved your life simply because—because you resemble in form and feature, in look and manner, the only man I love!"

A curious silence followed her words. The faint far whispering of the leaves on the trees outside seemed almost intrusively loud in such a stillness,—the placid murmur of the sea against the cliff below the Palace became well-nigh suggestive of storm. Lotys was suddenly conscious of an odd strained sense of terror,—she had spoken as freely and frankly as she would have spoken to any one of her own associates, —and yet she felt that somehow she had been over-impulsive, and that in a thoughtless moment she had let slip some secret which placed her, weak and helpless, in the King's power. The King himself stood immovable as a figure of bronze,—his eyes resting upon her with a deep insistence of purpose, as though he sought to wrest some further confession from her soul. The tension between them was painful,—almost intolerable,—and though it lasted but a minute, that minute seemed weighted with the potentialities of years. Forcing herself to break the dumb spell, Lotys went on hurriedly and half desperately:—

"You may smile at this," she said—"Men always jest with a woman's heart,—a woman's folly! But folly or no, I will not have you draw any false conclusions concerning me,—or flatter yourself that it was loyalty to you, or honour for your position that made me your living shield to-day. No!—for if you were not the exact counterpart of him who is dearer to me than all the world beside, I think I should have let you die! I think so—I do not know! Because, after all, you are not like him in mind or heart; it is only your outward bearing, your physical features that resemble his! But, even so, I could not have looked idly on, and seen his merest Resemblance slain! Now you understand! It is not for you, as King, that I have turned aside a murderer's weapon,—but solely because you have the face, the eyes, the smile of one who is a thousand times greater and nobler than you,—who, though poor and uncrowned, is a true king in the grace and thought and goodness of his actions,—who, all unlike you, personally attends to the wants of the poor, instead of neglecting them,—and who recognises, and does his best to remedy, the many wrongs which afflict the people of this land!"

Her sweet voice thrilled with passion,—her cheeks glowed,— unconsciously she stretched out her uninjured hand with an eloquent gesture of pride and conviction. The King's figure, till now rigid and motionless, stirred;—advancing a step, he took that hand before she could withhold it, and raised it to his lips.

"Madame, I am twice honoured!" he said, in accents that shook ever so slightly—"To resemble a good man even outwardly is something,—to wear in any degree the lineaments of one whom a brave and true woman honours by her love is still more! You have made me very much your debtor"— here he gently relinquished the hand he had kissed—"but believe me, I shall endeavour most faithfully to meet the claim you have upon my gratitude!" Here he paused, and drawing back, bowed courteously. "The way for your departure is clear," he continued;—"I have ordered a carriage to be in waiting at one of the private entrances to the Palace. Professor von Glauben, my physician, who has just attended you, will escort you to it. You will pass out quite unnoticed,—and be,—as you desire it—again at full liberty. Let the memory of the King whose life you saved trouble you no more,—except when you look upon his better counterpart!—as then, perchance, you may think more kindly of him! For he has to suffer!—not so much for his own faults, as for the faults of a system formulated by his ancestors."

Her intense eyes glowed with a fire of enthusiasm as she lifted them to his face.

"Kingship would be a grand system," she said, "if kings were true! And Autocracy would be the best and noblest form of government in the world, if autocrats could be found who were intellectual and honest at one and the same time!"

He looked at her observantly.

"You think they are neither?"

"*I* think? 'I' am nothing,—my opinions count for nothing! But History gives evidence, and supplies proof of their incompetency. A great king,—good as well as great,—would be the salvation of this present time of the world!"

Still he kept his eyes upon her.

"Go on!"—he said—"There is something in your mind which you would fain express to me more openly. You have eloquent features, Madame!— and your looks are the candid mirror of your thoughts. Speak, I beg of you!"

The light of a daring inward hope flashed in her face and inspired her very attitude, as she stood before him, entirely regardless of herself.

"Then,—since you give me leave,—I *will* speak!" she said; "For perhaps I shall never see you again—never have the chance to ask you, as a Man whom the mere accident of birth has made a king, to have more thought, more pity, more love for your subjects! Surely you should be their guardian—their father—their protector? Surely you should not leave them to become the prey of unscrupulous financiers or intriguing Churchmen? Some say you are yourself involved in the cruel schemes which are slowly but steadily robbing this country's people of their Trades, the lawful means of their subsistence; and that you approve, in the main, of the private contracts which place our chief manufactures and lines of traffic in the hands of foreign rivals. But I do not believe this. We—and by we, I mean the Revolutionary party—try hard not to believe this! I admit to you, as faithfully as if I stood on my trial before you, that much of the work to which we, as a party have pledged ourselves, consists in moving the destruction of the Monarchy, and the formation of a Republic. But why? Only because the Monarchy has proved itself indifferent to the needs of the people, and deaf to their protestations against injustice! Thus we have conceived it likely that a Republic might help to mend matters,—if it were in power for at least some twenty or thirty years,—but at the same time we know well enough that if a King ruled over us who was indeed a King,—who would refuse to be the tool of party speculators, and who could not be moved this way or that by the tyrants of finance, the people would have far more chance of equality and right under a Republic even! Only we cannot find that king!—no country can! You, for instance, are no hero! You will not think for yourself, though you might; you only interest yourself in affairs that may redound to your personal and private credit; or in those which affect 'society,' the most dissolute portion of the community,— and you have shown so little individuality in yourself or your actions, that your unexpected refusal to grant Crown lands to the Jesuits was scarcely believed in or accepted, otherwise than as a caprice, till your own 'official' announcement. Even now we can scarcely be brought to look upon it except as an impulse inspired by fear! Herein, we do you, no doubt, a grave injustice; I, for one, honestly believe that you have refused these lands to the Priest- Politicians, out of earnest consideration for the future peace and welfare of your subjects."

"Nay, why believe even thus much of me?" he interrupted with a grave smile; "May you not be misled by that Resemblance I bear, to one who is, in your eyes, so much my superior?"

A faint expression of offence darkened her face, and her brows contracted.

"You are pleased to jest!" she said coldly; "As I said before, it is man's only way of turning aside, or concluding all argument with a woman! I am mistaken perhaps in the instinct which has led me to speak to you as openly as I have done,—and yet,—I know in my heart I can do you no harm by telling you the truth, as others would never tell it to you! Many times within this last two months the people have sent in petitions to you against the heavy taxes with which your Government is afflicting them, and they can get no answer to their desperate appeals. Is it kingly—is it worthy of your post as Head of this realm, to turn a deaf ear to the cries of those whose hard-earned money keeps you on the Throne, housed in luxury, guarded from every possible evil, and happily ignorant of the pangs of want and hunger? How can you, if you have a heart, permit such an iniquitous act on the part of your Government as the setting of a tax on bread?—the all in all of life to the very poor! Have you ever seen young children crying for bread? I have! Have you ever seen strong men reduced to the shame of stealing bread, to feed their wives and infants? I have! I think of it as I stand here, surrounded by the luxury which is your daily lot,—and knowing what I know, I would strip these satin-draped walls, and sell everything of value around me if I possessed it, rather than know that one woman or child starved within the city's precincts! Your Ministers tell you there is a deficiency in the Exchequer,—but you do not ask why, or how the deficiency arose! You do not ask whether Ministers themselves have not been trafficking and speculating with the country's money! For if deficiency there be, it has arisen out of the Government's mismanagement! The Government have had the people's money,—and have thrown it recklessly away. Therefore, they have no right to ask for more, to supply what they themselves have wilfully wasted. No right, I say!—no right to rob them of another coin! If I were a man, and a king like you, I would voluntarily resign more than half my annual kingly income to help that deficit in the National Exchequer till it had been replaced;—I would live poor,—and be content to know that by my act I had won far more than many millions—a deathless, and beloved name of honour with my people!"

She paused. He said not a word. Suddenly she became conscious that her hair was unbound and falling loosely about her; she had almost forgotten this till now. A wave of colour swept over her face,—but she mastered her embarrassment, and gathering the long tresses together in her left hand, twisted them up slowly, and with an evident painful effort. The King watched her, a little smile hovering about his mouth.

"If I might help you!" he said softly—"but—that is a task for my Resemblance!"

She appeared not to hear him. A sudden determination moved her, and she uttered her thought boldly and at all hazards.

"If you do not, as the public report, approve of the financial schemes out of which your Ministers make their fortunes, to the utter ruin of the people in general," she said slowly; "Dismiss Carl Perousse from office! So may you perchance avert a great national disaster!"

He permitted himself to smile indulgently.

"Madame, you may ask much!—and however great your demands, I will do my utmost to meet and comply with them;—but like all your charming sex, you forget that a king can seldom or never interfere with a political situation! It would be very unwise policy on my part to dismiss M. Perousse, seeing that he is already nominated as the next Premier."

"The next Premier!" Lotys echoed the words with a passionate scorn; "If that is so, I give you an honest warning! The people will revolt,—no force can hold them back or keep them in check! And if you should command your soldiery to fire on the populace, there must be bloodshed and crime!—on your head be the result! Oh, are you not, can you not be something higher than even a king?—an honest man? Will you not open the eyes of your mind to see the wickedness, falsehood and treachery of this vile Minister, who ministers only to his own ends?—who feigns incorruptibility in order to more easily corrupt others?—who assumes the defence of outlying states, merely to hide the depredations he is making on home power? Nay, if you will not, you are not worth a beggar's blessing!—and I shall wonder to myself why God made of you so exact a copy of one whom I know to be a good man!"

Her breath came and went quickly,—her cheeks were flushed, and great tears stood in her eyes. But he seemed altogether unmoved.

"I' faith, I shall wonder too!" he said very tranquilly; "Good men are scarce!—and to be the copy of one is excellent, though it may in some cases be misleading! Madame, I have heard you with patience, and—if you will permit me to say so—admiration! I honour your courage—your frankness—and—still more—your absolute independence. You speak of wrongs to the People. If such wrongs indeed exist——"

"If!" interrupted Lotys with a whole world of meaning in the expression.

"I say, if they indeed exist, I will, as far as I may,—endeavour to remedy them. I, personally, have no hesitation in declaring to you that I am not involved in the financial schemes to which you allude—though I know two or three of my fellow-sovereigns who are! But I do not care sufficiently for money to indulge in specula-tion. Nevertheless, let me tell you, speculation is good, and even necessary in mat-ters affecting national finance, and I am confident—" here he smiled enigmatically, "that the country's honour is safe in the hands of M. Perousse!"

At this she lifted her head proudly and looked at him, with eyes that expressed so magnificent a disdain, that had he been any other than the man he was, he might have quailed beneath the lightning flash of such utter contempt.

"You are confident that the country's honour is safe!" she repeated bitterly; "I am confident that it is betrayed and shamed! And History will set a curse against the King who helped in its downfall!"

He regarded her with a vague, lingering gentleness.

"You are harsh, Madame!" he said softly; "But you could not offend me if you tried! I quarrel with none of your sex! And you will, I hope, think better of me some day,—and not be sorry—as perhaps you are now —for having saved a life so worth-less! Farewell!"

She offered no response. The silken portiere rustled and swayed,—the door opened and shut again quietly—he was gone. Left alone, Lotys dropped wearily on the sofa, and burying her head in the soft cushions, gave way to an outburst of tears and sobbed like a tired and exhausted child. In this condition Professor von Glauben, entering presently, found her. But his sympathy, if he felt any, was out-wardly very chill and formal. Another dose of his 'cordial,'—a careful examination and re-strapping of the wounded shoulder,—these summed up the whole of his consolation; and his precise cold manner did much to restore her to her self-posses-sion. She thanked him in a few words for his professional attention, without raising her eyes to his face, and quietly followed him down a long narrow passage which terminated in a small private door giving egress to the Royal pleasure-grounds,—and here a hired close carriage was waiting. Putting her carefully into this vehicle, the Professor then delivered himself of his last instructions.

"The driver has no orders beyond the citadel, Madame," he explained. "His Majesty begged me to say that he has no desire to seem inquisitive as to your place of residence. You will therefore please inform the coachman yourself as to where you wish to be driven. And take care of that so-much-wounded shoulder!" he added, relapsing into a kinder and less formal tone;—"It will pain you,—but there will be no inflammation, not now I have treated it!—and it will heal quickly, that I will guarantee—I, who have had first care of it!"

She thanked him again in a low voice,—there was an uncomfortable lump in her throat, and tears still trembled on her lashes.

"Remember well," said the Professor cheerily; "how very grateful we are to you! What we shall do for you some day, we do not yet know! A monument in the public square, or a bust in the Cathedral? Ha, ha! Goodbye! You have the blessing of the nation with you!"

She shook her head deprecatingly,—she tried to smile, but she could not trust herself to speak. The carriage rolled swiftly down the broad avenue and soon disappeared, and the Professor, having watched the last flash of its wheels vanish between the arching trees, executed a slow and somewhat solemn *pas-seul* on the doorstep where it had left him.

"Ach so!" he exclaimed, almost audibly; "The King's Comedy progresses! But it had nearly taken the form of Tragedy to-day—and now Tragedy itself has melted into sentiment, and tears, and passion! And with this very difficult kind of human mixture, the worst may happen!"

He re-entered the Palace and returned with some haste to the apartments of the King, whither he had been bidden.

But on arriving there he was met by an attendant in the ante-room who informed him that his Majesty had retired to his private library and desired to be left alone.

CHAPTER XXV
"I SAY—'ROME'!"

THE State prison was a gloomy fortress built on a wedge of rock that jutted far out into the ocean. It stood full-fronted to the north, and had opposed its massive walls and huge battlements to every sort of storm for many centuries. It was a relic of mediaeval days, when torture no less than death, was the daily practice of the law, and when persons were punished as cruelly for light offences as for the greatest crimes. It was completely honeycombed with dungeons and subterranean passages, which led to the sea,—and in one of the darkest and deepest of these underground cells, the wretched youth who had attempted the life of the King, was placed under the charge of two armed warders, who marched up and down outside the heavily-barred door, keeping close watch and guard. Neither they nor anyone else had exchanged a word with the prisoner since his arrest. He had given them no trouble. He had been carefully searched, but nothing of an incriminating nature had been found upon him,—nothing to point to any possible instigator of his dastard crime. He had entered the dungeon allotted to him with almost a cheerful air,—he had muttered half-inaudible thanks for the bread and water which had been passed to him through the grating; and he had seated himself upon the cold bench, hewn out of the stone wall, with a resignation that might have easily passed for pleasure. As the time wore on, however, and the reality of his position began to press more consciously upon his senses, the warders heard him sigh deeply, and move restlessly, and once he gave a cry like that of a wounded animal, exclaiming:—

"For Thy sake, Lord Christ! For Thy sake I strove—for Thy sake, and in Thy service! Thou wilt not leave me here to perish!"

He had been brought to the prison immediately after his murderous attack, and the time had then been about four in the afternoon. It was now night; and all over the city the joy-bells were clashing out music from the Cathedral towers, to express the popular thanksgiving for the miraculous escape and safety of the King. The echo of the chimes which had been ringing ever since sunset, was caught by the sea and thrown back again upon the air, so that it partially drowned the melancholy clang of the prison bell, which in its turn, tolled forth the dreary passing of the time for those to whom liberty had become the merest shadow of a dream. As it struck nine, a priest presented himself to the Superintendent of the prison, bearing a 'permit' from General Bernhoff, Head of the Police, to visit and 'confess' the prisoner. He was led to the cell and admitted at once. At the noise of a stranger's entrance, the criminal raised himself from the sunken attitude into which he had fallen on his stone bench, and watched, by the light of the dim lamp set in the wall, the approach of his tall, gaunt, black-garmented visitor with evident horror and fear. When,—with the removal of the shovel hat and thick muffler which had helped to disguise that visitor's personality,—the features of Monsignor Del Fortis were disclosed, he sprang forward and threw himself on his knees.

"Mercy!—Mercy!" he moaned—"Have pity on me, in the name of God!"

Del Fortis looked down upon him with contempt, as though he were some loathsome reptile writhing at his feet. "Silence!" he said, in a harsh whisper—"Remember, we are watched here! Get up!—why do you kneel to *me*? I have nothing to do with you, beyond such office as the Church enjoins!" And a cold smile darkened, rather than lightened his features. "I am sent to administer 'spiritual consolation' to you!"

Slowly the prisoner struggled up to a standing posture, and pressing both hands to his head, he stared wildly before him.

"'Spiritual consolation'!" he muttered-"'Spiritual'?" A faint dull vacuous smile flickered over his face, and he shuddered. "I understand! You come to prepare my soul for Heaven!"

Del Fortis gave him a sinister look.

"That depends on yourself!" he replied curtly—"The Church can speed you either way,—to Heaven, or—Hell!"

The prisoner's hands clenched involuntarily with a gesture of despair.

"I know that!" he said sullenly—"The Church can save or kill! What of it? I am now beyond even the power of the Church!"

Del Fortis seated himself on the stone bench.

"Come here!" he said—"Sit down beside me!"

The prisoner obeyed.

"Look at this!"—and he drew an ebony and silver crucifix from his breast—"Fix your eyes upon it, and try, my son,"—here he raised his voice a little—"try to conquer your thoughts of things temporal, and lift them to the things which are eternal! For things temporal do quickly vanish and disperse, but things eternal shall endure for ever! Humble your soul before God, and beseech Him with me, to mercifully cleanse the dark stain of sin upon your soul!" Here he began mumbling a Latin prayer, and while engaged in this, he caught the prisoner's hand in a close grip. "Act—act with me!" he said firmly. "Fool!—Play a part, as I do! Bend your head close to mine—assume shame and sorrow even if you cannot feel it! And listen to me well! *You have failed*!"

"I know it!"

The reply came thick and low.

"Why did you make the attempt at all? Who persuaded you?"

The wretched youth lifted his head, and showed a wild white face, in which the piteous eyes, starting from their sockets, looked blind with terror.

"Who persuaded me?" he replied mechanically—"No one! No single one,— but many!"

Del Fortis gripped him firmly by the wrist.

"You lie!" he snarled—"How dare you utter such a calumny! Who were you? What were you? A miserable starveling—picked up from the streets and saved from penury,—housed and sheltered in our College,—taught and trained and given paid employment by us,—what have *you* to say of 'persuasion'?—you, who owe your very life to us, and to our charity!"

Roused by this attack, the prisoner, wrenching his hand away from the priest's cruel grasp, sprang upright.

"Wait—wait!" he said breathlessly—"You do not understand! You forget! All my life I have been under One great influence—all my life I have been taught to dream One great Dream! When I talk of 'persuasion,' I only mean the persuasion of that force which has surrounded me as closely as the air I breathe!—that spirit which is bound to enter into all who work for you, or with you! Oh no!—neither you nor any member of your Order ever seek openly to 'persuade' any man to any act, whether good or evil—your Rule is much wiser than that!—much more subtle! You issue no actual commands—your power comes chiefly by suggestion! And *with* you,—working *for* you—I have thought day and night, night and day, of the glory of Rome!—the dominion of Rome!—the triumph of Rome! I have learned, under you, to wish for it, to pray for it, to desire it more than my own life!—do you, can you blame me for that? You dare not call it a sin;—for your Order represents it as a virtue that condones all sin!"

Del Fortis was silent, watching him with a kind of curious contempt.

"It grew to be part of me, this Dream!" went on the lad, his eyes now shining with a feverish brilliancy—"And I began to see wonderful visions, and to hear voices calling me in the daytime,—voices that no one else heard! Once in the College chapel I saw the Blessed Virgin's picture smile! I was copying documents for the Vatican then,—and I thought of the Holy Father,—how he was imprisoned in Rome, when he should be Emperor of all the Emperors,—King of all the Kings! I remembered how it was that he had no temporal power,—though all the powers of the earth should be subservient to him!—and my heart beat almost to bursting, and my brain seemed on fire!—but the Blessed Virgin's picture still smiled;—and I knelt down before it and swore that I,—even I, would help to give the whole world back to Rome, even if I died for it!"

He caught his breath with a kind of sob, and looked appealingly at Del Fortis, who, fingering the crucifix he held, sat immovable.

"And then—and then" he went on, "I heard enough,—while at work in the monastery with you and the brethren,—to strengthen and fire my resolution. I learned that all kings are, in these days, the enemies of the Church. I learned that they were all united in one resolve; and that,—to deprive the Holy Father of temporal power! Then I set myself to study kings. Each, and all of those who sit on thrones to-day passed before my view;—all selfish, money-seeking, sensual men!—not one good, true soul among them! Demons they seemed to me,—bent on depriving God's Evangelist in Rome of his Sacred and Supreme Sovereignty! It made me mad!—and

I would have killed all kings, could I have done so with a single thought! Then came a day when you preached openly in the Cathedral against this one King, who should by right have gone to his account this very afternoon!—you told the people how he had refused lands to the Church,—and how by this wicked act he had stopped the progress of religious education, and had put himself, as it were, in the way of Christ who said: 'Suffer little children to come unto Me!' And my dreams of the glory of Rome again took shape—I saw in my mind all the children,—the poor little children of the world, gathered to the knee of the Holy Father, and brought up to obey him and him only!—I remembered my oath before the Blessed Virgin's picture, and all my soul cried out: 'Death to the crowned Tyrant! Death!' For you said—and I believed it—that all who opposed the Holy Father's will, were opposed to the will of God!—and over and over again I said in my heart: 'Death to the tyrant! Death!' And the words went with me like the response of a litany,—till—till—I saw him before me to-day —a pampered fool, surrounded by women!—a blazoned liar!— and then—" He paused, smiling foolishly; and shaking his head with a slow movement to and fro, he added—"The dagger should have struck home!—it was aimed surely—aimed strongly!—but that woman came between—why did she come? They said she was Lotys!—ha ha!—Lotys, the Revolutionary sybil!—Lotys, the Socialist!—but that could not be,—Lotys is as great an enemy of kings as I am!"

"And an enemy of the Church as well!" said Del Fortis harshly—"Between the Church and Socialism, all Thrones stand on a cracking earth, devoured by fire! But make no mistake about it!—the woman was Lotys! Socialist and Revolutionary as she may be, she has saved the life of the King. This is so far fortunate—for you! And it is much to be hoped that she herself is not slain by your dagger thrust;—death is far too easy and light a punishment for her and her associates! We trust it may please a merciful God to visit her with more lingering calamity!"

As he said this, he piously kissed the crucifix he held, keeping his shallow dark eyes fixed on the prisoner with the expression of a cat watching a mouse. The half-crazed youth, absorbed in the ideas of his own dementia, still smiled to himself vaguely, and nervously plucked at his fingers, till Del Fortis, growing impatient and forgetting for the moment that they stood in a prison cell, the interior of which might possibly be seen and watched from many points of observation unknown to them, went up to him and shook him roughly by the arm.

"Attention!" he said angrily—"Rouse yourself and hear me! You talk like a fool or a madman,—yet you are neither—neither, you understand?—neither idiot-born nor suddenly crazed;—so, when on your trial do not feign to be what you are not! Such ideas as you have expressed, though they may have their foundation in a desire for good, are evil in their results—yet even out of evil good may come! The power of Rome—the glory of Rome—the dominion of Rome! Rome, supreme Mistress of the world! Would you help the Church to win this great victory? Then now is your chance! God has given you—you, His poor instrument,—the means to effectually aid His conquest,—to Him be all the praise and thanksgiving! It rests with you to accept His message and perform His work!"

The high-flown, melodramatic intensity with which he pronounced these words, had the desired effect on the stunned and bewildered, weak mind of the unfortunate lad so addressed. His eyes sparkled—his cheeks flushed,—and he looked eagerly up into the face of his priestly hypnotizer.

"Yes—yes!" he said quickly in a breathless whisper—"But how?—tell me how! I will work—oh, I will work—for Rome, for God, for the Blessed Virgin!—I will do all that I can!—but how—how? Will the Holy Father send an angel to take me out of this prison, so that I may be free to help God?"

Del Fortis surveyed him with a kind of grim derision, A slight noise like the slipping-back or slipping-to of a grating, startled him, and he looked about him on all sides, moved by a sudden nervous apprehension. But the massive walls of the cell, oozing with damp and slime, had apparently no aperture or outlet anywhere, not even a slit in the masonry for the admission of daylight. Satisfied with his hasty examination, he took his credulous victim by the arm, and led him back to the rough stone bench where they had first begun to converse.

"Kneel down here before me!"—he said—"Kneel, as if you were repeating all the sins of your life to me in your last confession! Kneel, I say!"

Feebly, and with trembling limbs, the lad obeyed.

"Now," continued Del Fortis, holding up the crucifix before him—"Try to follow my words and understand them! To-morrow, or the next day, you will be taken before a judge and tried for your attempted crime. Do you realise that?"

"I do!" The answer came hesitatingly, and with a faint moan.

"Have you thought what you intend to say when you are asked your reasons for attacking the King? Do you mean to tell judge and jury the story of what you call your 'persuasion' to dream of the dominion of Rome?"

"Yes—yes!" replied the lad, looking up with an eager light on his face—"Yes, I will tell them all,—just as I have told you! Then they will know,—they will see that it was a good thought of mine—it would have been a good sin! I will speak to them of the wicked wrongs done to you and your Holy Order,—of the cruelty which the Christian Apostle in Rome has to suffer at the hands of kings—and they will acknowledge me to be right and just;—they will know I am as a man inspired by God to work for the Church, the bride of Christ, and to make her Queen of all the world!"

He stopped suddenly, intimidated by the cruel glare of the wolfish eyes above him.

"You will say nothing of all this!" and Del Fortis shook the crucifix in his face as though it were a threatening weapon; "You will say only what *I* choose,—only what *I* command! And if you do not swear to speak as I tell you, I will kill you!—here and now—with my own hands!"

Uttering a half-smothered cry, the wretched youth recoiled in terror.

"You will kill me? You—*you*?" he gasped—"No—no!—you could not do that! you could not,—you are a holy man! I—I am not afraid that you will hurt me! I have done nothing to offend you,—I have always been obedient to you,—I have been your slave—your dog to fetch and carry!—and you should remember,—yes!—you should remember that my mother was rich,—and that because she too felt the call of God, she gave all her money to the Church, and left me thrown upon the streets to starve! But the Church rescued me—the Church did not forget! And I am ready to serve the Church in all and every possible way,—I have done my best, even now!"

He spoke with all the passionate self-persuasion of a fanatic, and Del Fortis judged it wisest to control his own fierce inward impatience and deal with him more restrainedly.

"That is true enough!" he said in milder accents;—"You are ready to serve the Church,—I do not doubt it;—but you do not serve it in the right way. No earthly good is gained to us by the killing of kings! Their conversion and obedience is what we seek. This king you would have slain is a baptised son of the Church; but beyond attending mass regularly in his private chapel, which he does for the mere sake of appearances, he is an atheist, condemned to the fires of Hell. Nevertheless, no advantage to us could possibly be obtained by his death. Much can be done for us by you—yes, *you*!—and much will depend on the answers to the questions asked you at your trial. Give those answers as *I* shall bid you, and you will win a triumph for the cause of Rome!"

The prisoner's eyes glittered feverishly,—full of the delirium of bigotry, he caught the lean, cold hand that held the crucifix, and kissed it fervently.

"Command me!" he muttered—"Command!—and in the name of the Blessed Virgin, I will obey!"

"Hear then, and attend closely to my words," went on Del Fortis, enunciating his sentences in a low distinct voice—"When you are brought before the judge, you will be accused of an attempt to assassinate the King. Make no denial of it,—admit it at once, and express contrition. You will then be asked if any person or persons instigated you to commit the crime. To this say 'yes'!"

"Say 'yes'!" repeated the lad—"But that will not be true!"

"Fool, does it matter!" ejaculated Del Fortis, almost savagely—"Have you not sworn to speak as I command you? What is it to you whether it is true or false?"

A slight shiver passed through the prisoner's limbs—but he was silent.

"Say"—went on his pitiless instructor—"that you were enticed and persuaded to commit the wicked deed by the teachings of the Socialist, Sergius Thord, and his followers. Say that the woman Lotys knew of your intention,—and saved the life of the King at the last moment, through fear, lest her own seditious schemes should be discovered and herself punished. Say,—that because you were young and weak and impressionable, she chose you out to attempt the assassination. Do you hear?"

"I hear!" The reply came thickly and almost inaudibly. "But must I tell these lies? I have never spoken to Sergius Thord in my life!—nor to the woman Lotys;—I know nothing of them or their followers, except by the public talk;—why should I harm the innocent? Let me tell the truth, I pray of you!—let me speak as my heart dictates!—let me plead for the Holy Father—for you—for your Order—for the Church!—"

He broke off as Del Fortis caught him by both hands in an angry grip.

"Do not dare to speak one word of the Church!" he said, "Or of us,—or of our

Order! Let not a single syllable escape your lips concerning your connection with us and our Society!—or we shall find means to make you regret it! Beware of betraying yourself! When you are once before the Court of Law, remember you know nothing of Us, our Work, or our Creed!"

Utterly bewildered and mystified, the unhappy youth rocked himself to and fro, clasping and unclasping his hands in a kind of nervous paroxysm.

"Oh why, why will you bid me to do this?" he moaned—"You know there are times when I cannot be answerable for myself! How can I tell what I shall do when I am brought face to face with my accusers?—when I see all the dreadful eyes of the people turned upon me? How can I deny all knowledge of those who brought me up, and nurtured and educated me? If they ask me of my home, is it not with you?— under your sufferance and charity? If they seek to know my means of subsistence, is it not through you that I receive the copying-work for which I am paid? You would not have me repudiate all this, would you? I should be worse than a dog in sheer ingratitude if I did not bear open testimony to all the Church has done for me!"

"Be, not worse than a dog, but faithful as a dog in obedience!" responded Del Fortis impressively—"And, for once, speak of the Church with the indifference of an atheist,—or with such marked coldness as a wise man speaks of the woman he secretly adores! Hold the Church and Us too sacred for any mention in a Court of criminal law! But serve the Church by involving the Socialist and Revolutionary party! Think of the magnificent results which will spring from this act,—and nerve yourself to tell a lie in order to support a truth!"

Rising unsteadily from his knees, the prisoner stood upright. By the flicker of the dim lamp, he looked deadly pale, and his limbs tottered as though shaken by an ague fit.

"What good will come of it?" he queried dully—"What good *can* come of it?"

"Great and lasting good will come of it!"—replied Del Fortis—"And it will come quickly too;—in this way, for by fastening the accusation of undue influence on Sergius Thord and his companions, you will obtain Government restriction, if not total suppression of the Socialist party. This is what we need! The Socialists are growing too strong—too powerful in every country,—and we are on the brink of trouble through their accursed and atheistical demonstrations. There will soon be serious disturbances in the political arena—possibly an overthrow of the Government, and a general election—and if Sergius Thord has the chance of advancing himself as a deputy, he will be elected above all others by an overpowering majority of the lower classes. *You* can prevent this!—you can prevent it by a single falsehood, which in this case will be more pleasing to God than a thousand mischievous veracities! Will you do it? Yes or No?"

The miserable lad looked helplessly around him, his weak frame trembling as with palsy, and his uncertain fingers plucking at each other with that involuntary movement of the muscles which indicates a disordered brain.

"Will you, or will you not?" reiterated Del Fortis in a whisper that hissed through the close precincts of the cell like the warning of a snake about to sting—"Answer me!"

"Suppose I say I will not!"—stammered the poor wretch, with trembling lips and appealing eyes—"Suppose I say I will not falsely accuse the innocent, even for the sake of the Church——?"

"Then," said Del Fortis slowly, rising and moving towards him;—"You had best accept the only alternative—this!"

And he took from his breast pocket a small phial, full of clear, colourless fluid, and showed it to him—"Take it!—and so make a quick and quiet end! For, if you betray you connection with Us by so much as a look,—a sign, or a syllable,—your mode of exit from this world may be slower, less decent, and more painful!"

The miserable boy wrung his hands in agony, and such a cry of despair broke from his lips as might have moved anyone less cruelly made of spiritual adamant than the determined servant of the cruellest 'religious' Order known. The dull harsh clang of the prison bell struck ten. The 'priest' had been an hour at the work of 'confessing' his penitent,—and his patience was well-nigh exhausted.

"Swear you will attribute your intended assassination of the King, to the influence of the Socialists!" he said with fierce imperativeness— "Or with this—end all your difficulties to-night! It is a gentle quietus!—and you ought to thank me for it! It is better than solitary imprisonment for life! I will give you absolution for taking it— provided I see you swallow it before I go!—and I will declare to the Church that I left you shrived of your sins, and clean! Half an hour after I leave you, you will sleep!—and wake—in Heaven! Make your choice!"

The last words had scarcely left his lips when the cell door was suddenly thrown open, and a blaze of light poured in. Dazzled by the strong and sudden glare, Del Fortis recoiled, and still holding the phial of poison in his hand, stumbled back against the half-fainting form of the poor crazed creature he had been terrorising, as a dozen armed men silently entered the dungeon and ranged themselves in order, six on one side and six on the other, while, in their midst one man advanced, throwing back his dark military cloak as he came, and displaying a mass of jewelled orders and insignia on his brilliant uniform. Del Fortis uttered a fierce oath.

"The King!" he muttered, under his breath—"The King!"

"Ay, the King!" and a glance of supreme scorn swept over him from head to foot, as the monarch's clear dark grey eyes flashed with the glitter of cold steel in the luminance of the torches which were carried by attendants behind him; "Monsignor Del Fortis! You stand convicted of the offence of unlawfully tampering with the conscience of a prisoner of State! We have heard your every word—and have obtained a bird's-eye view of your policy!—so that,—if necessary,—we will Ourselves bear witness against you! For the present,—you will be detained in this fortress until our further pleasure!"

For one moment Del Fortis appeared to be literally contorted in every muscle by his excess of rage. His features grew livid,—his eyes became almost blood-red, and his teeth met on his drawn-in under-lip in a smile of intense malignity. Baffled again!—and by this 'king,'—the crowned Dummy,—who had cast aside all former precedent, and instead of amusing himself with card-playing and sensual intrigue, after the accepted fashion of most modern sovereigns, had presumed to interfere, not only with the Church, but with the Government, and now, as it seemed, had acted as a spy on the very secrets of a so-called prison 'confession'! The utter impossibility of escaping from the net into which his own words had betrayed him, stood plainly before his mind and half-choked him with impotent fury,—till—all suddenly a thought crossed his brain like a flash of fire, and with a strong effort, he recovered his self-possession. Crossing his arms meekly on his breast, he bowed with a silent and profound affectation of humility, as one who is bent under the Royal displeasure, yet resigned to the Royal command,—then with a rapid movement he lifted the poison-phial he had held concealed, to his lips. His action was at once perceived. Two or three of the armed guards threw themselves upon him and, after a brief struggle, wrenched the flask from his hand, but not till he had succeeded in swallowing its contents. Breathing quickly, yet smiling imperturbably, he stood upright and calm.

"God's will and mine—not your Majesty's—be done!" he said. "In half an hour—or less—Mother Church may add to her list of martyrs the name of Andrea Del Fortis!—who died rather than sacrifice the dignity of his calling to the tyranny of a king!"

A slight convulsion passed over his features,—he staggered backward. The King, horror-stricken, signed to the prison warders standing by, to support him. He muttered a word of thanks, as they caught him by both arms.

"Take me where I can die quietly!" he said to them, "It will soon be over! I shall give you little trouble!"

A cold, weak, trembling hand clasped his. It was the hand of the King's wretched assassin.

"Let me go with you!" he cried—"Let me die with you! You have been cruel to me!—but you could not have meant it!—you were once kind!"

Del Fortis thrust him aside.

"Curse you!" he said thickly—"You are the cause—you—you are the cause of this damned mischief! You!—God!—to think of it!—you devil's spawn!—you cur!"

His voice failed him, and he reeled heavily against the sturdy form of one of the warders who held him—his lips were flecked with blood and foam. Shocked and appalled, no less at his words, than at the fiendish contortion of his features, the King drew near.

"Curse not a fellow-mortal, unhappy priest, in thine own passage towards the final judgment!" he said in grave accents—"The blessing of this poor misguided creature may help thee more than even a king's free pardon!"

And he extended his hand;—but with all the force of his now struggling and convulsed body, Del Fortis beat it back, and raised himself by an almost superhuman effort.

"Pardon! Who talks of pardon!" he cried, with a strong voice—"I do not need it—I do not seek it! I have worked for the Church—I die for the Church! For every one that says 'The King!'—I say, 'Rome'!"

He drew himself stiffly upright; his dark eyes glittered; his face, though deadly pale, scarcely looked like the face of a dying man.

"I say, 'Rome'!" he repeated, in a harsh whisper;—"Over all the world!—over all the kingdoms of the world, and in defiance of all kings—'Rome'!"

He fell back,—not dead,—but insensible, in the stupor which precedes death;—and was quickly borne out of the cell and carried to the prison infirmary, there to receive medical aid, though that could only now avail to soothe the approaching agonies of dissolution.

The King stood mute and motionless, lost in thought, a heavy darkness brooding on his features. How strange the impulse that had led him to be the mover and witness of this scene! By merest chance he had learned that Del Fortis had applied for permission to 'confess' the would-be destroyer of his life,—the life which Lotys had saved,—and acting—as he had lately accustomed himself to do—on a sudden first idea or instinct, he had summoned General Bernhoff to escort him to the prison, and make the way easy for him to watch and overhear the interview between priest and penitent,—himself unobserved. And from so slight an incident had sprung a tragedy,—which might have results as yet undreamed-of!

And while he yet mused upon this, General Bernhoff ventured respectfully to approach him, and ask if it was now his pleasure to return to the Palace? He roused himself,—and with a heavy sigh looked round on the damp and dismal cell in which he stood, and at the crouching, fear-stricken form of the semi-crazed and now violently weeping lad who had attempted his life.

"Take that poor wretch away from here!" he said in hushed tones—"Give him light, and warmth, and food! His evil desires spring from an unsound brain;—I would have him dealt with mercifully! Guard him with all necessary and firm restraint,—but do not brutalise his body more than Rome has brutalised his soul!"

With that he turned away,—and his armed guard and attendants followed him.

That self-same midnight a requiem mass was sung in a certain chapel before a silent gathering of black-robed stern-featured men, who prayed "For the repose of the soul of our dear brother, Andrea Del Fortis, servant of God, and martyr to the cause of truth and justice,—who departed this life suddenly, in the performance of his sacred duties." In the newspapers next day, the death of this same martyr and shining light of the Church was recorded with much paid-for regret and press- eulogy as 'due to heart-failure' and his body being claimed by the Jesuit brotherhood, it was buried with great pomp and solemn circumstance, several of the Catholic societies and congregations following it to the grave. One week after the funeral,—for no other ostensible cause whatever, save the offence of openly publishing his official refusal of a grant of Crown lands to the Jesuits,—the Holy Father, the Evangelist and Infallible Apostle enthroned in St. Peter's Chair, launched against the King who had dared to deny his wish and oppose his will, the once terrible, but now futile ban of excommunication; and the Royal son of the Church who had honestly considered the good of his people more than the advancement of priestcraft, stood outside the sacred pale,—barred by a so-called 'Christian' creed, from the mercy of God and the hope of Heaven.

CHAPTER XXVI
"ONE WAY,—ONE WOMAN!"

FOR several days after the foregoing events, the editors and proprietors of newspapers had more than enough 'copy' to keep them busy. The narrow escape of the King from assassination, followed by his excommunication from the Church, worked a curious effect on the minds of the populace, who were somewhat bewildered and uncertain as to the possible undercurrent of political meaning flowing beneath the conjunction of these two events; and their feelings were intensified by the announcement that the youth who had attempted the monarch's life,— being proved as suffering from hereditary brain disease,— had received a free pardon, and was placed in a suitable home for the treatment of such cases, under careful restraint and medical supervision. The tide of popular opinion was now divided into two ways,—for, and against their Sovereign-ruler. By far the larger half were against;—but the ban pronounced upon him by the Pope had the effect of making even this disaffected portion inclined to consider him more favourably,—seeing that the Church's punishment had fallen upon him, apparently because he had done his duty, as a king, by granting the earnest petitions of thousands of his subjects. David Jost, who had always made a point of flattering Royalty in all its forms, now let his pen go with a complete passion of toadyism, such as disgraced certain writers in Great Britain during the reigns of the pernicious and vicious Georges,—and, seeing the continued success of the rival journal which the King had personally favoured, he trimmed his sails to the Court breeze, and dropped the Church party as though it had burned his fingers. But he found various channels on which he had previously relied for information, rigorously closed to him. He had written many times to the Marquis de Lutera to ask if the report of his having sent in his resignation was correct,—but he had received no answer. He had called over and over again on Carl Perousse, hoping to obtain a few minutes' conversation with him, but had been denied an interview. Cogitating upon these changes,—which imported much,—and wishing over and over again that he had been born an Englishman, so that by the insidious flattery of Royalty he might obtain a peerage,—as a certain Jew associate of his concerned in the same business in London, had recently succeeded in doing,—he decided that the wisest course to follow was to continue to 'butter' the King;—hence he laid it on with a thick brush, wherever the grease of hypocrisy could show off best. But work as he would, the 'shares' in his journalistic concerns were steadily going down,—none of his numerous magazines or 'half-penny rags,' paid so well as they had hitherto done; while the one paper which had lately been so prominently used by the King, continued to prosper, the public having now learned to accept with avidity and eagerness the brilliant articles which bore the signature of Pasquin Leroy, as though they were somewhat of a new political gospel. The charm of mystery intensified this new writer's reputation. He was never seen in 'fashionable' society,—no 'fashionable' person appeared to know him,—and the general impression was that he resided altogether out of the country. Only the members of the Revolutionary Committee were aware that he was one of them, and recognised his work as part of the carrying out of his sworn bond. He had grown to be almost the right hand of Sergius Thord; wherever Thord sought supporters, he helped to obtain them,—wherever the sick and needy, the desolate and distressed, required aid, he somehow managed to secure it,—and next to Thord,—and of course Lotys, —he was the idol of the Socialist centre. He never spoke in public,— he seldom appeared at mass meetings; but his influence was always felt; and he made himself and his work almost a necessity to the Cause. The action of Lotys in saving the life of the King, had created considerable discussion among the Revolutionists, not unmixed with anger. When she first appeared among them after the incident, with her arm in a sling, she was greeted with mingled cheers and groans, to neither of which she paid the slightest attention. She took her seat at the head of the Committee table as usual, with her customary indifference and grace, and appeared deaf to the conflicting murmurs around her,—till, as they grew louder and more complaining and insistent, she raised her head and sent the lightning flash of her blue eyes down the double line of men with a sweeping scorn that instantly silenced them.

"What do you seek from me?" she demanded;—"Why do you clamour like babes for something you cannot get,—my obedience?"

They looked shamefacedly at one another,—then at Sergius Thord and Pasquin Leroy, who sat side by side at the lower end of the table. Max Graub and Axel Regor, Leroy's two comrades, were for once absent; but they had sent suitable and satisfactory excuses. Thord's brows were heavy and lowering,—his eyes were wild and unrestful, and his attitude and expression were such as caused Leroy to watch him with a little more than his usual close attention. Seeing that his companions expected him to answer Lotys before them all, he spoke with evident effort.

"You make a difficult demand upon us, Lotys," he said slowly, "if you wish us to explain the stormy nature of our greeting to you this evening. You might surely have understood it without a question! For we are compelled to blame you;—you who have never till now deserved blame,—for the folly of your action in exposing your own life to save that of the King! The one is valuable to us—the other is nothing to us! Besides, you have trespassed against the Seventh Rule of our Order —which solemnly pledges us to 'destroy the present monarchy'!"

"Ah!" said Lotys, "And is it part of the oath that the monarchy should be destroyed by murder without warning? You know it is not! You know that there is nothing more dastardly, more cowardly, more utterly loathsome and contemptible than to kill a man defenceless and unarmed! We speak of a Monarchy, not a King;—not one single individual,—for if he were killed, he has three sons to come after him. You have called me the Soul of an Ideal—good! But I am not, and will not be the Soul of a Murder-Committee!"

"Well spoken!" said Johan Zegota, looking up from some papers which he, as secretary to the Society, had been docketing for the convenience of Thord's perusal; "But do not forget, brave Lotys, that the very next meeting we hold is the annual one, in which we draw lots for the 'happy dispatch' of traitors and false rulers; and that this year the name of the King is among them!"

Lotys grew a shade paler, but she replied at once and dauntlessly.

"I do not forget it! But if lots are cast and traitors doomed,—it is part of our procedure to give any such doomed man six months' steady and repeated warning, that he may have time to repent of his mistakes and remedy them, so that haply he may still be spared;—and also that he may take heed to arm himself, that he do not die defenceless. Had I not saved the King, his death would have been set down to us, and our work! Any one of you might have been accused of influencing the crazy boy who attempted the deed,—and it is quite possible our meetings would have been suppressed, and all our work fatally hindered,—if not entirely stopped. Foolish children! You should thank me, not blame me! —but you are blind children all, and cannot even see where you have been faithfully served by your faithfullest friend!"

At these words a new light appeared to break on the minds of all present—a light that was reflected in their eager and animated faces. The knotted line of Thord's brooding brows smoothed itself gradually away.

"Was that indeed your thought, Lotys," he asked gently, almost tenderly—"Was it for our sakes and for us alone, that you saved the King?"

At that instant Pasquin Leroy turned his eyes, which till now had been intent on watching Thord, to the other end of the table where the fine, compact woman's head, framed in its autumn-gold hair, was silhouetted against the dark background of the wall behind her like a cameo. His gaze met hers,—and a vague look of fear and pain flashed over her face, as a faint touch of colour reddened her cheeks.

"I am not accustomed to repeat my words, Sergius Thord!" she answered coldly; "I have said my say!"

Looks were exchanged, and there was a silence.

"If we doubt Lotys, we doubt the very spirit of ourselves!" said Pasquin Leroy, his rich voice thrilling with unwonted emotion; "Sergius—and comrades all! If you will hear me, and believe me,—you may take my word for it, she has run the risk of death for Us!—and has saved Us from false accusation, and Government interference! To wrong Lotys by so much as a thought, is to wrong the truest woman God ever made!"

A wild shout answered him,—and moved by one impulse, the whole body of men rose to their feet and drank "to the health and honour of Lotys!" with acclamation, many of them afterwards coming round to where she sat, and kneeling to kiss her hand and ask her pardon for their momentary doubt of her, in the excitement and enthusiasm of their souls. But Lotys herself sat very silent,—almost as silent as

Sergius Thord, who, though he drank the toast, remained moody and abstracted.

When the company dispersed that night, each man present was carefully reminded by the secretary, Johan Zegota, that unless the most serious illness or misfortune intervened, every one must attend the next meeting, as it was the yearly "Day of Fate." Pasquin Leroy was told that his two friends, Max Graub and Axel Regor must be with him, and he willingly made himself surety for their attendance.

"But," said he, as he gave the promise, "what is the Day of Fate?"

Johan Zegota pointed a thin finger delicately at his heart.

"The Day of Fate," he said, "is the day of punishment,—or Decision of Deaths. The names of several persons who have been found guilty of treachery,—or who otherwise do injury to the people by the manner of their life and conduct, are written down on slips of paper, which are folded up and put in one receptacle, together with two or three hundred blanks. They must be all men's names,—we never make war on women. Against some of these names,—a Red Cross is placed. Whosoever draws a name, and finds the red cross against it, is bound to kill, within six months after due warning, the man therein mentioned. If he fortunately draws a blank then he is free for a year at least,—in spite of the fatal sign,—from the unpleasant duty of despatching a fellow mortal to the next world"—and here Zegota smiled quite cheerfully; "But if he draws a Name,—and at the same time sees the red cross against it, then he is bound by his oath to us to— *do his duty!*"

Leroy nodded, and appeared in no wise dismayed at the ominous suggestion implied.

"How if our friend Zouche were to draw the fatal sign," he said; "Would he perform his allotted task, think you?"

"Most thoroughly!" replied Zegota, still smiling.

And with that, they separated.

Meanwhile, during the constant change and interchange of conflicting rumours, some of which appeared to have foundation in fact, and others which rapidly dispersed themselves as fiction, there could be no doubt whatever of the growing unpopularity of the Government in power. Little by little, drop by drop, there oozed out the secrets of the "Perousse Policy," which was merely another name for Perousse Self- aggrandisement. Little by little, certain facts were at first whispered, and then more loudly talked about, as to the nature of his financial speculations;

and it was soon openly stated that in the formation of some of the larger companies, which were beginning to be run on the Gargantuan lines of the "American Trust" idea, he had enormous shares,—though these "Trusts" had been frequently denounced as a means of enslaving the country, and ruining certain trade- interests which he was in office to protect. Accusations began to be guardedly thrown out against him in the Senate, which he parried off with the cool and audacious skill of an expert fencer, knowing that for the immediate moment at least, he had a "majority" under his thumb. This majority was composed of persons who had unfortunately become involved in his toils, and were, therefore, naturally afraid of him;— yet it was evident, even to a superficial student of events, that if once the innuendoes against his probity as a statesman could be veraciously proved, this sense of intimidation among his supporters would be removed, and like the props set against a decaying house, their withdrawal would result in the ruin of the building. It was pretty well known that the Marquis de Lutera had sent in his resignation, but it was not at all certain whether the King was of a mind to accept it.

Things were in abeyance,—political and social matters whirled giddily towards chaos and confusion; and the numerous hurried Cabinet Councils that were convened, boded some perturbation among the governing heads of the State. From each and all of these meetings Ministers came away more gloomy and despondent in manner,—some shook their heads sorrowfully and spoke of "the King's folly,"— others with considerable indignation flung out sudden invectives against "the King's insolence!"—and between the two appellations, it was not easy to measure exactly the nature of the conduct which had deserved them. For the King himself made no alteration whatever in the outward character of his daily routine; he transacted business in the morning, lunched, sometimes with his family, sometimes with friends; drove in the afternoon, and showed himself punctiliously at different theatres once or twice in the evenings of the week. The only change more observant persons began to notice in his conduct was, that he had drawn the line of demarcation very strongly between those persons who by rank and worth, and nobility of life, merited his attention, and those who by mere Push and Pocket, sought to win his favour by that servile flattery and obsequiousness which are the trademarks of the plebeian and vulgarian. Quietly but firmly, he dropped the acquaintance of Jew sharks, lying in wait among the dirty pools of speculation;—with ease and absoluteness he 'let go' one by one, certain ladies of particularly elastic virtue, who fondly dreamed that they 'managed' him; and among these, to her infinite rage and despair, went Madame Vantine, wife of Vantine the winegrower, a yellow-haired, sensual "*femelle d'homme*," whose extravagance in clothes, and reckless indecency in conversation, combined with the King's amused notice, and the super- excellence of her husband's wines, had for a brief period made her 'the rage' among a certain set of exceedingly dissolute individuals.

In place of this kind of riff-raff of "*nouveaux riches*," and plutocrats, he began by degrees to form around himself a totally different *entourage*,—though he was careful to make his various changes slowly, so that they should not be too freely noticed and commented upon. Great nobles, whether possessed of vast wealth and estates, or altogether landless, were summoned to take their rightful positions at the Court, where Vantine the wine-grower, and Jost the Jew, no more obtained admittance;— men of science, letters and learning, were sought out and honoured in various ways, their wives and daughters receiving special marks of the Royal attention and favour; and round the icy and statuesque beauty of the Queen soon gathered a brilliant bevy of the real world of women, not the half-world of the '*femme galante*' which having long held sway over the Crown Prince while Heir-Apparent to the Throne, judged itself almost as a necessary, and even becoming, appendage to his larger responsibility and state as King. These excellent changes, beneficial and elevating to the social atmosphere generally, could not of course be effected without considerable trouble and heart-burning, in the directions where certain persons had received their dismissal from such favour as they had previously held at Court. The dismissed ones thirsted with a desire for vengeance, and took every opportunity to inflame the passions of their own particular set against the King, some of them openly declaring their readiness to side with the Revolutionary party, and help it to power. But over the seething volcano of discontent, the tide of fashion moved as usual, to all outward appearances tranquil, and absorbed in trivialities of the latest description; and though many talked, few dreamed that the mind of the country, growing more compressed in thought, and inflammable in nature every day, was rapidly becoming like a huge magazine of gunpowder or dynamite, which at a spark would explode into that periodically recurring fire-of-cleansing called Revolution.

Weighted with many thoughts, Sir Roger de Launay, whose taciturn and easy temperament disinclined him for argument and kept him aloof from discussion whenever he could avoid it, sat alone one evening in his own room which adjoined the King's library, writing a few special letters for his Majesty which were of too friendly a nature to be dealt with in the curt official manner of the private secretary. Once or twice he had risen and drawn aside the dividing curtain between himself and the King's apartment to see if his Royal master had entered; but the room remained empty, though it was long past eleven at night. He looked every now and again at a small clock which ticked with a quick intrusive cheerfulness on his desk,—then with a slight sigh resumed his work. Letter after letter was written and sealed, and he was getting to the end of his correspondence, when a tap at the door disturbed him, and his sister Teresa, the Queen's lady-in-waiting, entered.

"Is the King within?" she asked softly, moving almost on tiptoe as she came.

Sir Roger shook his head.

"He has been absent for some time," he replied,—then after a pause— "But what are you here for, Teresa? This is not your department!" and he took her hand kindly, noticing with some concern that there were tears in her large dark eyes;—"Is anything wrong?"

"Nothing! That is,—nothing that I have any right to imagine—or to guess. But—" and here she seemed a little confused—"I am commanded by the Queen to summon you to her presence if,—if the King has not returned!"

He rose at once, looking perplexed. Teresa watched him anxiously, and the expression of his face did not tend to reassure her.

"Roger," she began timidly—"Would you not tell me,—might I not know something of this mystery? Might I not be trusted?"

His languid eyes flashed with a sudden tenderness, as from his great and stately height he looked down upon her pretty shrinking figure.

"Poor little Teresa!" he murmured playfully; "What is the matter? What mystery are you talking about?"

"*You* know—you must know!" answered Teresa, clasping her hands with a gesture of entreaty; "There is something wrong, I am sure! Why is the King so often absent—when all the household suppose him to be with the Queen?—or in his private library there?" and she pointed to the curtained-off Royal sanctum beyond;

"Why does the Queen herself give it out that he is with her, when he is not?

Why does he enter the Queen's corridor sometimes quite late at night by the private battlement-stair? Does it not seem very strange? And since he was so nearly assassinated, his absences have been more frequent than ever!"

Sir Roger pulled his long fair moustache meditatively between his fingers.

"When you were a little girl, Teresa, you must have been told the story of Bluebeard;" he said; "Now take my advice!—and do not try to open forbidden doors with your tiny golden key of curiosity!"

Teresa's cheeks flushed a pretty rose pink.

"I am not curious;" she said, with an air of hauteur; "And indeed I am far too loyal to say anything to anyone but to you, of what seems so new and strange. Besides—the Queen has forbidden me—only it is just because of the Queen—" here she stopped hesitatingly.

"Because of the Queen?" echoed Sir Roger; "Why?"

"She is unhappy!" said Teresa.

A smile,—somewhat bitter,—crossed De Launay's face.

"Unhappy!" he repeated; "She! You mistake her, little girl! She does not know what it is to be unhappy; nothing so weak and slight as poor humanity affects the shining iceberg of her soul! For it *is* an iceberg, Teresa! The sun shines on it all day, fierce and hot, and never moves or melts one glittering particle!"

He spoke with a concentrated passion of melancholy, and Teresa trembled a little. She knew, as no one else did, the intense and despairing love that had corroded her brother's life ever since the Queen had been brought home to the kingdom in all her exquisite maiden beauty, as bride of the Heir-Apparent. Such love terrified her; she did not understand it. She knew it was hopeless,—she felt it was disloyal,— and yet—it was love!—and her brother was one of the truest and noblest of gentlemen, devoted to the King's service, and incapable of a mean or a treacherous act. The position was quite incomprehensible to her, for she was not thoughtful enough to analyse it,—and she had no experience of the tender passion herself, to aid her in sympathetically considering its many moods, sorrows, and inexplicable martyrdoms of mind-torture. She contented herself now with repeating her former assertion.

"She is unhappy,—I am sure she is! You may call her an iceberg, if you like, Roger!—men have such odd names for the women they are unable to understand!

But I have seen the iceberg shed tears very often lately!"

He looked at her, surprised.

"You have? Then we may expect the Pallas Athene to weep in marble? Well! What did you say, Teresa? That her Majesty commanded my presence, if the King had not returned?"

Teresa nodded assent. She was a little worried—her brother's face looked worn and pale, and he seemed moved beyond himself. She watched him nervously as he pushed aside the dividing curtain, and looked into the adjoining room. It was still vacant. The window stood open, and the line of the sea, glittering in the moon, shone far off like a string of jewels,—while the perfume of heliotrope and lilies came floating in deliciously on the cool night-breeze. Satisfied that there was as yet no sign of his Royal master, he turned back again,—and stooping his tall head, kissed the charming girl, whose anxious and timid looks betrayed her inward anxiety.

"I am ready, Teresa!" he said cheerfully; "Lead the way!"

She glided quickly on before him, along an inner passage leading to the Queen's apartments. Arriving at one particular door, she opened it noiselessly, and with a warning finger laid on her lips, went in softly,—Sir Roger following. The light of rose-shaded waxen tapers which were reflected a dozen times in the silver-framed mirrors that rose up to the ceiling from banks of flowers below, shed a fairy-like radiance on the figure of the Queen, who, seated at a reading-table, with one hand buried in the loosened waves of her hair, seemed absorbed in the close study of a book. A straight white robe of thick creamy satin flowed round her perfect form,— it was slightly open at the throat, and softened with a drifting snow of lace, in which one or two great jewels sparkled. As Sir Roger approached her with his usual formal salute,—she turned swiftly round with an air of scarcely- concealed impatience.

"Where is the King?" she demanded.

Startled at the sudden peremptory manner of her question, Sir Roger hesitated,—for the moment taken quite aback.

"Did I not tell you," she went on, in the same imperious tone; "that I made you responsible for his safety? Yet—though you were by his side at the time—you could not shield him from attempted assassination! That was left,—to a woman!"

Her breast heaved—her eyes flashed glorious lightning,—she looked altogether transformed.

Had a thunder-bolt fallen through the painted ceiling at Sir Roger's feet, he could scarcely have been more astounded.

"Madam!" he stammered,—and then as the light of her eyes swept over him, with a concentration of scorn and passion such as he had never seen in them, he grew deadly pale.

"Who, and what is this woman?" she went on; "Why was it given to *her* to save the King's life, while you stood by? Why was she brought to the Palace to be attended like some princess,—and then taken away secretly before I could see her? Lotys is her name—I know it by heart!"

Like twinkling stars, the jewels in her lace scintillated with the quick panting of her breath.

"The King is absent,"—she continued—"as usual;—but why are you not with him, also as usual? Answer me!"

"Madam," said De Launay, slowly; "For some few days past his Majesty has absolutely forbidden me to attend him. To carry out *your* commands I should be forced to disobey *his*!"

She looked at him in a suppressed passion of enquiry.

"Then—is he alone?" she asked.

"Madam, I regret to say—he is quite alone!"

She rose, and paced once up and down the room, a superb figure of mingled rage and pride, and humiliation, all comingled. Her eyes lighted on Teresa, who had timorously withdrawn to a corner of the apartment where she stood apparently busied in arranging some blossoms that had fallen too far out of the crystal vase in which they were set.

"Teresa, you can leave us!" she said suddenly; "I will speak to Sir Roger alone."

With a nervous glance at her brother, who stood mute, his head slightly bent, himself immovable as a figure of stone, Teresa curtseyed and withdrew.

The Queen stood haughtily erect,—her white robes trailing around her, —her exquisite face transfigured into a far grander beauty than had ever been seen upon it, by some pent-up emotion which to Sir Roger was well-nigh inexplicable. His heart beat thickly; he could almost hear its heavy pulsations, and he kept his eyes lowered, lest she should read too clearly in them the adoration of a lifetime.

"Sir Roger, speak plainly," she said, "and speak the truth! Some little time ago you said it was wrong for me to shut out from my sight, my heart, my soul, the ugly side of Nature. I have remedied that fault! I am looking at the ugly side of Nature now,—in myself! The rebellious side—the passionate, fierce, betrayed side! I trusted you with the safety of the King!"

"Madam, he *is* safe!" said Sir Roger quietly;—"I can guarantee upon my life that he is with those who will defend him far more thoroughly than I could ever do! It is better to have a hundred protectors than one!"

"Oh, I know what you would imply!" she answered, impatiently; "I understand, thus far, from what he himself has told me. But—there is something else, something else! Something that portends far closer and more intimate danger to him—"

She paused, apparently uncertain how to go on, and moving back to her chair, sat down.

"If you are the man I have imagined you to be," she continued, in deliberate accents; "You perfectly know—you perfectly understand what I mean!"

Sir Roger raised his head and looked her bravely in the eyes.

"You would imply, Madam, that one, who like myself has been conscious of a great passion for many years, should be able to recognise the signs of it in others! Your Majesty is right! Once you expressed to me a wonder as to what it was like 'to feel.' If that experience has come to you now, I cannot but rejoice,—even while I grieve to think that you must endure pain at the discovery. Yet it is only from the pierced earth that the flowers can bloom,—and it may be you will have more mercy for others, when you yourself are wounded!"

She was silent.

He drew a step nearer.

"You wish me to speak plainly?" he continued in a lower tone. "You give me leave to express the lurking thought which is in your own heart?"

She gave a slight inclination of her head, and he went on.

"You assume danger for the King,—but not danger from the knife of the assassin—or from the schemes of revolutionists! You judge him—as I do—to be in the grasp of the greatest Force which exists in the universe! The force against which there is, and can be no opposition!— a force, which if it once binds even a king— makes of him a life- prisoner, and turns mere 'temporal power' to nothingness; upsetting thrones, destroying kingdoms, and beating down the very Church itself in the way of its desires—and that force is—Love!"

She started violently,—then controlled herself.

"You waste your eloquence!" she said coldly; "What you speak of, I do not understand. I do not believe in Love!"

"Or jealousy?"

The words sprang from his lips almost unconsciously, and like a magnificent animal who has been suddenly stung, she sprang upright.

"How dare you!" she said in low, vibrating accents—"How dare you!"

Sir Roger's breath came quick and fast,—but he was a strong man with a strong will, and he maintained his attitude of quiet resolution.

"Madam!—My Queen!—forgive me!" he said; "But as your humblest friend—your faithful servant!—let me have my say with you now—and then—if you will—condemn me to perpetual silence! You despise Love, you say! Yes—because you have only seen its poor imitations! The King's light gallantries,—his sins of body, which in many cases are not sins of mind, have disgusted you with its very name! The King has loved—or can love—so you think,—many, or any, women! Ah! No—no! Pardon me, dearest Majesty! A man's desire may lead him through devious ways both vile and vicious,—but a man's *love* leads only one way to one woman! Believe it! For even so, I have loved one woman these many years!—and even so—I greatly fear—the King loves one woman now!"

Rigid as a figure of marble, she looked at him. He met her eyes calmly.

"Your Majesty asked me for the truth;" he said; "I have spoken it!"

Her lips parted in a cold, strained little smile.

"And—you—think," she said slowly; "that I—I am what you call 'jealous' of this 'one woman'? Had jealousy been in my nature, it would have been provoked sufficiently often since my marriage!"

"Madam," responded Sir Roger humbly; "If I may dare to say so to your Majesty, it is not possible to a noble woman to be jealous of a man's mere humours of desire! But of Love—Love, the crown, the glory and supremacy of life,—who, with a human heart and human blood, would not be jealous? Who would not give kingdoms, thrones, ay, Heaven itself, if it were not in itself Heaven, for its rapturous oblivion of sorrow, and its full measure of joy!"

A dead silence fell between them, only disturbed by a small silver chime in the distance, striking midnight.

The Queen again seated herself, and drew her book towards her. Then raising her lovely unfathomable eyes, she looked at the tall stately figure of the man before her with a slight touch of pity and pathos.

"Possibly you may be right," she said slowly, "Possibly wrong! But I do not doubt that you yourself personally 'feel' all that you express,— and—that you are faithful!"

Here she extended her hand. Sir Roger bowed low over it, and kissed its delicate smoothness with careful coldness. As she withdrew it again, she said in a low dreamy, half questioning tone:

"The woman's name is Lotys?"

Silently Sir Roger bent his head in assent.

"A man's love leads only one way—to one woman! And in this particular case that woman is—Lotys!" she said, with a little musing scorn, as of herself,—"Strange!"

She laid her hand on the bell which at a touch would summon back her lady-in-waiting. "You have served me well, Sir Roger, albeit somewhat roughly——"

He gave a low exclamation of regret.

"Roughly, Madam?"

A smile, sudden and sweet, which transfigured her usually passionless features into an almost angelic loveliness, lit up her mouth and eyes.

"Yes—roughly! But no matter! I pardon you freely! Good-night!"

"Good-night to your Majesty!" And as he stepped backward from her presence, she rang for Teresa, who at once entered.

"Our excommunication from the Church sits lightly upon us, Sir Roger, does it not?" said the Queen then, almost playfully; "You must know that we say our prayers as of old, and we still believe God hears us!"

"Surely, Madam," he replied, "God must hear all prayers when they are pure and honest!"

"Truly, I think so," she responded, laying one hand tenderly on Teresa's hair, as the girl caressingly knelt beside her. "And—so, despite lack of priestcraft,—we shall continue to pray,—in these uncertain and dangerous times,—that all may be well for the country,— the people, and—the King! Good-night!"

Again Sir Roger bowed, and this time altogether withdrew. He was strung up to a pitch of intense excitement; the brief interview had been a most trying one for him,—though there was a warm glow at his heart, assuring him that he had done well. His suspicion that the King had admired, and had sought out Lotys since the day she saved him from assassination, had a very strong foundation in fact;—much stronger indeed than was at present requisite to admit or to declare. But the whole matter was a source of the greatest anxiety to De Launay, who, in his strong love for his Royal master, found it often difficult to conceal his apprehension,—and who was in a large measure relieved to feel that the Queen had guessed something of it, and shared in his sentiments. He now re-entered his room, and on doing so at once perceived that the King had returned. But his Majesty was busy writing, and did not raise his head from his papers, even when Sir Roger noiselessly entered and laid some letters on the table. His complete abstraction in his work was a sign that he did not wish to be disturbed or spoken to;—and Sir Roger, taking the hint, retired again in silence.

CHAPTER XXVII

THE SONG OF FREEDOM

REVOLUTION! The flame-winged Fury that swoops down on a people like a sudden visitation of God, with the movement of a storm, and the devastation of a plague in one! Who shall say how, or where, the seed is sown that springs so swiftly to such thick harvest! Who can trace its beginnings—and who can predict its end! Tragic and terrible as its work has always seemed to the miserable and muddle-headed human units, whose faults and follies, whose dissoluteness and neglect of the highest interests of the people, are chiefly to blame for the birth of this Monster, it is nevertheless Divine Law, that, when any part of God's Universe-House is deliberately made foul by the dwellers in it, then must it be cleansed,—and Revolution is the burning of the rubbish,—the huge bonfire in which old abuses blazon their destruction to an amazed and terror-stricken world. Yet there have been moments, or periods, in history, when the threatening conflagration could have been stayed and turned back from its course,—when the useless shedding of blood might have been foregone—when the fierce passions of the people might have been soothed and pacified, and when Justice might have been nobly done and catastrophe averted, if there had been but one brave man,— one only!—and that man a King! But in nearly all the convulsive throes of nations, kings have proved themselves the weakest, tamest, most cowardly and ineffectual of all the heads of the time—ready and willing enough to sacrifice the lives of thousands of brave and devoted men to their own cause, but never prepared to sacrifice themselves. Hence the cause of the triumph of Democracy over effete Autocracy. Kings may not be more than men,—but, certes, they should never be less. They should not practise vices of which the very day-labourer whom they employ, would be ashamed; nor should they flaunt their love of sensuality and intrigue in the faces of their subjects as a 'Royal example' and distinctive 'lead' to vulgar licentiousness. The loftier the position, the greater the responsibility;—and a monarch who voluntarily lowers the social standard in his realm has lost more adherents than could possibly be slain in his defence on the field of honour.

The King who plays his part as the hero of this narrative, was now fully aware in his own mind and conscience of the thousands of opportunities he had missed and wasted on his way to the Throne when Heir-Apparent. Since the day of his 'real coronation,' when as he had expressed it to his thoughts, he had 'crowned himself with his own resolve,' he had studied men, manners, persons and events, to deep and serious purpose. He had learned much, and discovered more. He had been, in a moral sense, conquered by his son, Prince Humphry, who had proved a match for him in his determined and honourable marriage for love, and love only,—though born heir to all the conventions and hypocrisies of a Throne. He,—in his day,—had lacked the courage and truth that this boy had shown. And now, by certain means known best to himself, he had fathomed an intricate network of deception and infamy among the governing heads of the State. He had convinced himself in many ways of the unblushing dishonesty and fraudulent self-service of Carl Perousse. And—yet—with all this information stored carefully up in his brain he, to all appearances, took no advantage of it, and did nothing remarkable,—save the one act which had been so much talked about—the refusal of land in his possession to the Jesuits for a 'religious' (and political) settlement. This independent course of procedure had resulted in his excommunication from the Church. Of his 'veto' against an intended war, scarcely anything was known. Only the Government were aware of the part he had taken in that matter,—the Government and—the Money-market! But the time was now ripe for further movement; and in the deep and almost passionate interest he had recently learned to take in the affairs of the actual People, he was in no humour for hesitation.

He had mapped out in his brain a certain plan of action, and he was determined to go through with it. The more so, as now a new and close interest had incorporated itself with his life,—an emotion so deep and tender and overwhelming, that he scarcely dared to own it to himself,— scarcely ventured to believe that he, deprived of true love so long, should now be truly loved for himself, at last! But on this he seldom allowed his mind to dwell,—except when quite alone,—in the deep silences of night;—when he gave his soul up to the secret sweetness which had begun to purify and ennoble his innermost nature,—when he saw visioned before him a face,—warm with the passion of a love so grand and unselfish that it drew near to a likeness of the Divine;—a love that asked nothing, and gave everything, with the beneficent glory of the sunlight bestowing splendour on the earth. His lonely moments, which were few, were all the time he devoted to this brooding luxury of meditation, and though his heart beat like a boy's, and his eyes grew dim with tenderness, as in fancy he dreamed of joy that might be, and that yet still more surely might never be his,—his determined mind, braced and bent to action, never faltered for a second in the new conceptions he had formed of his duty to his people, who, as he now considered, had been too long and too cruelly deceived.

Hence, something like an earthquake shock sent its tremor through the country, when two things were suddenly announced without warning, as the apparent results of the various Cabinet Councils held latterly so often, and in such haste. The first was, that not only had his Majesty accepted the resignation of the Marquis de Lutera as Premier, but that he had decided—provided the selection was entirely agreeable to the Government—to ask M. Carl Perousse to form a Ministry in his place. The second piece of intelligence, and one that was received with much more favour than the first, by all classes and conditions of persons, was that the Government had issued a decree for the complete expulsion of the Jesuits from the country. By a certain named date, and within a month, every Jesuit must have left the King's dominions, or else must take the risk of a year's imprisonment followed by compulsory banishment.

Much uproar and discussion did this mandate excite among the clerical parties of Europe,—much indignation did it breed within that Holy of Holies situate at the Vatican,—which, having launched forth the ban of excommunication, had no further thunderbolts left to throw at the head of the recreant and abandoned Royalty whose 'temporal power' so insolently superseded the spiritual. But the country breathed freely; relieved from a dangerous and mischievous incubus. The educational authorities gave fervent thanks to Heaven for sparing them from long dreaded interference;—and when it was known that the excommunicated King was the chief mover in this firm and liberating act, a silent wave of passionate gratitude and approval ran through the multitudes of the people, who would almost have assembled under the Palace walls and offered a grand demonstration to their monarch, who had so boldly carried the war into the enemy's country and won the victory, had they not been held back and checked from their purpose by the counter- feeling of their disgust at his Majesty's apparently forthcoming choice of Carl Perousse as Prime Minister.

Swayed this way and that, the people were divided more absolutely than before into those two sections which always become very dangerous when strongly marked out as distinctly separated,—the Classes and the Masses. The comfortable wedge of Trade, which,—calling itself the Middle-class,—had up to the present kept things firm, now split asunder likewise,—the wealthy plutocrats clinging willy-nilly to the Classes, to whom they did not legitimately belong; and the men of moderate income throwing in their lot with the Masses, whose wrongs they sympathetically felt somewhat resembled their own. For taxation had ground them down to that particularly fine powder, which when applied to the rocks of convention and usage, proves to be of a somewhat blasting quality. They had paid as much on their earnings and their goods as they could or would pay;—more indeed than they had any reasonable right to pay,—and being sick of Government mismanagement, and also of what they still regarded as the King's indifference to their needs, they were prepared to make a dash for liberty. The expulsion of the Jesuits they naturally looked upon as a suitable retaliation on Rome for the excommunication of the Royal Family; but beyond the intense relief it gave to all, it could not be considered as affecting or materially altering the political situation. So, like the dividing waves of the Red Sea, which rolled up on either side to permit the passage of Moses and his followers—the Classes and the Masses piled themselves up in opposite billowy sections to allow Sergius Thord and the Revolutionary party to pass triumphantly through their midst, adding thousands of adherents to their forces from both sides;—while they were prepared to let the full weight of the billows engulf the King, if, like Pharaoh and his chariots, he assumed too much, or proceeded too far.

Professor von Glauben, seated in his own sanctum, and engaged in the continuance of his "Political History of Hunger," found many points in the immediate situation which considerably interested him and moved him to philosophical meditation.

"For,—take the feeling of the People as it now is," he said to himself; "It starts in Hunger! The taxes,—the uncomfortable visit of the tax-gatherer! The price of the loaf,—concerning which the baker, or the baker-ess, politely tells the customer that it is costly, because of the Government tax on corn; then from the bread, it is marvellous how the little clue winds upward through the spider-webs of Trade. The butcher's meat is dearer,—for says he—'The tax on corn makes it necessary for me to increase the price of meat.' There is no logical reason given,—the fact simply *is*! So that Hunger commences the warfare,—Hunger of Soul, as well as Hunger of body. 'Why starve my thought?' says Soul. 'Why tax my bread?' says Body. These tiresome questions continue to be asked, and never answered,—but answers are clamoured for, and the people complain—and then one fierce day the gods hear them grumble, and begin to grumble back! Ach! Then it is thunder with a vengeance! Now in my own so-beloved Fatherland, there has been this double grumbling for a long time. And that the storm will burst, in spite of the so-excellently-advertising Kaiser is evident! Hoch!—or *Ach*? Which should it be to salute the Kaiser! I know not at all,—but I admit it is clever of him to put up a special Hoarding-announcement for the private view of the Almighty God, each time he addresses his troops! And he will come in for a chapter of my history—for he also is Hungry!—he would fain eat a little of the loaf of Britain!—yes!—he will fit into my work very well for the instruction of the helpless unborn generations!"

He wrote on for a while, and then laid down his pen. His eyes grew dreamy, and his rough features softened.

"What has become of the child, I wonder!" he mused; "Where has she gone, the 'Glory-of-the-Sea'! I would give all I have to look upon her beautiful face again;—and Ronsard—he, poor soul—silent as a stone, weakening day after day in the grasp of relentless age,—would die happy,—if I would let him! But I do not intend to give him that satisfaction. He shall live! As I often tell him, my science is of no avail if I cannot keep a man going, till at least a hundred and odd years are past. Barring accidents, or self-slaughter, of course!" Here he became somewhat abstracted in his meditations. "The old fellow is brave enough,—brave as a lion, and strong too for his years;—I have seen him handle a pair of oars and take down a sail as I could never do it,—and—he has accepted a strange and difficult situation heroically. 'You must not be involved in any trouble by a knowledge of our movements.' So Prince Humphry said, when I saw him last,—though I did not then understand the real drift of his meaning. And time goes on— and time seems wearisome without any tidings of those we love!"

A tap at the door disturbed his mental soliloquy, and in answer to his 'Come in,' Sir Roger de Launay entered.

"Sorry to interrupt work, Professor!" he said briefly; "The King goes to the Opera this evening, and desires you to be of the party."

"Good! I shall obey with more pleasure than I have obeyed some of his Majesty's recent instructions!" And the Professor pushed aside his manuscript to look through his spectacled eyes at the tall equerry's handsome face and figure. "You have a healthy appearance, Roger! Your complexion speaks of an admirable digestion!"

De Launay smiled.

"You think so? Well! Your professional approval is worth having!" He paused, then went on; "The party will be a pleasant one to-night. The King is in high spirits."

"Ah!" And Von Glauben's monosyllable spoke volumes.

"Perhaps he ought not to be?" suggested Sir Roger with a slight touch of anxiety.

"I do not know—I cannot tell! This is the way of it, Roger—see!" And taking off his spectacles, he polished them with due solemnity. "If I were a King, and ruled over a country swarming with dissatisfied subjects,—if I had a fox for a Premier,— and was in love with a woman who could not possibly be my wife,—I should not be in high spirits!"

"Nor I!" said De Launay curtly. "But the fox is not Premier yet. Do you think he ever will be?"

Von Glauben shrugged his shoulders.

"He is bound to be, I presume. What else remains to do? Upset everything? Government, deputies and all?"

"Just that!" responded Sir Roger. "The People will do it, if the King does not."

"The King will do anything he is asked to do—now—" said the Professor significantly; "If the right person asks him!"

"You forget—she does not know—" Here checking himself abruptly, Sir Roger walked to the window and looked out. It was a fair and peaceful afternoon,—the ocean heaved placidly, covered with innumerable wavelets, over which the sea-birds flew and darted, their wings shining like silver and diamonds as they dipped and circled up and down and round the edges of the rocky coast. Far off, a faint rim of amethyst under a slowly sailing white cloud could be recognized as the first line of the shore of The Islands.

"Do you ever go and see the beautiful 'Gloria' girl now?" asked Sir Roger suddenly. "The King has never mentioned her since the day we saw her. And you have never explained the mystery of your acquaintance with her,—nor whether it is true that Prince Humphry was specially attracted by her. I shrewdly suspect——"

"What?"

"That he has been sent off, out of harm's way!"

"You are right," said the Professor gravely; "That is exactly the position! He has been sent off out of harm's way!"

"I heard," went on De Launay, "that the girl—or some girl of remarkable beauty had been seen here—actually here in the Palace— before the Prince left! And such an odd way he left, too—scuttling off in his own yacht without—so far as I have ever heard—any farewells, or preparation, or suitable companions to go with him. Still one hears such extraordinary stories——"

"True!—one does!" agreed the Professor; "And after proper experience, one hears without listening!"

De Launay looked at him curiously.

"The girl was certainly beautiful," he proceeded meditatively; "And her adopted father,—Rene Ronsard,—was not that his name?—was a quaint old fellow. A republican, too!—fiery as a new Danton! Well! The King's curiosity is apparently satisfied on that score,—but"—here he began to laugh—"I shall never forget your face, Von Glauben, when he caught you on The Islands that day!—never! Like an overgrown boy, discovered with his fingers in a jam-pot!"

"Thank you!" said the Professor imperturbably; "I can assure you that the jam was excellent—and that I still remember its flavour!"

Sir Roger laughed again, but with great good-humour,—then he became suddenly serious.

"The King goes out alone very often now?" he said.

"Very often," assented the Professor.

"Are we right in allowing him to do so?"

"Allowing him! Who is to forbid him?"

"Is he safe, do you think?"

"Safer, it would seem, my friend, than when laying a foundation-stone, with ourselves and all his suite around him!" responded the Professor. "Besides, it is too late now to count the possible risks of the adventure he has entered upon. He knows the position, and estimates the cost at its correct value. He has made himself the ruler of his own destiny; we are only his servants. Personally, I have no fear,—save of one fatality."

"And that?"

"Is what kills many strong men off in their middle-age," said Von Glauben; "A disease for which there is no possible cure at that special time of life,—Love! The love of boys is like a taste for green gooseberries,—it soon passes, leaving a disordered stomach and a general disrelish for acid fruit ever afterwards;—the love of the man- about-town between the twenties and thirties is the love of self;—but the love of a Man, after the Self-and-Clothes Period has passed, is the love of the full-grown human creature clamouring for its mate,—its mate in Soul even more than in Body. There is no gainsaying it—no checking it—no pacifying it; it is a most disastrous business, provocative of all manner of evils,—and to a king who has always been accustomed to have his own way, it means Victory or Death!"

Sir Roger gazed at him perplexedly,—his tone was so solemn and full of earnest meaning.

"You, for example," continued the Professor dictatorially, fixing his keen piercing eyes full upon him; "You are a curious subject,—a very curious subject! You live on a Dream; it is a good life—an excellent life! It has the advantage, your Dream, of never becoming a reality,— therefore you will always love,—and while you always love, you will always keep young. Your lot is an exceedingly enviable one, my friend! You need not frown,—I am old enough—and let us hope wise enough—to guess your secret—to admire it from a purely philosophic point of view—and to respect it!"

Sir Roger held his peace.

"But," continued the Professor, "His Majesty is not the manner of man who would consent to subsist, like you, on an idle phantasy. If he loves—he must possess; it is the regal way!"

"He will never succeed in the direction *you* mean!" said Sir Roger emphatically.

"Never!" agreed Von Glauben with a profound shake of his head; "Strange as it may seem, his case is quite as hopeless as yours!"

The door opened and closed abruptly,—and there followed silence. Von Glauben looked up to find himself alone. He smiled tolerantly.

"Poor Roger!" he murmured; "He lives the life of a martyr by choice! Some men do—and like it! They need not do it;—there is not the least necessity in the world for their deliberately sticking a knife into their hearts and walking about with it in a kind of idiot rapture. It must hurt;—but they seem to enjoy it! Just as some women become nuns, and flagellate themselves,—and then when they are writhing from their own self-inflicted stripes, they dream they are the 'brides of Christ,' entirely forgetting the extremely irreligious fact that to have so many 'brides' the good Christ Himself might possibly be troubled, and would surely occupy an inconvenient position, even in Heaven! Each man,—each woman,—makes for himself or herself a little groove or pet sorrow, in which to trot round and round and bemoan life; the secret of the whole bemoaning being that he or she cannot have precisely the thing he or she wants. That is all! Such a trifle! Church, State, Prayer and Power —it can all be summed up in one line—'I have not the thing I want— give it to me!'"

He resumed his writing, and did not interrupt it again till it was time to join the Royal party at the Opera.

That evening was one destined to be long remembered in the annals of the kingdom. The beautiful Opera-house, a marvel of art and architecture, was brilliantly full; all the fairest women and most distinguished men occupying the boxes and stalls, while round and round, in a seemingly never-ending galaxy of faces, and crowded in the tiers of balconies above, a mixed audience had gathered, made up of various sections of the populace which filled the space well up to the furthest galleries. The attraction that had drawn so large an audience together was not contained in the magnetic personality of either the King or Queen, for those exalted individuals had only announced their intention of being present just two hours before the curtain rose. Moreover, when their Majesties entered the Royal box, accompanied by their two younger sons, Rupert and Cyprian, and attended by their personal suite, their appearance created very little sensation. The fact that it was the first time the King had showed himself openly in public since his excommunication from the Church, caused perhaps a couple of hundred persons to raise their eyes inquisitively towards him in a kind of half-morbid, half-languid curiosity, but in these days the sentiment of Self is so strong, that it is only a minority of more thoughtful individuals that ever trouble themselves seriously to consider the annoyances or griefs which their fellow-mortals have to endure, often alone and undefended.

The interest of the public on this particular occasion was centred in the new Opera, which had only been given three times before, and in which the little dancer, Pequita, played the part of a child-heroine. The *libretto* was the work of Paul Zouche, and the music by one of the greatest violinists in the world, Louis Valdor. The plot was slight enough;—yet, described in exquisite verse, and scattered throughout with the daintiest songs and dances, it merited a considerably higher place in musical records than such works as Meyerbeer's "Dinorah," or Verdi's "Rigoletto." The thread on which the pearls of poesy and harmony were strung, was the story of a wandering fiddler, who, accompanied by his only child (the part played by Pequita), travels from city to city earning a scant livelihood by his own playing and his daughter's dancing. Chance or fate leads them to throw in their fortunes with a band of enthusiastic adventurers, who, headed by a young hare-brained patriot, elected as their leader, have determined to storm the Vatican, and demand the person of the Pope, that they may convey him to America, there to convene an assemblage of all true Christians (or 'New Christians'), and found a new and more Christ-like Church. Their expedition fails,—as naturally so wild a scheme would be bound to do,—but though they cannot succeed in capturing the Pope, they secure a large following of the Italian populace, who join with them in singing "The Song of Freedom," which, with Paul Zouche's words, and Valdor's music was the great *chef d'oevre* of the Opera, rousing the listeners to a pitch of something like frenzy. In this,—the last great scene,—Pequita, dancing the 'Dagger Dance,' is supposed to infect the people with that fervour which moves them to sing "The Freedom Chorus," and the curtain comes down upon a brilliant stage, crowded with enthusiasts and patriots, ready to fight and die for the glory of their country. A love-interest is given to the piece by the passion of the wandering fiddler-hero for a girl whose wealth places her above his reach; and who in the end sacrifices all worldly advantage that she may share his uncertain fortunes for love's sake only.

Such was the story,—which, wedded to wild and passionate music, had taken the public by storm on its first representation, not only on account of its own merit, but because it gave their new favourite, Pequita, many opportunities for showing off her exquisite grace as a dancer. She, while preparing for the stage on this special night, had been told that her wish was about to be granted—that she would now, at last, really dance before the King;—and her heart beat high, and the rich colour reddened in her soft childish face, as she donned her scarlet skirts with more than her usual care, and knotted back her raven curls with a great glowing damask rose, such as Spanish beauties fasten behind tiny shell-like ears to emphasise the perfection of their contour. Her thoughts flew to her kindest friend, Pasquin Leroy;—she remembered the starry diamond in the ring he had wished to give her, and how he had said, 'Pequita, the first time you dance before the King, this shall be yours!'

Where was he now, she wondered? She would have given anything to know his place of abode, just to send him word that the King was to be at the Opera that night, and ask him too, to come and see her in her triumph! But she had no time to study ways and means for sending a message to him, either through Sholto, her father, who always waited patiently for her behind the scenes,—or through Paul Zouche, who, though as *librettist* of the opera, and as a poet of new and rising fame, was treated by everyone with the greatest deference, still made a special point of appearing in the shabbiest clothes, and lounging near the side-wings like a sort of disgraced tramp all the time the performance was in progress. Neither of them knew Leroy's address;—they only met him or saw him, when he himself chose to come among them. Besides,—the sound of the National Hymn played by the orchestra, warned her that the King had arrived; and that she must hold herself in readiness for her part and think of nothing else.

The blaze of light in the Opera-house seemed more dazzling than usual to the child, when her cue was called,—and as she sprang from the wings and bounded towards the footlights, amid the loud roar of applause which she was now accustomed to receive nightly, she raised her eyes towards the Royal box, half-frightened, half-expectant. Her heart sank as she saw that the King had partially turned away from the stage, and was chatting carelessly with some person or persons behind him, and that only a statuesque woman with a pale face, great eyes, and a crown of diamonds, regarded her steadily with a high-bred air of chill indifference, which was sufficient to turn the little warm beating heart of her into stone. A handsome youth stared down upon her smiling,—his eyes sleepily amorous,—it was the elder of the King's two younger sons, Prince Rupert. She hated his expression, beautiful though his features were,—and hated herself for having to dance before him. Poor little Pequita! It was her first experience of the insult a girl-child can be made to feel through the look of a budding young profligate. On and on she danced, giddily whirling;—the thoughts in her brain circling as rapidly as her movements. Why would not the King look at her,—she thought? Why was he so indifferent, even when his subjects sought most to please him? At the end of the second act of the Opera a great fatigue and lassitude overcame her, and a look of black resentment clouded her pretty face.

"What ails you?" said Zouche, sauntering up to her as she stood behind the wings; "You look like a small thunder-cloud!"

She gave an unmistakable gesture in the direction of that quarter of the theatre where the Royal box was situated.

"I hate him!" she said, with a stamp of her little foot.

"The King? So do I!" And Zouche lit a cigarette and stuck it between his lips by way of a stop-gap to a threatening violent expletive; "An insolent, pampered, flattered fool! Yet you wanted to dance before him; and now you've done it! The fact will serve you as a kind of advertisement! That is all!"

"I do not want to be advertised through *his* favour!" And Pequita closed her tiny teeth on her scarlet under-lip in suppressed anger; "But I have not danced before him yet! I *will*!"

Zouche looked at her sleepily. He was not drunk—though he had,—of course,— been drinking.

"You have not danced before him? Then what have you been doing?"

"Walking!" answered Pequita, with a fierce little laugh, her colour coming and going with all the quick wavering hue of irritated and irritable Spanish blood, "I have, as they say 'walked across the stage.' I shall dance presently!"

He smiled, flicking a little ash off his cigarette.

"You are a curious child!" he said; "By and by you will want severely keeping in order!"

Pequita laughed again, and shook back her long curls defiantly.

"Who is that cold woman with a face like a mask and the crown of diamonds, that sits beside the King?"

It was Zouche's turn to laugh now, and he did so with a keen sense of enjoyment.

"Upon my word!" he exclaimed; "A little experience of the world has given you what newspaper men call 'local colour.' The 'cold woman with the face like a mask,' is the Queen!"

Pequita made a little grimace of scorn.

"And who is the leering boy?"

"Prince Rupert."

"The Crown Prince?"

"No. The Crown Prince is travelling abroad. He went away very mysteriously,—no one knows where he has gone, or when he will come back."

"I am not surprised!" said Pequita; "With such a father and mother, and such impudent-looking brothers, no wonder he wanted to get away!"

Zouche had another fit of laughter. He had never seen the little girl in such a temper. He tried to assume gravity.

"Pequita, you are naughty! The flatteries of the great world are spoiling you!"

"Bah!" said Pequita, with a contemptuous wave of her small brown hands. "The flatteries of the great world! To what do they lead? To *that*!" and she made another eloquent sign towards the Royal box;—"I would rather dance for you and Lotys, and Sergius Thord, and Pasquin Leroy, than all the Kings of the world together! What I do here is for my father's sake—*you* know that!"

"I know!" and Zouche smoked on, and shook his wild head sentimentally, —murmuring in a *sotto-voce*:

"What I do *here*, is for the need of gold,—
    What I do *there*, is for sweet love's sake only;
Love, ever timid *there*, doth *here* grow bold,—
    And wins such triumph as but leaves me lonely!"

"Is that yours?" said Pequita with a sudden smile.

"Mine, or Shakespeare's," answered Zouche indolently; "Does it matter which?"

Pequita laughed, and her cue being just then called, again she bounded on to the stage; but this time she played her part, as the stock phrase goes, 'to the gallery,' and did not once turn her eyes towards the place where the King sat withdrawn into the shadow of his box, giving no sign of applause. She, however, had caught sight of Sergius Thord and some of her Revolutionary friends seated 'among the gods,' and that was enough inspiration for her. Something,—a quite indefinable something,—a touch of personal or spiritual magnetism, had been fired in her young soul; and gradually as the Opera went on, her fellow- players became infected by it. Some of them gave her odd, half-laughing glances now and then,—being more or less amazed at the unusual vigour with which she sang, in her pure childish soprano, the few strophes of recitative and light song attached to her part;—the very prima-donna herself caught fire,—and the distinguished tenor, who had travelled all the way from Buda Pesth in haste, so that he might 'create' the chief role in the work of his friend Valdor, began to feel that there was something more in operatic singing than the mere inflation of the chest, and the careful production of perfectly-rounded notes. Valdor himself played the various violin solos which occurred frequently throughout the piece, and never failed to evoke a storm of rapturous plaudits,—and many were the half-indignant glances of the audience towards the Royal shrine of draped satin, gilding, and electric light, wherein the King, like an idol, sat,—undemonstrative, and apparently more bored than satisfied. There was a general feeling that he ought to have shown,—by his personal applause in public,—a proper appreciation of the many gifted artists playing that evening, especially in the case of Louis Valdor, the composer of the Opera itself. But he sat inert, only occasionally glancing at the stage, and anon carelessly turning away from it to converse with the members of his suite.

The piece went on;—and more and more the passion of Pequita's pent-up little soul communicated itself to the other performers,—till they found themselves almost unconsciously obeying her 'lead.' At last came the grand final act,—where, in accordance with the progress of the story, the bold band of 'New Christians' are fought back from the gates of the Vatican by the Papal Guard; and the Roman populace, roused to enthusiasm, gather round their defeated ranks to defend and to aid them with sympathy and support in their combat,—breaking forth all together at last in the triumphant 'Song of Freedom.' Truly grand and majestic was this same song,—pulsating with truth and passion,—breathing with the very essence of liberty,—an echo of the heart and soul of strong nations who struggle, even unto death, for the lawful rights of humanity denied to them by the tyrants in place and power. As the superb roll and swell of the glorious music poured through the crowded house, there was an almost unconscious movement among the audience,— the people in the gallery rose *en masse*, and at the close of the first verse, responded to it by a mighty cheer, which reverberated through and through the immense building like thunder. The occupants of the stalls and boxes exchanged wondering and half-frightened looks,— then as the cheer subsided, settled themselves again to listen, more or less spell-bound, as the second verse began. Just before this had merged into its accompanying splendid and soul-awakening chorus,— Pequita,—having obtained the consent of the manager to execute her 'Dagger Dance' in the middle of the song, instead of at the end,— suddenly sprang towards the footlights in a pirouette of extravagant and exquisite velocity—while,—checked by a sign from the conductor, the singers ceased. Without music, in an absolute stillness as of death, the girl swung herself to and fro, like a bell-flower in the breeze,—anon she sprang and leaped like a scarlet flame—and again sank into a slow and voluptuous motion, as of a fairy who dreamingly glides on tiptoe over a field of flowers. Then, on a sudden, while the fascinated spectators watched her breathlessly,—she seemed to wake from sleep,—and running forward wildly, began to toss and whirl her scarlet skirts, her black curls streaming, her dark eyes flashing with mingled defiance and scorn, while drawing from her breast an unsheathed dagger, she flung it in the air, caught it dexterously by the hilt again, twisted and turned it in every possible way,—now beckoning, now repelling, now defending,—and lastly threatening, with a passionate intensity of action that was well-nigh irresistible.

Caught by the marvellous subtlety of her performance, quite one half the audience now rose instinctively, all eyes being fixed on the strange evolutions of this whirling, flying thing that seemed possessed by the very devil of dancing! The King at last attracted, leaned slightly forward from his box with a tolerant smile,—the Queen's face was as usual, immovable,—the Princes Rupert and Cyprian stared, open- mouthed—while over the whole brilliant scene that remarkable silence brooded, like the sultry pause before the breaking of a storm. Triumphant, reckless, panting,—scarcely knowing what she did in her excitement,—Pequita, suddenly running backward, with the lightness of thistle-down flying before the wind, snatched the flag of the country from a super standing by, and dancing forward again, waved it aloft, till with a final abandonment of herself to the humour of the moment, she sprang with a single bound towards the Royal box, and there—the youthful incarnation of living, breathing passion, fury, patriotism, and exultation in one,—dropped on one knee, the flag waving behind her, the dagger pointed straight upward, full at the King!

A great roar,—like that of hundreds of famished wild beasts,—answered this gesture; mingled with acclamations,—and when 'The Song of Freedom' again burst out from the singers on the stage, the whole mass of people joined in the chorus with a kind of melodious madness. Shouts of 'Pequita! Pequita!' rang out on all sides,—then 'Valdor! Valdor!'— and then,—all suddenly,—a stentorian voice cried 'Sergius Thord!' At that word the house became a chaos. Men in the gallery, seized by some extraordinary impulse of doing they knew not what, and going they knew not whither, leaped over each other's shoulders, and began to climb down by the pillars of the balconies to the stalls,—and a universal panic and rush ensued. Terrified women hurried from the stalls and boxes in spite of warning, and got mixed with the maddened crowd, a section of which, pouring out of the Opera-house came incontinently upon the King's carriage in waiting,—and forthwith, without any reflection as to the why or the wherefore, smashed it to atoms! Then, singing again 'The Song of Freedom,'—the people, pouring out from all the doors, formed into a huge battalion, and started on a march of devastation and plunder.

Sergius Thord, grasping the situation from the first, rushed out of the Opera-house in all haste, anxious to avert a catastrophe, but he was too late to stop the frenzied crowd,—nothing could, or would have stopped them at that particular moment. The fire had been too long smouldering in their souls; and Pequita, like a little spark of fury, had set it in a blaze. Through private ways and back streets, the King and Queen and their sons, escorted by the alarmed manager, escaped from the Opera unhurt,—and drove back unobserved to the Palace in a common fiacre—and a vast multitude, waiting to see them come out by the usual doors, and finding they did not come, vented their rage and disgust by tearing up and smashing everything within their reach. Then, remembering in good time, despite their excitement, that the manager of the Opera had done nothing to deserve injury to himself or his property, they paused in this work of destruction, and with the sudden caprice of children, gave out ringing cheers for him and for Pequita;— while their uncertainty as to what to do next was settled for them by Paul Zouche, who, mounting on one of the pedestals which supported the columns of the entrance to the Opera, where his wild head, glittering eyes and eager face looked scarcely human, cried out:

"Damnation to Carl Perousse! Why do you idle here, my friends, when you might be busy! If you want Freedom, seek it from him who is to be your new Prime Minister!"

A prolonged yell of savage approval answered him,—and like an angry tide, the crowd swept on and on, gathering strength and force as it went, and pouring through the streets with fierce clamour of shouting, and clash of hastily collected weapons,—on and on to the great square, in the centre of which stood the statue of the late King, and where the house of Carl Perousse occupied the most prominent position. And the moon, coming suddenly out of a cloud, stared whitely down upon the turbulent scene,—one too often witnessed in history, when, as Carlyle says, 'a Nation of men is suddenly hurled beyond the limits. For Nature, as green as she looks, rests everywhere on dread foundations, and Pan, to whose music the Nymphs dance, has a cry in him that can drive all men distracted!'

In such distraction, and with such wild cry, the night of Pequita's long-looked-for dance before the King swept stormily on towards day.

CHAPTER XXVIII
"FATE GIVES—THE KING!"

NEWS of this fresh and more violent disturbance among the people brought the soldiery out in hot haste, who galloped down to the scene of excitement, only to find the mounted police before them, headed by General Bernhoff, who careering to and fro, cool and composed, forbade, 'in the name of the King!' any attempt to drive the mob out of the square. Swaying uneasily round and round, the populace yelled and groaned, and cheered and hissed; not knowing exactly whereunto they were so wildly moved, but evidently waiting for a fresh 'lead.' The house of Carl Perousse, with its handsome exterior and stately marble portico, offered itself as a tempting target to the more excitable roughs, and a stone sent crashing through one of the windows would have certainly been the signal for a general onslaught had not a man's figure suddenly climbed the pedestal which supported the statue of the late King in the centre of the square, and lifted its living visible identity against the frowning cold stone image of the dead. A cry went up from thousands of throats—'Sergius Thord!'—followed by an extraordinary clamour of passionate plaudits, as the excited people recognised the grand head and commanding aspect of their own particular Apostle of Liberty. He,—stretching out his hands with a gesture of mingled authority and entreaty,—pacified the raging sea of contradictory and conflicting voices as if by magic,—and the horrid clamour died down into a dull roar, which in its turn subsided into silence.

"Friends and brothers!" he cried; "Be calm! Be patient! What spirit possesses you to thus destroy the chances of your own peace! What is your aim? Justice? Ay—justice!—but how can you gain this by being yourselves unjust? Will you remedy

Wrong by injuring Right? Nay—this must not be!—this cannot be, with *you*, whose passion for liberty is noble,—whose love for truth is fixed and resolute,—and who seek no more than is by human right your own! This sudden tempest, by which your souls are tossed, is like an angry gust upon the sea, which wrecks great vessels and drowns brave men;—be something more than the semblance of the capricious wind which destroys without having reason to know why it is bent on destruction! What are you here for? What would you do?"

A confused shouting answered him, in which cries of 'Perousse!' and 'The King!' were most prominent.

Sergius Thord looked round upon the seething mass below him, with a strange sense of power and of triumph. He—even he—who could claim to be no more than a poor Thinker, speaker and writer,—had won these thousands to his command!—he had them here, willing to obey his lightest word,—ready to follow his signal wheresoever it might take them! His eyes glowed,—and the light of a great and earnest inspiration illumined his strong features.

"You call for Carl Perousse!" he said; "Yonder he dwells!—in the regal house he has built for himself out of the sweating work of the poor!" A fierce yell from the populace and an attempt at a rush, was again stopped by the speaker's uplifted hand; "Wait, friends—wait! Think for a moment of the result of action, before you act! Suppose you pulled down that palace of fraud; suppose your strong hands righteously rent it asunder;—suppose you set fire to its walls,—suppose you dragged out the robber from his cave and slew him here, before sunrise—what then? You would make of him a martyr!—and the hypocritical liars of the present policy, who are involved with him in his financial schemes,—would chant his praises in every newspaper, and laud his virtues in every sermon! Nay, we should probably hear of a special 'Memorial Service' being held in our great Cathedral to sanctify the corpse of the vilest stock-jobbing rascal that ever cheated the gallows! Be wiser than that, my friends! Do not soil your hands either with the body of Carl Perousse or his ill-gotten dwelling. What we want for him is Disgrace, not Death! Death is far too easy! An innocent child may die; do not give to a false-hearted knave the simple exit common to the brave and true! Disgrace!—disgrace! Shame, confusion, and the curse of the country,—let these be your vengeance on the man who seeks to clutch the reins of government!—the man who would drive the people like whipped horses to their ruin!"

Another roar answered him, but this time it was mingled with murmurs of dissatisfaction. Thord caught these up, and at once responded to them.

"I hear you, O People! I hear the clamour of your hearts and souls, which is almost too strong to find expression in speech! You cannot wait, you would tell me! You would have Perousse dragged out here,—you would tear him to pieces among you, if you could, and carry the fragments of him to the King, to prove what a people can do with a villain proposed to them as their Prime Minister!" Loud and ferocious shouts answered these words, and he went on; "I know—I understand!— and I sympathise! But even as I know you, you know me! Believe me now, therefore, and hear my promise! I swear to you before you all"—and here he extended both arms with a solemn and impressive gesture—"that this month shall not be ended before the dishonesty of Carl Perousse is publicly and flagrantly known at every street corner,—in every town and province of the land!—and before the most high God, I take my oath to you, the People,—that he shall never be the governing head of the country!"

A hurricane of applause answered him—a tempest of shouting that seemed to surge and sway through the air and down to the earth again like the beating of a powerful wind.

"Give me your trust, O People!" he cried, carried beyond himself with the excitement and fervour of the scene—"Give me yourselves!"

Another roar replied to this adjuration. He stood triumphant;—the people pressing up around him,—some weeping—some kneeling at his feet—some climbing to kiss his hand. A few angry voices in the distance cried out—'The King!'—and he turned at once on the word.

"Who needs the King?" he demanded; "Who calls for him? What is he to us? What has he ever been? Look back on his career!—see him as Heir- Apparent to the Throne, wasting his time with dishonest associates,— dealing with speculators and turf gamblers—involving himself in debt— and pandering to vile women, who still hold him in their grasp, and who in their turn rule the country by their caprice, and drain the Royal coffers by their licentious extravagance! Now look on him as the King, —a tool in the hands of financiers—a speculator among speculators— steeped to the very eyes in the love of money, and despising all men who do not bear the open blazon of wealth upon them,—what has he done for the people? Nothing! What will he ever do for the People? Nothing! Flattered by self-seekers—stuffed with eulogy by a paid Press—his name made a byword and a mockery by the very women with whom he consorts, what should we do with him in Our work! Let him alone!—let him be! Let him eat and drink as suits his nature—and die of the poison his own vices breed in his blood!—we want naught of him, or his heirs! When the time ripens to its full fruition, we, the People, can do without a Throne!"

At this, thousands of hats and handkerchiefs were tossed in the air,— thousands of voices cheered to the very echo, and to relieve their feelings still more completely the vast crowd once more took up 'The Song of Freedom' and began singing it in unison steadily and grandly, with all that resistless force and passion which springs from deep- seated emotion in the soul. And while they were singing, Thord, glancing rapidly about him, saw Johan Zegota close at hand, and to his still greater satisfaction, Pasquin Leroy; and beckoning them both to his side whispered his brief orders, which were at once comprehended. The day was breaking; and in the purple east a line of crimson showed where the sun would presently rise. A few minutes' quick organisation worked by Leroy and Zegota, and some few other of their comrades sufficed to break up the mob into three sections, and in perfect order they stood blocked for a moment, like the three wings of a great army. Then once more Thord addressed them:

"People, you have heard my vow! If before the end of the month Carl Perousse is not ejected with contempt from office, I will ask my death at your hands! A meeting will be convened next week at the People's Assembly Rooms where we shall make arrangements to approach the King. If the King refuses to receive us, we shall find means to make him do so! He *shall* hear us! He is our paid servant, and he is bound to serve us faithfully,—or the Throne shall be a thing of the past, to be looked back upon with regret that we, a great and free people, ever tolerated its vice and tyranny!"

Here he waited to let the storm of plaudits subside,—and then continued: "Now part, all of you friends!—go your ways,—and keep order for yourselves with vigilance! The soldiery are here, but they dare not fire!—the police are here, but they dare not arrest! Give them no cause even to say that it would have been well to do either! Let the spiritual force of your determined minds,—fixed on a noble and just purpose, over-rule mere temporal authority; let none have to blame you for murder or violence,—take no life,—shed no blood; but let your conquest of the Government,—your capture of the Throne,—be a glorious moral victory, out-weighing any battle gained only by brute force and rapine!"

He was answered by a strenuous cheer; and then the three great sections of the multitude began to move. Out of the square in perfect order they marched,—still singing; one huge mass of people being headed by Pasquin Leroy, the other by Johan Zegota,—the third by Sergius Thord himself. The soldiery, seeing there was no cause for interference, withdrew,—the police dispersed, and once again an out-break of popular disorder was checked and for a time withheld.

But this second riot had startled the metropolis in good earnest. Everyone be-came fully alive to the danger and increasing force of the disaffected community,—and the Government,—lately grown inert and dilatory in the transaction of business,—began seriously to consider ways and means of pacifying general clam-our and public dissatisfaction. None of the members of the Cabinet were much sur-prised, therefore, when they each received a summons from the King to wait upon him at the Palace that day week,—'to discuss affairs of national urgency,' and the general impression appeared to be, that though Carl Perousse dismissed the 'street rowdyism,' as he called it, with contempt, and spoke of 'disloyal traitors opposed to the Government,' he was nevertheless riding for a fall; and that his chances of obtaining the Premiership were scarcely so sure as they had hitherto seemed.

Meanwhile, Pequita, whose childish rage against the King for not noticing her dancing or applauding it, had been the trifling cause of the sudden volcanic erup-tion of the public mind, became more than ever the idol of the hour. The night after the riot, the Opera-house was crowded to suffocation,—and the stage was cov-ered with flowers. Among the countless bouquets offered to the triumphant little dancer, came one which was not thrown from the audience, but was brought to her by a messenger; it was a great cluster of scarlet carnations, and attached to it was a tiny velvet case, containing the ring promised to her by Pasquin Leroy, when, as he had said, she 'should dance before the King.' A small card accompanied it on which was written 'Pequita, from Pasquin!' Turning to Lotys, who, in the event of further turbulence, had accompanied her to the Opera that night to take care of her, and who sat grave, pale, and thoughtful, in one of the dressing-rooms near the stage, the child eagerly showed her the jewel, exclaiming:

"See! He has kept his promise!"

And Lotys,—sighing even while she smiled,—answered:

"Yes, dear! He would not be the brave man he is, if he ever broke his word!"

Whereat Pequita slipped the ring on her friend's finger, kissing her and whispering:

"Take care of it for me! Wear it for me! For tonight, at least!"

Lotys assented,—though with a little reluctance,—and it was only while Pequita was away from her, performing her part on the stage, that this strange lonely woman bent her face down on the hand adorned with the star-like gem and kissed it,—tears standing in her eyes as she murmured:

"My love—my love! If you only knew!"

And then the hot colour surged into her cheeks for sheer shame of herself that she should love!—she—no longer in her youth,—and utterly unconscious that there was, or could be any beauty in her deep lustrous eyes, white skin, and dull gold hair. What had she to do with the thoughts of passion?—she whose life was devoted to the sick and needy,—and who had no right to think of anything else but how she should aid them best, so long as that life should last! She knew well enough that love of a great, jealous, and almost savage kind, was hers if she chose to claim it—the love of Sergius Thord, who worshipped her both as a woman and an Intellect; but she could not contemplate him as her lover, having grown up to consider him more as a sort of paternal guardian and friend. In fact, she had thoroughly resigned herself to think of nothing but work for the remainder of her days, and to entirely forego the love and tenderness which most women, even the poorest, have the natural right to win; and now slowly,—almost unconsciously to herself,—Love had stolen into her soul and taken possession of it;—secret love for the man, who brave almost to recklessness, had joined his fortunes in with Sergius Thord and his companions, and had assisted the work of pushing matters so far forward, that the wrongs done to the poor, and the numerous injustices of the law, which for years had been accumulating, and had become part and parcel of the governing system of the country, now stood a fair chance of being remedied. She, with her quick woman's instinct, had perceived that where Sergius Thord, in his dreamy idealism, halted and was uncertain of results, Pasquin Leroy stepped into the breach and won the victory. And, like all courageous women, she admired a courageous man. Not that Thord lacked courage,—he had plenty of the physical brute force known as such,—but he had also a peculiar and uncomfortable quality of rousing desires, both in himself and others which he had not the means of gratifying.

Thus Lotys foresaw that, unless by some miraculous chance he obtained both place and power, and a share in the ruling of things, there was every possibility of a split in the Revolutionary Committee,—one half being inclined to indulge in the criminal and wholly wasteful spirit of Anarchy,—the other disposed to throw in its lot with the Liberal or Radical side of politics. And she began to regard Pasquin Leroy, with his even temperament, cool imperturbability, intellectual daring, and literary ability, as the link which kept them all together, and gave practical force to the often brooding and fantastic day-dreams of Thord, who, though he made plans night and day for the greater freedom and relief of the People from unjust coercion, had not succeeded in obtaining as yet sufficient power to carry them into execution.

It was evident, however, to the whole country that the times were in a ferment,—that the Government was growing more unpopular, and that Carl Perousse, the chief hinge on which Governmental force turned, was under a cloud of the gravest suspicion. Meetings, more or less stormy in character, were held everywhere by every shade of party in politics,— and strong protests against his being nominated as Premier were daily sent to the King. But to the surprise of many, and the annoyance of most, his Majesty gave no sign. The newspapers burst into rampant argument,—every little editor issued his Jovian 'opinion' on the grave issues at stake;—David Jost kept his Hebraic colours flying for the King,—judging that to flatter Royalty was always a safe course for most Jews;—while in the rival journal, brilliant essays, leaders and satires on the political situation, combined with point-blank accusations against the Secretary of State, (which that distinguished personage always failed to notice,) flew from the pen of the mysterious writer, Pasquin Leroy, and occupied constant public attention. Unlike the realm of Britain,—where the 'golden youth' enfeeble their intellects by the perusal of such poor and slangy journalism that they have lost both the art and wit to comprehend brilliant political writing,—the inhabitants of this particular corner of the sunny south were always ready to worship genius wherever even the smallest glimmer of it appeared,—and the admiration Leroy's writings excited was fast becoming universal, though for the most part these writings were extremely inflammable in nature, and rated both King and Court soundly. But with the usual indifference of Royalty to 'genius' generally, the King, when asked if he had taken note of certain articles dealing very freely with both him and his social conduct, declared he had never heard of them, or of their writer!

"I never," he said with an odd smile, "pay any attention to clever literature! I should be establishing a precedent which would be inconvenient and disagreeable to my fellow sovereigns!"

The time went on; the King met his Ministers on the day he had summoned them in private council,—and on the other hand Sergius Thord convened a mighty mass-meeting for the purpose of carrying a resolution formed to address his Majesty on the impending question of the Premiership. From the King's council, the heads of Government came away in haste, despair and confusion; from the mass-meeting whole regiments marched through the streets in triumphant and satisfied order.

After these events there came a night, when the sweet progress of calm weather was broken up by cloud and storm,—and when heavy thunder boomed over the city at long dull intervals, like the grinding and pounding of artillery, without any rain to cool the heated ether, which was now and again torn asunder by flashes of lightning. There was evidently a raging tempest far out at sea, though the land only received suggestions of this by the occasional rearing up of huge dark green billows which broke against the tall cliffs, plumed with mimosa and myrtle, that guarded the coast. Heavy scents of flowers were in the air—heavy heat weighed down the atmosphere,—and there was a languor in the slow footsteps of the men, who, singly, or in groups, arrived at the door of Sergius Thord's house to fulfil the dread compact binding upon them all in regard to the 'Day of Fate.' Pasquin Leroy and his two companions were among the first to arrive, and to make their way up the dark steep stairs to the Committee room, where, when they entered, they found the usual aspect of things strangely altered. The table no longer occupied its position in the middle of the floor; it was set on a raised platform entirely draped with black. Large candelabra, holding six lights each, occupied either end,—and in the centre one solitary red lamp was placed, shedding its flare over a large bronze vessel shaped like a funeral urn. The rest of the room was in darkness,—and with the gathering groups of men, who moved silently and spoke in whispers, it presented a solemn and eerie spectacle.

"Ah! You have now arrived," said Max Graub, in a cautious sotto voce to Leroy, "at the end of your adventures! Behold the number Thirteen! Six lights at one end, six lights at the other,—that is twelve; and in the centre the Thirteenth—the red Eye looking into the sepulchral urn! It is all up with us!"

Leroy said nothing,—but the face of the man called Axel Regor grew suddenly very pale. He drew Leroy a little aside.

"This is no laughing matter!" he said very earnestly; "Let me stand near you— let me keep close at your side all the evening!"

Leroy smiled and pressed his hand.

"My dear fellow!" he said; "Have no fear! Or if you have fear, do not show it! You stand in precisely the same danger as myself, or as any of us; you may draw the fatal Signal!—but if you do, I promise you I will volunteer myself in your place."

"*You*!" said Regor with a volume of meaning in the utterance; "You would stand in my place?"

"Why, of course!" replied Leroy cheerily; "Life is not such a wonderful business, that death for a friend's sake is not better!"

Regor looked at him, and a speechless devotion filled and softened his eyes. Certain words spoken to him by a woman he loved echoed through his brain, and he murmured:

"Nay, by the God above us, if death is in question, *I* will die rather than let *you* die!"

"That will depend on my humour!" said Leroy, still smiling; "You will require my permission to enter into combat with the last enemy before he offers challenge!"

Max Graub here approached them with a warning finger laid on his lips.

"Hush—sh—sh!" he said; "Think as much as you like,—but talk as little as you can! I assure you this is a most uncomfortable business!— and here comes the axis of the revolving wheel!"

They made way,—as did all the men grouped together in the room,—for the entrance of Sergius Thord and Lotys. These two came in together; and with a silent salute which included the whole Committee, ascended the raised platform.

Lotys was deadly pale; and the white dress she wore, with its scarlet sash, accentu-
ated that paleness. She appeared for once to move under the dominance of some
greater will than her own,—she moved slowly, and her head was bent,—and even
to Pasquin Leroy as she passed him, her faint smile of recognition was both sad and
cold. Once on the platform, she seated herself at the lower end of the funereally-
draped table; and leaning her head on one hand, seemed lost in thought. Thord took
his place at the opposite end,—whereupon Johan Zegota moving stealthily to the
door, closed it, locked it, and put the key in his pocket. Then he in turn mounted
the platform, and began in a clear but low voice to call the roll of the members of
the Committee.

Each man answered to his name in the same guarded tone; all without a single
exception were present;—and Zegota, having completed the catalogue, turned to
Thord for further instructions. The rest of the company then seated themselves,—
finding their chairs with some little difficulty in the semi-darkness. When the
noise of their shuffling feet had ceased, Thord rose and advanced to the front of the
platform.

"Friends," he said slowly; "You are here to-night to determine by the hand of
Chance, or Destiny, which of certain traitors among many thousands, shall meet
with the punishment his treachery deserves. In the list of those who are to-night
marked down for death is Carl Perousse;—happy the man that draws *that* name
and is able to serve as the liberator to his country! Another, is the Jew, David Jost,—
because it has been chiefly at his persuasion that the heads of the Government have
been tempted to gamble for their own personal motives with the secrets of State
policy. Another, is the Marquis de Lutera;—who though he has, possibly through
fear, resigned office, is to blame for having made his own private fortune,—as well
as the fortunes of all the members of his family,—out of the injuries and taxations
inflicted on the People. To his suggestion we owe the cruel price of bread,—the tax
on corn, a necessity of life;—on his policy rests the responsibility of opening our
Trades to such an over-excess of Foreign Competition and Supply that our native
work and our native interests are paralysed by the strain. To him,—as well as to Carl
Perousse, we owe the ridiculous urbanities of such extreme foreign diplomacies as
expose our secret forces of war to our rivals;—from him emanates the courteous
and almost servile attention with which we foolishly exhibit our naval and mili-

tary defences to our enemies. We assume that a Minister who graciously permits a foreign arsenal to copy our guns—a foreign dockyard to copy and to emulate our ships,—is a traitor to the prosperity and continued power of the country. Two of the great leaders in Trade are named on the Death-list;—one because, in spite of many warnings, he employs foreign workmen only; the other, because he 'sweats' native labour. The removal of all these persons will be a boon to the country—the clearing of a plague of rats from the national House and Exchequer! Lastly, the King is named;—because, —though he has rescued the system of National Education from Jesuit interference and threatening priestly dominance, he has turned a deaf ear to other equally pressing petitions of his People,—and also because he does nothing to either influence or guide society to its best and highest ends. Under his rule, learning is set at naught—Art, Science and Literature, the three saving graces which make for the peace, prosperity and fraternity of nations,—are rendered valueless, because no example is set which would give them their rightful prominence,—and wine, cards and women are substituted,—the three evil fates between which the honour of the Throne is brought into contempt. We should know and remember that Lotys, when she lately saved the life of the King, did,—as she herself can tell you,—plead personally with him to save the people from the despotic government of Carl Perousse and his pernicious 'majority';—but though she rescued the monarch at the risk of her own much more valuable existence—and equally at the risk of being misunderstood and condemned by this very Society to which her heart and soul are pledged,—he refused to even consider her entreaty. Therefore, we may be satisfied that he has been warned;—but it would seem that the warning is of no avail;—and whosoever to-night draws the name of the King must be swift and sure in his business!"

There was a deep pause. Suddenly Max Graub rose, his bulky form and great height giving him an almost Titanesque appearance in the gloom of the chamber. Raising one hand as a signal, he asked permission to speak, which was instantly accorded.

"To my chief, Sergius Thord, and my comrades," he said with a slight military salutation; "I wish to explain what perhaps they have already discovered,—that I am a poor and uncouth German,—not altogether conversant with your language,—and considerably bewildered by your social ethics;—so that if I do not entirely understand things as I should, you will perhaps pardon my ignorance, which includes other drawbacks of my disposition. But when death is in question, I am always much interested,—having spent all my days in trying to find out ways and means of combating man's chief enemy on his own ground. Because,— though I fully admit the usefulness of death as a cleanser and solvent; and as a means of clearing off hopelessly-useless persons, I am not at all sure that it is an advisable way to get rid of the healthy and the promising. I speak as a physician merely,—with an eye to what is called the 'stock' of the human race; and what I now want to know is this: On what scientific, ethical, or religious grounds, do you wish to get rid of the King? Science, ethics, and religion being only in the present day so many forms of carefully ministering to one's Self, and one's own particular humour, you will understand that I mean,—as concerns the 'happy dispatch' of this same King,—what good will it do to you?"

There was a silence. No one vouchsafed any explanation. After a considerable pause, Thord replied.

"It will do us no good. But it will show the country that we exist to revenge injustice!"

"But—is the King unjust?"

"Can you ask it?" replied Thord with a certain grave patience. "During your association with us, have you not learned?—and do you not know?"

"Sit down, Graub!" interrupted Pasquin Leroy suddenly; "I know the King's ways well enough,—and I can swear upon my honour that he deserves the worst that can be done to him!"

A murmur of sullen approval ran through the room, and somewhat lowering glances were cast at the audacious Graub, who had, by his few words, created the very undesirable impression that he wished, in some remote way, to interfere with the Committee solemnities in progress, and to defend the King from attack. He sat down again looking more or less crushed and baffled,—and Thord went on.

"We have little time to spend together to-night, and none to waste. Let each man come forward now, and take his chance,—remembering,—lest his courage fail him,—that whatever work is given him to do, this Committee are sworn to stand by him as their associate and comrade!—to defend him,—even at the risk of their own lives!—and to share completely in the consequences of whatever act he may be called upon to perform in the faithful following of his duty! Friends, repeat with me all together, the Vow of Fealty!"

At once every man rose,—and all lifting their right hands on high repeated in steady tones the following formula after their Chief,—

"We swear in the name of God, and by the eternal glory of Freedom! That whosoever among us this night shall draw the Red Cross Signal which destines him to take from life, a life proved unworthy,—shall be to us a sacred person, and an object of defence and continued protection! We guarantee to shield him at all times and under all circumstances;—we promise to fight for him against the utmost combined power of the law; —we are prepared to maintain an inviolate silence concerning his movements, his actions and their ultimate result,—even to the sufferance of imprisonment, punishment and death for his sake! And may the curse of the Almighty Creator of Heaven and Earth be upon us and our children, and our children's children, if we break this vow. Amen!"

The stern and impressive intensity with which these words were spoken sent a slight tremor along even such steel-like nerves as those of Pasquin Leroy, though he repeated the formula after Sergius Thord with the attentive care of a child saying a lesson. At its conclusion, however, a sudden thought flashed through his brain which brought a wonderful smile to his lips, and a rare light in his eyes, and touching the arm of Axel Regor, he whispered.

"Could anything be more protective to me,—*as you know me*,—than this Vow of Fealty? By my faith, a right loyal vow!"

The man he so questioned looked at him doubtfully. He did not understand. He himself had repeated the vow mechanically and without thought, being occupied in serious and uncomfortable meditation as to what possible dangerous lengths the evening's business might be carried. And, accustomed as he now was to the varying and brilliant moods of one whom he had proved to be of most varying and brilliant intelligence, his brain was not quick enough to follow the lightning- like speed of the chain of ideas,—all moving in a perfectly organised plan,—conceived by this daring, scheming and original brain, which had been so lately roused to its own powers and set in thinking, working order. He therefore merely expressed his mind's bewilderment by a warning glance mingled with alarm, which caused Leroy to smile again,— but the scene which was being enacted, now demanded their closest attention, and they had no further opportunity of exchanging so much as a word.

The Vow of Fealty being duly sworn, Sergius Thord stood aside, and made way for Lotys, who, rising from her seat, lifted the funeral urn from the table and held it out towards the men. She made a strange and weird picture standing thus,—her white arms gleaming like sculptured ivory against the dark bronze of the metal vase,—her gold hair touched with a blood-like hue from the reflection of the red lamp behind her,—and her face,—infinitely mournful and resigned,—wearing the expression of one who, forced to behold evil, has no active part in it. As she took up her position in the front of the platform, Thord again spoke.

"Let each man now advance and draw his fate! Whosoever receives a blank is exempt for another year;—whosoever draws the name of a victim must be prepared to do his duty!"

This order was at once obeyed. Each man rose separately and approaching Lotys, saluted her first, and then drew a folded paper from the vessel she held. But they moved forward reluctantly,—and most of their faces were very pale. When Pasquin Leroy's turn came to draw, he raised his eyes to the woman's countenance above him and marvelled at its cold fixity. She seemed scarcely to be herself,—and it was plainly evident that the part she was forced to play in the evening's drama was a most reluctant one.

At last all the lots were taken, and Johan Zegota lit up the gas-burners in the centre of the room. A sigh of relief came from the lips of many of the men who, on opening their papers found a blank instead of a name. But Leroy, unfolding his, sat in dumb amazement,—feeling, and not for the first time either, that surely God, or some special Providence, is always on the side of a strong man's just aim, fulfilling it to entire accomplishment. For to him was assigned the Red Cross, marked with the name of 'The King!' The words of Sergius Thord, uttered that very night, rushed back on his mind;—"Whosoever draws the name of the King must be swift and sure in his business!"

His heart beat high; he occupied at that moment a position no man in all the world had ever occupied before;—he was the centre of a drama such as had never before been enacted,—he had the greatest move to play on the chess-board of life that could possibly be desired;—and the greatest chance to prove himself the Man he was, that had ever been given to one of his quality. His brain whirled,—his pulses throbbed,— his eyes rested on Lotys with a passionate longing; something of the god-like as well as the heroic warmed his soul,—for Danger and Death stood as intimately close to him as Safety and Victory! What a strange, what a marvellous card he held in the game of life!—and yet one false move might mean ruin and an-nihilation! As in a dream he saw the members of the Committee go up, one by one, to Sergius Thord, who, as each laid their open papers before him, declared their contents. When Paul Zouche's paper was declared he was found to have drawn Carl Perousse, whereat he smiled grimly; and retired to his seat, walking rather un-steadily. Max Graub had drawn a blank,—so had Axel Regor,—so had Louis Valdor and many others.

At last it came to Leroy's turn, and as he walked up to the platform and as-cended it, there was a look on his face which attracted the instant attention of all present. His eyes were singularly bright,—his lithe handsome figure seemed taller and more erect,—he bore himself with a proud, even grand air,—and Lotys, moved at last from her chill and melancholy apathy, gazed at him as he approached, with eyes in which a profound sadness was mingled with the dark tenderness of many passionate thoughts and dreams. He laid down his paper before Thord, who, taking it up read aloud:

"Our friend and comrade, Pasquin Leroy, has received the Red Cross Signal."

Then pausing before uttering his next words he raised his voice a little, so that he might be heard by everyone in the room, and added slowly:

"To Pasquin Leroy, Fate gives—the King!"

A low murmur of deep applause ran through the room. Max Graub and Axel Regor sprang up with a kind of smothered cry, but Leroy stood immovable. Instead of returning to his seat as the others had done, he remained standing on the plat-form in front of the Committee table, between Lotys and Sergius Thord. A strange smile rested on his lips,— his attitude was inexplicable. Surveying all the men's faces which were grouped before him in a kind of chiaro-oscuro, he studied them for a moment, and then turned his head towards Thord.

"Sergius,—so far, I have served you well! Destiny has now chosen me out for even a greater service! May I speak a few words?"

Thord assented,—but a sudden sense of inquietude stirred in him as he saw that

Lotys had half risen, that her lips quivered, and that great tears stood in her eyes.

"She grieves!" he thought, sullenly, in his strange and confused way of balancing justice and injustice—"She grieves that the worthless life of the King she saved, is now to be taken by a righteous hand!"

Meanwhile Leroy faced the assembly.

"Comrades!" he said; "This is the first time I have assisted in the work of your Day of Fate,—the first time I have recognised how entirely Providence moves *with* you and *for* you in the ruling of your destinies! And because it is the first time, our Chief permits me to address you with the same fraternal liberty which was allowed to me on the night I became enrolled among you, as one of you! Since then, I have done my best to serve you—" here he was interrupted by applause —"and so far as it has been humanly possible, I have endeavoured to carry out your views and desires because,—though many of them spring from pure idealism, and are, I fear, impossible of realisation in this world,—they contain the seed of much useful and necessary reform in many institutions of this country. I have—as I promised you—shaken the stronghold of Carl Perousse;"—again the applause broke out, none the less earnest because it was restrained. "I have destroyed the press-power and prestige of that knavish Jew-speculator in false news, David Jost; and wherever the wishes of this Society could be fulfilled, I have honestly sought to fulfil them. On this night, of all nights in the year, I should like to feel, and to know, that you acknowledge me as your true comrade and faithful friend!"

At this, the whole of the company gave vent to an outburst of cheering.

"Do you doubt our love, that you ask of it?—or our gratitude that you seek to have it expressed?" said Thord, leaning forward to clasp his hand;—"Surely you know you have given new life and impetus to our work!—and that you have gained fresh triumph for our Cause!"

Leroy smiled,—but though returning his grasp cordially, he said nothing to him in person by way of reply, evidently preferring rather to address the whole community than one, even though that one was his acknowledged Chief.

"I thank you all!" he said in response to the acclamations around him. "I thank you for so heartily acknowledging me as your fellow-worker! I thank you for giving me your confidence and employing my services! Tonight—the most important night of my destiny—Fate has determined that I shall perform the greatest task of all you have ever allotted to me; and that with swiftness and sureness in the business I shall kill the King! He is my marked victim! I am his chosen assassin!" Here interrupting himself with a bright smile, he said: "Will someone restrain my two friends, Max Graub and Axel Regor from springing out of their seats? They are both extremely envious of the task which has been allotted to me!—both are disappointed that it did not fall to them to perform,—but I am not in the humour for arguing so nice a point of honour with them just now!"

A laugh went round the company, and the two delinquents thus called to order, and who had really been seeking in quite a wild and aimless way, to scramble out of their seats and make for the platform, resumed their places with heads bent low, lest those around them should see the deadly pallor of their countenances. Leroy resumed.

"I rejoice, friends and comrades, that I have been elected to the high task of removing from the Throne one who has long been unworthy of it! —one who has wasted his opportunities both in youth and middle-age,— and who, by his own fault in a great measure, has lost much of the love and confidence of his people! I am glad and proud to be the one chosen to put an end to the career of a monarch whose vices and follies—which might have suited a gambler and profligate—are entirely unbecoming to the Sovereign Ruler of a great Realm! I shall have no fear in carrying out my appointed duty to the letter! I here declare my acceptance of whatever punishment may be visited on one who removes from life a King who brings kingliness into contempt! And,—as our Chief, Sergius Thord, suggested to-night,—I shall be swift and sure in the business!—there shall be no delay!"

Here, as he spoke he drew a pistol from his pocket and turned the muzzle towards himself,—at which unexpected action there was a hasty movement of surprise, terror and confusion among the company.

"Gentlemen all! Friends! Brothers!—as you have been,—and are to me,— by the binding of our compact in the name of Lotys! It is the determination of destiny,—as it is your desire,—that I should kill the King! You have resolved upon it. You are sure that his death will benefit the country. You have decided not to take into consideration any of his possible good qualities, or to pity any of the probable sorrows and difficulties besetting him in the uneasy position he is compelled to occupy. You are quite certain among yourselves, that somehow or other his removal will bring about that ideal condition of society which many philosophers have written of, and which many reformers have desired, but which has till now, proved itself incapable of being realised. The King's death, you think, will better all existing conditions, and you wish me to fulfil not only the call of destiny, but your own desire. Be it so! I am ready to obey! I will kill the King at once!—here and now! I *am* the King!"

CHAPTER XXIX
THE COMRADE OF HIS FOES

THIS bold declaration, boldly spoken, had the startling effect of a sudden and sharp flash of lightning in dense darkness. Amazement and utter stupefaction held every man for the moment paralysed. Had a volcano suddenly opened beneath their feet and belched forth its floods of fire and lava, it could not have rendered them more helplessly stricken and speechless.

"I *am* the King!"

The words appeared to blaze on the air before them,—like the handwriting on the wall at Belshazzar's feast. The King! He,—their friend, their advocate, he—Pasquin Leroy,—the most obedient, the most daring and energetic of all the workers in their Cause—he—even he— was the King! Was it,—could it be possible! Their eyes—all riveted in fearful fascination upon him as he stood before them wholly at their mercy, but cool, dauntless, and smilingly ready to die,—had the wild uncomprehending stare of delirium;—the silence in the room was intense, breathless and terrible. Suddenly, like a lion roused, Sergius Thord, with a half-savage movement, sprang forward and seized him roughly by the arm.

"You,—you are the King?" he said; "You,—Pasquin Leroy?" and struggling for breath, his words almost choked him. "*You*! Enemy in the guise of friend! You have fooled us! You have deceived us—you—!"

"Take care, Sergius!" said the monarch smiling, as he gently disengaged himself from the fierce hand that clutched him; "This pistol is loaded,—not to shoot you with!—but myself!—at your command! It would be unfortunate if it went off and killed the wrong man by accident!"

His indomitable courage was irresistible; and Thord, relaxing his grasp, fell back in something like awe. And then the spell of horror and amazement that had struck the rest of the assemblage dumb, broke all at once into a sort of wild-beast clamour. Every man 'rushed' for the platform—and Max Graub and Axel Regor, taking swift and conscious possession of their true personalities as Professor von Glauben and Sir Roger de Launay, fought silently and determinedly to keep back the crowding hands that threatened instant violence to the person of their Royal master.

A complete hubbub and confusion reigned;—cries of "Traitor!" and "Spy!" were hurled from one voice to another; but before a single member of the Committee could reach the spot where stood the undaunted Sovereign whom they had so lately idolised as their friend and helper, and whom they were now ready to tear to pieces, Lotys flung herself in front of him, while at the same moment she snatched the pistol he held from his hand, and fired it harmlessly into the air. The loud report— the flash of fire,—startled all the men, who gaped upon her, thunderstruck.

"Through me!" she cried, her blue eyes flashing glorious menace; "Through me your shots! Through me your daggers! On me your destroying hands! Through my body alone shall you reach this King! Stand back all of you! What would you do? King or commoner, he is your comrade and associate! Sovereign or servant, he is the bravest man among you! Touch him who dare! Remember your Vow of Fealty!"

Transfigured into an almost sublime beauty by the fervour of her emotion, she looked the supreme incarnation of inspired womanhood, and the infuriated men fell back, dismayed and completely overwhelmed by the strong conviction of her words, and the amazing situation in which they found themselves.

It was true!—he, the King,—whom they had accepted and known as Pasquin Leroy,—was verily their own comrade! He had proved himself a thousand times their friend and helper!—they had sworn to defend him at the cost of their own lives, if need be,—to shelter and protect him in all circumstances, and to accept all the consequences of whatever danger he might run in the performance of his duty. His duty now,— according to the fatal drawing of lots,—was that he should kill the King; and he had declared himself ready to fulfil the task by killing himself! But—as he was their comrade—they were bound in honour to guard his life!

These bewildering and maddening thoughts coursed like fire through the brain of Sergius Thord,—the while his eyes, grown suddenly dark and bloodshot, rested wonderingly on the tall upright figure of the monarch, standing quietly face to face with the blood-thirsty Revolutionary Committee, entirely unmoved by their fierce and lowering looks, and on Lotys, white, beautiful and breathless, kneeling at his feet! A crushing sense of impotence and failure rushed over his soul like a storm wave,—his brain grew thick with the hurrying confusion, and a great cry, like that of a wounded animal, broke from his lips.

"My God! My God! All my life's work lost—in a single moment!"

The King heard. Gently, and with careful courtesy, raising Lotys from the position in which she had thrown herself to guard him from attack for the second time, he pressed her hands tenderly in his own.

"Trust me!" he whispered; "Have no fear! Not a man among them will touch me now!"

With a slight gesture he signed her back to the chair she had previously occupied. She sank into it, trembling from head to foot, but her eyes feverishly brilliant and watchful, were widely open and alert, ready to note the least movement or look that indicated further danger. Then the King addressed himself to Thord.

"Sergius, I am entirely in your hands! I wait your word of command! You are armed,—all my companions here are armed also! But Lotys has deprived me of the only weapon I possessed,—though there are plenty more in the room to be had on loan. What say you? Shall I kill the King? Or will you?"

Thord was silent. A strong shudder shook his frame. The King laid a firm hand on his shoulder.

"Friend!" he said in a low voice; "Believe me, I am your friend more than ever!— you never had, and never will have a truer one than I! All your life's work lost, you say? Nay, not so! It is gained! You conquered the People before I knew you,—and now you have conquered the People's King!"

Slowly Thord raised his great, dark, passionate eyes, clouded black with thoughts which could find no adequate expression. The look in them went straight to the monarch's heart. Baffled ambition,—the hunger of greatness,—the desire to do something that should raise his soul above such common ruck of human emmets as make of the earth the merest ant- hill whereon to eat and breed and die;—all this pent-up emotion swam luminously in the fierce bright orbs, which like mirrors, re-flected the picture of the troubled mind within. The suppressed power of the man, who, apart from his confused notions of 'liberty, equality, and fraternity' could resort to the sternest and most self-endangering measures for destroying what he considered the abuses of the law, had moved the King, while disguised as Pasquin Leroy, to the profoundest admiration for his bold character;—but perhaps he was never more moved than at this supreme moment, when, hopelessly entangled in a net of most unexpected weaving, the redoubtable Socialist had to confess himself vanquished by the simple friendship and service of the very monarchy he sought to destroy.

"Sergius," said the King again,—"Trust me! Trust me as your Sovereign, with the same trust that you gave to me as your comrade, Pasquin! For I am still your comrade, remember! Nothing can undo the oath that binds me to you and to the People! I have not become one of you to betray you; but to serve you! Our present position is certainly a strange one!—for by the tenets you hold, we should be sworn opponents, instead of, as we are, sworn friends! Political agitators would have set us one against the other for their own selfish ends; as matters stand, we are united in the People's Cause; and I may perhaps do you more good living than dead! Give me a chance to serve you even better than I have done as yet! Still,—if you judge my death would be an advantage to the country,—you have but to say the word! I have sworn,—and I am ready to carry out the full accomplishment of my vow! Do you understand? You are, by the rules of this Committee my Chief!—there are no kings here; and I am good soldier enough to obey orders! It is for you to speak!—straightly, plainly, and at once,—to the Committee,—and to me!"

"Before God, you are brave!" muttered Thord, gazing at him in reluctant admiration. "So brave, that it is almost impossible to believe that you can be a King!"

He smiled.

"Speak! Speak, my friend!" he urged; "Our comrades are watching our conference like famished tigers! Give them food!"

Thus adjured, Thord advanced, and confronted the murmuring, gesticulating crowd of men, some of whom were wrathfully expostulating with Johan Zegota, because he declined to unlock the door of the room and let them out, till he had received his Chief's commands to do so. Others were grouped round Paul Zouche, who had sat apparently stricken immovable in his chair ever since the King had declared his identity; and others showed themselves somewhat inclined to 'hustle'

Sir Roger de Launay and Professor von Glauben, who guarded the approach to the platform like sentinels,—though they were discreet enough to show no weapons of defence.

"Comrades!"

The rich, deep voice of their leader thrilled through the room, and brought them all to silence and attention.

"Comrades!" said Thord slowly,—his accents vibrating with the deepest emotion. "I desire and command you all to be satisfied that no wrong has been done to you! I ask you all to understand, fully and surely, that no wrong is intended to you! The man whom we have loved,—the man who has served us faithfully as Pasquin Leroy,—is still the same man, though the King! Rank cannot alter his proved friendship and service,— nor kingship break his bond! He is one of us,—signed and sealed in the blood of Lotys;—and as one of us he must, and will remain! Have I spoken truly?" he added, turning to the King, "or is there more that I should say?"

Before any reply could be given a hubbub of voices cried:—

"Explain! Confess! Bind him to his oath!"

Whereat the King, stepping forward a pace or two, confronted his would- be doubters and detractors with a dauntless composure.

"Explain? Confess? Friends, I will do both! but for binding me to my oath, there is no need,—for it is too strong a compact of faith and friendship ever to be broken! Would you have me remind *you* of your Vow of Fealty pronounced so solemnly this evening? Did you not swear that 'Whosoever among us this night shall draw the Red Cross Signal which destines him to take from life a life proved unworthy, shall be to us a sacred person, and an object of defence and continued protection'? As Pasquin Leroy, this vow applied to me,—as King, I ask no better or stronger pledge of loyalty!"

All eyes were fixed upon him as he spoke. For some moments there was a dead silence.

This silence was presently broken by a murmur of conflicting wonder, impatience and uncertainty,—deepening as it ran,—and then,—as the full situation became more and more apparent, coupled with the smiling and heroic calm of the monarch who had thus placed himself voluntarily in the hands of his sworn enemies, all their struggling passions were suddenly merged in one great wave of natural and human admiration for a brave man and a burst of impetuous cheering broke impulsively from every lip. Once started, the infection caught on like a fever,—and again and yet again the excited Revolutionists cheered 'for the King!'— till they made the room echo.

The tumult was extraordinary. Lotys sat silent, with clasped hands, her eyes dilated with feverish watchfulness and excitement,—the tempest of emotion in her own poor tortured soul, being of such a character which no words, no tears, no exclamations could possibly relieve. The memory of her interview with the King in his own Palace flashed across her like a scene limned in fire. She had no power to think—she was simply stunned and overwhelmed,—and held only one idea in her mind, and that was to save him at all costs, even at the sacrifice of her own life. Thord, carried away from his very self by the force of such a 'Revolution' as he had never planned or anticipated, stood more in the attitude of one who was trying to think, rather than of one who was thinking.

"For the King!" cried Johan Zegota, suddenly giving vent to the feelings he had long kept in check,—feelings which had made him a greater admirer of the so-called "Pasquin Leroy" than of Thord himself;—"For our sworn comrade, the King!"

Again the cheers broke out, to be redoubled in intensity when Louis Valdor added his voice to the rest and exclaimed:

"For the first real King I have ever known!"

Then the excitement rose to its zenith,—and amidst the tempest of applause, the King himself stood quiet, watching the turbulence with the thoughtful eyes of a student who seeks to unravel some difficult problem. Raising his hand gently, he, by this gesture created immediate silence,—and so, in this hush remained for an instant, leaning slightly against the Committee Table, draped as it was in its funereal black,—the lights at either end of it, and the red lamp in its centre flinging an unearthly radiance on his fine composed features. Long, long afterwards, his faithful servants, Sir Roger de Launay and Heinrich von Glauben retained a mental picture of him in that attitude,—the dauntless smile upon his lips,—the dreamful look in his eyes,—resting, as it seemed against a prepared funeral-bier, with the watch-lights burning for burial,—and the face of Lotys, pale as a marble mask, yet wearing an expression of mingled triumph and agony, shining near him like a star amid the gloom, while the tall form of Sergius Thord in the background loomed large,—a shadow of impending evil.

After a pause, he spoke.

"Comrades! I thank you for the expressed renewal of your trust in me. In my heart and soul, as a man, I am one of you and with you;—even though fate has made me a king! You demand an explanation—a confession. You shall have both! When I enrolled myself as a member of your Committee, I did so in all honesty and honour,—wishing to discover the object of your Cause, and prepared to aid it if I found it worthy. When I sealed my compact with you in the blood of Lotys, the Angel of our Covenant,"—here the cheering again broke out,—and Lotys, turning aside, endeavoured to restrain the tears that threatened to fall;—then, as silence was restored, he resumed;—"When as I say, I did this,—you will remember that on being asked of my origin and country, I answered that I was a slave. I spoke truly! There is no greater slave in all the length and breadth of the world than a king! Bound by the chains of convention and custom, he is coerced more violently than any prisoner,—his lightest word is misunderstood—his smallest action is misconstrued,—his very looks are made the subject of comment—and whether he walks or stands,—sits to give wearisome audience, or lies down to forget his sorrows in sleep, he should assuredly be an object of the deepest pity and consideration, instead of being as he often is, a target for the arrows of slander,—a pivot round which to move the wheel of social evil and misrule! The name of Freedom sounds sweet in your ears, my friends!—how sweet it is—how dear it is, we all know! You are ready to fight for it—to die for it! Then remember, all of you, that it is a glory utterly unknown to a king! Were he to take sword in hand and do battle for it unto the death, he could never obtain it;—he might win it for his country, but never for himself! Nothing so glorious as Liberty!—you cry! True!—but kings are prisoners from the moment they ascend thrones! And you never set them free, save in the way you suggested this evening;" and he smiled, "which way is still open to you—and—to me! But while you take time to consider whether I shall or shall not fulfil the duty which the drawing of lots on this Day of Fate has assigned to me,— whether you, on your parts, will or will not maintain the Vow of Fealty which we all have sworn together,—I will freely declare to you the motives which led me to depart from the conventional rule and formality of a merely 'Royal' existence, and to become as a Man among men,—for once at least in the history of modern sovereigns!"

He paused,—every eye was fixed upon him; and the stillness was so intense that the lightest breath might be heard.

"I came to the Throne three years ago," he resumed, "and I accepted its responsibilities with reluctance. As Heir-Apparent, you all know, or think you know, my career; for some of you have very freely expressed your convictions concerning it! It was discreditable,—according to the opinions formed and expressed by this Committee. No doubt it was! Let any man among you occupy my place;—and be surrounded by the same temptations,—and then comport himself wisely—if he can! Such an one would need to be either god or hero; and I profess to be neither. But I do not wish to palliate or deny the errors of the past. The present is my concern,—the present time, and the present People. Great changes are fermenting in the world; and of these changes, especially of those directly affecting our own country, I became actively conscious, shortly after I ascended the Throne. I heard of disaffections,— disloyalties; I gathered that the Ministry were suspected of personal self-aggrandisement. I learned that a disastrous policy was on foot respecting National Education—in which priestcraft would be given every advantage, and Jesuitry obtain undue influence over the minds of the rising generation. I heard,—I studied,—and finding that I could get no true answer on any point at issue from anyone of my supposed 'reliable' ministers, I resolved to discover things for myself. I found out that the disaffected portion of the metropolis was chiefly under the influence of Sergius Thord—and accordingly I placed myself in his way, and became enrolled among you as 'Pasquin Leroy'; his sworn associate. I am his sworn associate still! I am proud that he should call me friend;—and even as we have worked already for the People, so we will work still—together!"

No restraint could have availed to check the wild plaudits that broke out afresh at these words. Still thoughtfully and with grave kindness contemplating all the eager and excited faces upturned to him, the King went on.

"You know nearly all the rest. As Pasquin Leroy, I discovered all the shameful speculations with the public money, carried on by Carl Perousse,—and found that so far, at any rate, your accusations against him were founded in fact. At the first threatening suspicion of possible condemnation the Marquis de Lutera resigned,—

thus evidencing his guilty participation in the intended plunder. A false statement printed by David Jost, stating that I,—the King,—had revoked my decision concerning the refusal of land to the Jesuits, caused me to announce the truth of my own action myself, in the rival newspaper. Of my excommunication from the Church it is unnecessary to speak; a man is not injured in God's sight by that merely earthly ban. Among other things"—and he smiled,—"I found myself curiously possessed of a taste for literature!—and proved, that whereas some few monarchs of my acquaintance cannot be quite sure of their spelling, I could, at a pinch, make myself fairly well understood by the general public, as a skilled writer of polemics against myself!—as well as against the Secretary of State. This, so far as I personally am concerned, has been the humorous side of my little drama of disguise!—for sometimes I have had serious thoughts of appearing as a rival to our friend, Paul Zouche, in the lists of literary Fame!"

A murmur of wondering laughter ran round the room,—and all heads were turned to one corner, as the King, with the kindly smile still lighting up his eyes and lips, called:

"Zouche, are you there? Do you hear me?"

Zouche did hear. He had been sitting in a state of semi-stupor all the evening,—his chaotic mind utterly confused and bewildered by the events which had taken place;—but now, on being called, his usual audacious and irrepressible spirit came to his aid, and he answered:

"O King, I hear! O King, your Majesty would make the deaf to hear, and the dumb to speak! And if there is anything to be done to me for abominating you, O King, who had the impudence to offer me a hundred gold pieces a year for my poems, I, O King, will submit to the utmost terrors of the law!"

A burst of laughter long and loud, relieved the pent-up feelings of the company. The King laughed as heartily as the rest, and over the brooding features of Thord himself came the shadow of a smile.

"We will settle our accounts together later on, Zouche!" said the monarch gaily; "Meanwhile, I beg you to continue your harmless abomination of me at your leisure!"

Another laugh went round, and then the King resuming his speech continued:

"I have played two parts at once,—Revolutionist and King! But both parts are after all but two sides of the same nature. When I first came among you, I bade you all look at me well,—I asked you to note the resemblance I bore to the ruling Sovereign. I called myself 'the living copy of the man I most despise.' That was quite true! For there is no one I despise more utterly than myself,—when I think what I might have done with my million opportunities, and how much time I have wasted! You all scrutinised me closely;—and I did not flinch! You all accepted my service,—and I have served you well! I have noted every one of your desires. Where possible, I have sought to fulfil them. Every accusation you have brought against the Ministry has been sifted to the bottom, and proved down to the hilt. My publicly-proclaimed decision to nominate Carl Perousse as Premier was merely thrown out as a test to try the temper and quality of the nation. That test has answered its purpose well! But there is no need for fear,—Carl Perousse will never be nominated to anything but disgrace! All his schemes are in my hand, —I hold complete documentary proofs of his dishonesty and guilt; and the very day which you have chosen as that on which to appeal to the King against the choice of him as Prime Minister, will see him denounced by myself in person to the Government."

A storm of applause greeted this welcome announcement. For a moment all the men went mad with excitement, shouting, stamping and singing,— while again and yet again the cry: 'For the King!' echoed round and round in tempestuous cheering.

Sergius Thord gazed blankly at the Scene with a strange sense of being the dreaming witness of some marvellous drama enacted altogether away from the earth. He could hot yet bring himself to realise that by such a simple method as the independent working of one individual intelligence, all his own followers had been swept round to loyalty and love for a monarch, whom previously, though without knowing him, they had hated—and sworn to destroy! Yet, in very truth, all the hatreds and envys,—all the slanders and cruelties of the members of the human race towards each other, spring from ignorance; and when disaffected persons hate a king, they do so mostly because they do not know him, and because they can form no true opinion of his qualities or the various difficulties of his position. If the Anarchist, bent on the destruction of some person in authority, only had the culture and knowledge to recognise how much that person already suffers, by being in all probability forced to fulfil duties for which he has no heart or mind, he would stay his murderous hand, and pity rather than condemn. For the removal of one ruler only means the installation of another,— and the wild and often gifted souls of reformers, stumbling through darkness after some great Ideal which re-solves itself into a shadow and delusion the nearer one approaches to it, need to be tenderly dealt with from the standpoint of plainest simplicity and truth,—so that they may feel the sympathetic touch of human love and care emanating from those very quarters which they seek to assail. This had been the self-imposed mission of the King who had played the part of 'Pasquin Leroy';—and thus, fearing nothing, doubting nothing, and relying simply on his own strength, discretion, and determi-nation, he had gained a moral victory over the passions of his secret foes such as he had never himself anticipated. When silence was again restored, he proceeded:

"The various suggestions made in my presence during the time I have been a member of this Committee, will all be carried out. The present Government will naturally oppose every measure,—but I,—backed by such supporters as I have now won,—will elect a new Government—a new Ministry. When I began this bloodless campaign of my own, the present Ministry were on the edge of war. Determined to provoke hostilities with a peaceful Power, they were ready even with arms and am-munition, manufactured by a 'Company,' of which Perousse was the director and chief shareholder! Contracts for army supplies were being secretly tendered; and one was already secretly accepted and arranged for,—in which Carl Perousse and the Marquis de Lutera were to derive enormous interest;—the head of the concern being David Jost. This plan was concocted with devilish ingenuity,—for, if the war had actually broken out, the supplies of our army would have been of the worst pos-sible kind, in order to give the best possible profit to the contractors; and Jost, with his newspaper influence, would have satisfied the public mind by printing constant reiterations of the completeness and excellence of the supplies, and the entire con-tentment and jubilation of the men! But I awoke to my responsibilities in time to checkmate this move. I forbade the provocation intended;—I stopped the war. In this matter at least—much loss of life, much heavy expenditure, and much ill-will among other nations has been happily spared to us. For the rest,—everything you have been working for shall be granted,—if you yourselves will help me to realise your own plans! I want you in your thousands!—ay, in your tens of thousands!

I want you all on my side! With you,—the representatives of the otherwise un-voiced People, —I will enforce all the measures which you have discussed before me, showing good and adequate reason why they should be carried. The taxes you complain of shall be instantly removed;—and for the more speedy replenishment of the National Exchequer, I gladly resign one half my revenues from all sources whatsoever for the space of five years; or longer, if considered desirable. But I want your aid! Will you all stand by me?"

A mighty shout answered him.

"To the death!"

He turned to Thord.

"Sergius," he said, "my task is finished—my confession made! The next Order of this meeting must come from you!"

Thord looked at him amazedly.

"From me? Are you not the King?"

"Only so long as the People desire it!" replied the monarch gently; "And are you not the representative of the People?"

Thord's chest heaved. Burning tears stood in his eyes. The strangeness of the situation—the deliberate coolness and resolve with which this sovereign ruler of a powerful kingdom laid his life trustingly in his hands, was too much for his nerve.

"Lotys!" he said huskily; "Lotys!"

She rose at once and came to him, moving ghostlike in her white draperies, her eyes shining—her lips tremulous.

"Lotys," he said, "The King is in our hands! You saved his life once— will you save it again?"

She raised her bent head, and the old courageous light flashed in her face, transfiguring its every feature.

"It is not for me to save!" she replied in clear firm tones; "It is for you—and for all of us,—to defend!"

A ringing cheer answered her. Sergius Thord slowly advanced, and as he did so, the King, seeing his movement frankly held out his hand. For a moment the Socialist Chief hesitated—then suddenly yielding to his overpowering impulse, caught that hand and raised his dark eyes full to the monarch's face.

"You have conquered me!" he said, "But only by your qualities as a man —not by your authority as a king! You have won my honour—my respect— my gratitude—my friendship—and with these, so long as you are faithful to our Cause, take my allegiance! More I cannot say—more I will not promise!"

"I need no more!" responded the King cheerily, enclosing his hand in a warm clasp. "We are friends and fellow-workers, Sergius!—we can never be rivals!"

As he spoke, his glance fell on Lotys. She shrank from the swift passion of his gaze,—and her eyelids drooped half-swooningly over the bright star-windows of her own too ardent soul. Abruptly turning from both her and Thord, the King again addressed the company:

"One word more, my friends! It is arranged that you, with all your thousands of the People are to convene together in one great multitude, and march to the Palace to demand justice from the King. There is now no need to do this,—for the King himself is one of you!—the King only lives and reigns that justice in all respects may be done! I will therefore ask you to change your plan;—and instead of marching to the Palace, march with me to the House of Government. You would have demanded justice from the King; the King himself will go with you to demand justice for the People!"

A wild shout answered him; and he knew as he looked on the faces of his hearers that he had them all in his power as the servants of his will.

"And now, gentlemen," he proceeded; "I should perhaps make some excuses for my two friends, known to you as Max Graub and Axel Regor. I told you I would be responsible for their conduct, and, so far as they have been permitted to go, they have behaved well! I must, however, in justice to them, assure you that whereas I became a member of your Committee gladly, they followed my example reluctantly, and only out of fidelity and obedience to me. They have lived in the shadow of the Throne,—and have learned to pity,—and I think,—to love its occupant! Because they know,—as you have never known,—the heavy burden which a king puts on with his crown! They have, however, in their way, served you under my orders, and under my orders will continue to serve you still. Max Graub, or, to give him his right name, Heinrich von Glauben, has a high reputation in this country for his learning, apart from his position as Household Physician to our Court; —Axel Regor is my very good friend Sir Roger de Launay, who is amiable enough to support the monotony of his duty as one of my equerries in waiting. Now you know us as we are! But after all, nothing is changed, save our names and the titles we bear; we are the same men, the same friends, the same comrades!—and so I trust we shall remain!"

The cheering broke out again, and Sir Roger de Launay, who was quite as overwhelmed with astonishment at the courage and coolness of his Royal master as any Revolutionist present, joined in it with a will, as did Von Glauben.

"One favour I have to ask of you," proceeded the King, "and it is this: If you exempt me to-night from killing the King;" and he smiled,—"you must also exempt all the members of the Revolutionary Committee from any similar task allotted to them by having drawn the fatal Signal! Our friend, Zouche, for instance, has drawn the name of Carl Perousse. Now I want Zouche for better work than that of killing a rascal!"

Loud cheers answered him, and Zouche rising from his place advanced a little.

"Majesty!" he cried, "You are right! I hand your Majesty's intended Premier over to you with the greatest, pleasure in the world! Apart from the fact of your being the King, I am compelled to admit that you have common sense!"

Laughter and cheers resounded through the room again, and the King quietly turning round, extinguished the red lamp on the table. The thirteenth light was quenched; the Day of Fate was ended. As the ominous crimson flare sank out, a sudden silence prevailed, and the King fixed his eyes on Lotys.

"From you, Madame, must come my final exoneration! If you still condemn me as a King, I shall be indeed unfortunate! If you still think well of me as a man, I shall be proud! I have to thank you, not only for my life, but for having helped me to make that life valuable! As Pasquin Leroy, I have sought to serve you,—as King, I seek to serve you still!"

The silence continued. Every man present watched the visible emotion which swept every vestige of colour from the face of Lotys, and made her eyes so feverishly bright. Every man gazed at her as she rose from her chair and came forward a little to the front of the platform. It was with a strong effort that she raised her eyes to those of the King, and in that one glance between them, the lightning flash of a resistless love tore the veil of secrecy from their souls. But she spoke out bravely.

"I thank your Majesty!" she said; "I thank you for all you have done for us as our comrade and associate,—for all you will yet do for us as our comrade and associate still! It is better to be a brave man than a weak King—but it is best to be a strong man and a strong king both together! You have disproved the thoughts I had of you as King! You have ratified—" here she paused, while the colour suddenly sprang to her cheeks, and her breath came pantingly and quick,—"and strengthened the thoughts I had of you as our Pasquin!" Her eyes softened with tears, though she smiled. "We have believed in you; we believe in you still! All is as it was,—save in the one thing new,—that where we were banded together against the King, we are now united for, and with the King!"

These words were all that were needed to reawaken and confirm the enthusiasm of the Revolutionists, whose 'revolutionary' measures were now accepted and sworn to by the Crowned Head of the Realm. Thereupon, they gave themselves up to the wildest cheering.

"Comrades!" cried Paul Zouche, in the midst of the uproar; "There is one point you seem to have missed! The King,—God bless him!—doesn't see it,—Thord, glowering like an owl in his ivy-bush of hair, doesn't see it! It is only left to me to perceive the chief result of this evening's disclosures!"

All the men laughed.

"What is it, Zouche?" demanded Louis Valdor.

"Ay! What is it?" echoed Zegota.

"Speak, Zouche!" said the King; "Whatever strange conclusion your poetic brain discovers, doubt not but that we shall accept it,—from !"

"Accept it? I should think so!" cried Zouche; "You are bound to accept it whether you like it or not; there is no other way out of it!"

"Well, what is it?" repeated Zegota impatiently; "Declare it!"

"It is this;" said Zouche, "Simply this,—that, with the King as our comrade and associate, the Revolutionary Committee is no use! It is finished! There can be no longer a Revolutionary Committee!"

"That is true!" said the King; "It may henceforth be known as a new Parliament!"

Cheer after cheer echoed through the crowded room, and while the noise was at its height a knocking was heard outside and Sholto, the hunchback father of Pequita, demanded admittance. Zegota unlocked the door, and in a few minutes the situation was explained to the astonished landlord of the Revolutionary Committee quarters. Overwhelmed at the news, and full of gratitude for the kindness shown to his child, which he now knew had emanated from the King in person, he would have knelt to kiss the Royal hand, had not the monarch prevented him.

"No, my good Sholto!" he said gently; "Enough of such humility wearies me in the monotonous routine of Court life; and were it not for custom and prejudice, I would suffer no self-respecting man to abase himself before me, simply because my profession is that of King! Tell Pequita that I would not look at her, or applaud her dancing the other night, because I wished her to hate the King and to love Pasquin!—but now you must ask her for me, to love them both!"

Sholto bowed low, profoundly overcome. Was this the King against whom they had all been in league?—this simple, unaffected man, who seemed so much at home and at one with them all? Amazed and bewildered, he, by general invitation, mixed with the rest of the men, for each of whom the King had a kind and appreciative word, or a fresh pledge of his good faith and intention towards them and the reforms they sought to effect. Von Glauben was surrounded by a group of those among whom he had made himself popular; and a hundred eager questions were asked of both him and De Launay, who were ready enough to eulogise the daring of their Royal master, and the determination with which he had resolved on making his secret foes his open friends.

"After all," said Zegota deprecatingly, "it is not so much the King whom we were against, as the Government."

"Ah! You forget, no doubt," said Von Glauben, "that the King—any King— is usually a Dummy in the hands of Government, unless, as in the present instance, he chooses to become a living Personality for himself!"

"The King has created an autocracy!" said Louis Valdor; "and it will last for his lifetime. But after——!"

"After him,—if his eldest son, Prince Humphry, comes to the Throne,— the autocracy will be continued;" said Von Glauben decisively; "For he is a young man who is singularly fond of having his own way!"

The conversation now became general; and the big, bare, common room assumed in a few minutes almost the aspect of a Royal levee. This was curious enough,—and furnished food for meditation to Professor von Glauben, who was considerably excited by the dramatic denouement of the Day of Fate,—a climax for which neither he nor Sir Roger had been in the least prepared. He said something of it to Sir Roger who was watching Lotys.

"You look at the woman," he said; "I look at the man! Do you think this drama is finished?"

"Not yet!" answered De Launay curtly; "Nor is the danger over!"

The hum of talk continued; and the good feeling of friendship and unity of the assemblage was intensified with every cordial handshake. When the time came to break up, someone suggested that a carriage should be sent for to convey the King and his two companions to the Palace. Whereat the monarch laughed aloud and right joyously.

"By my faith!" he exclaimed; "You, my friends, would actually pamper me already, by offering me a luxury which you yourselves do not propose to enjoy! Ah, my friends, here comes in the mischief of the monarchical system! What of your 'Liberty, Equality, and Fraternity'? Do I ask to have anything different to yourselves? Can I not walk, even as you do? Have I not walked to, and from these meetings often? And even so, I purpose to walk now! If you are true Revolutionists—as I am—do not reverse your own theories! You complain,—and justly,—that a king is over-flattered; do not then flatter him yourselves by insisting on such convenience for him as he does not even demand at your hands!"

"You take us too literally, Sir," said Louis Valdor; "Even Revolutionists owe respect to their chief!"

"Sergius Thord is your Chief, my friend!" replied the monarch; "And, from a Revolutionary point of view, mine! But you have never thought of sending *him* anywhere in a carriage! Ah!—what children we are! What slaves of convention! 'Liberty, Equality and Fraternity' have been the ideals of ages;—yet despite them, we are always ready to follow a Leader,—and form ourselves into one body under a Head!"

"Provided the Head has brains in it!" said Zouche. "But otherwise—"

"You cut it off!" laughed the monarch—"and quite right too!"

They now began to separate. The hunchback Sholto explained that it was long after midnight, and that he had already put out all the lights in the basement.

Whereupon the King, turning to Sergius Thord said: "Farewell for the moment,

Sergius! Come to me at the Palace with the whole plan of the meeting you are now organising; I shall hold myself ready to fall in with your plans! Gather your thousands, and—leave the rest to me!"

Thord clasped his extended hand,—and was moved by a curious instinct to bend down low over it after the fashion of a courtier, but restrained himself almost by force. The men began to move; one after the other bade good-night to the King—then to Thord, and last to Lotys, who, drawing on her cloak, prepared to leave also.

"I will see you safely down the stairs," said the King smilingly, to her. "It is not the first time I have done so! How now, Zouche?"

Paul Zouche stood before him, his eyes full of a strange mingled pathos and scorn.

"I have to thank your Majesty," he said slowly, "for something I do not in the least value,—Fame! It has come too late! Had it been my portion three years ago, the woman I loved would have been proud of me, and I should have been happy! She is dead now—and nothing matters!"

The King was silent. There was something both solemn and pitiful about this wreck of manhood which was still kept alive by the fire of genius.

"With one word you might have saved me—and her!" he went on. "When you came to the Throne,—and all the wretched versifiers in the kingdom were scribbling twaddle in the way of 'Coronation odes' and medleys, I wrote 'The Song of Freedom' for your glory! All the people of the land know that song now!—but you might have known it then! For now it is too late!—too late to call her back;—too late to give me peace!"

He paused;—then—without another word—turned, and went out.

"Poor Zouche!" said the King gently; "I accept his reproach and understand it! He is right! The recognition of his genius is one of the thousand chances I have missed! But, as God lives, I will miss no more!"

A great quietude fell on the house as the Revolutionary Committee dispersed. The last to leave was the King, his two friends, and Lotys. Lotys declined all escort somewhat imperatively, refusing to allow Sergius Thord to see her to her own home.

"I must be alone!" she said; "Do you not understand! I want to think—I want to realise our change of position. I cannot talk to you, Sergius, —no—not till to-morrow—you must let me be!"

He drew back, chilled and hurt by her tone, but forbore to press his company on her. With another farewell to the King, he stood at the top of the long dark winding stair watching the group descend,—first Von Glauben, next De Launay,—thirdly, the King,—and lastly, Lotys.

"Good-night!" he called, as her white robes vanished in the gloom.

"Good-night!" she answered tremulously, as she disappeared.

And he, returning to the empty room, stared vacantly at the table draped with black, and the funeral urn set upon it,—stared at the empty chairs and bare walls, and listened as it were, to the midnight silence,—realising that he as Chief of the Revolutionary Committee, was no longer a chief but a servant!—and that the power he sought— that power which he had endeavoured to attain in order that he might make of Lotys, as he had said, 'a queen among women!' was only to be won through,—the King! The King knew all his secret plans and his aims,—he held the clue to the whole network of his Revolutionary organisation,—and the only chance he now had of ever arriving at the highest goal of his ambition was in the King's hands! Thus was he,— Socialist and Revolutionist,—made subject to the Throne; the very rules he had drawn up for himself and his Committee making it impossible that he could be otherwise than loyal, to a monarch who was at the same time his comrade!

Meanwhile, in the thick darkness of the hall below, while Von Glauben and De Launay were groping their way to the door which was cautiously held open by Sholto, Lotys, moving with hesitating steps down the stairs, felt rather than saw a head turned back upon her,—a flash of eyes in the darkness, and heard her name breathed softly:

"Lotys!"

She grew dizzy and uncertain of her footing; she could not answer. Suddenly a strong arm caught her,—she was drawn into a close, fierce, jealous clasp; warm lips caressed her hair, her brow, her eyes; and a voice whispered in her ear:

"You love me, Lotys! You love me! Hush!—do not deny it—you cannot deny it!—you know it, as I know it!—you have told me you love me! You love me, my Love! You love me!"

Another moment—and the King passed quietly out of the door with a bland 'Good-night' to Sholto, and joining his two companions, raised his hat to Lotys with a courteous salutation.

"Good-night, Madame!"

She stood in the doorway, shuddering violently from head to foot,— watching his tall figure disappear in the shadows of the street. Then stretching out her hands blindly, she gave a faint cry, and murmuring something inarticulate to the alarmed Sholto, fell senseless at his feet.

CHAPTER XXX
KING AND SOCIALIST

TO many persons of the servile or flunkey habit, the idea that a king should ever comport himself as an ordinary,—or extraordinary,—man, seems more or less preposterous; while to conceive him as endowed with dash, spirit, and a love of adventure is judged almost as absurd and impossible. The only potentate that ever appears, in legendary lore, to have indulged himself to his heart's content in the sport of adopting a disguise and going about unrecognised among his subjects, is the witty and delightful hero of the 'Arabian Nights' Entertainment,' Caliph Haroun Alraschid, who, as Tennyson describes him, had

> "Deep eyes, laughter-stirred
> With merriment of kingly pride;
> Sole star of all that place and time,
> I saw him in his golden prime.
> The good Haroun Alraschid!"

We accept Haroun; and acknowledge him to have been wise in the purport of his wanderings through the streets of the city,—gaining new experience with every hour, and studying the needs and complaints of his people for himself;—but if we should be told of a modern monarch doing likewise in our own day, we should mount on the stiff hobby-horse of our ridiculous conventionality, and accuse him of having brought the dignity of the Throne into contempt. Yet nothing perhaps can be more contemptible than a monarch who is too surrounded by flunkeyism to be a Man,—and, on the other hand, nothing could be more beneficial than the feeling that perhaps a monarch may be so much of a man after all that no one can be quite certain as to his whereabouts. It would be well if some rowdy 'clubs' could be restrained by the idea that the Sovereign of the Realm might step in unexpectedly,—or if the 'slums' could scarcely be able to tell when he might not be among their inmates, disguised as one of them, studying and knowing more in a day than his ministers would tell him in several years. It is generally admitted that no man is fit for a profession till he has thoroughly mastered its possibilities,—yet it is not too much to declare that in the profession of Sovereignty the few who practise it, have mastered it to so little purpose, that they are almost entirely blind to the singular advantages which they might obtain, not only for themselves, but for the entire world, if they chose to put forth their own individuality, and, instead of wasting their time on the scheming and self-seeking sections of Society, elected to try their powers on the working and trade communities of the nation. But throughout all history, the various careers of kings and emperors contain instructive lessons of Lost Opportunity. Allowing for the differences of climate and temperament, it may be taken for granted that no people of any country are constitutionally able to rise above a certain height of enthusiasm; and that when the high-water mark is reached, their enthusiasm cools, and a reaction invariably sets in. For this cause a monarch should never rely too much on the plaudits of the mob in a time of conquest, or public festival of jubilation. He should look upon such acclamation as the mere rising of a wave, which must in due time sink again,—and if he would know his people thoroughly, he should study that same shouting mob, not when it is affected by hysteria, but during its everyday level condition of stubborn and patient toil. So will he perhaps be able to lay his finger on the sore places of life, and to find out where the seed of mischief is planted, before it begins to grow. But he must give an individual interest to such work; no information must be obtained or given through this person or that person,—for the old maxim that 'if you want anything done, do it yourself' applies to kings as well as to all other classes of men.

That the old adage had been amply practised by one king at least, was soon known throughout the capital of the country over which the monarch here written of held dominion. Somehow, and by some means or other, the story oozed out bit by bit and in guarded whispers, that the King had 'trapped' Carl Perousse, as well as several other defaulting ministers,—and that, strange and incredible as it appeared, he himself was the very 'Pasquin Leroy' whose political polemics had created such a stir. Once started, the rumour flew;—some disbelieved it;—others listened, with ears stretched wide, greedy for more detail,—but presently the scattered threads of gossip became woven into a consecutive web of certainty so far as one point, at least, was concerned,—and this was, that the King would personally address his Parliament during the ensuing week on matters of national safety and importance. Such an announcement was altogether unprecedented, and excited the whole country's attention. Plenty of discussion there was, as to whether the King had any right to so address the members of the Government,—and some oracular journals were of the opinion that he was acting in an 'unconstitutional manner.' On the other hand, it was discovered and proved that there was no actual law forbidding the Sovereign to speak when any question of urgency appeared to call for his expressed opinion.

While this affair was being contested and argued, a considerable sensation was created by the news that the Marquis de Lutera had suddenly left the country,—ostensibly for his health, which, everyone was assured, had completely broken down. People shook their heads ominously, and wondered when the King would give M. Perousse the task of forming a new Ministry,—while they watched with deepening interest the progress of the various Government debates, which were carried on in the usual way, following the lines laid down by the absent Premier, Marquis de Lutera. Carl Perousse, confronted by a thousand difficulties, maintained his usual equable and audacious attitude, scouting with scorn the rumour that the Socialist writer, 'Pasquin Leroy' was merely a disguise adopted by the King himself,—and he was as cool and imperturbable as ever when one morning David Jost succeeded in finding him at home, and obtaining an audience.

"It was the King!" burst out Jost, as soon as he found himself alone with his ally; "It was the King himself who wore Lutera's signet, and came to me disguised so well that his own father would not have known him! The King himself, I say! And I told him everything!"

"More fool you!" returned Perousse quietly; "However, fools generally have to pay the price of their folly!"

"And knaves!" said Jost furiously; "But there is a power which cannot be controlled, even by kings or statesmen—and that is—the pen!"

"And do you think you can use the pen?" queried Perousse indolently; "Excellent Shylock, you know you cannot! You can pay others to use it for you! That is all!"

"I can make short work of *you* at any rate!" said Jost, his little eyes sparkling with rage; "For I see plainly enough now that even if our plans had succeeded, you would have left me in the lurch!"

"Of course!" smiled Perousse; "Are you so simple in the world's ways as not to be able to realise that such Jew pressmen as you are only made for the use of politicians? We drop you, when we have done with you! Go to London, Jost! Start a paper there! It is the very place for you! Get a Cardinal to back you up, with funds to be used for the 'conversion' of England! Or give a hundred thousand pounds to a hospital! You can become naturalised as an Englishman if you like; any country does for a Jew! And you will be a power of the realm in no time! They manage these sort of things capitally there!"

"By God!" said Jost; "I could kill you!"

"What for?" demanded Perousse; "Because you think I am going to be proved a political fraud? Wait and see! If the King denounces me, I am prepared to denounce the King!"

Jost stared, then laughed aloud.

"Denounce the King! You are bold! But you make up your sum with the wrong numerals this time! The King holds the complete list of your speculations in his hand,—he has got them through the agency of the Revolutionary Committee, to which your stockbroker's confidential clerk belongs! You fool! All your schemes— all your 'companies' are known to him root and branch—and you say you will 'denounce' him! If you do, it will be a real comedy!—the case of a thief denouncing the officer who has caught him red-handed in the act of thieving!"

With this parting shot, he made a violent exit. Perousse left alone, dismissed him, with all other harassments from his mind; for being entirely without a conscience, he had very little care as to the results of the King's reported intentions. He was preparing a brilliant speech, which he intended to deliver if occasion demanded; and on his own coolness, mendacity and pluck, he staked his future.

"If I fail," he said to himself; "I will go to the United States, and end by becoming President! There are many such plans open to a man of resources!"

During the ensuing few days there were some extra gaieties at the Palace,—and the King and Queen were seen daily in public. Everywhere, they were greeted with frantic outbursts of cheering, and the recent riotous outbreaks seemed altogether forgotten. The Opera was crowded nightly, and undeterred by the fear of any fresh manifestations of popular discontent, their Majesties were again present. This time the King was the first to lead off the applause that hailed Pequita's dancing. And how her little feet flew!—how her eyes sparkled with rapture—how the dark curls tossed, and the cherry lips smiled! To her the King remained Pasquin!—a kind of monarch in a fairy tale, who scattered benefits at a touch, and sunshine with a glance, and who deserved all the love and loyalty of every subject in the kingdom! But she had never had any idea of 'Revolution,' poor child!—save such a revolving of chance and circumstance as should enable her father to live in comfort, without anxiety for his latter days. And perhaps at the bottom of all political or religious fanaticism we should find an equally simple root of cause for the effect.

The day at last came when Sergius Thord held his mighty 'mass meeting,' convened in the Cathedral square,—all ready for marching orders. No interference was offered either from soldiery or police; and the people came pouring up from every quarter of the city in their thousands and tens of thousands. By noon, the tall lace-like spire of the Cathedral towered above a vast sea of human heads, which from a distance looked like swarming bees; and as the bells struck the hour, Thord, mounting the steps of a monument erected to certain heroes who had long ago fallen in battle, was greeted with a roar of acclamation like the thunder of heaven's own artillery. But even while the multitude still shouted and cheered, the sight of another figure, which quietly ascended to the same position, caused a sudden hush,—a gradually deepening silence of amazement and awe,—and then finally swift recognition.

"The King!" cried a voice.

"Pasquin Leroy!" shouted another, who was answered by yells and shrieks of derision.

"The King!" was again the cry. And as the vast crowd circled round and round, its million eyes wonderingly upturned, Sergius Thord suddenly lifted his cap and waved it:

"Ay! The King!" His voice rang over the heads of the people with a rich thrill of command. "The King, who here declares himself the friend of our Cause! The King, who is with us to-day of his own will, at his own request, by his own choice!—without escort,—unarmed—defenceless! The King! The King who has resolved to go with us, and demand justice for his overtaxed and suffering subjects! The King, who is one with us!— who seeks no greater kingliness than that of being loved and trusted by his People!"

The surprise of this announcement was so truly overpowering, that for the moment the mighty mass of men stood inert; then,—as the situation flashed upon them, such a thunder of cheering broke out as seemed to make the very earth rock and the houses in the square tremble. The King himself, standing by Thord, grew pale as he heard it, and his eyes were suffused with something like tears.

"By Heaven!" he murmured; "The love of this people is worth having!"

"Did you ever doubt it?" queried Thord slowly, eyeing him with a touch of wonder not unmixed with jealousy; "There is only one power which keeps a king on his throne—the confidence of the nation! You had nearly lost that! For though there is nothing so easy to win, there is nothing so easy to lose!"

"True!" said the monarch, his eyes still resting tenderly on the excited multitude below him. "I have deserved little at the people's hands—but perhaps—when I am gone—" he paused abruptly, then with a smile added—"Give us our marching orders, Sergius!"

Thord obeyed,—and very soon, under his command, the huge multitude arranged itself in blocks, or regiments, perfectly organised in different companies, and entirely prepared to keep order. Dividing into equal lines they made way quickly and with enthusiasm as they perceived the King's charger, which, richly caparisoned, had been brought for his Majesty at Thord's own earnest request.

When all was ready, the King sprang into the saddle, and gathering the reins in one hand, sat for a moment bare-headed, the people surging round him with repeated outbursts of applause. Without a weapon,— without a single man of his own household to bear him company,—without any armed escort,—he remained there enthroned;—the centre,—not of 'society,'—but of the People, who gathered round him as their visible Head, with as much shouting and enthusiasm and worship, as if he had, in his own person, made the conquest, single-handed, of a hundred nations! Never, in his most gorgeous apparel,—never, even when robed and crowned in state, had he looked so noble; never had he seemed so worthy of the highest honour, reverence and admiration, as now! At a signal from Thord, who led the way on foot, the thousands of the city began to march to the House of Government, all gathering round one principal figure, that of their King. A group of workmen constituted themselves his body-guard, protecting his proudly-stepping charger from so much as a stone that might startle it or check its progress, and thus—liberated from the protection of flunkeys and flatterers,— the monarch, surrounded by his true subjects advanced together as one Body, to challenge and overthrow a fraudulent Ministry, whose measures had been drawn up and passed, not for the good of the country, but for the financial advantage and protection of themselves.

Never was such a wondrous sight seen, as that almost interminable procession through the broad thoroughfares of the city, headed by a Socialist, and centred by a King! No Royal ceremonial, overburdened with snobbish conventionalities and hypocritical parade, ever presented so splendid and imposing a sight as that concentrated mass of the actual people,—the working muscle and sinew of the land's common weal, marching in steady and triumphant order,—surging like the billows of the sea around that brave ship, their Sovereign, cheering him to the echo, and waving around him the flags of the country, while he, still bare-headed, rode dauntless in their midst looking every inch a king!— more kingly indeed than he had ever seemed, and more established in the affections of his subjects than any living monarch of the time. So was he brought with ceaseless acclamation to the Government House, where, as all knew, he purposed denouncing Carl Perousse;—and thus did he assert in his own person that a king, supported by a nation, is more powerful than any government built up by mere party agency!

And even so, at his best and bravest, two women looked upon him and loved him! One, from the outskirts of the great crowd where, shrouded close in her veil, she waited tremblingly near the Government buildings, and saw him alight from his charger, and enter there, amid the wild shoutings of the populace,—the other, from a high window in the Royal Palace, where she leaned watching the crowd,— the sunlight catching the diamonds at her breast and sparkling in her proud cold eyes. And over the whole city rang the continuous and exultant cry:

"The King! The King!"

And perhaps only one soul, prophetic in instinct, foresaw any terror in the triumph!—only one voice, low and tremulous and weighted with tears and prayers, murmured:

"Ah, dear God! Would he were not a King!"

CHAPTER XXXI
A VOTE FOR LOVE

NEXT day it was known through the length and breadth of the city that the King, so long judged as a political Dummy, had proved himself a living, acting authority. Every journal in city and province led off its news under the one chief heading,—'The King's Speech.' The King had spoken;—and with no uncertain voice. Cool, brilliant in wording, concise in statement,—cuttingly correct in facts, convincing in argument, his unexpected denouncement of Carl Perousse, and the Perousse 'majority,' swept the Government off their feet by its daring courage, and still more daring veracity. Documentary evidence of the dishonourable speculations with the public money which had been so freely indulged in by the Secretary of State, aided and abetted by the Premier, was handed by the King in person to the authorities whose business it was to examine such proofs,—the dishonourable measures used to retain the 'majority' were fully exposed, and the whole House stood thunderstruck and mentally paralysed, under the straight accusation and merciless condemnation launched at their own lax tolerance of such iniquitous practices, by their reigning monarch. With perfect dignity and impressive calm, the King quietly demanded whether M. Carl Perousse would be pleased to explain his actions? Whether he had anything to say in response to the charges brought against him? To this last query, after a dead silence, during which every eye was fixed on the defaulting Minister, who, in the course of the Royal speech had seen every bulwark of his own intended defence torn away from him, Perousse, with an ashy white countenance answered:

"Nothing!"

And the silence around him continued; a silence more expressive than any outspoken word of scorn.

But more surprises were in store for the Ministry, which found itself thus suddenly overthrown. The King announced the marriage of his son, the Crown Prince, to 'a daughter of the People'! Boldly, and with an ardent passion of truth lighting up every feature of his handsome countenance, he stated this overwhelming piece of news in a perfectly matter-of-fact way, adding, that in consequence of the step taken,—a step which he did not himself in any way regret,—the Crown Prince asked to be allowed to resign the Throne in favour of his brother Rupert.

"Unless," continued his Majesty, "the Nation should be proved ready to accept the wife he has chosen. It is needless to add that my son has married without my consent, and this is the reason of his present absence from the country. If the Nation accepts his wife, he will return to the Nation; if not, I am bound to say, knowing his mind, that there is nothing to be done, but to declare Prince Rupert Heir to the Throne. This, however, I personally desire may be left to the consideration and vote of the people!"

And when the House rose on that astonishing afternoon, they knew they were no longer a House,—they knew the Government was entirely overthrown, and that there would be a new Ministry and a General Election. They had to realise also, that their 'Bills' for imposing fresh taxes on the people were mere waste paper,—and they heard likewise with redoubled amazement that the King had decided to resign half his revenues for the space of five years, to assist the deficit in the National Exchequer.

At the conclusion of the whole unprecedented scene, they saw the King received, as it were, into the arms of a frenzied crowd, numbering many tens of thousands, which spread round all the Government buildings, and poured itself in thick streams through every street and thoroughfare, and they had to accept the fact that their 'majority' was reduced to a minority so infinitesimal, amid the greater wave of popular resolve, that it was not worth counting.

Carl Perousse, leaving the House by a private door of egress, shamed, disgraced and crestfallen as he was, dared not trust the very sight of himself to such an overwhelming multitude, and managed by lucky chance to escape unobserved. He was assisted in this manoeuvre by General Bernhoff. The Chief of the Police perceived him slinking cautiously along the side-wall of an alley where the crowd had not penetrated, and helped him into a passing cab that he might be driven rapidly and safely to his home.

"You will no doubt excuse me"—said the General with a slight smile— "for not having acted more rigorously in the matter of the suspected 'Pasquin Leroy'! I am afraid I should never have summed up sufficient impudence to ask the King to sign a warrant against himself!"

Perousse muttered an inarticulate oath by way of reply. He realised fully that the game for him was lost. His speech of defence, so carefully prepared had been useless, for he could not have uttered it in the face of the damnatory evidence against him pronounced by the King, and verified by his own public actions. Yet his audacity had not, in the main, deserted him. He knew that, owing to his proved defalcations and fraudulent use of the public money, his own property would be confiscated to the Crown,—but he had always kept himself well prepared for emergencies, and had invested in foreign securities under various assumed names. Turning his attention to America, he felt pretty sure he could do something there,—but so far as his own country was concerned, he submitted to the inevitable, feeling that his day was done.

"The Jew is always triumphant!" he said, as he opened Jost's newspaper next morning, and read a full account of the proceedings in the House, described with all the 'colour' and gush of Jost's most melodramatic reporter. "There is no doubt a 'leader' on my 'unhappy position' as a fallen, but once trusted Minister!"

He was right; there was! A gravely-reproachful, sternly-commiserating 'leader,' wherein the apparently impeccable and highly conscientious writer 'deplored' the laxity of those who supported M. Carl Perousse in his 'regrettable' scheme of self-aggrandisement.

"The rascal!" ejaculated Perousse, as he read. "If I ever get a fresh start in the United States or South Africa, I'll put him on a gridiron, and roast him to slow music!"

Meanwhile the whole country went mad over the King. No man was ever so idolised; no man was ever made the centre of more hero-worship. In all the excitement of a General Election, the wave of loyalty rose to its extremest height, and no candidate that was not ready to follow the lines of reform laid down by the monarch, had a ghost of a chance of being returned as a deputy. With the abolition of the tax on bread, the popular jubilation increased; bonfires were lit on every hill,—rockets flared up star-like from every rocky point upon the coast, and the Nation gave itself entirely up to joy.

All the long dormant sentiment of the multitude was roused to a fever- heat by the story of Prince Humphry's marriage, and he too, next to his father, became a veritable hero of romance in the eyes of the people, for whom Love, and all pertaining to love-matters form the most interesting part of life. Following his announcement in the House, the King issued a 'manifesto,' setting forth the facts of his son's union with 'One Gloria Ronsard, of The Islands,' and requesting the vote of the people for, or against, the Prince as Heir-Apparent to the Throne.

The result of this bold and candid reliance on the Nation was one which could never have been foreseen by so-called 'diplomatic' statesmen, who are accustomed to juggle with simple facts, and who strive to cover up and conceal the too distinct plainness of truth. An electric thrill of chivalrous enthusiasm pulsated through the entire country; and the unanimous vote of the people was returned to the King in entire favour of the Crown Prince and his chosen bride. Perhaps no one was more astonished at this than the King himself. He had been prepared for considerable friction; he had been quite sure of opposition on the part of 'Society,' but, Society, moved for once from its usual selfishness by the boldness and daring of a heroic king, had ranked itself entirely on his side, and was ready and even anxious to accept in Prince Humphry a new kind of 'Cophetua,' even if he had chosen to wed a beggar-maid! And it so chanced that there were many persons who had seen Gloria,— and among these was Sergius Thord, He had not only seen her, but known her;—he had studied her character and qualities,—and was aware that she possessed one of the most pure and beautiful of womanly souls;—and though taken by surprise at the discovery that the young 'sailor' she had wedded was no other than the Crown Prince, yet, after the experience he had personally gone through with one 'Pasquin Leroy,' he could scarcely feel that any news, even of the most wonderful kind, was so wonderful after all! So that, as soon as he learned the truth, he brought all his enormous 'following' into unanimity as regarded the Prince's romantic love-story; and ere long there was not one in the metropolis at least, who did not consider the marriage a good thing, and likely to weld even more closely together the harmonious relationship between people and Throne.

And so it chanced, that even while the General Election was still going on all over the country, an incessant popular clamour was made for the instant return of the Prince to his native land. The papers teemed with suggestions as to the 'welcoming home' of the young hero of romance and his bride, and Professor von Glauben, mentally giddy with the whirl of events, was nevertheless triumphantly elated.

"Now that you know everything," he said to Sir Roger de Launay, "I hope you are satisfied! My 'jam-pot' that you spoke of, has turned out to be a special Sweetmeat for the whole nation!"

"I am very much surprised, I confess!" said Sir Roger slowly; "I should hardly have thought such a love-story possible in these modern days. And I should certainly never have given the nation credit for so much sentiment!"

"A nation is always sentimental!" declared the Professor; "What does a Government exist for? Merely to keep national sentiment in order. Ministers know well enough, that despite the various 'Bills' brought in for material advantage and improvement, they have always to deal with the imaginative aspiration of the populace, rather than their conception of logic. For truly, the masses have no logic at all; they will not stop to count the cost of an Army, but they will shout themselves hoarse at the sight of the Flag! The Flag is the Sentiment; the Army is the Fact. The King has secured all the votes of the nation on a question of Sentiment only,—but there is this pleasant scientific 'fact underlying the sentiment,—Gloria is fit to be the mother of kings! And that is what I will not say of any royally-born woman I know!"

Sir Roger was silent.

"Consider our present Queen as a mother only!" he went on; "Beautiful and impassive as a snow-peak with the snow shining upon it! What of her sons? The Crown Prince is the best of them,—but he has only been saved from inherited mischief by his love for Gloria. The other two boys, Rupert and Cyprian, will probably be selfish libertines!"

Sir Roger opened his eyes in astonishment.

"Why do you say that?" he asked; "They are harmless lads enough! Cricket and football are enough to make them happy."

"For the present, no doubt!" agreed Von Glauben; "But it sometimes happens that the young human animal who expends all his brains on kicking a football, is quite likely to expend another sort of force when he grows up, in morally kicking other things! At least, that is how I regard it. The over-cultivation of physical strength leads to mental callousness and brutality. These are scientific points which require discussion,—not with you,—but with a scientist. Nothing should be overdone. Too much enervation and lack of athleticism leads to moral deterioration certainly,—but so does too much 'sport' as they call it. There is a happy medium to be obtained on both sides, but human beings generally miss it. Prince Humphry, born of a beautiful, introspective, selfish—yes, I repeat it!—selfish mother, would, if he had married a hard-natured, cold and conventional wife, probably have been the most indifferent, casual, and careless sovereign that ever reigned; but, united as he is to a trusting, warm-hearted, loving, womanly woman like Gloria, he will probably make himself the idol of the Nation."

"Not more so than his father is!" said Sir Roger, with a smile.

"Ach so! That would be difficult, I grant you!" agreed the Professor; "As I told you, Roger, at the beginning of this drama in which we have both played our little parts; no harm ever came undeservedly to a brave man with a good conscience!"

"True! And no harm has come to the King—as yet!" said Sir Roger thoughtfully. "But I sometimes fear one man——!"

"Sergius Thord?" suggested Von Glauben; "To speak honestly, so do I! But I watch him—I watch him closely! He loves Lotys, as a tiger loves its mate,—and if he should ever suspect——!"

"Hush!" said Roger quickly; "Do not speak of it! I assure you I am always on guard!"

"Good! So am I! But Thord is too busy just now climbing the hill to look either backward or aside. When he reaches the summit, it is possible he may see the whole landscape at a glance!"

"He will reach the summit very soon!" said De Launay; "His election as deputy for the city, is certain. From the moment he announced himself as candidate, there has been no opposition."

"He will be returned by an overwhelming majority," said the Professor; "And he will gain all the power he has been working for. Also, with the power, he will obtain all the difficulty, responsibility, disappointment and bitterness. Power is a dangerous possession, unless it is accompanied by a cool head; and in that our friend Sergius Thord is lacking. He is a creature of impulse—and a savage creature too!—a half-educated genius,—than which nothing in the shape of humanity is more desperately difficult to manage!"

"Lotys can manage him!" said Sir Roger.

"That depends!" And the Professor rubbed his nose irritably. "Women are excellent diplomatists up to a certain point, but their limit is reached when they fall in love! Passion and enthusiasm transform them into quite as absurd fools as—men!"

Sir Roger smiled, and changed the subject.

But in a few days, what had been foreshadowed in their conversation came true. One of the chief results of the General Election was the triumphal return of Sergius Thord as Deputy for the Metropolis by an enormous majority; and in the evening of the day on which the polling was declared, great crowds assembled beneath the windows of his house, —that house so long known as the quarters of the Revolutionary Committee,—roaring themselves hoarse with acclamation. He was, of course, called out before them to speak,—and he yielded to the clamorous demand, as perforce he was bound to do, but strangely enough, with extreme reluctance.

A certain vague weariness depressed his spirits; his undisputed election as one of the most important Government-representatives of the people, lacked the savour of the triumph he had expected;—and like all those who have worked for years to win a coveted post and succeed at last in winning it, he was filled with the fatal satiety of accomplishment. Power,—temporal power,—was after all not so great as it had seemed! He had climbed—he had striven; but all the joy was contained in the climbing and the striving. Now that he had gained his point there seemed nothing left to prick afresh his flagging ambition. Nevertheless, he succeeded in addressing his enthusiastic followers and worshippers with something of his old fervour and fire,—sufficiently well, at any rate, to satisfy them, and send them off with renewed shouts of exultation, expressive of their continued reliance on his courage and ability. But, when left alone at last, his heart suddenly failed him.

"What is the use of it!" he thought wearily; "True, I now represent the city,—I lead its opinions—I am its mouth-piece for the State,—and the wrongs and injuries done to the million are mine to bring before the Government; and my business it will be to force remedial measures for the same. But what then? There will be, there must be, constant discussion, argument, contradiction,—for there are always conflicting opinions in every aspect of human affairs,—and it will be my work to put down all contradiction,—all opposition,—and to carry the People's Cause with a firm hand. Yet—after all, if I succeed, it will be the King's doing,—not mine! To him I partly owe my present power; the power I had before, was *all* my own!"

Sullen and silent he brooded on the changes in his fortunes with no very satisfied mind. While he could not, as a brave man, refuse his respect and homage to the monarch who had quietly made himself complete master of the 'Revolutionary' organisation, and who had succeeded in turning thousands of disaffected persons into ardent Loyalists, he was nevertheless troubled by a lurking suspicion that Lotys had secretly known and favoured the King's scheme. Vaguely ashamed in his own mind of the idea, he yet found himself giving way to it now and again, as he remembered how she had defended his life,—not once but twice,—and how she had often frankly declared her admiration for the unselfishness, heroism, and tireless energy of the so-called 'Pasquin Leroy.' After much perplexed meditation, he came at last to one resolve.

"She must be my wife!" he said, his eyes gleaming with a sudden fire of passion and determination combined; "If,—as she says,—she does not love me, she must learn to love me! Then, all will be well! With her, it is possible I may reach still greater heights; without her, I can do nothing!"

Meantime, while the results of the Election to what was now called 'The Royal Government,' were being daily recorded in all parts of the world, and the King himself, from a selection of the ablest and most honourably-proved men of the time, was forming a new Ministry, the news of these radical changes in the kingdom's affairs, spreading rapidly everywhere by cable, as news always spreads nowadays, reached a certain far corner in one of the most beautiful provinces of India,—a corner scarcely known to the conventional traveller,—where, in a wondrous palace, lent to them by one of the most civilised and kindly of Oriental potentates,—a palace surrounded by gardens that might have been a true copy of the fabled Eden, Prince Humphry and the fair 'Gloria' of his life, were passing a happy, 'hidden-away' time of perfect repose.

The evening on which they learned that their own nation demanded their return was 'like the night of Al-Kadir, better than a thousand months.' All day long the heat had been intense,—and they had remained indoors enjoying the coolness of marble courts and corridors, and plashing fountains,—but with the sunset a soft breeze had sprung up, and Gloria, passing into the shadiest corner of the gardens, had laid herself down in a silken hammock swung between two broad sycamore trees, and there, gently swaying to and fro, she watched her husband reading the various European journals that had arrived for his host by that day's mail. Beautiful always, she had grown lovelier than ever in these halcyon days of rest, when 'Love took up the harp of Life and smote on all the chords with might; Smote the chord of Self, that, trembling, pass'd in music out of sight.' To her native grace she now united a distinctive dignity which added to her always gracious and queenly charm, and never had she looked more exquisite than now, when rocking gently in the suspended network of woven turquoise silk fringed with silver, she rested her head against cushions of the same delicate hue, and turned her expressive eyes enquiringly towards her husband,— wondering what kept him so silent, and what was the cause of the little line of anxiety which furrowed his brow. Clad in a loose diaphanous robe of white, with a simple band of silver clasping it round her supple form, her rich hair caught carelessly back with a knot of scarlet passion-flowers, she looked a creature too fair for earth, a being all divine; and the Prince presently turning his glances towards her, evidently thought so, from the adoring tenderness with which he bent over her and kissed the ripe, red, smiling lips which pouted so deliciously to take the offered caress.

"They want us back, my Gloria!" he said; "The Nation asks for me—and for *you*!"

She raised herself a little on one arm.

"Do they know all?"

"Yes! The King, my father, has announced everything concerning our marriage, not only to the Government, but by special 'manifesto' to the People. I did not think he would be so brave!"

"Or so true!" said Gloria, her eyes darkening and deepening with the intensity of her thought. "Let me read this strange news, Humphry!"

He gave her the papers,—and a few tears sparkled on her lashes like diamonds and fell, as with a beating heart she read of the complete triumph of the King over the Socialist and Revolutionary party,—of his march with the multitude to the Government House,—of his bold denunciation of Carl Perousse, ending in the utter overthrow of a fraudulent Ministry,—and of his determination to renounce for five years, one half his royal revenues in order to personally assist the deficit in the National Exchequer.

"He is, in very truth a King!" she said, looking up with flushed cheeks and sparkling eyes,—"Surely the noblest in the world!"

Prince Humphry's face expressed wonderment as well as admiration.

"I have been utterly mistaken in him,"—he confessed,—"Or else, something has greatly changed his ideas. I should never have deemed him capable of running so much risk of his position, or of showing so much heroism, candour and self-sacrifice. All my life I have been accustomed to see him more or less indifferent to everything but his own pleasure, and more or less careless of the griefs of others; but now it seems as if he had kept himself back on purpose, only to declare his true character more openly and boldly in the end!"

Gloria read on, with eagerness and interest, till she came to the King's 'manifesto' regarding his son's marriage with 'a daughter of the People.' She pointed to this expression with the tapering, rosy point of her delicate little finger.

"That is me!" she said; "I *am* a daughter of the People! I am proud of the name!"

"You are my wife!" said the Prince; "And you are Crown Princess of the realm!"

She looked meditative.

"I am not sure I like that title so well!" she said surveying him archly under the shadow of her long lashes; "Indeed—if *you* were not Crown Prince,—I should not like it at all!"

Prince Humphry smiled, and tenderly touched the scarlet passion-flowers in her hair.

"But as I am Crown Prince, you will try to put up with it, my Gloria!" and he kissed her again. "We must return home, Sweetheart!—and as speedily as possible,—though I am sorry our restful honey-time is over!"

Gloria looked wistfully around her,—over the long smooth undulating lawns, the thickets of myrtle and orange, the lovely deep groves of trees, and away to the peaks of the distant dark blue hills, over which a great golden moon was slowly rising.

"I am sorry too!" she said; "I could live always like this, in peace with you, far, far away from all the world! Hark!"

She held up her hand to invite attention, as the delicious warble of a nightingale, or 'bul-bul' broke the heated silence into liquid melody. Her lover-husband took that little uplifted hand, and drawing it in his own, kissed it fondly,—and so for a moment they were very quiet, while the little brown bird of music poured from its palpitating throat a cadence of heart-moving song. Gradually, the golden splendour of the Indian moonlight widened through the trees, enveloping them in its clear luminous radiance; and the two beautiful human creatures, gazing into each other's eyes with all the unspeakable rapture of a perfect love, touched that wondrous height of pure mutual passion which makes things temporal seem very far off, and things eternal very near.

"If life could always be like this," murmured Gloria; "We should surely understand God better! We should feel that He truly loved us, and wished us to love each other! Ah, if only all the world were as happy as I am!"

"You will help to make a great part of it so, my beloved!" said the Prince; "You will bring with you into our kingdom, comfort for the sorrowful, aid to the poor, sympathy for the lonely, thought for all! You will forget nothing that calls for your remembrance, my Sweet! And one nation at least, will know what it is to have a true woman's love to light up the darkness of a Throne!"

That night a cable message was sent by the Prince to his father, stating his intention to return home immediately. The Oriental potentate who had generously placed his palace at the Royal lovers' disposal, and had religiously preserved the secret of their identity and whereabouts, being himself much fascinated and interested by the romance of their story, now commanded festivals and illuminations for their entertainment before their departure, and within a fortnight of the despatch of his message, the Prince's yacht had left the mystic shores of the East, and started on its homeward journey.

The news that the Crown Prince was returning with his bride, set all the country in a flutter of excitement, and the General Election being concluded, and the meeting of the new Government being deferred until after the Heir-Apparent's return, the people of every city and town and province set themselves busily to work to prepare suitable festivities for the homecoming of the Royal pair. At The Islands especially the spirit of enthusiasm was complete—all sorts of ideas for fetes and sports, and bonfires and illuminations, exercised the minds of the simple fisher-folk, who were wild with joy at the singular destiny that had befallen their 'waif of the sea' as they were wont to call the beautiful girl who had grown up among them,— and the aged Rene Ronsard was made the centre of their interest and attention,— even of their adulation. But Ronsard had grown very listless of late. His age began to tell heavily upon him, and the news that Gloria was returning in all triumph as Crown Princess, moved him but little.

"She would have been happier as a simple sailor's wife!" he averred, when Professor von Glauben, who visited him constantly, sought to rouse him from the apathy into which he appeared to have sunk. "The greater the position, the heavier the burden!—the more outwardly brilliant the appearance of life, the deeper its secret bitterness!"

"But Gloria has Love with her, my friend!" urged the Professor; "And Love makes the bitterest things sweet!"

Ronsard's aged eyes sparkled faintly.

"Ay, Love!" he echoed; "A dream—a delusion—and a snare! Unless it be a love strong enough to drag one down to death!—and then it is the strongest power in the world! It is a terror and a martyrdom,—and in nothing shall its desire be thwarted! If It calls—even kings obey!"

CHAPTER XXXII
BETWEEN TWO PASSIONS

SLOWLY, and with hesitating steps, Sergius Thord mounted the long flight of stairs leading to the quiet attic which Lotys called 'home.' Here she lived; here she had chosen to live ever since Thord had made her, as he said, the 'Soul of the Revolutionary Ideal.' Here, since the King had conquered the Revolutionary Ideal altogether, and had made it a Loyalist centre, did she dwell still, though she had now some thoughts of yielding to the child Pequita's earnest pleading, and taking up her abode with her and her father, in a pretty little house in the suburbs which, since Pequita's success as *premiere danseuse* at the Opera, Sholto had been able to afford, and to look upon as something like a comfortable dwelling-place. For with the election of Thord to the dignity of a Deputy, had, of course, come the necessity of resigning his old quarters where his 'Revolutionary' meetings had been held,—and he now resided in a more 'respectable' quarter of the city, in such sober, yet distinctive fashion as became one who was a friend of the King's, and who was likely to be a Minister some day, when he had further proved his political mettle. So that Sholto had no longer any need to try and eke out a scanty subsistence by letting rooms to revolutionists and 'suspects' generally,—and Thord himself had helped him to make a change for the better, as had also the King.

But Lotys had not as yet moved. She had lived so long among the desperately poor, who were accustomed to go to her for sympathy and aid, that she could not contemplate leaving so many sick and suffering and sorrowful ones alone to fight their bitter battle. So had she said, at least, to Thord, when he had endeavoured to persuade her to establish herself in greater comfort, and in a part of the city which had a 'better-class' reputation. She had listened to his suggestions with a somewhat melancholy smile.

"Once,—and not so very long ago,—for you there was no such thing as the 'better-class,' Sergius!" she said; "You were wont to declare that rich and poor alike were all one family in the sight of God!"

"I have not altered my opinion," said Thord, a slight flush colouring his cheek; "But—you are a woman—and as a woman should have every care and tenderness."

"So should my still poorer sisters," she replied; "And it is for those who have least comfort, that comfort should be provided. I am perfectly well and happy where I am!"

Remembering her fixed ideas on this point, there was an uneasy sense of trouble in Thord's mind as he ventured again on what he feared would be a fruitless errand.

"If I could command her!" he thought, chafing inwardly at his own impotence to persuade or lead this woman, whose character and will were so much more self-contained and strong than his own. "If I could only exercise some authority over her! But I cannot. What small debt of gratitude she owed me as a child, has long been cleared by her constant work and the assistance she has given to me,—and unless she will consent to be my wife, I know I shall lose her altogether. For she will never submit to live on money that she has not earned."

Arrived at the summit of the staircase he had been climbing, he knocked at the first door which faced him on the uppermost landing.

"Come in!" said the low, sweet voice that had thrilled and comforted so many human souls; and entering as he was bidden, he saw Lotys seated in a low chair near the window, rocking a tiny infant, so waxen-like and meagre, that it looked more like a corpse than a living child.

"The mother died last night," she said gently, in response to his look of interrogation; "She had been struggling against want and sickness for a long time. God was merciful in taking her at last! The father has to go out all day in search of work,—often a vain search; so I do what I can for this poor little one!"

And she bent over the forlorn waif of humanity, kissing its pale small face, and pressing it soothingly to her warm, full breast. She looked quite beautiful in that

Madonna-like attitude of protection and love,— her gold hair drooping against the slim whiteness of her throat,—her deep blue eyes full of that tenderness for the defenceless and weak, which is the loveliest of all womanly expressions.

Sergius Thord drew a chair opposite to her, and sat down.

"You are always doing good, Lotys!" he said, with a slight tremor in his voice; "There is no day in your life without its record of help to the helpless!"

She shook her head deprecatingly, and went on caressing and soothing the tiny babe in silence.

After a pause, he spoke again.

"I have come to you, Lotys, to ask you many things!"

She looked up with a little smile.

"Do you need advice, Sergius? Nay, surely not!—you have passed beyond it—you are a great man!"

He moved impatiently.

"Great? What do you mean? I am Deputy for the city, it is true—but that is not the height of my ambition; it is only a step towards it."

"To what do you aspire?" she queried. "A place in the Ministry? You will get that if you wait long enough! And then—will you be satisfied?"

"No—I shall never be satisfied—never till—"

He broke off and shifted his position. His fierce eyes rested tenderly upon her as she sat holding the motherless infant caressingly in her arms.

"You have heard the latest news?" he asked presently, "That Carl Perousse has left the country?"

"No, I have not heard that," said Lotys; "But why was he allowed to go without being punished for his dishonesty?"

"To punish him, would have involved the punishment of many more associated with him," replied Thord; "His estates are confiscated;—the opportunity was given him to escape, in order to avoid further Ministerial scandals,—and he has taken the chance afforded him!"

She was silent.

"Jost too has gone," pursued Thord; "He has sold his paper to his chief rival. So that now both journals are amalgamated under one head, and work for the same cause—our cause, and the King's."

Lotys looked up with a slight smile.

"It is the same old system then?" she said. "For whereas before there was one newspaper subsidised by a fraudulent Ministry, there are now two, subsidised by the Royal Government;—with which the Socialist party is united!"

He frowned.

"You mistake! We shall subsidise no newspaper whatever. We shall not pursue any such mistaken policy."

"Believe me, you will be compelled to do so, Sergius!" she declared, still smiling; "Or some other force will step in! Do you not see that politics always revolve in the same monotonous round? You have called me the Soul of an Ideal,—but even when I worked my hardest with you, I knew it was an Ideal that could never be realised! But the practice of your theories led me among the poor, where I felt I could be useful,— and for this reason I conjoined what brains I had, what strength I had, with yours. Yet, no matter how men talk of 'Revolution,' any and every form of government is bound to run on the old eternal lines, whether it be Imperial, Socialistic or Republican. Men are always the same children—never satisfied,—ever clamouring for change,—tired of one toy and crying for another,—so on and on,—till the end! I would rather save a life"—and she glanced pityingly down upon the sleeping infant she held-"than upset a throne!"

"I quite believe that;" said Sergius slowly; "You are a woman, most womanly! If you could only learn to love——"

He paused, startled at the sudden rush of colour that spread over her cheeks and brow; but it was a wave of crimson that soon died away, leaving her very pale.

"Love is not for me, Sergius!" she said; "I am no longer young. Besides, the days of romance never existed for me at all, and now it is too late. I have grown too much into the habit of looking upon men as poor little emmets, clambering up and down the same tiny hill of earth,—their passions, their ambitions, their emotions, their fightings and conquests, their panoply and pride, do not interest me, though they move me to pity; I seem to stand alone, looking beyond, straight through the glorious world of Nature, up to the infinite spaces above, searching for God!"

"Yet you care for that waif?" said Thord with a gesture towards the child she held.

"Because it is helpless," she answered; "only that! If it ever lives to grow up and be a man, it will forget that a woman ever held it, or cherished it so! No wild beast of the forest—no treacherous serpent of the jungle, is more cruel in its inherited nature, than man when he deals with woman;—as lover, he betrays her,—as wife, he neglects her,—as mother, he forgets her!"

"You have a bad opinion of my sex!" said Thord, half angrily; "Would you say thus much of the King?"

She started, then controlled herself.

"The King is brave,—but beyond exceptional courage, I do not think he differs from other men."

"Have you seen him lately?"

"No."

The answer came coldly, and with evident resentment at the query. Thord hesitated a minute or two, looking at her yearningly; then he suddenly laid his hand on her arm.

"Lotys!" he said in a half-whisper; "If you would only love me! If you would be my wife!"

She raised her dark-blue pensive eyes.

"My poor Sergius! With all your triumphs, do you still hanker for a wayside weed? Alas!—the weed has tough roots that cannot be pulled up to please you! I would make you happy if I could, dear friend!—but in the way you ask, I cannot!"

His heart beat thickly.

"Why?"

"Why? Ask why the rain will not melt marble into snow! I love you, Sergius— but not with such love as you demand. And I would not be your wife for all the world!"

He restrained himself with difficulty.

"Again—why?"

She gave a slight movement of impatience.

"In the first place, because we should not agree. In the second place, because I abhor the very idea of marriage. I see, day by day, what marriage means, even among the poor—the wreck of illusions—the death of ideals—the despairing monotony of a mere struggle to live—"

"I shall not be poor now;" said Thord; "All my work would be to make you happy, Lotys! I would surround you with every grace and luxury— with love, with worship, with tenderness! With your intelligence and fascination you would be honoured,—famous!"

He broke off, interrupted by her gesture of annoyance.

"Let me hear no more of this, Sergius!" she said. "You were very good to me when I was a castaway child, and I do not forget it. But you must not urge a claim upon me to which I cannot respond. I have given some of the best years of my life to assist your work, to win you your followers,—and to advance what I have always recognised as an exalted, though impossible creed—but now, for the rest of the time left to me, I must have my own way!"

He sprang up suddenly and confronted her.

"My God!" he cried. "Is it possible you do not understand! All my work —all my plans—all my scheming and plotting has been for you—to make you happy! To give you high place and power! Without you, what do I care for the world? What do I care whether men are rich or poor— whether they starve or die! It is you I want to serve—you! It is for your sake I have desired to win honour and position. Have pity on me, Lotys! Have pity! I have seen you grow up to womanhood—I have loved every inch of your stature—every hair of the gold on your head—every glance of your eyes—every bright flash of your intelligent spirit! Oh, I have loved you, and love you, Lotys, as no man ever loved woman! Everything I have attempted—everything I have done, has been that you might think me worthier of love. For the Country and the People I care nothing—nothing! I only care for you!"

She rose, holding the sleeping child to her like a shield. Her features seemed to have grown rigid with an inflexible coldness.

"So then," she said, "You are no better than the men you have blamed! You confess yourself as false to the People as the Minister you have displaced! You have served their Cause,—not because you love them, but simply because you love Me!—and you would force me to become your wife, not because you love Me, so much as you love Yourself! Self alone is at the core of your social creed! Why, you are not a whit higher than the vulgarest millionaire that ever stole a people's Trade to further his own ends!"

"Lotys! Lotys!" he cried, stung to the quick; "You judge me wrongly—by Heaven, you do!"

"I judge you only by your own words;" she answered steadily; "They condemn you more than I do. I thought you were sincere in your love for the People! I thought your work was all for them,—not for me! I judged that you sought to gain authority in order to remedy their many wrongs;—but if, after all, you have been fighting your way to power merely to make yourself, as you thought, more acceptable to me as a husband, you have deceived me in the honesty of your intentions as grossly as you have deceived the King!"

"The King!" he cried; "The King!"

She flashed a proud and passionate glance upon him—and then—he suddenly found himself alone. She had left the room; and though he knew there was only one wall, one door between them, he dared not follow.

Glancing around him at the simple furniture of the chamber he stood in, which, though only an attic, was bright and fresh and sweet, with bunches of wildflowers set here and there in simple and cheap crystal vases, he sighed heavily. The poor and 'obscure' life was perhaps, after all, the highest, holiest and best! All at once his eyes lighted on one large cluster of flowers that were neither wild nor common, a knot of rare roses and magnificent orchids, tied together with a golden ribbon. He looked at them jealously, and his soul was assailed by sudden resentment and suspicion. His face changed, his teeth closed hard on his under lip, and he clenched his hand unconsciously.

"If it is so—if it should be so!" he muttered; "There may be yet another and more complete Day of Fate!"

He left the room then, descending the stairs more rapidly than he had climbed them, and as he went out of the house and up the street, he stumbled against Paul Zouche.

"Whither away, brave Deputy?" cried this irresponsible being; "Whither away? To rescue the poor and the afflicted?—or to stop the King from poaching on your own preserves?"

With a force of which he was himself unconscious, he gripped Zouche by the arm.

"What do you mean?" he whispered thickly;—"Speak! What do you know?"

Zouche laughed stupidly.

"What do I know?" he echoed; "Why, what should I know, blockhead, save what all who have eyes to see, know as well as I do! Sergius, your grasp is none of the lightest; let me go!" Then as the other's hand fell from his arm, he continued. "It is you who are the blind man leading the blind! You—who like all thick-skulled reformers, can never perceive what goes on under your own nose! But what does it matter? What does anything matter? I told you long ago she would never love you; I knew long ago that she loved his Majesty, 'Pasquin Leroy!'"

"Curse you!" said Thord suddenly, in such low infuriated accents that the oath sounded more like a wild beast's snarl. "Why did you not tell me? Why did you not warn me?"

Zouche shrugged his shoulders, and began to sidle aimlessly along the roadway.

"You would not have believed me!" he said; "Nobody believes anything that is unpleasant to themselves! If you had not some suspicion in your own mind, you would not believe me now! I am foolish—you are wise! I am a poet—you are a re-former! I am drunk—you are sober! And with it all, Lotys is the only one who keeps her head clear. Lotys was always the creature of common-sense among us; she understood you—she understood me—and better than either of us—she understood the King!"

"No, no!" whispered Thord, more to himself than his companion; "She could not—she could not have known!"

"Now you look as Nature meant you to look!" exclaimed Zouche, staring wildly at him; "Savage as a bear;—pitiless as a snake! God! What men can become when they are baulked of their desires! But it is no use, my Sergius!—you have gained power in one direction, but you have lost it in another! You cannot have your cake, and eat it!" Here he reeled against the wall,—then straightening himself with a curious effort at dignity, he continued: "Leave her alone, Sergius! Leave Lotys in peace! She is a good soul! Let her love where she will and how she will,—she has the right to choose her lover,—the right!—by Heaven!—it is a right denied to no woman! And if she has chosen the King, she is only one of many who have done the same!"

With a smothered sound between a curse and a groan, Thord suddenly wheeled round away from him and left him. Vaguely surprised, yet too stupefied to realise that his rambling words might have worked serious mischief, Zouche gazed blinkingly on his retreating figure.

"The same old story!" he muttered, with a foolish laugh; "Always a woman in it! He has won leadership and power,—he has secured the friendship of a King,—but if the King is his rival in matters of love— ah!—that is a worse danger for the Throne than the spread of Socialism!"

He rambled off unthinkingly, and gave the only part of him which remained still active, his poetic instinct, up to the composition of a delicate love-song, which he wrote between two taverns and several drinks.

Late in the afternoon—just after sundown—a small close brougham drove up to the corner of the street where stood the tenement house,—divided into several separate flats,—in which the attic where Lotys dwelt was one of the most solitary and removed portions. The King alighted from the carriage unobserved, and ascended the stairs on which Sergius Thord's steps had echoed but a few hours gone by. Knocking at the door as Sergius had done, he was in the same way bidden to enter, but as he did so, Lotys, who was seated within, quite alone, started up with a faint cry of terror.

"You here!" she exclaimed in trembling accents; "Oh, why, why have you come! Sir, I beg of you to leave this place!—at once, before there is any chance of your being seen; your Majesty should surely know——!"

"Majesty me no majesties, Lotys!" said the King, lightly; "I have been forbidden this little shrine too long! Why should I not come to see you? Are you not known as an angel of comfort to the sorrowful and the lonely?—and will you not impart such consolation to me, as I may, in my many griefs deserve? Nay, Lotys, Lotys! No tears!—no tears, dearest of women! To see you weep is the only thing that could possibly unman me, and make even 'Pasquin Leroy' lose his nerve!"

He approached her, and sought to take her hand, but she turned away from him, and he saw her bosom heave with a passion of repressed weeping.

"Lotys!" he then said, with exceeding gentleness; "What is this? Why are you unhappy? I have written to you every day since that night when your lips clung to mine for one glad moment,—I have poured out my soul to you with more or less eloquence, and surely with passion!—every day I have prayed you to receive me, and yet you have vouchsafed no reply to one who is by your own confession 'the only man you love'! Ah, Lotys!—you will not now deny that sweet betrayal of your heart! Do you know that was the happiest day of my life?—the day on which I was threatened by Death, and saved by Love!"

His mellow voice thrilled with its underlying tenderness;—he caught her hand and kissed it; but she was silent.

With all the yearning passion which had been pent up in him for many months, he studied the pure outlines of her brow and throat—the falling sunlight glow of her hair—the deep azure glory of the pitying eyes, half veiled beneath their golden lashes, and just now sparkling with tears.

"All my life," he said softly, still holding her hand; "I have longed for love! All my life I have lacked it! Can you imagine, then, what it was to me, Lotys, when I heard you say you loved my Resemblance,—the poor Pasquin Leroy!—and even so I knew you loved me? When you praised me as Pasquin, and cursed me as King, how my heart burned with desire to clasp you in my arms, and tell you all the truth of my disguise! But to hear you speak as you did of me, so unconsciously, so tenderly, so bravely, was the sweetest gladness I have ever known! I felt myself a king at last, in very deed and truth!—and it was for the love of you, and because of your love for me, that I determined to do all I could for my son Humphry, and the woman of his choice! For, finding myself loved, I swore that he should not be deprived of love. I have done what I could to ensure his happiness; but after all, it is your doing, and the result of your influence! You are the sole centre of my good deeds, Lotys!—you have been my star of destiny from the very first day I saw you!—from the moment when I signed my bond with you in your own pure blood, I loved you! And I know that you loved me!"

She turned her eyes slowly upon him,—what eyes!—tearless now, and glittering with the burning fever of the sad and suffering soul behind them.

"You forget!" she said in hushed, trembling accents; "You are the King!"

He lifted her hand to his lips again, and pressed its cool small palm against his brows.

"What then, my dearest? Must the King, because he is King, go through life unloved?"

"Unless the King is loved with honour," said Lotys in the same hushed voice; "He must go unloved!"

He dropped her hand and looked at her. She was very pale—her breath came and went quickly, but her eyes were fixed upon him steadily,—and though her whole heart cried out for his sympathy and tenderness, she did not flinch.

"Lotys!" he said; "Are you so cold, so frozen in an ice-wall of conventionality that you cannot warm to passion—not even to that passion which every pulse of you is ready to return? What do you want of me? Lover's oaths? Vows of constancy? Oh, beloved woman as you are, do you not understand that you have entered into my very heart of hearts—that you hold my whole life in your possession? You—not I—are the ruling power of this country! What you say, that I will do! What you command, that will I obey! While you live, I will live—when you die, I will die! Through you I have learned the value of sovereignty,— the good that can be done to a country by honest work in kingship,— through you I have won back my disaffected subjects to loyalty;—it is all you—only you! And if you blamed me once as a worthless king, you shall never have cause to so blame me again! But you must help me,—you must help me with your love!"

She strove to control the beating of her heart, as she looked upon him and listened to his pleading. She resolutely shut her soul to the persuasive music of his voice, the light of his eyes, the tenderness of his smile.

"What of the Queen?" she said.

He started back, as though he had been stung.

"The Queen!" he repeated, mechanically—"The Queen!"

"Ay, the Queen!" said Lotys. "She is your wife—the mother of your sons! She has never loved you, you would say,—you have never loved her. But you are her husband! Would you make me your mistress?"

Her voice was calm. She put the plain question point-blank, without a note of hesitation. His face paled suddenly.

"Lotys!" he said, and stretched out his hands towards her; "Lotys, I love you!"

A change passed over her,—rapid and transfiguring as a sudden radiance from heaven. With an impulsive gesture, beautiful in its wild abandonment, she cast herself at his feet.

"And I love you!" she said. "I love you with every breath of my body, every pulse of my heart! I love you with the entire passion of my life! I love you with all the love pent up in my poor starved soul since childhood until now!—I love you more than woman ever loved either lover or husband! I love you, my lord and

King!—but even as I love you, I honour you! No selfish thought of mine shall ever tarnish the smallest jewel in your Crown! Oh, my beloved! My Royal soul of courage! What do you take me for? Should I be worthy of your thought if I dragged you down? Should I be Lotys,—if, like some light woman who can be bought for a few jewels,—I gave myself to you in that fever of desire which men mistake for love? Ah, no!—ten thousand times no! I love you! Look at me,—can you not see how my soul cries out for you? How my lips hunger for your kisses—how I long, ah, God! for all the tenderness which I know is in your heart for me,—I, so lonely, weary, and robbed of all the dearest joys of life!—but I will not shame you by my love, my best and dearest! I will not set you one degree lower in the thoughts of the People, who now idolise you and know you as the brave, true man you are! My love for you would be poor indeed, if I could not sacrifice myself altogether for your sake,—you, who are my King!"

He heard her,—his whole soul was shaken by the passion of her words.

"Lotys!" he said,—and again—"Lotys!"

He drew her up from her kneeling attitude, and gathering her close in his arms, kissed her tenderly, reverently—as a man might kiss the lips of the dead.

"Must it be so, Lotys?" he whispered; "Must we dwell always apart?"

Her eyes, beautiful with a passion of the highest and holiest love, looked full into his.

"Always apart, yet always together, my beloved!" she answered; "Together in thought, in soul, in aspiration!—in the hope and confidence that God sees us, and knows that we seek to live purely in His sight! Oh, my King, you would not have it otherwise! You would not have our love defiled! How common and easy it would be for me to give myself to you!—as other women are only too ready to give themselves,— to take your tenderness, your care, your admiration,—to demand your constant attendance on my lightest humour!—to bring you shame by my persistent companionship!—to cause an open slander, and allow the finger of scorn to be pointed at you!—to see your honour made a mockery of, by base, persons who would judge you as one, who, notwithstanding his brave espousal of the People's Cause, was yet a slave to the caprice of a woman! Think something more of me than this! Do not put me on the level of such women as once brought your name into contempt! They did not love you!—they loved themselves! But I—I love you!

Oh, my dearest lord, if self were concerned at all in this great love of my heart, I would not suffer your arms to rest about me now!— I would not let your lips touch mine!—but it is for the last time, beloved!—the last time! And so I put my hands here on your heart—I kiss your lips—I say with all my soul in the prayer—God bless you!—God keep you!—God save you, my King! Though I shall live apart from you all my days, my spirit is one with yours! God will know that truth when we meet—on the other side of Death!"

Her tears fell fast, and he bent over her, torn by a tempest of conflicting emotions, and kissing the soft hair that lay loosely ruffled against his breast.

"Then it shall be so, Lotys!" he murmured, at last. "Your wish is my law!—it shall be as you command! I will fulfil such duties as I must in this world,—and the knowledge of your love for me,—your trust in me,—shall keep me high in the People's honour! Old follies shall be swept away—old sins atoned for;—and when we meet, as you say, on the other side of Death, God will perchance give us all that we have longed for in this world—all that we have lost!"

His voice shook,—he could not further rely on his self-control.

"I will not tempt you, Lotys!" he whispered—"I dare not tempt myself! God bless you!"

He put her gently from him, and stood for a moment irresolute. All the hope he had indulged in of a sweeter joy than any he had ever known, was lost,—and yet—he knew he had no right to press upon her a love which, to her, could only mean dishonour.

"Good-bye, Lotys!" he said, huskily; "My one love in this world and the next! Good-bye!"

She gazed at him with her whole soul in her eyes,—then suddenly, and with the tenderest grace in the world, dropped on her knees and kissed his hand.

"God save your Majesty!" she said, with a poor little effort at smiling through her tears; "For many and many a long and happy year, when Lotys is no more!"

With a half cry he snatched her up in his arms and pressed her to his heart, showering kisses on her lips, her eyes, her hair, her little hands!—then, with a movement as abrupt as it was passion-stricken, put her quickly from him and left her.

She listened with straining ears to the quick firm echo of his footsteps departing from her, and echoing down the stairs. She caught the ring of his tread on the pavement outside. She heard the grinding roll of the wheels of his carriage as he was rapidly driven away. He had gone! As she realised this, her courage suddenly failed her, and sinking down beside the chair in which he had for a moment sat, she laid her head upon it, and wept long and bitterly. Her conscience told her that she had done well, but her heart—the starving woman's heart,— was all unsatisfied, and clamoured for its dearest right—love! And she had of her own will, her own choice, put love aside,—the most precious, the most desired love in the world!—she had sent it away out of her life for ever! True, she could call it back, if she chose with a word—but she knew that for the sake of a king, and a country's honour, she would not so call it back! She might have said with one of the most human of poets:

> "Will someone say, then why not ill for good?
> Why took ye not
> your pastime? To that man
> My word shall answer, since I knew the Right
> And did it."[1]

A shadowy form moving uncertainly to and fro near the corner of the street, appeared to spring forward and to falter back again, as the King, hurriedly departing, glanced up and down the street once or twice as though in doubt or questioning, and then walked to his brougham. The soft hues of a twilight sky, in which the stars were beginning to appear, fell on his face and showed it ashy pale; but he was absorbed in his own sad and bitter thoughts,—lost in his own inward contemplation of the love which consumed him,—and he saw nothing of that hidden watcher in the semi-gloom, gazing at him with such fierce eyes of hate as might have intimidated even the bravest man. He entered his carriage and was rapidly driven away, and the shadow,—no other than Sergius Thord,—stumbling forward,—his brain on fire, and a loaded pistol in his hand,—had hardly realised his presence before he was gone.

"Why did I not kill him?" he muttered, amazed at his own hesitation; "He stood here, close to me! It would have been so easy!"

He remained another moment or two gazing around him at the streets, at the

---

1   Tennyson

roofs, at the sky, as though in a wondering dream,—then all at once, it seemed as if every cell in his brain had suddenly become superhumanly active. His eyes flashed fury,—and turning swiftly into the house which the King had just left, he ran madly up the stairs as though impelled by a whirlwind, and burst without bidding, straight into the room where Lotys still knelt, weeping. At the noise of his entrance she started up, the tears wet on her face.

"Sergius!" she cried.

He looked at her, breathing heavily.

"Yes,—Sergius!" he said, his voice sounding thick and husky, and unlike itself. "I am Sergius! Or I was Sergius, before you made of me a nameless devil! And you—you are Lotys!—you are weeping for the lover who has just parted from you! You are Lotys—the mistress of the King!"

She made him no answer. Drawing herself up to her full height, she flashed upon him a look of utter scorn, and maintained a contemptuous silence.

"Mistress of the King!" he repeated, speaking in hard gasps; "You,— Lotys,— have come to this! You,—the spotless Angel of our Cause! You!—why,—I sicken at the sight of you! Oh, you fulfil thoroughly the mission of your sex!—which is to dupe and betray men! You were the traitor all along! You knew the real identity of 'Pasquin Leroy'! He was your lover from the first,—and to him you handed the secrets of the Committee, and played Us into his hands! It was well done—cleverly done!—woman's work in all its best cunning!—but treachery does not always pay!"

Amazed and indignant, she boldly confronted him.

"You must be mad, Sergius! What do you mean? What sudden accusations are these? You know they are false—why do you utter them?"

He sprang towards her, and seized her roughly by the arm.

"How do I know they are false?" he said. "Prove to me they are false! Who saved the King's life? You! And why? Because you knew he was 'Pasquin Leroy'! How was it he gained such swift ascendancy over all our Committee, and led the work and swayed the men,—and made of me his tool and servant? Through you again! And why? Because you knew he was the King! Why have you scorned me—turned from me—thrust me from your side—denied my love,—though I have loved and cared for you from childhood! Why, I say? Because you love the King!"

She stood perfectly still,—unmoved by his frantic manner—by the glare of his bloodshot eyes, and his irrepressible agony of rage and jealousy. Quietly she glanced him up and down.

"You are right!" she said tranquilly; "I do love the King!"

A horrible oath broke from his lips, and for a moment his face grew crimson with the rising blood that threatened to choke the channels of his brain. An anxious pity softened her face.

"Sergius!" she said gently, "You are not yourself—you rave—you do not know what you say! What has maddened you? What have I done? You know my life is free—I have a right to do with it as I will, and even as my life is free, so is my love! I cannot love where I am bidden—I must love where Love itself calls!"

He stood still, staring at her. He seemed to have lost the power of speech.

"You have insulted me almost beyond pardon!" she went on. "Your accusations are all lies! I love the King,—but I am not the King's mistress! I would no more be his mistress than I would be your wife!"

Slowly, slowly, his hand got at something in his pocket and clutched it almost unconsciously. Slowly, slowly, he raised that hand, still clutching that something,—and his lips parted in a breathless way, showing the wolfish glimmer of white teeth within.

"You—love—the King!" he said in deliberate accents. "And you dare— you dare to tell me so?"

She raised her golden head with a beautiful defiance and courage.

"I love the King!" she said—"And I dare to tell you so!"

With a lightning quickness of movement the hand that had been groping after an unseen evil now came out into the light, with a sudden sharp crash, and flame of fire!

A faint cry tore the air.

"Ah—Sergius!—Sergius! Oh—God!"

And Lotys staggered back—stunned, deafened—sick, dizzy——

"Death, death!" she thought, wildly; "This is death!"

And, with a last desperate rallying of her sinking force, as every memory of her life swept over her brain in that supreme moment, she sprang at her murderer and wrenched the weapon from his hand, clutching it hard and fast in her own.

"Say—say I did it—myself—!" she gasped, in short quick sobs of pain; "Tell the King—I did it myself—myself! Sergius—save your own life!—I—forgive!"

She reeled, and with a choking cry fell back heavily—dead! Her hair came unbound with her fall, and shook itself round her in a gold wave, as though to hide the horror of the oozing blood that trickled from her lips and breast.

With a horrid sense of unreality Thord stared upon the evil he had done. He gazed stupidly around him. He listened for someone to come and explain to him what had happened. But up in that remote attic, there was no one to hear either a pistol-shot or a cry. There was only one thing to be understood and learnt by heart,—that Lotys, once living, was now dead! Dead! How came she dead? That was what he could not determine. The heat of his wild fury had passed,—leaving him cold and passive as a stone.

"Lotys!"

He whispered the name. Horrible! How she looked,—with all that blood!— all that golden hair!

'Tell the King I did it myself!' Yes—the King would have to be told— something! Stooping, he tried to detach the pistol from the lifeless hand, but the fingers, though still warm were tightened on the weapon, and he dared not unclasp them. He was afraid! He stood up again, and looked around him. His glance fell on the knot of regal flowers he had noticed in the morning,—the great roses,—the voluptuous orchids—tied with their golden ribbon. He took them hastily and flung them down beside her,—then watched a little trickling stream of blood running, running towards one of the whitest and purest of the roses. It reached it, stained it,—and presently drowned it in a little pool. Horrified, he covered his eyes, and staggered backward against the door. The evening was growing dark,—through the small high window he could see the stars beginning to shine as usual. As usual,—though Lotys was dead! That seemed strange! Putting one hand behind him, he cautiously opened the door, still keeping his guarded gaze on that huddled heap of clothes, and blood, and glittering hair which had been Lotys.

"I must get home," he muttered. "I have business to attend to—as Deputy to the city, there is much to do—much to do for the People! The People! My God! And Lotys dead!"

A kind of hysteric laughter threatened him. He pressed his mouth hard with his hand to choke back this strange, struggling passion.

"Lotys! Lotys is dead! There she lies! Someone, I know not who, killed her! No,—no! She has killed herself,—she said so! There she lies, poor Lotys! She will never speak to the People—never comfort them,— never teach them any more— never hold little motherless infants in her arms and console them,—never smile on the sorrowful, or cheer the sick—never! 'I love the King!' she said,—and she died for saying it! One should not love kings! 'Tell the King I did it myself!' Yes, Lotys!—lie still—be at peace—the King shall know—soon enough!"

Still muttering uneasily to himself, he went out, always moving backwards— and with a last look at that fallen breathless form of murdered woman, shut the door stealthily behind him.

Then, stumbling giddily down the stairs, he wandered, blind and half crazed, into the darkening night.

CHAPTER XXXIII
SAILING TO THE INFINITE

GREAT calamities always come suddenly. With the swiftness of lightning they descend upon the world, often in the very midst of fancied peace and security,—and the farcical, grinning, sneering apes of humanity, for whom even the idea of a God has but furnished food for lewd jesting, are scattered into terror-stricken hordes, who are forced to realise for the first time in their lives, that whether they believe in Omnipotence or no, an evident Law of Justice exists, which may not be outraged with impunity. Sometimes this Law works strangely,—one might almost say obliquely. It sweeps away persons whom we have judged as useful to the community, and allows those to remain whom we consider unnecessary. But 'we,'—all important 'we,'—are not allowed to long assert or maintain our petty opinions against this unknown undetermined Force which makes havoc of all our best and most carefully conceived arrangements. For example, we are not given any practical reason why Christ,—the Divine Man,—was taken from the world in His youthful manhood, instead of being permitted to live to a great age for the further benefit, teaching, and sanctification of His disciples and followers. Pure, sinless, noble, and truly of God, He was tortured and crucified as though He were the worst of criminals. And apart from the Church's explanation of this great Mystery, we may take it as a lesson that misfortune is like everything else, two-sided;—it falls equally upon the ungodly and the godly,—with merely this difference—that when it falls on the ungodly it is, as we are reluctantly forced to admit, 'the act of God'—but when it falls on the godly, it is generally the proved and evident work of Man.

In this last way, and for no fault at all of her own, had cruel death befallen Lotys. Such as her career had been, it was unmarked by so much as a shadow of selfishness or wickedness. From the first day of her life, sorrow had elected her for its own. She had never known father or mother;—cast out as an infant in the street, and picked up by Sergius Thord, she had secured no other protector for her infancy and youth, than the brooding, introspective man, who was destined in the end to be her murderer. As a child, she had been passionately grateful to him; she had learned all she could from the books he gave her to study, and with a quick brain, and a keen sense of observation, she had become a proficient in literature, so much so indeed, that more than one half the Revolutionary treatises and other propaganda which he had sent out to different quarters of the globe, were from her pen. Her one idea had been to please and to serve him,—to show her gratitude for his care of her, and to prove herself useful to him in all his aims. As she grew up, however, she quickly discerned that his affection for her was deepening into the passion of a lover; whereupon she had at once withdrawn from his personal charge, and had made up her mind to live alone and independently. She desired, so she told him, to subsist on her own earnings,—and he who could do nothing successfully without her, was only too glad to give her the rightful share of such financial results as accrued from the various workings of the Revolutionary Committee,—results which were sometimes considerable, though never opulent. And so she had worked on, finding her best happiness in succouring the poor, and nursing the sick. Her girlhood had passed without either joy or love,—her womanhood had been bare of all the happiness that should have graced it. The people had learned to love her, it is true,—but this more or less distantly felt affection was far from being the intimate and near love for which she had so often longed. When at last this love had come to her,—when in 'Pasquin Leroy' she thought she had found the true companion of her life and heart,—when he had constantly accompanied her by his own choice, on her errands of mercy among the poor; and had aided the sick and the distressed by his own sympathy and tenderness, she had almost allowed herself to dream of possible happiness. This dream had been encouraged more than ever, after she had saved the King from assassination. 'Pasquin Leroy' had then become her closest comrade,—always at hand, and ever ready to fulfil her slightest behest;—while from his ardent and eloquent glances,—the occasional lingering pressure of his hand, and the hastily murmured words of tenderness which she could not misunderstand, she knew that he loved her. But when he had disclosed his real identity to be that of the King himself, all her fair hopes had vanished!—and her spirit had shrunk and fallen under the blow. Worse than all,—when she learned that this great and exalted Personage, despite his throned dignity, did still continue to entertain a passion for herself, the knowledge was almost crushing in its effect upon her mind. Pure in soul and body, she would have chosen death any time rather than dishonour; and in the recent developments of events she had sometimes grown to consider death as good, and even desirable. Now death had come to her through the very hand that had first aided her to live! And so had she fulfilled the common lot of women, which is, taken in the aggregate, to be wronged and slain (morally, when not physically) by the very men they have most unselfishly sought to serve!

The heavy night passed away, and all through its slow hours the murdered creature lay weltering in her blood, and shrouded in her hair,—looked at by the pitiless stars and the cold moon, as they shed their beams in turn through the high attic window. Morning broke; and the sun shot its first rays down upon the dead,—upon the fixed white countenance, and on the little hand grown icy cold, but clenched with iron grip upon the pistol which had been so bravely snatched in that last moment of life with the unselfish thought of averting suspicion from the true murderer. With the full break of day, the mistress of the house going to arouse her lodgers, came up the stairs with a bright face, cheerfully singing, for her usual morning chat with Lotys was one of her principal pleasures. Knocking at the door, and receiving no answer, she turned the handle and pushed it open,—then, with a piercing scream of horror, she rushed away, calling wildly for help, and sending frantic cries down the street.

"Lotys! Lotys! Lotys is dead!"

The news flew. The houses poured out their poverty-stricken occupants from garret to basement; and presently the street was blocked with a stupefied, grief-stricken crowd. A doctor who had been hastily summoned, lifted the poor corpse of her whose life had been all love and pity, and laid it upon the simple truckle-bed, where the living Lotys had slept, contented with poverty for many years; and after close and careful examination pronounced it to be a case of suicide. The word created consternation among all the people.

"Suicide!" they murmured uneasily; "Why should she kill herself? We all loved her!"

Ay! They all loved her!—and only now when she was gone did they realise how great that love had been, or how much her thought and tenderness for them all, had been interwoven with their lives! They had never stopped to think of the weariness and emptiness of her own life, or of the longing she herself might have had for the love and care she so freely gave to others. By and by, as the terrible news was borne in upon them more convincingly, some began to weep and wail, others to kneel and pray, others to recall little kindnesses, thoughtful deeds, unselfish tendernesses, and patient endurances of the dead woman who, friendless herself, had been their truest friend.

"Who will tell Sergius Thord?" asked a man in the crowd; "Who will break the news to him?"

There was an awe-stricken silence. No one volunteered such heart- rending service.

"Who will tell the King?" suddenly exclaimed a harsh voice, that of Paul Zouche, who in his habit of hardly ever going to bed, had seen the crowd gather, and had quickly joined it. "Lotys saved his life! He should be told!"

His face, always remarkable in its thin, eager, intellectual aspect, looked ghastly, and his eyes no longer feverish in their brilliancy, were humanised by the dew of tears.

"The King!"

The weeping people looked at one another. The King had now become a part of their life and interest,—he was one with them, not apart from them as once he had been; therefore he must have known how Lotys had loved them. Yes,—someone should surely tell the King!

"The King must be informed of this," went on Zouche; "If there is no one else to take the news to him,—I will!"

And before any answer could be given, or any suggestion made, he was gone.

Meanwhile, no person volunteered to fetch Sergius Thord. Every man who knew him, dreaded the task of telling him that Lotys was dead, self- slain. Some poor, but tender-hearted women sorrowfully prepared the corpse for burial, removing the bloodstained clothes with gentle hands, smoothing out and parting on either side the glorious waves of hair, while with the greatest care and difficulty they succeeded by slow degrees in removing the pistol so tightly clenched in the dead hand. While engaged in this sad duty, they found a sealed paper marked 'My Last Wish,' and this they put aside till Thord should come. Then they robed her in white, and laid white flowers upon her breast; and so came in turns by groups of tens and twenties to kneel beside her and kiss her hands and say prayers, and weep for the loss of one who had never uttered a harsh word to any poor or sorrowful person, but whose mission had been peace and healing, love and resignation, and submission to her own hard fate until the end!

Meantime Zouche, who had never been near any Royal precincts before, walked boldly to the Palace. All irresolution had left him;—his step was firm, his manner self-contained, and only his eyes betrayed the deep and bitter sorrow of his soul. He was allowed to pass the sentinel at the outer gates, but at the inner portico of the Palace he was denied admittance. He maintained his composure, however, and handed in his written name.

"If I cannot see the King, I must see Sir Roger de Launay!" he said.

At this the men in authority glanced at one another, and began to unbend;— if this shabby, untidy being knew Sir Roger de Launay, he was perhaps someone of importance. After a brief consultation together, they asked him to wait while a messenger was despatched to Sir Roger.

Zouche, with a curious air of passive toleration sat quietly on the chair they offered, and waited several minutes glancing meanwhile at the display of splendour and luxury about him with an indifference bordering on contempt.

"All this magnificence," he mused; "all this wealth cannot purchase back a life, or bring comfort to a stricken heart! Nor can it vie with a poet's rhyme, which, often unvalued, and always unpaid for, sometimes outlasts a thousand thrones!"

Here, seeing the tall figure of Sir Roger de Launay coming between him and the light, he rose and advanced a step or two.

"Why, Zouche," said Sir Roger kindly, greeting him with a smile; "You are up betimes! They tell me you want to see the King. Is it not a somewhat early call? His Majesty has only just left his sleeping- apartment, and is busy writing urgent letters. Will you entrust me with your message?"

Paul Zouche looked at him fixedly.

"My message is from Lotys!" he said deliberately; "And it must be delivered to the King in person!"

Vaguely alarmed, Sir Roger recoiled a step.

"You bring ill news?" he whispered.

"I do not know whether it will prove ill or well;" answered Zouche wearily; "But such news as I have, must be told to his Majesty alone."

Sir Roger paused a moment, hesitating; then he said:

"If that is so—if that must be so,—then come with me!"

He led the way, and Zouche followed. Entering the King's private library where the King himself sat at his writing-desk, Sir Roger announced the unexpected visitor, adding in a low tone that he came 'from Lotys!'

The King started up, and threw down his pen.

"From Lotys!" he echoed, while through his mind there flew a sudden sweet hope that after all the star was willing to fall!—the flower was ready to be gathered!—and that the woman who had sent him away from her the day before, had a heart too full of love to remain obdurate to the pleadings of her kingly lover!—"Paul Zouche, with a message from Lotys? Let him come in!"

Whereupon Zouche, bidden to enter, did so, and stood in the Royal presence unabashed, but quite silent. An ominous presentiment crept coldly through the monarch's warm veins, as he saw the dreary pain expressed on the features of the man, who had so persistently scorned him and his offered bounty,—and with a slight, but imperative sign, he dismissed Sir Roger de Launay, who retired reluctantly, full of forebodings.

"Now Zouche," he said gently; "What do you seek of me? What is your message?"

Zouche looked full at him.

"As King," he answered, "I seek nothing from you! As comrade"—and his accents faltered—"I would fain break bad news to you gently—I would spare you as much as possible—and give you time to face the blow,— for I know you loved her! Lotys——"

The monarch's heart almost stood still. What was this hesitating tone— these great tears in Zouche's eyes?

"Lotys!" he repeated slowly, and in a faint whisper; "Yes, yes—go on! Go on, comrade! Lotys?"

"Lotys is dead!"

An awful stillness followed the words. Stiff and rigid the King sat, as though stricken by sudden paralysis, giving no sign. Minute after minute slipped away,—and he uttered not a word, nor did he raise his eyes from the fixed study of the carpet at his feet.

"Lotys is dead!" went on Zouche, speaking in a slow monotonous way. "This morning, the first thing—they found her. She had killed herself. The pistol was in her hand. And they are laying her out with flowers,—like a bride, or a queen,—and you can go and see her at rest so,—for the last time,—if you will! This is my message! It is a message from the dead!"

Still the King spoke not a word; nor did he lift his eyes from his brooding observation of the ground.

"To be a great King, as you are," said Zouche; "And yet to be unable to keep alive a love when you have won it, is a hard thing! She must have killed herself for your sake!"

No answer was vouchsafed to him. He began to feel a strange pity for that solemn, upright figure, sitting there inflexibly silent,—and he approached it a little nearer.

"Comrade!" he said softly; "I have hated you as a King! Yes, I have always hated you!—even when I found you had played the part of 'Pasquin Leroy,' and had worked for our Cause, and had helped to make what is now called my 'fame'! I hated you,—because through it all, and whatever you did for me, or for others, it seemed to me you had never known hunger and cold and want!—never known what it was to have love snatched away from you! I watched the growth of your passion for Lotys —I knew she loved you!—and had you indeed been the poor writer and thinker you assumed to be, all might have been well for you both! But when you declared yourself to be King, what could there be for such a woman but death? She would never have chosen dishonour! She has taken the straight way out of trouble, but—but she has left *you* alone! And I am sorry for you! I know what it is—to be left alone! You have a palace here, adorned with all the luxuries that wealth can buy, and yet you are alone in it! I too have a palace,—a palace of thought, furnished with ideals and dreams which no wealth can buy; and I am alone in it too! I killed the woman who loved me best; and you have done the same, in your way! It is the usual trick of men,—to kill the women who love them best, and then to be sorry for ever afterwards!"

He drew still nearer—then very slowly, very hesitatingly, dropped on one knee, and ventured to kiss the monarch's passive hand.

"My comrade! My King! I am sorry for you now!"

For answer, his own hand was suddenly caught in a fierce convulsive grip, and the King rose stiffly erect. His features were grey and drawn, his lips were blood-less, his eyes glittering, as with fever. Stricken to the heart as he was, he yet forced himself to find voice and utterance.

"Speak again, Zouche! Speak those horrible, horrible words again! Make me feel them to be true! Lotys is dead!"

Zouche, with something like fear for the visible, yet strongly suppressed an-guish of the man before him, sighed drearily as he repeated——

"Lotys is dead! It is God's way—to kill all beautiful things, just as we have learned to love them! She,—Lotys,—used to talk of Justice and Order,—poor soul!—she never found either! Yet she believed in God!"

The King's stern face never relaxed in its frozen rigidity of woe. Only his lips moved mutteringly.

"Dead! Lotys! My God!—my God! To rise to such a height of hope and good—and then—to fall so low! Lotys gone from me!—and with her goes all!"

Then a sudden delirious hurry seemed to take possession of him.

"Go now, Zouche!" he said impatiently—"Go back to the place where she lies—and tell her I am coming! I must—I will see her again! And I will see you again, Zouche!—you too!" He forced a pale smile—"Yes, poor poet! I will see you and speak with you of this—you shall write for her a dirge!—a threnody of passion and regret that shall make the whole world weep! Poor Zouche!—you have had a hard life—well may you wonder why God made us men! And Lotys is dead!"

He rang the bell on his desk violently. Sir Roger de Launay at once returned,—but started back at the sight of his Royal master's altered countenance.

"Have the kindness, De Launay"—said the King hurriedly, not heeding his dis-mayed looks—"to place a carriage at the disposal of our friend Zouche! He has much business to do;—sad news to bear to all the quarters of the city—he will tell you of it,—as he has just told me! Lotys,—you know her!—Lotys, who saved my life at the risk of her own,—Lotys is dead!"

Sir Roger recoiled with an ejaculation of horror and pity.

"It is sudden—and—and strange!" continued the King, still speaking in the same rapid manner, and beginning to push aside the various letters and documents on his table—"It is a kind of darkness fallen without warning!—but—such tragedies always do happen thus—unpreparedly! Lotys was a grand creature,—a noble and self-sacrificing woman—the poor will miss her—yes—the poor will miss her greatly!——"

He broke off, and with a speechless gesture of agonised entreaty, intimated that he must be left alone. De Launay hustled Zouche out of the apartment in a kind of impotent fury.

"Why have you brought the King such news?" he demanded—"It will kill him!"

"He has killed *her*!" returned Zouche, grimly—"If he had never crossed her path, she would have been alive now! Why should not a King suffer like other men? He does the same foolish things,—he has his private loves and hatreds in the same foolish manner,—why should he escape punishment for his follies? It is only in suffering that he grows human,—stripped by grief and pain of his outward pomp and temporal power, he even becomes lovable! God save us from this bauble of 'power'! It is what Sergius Thord has worked for all his life!—it is what this King claims over his subjects—and yet—both monarch and reformer would give it all for the life of one woman back again! Look you, the King has had a dozen or more mistresses, and Heaven knows how many bastards—but he has only loved once! And it is well that he should learn what real love means,—Sorrow always, and Death often!"

That afternoon the whole city knew of the tragic end of Lotys. Nothing else was thought of, nothing else talked of. Thousands gathered to look up at the house where her body lay, stiffening in the cold grasp of death, and a strong body of police were summoned to guard all the approaches to the premises, in order to prevent a threatening 'crush' and disaster among the increasing crowd, every member of which sought to look for the last time on the face of her who had unselfishly served them and loved them in their hours of bitterest need. The sight of Sergius Thord passing through their midst, with bent head, and ashy, distraught countenance, had not pacified the clamorous grief of the people, nor had it elicited such an outburst of sympathy for him as one might have thought would have been forthcoming. An idea had gotten abroad that since his election as Deputy for the city, he had either neglected or set aside the woman who had assisted him to gain his position. It was a wrong idea, of course,—but the trifling fact of his having taken up his abode in a more 'aristocratic' part of the metropolis, while Lotys had still remained in the 'quarter of the poor,' was sufficient to give it ground in the minds of the ignorant, who are always more or less suspicious of even their best friends. Had they made a more ominous guess,—had they imagined that Sergius Thord was the actual murderer of the woman they had idolised, there would have been no remembrance whatever of the work he had done to aid them in the various reforms now being made for their benefit;—they would have torn him to pieces without a moment's mercy. The rough justice of the mob is a terrible thing! It knows nothing of legal phraseology or courtesy—it merely sees an evil deed done, and straightway proceeds to punish the evil-doer, regardless of consequences. Happily for the sake of peace and order, however, no thought of the truth, no suspicion of the real cause of the tragedy occurred to any one person among the sorrow-stricken multitude. A faint, half-sobbing cheer went up for the King, as his private brougham was recognised, making its way slowly through the press of people,—and it was with a kind of silent awe, that they watched his tall figure alight and pass into the house where lay the dead. Sergius Thord had already entered there,—the King and his new Deputy would meet! And with uneasy movements, rambling up and down, talking of Lotys, of her gentleness, patience and never-wearying sympathy for all the suffering and the lonely, the crowds collected, dispersed, and collected again,—every soul among them heavily weighted and depressed by the grief and the mystery of death, which though occurring every day, still seems the strangest of fates to every mortal born into the world.

Meantime, the King with slow reluctant tread, ascended into the room of death. Sergius Thord stood there,—but his brooding face and bulky form might have been but a mote of dust in a sunbeam for the little heed the stricken monarch took of him. His whole sight, his whole soul were concentrated on the white recumbent statue with the autumn-gold hair, which was couched in front of him, strewn with flowers. That was Lotys—or rather, that had been Lotys! It was now a very beautiful, still, smiling Thing,—its eyes were shut, but the eyelashes lay delicately on the pallid cheeks like little fringes of dark gold, tenderly slumbrous. Those eyelashes matched the hair—the soft, silken hair—so fine—so lustrous, so warm and bright!—the hair was surely yet living! With a shuddering sigh, the King bent over the piteous sight,—and stooping lower and lower still, touched with trembling lips the small, crossed hands.

As he did this, his arm was caught roughly, and Thord thrust him aside.

"Do not touch her!" he muttered hoarsely—"Let her rest in peace!"

Slowly the King raised his face. It was ashen grey and stricken old. The dark, clear, grey eyes were sunken and dim,—the light of hope, ambition, love and endeavour, was quenched in them for ever.

"Was she unhappy, that she killed herself?" he asked, in a hushed voice.

Thord drew back, shuddering. Those sad, lustreless eyes of his Sovereign seemed to pierce his soul! He—the murderer of Lotys—could not face them! A vague whirl of thoughts tormented his brain,—he had heard it said that a murdered person's corpse would bleed in the presence of the murderer,—would the dead body of Lotys bleed now, he wondered dully, if he waited long enough? If so— the King would know! He started guiltily, as once more the sad, questioning voice broke on his ears.

"Was she unhappy, think you? You knew her better than I!"

Huskily, and with dry lips, Thord forced an answer.

"Nay, it is possible your Majesty knew her best!"

Again the sunken melancholy eyes searched his face.

"She was endowed with genius,—rich in every good gift of womanhood! I would have given my life for hers—my kingdom to spare her a moment's sorrow!" went on the King; "But she would have nothing from me— nothing!"

"Nothing,—not even love!" said Thord recklessly.

"That she had, whether she would or no!"—replied the King, slowly,— "That she will have, till time itself shall end!"

Thord was silent. A passion of mingled fury and remorse consumed him,— his heart was beating rapidly,—there were great pulsations in his brain like heavy hammer-strokes,—he was afraid of himself, lest on a savage impulse he should leap like a beast of prey on this grave composed figure,—this King,—who was his acknowledged ruler,—and kill him, even as he had killed Lotys! And then,—he thought of the People! —the People by whose great force and strong justice he had sworn to abide!—the People who had worshipped and applauded him,—the People who, if they ever knew the truth of him and his crime, would snatch him up and tear his body to atoms, as surely as he stood branded with Murder in God's sight this day! With a powerful effort he rallied his forces, and drawing from his breast the small folded paper which had been found on the body of Lotys, and which was inscribed with the words 'My Last Wish,' he held it out to the King.

"Then your Majesty will perhaps grant her the burial she here demands?" he said—"It is a strange request!—but not difficult to gratify!"

Taking the paper, the monarch touched it tenderly with his lips before opening it. In all the blind stupefaction of his own grief, he was struck by the fact that there was something strained and unnatural about Thord's appearance,—something wild and forced even in his expression of sorrow. He studied his face closely, but to no purpose; —there was no clue to the mystery packed within the harsh lines of those dark, fierce features,—he seemed no more and no less than the same brood-ing, leonine creature that had mercilessly planned the deaths of men in his own Revolutionary Committee. There was no touch of softness in his eyes,—no tears, even at the sight of Lotys smiling coldly in her flower-strewn shroud. And now, unfolding her last message, the King beheld it thus expressed:

"To THOSE WHO SHALL FIND ME DEAD

"I pray you of your gentle love and charity, not to bury my body in the earth, but in the sea. For I most earnestly desire no mark, or remembrance of the place where my sorrows, with my mortal remains, shall be rendered back to nature; and kinder than the worms in the mould are the wild waves of the ocean which I have ever loved! And there,—at least to my own thoughts,—if any spiritual part of me remains to watch my will performed,—shall I be best pleased and most grateful to be given my last rest. LOTYS."

This document had been written and signed some years back, and had, there-fore, nothing to do with any idea of immediate departure from the world, or pre-meditated suicide. And once again the King looked searchingly at Thord, as he returned him the paper.

"Her will shall be performed!" he said—"And in a manner befitting her memory,—befitting the love borne to her by a People—and—a King!"

He paused,—then went on softly.

"To you Sergius, my friend and comrade!—to you will be entrusted the task of committing this sweet casket of a sweeter soul to the mercy of the waves!—you, the guardian of her childhood, the defender of her womanhood, the protector of her life——"

"O God! No more—no more!" cried Thord, suddenly falling on his knees by the couch of the dead—"No more—in mercy! I will do all—all! But leave me with her now!—leave me alone with her, this last little while!"

And breaking into great sobs, he buried his head among the death- flowers in an utter abandonment of despair.

Silently the King watched him for a little space. Then he turned his eyes towards the pale form of the woman he had loved, and who had taught him the noblest and most selfless part of love, sleeping her last sleep, with a fixed sweet smile upon her face.

"We shall meet again, my Lotys!" he whispered—"On the other side of Death!"

And so,—with the quiet air of one who knows a quick way out of difficulty, he departed.

Some five days later, a strange and solemn spectacle was witnessed by thousands of spectators from all the shores and quays of the sea-girt city. A ship set sail for the Land of the Infinite!—a silent passenger went forth on a voyage to the borders of the Unknown! Coffined in state,—with a purple velvet pall trailing its rich folds over the casket which enshrined her perished mortality,—and with flowers of every imaginable rareness, or wildness, scattered about it,—the body of Lotys was, with no religious or formal ceremony, placed on the deck of a sailing-brig, and sent out to the waves for burial. So Sergius Thord had willed it; so Sergius Thord had planned it. He had purchased the vessel for this one purpose, and with his own hands he had strewn the deck with blossoms, till it looked like a floating garden of fairyland. Garlands of roses trailed from the mast,—wreaths from every former member of the now extinct 'Revolutionary Committee' were heaped in profusion about the coffin which lay in the centre of the deck,—the sails were white as snow, and one of them bore, the name 'Lotys' upon it, in letters of gold. It was arranged that the brig should be towed from the harbour, and out to sea for about a couple of miles,—and when there, should be cut free and set loose to the wind and tide to meet its fate of certain wreckage in the tossing billows beyond. In strange contrast to this floating funeral were the brilliant flags and gay streamers which were already being put up along the streets and quays, as the first signs of the city's welcome to the Crown Prince and his bride, who were expected to arrive home somewhere within the next ten days. Eager crowds watched the unique ceremony, unknown save in old Viking days, of sending forth a dead voyager to sail the pitiless seas; and countless numbers of small boats attended the funeral vessel in a long flotilla,— escorting it out to that verge where the ocean opened widely to the wider horizon, and spread its high road of silver waves invitingly out to the approaching silent adventurer. Comments ran freely from lip to lip,—Sergius Thord had been seen, pale as death, laying flowers on the deck to the last,—the King,—yes!—the King himself had sent a wreath, as a token of remembrance, to the obsequies of the woman who had saved his life,—the purple velvet pall, with its glittering fringes of gold, had been the gift of the city of which Thord was the lately-elected Deputy,—Louis Valdor had sent that garland of violets,—the great wreath of roses which lay at the head of the coffin, was the offering of the famous little dancer, Pequita, who, it was said, now lay sick of a fever brought on by grief and fretting for the loss of her best friend,—and rich and poor alike had vied with one another in assisting the weird beauty of this exceptional and strange burial, in which no sexton was employed but the wild wind, which would in due time scoop a hollow in the sea, and whirl down into fathomless deeps all that remained of a loving woman, with the offerings of a People's love around her!

From the Palace windows the Queen watched the weird pageant, with straining eyes, and a sense of relief at her heart. This unknown rival of hers,—this Lotys—was dead! Her body would soon be drifting out on the wild waste of waters, to be caught by the first storm and sunk in the depths of eternal silence. She was glad!—almost she could have sung for joy! The colour mantled on her fair cheeks,—she looked younger and more beautiful than ever. She had learned her long- neglected lesson,— the lesson of, 'how to love.' And to herself she humbly confessed the truth—that she loved no other than her husband! The King had now become the centre of her heart, as he had become the centre of his People's trust. And she watched the vessel bearing the corpse of Lotys, gliding, gliding over the waves—she tracked the circling concourse of boats that went with it—and waited, with quickened breath and eager eyes, till she saw a sudden pause in the procession—when, riding lightly on a shining wave, the funeral-ship seemed to stop for an instant—and then, with a bird-like dip forward, scurried out with full, bulging sails to the open sea! The crowding spectators began to break up and disperse—the flotilla of attendant boats turned back to shore—the dead woman who had held such magnetic influence over the King, was gone!—gone for ever into the watery caverns of endless death!

It was with a light heart that the Queen at last rose from her watch at the window, and prepared to array herself for the return of her sovereign lord. Her eyes sparkled, her lips smiled; she looked the very incarnation of love and tenderness. The snow-peak had melted at last, and underneath the ice, love's late violets had begun to bloom! She glanced once more out at the sea, where the vanishing death-ship now seemed but a speck on the far horizon, and saw a bank of solemn purple clouds darkening the golden sunset line,—clouds that rose up thickly and swiftly, like magic mountains conjured into sudden existence by some witch in a fairy tale. A gust of wind shook the lattice—and moaned faintly through the chinks of the door.

"There will be a storm to-night!" she said musingly, her eyes following the dispersing crowds, as they poured along the terrace from the shore, or climbed up from the quays to the higher streets of the town:—"There will be a storm!—and the woman who was called Lotys, will know nothing of it! The vessel she sails in will be crushed like a shell in the teeth of the blast, and her body will sink like a stone in the angry sea! So will she sleep—so does her brief power over the King come to an end!"

Turning, she smiled at her lady-in-waiting, Teresa de Launay, who had also watched the sea funeral of Lotys with wondering and often tear- filled eyes.

"How the people must have loved her!" the girl murmured softly; "No poor person or child came to these strange obsequies without flowers!— many wept— and some swear there is no happiness at all for them now, without Lotys! She must have been a sweet, unselfish woman!"

The Queen was silent.

"Since she saved the life of our lord the King, I have often thought of her!"

went on Teresa—"I have even hoped to see her! Dearest Madam, would you not have been glad to thank her once before she died?"

The Queen's face hardened.

"She only did her duty!" was the cold answer—"Every subject in the realm would be proud to have the chance of being the King's defender!"

At that moment the door opened, and Sir Roger de Launay entered,—then drew back in some surprise and hesitation.

"I crave your pardon, Madam!" he said, bowing low—"I thought the King was here!"

"Truly the King should be here by now,"—replied the Queen gently—"But he is doubtless detained among the people, who wait upon his footsteps, as though he were a demi-god!" She smiled happily. "He went out to see yonder strange funeral pageant—and left no word of the hour of his return."

Sir Roger looked perplexed. The Queen noticed his expression of anxiety.

"Stay but a moment, Sir Roger," she added—"Now I remember, he bade me at sunset, go to my own room and fetch a packet I would find from him there,—he may be waiting for me now!"

She retired, the radiant smile still upon her face, and Sir Roger looked at his sister with concern for her tearful eyes.

"Weeping, Teresa?" he said—"What is the trouble?"

"Nothing!" she answered quickly—"Only a presentiment of evil! That funeral-ship has made me sad!"

Sir Roger said nothing for the moment. He was too preoccupied with his own forebodings to give much heed to hers. He walked to the window.

"There will be a storm to-night!" he said. "Look at those great clouds! They are big with thunder and with rain!"

"Yes!" murmured Teresa—"There will be a storm—Madam!"

She turned with a cry to feel the Queen's grip on her shoulder—to see the Queen, white as marble, with blazing eyes, possessed by a very frenzy of grief and terror. A tragic picture of despairing Majesty, she confronted the startled De Launay with an open paper in her hand.

"Where is the King?" she demanded, in accents that quivered with fear and passion. "From you, Sir Roger de Launay, must come the answer! To you, his friend and servant, I trusted his safety! And of you I ask again—Where is the King?"

Stupefied and stunned, Sir Roger stared helplessly at this enraged splendour of womanhood, this embodied wrath of royalty.

"Madam!" he stammered,—"I know nothing—save that the King has been sorely stricken by a great sorrow—"

She looked at him with flashing eyes.

"Sorrow for what?—for whom?"

De Launay gazed at her amazedly;—why did she ask of what she knew so well?

"Madam, to answer that is not within my province!"

She was silent, breathing quickly. Great tears gathered on her lashes, but did not fall.

"When saw you his Majesty last?"

"But three hours since, Madam! He bade me leave him alone, saying he would walk a while in the further grounds away from the sight of the sea. He had no mind, he said, to look upon the passing away of Lotys!"

A strange grey pallor crept over the Queen's face. She stood proudly erect, yet tottered as though about to fall. Teresa de Launay ran to her in terror.

"Dearest Madam!" cried the trembling girl—"Be comforted! Be patient! The King will come!"

"He will never come!" said the Queen in a low choked voice;—"Never again— never, never again! I feel—I know—that I have lost him for ever! He has gone—but where?—O God!—where!"

"Madam!" said Sir Roger, shaken to the soul by the sight of her suppressed agony—"That paper in your hand—"

"This paper," she said, with a convulsive effort at calmness, "makes me Regent till the return of my son, the Crown Prince—and—at the same time—bids me farewell! Farewell!—and why farewell? Oh, faithless servant!" and she advanced a step, fixing her burning eyes on the stricken De Launay—"I thought you loved me!"

His face flushed—his lips quivered.

"As God lives, Madam, I yield to no one in my love and service of you!"

"Then find the King!" and she stretched out her arm with a gesture of authority—"Bring back to me my husband!—the one man of the world!— the one man

I have learned to love! Follow the King!—whether on land or sea, whether alive or dead,—in heaven or hell, follow him! Your place is not with me—but by your master's side! If you know not whither he has fled, make it your business to learn!— and never let me see your face again till *his* face shines beside yours, like sunshine against darkness!—till his eyes, his smile make gladness where your presence without him is a mocking misery! Out of my sight! And nevermore return again, save in your duty and attendance on the King!"

"Madam,—Madam!" exclaimed Teresa—"Would you condemn my brother to a lasting banishment? What if the King were dead?"

"Dead!" The word left the Queen's lips in a sharp sob of pain—"The King cannot die!—he is too strong—too bold and brave! He has met death ere now and conquered it! Dead? No—that is not possible—that could not be!"

She turned again upon Sir Roger, standing mute and pale, a very statue of despair.

"I give you a high mission!" she said—"Fulfil it!"

He started from his unhappy reverie.

"Be sure that I will do so!" he said—"I will—as your Majesty bids me— follow the King! And—till the King returns with me—I also say farewell!"

Catching his sister in his arms, he kissed her with a murmured blessing—and profoundly saluting the woman for whose love's sake his very life was now demanded, he left the room.

"Roger, Roger!" cried Teresa in an anguish, as the sound of his footsteps died away—"Come back! Come back!"

And falling on her knees by the Queen's side, she burst into wild weeping.

"If the King has gone for ever, my brother is gone too," she sobbed— "Oh, dearest Majesty, have you no heart?"

"None!" said the Queen with a strained smile, while the slow, hot tears began to fall from her aching eyes—"None! What heart I had is gone! It follows the King!"

CHAPTER XXXIV
ABDICATION

A GREAT storm was gathering. The heavy purple clouds which had arisen in the west at sunset, when all that was mortal of Lotys had been sent forth to a lonely burial in the sea, had gradually spread over the whole sky, darkening in hue as they moved, and rolling together in huge opaque masses, which presently began to close in and become denser as the night advanced. By and by a wild wind awoke, as it were, from the very cavities of ocean, and the waves began to hiss warnings all along the coast, and to rise higher and higher over each other's shoulders as the gale steadily increased. Rene Ronsard, sitting in his cottage, feeble and somewhat ailing, heard the beginnings of the tempest with long-accustomed ears. He was depressed in spirit, yet not altogether solitary, for he had with him a kindly companion in Professor von Glauben. The Professor had been one of the many who had attended the strange funeral-pageant of the afternoon, not only out of interest in, and regret for, the fate of the woman whose unique character he had admired, and whose difficult position he had pitied; but also because he had suffered from an unpleasant presentiment to which he could give no name. If he could have described his forebodings at all, he would have said they were more or less connected with the King,—but how or why, he would not have been able to explain, save that since the death of Lotys, his Sovereign master had no longer looked the same man. Stricken as with a blight, and grown suddenly old, his manner and appearance were as of one devoured by a secret despair,—a corroding disease,—of which the end could only be disastrous. Overcome by the pain and distress of being the constant witness of a sorrow which he felt to the heart, yet could not relieve, the Professor, on returning from the scene of Lotys's impressive funeral, had put ashore on The Islands, instead of going back to the mainland. He had sought permission from the King to remain with Ronsard for the night,—and the permission had been readily, almost eagerly granted. The King, indeed, had seemed glad to be relieved of the too anxious solicitude of his physician, who, he knew, was well aware of the concealed agony of mind which tortured and well-nigh maddened him,—and the Professor, keenly observant, was equally conscious that, under the immediate circumstances, his attendance might seem more of an intrusion than a duty.

"De Launay was not far wrong when he prophesied danger for the King as the result of his beginning to think for himself;" he mused—"Yet it has come—this danger—in a different way to that in which we expected it! It is a bold move for the ruler of a country to make personal examination into the needs of his people,—but it is seldom that, while engaged in such a task, the ruler himself becomes ruled, by a stronger force than even his own temporal power!"

And now, sitting with old Rene Ronsard, by a fire which had been kindled on this somewhat chilly night for his better comfort, he was, despite the impression of sadness and disaster which hung upon his mind as darkly as the clouds were hanging in heaven, doing his best to rouse both himself and his companion to greater cheerfulness. The wind, shaking the lattice, and now and then screaming dismally under the door, did not inspire him to gaiety, but his thoughts were principally for Ronsard, who was inclined to yield to an overpowering despondency.

"This will never do, Ronsard!" he said after a pause, during which he had noticed a tear or two steal slowly down the old man's furrowed cheek; "What sort of a welcome will such a face as yours be to our Crown Princess Gloria? She will soon be here; think of it! And what a triumphant entry she will make, acclaimed by the whole nation!"

"I shall not be wanted in her life!" said Ronsard, slowly. "After all, I am nothing to her, and have no claim upon her. I found her, as a poor man may by chance find a rare jewel,—that the jewel is afterwards found worthy to be set in a king's crown, is not the business of that same poor man. He who merely hews a diamond out of the mine, is not the maker of the diamond!"

"Gloria loves you!" said the Professor; "And she will love you always!"

Ronsard smiled faintly.

"My friend, I understand, and I accept the law of change!" he said. "To me, as to all, it must come! The old must die, and the young succeed them. As for me, I shall be glad to go—the sooner the better, I truly think, for then none will taunt my Gloria with the simple manner of her bringing up;—none will remember aught, save her exceeding beauty, or blame her that the sun and sea were her only known parents. And if we credit legend, hers is not the first birth of loveliness from the bosom of the waves!"

Here the wind, tearing round the rafters, rattled and roared for a space like a demon threatening the whole construction of the house, and then went galloping away with a shriek among the pines down to the shore.

"A wild night!" said the Professor, with a slight shiver. "Alas! poor Lotys!—poor 'Soul of an Ideal' as Sergius Thord called her,—her frail mortal tenement will soon be drawn down to the depths in such a storm as this!"

"I never saw her!" said Ronsard musingly; "Thord I have seen often. Lotys was to me a name merely,—but I knew it was a name to conjure with—a name beloved of the People. Gloria longed to see her,—she had heard of her often."

"She was a psychological phenomenon," said the Professor slowly; "And I admit that her composition baffled me. No one have I ever seen at all like her. She was beautiful without any of the accepted essentials of beauty—and it is precisely such a woman as that who possesses the most dangerous fascination over men—not over boys—but over men. She had a loving, passionate, feminine heart, with a masculine brain,—the two together are bound to constitute what is called Genius. The only thing I cannot understand is the unexpected weakness she displayed in committing suicide. That I should never have thought of her. On the contrary, I should have imagined, knowing as much of her as I did, that the greater the sorrow, the greater the fight she would have made against it."

A silence fell between them, filled by the thundering noise of the wind.

"Where is Thord?" asked Ronsard presently.

"I do not know. The last I saw of him was on board the vessel that bore her coffin;—he was laying flowers on the deck. He was not, I think, in any of the smaller boats that accompanied it; he must have returned with the crowd on shore. He has his duties as Deputy for the city now, we must remember!"

Ronsard's eyes flashed with a glimmer of satire in the firelight.

"If it had not been for Lotys, he would not be a Deputy, or anything else,—save perchance a Communist or an Anarchist!" he said; "he used to be one of the fiercest malcontents in all the country when I first came here. Many and many is the time I have heard him threaten to kill the King!"

"Ah!" said the Professor meaningly, the while he bent his eyes on the flickering fire.

Again a silence fell. The wind roared and screamed around the building, and in the pauses of the gale, the minutes seemed weighted with a strange dread. Every tick of the clock sounded heavy and long, even to the equable-minded Professor. The storm outside was growing louder and even louder, and his thoughts, despite himself, turned to the ocean- wildernesses over which Prince Humphry's home-returning vessel must be now on its way—while that other solitary barque, un-helmed and unmanned, whose sail bore the name of 'Lotys' was also voyaging, but in a darker direction, down to death and oblivion, carrying with it, as he feared, all the love and heart of a King! Suddenly a loud knocking at the door startled them; and as Ronsard rose from his chair, amazed at the noise and Von Glauben did the same with more alacrity, a man with wind blown hair and excited gestures burst into the little room.

"Ronsard!" he cried; "The King—the King!"

He paused, gasping for breath. Ronsard looked at him wonderingly. His clothes were saturated with sea-water,—his face was pale—and his eyes expressed some fear that his tongue seemed incapable of uttering. He was one of the coral-fishers of the coast, and Ronsard knew him well.

"What ails you, man?" he asked; "What say you of the King?"

Holding the door of the cottage open with some difficulty, the coral- fish-er pointed to the sky overhead. It was flecked with great masses of white cloud, through which the moon appeared to roll rapidly like a ball of yellow fire. The wind howled furiously, and the pines in the near distance could be seen bending to and fro like reeds in its breath, while the roar of the sea beyond the rocks was fierce and deafening.

"It is all storm!" cried the man, excitedly; "The billows are running mountains high!—there is no chance for him!"

"No chance for whom?" demanded Von Glauben, impatiently; "What would you tell us? Speak plainly!"

"It was the King!" said the coral-fisher again, trying to express himself more collectedly—"I saw his face lit up by the after-glow of the sky—white—white as the foam on the wave! Listen! When the body of the woman Lotys was borne away on that vessel, a man came to me out of the thickest of the crowd (I was on one of the furthest quays)—and offered me a purse of gold to take him out to sea—and to steer him in such a way that we should meet the funeral barque just as she was cut adrift and sent forth to be wrecked in the ocean. I did not know him then. He kept his face hidden,—he spoke low, and he was evidently in trouble. I thought he was a lover of the dead woman, and sought perhaps to comfort himself by looking at her coffin for the last time. So I consented to do what he asked. I had my sailing skiff, and we went at once. The wind was strong; we sailed swiftly—and at the appointed place—" He paused to take breath. Ronsard seized him by the arm.

"Quick! Go on—what next?"

"At the appointed place when the vessel stopped,—when her ropes were cut and she afterwards sprang out to sea, I, by his orders, ran my skiff close beside her as she came,—and before I knew how it happened, my passenger sprang aboard her—Ay!—with a spring as light and sure as the flight of a bird! 'Farewell!' he said, and flung me the promised gold; 'May all be prosperous with you and yours!' And then the wind swooped down and bore the ship a mile or more ere I could follow it; but the strong light in the west fell full upon the man's face—and I saw—I knew it was the King!"

"Gott in Himmel! May you for ever be confounded and mistaken!" exclaimed Von Glauben,—"I left the King in his own grounds but an hour before I myself started to witness this accursed sea-funeral!"

"I say it was the King!" repeated the man emphatically. "I would swear it was the King! And the vessel going out to meet the storm tonight, holds the living, as well as the dead!"

With a sudden movement, as active as it was decided, old Ronsard went to a corner in the room and drew out a thick coil of rope with an iron hook at the end, and slinging it round his waist with the alert quickness of youth, made for the open door.

"Where is your skiff?" he demanded.

"Ashore down yonder;" answered the coral-fisher; "But you—what are you going to do? You cannot sail her in such a night as this!"

"I will adventure!" said Ronsard. "If, as you say, it was the King, I will save him if he can be saved! Once a King's life was nothing to me; now it is something! The tide veers round these Islands, and the vessel on which they have placed the body of Lotys, can scarcely drift away from the circle till morning, unless the waves are too strong for it—"

"They are too strong!" cried the coral-fisher; "Ronsard, believe me! There is no rain to soften or abate the wind—and the sea grows greater with every breath of the rising gale!"

"I care nothing!" replied Ronsard; "Let be! If you are afraid, I will go alone!"

At these words, the Professor suddenly awoke to the situation.

"What would you attempt, Ronsard?" he exclaimed; "You can do nothing! You are weak and ailing!—there is no force in you to combat with the elements on such a night as this—"

"There *is* force!" said Ronsard; "The force of my thirst for atonement! Let me be, for God's sake! Let me do something useful in my life!—let me try to save the King! If I die, so much the better."

"Then I will go with you!" said Von Glauben, desperately.

Ronsard shook his head.

"You? No, my friend! You will not! You will remain to welcome Gloria— to tell her that I loved her to the last!—that I did my best!"

He seemed to have grown young in an instant,—his eyes flashed with alertness and vigour, and instead of an old decaying man, full of cares and despondencies, he seemed like a bold adventurer, before whom a new land of promise opens. Von Glauben looked at him, and in a moment made up his mind. He turned to the coral-fisher.

"What think you truly of the night, my friend? Is it for life or death we go?"

"Death! Certain death!" answered the man; "It is madness to set sail in such a storm as this!"

"You are married, no doubt? And little ones eat your earnings? Ach so! Then you shall not be asked to go with us. Ronsard, I am ready! I can pull an oar and manage a sail, and I am not afraid of death by drowning! For Gloria's sake, let me go with you!"

"For Gloria's sake, stay here!" cried Ronsard; and with an abrupt movement he escaped Von Glauben's hold, and ran with all the speed of a boy out of the cottage into the garden beyond.

Von Glauben rushed after him, but found himself in the thicket of pines, trapped and hemmed in by the darkness of their stems and branches. The wind was so fierce and strong, that he could scarcely keep his feet,—every now and again the moon flew out of a great cloud- pinnacle and glared on the scene, but not with sufficient clearness to show him his way. Yet he knew the place well—often had he and Gloria trodden that path down to the sea, and yet to-night it seemed all unfamiliar. How the sea roared! Like a thousand lions clamouring for prey! Against the rocks the rising billows hissed and screamed, rattling backward among stones and shells with the grinding noise of artillery wagons being hastily dragged off a lost field of battle.

"Ronsard!" he called as loudly as he could, and again "Ronsard!" but his voice, big and stentorian though it was, made but the feeblest wail in the loud shriek of the wind. Yet he stumbled on and on, and by slow and difficult degrees found his way down to the foot of the high rocks which formed a pinnacled wall between him and the sea,—the rocks he had so often climbed with Gloria, and of which she had sung in such matchless tones of triumph and tenderness.

> Here, by the sea.
> My King crown'd me!
> Wild ocean sang for my Coronation,
> With the jubilant voice of a mighty nation!

The memory of this song came back to his ears in a ringing echo, amid the howling of the boisterous wind, which now blew harder and harder, scattering masses of blown froth from the waves in his face, with flying sand and light shells, and torn-up weed. Scarcely able to stand against it, he paused to get his breath, realising that it would be worse than useless to climb the rocks in the teeth of such a gale, or try to reach the old accustomed winding way down to the shore. He endeavoured to collect his scattered wits;—if the ceaseless onslaught of the storm would only have allowed him to think coherently, he fancied he might have found another and easier path to lead him in the direction whither Ronsard, in his mad, but heroic impulse, had gone. But the gale was so terrific, and the booming of the great waves on the other side of the rocky barrier so awful, that it seemed as if the water must be rolling in like a solid wall, bent on breaking down the coast, and grinding it to powder. His heart ached heavily;—tears rose to his eyes.

"What a grain of dust I am in this world of storm!" he ejaculated; "Here I stand,—a strong man, utterly useless! Powerless to save the life I would die to serve! But maybe the story is not true!—the man can easily have been mistaken! Surely the King would not give up all for the sake of one woman's love!"

But though he said this to himself, he knew that such things have been; indeed, that they are common enough throughout all history. He had not studied humanity to so little purpose as not to be aware that there are certain phases of the passion of love which make havoc of a man's wisest and best intentions; and that even as Marc Antony lost all for Cleopatra's smile, and Harry the Eighth upset a Church for a woman's whim, so in modern days the same old story repeats itself; and no matter how great and famous the position of a king or an emperor, he may yet court and obtain his own ruin and disaster, ay, lose his very Throne for love;—deeming it well lost!

Restless, miserable and troubled by the confusion of his thoughts, which seemed to run wild with the wild wind and the thundering sea, the unhappy Professor retraced his steps to the cottage, hoping against hope that Ronsard, physically unable to cope with the storm, would have returned, baffled in his reckless attempt to put forth a boat to sea. But the little home was silent and deserted. There was the old man's empty chair;—the clock against the wall ticked the minutes away with a comfortable persistence which was aggravating to the nerves; the fire was still bright. Before entering, Von Glauben looked up and down everywhere outside, but there was no sign of any living creature.

Nothing remained for him to do but to resign himself passively to whatsoever calamity the Omnipotent Forces above him chose to inflict,— and utterly weary, baffled and helpless, he sank into Ronsard's vacant chair, unconscious that tears were rolling down his face from the excess of his anxiety and exhaustion. The shrieking of the wind, the occasional glare of the moonlight through the rattling lattice windows, and the apparent rocking of the very rafters above him thrilled him into new and ever recurring sensations of fear—yet he was no coward, and had often prided himself on having 'nerves of steel and sinews of iron.' Presently, he began to see quaint faces and figures in the glowing embers of the fire; old scraps of song and legend haunted him; fragments of Heine, mixed up with long-winded philosophical phrases of Schopenhauer, began to make absurd contradictions and glaring contrasts in his mind, while he listened to the awful noises of the storm; and the steady ticking of the clock on the wall worried him to such an almost child-ish degree, that had he not thought how often he had seen Gloria winding up that clock and setting it to the right hour, he could almost have torn it down and broken it to pieces. By and by, however, tired Nature had her way, and utterly heavy and worn out in mind and body, and weary of the disturbed and incoherent thoughts in his brain, he lay back and closed his eyes. He would rest a little while, he said to himself, and 'wait.' And so he gradually fell asleep, and in his sleep wrote, so he imagined, a whole eloquent chapter of his 'Political History of Hunger' in which he described Sergius Thord as a despot, who, after proving false to the cause of the People, and grinding them down by unlimited taxation such as no Government had ever before inflicted, seized the rightful king of the country, and sent him away to be drowned in company with a woman of the People, whose body was fastened to his by ropes and iron chains, in the fashion of 'Les Noyades' of Nantes. And he thought that the King rejoiced in his doom, and said strange words like those of the poet who sang of a similar story:

> "For never a man like me
> Shall die like me till the whole world dies,
> I shall drown with her, laughing for love, and she

Mix with me, touching me, lips and eyes!"Meanwhile, Ronsard, true to the instinct within him, had fulfilled his intention and had put out to sea. The fish-erman who had brought the tidings which had moved him to this desperate act, was too much of a hero in himself to let the old man venture forth alone,—and so, following him down to the shore, had, despite all commands and entreaties to the contrary, insisted on going with him. The sailing skiff he owned was a strong boat, stoutly built,—and at first it seemed as if their efforts to ride the mountainous billows would be crowned with success. Old Rene had a true genius for the man-agement of a sail; his watchfulness never flagged:—his strenuous exertions would have done credit to a man less than half his age. With delicate precision he guided the ropes, as a jockey might have guided the reins of a racehorse, and the vessel rose and fell lightly over the great waves, with such ease and rapidity, that the man who accompanied him and took the helm, an experienced sailor himself, began to feel confident that after all the voyage might not be altogether futile.

"The sea may be calmer further out from land!" he shouted to Rene, who nod-ded a quiet aquiescence, while he kept his eyes earnestly fixed on the horizon, which the occasional brightness of the moon showed up like a line of fretted silver. Everywhere he scanned the waves for a glimpse of the fatal vessel bearing Death— and perhaps Life—on board; but over the whole expanse of the undulating hills and valleys of wild water, there was no speck of a boat to be seen save their own. They swept on and on, the wind aiding them with savage violence—when suddenly the man at the helm shouted excitedly:

"Ronsard! See yonder! There she sails!"

With an exclamation of joy, Ronsard sprang up, and looking, saw within what seemed an apparently short distance, the drifting funeral-barque he sought. So far she seemed intact; her sails were bellying out full to the wind, and she was rising and plunging bravely over the great breakers, which rolled on in interminable ar-ray, one over the other,— with rugged foam-crests that sprang like fountains to the sky. A five or ten minutes' run with the wind would surely bring them alongside,— and Ronsard turned with an eager will to his work once more. Over the heads of the monstrous waves, rising with their hills, sinking in their valleys, he guided the few yielding planks that were between him and destruction, trimming the straining sail to the ferocious wind, and ever keeping his eyes fixed on the vessel which was the object of his search,—the sole aim and end of his reckless voyage, and which seemed now to recede, and then to almost disappear, the more earnestly he strove to reach it.

"To save the King!" he muttered—"To save—not to kill! For Gloria's sake!—to save the King!"

A capricious gust from the beating wings of the storm swooped down upon him sideways, as he twisted the ropes and tugged at them in a herculean effort to balance the plunging boat and keep her upright,—and in the loud serpent-like hiss of the waves around him, he did not hear his companion's wild warning cry—a cry of despair and farewell in one! A toppling dark-green mass of water, moving on shoreward, lifted itself quite suddenly, as it were, to its full height, as though to stare at the puny human creatures who thus had dared to oppose the fury of the elements, and then, leaping forward like a devouring monster, broke over their frail skiff, sweeping the sail off like a strip of ribbon, snapping the mast and rolling over and over them with a thousand heads of foam that, spouting upwards, again fell into dark cavernous deeps, covering and dragging down everything on the surface with a tumult and roar! It passed on thundering,—but left a blank behind it. Skiff and men had vanished,—and not a trace of the wreck floated on the angry waves!

For one blinding second, Ronsard, buffeting the wild waves, saw the face of Gloria,—that best-beloved fair face,—angelic, pitying, loving to the last,—shine on him like a star in the darkness!—the next he was whelmed into the silence of the million dead worlds beneath the sea! So at last he paid his life's full debt. So, at last his atonement was fulfilled. If it was true,—as he had in an unguarded moment confessed,—that he had once killed a King, then the resistless Law of Compensation had worked its way with him,—inasmuch as he had been forced to render up what he cherished most,—the love of Gloria,—to the son of a King, and had ended his days in an effort to save the life of a King! For the rest, whatever the real nature of his long-hidden secret,—whatever the extent of the torture he had suffered in his conscience, his earthly punishment was over; and the story of his past crime would never be known to the living world of men. One sinner,—one sufferer among many millions, he was but a floating straw on the vast whirlpools of Time,—and whether he prayed for pardon and obtained it, whether he had worked out his own salvation or had lost it, may not be known of him, or of any of us, till God makes up the sum of life, in which perchance none of even the smallest numerals shall be found missing!

Wilder grew the night, and more tempestuous the sea, while the sky became a mountainous landscape of black and white clouds fitfully illumined by the moon, which appeared to run over their fleecy pinnacles and sable plains like some scared white creature pursued by invisible foes: The vessel on which the corpse of Lotys lay, palled in purple, and decked with flowers, flew over the waves, to all seeming with the same hunted rapidity as the moon rushed through the heavens,— and so far, though her masts bent reed-like in the wind, and her sails strained at their cordage, she had come to no harm. Tossed about as she was, rudderless and solitary, there was something almost miraculous in the way she had weathered a storm in which many a well-guided ship must inevitably have gone down. The purple pall with its heavy fringe of gold, that shrouded the coffin she carried, was drenched through and through by the sea, and the flowers on the deck were beaten and drowned in the salt spray that dashed over them.

But amid all the ruined blossoms of earth, by the side of the dead, and full-fronted to the tempest, stood one living man, for whom life had no charm, and death no terror—the King! What had been reported of him was true—he had resigned his Throne and left his kingdom for the sake of adventuring forth on this great voyage of Discovery,—this swift and stormy sail with Lotys to the Land of the Unknown! Whether it was a madness, or a sick dream that fevered his blood, he knew not— but once the woman he loved was dead, every hope, every ambition in him died too—and he felt himself to be a mere corpse of clay, unwillingly dragged about by a passionate soul that longed, and strove, and fought in its shell for larger freedom. All his life, so to speak, save for the last few months, he had been a prisoner;—he had never, as he had himself declared, known the sweetness of liberty;—but for the sake of Lotys,—had she lived,—he would have been content to still wear the chains of monarchy, and would have endeavoured to accomplish such good as he might, and make such reforms as could possibly benefit his country. But, after all, it is only a 'possibility 'that any reforms will avail to satisfy any people long; and he was philosopher and student enough to know that whatsoever good one may endeavour to do for the wider happiness and satisfaction of the multitude, they are as likely as not to turn and cry out—"Thy good is our evil! Thy love to us is but thine own serving!"—and so turn and rend their best benefactors. With the loss of Lotys, he lost the one mainspring of faith and enthusiasm which would have helped him to match himself against his destiny and do battle with it. A great weariness seized upon him,—a longing for some wider scope of action than such futile work as that of governing, or attempting to govern, a handful of units whose momentary Order was bound, in a certain period of time to lapse into Disorder—then into Order again, and so on till the end of all.

Hence his resolve to sail the seas with Lotys to that 'other side of Death' of which she had spoken,—that 'other side' which an inward instinct told him was not Death, but Life! He could not of himself analyse the emotions which moved him. He could not take the measure of his grief; it was too wide and too painful. He might have said with Heine: "Go, prepare me a bier of strong wood, longer than the bridge at Mayence, and bring twelve giants stronger than the vigorous St. Christopher of Cologne Cathedral on the Rhine;—they will carry the coffin and fling it in the sea,—so large a coffin needs a large grave! Would you know why the bier must be so long and large? With myself, I lay there at the same time all my love and my sorrow!"

Sovereignty,—a throne,—a kingdom,—even an Empire—seemed poor without love to grace them. Had he never known the pure ideal passion, he would still have missed it;—but having known it—having felt its power environing him day and night with a holy and spiritual tenderness, he could not but follow it when it was withdrawn—follow it, ay, even into the realms of blackest night! Like the 'Pilgrim of Love,' delineated by one of the greatest painters in the world, he recked nothing of the darkness closing in,—of the pain and bewilderment of the road, which could only lead to interminable, inexplicable mystery;—he felt the hand of the great Angel upon him— the Angel of Love whom alone he cared to serve,—and if Love's way led to Death, why then Death would be surely as sweet as Love! A great and almost divine calm had taken possession of him from the moment he had fulfilled his intention of boarding the ship which carried away from him all that was mortal of the woman he had secretly idolised. The wild turbulence of Nature around him had only intensified his perfect content. He had pleased himself by taking care of the sleeping Lotys— such tender care! He had tried to shield her coffin from the onslaughts of the fierce waves; he had protected many of the funeral flowers from destruction, and had lifted the gold fringe of the purple pall many and many a time out of the drenching spray cast over it. There was a strange delight in doing this. Lotys knew! That was his chief reflection. And 'on the other side of Death,' as she had said, they would meet—and to that 'other side' they were sailing together with all the speed Heaven's own forces could give to their journey. Oh, that 'other side'! What brightness, what peace, what glory, what mutual comprehension, what deep and perfect and undisturbed love would be found there! He smiled as he watched the swollen and angry sea,—the rising billows shouldering each other and bearing each other down;—how much grander, how much more spiritual and near to God, he thought, was this conflict of the elements, than the petty wars of men!—their desires of conquest, their greed of gold, their thirst for temporal power!

"My Lotys!" he said aloud; "You knew the world! You knew the littleness of worldly ambition! You knew that there is only one thing worth living and dying for, and that is Love! Your heart was all love, my Lotys! Deprived of love for yourself, you gave all you had to those who needed it, and when you found my love for you might do me harm in the People's honour, you sacrificed your life! Alas, my Lotys! If you could but have realised that through you, and the love of you, I a King, who had long missed my vocation, could alone be truly worthy of sovereignty!"

He laid his hand on her coffin with a tender touch, as though to soothe its quiet occupant.

"My beloved!" he said, "We shall meet very soon!—very soon now! 'on the other side of death'—and God will understand,—and be pitiful!"

The storm now seemed to be at its height. The monstrous waves, as they arose to combat the frail vessel in her swift career, made a bellowing clamour, and once or twice the ship reeled and staggered, as though about to lurch forward and go under. But the King felt no fear,—no horror of his approaching fate. He watched the wild scene with interest, even with appreciation,—as an artist or painter might watch the changes in a landscape which he purposes immortalising. His past life appeared to him like a picture in a magic crystal,—blurred and uncertain,—a mist of shapes without decided meaning or colour. He thought of the beautiful cold Queen, his wife,—and wondered whether she would weep for his loss.

"Not she!"—and he almost smiled at the idea—"Perhaps there will be a ballad written about it—and she will listen, unchanged, unmoved—as she listened that night when her minstrels sang:

> 'We shall drift along till we both grow old—
> Looking back on the days that have passed us by,
> When "what might have been," can no longer be,—
> When I lost you and you lost me!'

That was a quaint song—and a true one! She will not weep!"

Then he went over in memory the various scenes of his life—brilliant, useless, and without results—when he was Heir-Apparent;—he thought of his two young sons, Rupert and Cyprian, who were as indifferent to him as young foals to their sire,—and anon, his mind turned more tenderly to his eldest-born, Prince Humphry, and the fair girl he had so boldly wedded,—the happy twain, who, returning homeward, would find the Throne ready for their occupancy, and a whole nation waiting to welcome them.

"God bless them both!" he said aloud, lifting his calm eyes to the wild heavens—"They have the one shield and buckler against all misfortune— Love! And I thank God that I have not the sin upon my conscience of having broken that shield away from them; or of having forced their young lives asunder! Wiser than I, they took their own way and kept it!—may they so keep it always!"

Then a thought of 'the People' came to him—the People who had latterly taken to idolising him, and making of him a hero greater than any monarch whose deeds have ever been glorified since history began.

"They will forget!" he said—"Nowadays Nations have short memories! Battles and conquests, defeats and victories pass over the national mind as rapidly and changefully as the clouds are flying over the sky to-night!—the People remember neither their disgraces nor their triumphs in the life of individual Self which absorbs each little unit. Their idolatry of one monarch quickly changes to their idolatry of another! I shall perhaps be regretted for six months as my father was— and then— consigned with my ancestors to oblivion! Nothing so beautiful or so gladdening to the heart of a Monarch as the love of his People!— but—at the same time—nothing so changeable or uncertain as such love!—nothing so purely temporal! And nothing so desperately sad, so irremediably tragic as the death of kings!"

Rapidly he reviewed the situation—the new Ministry, the new Government members were elected—and business would begin again immediately after the Crown Prince's return. All the reforms he had been prepared to carry out, would be effected,—and then would come the new King's Coronation. What a dazzling picture of resplendent beauty would be seen in Gloria, robed and crowned! His heart beat rapidly at the mere contemplation of it. For himself he had no thought—save to realise that the strange manner of his disappearance from his kingdom would probably only awaken a sense of resentment in 'society,' and a vague superstition among the masses, who would for a long time cling to the belief that he was not dead, but that like King Arthur he had only gone to the 'island valley of Avillion' to "heal him of his grievous wound,"—from which deep vale of rest he would return, rejoicing in his strength again. Sergius Thord would know the truth—for to Sergius Thord he had written the truth. And the letter would reach him this very night— this night of his last earthly voyage.

"When his great sorrow has abated," he said, "he too will forget! He has all his work to do—all his career to make—and he will make it well and nobly! Even for his sake, and for his future, it is well that I am gone—for if he ever came to know,— if he were to guess even remotely, through Zouche's ravings, or some other means, the reason why Lotys killed herself, he would hate me,—and with justice! He loves the People—he will serve their Cause better than I!"

The moon stared whitely out of a cloud just then,—and to his amazement and awe, he suddenly perceived the black shadow of a man lifting itself slowly, slowly from the hold of the ship, like a massive bulk, or ghost in the gloom. Unable to imagine what this might be, or how any other human creature save himself would venture to sail with the dead on a voyage whose end could be but destruction, he advanced a step towards that looming shape, and started back with a cry, as he recognised the very man he had been thinking of—Sergius Thord!

"Sergius!" he cried aghast.

"King!" and Thord looked scarcely human in the pale fleeting moonbeams, as he too stared in half-maddened wonder at the face and form of a companion on this dread journey such as he had never expected to see. "What do you here in the midst of the sea and the storm? You should be at home!—playing the fool in your Palace!—giving audiences on your throne!—you—you have no right to die with Lotys, whom I loved!"

"With Lotys whom you loved!" echoed the King; "You loved her—true! But I loved her more!"

"You lie!" said Thord, furiously; "No man—no King,—no Emperor of all the world, could ever have loved Lotys as I loved her! These great waves waiting to devour us—dead and living together—are not more insatiate in their passion for us than I in my passion for Lotys! I loved her!—and when she scorned me—when she rejected me,—when she openly confessed that she loved you—the King—what

remained for her but death! Death, rather than dishonour at your Royal hands, Sir!"
And he laughed fiercely—a laugh with the ring of madness in it. "I rescued her as
a child from starvation and misery—and so I may say I gave her her life. What I
gave, I took again—I had the right to take it! I would not see her shamed by you—
dishonoured by you—branded by you!—I did the only thing left to me to save her
from you—I killed her!"

With a loud cry the King, no longer so much king as man, with every passion
roused, sprang at him.

"You killed her? Oh, treacherous devil! They said she killed herself!"

"Hands off!" cried Thord, suddenly pointing a pistol at him; "I will shoot you
as readily as I shot her if you touch me! She killed herself you think? Oh, yes—in a
strange way! Her last words were: 'Say I did it myself! Tell the King I did it myself!'
A lie! All women are fond of lying. But her lie was to protect Me! Her last thought
was for my defence,—not yours! Her last wish was to save Me, not you!—King
though you are—lover though you craved to be! I say I murdered her! This is my
Day of Fate,—the day on which it seems that Heaven itself has drawn lots with me
to kill a King! Why did I ever relax my hate of you? It was inborn in me—a part
of me,—my very life, the utmost portion of my work! I called you friend;—I curse
myself that I ever did so!—for from the first you were my enemy—my rival in the
love of Lotys! What did I care for the People? What did you? We were both at one
in the love of the same woman! And now I am here to die with her alone! Alone, I
say—do you hear me? I will be alone with her to the last—you shall not share with
us in our sea burial! I will die beside her,—all, all alone!—and drift out with her to
the darkness of the grave, to meet my fate with her—always with her,—whether
her spirit lead me to Hell or to Heaven!"

His insensate frenzy was so desperate, so terrible, that by its very force the
strange mental composure of the King became intensified. Quietly folding his arms,
he took his stand by the coffin of the dead in silence. The dashing spray that leaped
at the masts of the vessel,— the wind that scooped up the billows into higher and
higher pinnacles of emerald green, might have been soundless and powerless, for all
he seemed to hear or to heed.

"Why are you with us?" cried Thord again—"How came you on this ship,
where I thought I had hidden myself alone with her, voyaging to Death? Could you

not have left her to me?—you who have a throne and kingdom —I, to whom she was all my life!"

"I came—as you have come"—answered the King—"to die with her—or rather not to die, but to find Life with her! She loved me!"

With a savage curse, Thord raised the pistol he held. The King looked him full in the eyes.

"Take good aim, Sergius!" he said tranquilly—"For here between us lies Lotys— the silent witness of your deed! Go hence, if you must, with two murders on your soul! There is no escape from death for either you or me, take it how we may;—and I care not at all how I meet it, whether at your hands or in the waves of the sea! Give me the same death you gave to Lotys! I ask no better end! For so at least shall we meet more quickly!"

Half choked with his fury, Thord looked at him with fixed and glassy eyes. He was jealous of death!—jealous that death should of itself seem to reunite Lotys and the man she had loved more closely together! Standing erect by the purple pall that covered the one woman of the world to them both, the King looked 'every inch a king,'—the incarnation of pride, love, resolve and courage. With a sudden wild-beast cry, Thord sprang at him and caught his arm with one hand, the pistol grasped in the other.

"Too near!" he gasped; "You shall not stand too near her!—you shall not die so close to her!—you shall not have the barest chance of resting where she sleeps!"

He fell back, as the King's calm eyes regarded him steadfastly, imperiously, almost commandingly, without a trace of fear. He trembled.

"Do not look so!" he muttered; "I cannot kill you!—not if you look so!—"

Raising the pistol, he took apparent aim. The King stood unmoved, only murmuring softly to himself: 'On the other side of Death, my Lotys!— On the other side!'

There was a loud report, a crash in his ears—then—as he staggered back, stunned by the shock, he saw that he was untouched, unhurt. Thord had turned the pistol against his own breast, and reeling backward, with a last supreme effort, dragged his sinking body to the vessel's edge.

"God save your Majesty!" he cried wildly; "Tell Lotys I did it myself! God knows that is true!"

The wild waves, clambering up over the deck rushed at him, and an enormous foam-crested billow, higher and stronger than all the rest, beat at the mast of the vessel and snapped it in twain. It came down, dragging the sail with it in a tangle of cordage, and with that sail the name of 'Lotys' inscribed upon it was whirled furiously out to sea. The body of the vessel, now netted in a mass of ropes and rigging, began to roll helplessly in the trough of the waves, and the corpse of Thord, sinking under it as it plunged, was swept away like a leaf in the storm! Gone, his wild heart and wilder brain!—gone his restless ambition,—gone his unsatisfied love— his fierce passions, his glimmerings of a noble nature which if trained and guided, might have worked to noblest ends. Like many would-be leaders of men, he could not lead himself—like many who seek to control law, and revolutionise the world, he had been unable to master his own desperate soul. He was not the first,—he will not be the last,—who for purely personal ends has sought to 'serve the People'! The disinterested, the impersonal and unselfish Leader has yet to come,—and if he ever does come, it is more than probable that those for whom he gives his life, will be the first to crucify his soul, and cry 'Thou hast a devil!'

Death was now sole commander of the ocean that night! And the King of a mere little earth-country, realised to the full that he stood irrevocably face to face with the last great Enemy of Empires. Yet never had he looked more truly imperial,—never more superbly the incarnation of life! A mighty exultation began to stir within him—a consciousness that he, despite all the terrors of the grave, would still come forth the conqueror! The waves, leaping at him, were friends, not foes,—the moon shedding ghostly glamours on the watery wilderness, smiled as though she knew that he would soon be a partaker in the secrets of all Nature, and solve the mystery of existence,— there was a singing in his ears as of voices triumphant, which swelled with the passion of a mighty anthem,—and with the quietest mind and calmest brain he found himself musing on life and death as if he were already a witness apart, of their strange phenomena. Thord's appearance on the same ship in which he and Lotys were passengers, seemed to him quite simple and natural,—Thord's death moved him to a certain grave compassion,—but the whole swift circumstance had been so dreamlike, that he had no time to think of it, or regret it,—and the only active consciousness his mind held was that he and Lotys were journeying to 'the other side';—that 'other side' which he now felt so near and sure, that he could almost declare he saw the living presence of the woman he loved arisen from the dead and standing near him!

The ocean widened out interminably, and he saw, looking ahead, a great heap of gigantic billows, leaping, sparkling, tossing, climbing over each other in the fitful light of the moon, like huge sea-monsters waiting to devour and engulf him. He smiled as he felt the yielding craft on which he stood swirl towards those breakers, and begin to part asunder,—so would he have smiled on a battlefield facing his foes, and fronted with fiery cannon! The glory of Empire,—the splendour of Sovereignty,—the pride and panoply of Temporal Power! How infinitely trivial seemed all these compared with the mighty force of a resistless love! How slight the boasted 'supremacy' of man with his laws and creeds, matched against the wrath of the conflicting sea,—the sure and swift approach of inexorable Death! Under the depths of the ocean which this ruler of a kingdom traversed for the last time, lay a lost Continent,—fallen dynasties—forgotten civilisations, wonderful and endless— kings and queens and heroes once famous—and now as blotted out of memory as though they had never been!

> "If thou could'st see a thousand fathoms down,
> Thou would'st behold 'mid rock and shingle brown—
> The shapeless wreck of temple, tower and town,—
> The bones of Empires sleeping their last sleep,
> Their names as dead as if they never bore
>   Crown or dominion!"

With keen and watchful eyes he measured the swiftly lessening distance between him and the glittering, tumbling whirlpool of waves—he felt the weight of the wind bearing against the drifting vessel—the end was very near! Standing by the dead Lotys, he prayed silently—prayed strangely,—in words borrowed from no Church formula, but as they came, straight from his heart—prayed that God might not be a Dream—that Love might not be a Snare—and Death might not be an End! So do we all pray when the last dread moment of dissolution comes—when no priest's assurance can comfort us—and when the greatest King in the world is but a poor ordinary human soul, ignorant and forlorn, shuddering on the verge of eternal Judgment!

A mountainous billow broke over the deck, half stunning him with the shock of its cold onslaught, and sweeping the coffin of Lotys almost over the edge of the vessel. He threw himself beside that dreary casket, fastening his own body with strong rope knotted many times, to its heavy leaden mass, resolved to sink with it painlessly, and without a struggle. So,—in perfect passiveness,—he awaited his end. Suddenly,—as if a bell had chimed in the distance, or a voice had sung some old familiar song in his ears,—he saw, clearly visioned in all the flying spray of the tempest a face!—not the face of Lotys—but a soft, childish, piteous little countenance, framed in curling tendrils of hair, with trusting sweet eyes, raised to his own in holiest, simplest confidence! So pure, so fair a face!—so pathetically loving!— where had he seen it before? All at once he remembered,—and sprang up with a sharp cry of pain. Why, why had this frail ghost of the past flown out of the darkness of sea and storm to confront him now? The ghost of his first young love!—the clinging, fond, credulous creature who had gone to her death uncomplainingly for his sake—with only the one little cry of farewell—'My love! Forgive me!' Why should he think of her?—why should he see her before him at this supreme moment when Death stared him in the face, and his spirit hovered on the edge of Infinity? "Vengeance is mine!—I will repay, saith the Lord!" His first love!—so lightly won—so cruelly betrayed! Tears rushed to his eyes,— he thought of the wrong done to a perfectly pure and blameless life—a wrong he had forgotten in all these years—till now!

"Oh God!" he cried aloud—"Forgive me! Forgive my weakness, my selfishness, my many wasted years! Let not her face forever come between thy redeeming Angel, Lotys, and my soul!"

The tumultuous breakers rushing now with a great swoop at the vessel, snatched and tore at him. He nerved himself to look again,—once again, and for the last time, across the great wilderness of warring waters! The moon now shone brightly,—the clouds were parting on either side of her, rolling up in huge masses, white and glistening as Alpine peaks of snow—the wind had not lessened, and the fury of the sea was still unabated. But the fair childish face had vanished,—and only the clear salt spray dashed in his eyes and blinded them,—only the salt waves clambered round him, drawing him towards them in a cold embrace!

"'On the other side,' my Lotys!" he said—"God be merciful to us both!— 'on the other side'!"

For one moment the breaking vessel paused shudderingly on the edge of the seething whirlpool of waves, which, meeting in a centre of tidal commotion, leaped at her, and began steadily to suck her down. For one moment the moonbeams fell purely on the calm upturned face of the King, who like others allied to him in kingship throughout history, had esteemed mere sovereignty valueless at the cost of Love! For kings,— though surrounded with flatterers and sycophants who seek to make them imagine themselves somewhat more than human,—are but men, with all men's vain sins and passions, mad weaknesses and wild dreams; and when they love, they love as foolishly as commoners,—and when they die, as die they must, there is no difference in the actual way of death than is known to a pauper. More gold and purple on the one side,—more straw and sackcloth on the other,—but the solemnity and equality of Death itself, is the same in both. And as this dying King well knew, the People care little who governs them, provided bread is cheap, and labour well paid. He is greatest who gives them most,—and he is the most applauded who allows them the most liberty of action! The personality, the complex nature, the character, the temptations, the mind-sufferings of a King, as man merely, are less than nothing to the multitude who run to follow and to cheer him. If he were once to complain, he would be condemned;—and if he asked from his crowding flatterers the bread of sympathy, they would give him but a stone!

The moon smiled—the stars flashed fitfully through the clouds,—and all through the length and breadth of ocean there seemed to come the sound of a great psalmody, rising and filling the air. It surged on the King's ears, as with hands clasped on the drenched lilies strewn over the sleeping Lotys, he welcomed the coming Unveiling of the Beyond! And then—the waters rose up, and caught living and dead together, and dragged them down with a triumphal rush and roar,—down, down to that grand Unconsciousness,—that sublime Pause in the chain of existence,— that longer Sleep, from which we shall wake refreshed and strong again,—ready to learn Where we have failed, Why we have loved, and How we have lost. But of things temporal there shall be no duration,— neither Sovereignty nor Supremacy, nor Power; only Love, which makes weak the strongest, and governs the proudest;— and of things eternal we know naught save that Love, always Love, is still the centre of the Universe, and that even to redeem the sins of the world, God Himself could find no surer way than through Love, born of Woman into Life.

*   *   *   *   *

Days passed,—and angry Ocean gradually smoothed out its frowning furrows, spreading a surface darkly-blue and peaceful, under a cloudless arch of sky. And one night,—when the moon, like a golden cup in heaven, emptied her sparkling wine of radiance over the gently heaving waves, a fair ship speeding swiftly with all the force of steam and sail, with flags fluttering from every mast, and sounds of music echoing from her lighted saloons, came flying over the billows like a glorious white-winged bird soaring to its home on an errand of joy. On her deck stood Gloria,—happily ignorant of all calamity,—watching with dreamy, thoughtful eyes the lessening lengths of sea between her and the land she loved. The Crown Prince, her husband,—now King, though he knew it not,—stood beside her;—his handsome face brightened by a smile which expressed his heart's elation, his soul's deep peace and inward content. Naught knew these wedded lovers of the strange reception awaiting them; of the half-mourning, half-rejoicing people,— of national flags suddenly veiled in crape,—of black funeral-streamers set distractedly amidst gay bridal garlands;—of a widowed Queen, broken-hearted and despairing, weeping vainly for the love she had so long misprized, and had learned too late to value,—of a Crown resigned,—of the lost Majesty and hero of a nation's idolatry;—of the death of Ronsard, and the inexplicable disappearance of the famous Socialist leader, Sergius Thord,—and of all the strange and tragic history of vanished lives, even to that of Sir Roger de Launay whom no man ever saw again,—which it fell to their faithful friend, Heinrich von Glauben to relate, with passionate grief and many tears. They knew nothing. They only saw home and the future before them, shining in bright hues of hope and promise; for Love was with them,—and through Love alone—love for the nation, love for the people, love for each other,—they purposed, God willing, to faithfully fulfil whatever destiny might be theirs, whether fortunate or disastrous! Thus minded, they could see no evil in the world,—no mischief,—no ominous crossings of Fate,—they had all earth and all heaven in each other! And the gay ship bearing them onward, danced over the smiling, singing, siren waves, as if she too had a human heart to feel and rejoice!—and in her swift course swept lightly over the very spot, now tranquil and radiant, where but a short while since, the body of Lotys had gone down, companioned by the King. Gloria leaning over the deck-rail looked dreamily into the sparkling water.

"The storm we met has left no trace!" she said; "It was but a passing hurricane!"

Her husband came to her side, and they stood together in silence. Sweet harmonies floating upwards from the saloon below, where a company of musicians and singers were stationed to charm the evenings of the Royal pair with 'sounds more dulcet than Heaven's own dulcimers' held them attentive. The tender tones of an undetermined melody rose and fell on the quiet air,—they listened, drawing closer and closer to each other, till it seemed as if but one heart beat between them,—as if but one Soul aspired,—Archangel-like,—from their two lives to Heaven! And Gloria, with a sigh of perfect happiness, murmured softly,—

"How beautiful the night! How calm the sea!"

So sped they onward,—with Love to steer them; with Love to bring them safely through the brief cloud of sorrow and wonder hanging over the kingdom to which they wended,—with Love to guide their lives through all difficulty and danger, and to give them all the good that Love alone can give! For whether the days be dark or bright,—whether tempest fills the air, or sunshine illumines the sky,—whether we are followed with fair blessing from friends, or pursued with the hate, envy and slander of injurious foes,—whether we drown by choice in tempestuous waters of passion, or float securely to the shores of peace,—whether our ships are bound for Death or for Life, we are safe in the hands of Love! And in the midst of what the world deems storm and wreckage, we can gaze into the deeper depths of God's meaning with trustful eyes, and sail on our voyage fearlessly,—on, even to the Grave and beyond it!—for with Love at the helm, how beautiful is the Night!—how calm the Sea!

THE END

The Codes Of Hammurabi And Moses
W. W. Davies

QTY

The discovery of the Hammurabi Code is one of the greatest achievements of archaeology, and is of paramount interest, not only to the student of the Bible, but also to all those interested in ancient history...

Religion **ISBN:** *1-59462-338-4*

Pages:132
MSRP $12.95

The Theory of Moral Sentiments
Adam Smith

QTY

This work from 1749. contains original theories of conscience amd moral judgment and it is the foundation for systemof morals.

Philosophy ISBN: *1-59462-777-0*

Pages:536
MSRP $19.95

Jessica's First Prayer
Hesba Stretton

QTY

In a screened and secluded corner of one of the many railway-bridges which span the streets of London there could be seen a few years ago, from five o'clock every morning until half past eight, a tidily set-out coffee-stall, consisting of a trestle and board, upon which stood two large tin cans, with a small fire of charcoal burning under each so as to keep the coffee boiling during the early hours of the morning when the work-people were thronging into the city on their way to their daily toil...

Childrens ISBN: *1-59462-373-2*

Pages:84
MSRP $9.95

My Life and Work
Henry Ford

QTY

Henry Ford revolutionized the world with his implementation of mass production for the Model T automobile. Gain valuable business insight into his life and work with his own auto-biography... "We have only started on our development of our country we have not as yet, with all our talk of wonderful progress, done more than scratch the surface. The progress has been wonderful enough but..."

Biographies/ ISBN: *1-59462-198-5*

Pages:300
MSRP $21.95

www.bookjungle.com *email: sales@bookjungle.com fax: 630-214-0564 mail: Book Jungle PO Box 2226 Champaign, IL 61825*

The Art of Cross-Examination
Francis Wellman

QTY

I presume it is the experience of every author, after his first book is published upon an important subject, to be almost overwhelmed with a wealth of ideas and illustrations which could readily have been included in his book, and which to his own mind, at least, seem to make a second edition inevitable. Such certainly was the case with me; and when the first edition had reached its sixth impression in five months, I rejoiced to learn that it seemed to my publishers that the book had met with a sufficiently favorable reception to justify a second and considerably enlarged edition. ..

Reference   ISBN: *1-59462-647-2*

Pages:412

MSRP $19.95

On the Duty of Civil Disobedience
Henry David Thoreau

QTY

Thoreau wrote his famous essay, On the Duty of Civil Disobedience, as a protest against an unjust but popular war and the immoral but popular institution of slave-owning. He did more than write—he declined to pay his taxes, and was hauled off to gaol in consequence. Who can say how much this refusal of his hastened the end of the war and of slavery ?

Law   ISBN: *1-59462-747-9*

Pages:48

MSRP $7.45

Dream Psychology Psychoanalysis for Beginners
Sigmund Freud

QTY

Sigmund Freud, born Sigismund Schlomo Freud (May 6, 1856 - September 23, 1939), was a Jewish-Austrian neurologist and psychiatrist who co-founded the psychoanalytic school of psychology. Freud is best known for his theories of the unconscious mind, especially involving the mechanism of repression; his redefinition of sexual desire as mobile and directed towards a wide variety of objects; and his therapeutic techniques, especially his understanding of transference in the therapeutic relationship and the presumed value of dreams as sources of insight into unconscious desires.

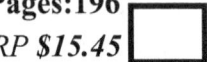

Psychology   ISBN: *1-59462-905-6*

Pages:196

MSRP $15.45

The Miracle of Right Thought
Orison Swett Marden

QTY

Believe with all of your heart that you will do what you were made to do. When the mind has once formed the habit of holding cheerful, happy, prosperous pictures, it will not be easy to form the opposite habit. It does not matter how improbable or how far away this realization may see, or how dark the prospects may be, if we visualize them as best we can, as vividly as possible, hold tenaciously to them and vigorously struggle to attain them, they will gradually become actualized, realized in the life. But a desire, a longing without endeavor, a yearning abandoned or held indifferently will vanish without realization.

Pages:360

Self Help   ISBN: *1-59462-644-8*

MSRP $25.45

The Rosicrucian Cosmo-Conception Mystic Christianity *by Max Heindel* ISBN: *1-59462-188-8* **$38.95**
The Rosicrucian Cosmo-conception is not dogmatic, neither does it appeal to any other authority than the reason of the student. It is, not controversial, but is: sent forth in the, hope that it may help to clear.. New Age/Religion Pages 646

Abandonment To Divine Providence *by Jean-Pierre de Caussade* ISBN: *1-59462-228-0* **$25.95**
"*The Rev. Jean Pierre de Caussade was one of the most remarkable spiritual writers of the Society of Jesus in France in the 18th Century. His death took place at Toulouse in 1751. His works have gone through many editions and have been republished...* Inspirational/Religion Pages 400

Mental Chemistry *by Charles Haanel* ISBN: *1-59462-192-6* **$23.95**
Mental Chemistry allows the change of material conditions by combining and appropriately utilizing the power of the mind. Much like applied chemistry creates something new and unique out of careful combinations of chemicals the mastery of mental chemistry... New Age Pages 354

The Letters of Robert Browning and Elizabeth Barret Barrett 1845-1846 vol II ISBN: *1-59462-193-4* **$35.95**
by Robert Browning and Elizabeth Barrett Biographies Pages 596

Gleanings In Genesis (volume I) *by Arthur W. Pink* ISBN: *1-59462-130-6* **$27.45**
Appropriately has Genesis been termed "the seed plot of the Bible" for in it we have, in germ form, almost all of the great doctrines which are afterwards fully developed in the books of Scripture which follow... Religion/Inspirational Pages 420

The Master Key *by L. W. de Laurence* ISBN: *1-59462-001-6* **$30.95**
In no branch of human knowledge has there been a more lively increase of the spirit of research during the past few years than in the study of Psychology, Concentration and Mental Discipline. The requests for authentic lessons in Thought Control, Mental Discipline and... New Age/Business Pages 422

The Lesser Key Of Solomon Goetia *by L. W. de Laurence* ISBN: *1-59462-092-X* **$9.95**
This translation of the first book of the "Lernegton" which is now for the first time made accessible to students of Talismanic Magic was done, after careful collation and edition, from numerous Ancient Manuscripts in Hebrew, Latin, and French... New Age/Occult Pages 92

Rubaiyat Of Omar Khayyam *by Edward Fitzgerald* ISBN:*1-59462-332-5* **$13.95**
Edward Fitzgerald, whom the world has already learned, in spite of his own efforts to remain within the shadow of anonymity, to look upon as one of the rarest poets of the century, was born at Bredfield, in Suffolk, on the 31st of March, 1809. He was the third son of John Purcell... Music Pages 172

Ancient Law *by Henry Maine* ISBN: *1-59462-128-4* **$29.95**
The chief object of the following pages is to indicate some of the earliest ideas of mankind, as they are reflected in Ancient Law, and to point out the relation of those ideas to modern thought. Religion/History Pages 452

Far-Away Stories *by William J. Locke* ISBN: *1-59462-129-2* **$19.45**
"*Good wine needs no bush, but a collection of mixed vintages does. And this book is just such a collection. Some of the stories I do not want to remain buried for ever in the museum files of dead magazine-numbers an author's not unpardonable vanity...*" Fiction Pages 272

Life of David Crockett *by David Crockett* ISBN: *1-59462-250-7* **$27.45**
"*Colonel David Crockett was one of the most remarkable men of the times in which he lived. Born in humble life, but gifted with a strong will, an indomitable courage, and unremitting perseverance...* Biographies/New Age Pages 424

Lip-Reading *by Edward Nitchie* ISBN: *1-59462-206-X* **$25.95**
Edward B. Nitchie, founder of the New York School for the Hard of Hearing, now the Nitchie School of Lip-Reading, Inc, wrote "LIP-READING Principles and Practice". The development and perfecting of this meritorious work on lip-reading was an undertaking... How-to Pages 400

A Handbook of Suggestive Therapeutics, Applied Hypnotism, Psychic Science ISBN: *1-59462-214-0* **$24.95**
by Henry Munro Health/New Age/Health/Self-help Pages 376

A Doll's House: and Two Other Plays *by Henrik Ibsen* ISBN: *1-59462-112-8* **$19.95**
Henrik Ibsen created this classic when in revolutionary 1848 Rome. Introducing some striking concepts in playwriting for the realist genre, this play has been studied the world over. Fiction/Classics/Plays 308

The Light of Asia *by sir Edwin Arnold* ISBN: *1-59462-204-3* **$13.95**
In this poetic masterpiece, Edwin Arnold describes the life and teachings of Buddha. The man who was to become known as Buddha to the world was born as Prince Gautama of India but he rejected the worldly riches and abandoned the reigns of power when... Religion/History/Biographies Pages 170

The Complete Works of Guy de Maupassant *by Guy de Maupassant* ISBN: *1-59462-157-8* **$16.95**
"*For days and days, nights and nights, I had dreamed of that first kiss which was to consecrate our engagement, and I knew not on what spot I should put my lips...*" Fiction/Classics Pages 240

The Art of Cross-Examination *by Francis L. Wellman* ISBN: *1-59462-309-0* **$26.95**
Written by a renowned trial lawyer, Wellman imparts his experience and uses case studies to explain how to use psychology to extract desired information through questioning. How-to/Science/Reference Pages 408

Answered or Unanswered? *by Louisa Vaughan* ISBN: *1-59462-248-5* **$10.95**
Miracles of Faith in China Religion Pages 112

The Edinburgh Lectures on Mental Science (1909) *by Thomas* ISBN: *1-59462-008-3* **$11.95**
This book contains the substance of a course of lectures recently given by the writer in the Queen Street Hall, Edinburgh. Its purpose is to indicate the Natural Principles governing the relation between Mental Action and Material Conditions... New Age/Psychology Pages 148

Ayesha *by H. Rider Haggard* ISBN: *1-59462-301-5* **$24.95**
Verily and indeed it is the unexpected that happens! Probably if there was one person upon the earth from whom the Editor of this, and of a certain previous history, did not expect to hear again... Classics Pages 380

Ayala's Angel *by Anthony Trollope* ISBN: *1-59462-352-X* **$29.95**
The two girls were both pretty; but Lucy who was twenty-one who supposed to be simple and comparatively unattractive, whereas Ayala was credited, as her Bombwhat romantic name might show, with poetic charm and a taste for romance. Ayala when her father died was nineteen... Fiction Pages 484

The American Commonwealth *by James Bryce* ISBN: *1-59462-286-8* **$34.45**
An interpretation of American democratic political theory. It examines political mechanics and society from the perspective of Scotsman James Bryce Politics Pages 572

Stories of the Pilgrims *by Margaret P. Pumphrey* ISBN: *1-59462-116-0* **$17.95**
This book explores pilgrims religious oppression in England as well as their escape to Holland and eventual crossing to America on the Mayflower, and their early days in New England... History Pages 268

QTY

The Fasting Cure *by Sinclair Upton*　　　　　　　　　ISBN: *1-59462-222-1*　**$13.95**
In the Cosmopolitan Magazine for May, 1910, and in the Contemporary Review (London) for April, 1910, I published an article dealing with my experiences in fasting. I have written a great many magazine articles, but never one which attracted so much attention... New Age/Self Help/Health Pages 164

Hebrew Astrology *by Sepharial*　　　　　　　　　　　ISBN: *1-59462-308-2*　**$13.45**
In these days of advanced thinking it is a matter of common observation that we have left many of the old landmarks behind and that we are now pressing forward to greater heights and to a wider horizon than that which represented the mind-content of our progenitors... Astrology Pages 144

Thought Vibration or The Law of Attraction in the Thought World ISBN: *1-59462-127-6*　**$12.95**
by William Walker Atkinson　　　　　　　　　　　　　　　Psychology/Religion Pages 144

Optimism *by Helen Keller*　　　　　　　　　　　　　ISBN: *1-59462-108-X*　**$15.95**
Helen Keller was blind, deaf, and mute since 19 months old, yet famously learned how to overcome these handicaps, communicate with the world, and spread her lectures promoting optimism. An inspiring read for everyone... Biographies/Inspirational Pages 84

Sara Crewe *by Frances Burnett*　　　　　　　　　　　ISBN: *1-59462-360-0*　**$9.45**
In the first place, Miss Minchin lived in London. Her home was a large, dull, tall one, in a large, dull square, where all the houses were alike, and all the sparrows were alike, and where all the door-knockers made the same heavy sound... Childrens/Classic Pages 88

The Autobiography of Benjamin Franklin *by Benjamin Franklin*　ISBN: *1-59462-135-7*　**$24.95**
The Autobiography of Benjamin Franklin has probably been more extensively read than any other American historical work, and no other book of its kind has had such ups and downs of fortune. Franklin lived for many years in England, where he was agent... Biographies/History Pages 332

Name	
Email	
Telephone	
Address	
City, State ZIP	

☐ **Credit Card**　　　　　☐ **Check / Money Order**

Credit Card Number	
Expiration Date	
Signature	

Please Mail to:　Book Jungle
PO Box 2226
Champaign, IL 61825
or Fax to:　　　630-214-0564

ORDERING INFORMATION

web: *www.bookjungle.com*
email: *sales@bookjungle.com*
fax: *630-214-0564*
mail: *Book Jungle PO Box 2226 Champaign, IL 61825*
or PayPal *to sales@bookjungle.com*

Please contact us for bulk discounts

DIRECT-ORDER TERMS

**20% Discount if You Order
Two or More Books**
Free Domestic Shipping!
Accepted: Master Card, Visa,
Discover, American Express